a life of her own

Joan G. Hauser

Beach Plum Press

Northport, NY

ISBN: 0615998143
ISBN-13: 978-0615998145

Library of Congress Control Number: 2014936983

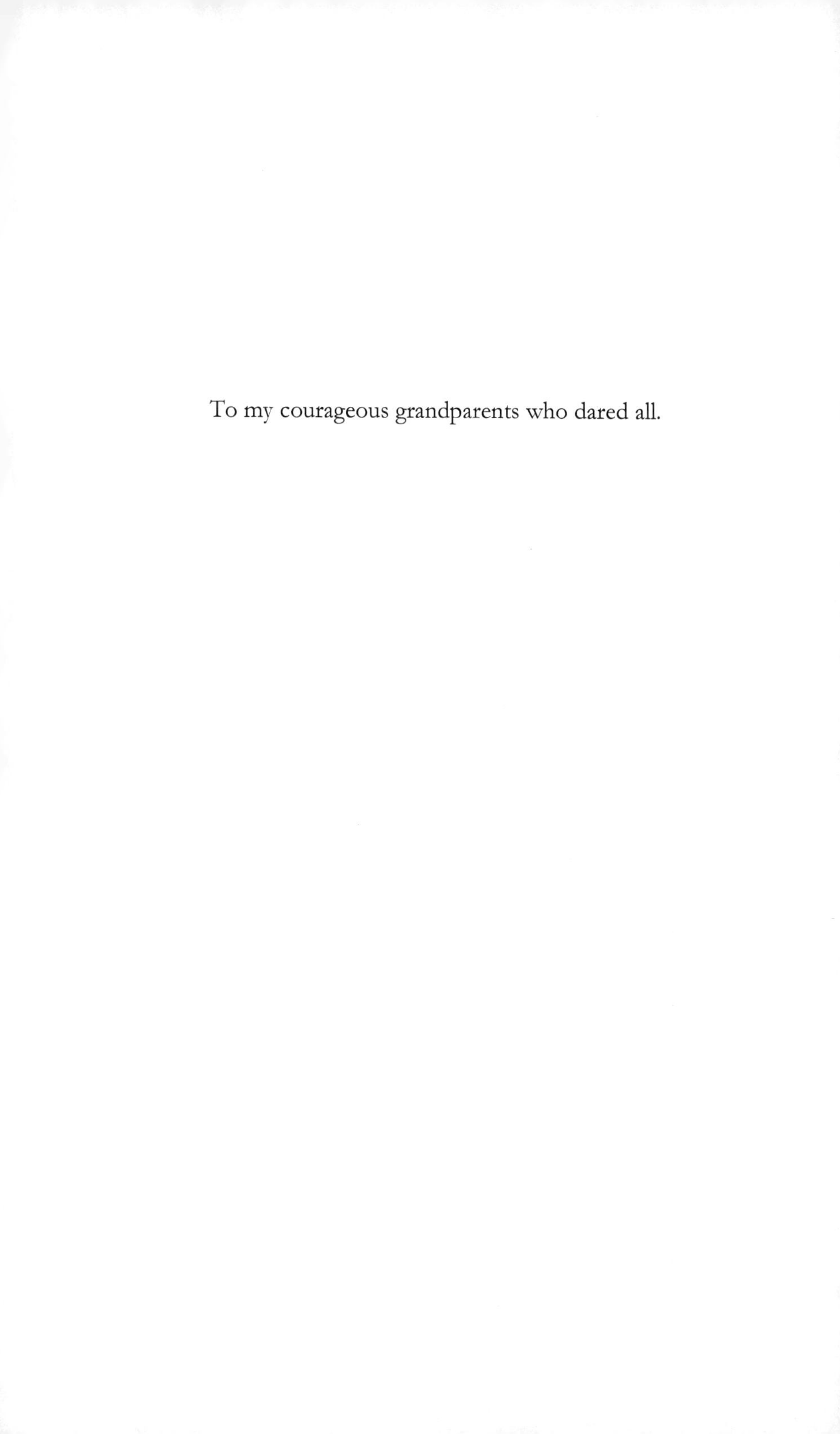
To my courageous grandparents who dared all.

PREFACE

This book was inspired by my attempt to understand the experiences of a whole generation and most particularly, my grandparents, who came to this country as immigrants in the beginning of the twentieth century. Sadly, I have no first-hand knowledge of their journey. With a leap of imagination and much research, I hope I have created characters they would recognize.

My parents "succeeded" and I grew up in a prosperous suburb with a life far removed from that of my grandparents. They lived far away, spoke English badly, and rarely visited. When they did, they did not speak of the past. Their accents and their old-fashioned ways seemed at odds with the melting pot theory of assimilation we were then taught.

It was only many years later, after their death and the death of my parents, that I felt compelled to research the world they had known. I deeply regretted not knowing more about their lives. How could I understand my own if I didn't understand theirs? An important theme in my book is the importance of keeping the memory of the past for one's children and grandchildren. Overshadowing all is my awareness that neither my parents nor I would be here if my grandparents hadn't had the courage to leave the Old World long before the advent of Hitler.

One of my grandmothers, Dora Hurwitch, left a short recording about her arrival in this country, which became my starting point. I researched the period exhaustively, setting the story in New York rather than Massachusetts where they had lived.

Accounts of life in the *shtetl*, of immigrant life on the Lower East Side, and of the fire at Triangle Shirtwaist Factory and its aftermath are based on documents from the time as well as later histories. A member of the staff at the Yiddish Book Center in Amherst, Massachusetts, was good enough to glance at some of the Yiddish phrases I use in the beginning of the book and make corrections.

I believe the immigrant experience is a universal one, regardless of country of origin. Today in America, we embrace differences rather than trying to eliminate them, but current problems make life more difficult for newcomers in other ways. I know the impetus for all immigrants is the need to feel safe, free, and successful, just as it was for my grandparents.

I'd especially like to thank my brilliant granddaughter, Celia Abernathy, who helped me publish this book as well as editing and suggesting revisions. My daughter, Betsy Abernathy, helped me lay out the original manuscript so it was in a workable form. My son, Andrew Aiello-Hauser, created a cover I love, with technical assistance from my granddaughter, Rose Abernathy. As always, my husband, Dick, was my first reader and chief encourager throughout this work.

CHAPTER 1

Like tangled *tzitzit*, the fringes on a prayer shawl, the *shtetl*'s unpaved streets curved in and out, criss-crossing the edges of the market square. In this early spring afternoon, each ramshackle wooden house seemed insubstantial, perched precariously above the river of black mud that appeared every year as the snow melted. Later, when the weather became warmer, the road would turn to dust, sending clouds of yellow grit billowing into the air when trodden.

Minna Ruben waited, framed sharply in the doorway of one of the smallest houses on one of the smallest streets. Her bare toes curled around the gobbets of mud that had collected upon the doorsill. She wore a loose drab dress, its hem dipping unevenly over her mud-streaked legs. Carelessly, she had tossed a rusty black shawl with frayed edges over her narrow shoulders. The only touches of color were a long fat braid of dull auburn cascading down to her waist and the startling gray-green of her eyes.

She turned to the open door behind her and called impatiently, "Come on, Chava! We have to hurry. Mama will be angry."

As she waited for a reply, she shifted the long wooden pole and the two empty buckets she carried from one hand to the other.

Inside the house, her sister Chava sat upon the sand-covered floor of the largest of its two rooms. Slowly, she slid on her boots. At fourteen, four years older than Minna, she no longer cared to leave the house barefooted. She hummed to herself as she tied her laces, her eyes dreamy and her lips curving in a slight smile.

Minna peered back into the house. For one startling moment, she saw Chava as a stranger would…glossy black hair gleaming in the sunlight pouring through the open door…blue sky eyes…dimples flickering as she smiled… a soft curving shape even in her faded dress.

She's beautiful, Minna thought. My sister is beautiful.

As Minna watched, Chava stood up and drifted to the open door. Shutting it behind her, she stepped down onto the street, placing her feet carefully to avoid the deepest mud puddles. Gracefully, she took the two buckets from her sister.

As they walked towards the well in the center of the market square, Minna sneaked glances at Chava. Was this the same sister who sang her to sleep, who burst into tears when Mama lost her temper, who had played barefoot in the street with her? For the first time, she noticed how everyone turned to look at Chava as they approached the well. Russian peasants, carrying their produce to the market, stared in open admiration. *Yeshiva bocher*, young Jews who attended *shul* and studied the Torah, eyed her secretively. Women looked her full in the face, smiling in delight or frowning enviously.

Minna put her arm around Chava's waist and looked up at her wistfully.

"Chava?" she asked, as if to a stranger.

Chava tweaked her braid. "What's the matter? You look as if you've lost your best friend. Did you have a fight with Hodel-next-door? She is your best *chaver*, isn't she?"

Minna smiled, relieved. Chava was still herself. Nothing had changed. "Of course, she is. We didn't have a fight. Everything's fine!" She tugged at Chava's hand. "Come on. Let's go. You're too slow."

As they reached the cobblestones of the market square, Pearl, their little sister, ran up to them. "Mama wants you," she said importantly, tugging on her long braid. "She says to come and see her before you go to the well."

Minna looked down at her. "Calm down! You don't have to be so bossy!"

"We're coming! We're coming!" Chava said as they turned to follow Pearl, weaving their way through the stalls, shops, and peddlers.

They could see Mama across the square. She stood behind her

stall, a rickety wooden stand festooned with brightly colored ribbons and trimmings. She waved at them, motioning them to hurry, and turned back to her customer. She smiled and talked as she cajoled a young Russian peasant girl. Her brown eyes snapped. A long lock of dark hair crept out from under the scarf she wore to hide it. Holding a shiny red ribbon in the air, she stroked it lovingly as she spoke.

As they approached, they could hear Mama's words. "…a red ribbon to show off your pretty face. There's someone special, I know there is. Does he like red? What will he say when he sees it?"

The girl blushed and touched the ribbon.

The gnarled old woman in the next stall, nestled amongst her straw brooms, smiled at Chava as she passed. Turning to Mama, she called, "It's truly spring when your beautiful daughter comes by. Like a princess, she is."

"I couldn't say, *kineahora*," Mama replied quickly, flicking her hand to ward off the evil spirits who could become jealous when they heard such praise.

Aware that she no longer had Mama's full attention, the young girl reached in her pocket and took out a few coins. "I'll take it," she said.

Mama accepted the money and quickly rolled the ribbon. "May it bring you joy," she called after the girl as she hurried away, ribbon in hand.

Mama turned to the girls, her smile falling away. Arms akimbo, she examined them. Chava fidgeted and Minna curled one dirty foot behind the other. Pearl stood next to Mama, looking up at her.

After what seemed like a long time, Mama nodded and said, "Tonight is a special night. We have a guest for dinner so you must hurry at the well."

Minna looked at Chava. She was usually the first to ask questions and demand answers. Today, she looked away, blushing.

Minna frowned. Maybe… She looked at Mama and demanded, "Who is coming? Who is it?"

Pearl hugged herself and jumped up and down. "I know! I know!" she crooned triumphantly.

Mama drew herself up, glaring at Pearl. "I'll tell when I'm ready," she snapped and stared at Chava. "And you…you have no questions?"

Chava shook her head.

A group of housewives approached the stall. Mama waved her hands impatiently at the girls. "Go! Go! Get water. After, stop and pick some flowers for your hair, Chava. I'll be home early to put fresh sand on the floor and cook dinner. Go! Go!" She shooed them away and turned to her customers with a smile.

Minna tried to coax Pearl to come with them, but Mama, as usual, understood her motives. "She'll tell you nothing!" she hissed, sending the little girl over to the corner to straighten out a tangle of ribbons.

Chava walked so briskly Minna could barely keep up with her. She trotted as fast as she could, balancing the long wooden pole in both hands. They reached the well before she had a chance to question her about Mama's mysterious visitor.

The usual group of small children giggled and played around it. A water carrier leaned against a nearby building, his *yarmulke* slightly askew on the top of his head. For a small sum, he'd carry water back to their home, but this was a luxury the girls could not afford. Recognizing them, he relaxed, tilted his head back, and closed his eyes.

As they were bending over the well to fill their two buckets, Minna whispered to Chava, "Who is coming? Why did you blush? And why did Mama tell you to put flowers in your hair? She never…"

Chava blushed again. "I'll tell you when we see Bubbe. I want to talk to her, anyway. I'll take a few of the forget-me-nots growing at her grave for my flowers. I know she won't mind."

Minna nodded. As long as she could remember, Bubbe, her mother's mother, had lived with the family. Last year, she had died suddenly while scouring a large brass samovar, her pride and joy. A cozy dumpling of a woman, she was considered so good and so wise that neighbors often asked her advice. Now that she was gone, members of the family sometimes visited the cemetery to consult with her and beg her help from "up there." Minna and Chava went often. They missed her and, as always, preferred to tell her rather than Mama their problems.

They left the well, balancing the two full buckets on the long pole Minna had been carrying. Each held an end. Through long practice, they moved quickly through the market square without spilling a drop.

They skimmed along until a blonde young man ran towards

them and careened into Chava, tipping the pails and spilling the water. She stumbled and fell. Shocked, she looked up at the man.

Minna set down her end of the pole, retrieved the buckets, and advanced angrily. "Why don't you watch where you're going?" she yelled. "Now we have to go back to the well."

The man helped Chava up. He was well dressed in a velvet jacket with a brightly colored silk scarf wound around his neck. He looked into Chava's eyes and said, in Russian, "I'm sorry. I was in a hurry."

Chava blushed.

Minna bit her lip. From the way he was dressed, she knew immediately that he must be the son of one of the more prosperous local landowners. How could she have yelled at him? She had been taught to be careful around the Russians and the *goyim*. "They'd just as soon kick you as smile" was the saying.

'You're a little beauty!" the man said, ignoring Minna and smiling at Chava. 'You're beautiful."

Chava smiled, showing her dimples and looked away modestly.

Minna moved closer to her sister and took her hand protectively.

"What's your name?" he asked.

"Chava," she replied.

"Chava," he repeated. He held out his hand. "Give me the buckets. I'll fill them for you."

Chava handed him hers and reached for Minna's.

Minna wanted to say "never mind" but Chava took hers and held it out to him. His hands lingered on hers as he grasped the handles.

With a bucket in each hand, he raced back to the well, scattering passersby in his wake.

"What are you doing, talking to him like that? You know what happened to Rachel. You can't trust the *goyim.*"

Rachel, a neighbor of theirs, had been betrayed by the son of a local farmer. When he refused to marry her because she was "only a Jew," she was sent away in disgrace. Later, they were told she had died giving birth.

Chava shook her head and smiled softly. "All I said was my name. Don't worry, Minna. It's all right."

"What if Mama or Tata saw you?"

"I don't care. He's just being polite. It doesn't mean anything."

"I didn't notice him being so polite to me," Minna said suspiciously.

He hurried back to them, holding a bucket in each hand. Minna watched him carefully as he approached. He did seem to have a kind face. Still, she shivered, sure there was danger in the encounter.

He set the buckets down. Minna inserted the pole and gesturing to Chava to pick up her end, raised the stick to her shoulder. He watched with a smile.

"Thank you," Chava said.

"We'll meet again," he replied. Bowing slightly, he turned away.

Chava looked after him. Then, settling the pole comfortably, she led the way to the cemetery.

At Bubbe's grave with its small stone and elaborate Hebrew inscription, they set the pails down gently and sat upon the grass. Clumps of newly emerging forget-me-nots surrounded the stone.

Chava leaned forward. "We're having a guest tonight, Bubbe, and I think I know who it is. I think it's the *shadchen* and…maybe…he's going to propose a match for me. I hope…I hope…" she glanced at Minna. "Well, you know what I hope. Remember me in your prayers, Bubbe, as I remember you."

Minna's mouth fell open. "Already! A match! Oh, Chava!"

She, too, faced the grave and spoke to Bubbe. "You will be there tonight, Bubbe, to see what happens. Something else happened today, but I'll tell it to you next time. Remember me in your prayers, Bubbe, as I remember you." She almost gabbled the words in her hurry to talk to Chava.

She turned and faced her. "But…I'll miss you when you go," she wailed.

Chava stroked her hair. "Don't worry, I won't forget you. You'll come and visit me in my new home. Maybe I'll marry a rich man, a *shayner Yid*, and I'll have a big house with my own carriage. Or maybe a *yeshiva bokher* and he'll be wise and good. All day, he'll study Torah like Tata and people will come from miles around to learn from him. Maybe he'll be handsome, too," she added hopefully.

"But Chava," Minna said, "you have no dowry. How can you marry a rich man? You have nothing to bring to the marriage."

Chava laughed softly and Minna noted again the deep blue of her eyes and the softness of her skin. "You're so beautiful," she continued, "You probably did catch someone's eye. Someone's dying for love of you!" She jumped up and bowed to her sister. "Maybe it's Enos, the watchmaker's son or Jacob, the rabbi's son. Maybe it's a prince in disguise!"

Chava shook her head. 'How can I know? Except there are no princes around here." Leaning forward, she started to pick a nosegay of forget-me-nots. Her expression was thoughtful.

"What if it's the butcher?" Minna said dramatically. "He's old and he already has four children. What if…"

Chava shook her head fiercely "What if this? What if that? There's no point in worrying till we know."

Minna realized that Chava was nervous despite her seeming calm. She flopped down on the ground next to her and touched her hand. "What do you think it's like?" she asked. "Being married, I mean."

Chava laid down her flowers. "I suppose…" she began, "it must be…" She shook her head. "Like Mama, I guess," she finished weakly.

Minna frowned. Chava was the older sister. She was supposed to know all the answers. Yet she sounded uncertain. "What if you don't like him?" she whispered.

"Love can come after," Chava replied nervously. Jumping up, she grabbed her end of the pole. "Let's go home. I want to go home."

Although they hurried, Mama and Pearl were already there by the time they reached the house. Mama was raking out the floor and Pearl was helping her by strewing new sand to make it look clean. On the stove, a large pot was simmering.

"It's chicken," Mama said proudly. "Rivka, the neighbor, gave me the carcass and a little meat. It's almost a golden soup. Then, potato pancakes with *tsimmes*. Set the table, Minna. Chava, change into your other dress."

Chava scurried into the tiny second room shared by all three girls and their brother, Yussel.

Minna carefully cleared her father's books from the only table in the room. She stacked them on their other major piece of furniture, a large chest that had been part of Mama's dowry. Painstakingly, she assembled the knives, forks, and spoons and drew the motley collection of stools and wooden chairs they used around the scarred table. Luckily, there was one extra for their guest.

Mama had already rolled up the featherbed she and Tata shared. Minna took it into the little bedroom and laid it on top of hers in the corner. She plumped herself down onto it and watched Chava as she pulled her dress over her head.

It was dyed a deep blue, to match Chava's eyes. Mama's best ribbons outlined the neck and sleeves. Minna could remember long evenings of sewing and her own painstaking task of picking out the bastings as each section was done.

Chava spun around. She smoothed the bodice, her hand lingering at her waist as she patted the soft fabric. Picking up the small cracked mirror that hung from a nail on the wall, she arranged Bubbe's forget-me-nots in her hair, smiling at herself in the mirror.

"What do you think?" she asked. "How do I look?"

Minna was speechless.

"How do I look?" Chava repeated, her voice quavering.

Minna stood up and touched Chava's hair. "You look beautiful," she said. "You look…perfect."

Pearl ran into the room. "Tata and Yussel are here," she said importantly. She stopped in front of Chava. "Oh," she sighed. "You look beautiful."

Chava ducked her head modestly and smiled benevolently, almost like a queen saluting her subjects, Minna thought. She stared after her sister as she left the room. Peeking into the cracked mirror, she sighed. Would she ever be a queen?

As they entered the other room, Minna could hear Tata grumbling at the dispersal of his books. Usually when he came home from *shul*, he'd sit at the table and read. Yussel, as always, awaited Tata's decision. He stood in the middle of the room balancing a huge stack of volumes. Mama, almost beside herself, stomped over to Yussel took the top book, and carefully put it with the others Minna had placed on the chest. Yussel eyed Tata anxiously.

Tata gestured angrily and turned his back on both Yussel and Mama. As he did, he noticed Chava for the first time. His stern blue eyes, the same color as hers, narrowed as he examined her.

Chava blushed, awaiting his verdict.

After what seemed like a long time, he nodded. "You look well, *tochter*," he said gravely. "May God be praised."

Chava returned his gaze and timidly essayed a smile.

Tata nodded. 'It is good," he said.

Yussel meticulously set down the books he was holding and stroked a non-existent beard, demonstrating his newly acquired dignity as a man of thirteen years and three months. Emulating Tata, he nodded. "You look well, Chava."

Then he laughed and added, "I hope you're ready to marry Israel, the *schnorrer*. I hear he's looking for a wife to help him beg in the streets."

Chava pretended to slap him.

As he ducked, Mama sucked in her breath. "Don't say that, my son. Do you want to bring a *kineahora* on your sister?"

"I take it back," he said hastily. "May God be praised."

Tata closed his eyes and bowed his head. "Hear me, O Lord, our God. Only this I ask. Let Chava, my daughter, find a good husband, one that will never remind her she had no bridal portion."

Mama bowed her head in acquiescence. Then she looked around the room proudly. "I am so proud I *kvell* when I look at my family. I only wish, Chava, your brothers Moishe and Isaac could be here, may God rest their souls. Only a week old when they died, the little angels. I tell you, the *shadchen*, Reb Jacobs, should only know what it is to feel such *naches*."

Tata shook his head. "Pride is pride. Maimonides says…"

Minna stopped listening. Once she heard the name, Maimonides, she knew that whatever was said would be unpleasant. Instead, she ran to the door to see if Reb Jacobs was coming.

Mama motioned her back. "Hst, child. Do you want him to think we are anxious to see him? No, here we sit, like kings of old, waiting for him to come."

Suddenly, there was a loud thumping at the door. Assuming it was Reb Jacobs, Minna looked at Mama for permission to open it. Mama held up her hand for a few seconds. Minna waited.

Chava hurried over to the stove and began to stir the soup nervously. Yussel smiled and Pearl began to giggle. Only Tata maintained his dignity. He put his hands behind his back and gazed off into the distance. A visit from Reb Jacobs, his visage proclaimed, was nothing special in his life.

The thumping grew louder. Finally, Mama nodded and Minna opened the door, thinking that Reb Jacobs must be very eager to see them to knock so loudly.

Minna had barely begun to turn the knob when the door was flung open. Rivka, their neighbor, tumbled in. Her eyes were wide with fright. 'It's Kishinev all over again. They're coming! They're coming! They'll kill us all. *Oy vey'z mir*! For this, I was born a Jew. They're coming, I tell you. Hide! Hide!"

Mama didn't understand. She tried to look past Rivka to see Reb Jacobs, saying angrily, "What do you mean, Kishinev? What's Kishinev here?"

Rivka stamped upon the floor, almost dancing in her impatience. "Listen!" she cried. "Listen, you can hear them at the other end of the street. And I'm all alone tonight. It's a pogrom, I tell you! 49 killed in Kishinev and..." Her voice rose. "They're coming! They're coming!"

"Stay here with us," Mama said automatically.

She looked around the room, shaking her head as she eyed the table, all set, Chava dressed in her best, the others, their faces shocked. "What to do? What to do?" she demanded, looking at Tata.

In the sudden silence, they could hear the noise of the crowd. To Minna, it sounded like an explosive winter storm. She remembered the noise of the wind wailing, the tree branches whipping against the house, and the hail banging against the roof as loud as bullets—and how frightened she had been. This was worse. She put her hands over her ears to shut out the sound of screams, men's voices yelling, the thumping of the horses hooves as they approached. Trembling, she jerked backwards, crouching away from the door. They'll kill us, she thought. They'll kill us.

"I must go to the *shul*," Tata said, speaking rapidly. "We have to protect the Torah. Yussel will come with me. Otherwise, they will desecrate the word of the Lord. Wife, take the girls and go to the graveyard. Hide among the stones and you'll be safe. The peasants, they're superstitious. They won't dare disturb the dead. Go now!"

Mama shook her head violently. "No! No! Come with us. Don't leave us alone. I'm afraid. They came when I was a child..."

Tata stood up, straighter than ever. His cold eyes bore into Mama's. "Go, woman! You're not a child now. Your place is with your daughters. Guard them well. My place is with the men, protecting God's word."

"Your place is with us, your family," Mama whispered hoarsely.

"You'll be killed. We'll all be killed. Let us at least die together."

As Minna waited for Tata's answer, it seemed as if time had stopped. It was so still in the room that the sounds from outside were magnified, filling every corner with fear and dread.

Tata shook his head stubbornly and turned to leave. Yussel remained standing until Tata gestured to him fiercely. Like a sleepwalker, the boy went slowly to his side.

"May God be with you," Tata said as he went out to the street followed by his son, a pale shadow

Mama clenched her hands, smoothing her apron, pulling at it and smoothing it again. She looked around the room wildly.

The sound of voices came closer. Minna heard a sharp scream as clearly if it were next door. Was it her friend Hodel's voice? Suddenly she could move again. She grabbed Chava's hand as she stood paralyzed, and pulled her over to Mama.

Tugging at her mother's skirt, she said urgently, "We have to go now. Tata said we should go. Come, Mama, let's go to Bubbe. She'll protect us." Her voice rose.

Mama started, clenched her apron, and seemed to waken. She took Minna's hand and gestured at Chava, Pearl, and Rivka. "Yes, we must go. Come now. We must leave." She spoke so softly they had to lean towards her to hear her words over the noise from outside.

Mama walked out of her house as if it belonged to a stranger. She didn't even stop to take the golden soup off the fire. Moving blindly, she stumbled and allowed herself to be led away by Minna.

They stood for a moment in the darkened street, shocked by its sudden unfamiliarity. Minna felt something soft strike her face. She flailed at it wildly, plucking at her forehead. She grasped it and saw what it was a feather. When she looked up, she could see more, swirling around them.

She remembered Bubbe had once told her, "They cut the feather beds, the *goyim.* The streets were white, like winter in July." Her eyes had filled, as she remembered the daughter who had been killed. "God forbid you should ever see such a thing," she had added.

I see it, Bubbe, Minna thought fiercely. Her courage rose defiantly as she remembered those words and knew this had happened before. Firmly, she led Mama and the others down the street, away from the approaching mob.

Everyone was in their way. Running. They were all running. Children cried, women called desperately, men pushed others aside to make way for themselves and their families. Blinding drifts of goose down feathers cascaded through the air but nothing could obscure the panic on each person's face. The confusion was suffocating.

Somehow, Minna kept moving, weaving in and out, through the crowds, behind the houses, pulling at Mama urgently. Looking back, she could see Chava, Pearl, and Rivka following.

They turned a corner and, for a moment, they were alone. Mama stopped. "Are we all here?" she panted. "I won't move until I know we're all here."

"I'm here, Mama," Chava whispered. "I'm here."

"I'm here," said Rivka.

There was a pause as they waited to hear Pearl's voice. In the distance, they could hear shouting in Russian and screams in Yiddish. "Dirty Yid!" Minna heard someone call. She brushed the feathers out of her eyes and peered tensely at the corner.

Mama jerked her hand from Minna's. "Pearl! My baby!' she screamed. "They'll kill her, the *goyim*. I saw them! I saw what they did to my sister … I have to go back and find her."

Minna gripped her arm, holding it with all her force. "Don't go, Mama," she rasped, her voice dry with fear.

Chava stepped forward. "Don't worry, Mama, I saw her right behind us. I'll go get her. We'll meet you by Bubbe." She spoke with such assurance no one doubted her. Automatically, they turned toward the graveyard.

Mama stopped again and looked back. "Are you sure she's right behind us?"

"Yes, Mama. Just two steps behind. We must have lost her at the last turning. Now go! Go!" Without waiting for an answer, Chava turned and ran back the way they had come.

Silently, Minna, Mama, and Rivka raced on. The two women were panting by the time they reached Bubbe's grave. They flung themselves on the ground, huddled behind her small gravestone. It was quieter now. The sounds from the village were muted, although occasionally they could hear an indescribable scream.

Mama spoke to Bubbe in a whisper. "Mama, I beg of you, helps us. Beg the Lord God to preserve us. Is my Angel watching over me, Mama? The other time, when I hid in the rain barrel and I saw them take Emma, my little sister…and what they did… Help us, Mama. Speak to the holy angels. Save my children. Save me, Mama. I'm afraid, Mama. God preserve us."

Listening to Mama's words, Minna was terrified. Mama was never afraid, not even when Tata yelled at her. She gripped the gravestone, clinging to it with all her might.

Peering through the darkness, she looked for Pearl and Chava. Several times, she started to jump up, certain she heard their voices or could see them as vague shapes in the distance. Each time, she sank back, disappointed. Finally, she leaned against Bubbe's stone, welcoming its familiar roughness. 'Help us, Bubbe, help us,' she thought, repeating the words like an incantation.

Rivka lay upon the ground, her shawl over her head, whimpering.

Mama screamed, "Where are they? My Pearl and my Chava! Where are they? Oh, God, hear my words. I didn't complain to You when You took Moishe and Isaac. Thy will be done. But, save my girls! I beg of you, hear a mother's prayer, O Lord." She stood abruptly as if ready to go and look for them, but Minna pulled her down.

"They're coming, Mama. I think I hear them coming. Wait and see. They'll be here soon. You'll see," Minna repeated soothingly, although her voice kept breaking.

Mama looked down at her, seeming to see her for the first time. Awkwardly, she held out her arms. After a slight hesitation, Minna crept timidly into them. Mama never held her, not since she was a baby.

Mama rocked back and forth with Minna, murmuring, "You're the brave one. Don't worry. It will be all right …"

Every few minutes, she jumped up and looked frantically through the night. Then she crouched down again, putting her arms around Minna as if seeking reassurance from the warmth of her body.

When Mama finally stood up and began to move away, Minna almost fell over. Painfully, she struggled to her feet, her body stiff and sore.

"We can't wait any longer. It's time to go home now, Minna," Mama said. "We'll find them both there, waiting for us. Then Tata and Yussel will come back and Reb Jacobs will come and we'll sit to dinner like kings. Yes, I'm sure they'll be waiting for us now."

Mama spoke so calmly, Minna was lulled into belief. Unhesitatingly, she followed as they left the cemetery and walked towards home. Rivka refused to come with them. She remained hiding behind Bubbe's grave, still moaning under her shawl.

The streets on the way home were unrecognizable, even though the storm seemed to have passed. Instead of loud Russian curses, there were wails and cries in Yiddish. Broken beds, upturned pots, ripped clothing, and shredded prayer shawls filled the streets. All was covered in a light dusting of white down. Fires, from over-turned stoves and candles, glowed ominously.

Most doors were open. As they moved swiftly towards home, Minna could see women sobbing and children screaming. The men, silent and abashed, beat at the fires and *davened* in prayer among the wreckage.

At one house, a child lay upon the floor, her leg twisted under her. She was alone. Although she said not a word, the tears streamed down her face. Automatically, she wiped them and touched her leg, repeating the actions over and over. Minna wanted to stop and help her, but Mama pulled her forward, walking more and more rapidly as they approached their own street.

They could see their house from a distance. The front door was wide open. On the sill lay a bundle of clothes. That's strange, Minna thought, beginning to run.

As she came closer, she could see it was Pearl, huddled, half-sitting, on the threshold. Her legs dragged in the mud and her arms clutched the doorframe. She pressed her face against the wall.

Mama ran to her. "Pearl! Pearl! Are you all right?" She gently turned her daughter's face away from the wall and wiped away the mud and tear stains.

"Are you all right?" she asked insistently.

Almost imperceptibly, Pearl nodded.

"Watch her," Mama said to Minna. "I'll find Chava."

Slowly, heavily, she walked into the house.

Minna, her arms around Pearl, listened. At first, she heard nothing but Mama's footsteps, a faint thumping noise as she stepped onto the dirt floor. Then she heard a strange sound, the same sound she had heard once before when she had seen the *shochet* slaughter a cow. It was the sound the beast made as the knife pierced its skin, a loud exhalation of air as if its very soul had parted from its body.

Minna set Pearl down carefully and entered the house on trembling legs. At first, all she saw was the table she had set so carefully that afternoon. It was overturned onto the floor, the dishes, knives, forks, and spoons scattered throughout the room. The beautiful clean sand that Mama and Pearl had raked so neatly was roiled and trampled, yet the golden soup was still bubbling on the stove.

Minna saw Mama. She was on the other side of their upside down table, sitting on the dirty floor, bent over something. Her head was bowed over her lap, her face anguished. What was it? It looked like the head of a doll lying there, but it couldn't be. They had no doll like that. Mama stroked its hair as tears fell from her eyes.

Minna moved closer, shaking her head. It must be a dream, she thought. Bubbe, make it be a dream, she pleaded.

Then she saw one of Chava's legs half under the table. Was it Chava there, sprawled on the floor, her skirt pulled up and her legs apart? There was so much blood. Blood on her legs, on the floor, and on her head. Minna saw it, a rich, red puddle.

Minna forced herself to look at her sister's pallid face. Had all her blood drained from her face as it seeped into the floor and Mama's skirt? Her blue eyes were no longer bright and her hair, her thick, glossy black hair, was matted and tangled.

Mama caressed her pale cheeks and stroked the snarled locks. "My God, what have they done? My beauty! What have they done to you, my baby?" she murmured.

Minna bent over her sister. She saw Chava's lips move weakly. It was only by holding her breath that she could hear her words, spoken in an almost inaudible voice.

"Mama?"

"Yes, my darling. I'm here. You don't have to be afraid any more. It's all over now."

"Mama, they hurt me… Then they hit my head…" Her voice faded.

Minna leaned closer.

"The men…" Chava saw Minna. "Minna, it was the same …" She closed her eyes and her mouth fell open.

Mama kept stroking her. "It was a *kineahora*, my darling. I was too proud of you. The sin is mine. But you'll be all right now, my beauty. I'll take care of you."

Mama bent to kiss Chava's forehead. She remained for a moment, her lips against her head. Wearily, she looked up. "She's cold. My Chava is so cold," she said softly. She leaned her cheek close to her mouth. Frantically, she touched her wrist and felt for a pulse.

Minna watched, frozen in horror.

Finally, Mama shook her head and laid Chava's hand gently down. Kissing her on the lips, she whispered, "So you have gone, my Chava. You have gone to be with Bubbe and your brothers. May God welcome you to His palace." She smoothed Chava's head once more and stood up.

Then she screamed. "She's dead! My daughter, she is dead, killed by the *goyim*! They killed Chava!" She plucked at her dress, ripping it. "My Chava…my beauty… It was for this, I bore you and fed you my milk? It was for this, so the devils could kill you?"

Minna thought she would never be able to move again. Aghast, she watched Mama, unaware of the tears falling from her eyes. Everything was blurry.

Then she heard a different noise. It seemed doubly loud because the only other sound, the only sound in the whole world was Mama, screaming. With difficulty, she looked up. Tata and Yussel were in the room.

Mama whipped her head around to face them. "So, you saved your precious Torah while your daughter lies dead before you," she screamed at Tata. "Your daughter, she was like the spring come to us, lies here defiled by the *goyim*. Dead…she's dead…my Chava's dead! I wasn't there! I could have hidden her… I could have said to the devils, 'Take me, I'm an old woman. I've had my life. Take me and leave my daughter.' I could have saved her, but I wasn't here. And you, old man, you ran to your books, as you always run to your books. I spit on you! What are dead books to the life of my daughter, my beauty?"

"The Lord giveth and the Lord taketh away." Tata began to pray, muttering in Hebrew and *davening* back and forth. Minna thought she saw tears in his eyes, but afterwards, she was never sure.

Yussel's face twisted. He turned away, pushing his face against the wall as if to burrow into it. His shoulders shook as he sobbed silently.

Minna looked at Chava again. What had she meant when she

said, "It was the same…?"

Scattered over the floor were the forget-me-nots they had gathered at Bubbe's grave. Chava lay still, now untouchable. Gone was the warm-voiced sister, the laughing friend, the beauty… Minna stopped to pluck a forget-me-not crushed by a heavy boot from the floor. She stroked it tenderly, trying to straighten its wilted petals to no avail. Head bowed, she let it drop. Slowly, she turned and stumbled out of the room.

As she went through the outer doorway, Minna almost tripped over Pearl. She had not moved. She lay across the doorsill, her head buried in her arms. Minna sat down next to her and put her arms around her. They clung together in silence.

Finally, Pearl spoke. "I fell down. Then I lost you, so I ran back to the house. I was so scared. Chava came back for me. When she heard them coming, she hid me in the old rain barrel, just like Mama did when she was a little girl. But she didn't have time to hide herself. I could hear it. I could hear it all. Chava screamed. She screamed so, Minna. I didn't know what to do."

Minna hugged her sister tighter.

"I … I was afraid to help her. So, I stayed in there, hiding … and I listened … I was afraid, Minna. I could have …"

Minna put her hand under Pearl's chin and turned her face upwards, knowing instinctively how important her next words were. Looking into her sister's eyes, she said firmly, each word clear and strong, "You could have done nothing. You're too little. You would have been killed, too."

Pearl shivered.

Minna thought to herself, if it had been me, could I have done anything? Could I have saved Chava if I had gone back?

Minna felt something pushing her away. She looked up, startled. It was Mama. She shook Pearl, screaming, "It was you! It was you she went back for! Because of you, your sister lies dead on the floor. Like my sister before her, Chava's dead… My Chava's dead…and it's your fault!"

Pearl fainted, her small body becoming limp. Mama didn't even look. She turned and went back inside.

Minna wanted to pick her up, but she was frozen in place, unable to move her arms or her legs. Straining, she tried to move, sobbing in frustration. Yussel came and lifted Pearl easily. Carrying her in his arms, he went next door to a neighbor's to ask for help.

Slowly, Minna's paralysis ebbed. Finally she stood up and followed them.

When Pearl sat up, her eyes wavered. She hid her face in shame.

"It's all right," Minna repeated. "I know it wasn't your fault. You could have done nothing."

Pearl looked at Yussel for his judgment.

He nodded. "You could have done nothing."

Yussel thanked the neighbor and took Pearl home. Now there were many women crying and wailing over Chava's body. Tata and a group of men prayed in one corner of the room.

Pearl hid behind Minna as they approached Mama, but she didn't even look up. The two girls hovered uncertainly at the edge of the circle of women. After waiting for a moment, Minna took Pearl's hand and led the way into their bedroom. It was just as it had been before. The Russians, it seemed, hadn't bothered to enter. In the corner, Chava's old dress was flung upon the featherbed, just as she had left it.

Minna fixed their bed and lay down with Pearl. The two girls huddled together, their arms around each other. Chava had always slept with them. As they usually did, they rolled to one side, to make room for her.

Minna shut her eyes. Then she opened them suddenly. She looked around the room, praying it had all been a dream. Chava would be there, next to her in the bed. She'd laugh and… From the next room, she could hear the women wailing and the men praying. It was true. It was all true. She shut her eyes again.

All night, she dozed, and then awakened in terror. Only the anguished sounds of the mourners in the next room were real. And Pearl, clasped in her arms. Finally, near dawn, she slept.

When Minna opened her eyes the next morning, she saw Mama kneeling by the bed. "Are you all right, both of you?" she asked. "I couldn't find you in the night. Yussel said to look in here. Are you all right?"

Minna eyed at her cautiously, remembering the words she had screamed at Pearl last night. Her voice sounded as it usually did. Her hair hung down her back instead of in its usual neat bun, her eyes were red and puffy, but otherwise, she was Mama, as always.

Pearl shrank from her, but Mama didn't even notice. She continued speaking, as if to herself. "It is…it must be…God's will that we have lost our Chava. Now she'll keep the angels company."

She stood up. "Come, girls. It's time to get up. Soon, we'll be taking Chava to lie beside Bubbe."

Minna and Pearl sat up.

"I've been sewing Chava's white linen shroud all night. The ladies of the Hevra Kadisha have been here and they've performed *tahara.* They've cleansed and purified Chava so she'll meet God as she came into the world. Reb Kilem gave us a coffin. Chava need not be buried on a board, as Bubbe was." Mama's voice broke. 'Now we'll follow Chava to her eternal home in the graveyard and lay her to rest. May God welcome her diamond soul."

Minna and Pearl followed Mama into the other room. They entered reluctantly, rubbing their eyes and straightening the dresses they had slept in. Minna grasped Pearl's hand tightly. She knew her sister would never forget Mama's words of last night. Yet Mama was oblivious. She shook her head.

The two girls gazed around the room. The table had been righted, the plates and flatware put away. All the chairs and stools that were unbroken had been stacked in one corner of the room. Mama's dowry chest had a big gash in it, but otherwise, it was undamaged.

Near the door, they saw a large wooden coffin held together by wooden pegs perched on the floor. Gathered around it ready to pick it up and carry it to the graveyard were Tata, Yussel, and other men from the *shul.* The women waited, their heads bowed, to follow Chava to her final resting place.

Minna and Pearl waited, too. They found themselves standing next to the old broom seller. She nodded at the girls, saying sadly, "She was like the spring, your sister."

Minna looked at the coffin. How could Chava be there, in a wooden box? Chava, who had danced in the wind and felt the sunshine upon her face? Minna blinked her eyes to stop the tears. That's not her, she thought. The wailing of the women grew louder.

Like a mechanical doll, Minna followed the procession, holding Pearl's hand as they walked together. Both girls were mute as the women lamented. Mama was the loudest. She sobbed and cried out, her head bent like an old woman's. As they passed other houses, the families within came to their doors and bowed in respect. Many joined the procession.

At the cemetery, Chava's coffin was laid upon the grass next to

Bubbe's stone. The rabbi, joined by the men, said *Kaddish.* Behind them, the women wept loudly.

After the prayers, each man took a shovel and began to dig the grave. Mama took a shovel, too. Minna waited till Yussel had finished. Then she held out her hand for his shovel.

As she dug into the soft earth, flinging the green grass to the side, she thought of yesterday. She remembered how she and Chava had sat by Bubbe's grave, picking a garland of forget-me-nots. I'll never forget you, Chava, she thought, not if I live to be a hundred years old.

After the grave was dug, Chava's coffin was set into the earth. Those with shovels covered the grave with dark, rich soil. Each shovelful made a heavy sound that reverberated in Minna's ears. For a moment, she felt Chava was being smothered, dying anew under the earth's blanket. She imagined she could hear Chava's voice, crying, "Let me out! Let me out!"

After the coffin was completely covered, the mourners left the grave, their steps heavy and their heads bowed. Minna watched them go. Mama held Pearl's hand and leaned on Yussel's shoulder, her body shaking with the force of her sobs. Pearl was pale and stoic. Tata walked alone, straight and proud, only his head inclined as he muttered words in Hebrew.

Minna stayed behind for a few moments, knowing the neighbors would stay with Mama. Even though every family had been scarred by the pogrom, Chava was the only young girl to die. The whole village shared their grief.

Once she was home, Minna knew she would have to remain there for seven days of mourning as they sat *shiva* for Chava. She crept to Bubbe's grave and sat in her favorite position by the side of the stone with her head against it. She had sat that way last night. Now, as then, she sought comfort.

"You and Chava are together now, Bubbe," Minna said out loud. As she spoke the words, she felt a surge of pain and she began to sob. For a long time, she lay against the grave, grieving.

Finally she sat up. "I'll be the big sister now, Bubbe. I'll take care of Pearl and help Mama." Her eyes filled with tears. Still catching her breath, she bent over and picked a bouquet of forget-me-nots.

As Minna gazed at the delicate blue flowers, she felt anew the injustice of Chava's death. The soft spring wind and the lush smell of the new green grass seemed an insult. Picturing Chava as she had been the day before, her hand clenched, nearly crushing the flowers,

Nothing will ever be the same, she thought.

In her mind, she heard Bubbe replying, 'So what, little Minna. Do you want the whole world to stop? Thanks be to God, life goes on.'

I won't thank God, Minna thought. I'll never thank God. God is cruel, like the *goyim*, and like Mama was last night. God is like Tata. He doesn't help.

She opened her hand, allowing the flowers to fall gently onto the raw dirt above Chava's grave. "These are for you, Chava. May you dance with the angels."

The family sat *shiva* for Chava for a week. They remained at home, expressing their sorrow the traditional way. Minna wore no shoes, ripped her dress, sat upon the floor rather than upon a chair, and did not comb her hair or look into a mirror. Tata, Yussel, and eight other men made a *minyan* twice a day to pray for Chava's soul.

Mama was silent. Occasionally, she spoke to others, but even then she seemed far away. She paused before she replied to a question or a comment, as if returning from a far country. She rarely cried, and hardly slept.

Pearl, poor Pearl, was equally quiet. She watched Mama anxiously, always the first to jump up and help. Minna knew she still blamed herself for Chava's death.

She tried to talk to her about it several times, but Pearl was unresponsive. Only Mama, Minna thought, can make it all right. Yet she could say nothing to her. All she could do was to watch out for her sister. Every night in bed, she held her tightly before they fell asleep.

Tata was as he had always been. It was Yussel who was different. He had always been separated from his sisters. As the only boy, he had been favored. He had received better portions of food and like Tata, stood above all household duties. Now he sat with Pearl, helped Mama, and had long talks with Minna about Chava. He no longer copied everything Tata did or pretended to finger his beard like a man. Instead, Minna thought, it's as if he really has become a man.

It was Yussel that Minna told about Chava's last words. "'It was the same…' That's what she said. Maybe she meant that blonde man, the one who brought us water. Maybe he was one of the murderers. I didn't like him from the beginning."

"You'll tell me if you see him again?" Yussel asked grimly.

Minna hesitated. "Why? What will you do?"

"I don't know. I'll do something. I must, for Chava."

"You can do nothing, Yussel. We don't know that's what she meant. Even if she did, what can we do? There's no one to tell. There's no one who will listen. It will just be the worse for us and for everyone in the village. There's no justice here for her."

"Tell me when you see him," Yussel repeated stubbornly.

Minna decided she would look out for the man, but she wouldn't tell Yussel. What was the good? There was no way they could punish him. Yussel would be the only one to suffer.

Sometimes, Minna was so angry that she wanted revenge no matter what it cost. The thought of it was like a fire burning. She pictured herself accusing the man. She saw the whole village stoning him, calling him vile names. On other occasions, she convinced herself to be cautious and reserve judgment. In the end, she decided to wait and see. In any case, she could do nothing until she saw him.

After the week of intense mourning, Minna found she was busier than she had ever been. Mama had to go to her stall every day, for it was her work that supported the family. So it was Minna, forced to assume Chava's responsibilities as well as her own, who helped prepare the food, fetched the water, cleaned the house, washed the clothes in the river, and looked after Pearl.

She often tried to speak to Pearl about Chava's death but her sister remained uncharacteristically silent. Only occasionally, did she forget and tease Minna in the old way or laugh aloud. With Mama, she was timid and wordless.

In the mornings, Minna and Pearl resumed their lessons with Tata. Although he considered it unnecessary and improper for them to learn Hebrew, they were taught to read and write in Yiddish. He was a stern as ever, striking them on the hands with a stick when they did not pay attention and striking them even harder when they made mistakes. Yet his expression never changed. As always, he did not share in the family's daily routine.

The days were punctuated by the saying of *Kaddish*, the prayer for Chava's soul, every morning and every evening. At those times, and at night, before she closed her eyes, Minna allowed the realization of her death to touch her. Memories of her sister and all they had shared overwhelmed her in an unbearable flood of loss and regret. During the rest of day, she did not have time to mourn. There was too much to be done.

CHAPTER 2

After many long weary weeks, Mama came home from the market place with a new expression on her face. Minna was reminded of the time she had decided to sell ribbons instead of the more traditional baskets at her stall. She had looked the same way when she first broached her idea. Perhaps, Minna thought, Mama is hatching a new plan.

At dinner, as Tata was leaving the table, Mama held up her hand. "Stay, my *mann*. I have something I wish to say."

Reluctantly, Tata sat back in his chair. The others waited.

"I have been thinking," she began slowly. "Ever since Chava…I have been thinking. And I have decided something. I have decided we must leave this land of sorrow, where children are killed and we are ashamed to hold our heads up in the streets. We must leave and go to *der goldener medina*, the golden land. We must go to America."

Mama spoke quickly. "So many have gone…the shoemaker and his family…the seller of straw and his family…the peddler, and his brother… Neighbor Rivka told me of a letter she had from her son. He says he has chicken every day and a carpet of velvet on his floors as rich as the *shayner Yiden* here have on their tables. But most of all, he is a *mensch* when he walks the street. He says everyone is free to come and go as they please."

She leaned forward and spoke firmly. "I won't be afraid anymore. I won't see my children killed. I want them to be *Amerikane kinder*, to grow up healthy and strong. I think …"

Tata stood up abruptly, his voice harsh and angry. "What are you to suggest such a *farposhket* idea? Are you a crazy woman? To leave and go to the land of the Godless! Are we to go running in search of velvet? What is *gelt* to us?" He spat the words out.

Mama stood up. "I care about the *kinder*. I, a mother, I can only say what I know." She hit her chest. "Here, there is no life. There is only death for them and for us."

Tata marched out of the house in a fury, slamming the door. Minna, Pearl, and Yussel remained seated, their eyes wide with questions.

Mama watched Tata leave, her lips pinched and her color rising. She said slowly and firmly, "We will go to *der goldener medina*." She rose and began clearing the plates. No one dared say a word.

After they had helped Mama, the three children went into their room. They sat together on the featherbed, Pearl leaning against Minna and Yussel sitting next to them.

"What do you think, Yussel?" Minna asked.

"I think Mama is right. We must leave here. Soon I'll have to enlist in the Tsar's army. I'll be a soldier for the rest of my life…at least, until I'm killed. And you, both of you, might suffer as Chava did."

Pearl huddled closer to Minna.

Minna hugged her. "But … what do you think it's like? Are the streets really paved in gold? Is everyone a *shayner Yid* there, with velvet carpets and chicken every day? And Yussel, why is Tata so angry?"

Yussel considered her questions. "I don't know about the streets, the velvet or the chicken, but I think it is a place to be free … to be a *mensch*. They don't have *shtetls* there. Jews and everybody can go wherever they want. That's what I heard. And Tata… I think he's afraid."

"Afraid? Tata?"

"It must be very different there. I've noticed before when Tata doesn't know about something, the first thing is, he hates it." He looked at Minna. "God must live in America, too, don't you think?"

Minna was silent.

"Yes, of course, he does." Yussel answered himself. "God is everywhere."

"I'm afraid, too," Pearl whispered. "How will I visit Bubbe and Chava in America?"

Minna's eyes filled with tears. Chava, she thought. Who will plant the flowers on your grave and talk to you if we leave. You'll be alone. And Bubbe … How can I manage without you?

"They'll be with us," Yussel said dubiously. "Like the angels, I'm sure they can be anywhere, for they live in the sky. We'll have to get used to speaking to them in America instead of by their stones on the green grass."

"Oh." Pearl sighed, content.

The next day, Minna went to Chava's grave after filling her water bucket at the well. Already, the forget-me-nots she had transplanted a few weeks ago had taken root. Their leaves helped to disguise the rough earth.

Chava, she thought, what if we go to America and leave you behind? Will we lose you? Will you lose us? She looked over at Bubbe's grave questioningly.

Bubbe's words came into her thoughts as clear as a bell. 'So, little Minna, where I am, sitting with the angels, you think it makes a difference whether you're here or there? You think you could leave me behind if such a great adventure comes your way? Chava will come, too. Where else do we belong, but with our family? We'll always be with you — here or in *der goldener medina*.'

Minna smiled. Then she continued in a low voice, "Last night, Tata and Mama were as silent as stars in the sky. This morning, he left without saying a word and Mama's eyes were red. Maybe we won't go, after all."

'Child,' Bubbe said, 'When your Mama makes up her mind, it's as good as done.'

It was true. When Mama did make up her mind, it always happened. She remembered the time she decided Chava should have a blue dress to match her eyes, the time she took Minna to the Rabbi for a special blessing when she was so sick with fever, the time she managed to buy Yussel a new pair of boots.

"We'll go. I think we really will go," Minna said aloud.

She stood up and went to the small, wooded glade behind the cemetery. With a stick, she dug some violets and planted them with the forget-me-nots on Chava's grave. She smoothed the dirt gently and sprinkled water upon it. Picking up her now half-empty bucket, she trotted off to the well again.

Whenever she went there to fill her bucket, Minna looked for the blonde man, but she never saw him. Each day, her anger grew, although she still hadn't decided what she'd do if he actually did appear. As time passed, he became a *dybbuk* in her mind, a terrifying evil spirit, whose power grew more menacing daily.

It's because he's a *goy*, Mina thought. They're all the same. She found herself distrusting and hating the other peasants she saw in the market place, although a few had been kind to her. Sometimes she felt that being a Jew was a punishment. Sometimes she blamed the *goyim* and sometimes she blamed God, Who had made the Jews.

Although she never talked about her anger at God, one sunny afternoon at the graveyard, she did tell Bubbe about her hatred of the *goyim*. Bubbe replied with words she had used in the past. 'So *nu*, there's good and there's bad, even among the *goyim*. I've told you a hundred times about the woman in Vilna who was so kind to me and the *goyishe* lawyer who helped your Zayde when we first married. People are people and in *der goldener medina*, they are still people. It may be different there, but they still have the *goy* and the Jew. If they can't get along there, where's the hope? Don't make up your mind yet, little Minna. You have, God willing, many more years before you join me. Much will happen to you. The *goy* and the Jew — remember this — both are born in pain, both die in sorrow. So how different are they?"

Minna often thought of Bubbe's words and wondered if she was right. Yet she never stopped looking for the man. Her anger against him remained constant. Yussel asked her more than once if she had seen him, but she could always answer "no" honestly.

Tata and Mama continued to talk about America. Or rather, Mama talked and Tata left the house. When he started remaining in order to voice his objections, the others felt it was a positive sign.

Tata said such things as, "How will we go to this promised land? *Gelt* doesn't grow in the fields. We'll have to purchase tickets for the boat, pay off the police so we can sneak across the border, and provide food for the long journey. Every one knows that the food on the boat is *trayf*, poisonous to us. Already, we'll become like the *goyim*. And in this magical land, where shall we go? What will we do? It is written that the troubles you know are better than the troubles you don't know. Shall we travel across the world to starve when we have a life here?"

Each time, Mama replied by saying, "The Lord will provide."

Minna worried. It was well and good to say that the Lord would provide, but what did that mean? Had He provided so well before?

One warm summer evening, Mama arrived home late with a triumphant expression on her face. All through the blessing, Minna watched her, trying to guess what had happened. The others, noticing the gleam in Mama's eyes, watched her too, anticipating a pronouncement.

As soon as they began to eat, Mama leaned forward in her seat. "I have news!" she exclaimed, in an electrifying tone.

The three children put down their forks and looked at her. Tata stared at her dubiously, but he, too, waited to hear what she had to tell.

With a flourish, Mama pulled a letter out of the inner pocket of her dress. "I have received a letter," she said importantly. "A letter from America!"

All were stunned. A letter from America! It was as if a holy angel had come to dinner. A letter from America at their table! Reverently, they examined the envelope she passed around the table. Minna touched the bright stamps gingerly.

Mama cleared her throat. "I wrote to my cousin Avraim, Bubbe's sister's son, in New York, and he wrote back! He says he's doing very well. Already he owns a store!"

Minna gasped. She could remember Avraim, a tall, slim youth who was considered a *grauber jung*, a vulgar fellow, because he could not learn Torah. Three years ago, he had gone to America and the consensus of the family, except for his mother, was "good riddance!" If he, the *grauber jung*, already had a store, who was to say what they might not do? Even Tata looked more optimistic than he had before.

There was a long silence, as everyone absorbed Mama's news.

Tata cleared his throat. "A store, eh? That *grauber jung* already has a store? Well, well…"

"He says he'll pay our passage if we agree to work in the store with him for a year. He remembers my ribbons! He'll find us a place to live, too. He wants us all to work in the store."

"It must be a very big store," Yussel mused, awestruck.

"Well, if it's family, that's a different story. Then we're not alone in a strange land," Tata said pensively.

That was all the encouragement Mama needed. She continued triumphantly. "I've found out all we need is enough money to get to Hamburg for the boat, including extra to pay off the police so we can get across the border into Germany. If we try to get passports, it'll take months, a trip to the city, and more money. Instead, we'll go in a cart and take the train to Hamburg. But we also have to have money when we land. I have been figuring…and I think if we sell the stall, the house, and my dowry chest—we can't bring it with us, anyway—we might have, *eppes*, just enough."

Tata was silent. He didn't, as before, leave the house or yell. He simply listened as Mama continued. Their journey began to seem real.

Minna nudged Yussel, as if to say, "See, we are going." It was exciting to listen to Mama talk of what she would sell, who would buy, and how much *gelt* they needed. She wanted to stand up and shout "Hooray!" At the same time, it was frightening.

After Minna, Yussel, and Pearl were in bed, Mama and Tata continued talking far into the night. As they calculated costs and planned for the journey, Minna listened, unable to fall asleep.

Once she heard Tata say, "We should sell everything? Suppose America is not a golden land. Suppose it's not good to us. What then? There will be nothing to come home to."

Mama replied by once again painting her picture of their life in America. "You'll have a separate room for your studies," she promised. "After we find our feet, I'll buy a little store like Cousin Avraim, and you can sit, like King David, in your library. You'll be known as a *tzaddik*, a holy Jew, and scholars will come from miles around to sit at your feet. Who else is so wise?"

Tata said nothing.

Mama continued, her voice becoming more insistent. "Here, you are known as the wisest man in the shtetl next to the Rabbi, and even he consults you. In America, they have need of your wisdom more. I can see it. There'll be lines outside our house for you. I'll *kvell* to be married to such a man! So *nu*, for a year we'll all work and save our money. Then, your library will come. Yussel, too, will be a man of learning. The girls, they will marry like princesses …"

"And you?" Tata asked harshly. "What of you?"

"I'll be happy as the Queen of Sheba. All day long, I'll dance and sing when I think of my family. You'll see how it will be."

"I will have to take all my books with me. I can't leave my books behind. Who's to say what books they have there, in that strange land."

"We'll pack them," Mama soothed. "They'll go into a large straw trunk. The lady in the stall next to mine has just the thing. In between, we'll put our featherbeds and clothes, so your books, they'll be protected. We'll take them all, every single one."

"Well..."

"Don't worry," Mama said softly. "I'll take care of everything. I know it is good to leave. I am sure."

Minna closed her eyes. She had confidence in Mama's ability to arrange their lives. As she lay in the dark, she tried to imagine America.

The pictures in her mind kept getting mixed up with an illustration in a book she had once picked up at the bookseller's stall. The old man who owned it was kind and let her spend hours poring over his wares. This particular picture, from a book in an unknown language, showed tall golden buildings on a wide green hill surrounded by a brilliant blue sky. The spires of the buildings sparkled like diamonds against the sky. In the far distance, a beautiful woman rode a graceful white horse. Her long golden hair floated in the wind behind her. Minna had gazed at the picture for a long time. When she went back the next day, the book was gone and she never saw it again, yet she remembered every detail clearly.

Tonight, it came to her mind as clear and sharp as if she were still holding it in her hands. Maybe America, she thought, is like the picture, and everything will be clean, new, and beautiful. All the people will look like kings and queens and we'll live in golden palaces. She smiled as she fell asleep.

Once the money for the tickets arrived from Cousin Avraim, and the news of their departure became common knowledge, the family was invaded. Many salesmen arrived to sell them tickets "direct to New York." Even at the cheapest cost of $34 per person, the commission for a whole family was well worth their efforts. Each tried to persuade Mama that his tickets were the cheapest, his boat the cleanest and safest. Each had horror stories to tell of the other boats and agents.

Mama listened carefully. She had heard stories of other families landing in London instead of New York City and of deathly illness in the filth of the boats. After she listened to what each agent had to say, she asked questions. Then she visited every family who had a relative in America to ask their opinion of the various boat lines. Finally, she made her decision.

After she bought the tickets, she stored them in her dowry

chest, a place of great honor. They were often taken out and examined by members of the family. It seemed miraculous to Minna that such flimsy bits of paper could take them so far away.

Although it was many weeks before they were prepared to leave, the time passed quickly. Mama sold the stall, the house, and her chest. She added the stools and the table—indeed, almost everything except for her biggest, sturdiest cooking pot and their featherbeds. The rest of their possessions were to be taken away on the day of their departure.

One evening, Mama marched ceremoniously to the back yard, took a large ladle and scraped a small hole under their one scrawny tree. She reached in and pulled out a battered tin box wrapped carefully with a piece of old cloth. On the table in front of the whole family, she opened the box. It contained many kopecks, dull and lusterless with age.

"I've saved a little through the years," she said modestly. "A *bissel* here, a *bissel* there, it adds up."

With the extra money, Mama was able to hire *el mole rachamim*, women who would say prayers over the family graves. She left enough money for five years, promising to send more from America and binding the women with an unbreakable oath. Then she went alone to the cemetery. She spent several hours there, and Minna assumed that she, like the rest of the family, was saying farewell.

In the last days before their departure, Minna and Pearl went to the cemetery often. Pearl was silent during these visits, huddling on the ground near Chava's grave. Often, large tears rolled down her cheeks. Minna, on the other hand, had far too much to say. Over and over, she begged Bubbe to confirm that she and Chava would accompany the family to *der goldener medina.* Always, she left feeling reassured, although within a few hours, she'd again feel that she was abandoning the two she loved best in the world.

Finally, it was the night before they were to start their travels. Mama had been cooking for days, making enough *kuchlech*, diamond-shaped wafers made of sugar, flour, and water, to take with them to eat on the way and on the boat in case their food was not *kosher* as had been promised. Part of their luggage was a tremendous sack holding pounds of kuchlech. Finally, Mama put the last one in and tied it at the neck with a strong leather thong.

When Mama had begun cooking the *kuchlech*, the scent had

been enticing. They had all wanted a taste. By the time she was finished, the sweet odor pervading the house had become hateful. They dreaded eating the wafers on their trip. It was odd, Minna thought, how one could become sick of something without even tasting it.

Tata kept opening the huge straw trunk to make sure his books had been packed properly. Yussel made it his job to wrap and carry the heavy brass candlesticks that Mama lit every Friday night for the Sabbath. Pearl had inherited one bedraggled doll from her two sisters. She carried it everywhere, afraid it would be left behind when they departed.

Minna had two treasures. One was a china cup given to her by Bubbe. Although its rim was slightly cracked, it had a painting of forget-me-nots upon its side. Minna had never used it, but she often took it out to admire. For the trip, she wrapped it carefully in a large clean rag and put it with her clothing.

Her other treasure was a new dress, re-made from the one Chava had left on the bed. Chava's beautiful blue dress had been stained with her blood, so Mama had burned it. Then the two of them had worked long hours re-sewing and cutting down her old one. It was made of a heavy, wool-like material, too hot for summer, but Minna was happy to wear it. When she did, Chava seemed closer.

That evening, they attended a farewell dinner given by friends and neighbors. It was an occasion for many prayers, toasts, and tears. Minna and her best friend, Hodel, whispered sadly to each other all evening. The only toast Minna could remember the next day was given by the Rabbi. A strong-faced, gray-haired man, he said to Tata, "May you and your family remain faithful to the old ways in the new land." Then he prayed for their health and happiness.

When the evening was almost over, Minna slipped out to say farewell to Chava and Bubbe one more time. At twilight, the cemetery was cool and peaceful compared to the noisy, overheated room she had just left.

Kneeling on the grass between the two graves, Minna touched each, committing to memory its texture and shape. She breathed the fresh grass smell of the cemetery and patted the forget-me-nots still blooming above each grave, memorizing every part of her surroundings.

"Although you will be with me, I'll miss seeing you here," she said softly. "Someday, when I'm old, I'll come back and plant more flowers." She bowed her head and kissed the familiar stones. "Farewell," she whispered.

The next morning, the family started out bright and early. They borrowed an old cart and a sad-looking horse to carry them to the nearest railroad station, where they would continue their journey. Pearl was allowed to sit in the cart with the luggage because she was so light. Clutching her doll tightly, she sat up straight, pale and determined, as she stared at the road ahead.

The rest of the family walked behind. Yussel led the plodding horse, to be picked up by a friend of its owner arriving on the same train. Tata kept a protective hand on the box containing his books. Mama walked firmly, her steps steady and unfaltering. A small cloth pouch, containing the precious tickets and the family's money, hung around her neck inside her dress.

Minna ran back and forth from the front to the back of the cart. The whole village had assembled to watch them leave and one of them yelled, "Don't run so much, Minna. You'll be worn out before you get to Hamburg!"

Minna, too excited to heed the words, waved at their neighbors, helped Yussel load the horse, and whispered to Pearl. Only when Hodel ran out to say a last farewell did her eyes fill with tears.

Hodel hugged her and thrust a small bouquet into her hands. "Some forget-me-nots to take to America," she said.

Minna held the flowers tightly to her chest and turned away from the village. A long, steep hill led towards the station. As the family reached the top, they stopped and looked back. There, below, the whole *shtetl* was spread out, perfect in every detail yet tiny as a child's miniature.

In the distance, they could see their friends turning and making their way back to their homes. The market square with its stalls, the well, the street where they lived, the graveyard…all were sharply etched against the sky.

As they watched, a slight breeze caused the dust to rise. A shifting curtain of tan and yellow obscured their view, hiding the small world they were leaving. As the dust settled back upon the road, the *shtetl* could be seen again, as faded and indistinct as a sepia print. The family turned and silently continued their journey.

CHAPTER 3

Minna's first glimpse of the train startled her. It appeared to be a monster, roaring as it screeched to a grating stop at the station. Steam billowed from its mouth. Suspiciously, Minna watched the passengers getting off. To her surprise, they seemed to be in good spirits, many of them laughing and talking.

All the Rubens tried to push the straw box with Tata's books to the train. Grunting and groaning, they had almost reached the train steps when a conductor intervened.

"And where do you think you're taking that?" he asked sternly.

"They're my books, your honor," Tata mumbled, hugging the box protectively.

"Not allowed! If you want to bring that…box…on the train, you'll have to take it to the baggage car."

Tata looked desperately at Mama. She stepped forward. Meekly touching the conductor's coat sleeve, she started to explain about the books in Russian. "So you see," she concluded, "we have to take them with us."

The conductor pulled out a large watch and consulted it gravely. "Like it or not, the box must go in the baggage car. You have three minutes till the train leaves."

Mama looked at Tata despairingly. Luckily, he hadn't entirely trusted the straw box. His most important books were in a separate sack. This he clutched to himself so ferociously that even the conductor dared not say a word.

The official spotted the large bag of *kuchlech*. 'That's for the baggage car, too," he boomed.

"It's our food," Mama screamed. "Do you want my children to

starve? For days, we are to ride without food?" Without waiting for an answer, she dragged the bag up the steps of the train. Minna and Pearl rushed to help.

The whistle blew. Glaring at them, the conductor shrugged and pointed toward the back of the train. Tata and Yussel strained to push the box to the baggage car while the conductor lounged against the station sign. Passengers already on the train gazed at them disinterestedly. Finally, a few young men waiting at the station lounged over to lend a hand.

Minna, now sitting inside with Mama, Pearl, and the *kuchlech*, peered through the window. One of the young men who helped with the box looked familiar. She leaned out to see him more clearly. Although the men grouped around Tata's box were already at the other end of the platform, she could tell he was blonde. Could it be he, Chava's man, the devil?

Abruptly, Mama yanked her inside. "What are you—a *meshugge* daughter? Do you want to get killed? Put your head inside and stay still," she yelled.

Minna sat back in her seat, her neck rigid as she tried to look out the window without attracting Mama's attention. She stared grimly at as much of the narrow platform as she could see, but the man was out of sight. She'd never know.

Suddenly, with a last blast of its whistle, the train started with a jerk. "*Gottenyu*!" Mama cried. She jumped up and stared out the window. "I don't see them," she moaned, wringing her hands.

The conductor who had spoken to them before came into the car. "What's the matter this time?" he demanded.

"My man, my *zun*," Mama screamed frantically. "Where are they? They're not on the train."

"They're coming," the conductor said angrily and hurried down the aisle.

Mama stared after him. "How can they be coming if they're not here?" she asked, her voice rising. Nervously, she touched the outside of her dress to make certain that the pouch with their tickets and money was still there.

A man sitting across the aisle said calmly, "Don't worry. They're probably walking up inside the train."

"Inside the train?" Mama gasped. "You can walk all the way inside the train? From the baggage car you can walk?"

The man nodded condescendingly. "Haven't you ever been on a

train before?"

Mama shook her head.

Minna shivered. If Tata and Yussel were lost and Mama had never been on a train before… She clutched Mama's dress nervously. How would they ever get to America if they weren't all together?

Automatically, Mama pushed her hand away and turned to stare at the far end of the car, watching for Tata and Yussel. Her hands clenched, she held herself stiffly, her whole body expressing her apprehension.

Finally, Tata appeared, followed by Yussel. They swayed with the movement of the train. As they came closer, Minna saw the same fearful look in their eyes as had been in Mama's.

"You're here! I thought you'd been left behind," Mama cried.

"We walked up the train," Tata said, attempting an air of nonchalance.

Yussel made no pretense. His nervousness was evident. When he sat down next to Minna, she noticed large drops of perspiration under his *yarmulke*. She patted his hand and directed his gaze to the window.

Pearl stood against Minna's legs and the three of them watched the houses and farms flashing by. Tata carefully stored his sack of books on the rack across from him, standing up to make sure it was wedged securely every time the train rounded a curve. Mama leaned back in her seat, holding tightly to the neck of the bag of *kuchlech*, as if for security.

The train ride took many days. The family ate and slept on the same narrow seats. Drinks and fruit could be purchased at each station and that, with the kuchlech and some cheese, was ample food.

By the time they reached the end of their journey near the German border, everyone was glad to disembark. Minna especially wanted to run and jump. "I've been sitting for my whole life," she complained.

At first, the ground heaved and rocked under her feet. Minna clutched at Yussel's arm in dismay.

He shook his head. He was having the same problem. "I think it's always like this after a long journey," he explained.

Tata's straw box had already been pushed out upon the platform. Luckily, it had not broken. By piling the sack of *kuchlech* and all their other bags and parcels on top of it, the family discovered they could just barely manage to half-push, half-carry their possessions. They stopped often to rest.

Mama had the name and address of a man who would take them across the border into Germany for a modest payment. She looked at the others. "You stay here at the station," she commanded. "I'll go find the man."

It took a few hours. By the time she returned, Minna had discovered she could run and skip again although the earth still shivered under her feet. They had begun to worry when Mama finally reappeared, followed by a shabby looking man who inclined his head toward them.

"This is Leopold," Mama said. "He'll take us where we want to go," she added quietly, after making sure that the platform was deserted.

"First of all," Leopold insisted, "You must send the straw basket ahead of you. Here at the station, you can check it through to Hamburg. It will arrive before you, so you can pick it up when you get off the German train." It was apparent from his reassuring tone that Leopold had said the same things many times to other refugees.

"Those are my books." Tata shook his head stubbornly. 'They go with me."

"Books, *schnooks*! You want to go to *der goldener medina*, don't you? If you want me to take you, you can't carry that big box with you." Leopold folded his arms, leaned back on his heels, and began to whistle under his breath. "Make up your mind. It's one or the other," he added.

Tata started forward angrily, but Mama stopped him. Her hand upon his arm, she led him aside, talking earnestly in whispers. The three children watched anxiously. Were they to return home because of Tata's books?

Finally he nodded.

Hurriedly, before Tata could change his mind, Mama gestured to Leopold. The two of them walked over to the ticket window inside the station and arranged to send the straw box ahead. Mama turned her back and added the receipt to her secret pouch.

Crossing the border was not at all the way Minna had thought it would be. She had imagined a tall stone wall guarded by soldiers for the whole distance between Russian and Germany. Several times, she had asked Mama how they were to cross such a barrier, but the only answer she had ever received was, "The man. The man will help us."

As they followed Leopold, Minna still wondered. Would they have to climb the wall? Perhaps they would dig under it or make a hole in it. Either way, it would take a long time. She gripped Pearl's hand, so she could help her when the time came.

Leopold led the family along a winding path to the forest. They walked for hours. Several times they heard rifle shots in the distance.

Leopold smiled at the shots. "That's good. That's the frontier post. If they're shooting there, we're safe here."

Minna was still looking for the impassable boundary wall when Leopold stopped. "You're in Germany now," he said. "We have crossed the border."

Minna looked around. It wasn't any different.

Mama must have had the same doubts, for she refused to pay Leopold until she had proof that they were really in Germany.

Finally Leopold pointed impatiently at Yussel. "All right," he snapped. "Send the boy further up the road and he'll see a sign in German."

"How will I know it's German?" Yussel asked.

"The letters will be different. Now run, boy, run! I don't have all day to stand and wait for you."

Yussel looked at Mama for permission. She gestured to him, so he ran down the road. In no time at all, he was back, panting so hard he couldn't speak. Instead, he nodded.

Mama paid Leopold. He gave them directions to the train station and slid back into the woods.

Before he disappeared, he stopped and called back, "*Sholom Aleichem.*"

"*Aleichem Sholom*," Minna called after him.

As the family walked several miles to the railroad station, Minna looked around dubiously. It didn't seem possible they were in a different country. So far, she thought, Germany is the same as home. For the first time, she began to wonder if America would be like home, too. She stifled her doubts. She forced herself to remember the picture of the castle and the lady.

The train in Germany was very much like the train in Russia, except that it was cleaner and the conductors spoke German instead of Russian. German, Minna learned, was a lot like Yiddish. This made her feel a slightly more comfortable.

The trip took several days. They arrived in Hamburg in the middle of a summer storm. The *kuchlech* bag was appreciably lighter and their clothing more crumpled. Again, the ground rocked as they walked.

After picking up the straw box, the family managed to lug it to the Jewish Immigration House, where they were assisted by a group of volunteers from an organization called Hiverein. They were given rolls and coffee. After registering for their ship, it was suggested they board immediately, as departure was at first light tomorrow morning.

This part of the trip was a blur to Minna. Tired and stiff from so many days on the train, she struggled on, pulling Pearl with her. The rain poured down, making it impossible to see more than a few feet ahead. She followed Yussel blindly, hardly noticing the city streets as she worried about the ship. She wondered, would it be like the train with many cars so that one could walk from one end to the other? How, she asked herself, did one ship stop from bumping into another ship? She knew, of course, that the ocean was made of water, like the river at home, but when people told her it was larger than the whole country of Russia, she didn't believe them. That was impossible! The best she could do was to picture a very wide river with banks on both sides. The boat, she thought, would sail down the middle until they arrived in America.

When they finally saw the ship, Minna was amazed. "It's so big," she marveled.

Mama, on the other hand, felt it was all too small. "On this, I cross the ocean? *Gottenyu*, we'll be tossing like the salt in my salt box when I stir it in the soup," she exclaimed.

"Since when have you become an expert on the sea?" Tata asked. "God willing, we'll arrive at this promised land of yours. If God, He is not willing, we could go on a ship the size of Ararat and still sink into the sea."

Mama nodded grimly.

Yussel gripped his burden tightly and set his mouth. He put his arm around Minna. Minna was grateful for his support, even though she realized Yussel, too, was afraid and unable to speak.

Two sailors hoisted their luggage aboard and led them farther and farther down to what seemed to be the very bottom of the ship. On the deck, the rain almost obscured any sight of the water far below, so, as they kept descending, it was hard to realize they were actually on a boat. It might have been a giant building, Minna thought, if there was such a thing, a building so big.

One thing that made it very different from any place she had ever been was the unpleasant odors that became more pronounced as they descended deeper and deeper. There was a salty tar-like smell, which she found out later was the ropes, and, as they came closer, a heavy, stagnant odor that was somehow familiar.

As they entered a very large room, Minna identified the familiar odor. It was the smell of many people crowded together, of rotting food, of babies, and of the pit in the back of the house where they dumped their night soil, yet it was stronger than anything that Minna had before experienced. It was so thick, she thought, drawing back, it was like a wall barring their path.

Even Mama halted in dismay, momentarily overcome by the noise, the darkness, and the powerful odor. There was so much confusion that Minna couldn't register where they were going. She and Pearl followed Yussel as he followed Tata, who followed Mama. They passed rows and rows of berths, all filled with people. Later, Minna was to learn this was called a compartment. Three hundred fellow passengers were jammed into a small iron-floored room furnished with rows of bunks two tiers high. For now, it seemed impossible to make sense of anything she saw.

Finally, they stopped. One of the sailors pointed out their bunks, a place for their luggage, a small cabinet for food storage, and a clothes rack. Grimacing, the men dropped the straw box and hurried away.

The family hesitated, bewildered. The other passengers stared at them. Finally, ignoring the curious eyes, Mama assigned each of them to a bunk. Pearl was to sleep above Minna, Tata above Mama, and Yussel above a young boy who looked to be about Minna's age. He smiled as Yussel clambered over his head to inspect his bunk.

Stored in each berth was a tin lunch pail fitted with a cover that became a tin dish, a tin cup, a fork, and a spoon. The mattress, Minna noticed, as she lay upon it experimentally, emitted a strange, crackling sound.

"It's stuffed with dried seaweed and straw," the boy in the next bunk said, poking his head out at Minna. "That's why it makes that sound. That's why it smells, too."

"Oh."

"My name's Yankel. What's yours?"

Minna looked at Mama for permission to answer, but she was sitting wearily on her bunk, lost in thought.

"It's Minna," she replied shyly.

"*Oyf Kapores*!" he exclaimed. "This is some mess, isn't it?"

Minna, feeling slightly more comfortable as she sat in what was to be her own bunk, looked around surreptitiously. Almost every berth was filled. Across from her family was a woman with her husband and a small baby. Farther down, she saw a group of young men with strange clothing, speaking a language she didn't know. On the other side of the couple with the baby, another young man sat upon his bunk playing a concertina and singing softly. Above him, an old man mumbled aloud as he read and chanted in Hebrew. Minna could hear groups of people singing, others praying, infants crying, women chattering and men's voices raised as if in disagreement. She turned away and faced the wall.

Yankel reached across the side of his berth to hers and patted her arm reassuringly. "Don't worry," he said. "You'll get used to it. I've been here for a whole day and I hardly hear the noise any more." Deep circles under his eyes belied this statement.

Pearl crept down from her upper berth and sat next to Minna. She looked as if she was about to cry.

Minna forced herself to smile. "How many of these people do you think we'll know by the time we land?" she asked.

Pearl buried her head in Minna's lap.

"You look just like my little sister," Yankel said. "She's still at home in Russia, but I'm going to earn enough *gelt* so I can send for her soon. My father and I, we're going over first," he added proudly.

Pearl looked up.

"This is Pearl." Minna introduced. Then she pointed over Yankel's head. "That's my brother, Yussel."

Yussel, hearing the conversation, climbed down and stood protectively next to his sisters. After looking Yankel up and down, he asked, "Your name's Yankel?"

Yankel nodded.

"You're from Russia, too, eh? That means you're a *landsman*—or almost, anyway."

Mama looked up.

"Mama," Minna said, "this is Yankel. He's from Russia, too."

Mama examined Yankel. "So, where's your family?" she asked.

"My Mama's with the holy angels. My Tata's over there." Yankel pointed at the man Minna had already noticed, reading and chanting in Hebrew. "My sisters are with Bubbe until we can send for them. We're going first, you see."

By now, Tata had put his sack of books carefully down on his bunk. He took one out and held it caressingly. Yankel's father, not as oblivious as he had seemed, spoke to Tata in Hebrew. Tata replied. Immediately, the two men were immersed in conversation. Tata held out the book in his hands and Yankel's father scrutinized it with interest.

Yankel, who had been watching, breathed a sigh of relief. "I can see your father is a learned man, too. They'll talk together and build each *pilpul* until it becomes a mountain. Better your father than me!" Yankel smiled at Minna.

Minna smiled back. She began to describe their journey to Hamburg, gesturing widely as she spoke.

Mama asked the young mother where the washroom was.

She pointed to the right and shook her head. "I wouldn't call it a washroom," she sighed. "It's got cold salt water and only six toilets for all the ladies in this compartment. And the smell! It's better to use it at night, believe me. It's less crowded then."

Mama thanked her and went off to see for herself.

When she returned, her face was pale. "Feh! That place! It's *schmutzig* and it smells. I'll go back with you, Minna and Pearl, and then we should all try to sleep. It's late and we sail for America tomorrow."

Minna and Pearl followed Mama. It was disgusting, Minna thought. The toilets were like trenches. Running water was a novelty, but when it trickled out cold and salty, Minna knew she would prefer twenty trips to the well and Mama's stove to heat it in.

Everyone slept in their clothes. "At least for tonight," Mama had decided, looking at their neighbors. Later, they learned to hang a blanket over their bunks. That way, a minimum of privacy was achieved, although the sleeper's air became almost unbearably rancid and stagnant.

Despite the noise and the proximity of her new friend, Yankel,

Minna fell asleep almost immediately. Her last thought before she closed her eyes was to wonder how the sailors gathered seaweed to stuff her mattress. Perhaps they have seaweed farms, she decided drowsily.

First thing in the morning, Minna shut her eyes and talked to Bubbe and Chava in an undertone. There was so much noise in the compartment she knew no one else would hear her. "So, here we are," she said. "Two more weeks and we'll be in America. I didn't know so many people could fit in one place. I can hear the baby crying across from us and Tata saying his morning prayers from above. I keep thinking of *der goldener medina* and wondering what it will be like. Soon, we'll have our own little house or maybe, we'll have a palace." She had to laugh, picturing her family in a palace. "I miss you. Please stay with me so I won't be afraid." There was a pause and then she added, "I've found a new friend. His name's Yankel."

She jumped out of bed and looked overhead to see if Pearl was up yet. No, she was fast asleep. Mama was not in her bed and Yussel was gone, too. Yankel sat up. He, too, had slept in his clothes.

"Good morning," he said. "We're under weigh already."

"You mean, we're on the ocean?" Minna's voice rose.

"Not yet. We have to leave the harbor first. Can't you hear the throbbing of the motor?"

Minna stood up. Now she could hear the sound of motors and feel vibrations under her feet. The air in the compartment seemed even closer than it had last night.

"Can we go outside and watch?" she asked.

"I don't know."

"Let's try," Minna suggested, after checking on Pearl again. She followed Yankel as he threaded his way through the tiers of bunks. At the entrance to the compartment, a sailor stood guard.

"Can we go out?" Yankel asked.

The sailor shook his head, signifying that he didn't understand.

Yankel gestured at Minna and himself and then pointed upwards.

The sailor shook his head firmly.

The two of them headed slowly back to their bunks. Minna felt disheartened. Yankel hung his head.

On the way, they met Mama, who was carrying her tin pail

carefully. "The food is *kosher*," she said. "We can try to eat it, although it looks terrible." She extended the pail.

Minna sniffed and turned away in disgust. It was hard to tell exactly what was inside. Whatever it was certainly didn't look worth eating.

"I'll get hot water later and we'll have some tea," Mama said. Then she realized where Minna was. "What are you doing here? You should stay by your bunk."

"We thought we'd step out on deck," Yankel explained.

"Step out on deck!" Mama laughed bitterly. "Until we land, we are only allowed out of our compartment a few times. The fancy passengers above would be offended by the sight of us. Like cattle, we'll be led to the air. I heard all about it from the lady next to me on line for food."

Minna sighed. The two weeks were going to pass very slowly.

However, by the end of the day she felt better. Mama realized it was foolish to insist that Minna stay by her bunk, so she was able to meet some of the other passengers. One of them promised to start teaching her English from a book she owned. Mrs. Horowitz, across the way, was delighted for any help she could give with the baby. She even found a bubbe to talk to, a round, grandmotherly woman, who was joining her family in America.

Tata insisted on continuing her lessons, although Minna objected.

"Why study Yiddish if we're going to America?" she asked indignantly.

Tata frowned at her. "You may become an *Amerikane kinder*, but you will speak the language of your forefathers."

Although Minna disagreed, she had no choice. She felt better when she saw that Yankel had lessons in Hebrew just as arduous as Yussel's.

As the time passed, Minna found that she spent most of her free time with Yankel, talking and exploring. Pearl, given a choice of remaining in her bunk or following Yankel and Minna, clung to her sister. She participated by listening shyly and, as she became more comfortable with Yankel, smiling at his attempts to make her laugh.

Yussel made friends with a group of young men who had walked all the way from Rumania to Hamburg. When he wasn't talking with them, learning their songs and hearing the stories of their trip, he was reading Torah with Tata.

One night, Minna asked Yussel about them. "What are they like?" she asked.

"They're very brave," Yussel replied. "They decided on their own they wanted to go to the New World. When their parents' wouldn't come, they left, anyway. They gave shows along the way to pay for their trip. Ephraim said that all through Rumania, the *goyim* peasants helped them, even though they are Jews. They plan to start a communal farm in a place called New Jersey."

Minna listened, fascinated.

"I admire them," Yussel burst out. "They're searching for a new way to live. They're not bound by the old rules."

"What do you mean?" Minna asked in a shocked tone. What could that be, to live in a new way?

"My friend, Ephraim, for example," Yussel continued. "His father insisted that he read Torah and be a *Yeshiva bokher*. But he had a friend who gave him other books to read. He learned about something called a commune, where no one is rich or poor because they all help each other. His father beat him for his ideas, so Ephraim left with the others. He doesn't even pray anymore."

"But…is he a Jew after all?"

"He says he thinks of himself as Jew, but he doesn't believe in God. If there was a God, he says, there wouldn't be any pogroms, or pain, or suffering."

Minna's eyes lit up. Here was someone who felt the way she did. No one, not even Yussel or Yankel, knew how angry she was at God.

Encouraged, Yussel went on. "He's a good person, Minna. He has courage and he cares about others. I know Tata won't understand, but I believe in him and his friends. They're right to try new ways. How else can you know what's a good way for you?"

"But the Torah, Yussel. Do you think the Torah is wrong?"

"Well… Of course, it's not wrong. But maybe it's only one way. What if there are other ways? Was it right for Tata and me to save the Torah while Chava died?" he asked fiercely. "How can it be right to save a book over a person?"

Minna wanted to shout, "I agree!" but aware that Yussel was actually talking to himself, she said nothing.

"Ephraim says that in the New World, things will become clearer to me. Meanwhile, it's good I can talk to someone like him.

I'm a man now, after all, and I have to make my own decisions. Tata can't decide everything for me."

"Does he know what you're thinking?" Minna asked.

Yussel shook his head. "Not yet." He hesitated. "Why say anything till I know where my heart is? In America, we'll see."

Minna agreed with him whole-heartedly. It was always better to avoid Tata's cold and terrifying wrath.

Her friendship with Yankel grew stronger each day. There was something endearing about the contrast between his confident manner and his sad eyes. Even Mama liked him.

Yankel's Tata, Minna noticed, instructed him sternly in Torah but otherwise left him to his own devices. Even Tata, Minna thought, talks to us more than Yankel's father talks to him. Maybe that's one of the reasons for his sad eyes.

Then one day, he said quietly, "I miss my mama. She died only six months ago. Everything changed after that. Tata only prays now. Bubbe was always yelling at me to do this and do that. She says my mama must have been a saint to put up with me. But Mama didn't act that way. She joked with me and sang songs. On my birthday, she made me a special treat. Every year, she did."

"Why don't you talk to your mama?" Minna asked.

"What do you mean?"

Minna told him how she talked to Bubbe and Chava. "I know they're always with me. They're my angels now. They're watching and protecting me wherever I go or whatever I do. The important thing is, they left *der alter heym* with us. They're coming to America, too."

"You mean my mama is here now?" Yankel looked around the room.

"You have to feel she's here," Minna explained, "and then she will be. Don't you think your mama would be watching you? How could she say goodbye to you so easily?"

Yankel sighed. "But, she did say goodbye." Then he thought about it. "If I could talk to her, if she were here with me…" He smiled. "I'll try it, just like you say, Minna. Thanks."

Another time, he told Minna of his plans for the future. "I'm going to make so much *gelt* in the New World. Then I'm going to send for my sisters. We'll live in a big house and eat white bread every day. When we're sick, the doctor will come immediately. For Mama, he came too late. It shouldn't take me too long, do you think?" He looked at Minna anxiously.

"I don't know." She shook her head. "They say the streets are paved with gold. Can you just reach down and pick up a nugget? I don't think it could be true, do you?"

Yankel shook his head. "I don't know what's true and what's not. I do know it'll be better than it was at home. It has to be," he added fiercely. "I'll make it be!"

"Where are you going to?" Minna asked.

"My Uncle Moishe, he's promised to take us. He lives on Hester Street in New York City. What he does, I don't know, but I suppose we'll help him."

"We're going to New York City, too," Minna said happily. "So, we'll see you. We're going to work in Cousin Avraim's store."

"So *nu*, we'll both get rich," Yankel laughed. "We'll meet on the streets and we'll bow to each other. We won't even remember this ship. The skies will be blue when we live in New York."

They both felt their lives would begin again when they landed in America. They spent long hours trying to imagine how they would live and how quickly they could amass enough *gelt* to make their dreams come true.

Minna told him about the picture she saw in her mind when she imagined *di goldeneh medina.* Although Yankel scorned her vision at first, he asked her to describe it to him over and over again. He listened intently when she did, memorizing her words.

A few days before they were to land in New York, the ship ran into bad weather. The boat rocked and the pungent smell of vomit was added to the already overwhelming odors in the compartment. People tried to use their dinner pails, but many were too nauseous. The floors were slippery with regurgitated food.

Minna felt queasy, particularly when she looked around at the others who were sick. Somehow, she managed to contain herself. Fortunately, Pearl slept through the worst of the storm. It was Mama who was the most affected. She lay in her bunk, moaning faintly.

It became Minna's responsibility to take care of her. She sat by her for hours, stroking her hand, wiping her brow with a damp cloth, and holding the pail when she was sick. For two days, Mama lay there, helpless.

Minna realized, as she ministered to her mother's needs, how much they all relied upon her. In the long, difficult hours, it became clear to her that Mama was the one they turned to in time of trouble. Facing America without her, Minna realized, would be impossible. Poor Yankel, she thought. He has only himself. His Tata is like ours.

With this realization came increased respect for Mama. Minna said to Bubbe, 'So, *nu*, she's angry. So, she doesn't hug us often the way you did. She shows she cares in her own way, doesn't she?'

Minna pictured Bubbe smiling as she said, 'You're beginning to grow up, Minna. To be strong is a mother's duty. Later, for the grandchildren, it's easy to give a kiss or a sugar cake, especially when their fate is in the hands of another. Life is not all flowers and sunshine.'

The day before the ship was to land, the waters calmed. For the first time in three days, Mama enjoyed a good night's sleep. In the morning, she sat up, pale but collected.

Minna smiled at her. "I'm glad you're better, Mama."

"I thought the Angel of Death was calling me," Mama replied weakly. She patted Minna's shoulder and mumbled, "You're a good daughter." Embarrassed, she changed the subject. "We have to get ready to land. Let's get our clothes together. We must look well for the inspectors."

The inspectors! They were all afraid of the inspectors at Ellis Island. Everyone had at least one story about a relative who had been refused admission to America. Some worried about money. It was said you had to have fifty dollars to land. No one had that much. Others touched their eyes fearfully. Trachoma, an infectious eye disease, was guaranteed to keep someone from entering the country.

Mr. Horowitz said proudly, "I have a job promised."

"That's not so good, maybe," said Mr. Fishbein from the next bunk. "I heard it's against the law to have labor pre-contracted. That's taking work away from the Americans."

"I have a job promised," Mr. Horowitz repeated nervously.

Mrs. Moskowitz, the nice bubbe that Minna often spoke to, had other fears. "I woke up this morning and my eye felt grainy. What if I have trachoma? They won't let me stay. I'll die, going back on the boat. And if I don't, then I'll starve to death in *der alter heym*. I sold everything to make this journey," she wailed.

Minna looked at her eyes. "They look fine. I don't think you have anything to worry about."

Yankel had no fears. "I'm young, I'm healthy, and I have Uncle Moishe. They'll take me," he boasted.

Mama concentrated all her efforts on sponging their clothes and re-packing their possessions. There was just enough *kuchlech* left for one more meal. No longer would they have to carry the bulky sack.

Mama instructed the children as she prepared them for the ordeal. Determined they would at least be clean, she stood over them as they scrubbed with cold salt water. "Remember, be sure to answer all the questions they ask you. Cousin Avraim has vouched for us, so we shouldn't have any problems unless one of us is ill…or … …" She looked at their eyes and ears nervously.

The stewards entered, ruthlessly hosed down the floor and even cleaned out the toilets. Someone whispered that other inspectors would come to examine the boats. Maybe America is a land of inspectors, Minna thought.

When the day of arrival finally dawned, all the passengers were allowed on deck to catch their first glimpse of America. Minna, Pearl, and Yankel hung over the railing. Yussel, as befitted his greater dignity, stood behind them, next to Mama and Tata.

"Ephraim says that coming to a new country is like being born again," Yussel said. "When we are first born, he says, we are too small to remember. But now, we can experience every sensation. We must never forget, so we can tell our children about our second birth."

Minna agreed. She was sure their lives would be completely new and different after they landed.

Although everyone was staring at the horizon, it was Pearl who first saw the trees of Staten Island. "I see trees!" she screamed.

Everyone looked, savoring their first sight of land.

"*Gottenyu*! There are trees there!" someone yelled.

As the ship traveled farther into the harbor, they saw many other boats. Some seemed like huge floating palaces, filled with people. Others were small fishing boats and tugs. Minna found that if she waved, the people on the boats waved back. She began to hope that New York City might be a friendly place.

"Those are ferry boats," said the man next to her, pointing at the largest ones.

"Ferry boats!" Yankel laughed. "In America, the ferry boats are like ocean liners."

Minna's mouth fell open when she saw the Manhattan skyline.

She had never seen so many tall buildings. How can people climb to the top, she wondered, looking at the tallest. To think of walking so high up in the air!

Even Tata put aside his books and pushed his way to the rail. As they came closer to the shore, he patted Mama's arm. "So, here we are. When do they bring us the pails heaped with gold?"

Mama was too anxious to do more than nod. She looked only at her family, examining each one in turn. Desperately, she scrutinized them for infirmities.

Yankel's Tata, his nose still in his book, stood at the rail, too. He looked up as they approached a gigantic statue on an island in the middle of the water. "It's the lady!" he exclaimed.

The cry was repeated by others standing at the rail. "It's the lady!" they said, in differing languages and in varying accents. The tone of awe was common to all.

Minna looked at the lady, turning her head to keep her in view as they steamed past. Her face looked strong, yet kind, Minna thought. She had heard of the Statue of Liberty before, but she had not imagined that it dominated the harbor. It must be a good country, Minna thought, or else they wouldn't have a lady like that to greet us first thing.

When they came near to the Hudson River pier, Minna shrieked, "Look! I see a cat!" There, on the pier, was a gold and white tabby cat, lying in the sun and licking its flanks.

To Minna, this was miraculous. That people in America should have cats just they way they did at home! She stared at the cat. Yes, it was the same. This is a real place, she thought. Standing at the rail, she began to reconstruct her picture of America. That they should have cats!

Mama gripped Yussel's shoulder nervously. “Come!" she cried. "We must get our luggage so we’ll be ready to land. Come on! Soon, we'll be off this boat! "

Her words started an exodus back to the berths. People milled around, pushing and shoving, as they searched for family members. No one wanted to be unprepared for the next step—the dreaded inspectors. Children cried, mothers straightened clothing, fathers began to count heads and pieces of luggage. All was chaos.

After what seemed like hours, all the passengers, pushing and carrying their luggage, were herded back to the deck of the ship. There they waited to board the ferry that would take them directly to Ellis Island. Ellis Island! Faces grew taut, eyes narrowed.

"This is the Day of Judgment!" someone called.

"Only God knows," was the reply.

Minna, wearing Chava's old dress, felt her sister's presence. "Here we are," she said softly. "We made it!"

Pearl held onto the edge of Minna's dress. Mama, Tata, and Yussel stood guard over the wicker trunk. Perched on top were Mama's best pot and several other sacks of belongings.

As the ferry approached Ellis Island, a gasp escaped the waiting crowd. The building's elaborate towers and elegant copper spires embellished by brilliant white trimming against red brick made it seem royal. Flying proudly in front was a large American flag.

"This is where we go?" Minna heard someone say. "It's a palace."

"Some palace!" another person replied. "Underneath, there may be dungeons for the ones they send back."

Men started gabbling prayers and women held their children tightly. Upon everyone's face was the greatest apprehension. What if a whole family failed to pass inspection? Worse yet, what if one of a family was refused? Would some go and some stay? As they pushed out of the ferry, most were fearfully silent.

They were herded into a huge room. There they left their luggage. Each person was numbered and tagged by name and nationality. In an endless line, they ascended the stairs to the dreaded inspection rooms. At the top of the stairs, they broke into a series of smaller lines. Mothers were separated from older children, husbands from wives. All were to be examined separately.

Minna stood as tall as she could. "Stay with me, Bubbe and Chava," she murmured. What if she had to return and the rest of the family stayed in America? What if Mama couldn't stay? What would happen to them?

The first doctor looked her over and nodded. She had noticed that some of people ahead of her had chalk marks on their clothes. She worried because she didn't have the marks. Did that mean she had already failed some kind of test? Later, she found out that the chalk marks signified serious disease or the need for further examination.

Next, Minna was asked by a Yiddish-speaking interpreter what her name was and whether she thought the weather was good. She answered boldly, wondering why they needed to know about the weather. Surely, they could look out the windows and see for themselves.

Every few minutes, Minna looked behind her, craning her head, to make sure that her family was following. As she moved forward, she didn't want to lose them. She was relieved to see that none of them had chalk marks either. At least we're all the same, she thought, reassured.

Minna was examined by several other doctors. The worst was the "eye doctor". He held a stick in his hand. By flourishing it, he forced Minna to look into his eyes. Then, with his thumb and his forefinger, he caught her eyelash, turned it back and peered into one eye and then the other to see if she had trachoma. Minna bit her lip, so as not to scream. He nodded and passed her on.

After that, she was told to wait for her family. "Children with parents," the interpreter said.

As she waited, she gazed down at the large room below. It looked like a giant spider web, with rows and rows of weary immigrants radiating outward from its center. On the wall, she saw notices, some of them written in three languages. Above, on a higher level, she saw well-dressed spectators pointing at the people below. Perhaps, she thought, Cousin Avraim is waiting for us there.

Finally the family was reunited. They talked loudly so they could hear each other over the din, expressing their relief as they waited to see the last inspector.

"What did he say to you?" Minna asked Pearl.

"He asked me what color my dress was. I said, 'Gray, of course.' Then he laughed. I don't see why he couldn't tell the color himself," Pearl replied.

"You silly! He wanted to know if you were *krenk* in the *kopf*," Yussel laughed. "He asked me how much two and two were."

Mama looked at her children. "So, we're all here. Thanks be to God, I have a healthy family."

Tata davined, his eyes closed, shutting out both Ellis Island and the New World.

Suddenly, Yankel caught up with them, his face distraught. "My Tata can't stay!" he cried. "He has to go back! They took him away."

"They took him away?" The family gathered around Yankel. "What's the matter with him?"

"He has tuberculosis, they said. That's what my mama died

from. He said to me, 'Go, my *zuhn.* Go to the New World, or you, too, will die of this. Work so you can send for your sisters.' Then they took him away to be sent back to the boat." Yankel began to cry.

Minna took Yankel's hand and squeezed it as hard as she could. "Don't worry," she said. "Your uncle will take care of you. We'll be here, too."

Pearl touched Yankel's sleeve sympathetically.

Yussel put his arm around the boy's shoulder.

Tata looked at Yankel. "He's a good man, your Tata. He was right in what he said. If one can be saved in the sight of the Lord, let that one be saved."

"Are you sure?" Yankel quavered.

Tata nodded. "You must fulfill your father's wishes, so saith the Lord."

As they were talking to Yankel, a woman approached. She handed Mama a card written in Yiddish, German, and English. Mama glanced at it and handed it to Minna to read aloud.

Minna cleared her throat. "'Warning,'" she read. "'Beware of any person who gives you addresses, offers you easy, well-paid work, or even marriage. There are many evil men and women who have in this way led girls to destruction. Always inquire for the persons whose names are given on the other side of this card, who will find out the truth for you, who will advise you, and give you all necessary information or aid.' It's signed, 'The Council of Jewish Women,'" Minna concluded.

The woman smiled. "You'll see my name on the other side of the card," she said. "I'm Mrs. Rosenblatt. I'm here to help those arriving in this country. Do you have any questions?"

Minna noticed although she spoke Yiddish, her accent was different from theirs. Her clothing was different, too, but whether it was the quality or the style, Minna couldn't say. She examined her avidly, for this was the first American woman she had seen up close. Maybe everyone in America speaks Yiddish, she thought hopefully.

Yankel stepped forward. "My Tata can't stay," he wailed. "We came all this way and now he has to go back. He told me to stay in America. I'll be met by my uncle …"

Mrs. Rosenblatt looked worried. "How old are you?"

Yankel hesitated. Minna knew he was deciding whether to lie.

Then he realized it was already written down in his papers. "I'm ten," he said.

"Unaccompanied children are not usually admitted, but in this case, it may be all right. Your uncle will take responsibility for you?" Mrs. Rosenblatt asked.

"I...I'm sure he will," Yussel stated as definitely as he could. It was obvious that he had some doubts.

"Is he here waiting for you and your father?"

"I think so. He said he would be. Tata made all the plans."

"Give me your uncle's name and I'll find out for you."

Yankel told her Uncle Moishe's full name. He added his address, which he had memorized. As she hurried away, he looked after her anxiously.

Before she had gone too far, Mrs. Rosenblatt called back, "Stay in line until I return!"

Yankel nodded.

Minna pulled Mama, who had been very quiet, over to the side. "Can't we take Yankel if his uncle won't? He doesn't eat much, and I know he'd work hard."

Mama stepped back. "How can I take on another mouth to feed? It's enough if we are well and healthy. To take charge of Yankel is to accept a debt from his dead mother, may God rest her soul. As we enter a strange land, I cannot make such a promise to the dead." She turned her head away.

In desperation, Minna approached Tata. "Can't we take Yankel?" she asked.

Tata shook his head. "It is written that each shall take care of his own. Charity is blessed, but I won't take another man's son for mine."

Yussel stepped forward impatiently. "I am a man. Yankel will be my responsibility. I know Ephraim would do the same."

Minna beamed at him.

Tata glared. "A son to stand against a father! Is this what the new land does? I forbid you, I, your father."

Yussel clenched his fists. "It could be me," he muttered. "I could be all alone with no one to stand up for me."

"But you're not," Mama stated loudly. "We're your family. You must obey our wishes."

Yussel shook his head and motioned to Yankel. Minna went and stood next to her brother. Pearl followed.

Yankel looked at them. Then he eyed Mama and Tata. "No," he said, finally. "Wait till the woman comes back."

The line moved slowly. Minna kept watching for Mrs. Rosenblatt, hoping it would not be their turn to be called before she returned. She forgot her own fears as she worried about Yankel.

At last, they were near the head of the line. There were only five people in front of them. Minna began to cry. 'It isn't fair! You can't go back! You came all the way, just as we did!"

Mama and Tata stared straight ahead.

Yussel cleared his throat.

Abruptly, Yankel called out, "I'm here! I'm here!"

Mrs. Rosenblatt pushed her way through the crowded line. "It's all right," she smiled. "I found your uncle. He says he'll take charge of you. I'll go in with you to tell the inspector."

Yankel clutched Mrs. Rosenblatt's hands. "Thank you, thank you," he babbled. "May the Lord bless you."

Mrs. Rosenblatt stepped back. Minna, watching, thought she didn't want Yankel to touch her. "I'm here to help," she explained. "It's the least I can do."

Relieved, the family smiled and laughed.

"It's a *broche,* a blessing," Mama said.

Tata patted Yankel's shoulder, "The Lord be with you," he said.

Minna and Pearl each gave him a hug and Yussel shook his hand heartily.

Yankel beamed at Yussel and Minna. "I won't ever forget," he promised.

Now they were at the head of the line. It was their turn to see the last inspector. First Tata went in. Yussel followed. Last of all, Mama and the two girls were called.

They entered a small stall. The inspector, through an interpreter, asked Mama many questions, checking the answers against a large ledger.

"What country are you from?"

"Do you have a place to go?"

"Has there ever been insanity in your family?"

"How long have you been married?"

"Who paid your passage?"

"Do you have any money?"

Mama must have answered the questions correctly, for she and the girls were waved through. As they hurried out, exhausted from the long ordeal, Minna lagged behind, walking slowly in the hope of seeing Yankel.

Finally, as they were about to turn a corner to go down the stairs to reclaim their luggage, she saw him come through another stall, his eyes aglow. He ran to catch up with them.

"It's all right!" he cried. "My uncle is waiting. I have to get my luggage and find him. I'll look for you in New York City." He gave Minna a farewell wave and disappeared, worming his way through the crowd.

Now Minna felt she could be completely happy. She saw her joy reflected on the faces of her family. We've done it! she thought triumphantly. Now we begin our new life. We're in America and we're invited to stay!

CHAPTER 4

As they entered the large room downstairs to claim their luggage, the Rubens recognized many others from the boat. Most were beaming. Regardless of what might happen in the future, they had passed the first test. They were still here. A few, relatives of those forbidden to land, were weeping. They stood, bewildered, before a pile of sacks, straw boxes, and bundles, unable to decide how to divide what was to stay and what was to go back.

Together, the whole family pushed the heavy straw box outside. At last, they could step on American soil as welcome visitors. Minna remembered again what Yussel had said about this being a second birth. She looked around, trying to fix the scene in her mind so she would never forget.

Americans, standing on the dock by the ferry, eagerly scanned the faces of passers-by. New arrivals, emerging from the building laden with baggage, looked around hopefully. Some were embraced by friends or relatives. Others sat upon their boxes and clutched their sacks, waiting.

The water sparkled in the sun. Across the river, Minna saw many large buildings. She stared at them. It looked as if none were made of wood. The polished stone gleamed as it reflected the sunlight.

"What a country!" she exclaimed. "Look! All the buildings are made of stone. They can never burn down."

She stared at the Americans waiting by the ferry. They looked vaguely familiar. Although they were dressed differently than the villagers in *der alter heym*, their faces were similar. Minna watched them carefully to see if they really did hold their heads higher because they were Americans.

The family sat with the others who were anxiously waiting. "He said he would meet us." Mama reached into her secret pouch and took out Cousin Avraim's well-worn letter. Sitting upon the straw box, she scanned it. "Yes, he says he will meet us, or have someone meet us."

"Have someone meet us? How will we know who he is?" Yussel asked anxiously.

Even Tata laid aside his book and looked around for a moment before he picked it up again.

Suddenly, Mama jumped up. "Cousin Avraim!" she shrieked, holding out her arms with a look of profound relief.

Minna peered at the man coming towards them. She shook her head. This couldn't be Cousin Avraim. He looked so different. He no longer had a beard or payos. He wore a western suit, and on his finger, a diamond ring glittered in the sun. In the *shtetl*, Cousin Avraim had been the palest and thinnest of all the young men. Now his plump face was ruddy and he walked with careless ease.

Yet, as he approached, he looked just as excited as they felt. "Cousin Ruchel!" he called to Mama. "You've come!"

Mama took his hands and squeezed them. Then she stepped back and looked him up and down. "You look like a real *Amerikaner*," she said admiringly.

Cousin Avraim laughed. "You will, too. It happens soon enough." He extended his hand to Tata. "How are you, Cousin Dovidl? I am glad to see you."

Before Tata could do more than shake his hand and begin to answer, Cousin Avraim turned to Yussel. "Yussel! You look like a nice strong fellow. Just what I need in my business."

Then he beamed at the two girls. 'My, you have grown, Minna. You are beginning to look like Chava."

Minna was flattered, although she couldn't believe it was true. She blushed.

"And this must be Pearl," Cousin Avraim smiled and patted her on the head.

"Come," he insisted, bustling about their luggage. "Let's go! In America, time is money. Later, you'll tell me all about the family and your trip."

Without further ado, he led them to the ferry. "We'll go to the Battery," he explained, "and then we'll take a subway."

Mama nodded, mesmerized by Cousin Avraim's seeming prosperity and the unfamiliar sights and sounds.

Minna was afraid of the Elevated. A train high above the ground! She thought they might never find their way back down to the street. Suppose, she worried, the train fell off the tracks and they were dashed to death below.

Despite her English lessons on the boat, the sounds that reached Minna's ears and the signs she saw were completely alien to her. She could recognize nothing of what she had learned.

Cousin Avraim shepherded them out of the train. Leading the way to a tall, steep, staircase, he started down. They followed him as quickly as they could, pushing, pulling, and lugging the straw box. Others passed them, hurrying frantically down the stairs to the street. They were pushed and shoved until it seemed they would be unable to keep their balance.

"So, there's a fire?" Mama asked. "The Tsar, he has died?"

Cousin Avraim laughed. "This is America. Everyone hurries."

"Hurries and pushes!" Tata grumbled.

Finally, they reached the street. "This is Essex Street," Cousin Avraim proclaimed. "I've taken an apartment for you on Allen Street, so we'll have to walk a few blocks. Then, as soon as I take you there, I'll return to my store." His tone was proud as he said the last two words. "I'll come back tonight to see you. Tomorrow, you'll see the shop."

He hurried ahead. The family struggled to keep up with him, buffeted to and fro as others tried to pass them. The air rang with Yiddish words and phrases.

The street, Minna noticed, was crammed with pushcarts. At each one, a man or a woman stood, bargaining with their customers, describing their wares in a loud voice, or simply gossiping with the other merchants. It looked like home, Minna thought, except she had never seen so many sellers and buyers in one place or heard so many voices talking at the same time.

As their small procession wound its way through the people and stalls, some of the passers-by made comments.

"So, new arrivals," smiled one brawny man festooned with suspenders, all of them for sale.

"That's all we need—more greenhorns," added a plump woman

good-humoredly.

The tone was friendly although no one in the family liked being identified as a newcomer. Cousin Avraim nodded at acquaintances, sometimes replying to their joking comments and sometimes simply shrugging and pushing his way forward. Once he stopped to discuss business with another man.

Tata brightened when he saw a stall with books for sale. The man behind the stall, dressed, like Tata, in traditional coat and hat, beckoned. Tata actually stopped, gazing at the books longingly, but Mama urged him on.

Minna noticed many unfamiliar things being sold. The food looked delicious, particularly after their trip on the boat. There was one stall, she saw, selling only nuts. Another had large chunks of halvah, the candy she loved. Peddlers roasted what looked like potatoes except the skin seemed thinner and the insides were orange. A man carrying a huge bronze container on his back offered drinks for a penny. Minna caught a glimpse of someone buying a drink. The man leaned forward and the liquid, whatever it was, poured into a glass. Other pushcarts were filled with fresh fruit, vegetables, meats, and fish.

Listening to the Yiddish words, Minna wondered, does everyone speak Yiddish here? Are there more Jews in New York City than at home?

Pearl held Minna's hand, trotting along by her side. Yussel and Tata strained under the weight of the straw box, but had enough energy to stare at everything as they passed. "I like this place," he said to Minna.

Cousin Avraim hurried on, not stopping or looking back. He lunged through walls of people confidently, halting frequently to pull out his big gold watch, which he inspected importantly.

Mama followed him desperately, helping with the straw box and continually looking around to make sure all of her family was with her. "Hurry! Hurry!" she hissed.

Minna saw not one tree, blade of grass, or flower. The roads were paved in a black, tarry material she later learned was called asphalt. The houses all seemed to be made of brick or stone. Many of them had steps leading down to the street. Upon these steps, Minna noticed mothers, children, old men bent over books, exhausted shoppers, and many others. Some tilted their faces upwards to catch the sun while others fanned themselves busily as they chatted.

Finally, panting and exhausted, the family stopped behind Cousin Avraim at one of the stoops. He pointed up the stairs. "It's up there, two more flights." Taking a key out of his pocket, he handed it to Mama. 'Here's the key. It's number eleven." Pulling out his watch again, he consulted it ostentatiously. "I'll see you in six hours—after my shop closes. Knock on your neighbor's door if you have any questions. Her name's Mrs. Perlman and she'll tell you everything you need to know." He spoke rapidly, overwhelmed by his need to return to his store. "I'll be back later. I must go now…my store…" With these words, he started down the road. As he turned the corner, he yelled back, his voice almost lost in the noises of the street, "Welcome to America!"

They stared after him, stunned at his abrupt departure. Mama was the first to step forward. She led the way, gripping the key tightly, to the front door at the top of the stoop. Clumsily, she opened it.

Yussel followed at her heels, helping Tata push the straw box. When he saw the almost vertical steps leading up to the second floor, his face fell. "We'll never do it," he warned.

"Oh yes, we will!" Mama grabbed one end of the straw box and led the way.

It was such hard work getting their possessions to the top of the second flight of stairs, Minna didn't have a chance to notice anything along the way. Panting, she looked around the hallway as they reached the top. It was dark and hot. The fetid air clung to their hair and their bodies.

Minna smelled rotting garbage. "It's like the boat," she whispered.

Mama paid no attention. She marched over to the door that said 11 on it. Holding up the key, she inserted it into the lock, turned it, and boldly pushed the door open.

Minna, standing aside so Tata and Yussel could push the straw box into the apartment, scrutinized the other doors in the hallway. One had no number on it and the other was labeled 12. Emanating from 12, Minna could hear the sound of whirring machinery and crying children.

One by one, the family filed into their new home, with Mama in the lead. Suddenly she stopped. They halted behind her, dismayed.

They were in a small, dark room, about 10 feet by 11 feet. A single window overlooking a tiny backyard provided the only light.. A closer look out the window showed lines of drying clothing suspended above overflowing garbage cans. Grubby children dressed in what looked like rags laughed and screamed as they chased each other in the dirt.

Mama pursed her lips and walked through the room to another door, which opened into a tiny kitchen ventilated by a narrow airshaft. Shaking her head, she looked at the range, the sink, and two glass-doored cabinets.

Then Minna saw another door at the side of the kitchen. She opened it. Inside, there was a closet-sized bedroom about the width and size of their old one. She held the door open for Mama, who walked in and out quickly.

"At least," Mama said grimly, "at home, we had windows. There's no window at all in the bedroom and a black hole in the kitchen."

Mama's words released the others from their self-imposed silence.

"I appreciate my beautiful library—so private and secluded," Tata sneered.

"Do we have to walk up and down all those stairs every time we get water?" Pearl asked.

Yussel went to the one window and stood looking out at the backyard. He said nothing.

Minna gazed at Mama apprehensively, waiting to see what she would do.

"Wait, Tata. The Temple wasn't built in a day, you know." Mama squared her shoulders. "You'll have your study, never fear."

"Pearl," she continued, "there's water out in the hall, I'm sure. See, we have a sink for the basin right here! The toilet's probably out in the hall, too. Why don't you and Minna go and see if you can find it."

Minna and Pearl walked into the hall. After a moment of indecision, Minna opened the unmarked door. There was a toilet and a sink with a faucet for cold water. "Look, Pearl," she said. "We'll never have to go outside in the middle of the night again."

Pearl tried to smile. "It's so dark, though. It's no bigger than our old house. It's even smaller. I thought we were going to live like millionaires."

Stepping back into the hall, Minna was about to answer her when the door of number 12 opened. A girl her own age stepped out.

She smiled at Minna and Pearl. "Hello. Are you our new neighbors?"

Minna nodded. The girl wore a short dress covered by a checked pinafore. Her legs were covered by long black stockings and on her feet, she wore high-buttoned boots. Her blonde hair was braided into two braids, not one. Each was decorated with a bright blue ribbon. Immediately, Minna realized that her new dress, Chava's old one, was wrong.

"My name's Debbie."

"Debbie? I've never heard that name," Minna commented, without stopping to think. She flushed.

"Debbie's an American name," the girl said proudly. "My name used to be Dvora, but Miss Hagerty, my teacher, calls me Debbie so I decided that's going to be my name from now on."

Minna was amazed. In America, people could decide their own names! She was thinking this over when she realized Debbie was waiting for an answer.

"My name's Minna," she said. "That's my sister, Pearl. You're the first real American I've talked to."

Debbie laughed. "I've only been here for about a year. I was a greenhorn, too, when I first came. Don't worry, you'll soon see what it's like."

"Do you speak English, too?"

"Of course," Debbie replied. "We have to in school. You'll learn it quick enough." She turned towards number 11. "Mama asked me to come over and see if I could show you anything."

Minna and Pearl followed Debbie back to their apartment. The door was open. Tata, Yussel, and Mama were in the same position, as if they hadn't moved at all.

"Mama," Minna said, catching up with Debbie, "this is our neighbor, Debbie. She came to show us everything."

Debbie blushed. "My mama sent me to see if I could be any help."

"Thank you," Mama replied. "One thing I was wondering… Where's the wood for the stove?"

"There is no wood," Debbie explained. "This is a gas stove. Here, I'll show you. You just turn the handle and light a match."

She lit the stove while the whole family watched her in amazement.

"*Gottenyu*!" Minna exclaimed.

"You see," Mama said triumphantly, "we have a stove with no chopping of wood. And," she turned to Minna, "you found the toilet?"

Minna nodded.

"So, there's a toilet and water right next door."

"You have gas lights in the front room, too," Debbie said, pointing out the gas jet. "In the little room, there's nothing. We use a candle."

"Gas lights in the living room!" Mama exclaimed, her voice rising in false heartiness.

It was clear to all of them, even Debbie, that Mama was making the best of things. Impulsively, Debbie touched Mama's hand. "Come," she insisted. "Why don't you walk across the hall and meet my Mama? She said to bring you over. She can't come because she's sewing. She has to finish three pieces by tonight."

The whole family followed Debbie across the hall. She opened her door and they stopped in amazement. Although both apartments were identical, this one was filled to bursting with children and furniture.

A plump motherly looking woman, bent over the sewing machine. When she heard them, she jumped up. "I'm Hodl Perlman. I'm glad to welcome you."

Mama looked at her anxiously. “I'm Ruchel Ruben and this is my husband, Dovidl. These are my children.”

Mrs. Perlman nodded sympathetically. "*Nu*, I know just how you feel. I felt the same when we came. But, it's better than you think. It's no palace, some neighbors aren't so good, but we're working, the children, too, and we have a boarder. One day, please God, we'll leave the city and go to the Bronx, where grass grows and flowers bloom." She gestured toward the other room. "Come and see my kitchen. It looks better when your own things are in it."

They followed her, crowding into the small kitchen so there was scarcely room to move. It did look cheery, Minna thought, with a red and white checked oilcloth on the table and a pot boiling on the stove. Gaslight provided a soft glow. A young man was seated at the table, poring over an open book.

"This is my boarder," Mrs. Perlman said. "His name is Irving

Fishbein. He goes to City College," she added proudly.

Irving looked up for a moment, smiled, and turned back to his book.

As Mama looked around the kitchen, her face brightened. "What we need to do," she said energetically, "is to clean. Once our new home is clean …"

"It's a good apartment for here," Mrs. Perlman assured them. "It's reasonable. It only costs nine dollars a month and there's room for a boarder. Some people can't find anything. Of course, the neighborhood…" She leaned forward and whispered to Mama, who looked appalled. "But if we don't bother them, they don't bother us," she concluded cheerfully.

Mama had clearly stopped trying to assimilate new information. "Soap!" she muttered. "I brought soap to use on the boat. I have rags. I just need some hot water … Then we'll need food…"

She looked at Mrs. Perlman inquiringly.

"You can buy food down the street from the stalls, and a kitchen table and chairs, too. They'll change money for you, too. Just don't let those *gonifs* take advantage because you're new. You have to bargain."

Mama's eyes gleamed. She smiled warmly at Mrs. Perlman. "Thank you, Missus. Thank you very much."

She stepped briskly out the door. Minna could tell from her expression that she was mentally scrubbing the floors.

As soon as they returned to their apartment, Mama rolled up her sleeves, found a clean apron, and began to delegate tasks. "We have a little money left," she began. "Yussel, you and Tata go out and buy some food for supper, maybe a little chicken. Don't spend too much," she warned, "because with what's left over, see how much furniture you can buy. We need a table and chairs right away. The feather beds can go on the floor … "

Tata looked dubious, but Yussel held out his hand for the money eagerly. "Don't worry, Mama," he promised. "I like to bargain. You'll be surprised with all I can get."

Mama looked into his eyes. "Don't be foolish, Yussel. Make good choices. There are some who would buy books with our little money," she frowned at Tata, "but we must eat." She gave Yussel a clap on the shoulder and turned to Minna.

Yussel hurried out the door, followed by Tata, who seemed oblivious to the whole conversation.

"Now," Mama addressed Minna and Pearl. "Now, we get to work! Minna—you fill the pot with water from the hall. Pearl, you help me turn on the stove."

Minna hurried to fill the pot. She was sorry she hadn't had more time to talk to Debbie. She hadn't even said goodbye. Maybe I'll see her tomorrow, Minna thought as she filled the heavy pot.

By the time Tata and Yussel returned, proudly dragging a table, chairs, and a bright red oilcloth, the apartment was spotless. "Now it will be our dirt," Mama said triumphantly. "That I can live with!"

The table was placed in the kitchen. It was, Minna thought, a little rickety, but Mama seemed pleased. With the addition of the red oilcloth, the kitchen looked brighter. Mama turned up the gaslight and a warm light suffused the room.

"So, *nu*, we have a beautiful table, a fancy cloth, and excellent chairs. For supper, what then? What kind of food did you buy?" she asked.

Tata, actually smiling, reached into the sack he was carrying and extricated a large piece of chicken, some vegetables, some flour, and some chicken fat in a container. With a flourish, he set them upon the table.

Mama beamed. Everything was ready. The few dishes and seasonings she had brought were in the glass-doored cupboard, her pot was on the stove, and her kitchen knife was upon the sink. Nonchalantly, she lit a match and turned on the stove.

"Look, Yussel!" Minna nudged her brother. "Look at our room!"

The two girls had spread the feather beds they had brought upon the floor. Between their side and Yussel's, they had hung a sheet, to provide a modicum of privacy.

"What was it like?" Pearl asked timidly.

"It was like home, only much bigger. There were so many people and so many things for sale, but everyone speaks Yiddish and most were friendly. They kept calling us greenhorns, though."

"What did Tata do?" Minna asked. She couldn't imagine him bargaining.

Yussel shook his head. "He went to the book stall. We passed it, he stopped to talk to the owner, and that was that. Finally, I went and bought everything. I picked him up on the way back. Actually," he continued thoughtfully, "I like bargaining. I think I'm going to enjoy working for Cousin Avraim."

"But your studies, Yussel?"

"It's different here. There's no *gelt* lying around, but everyone works hard. I can tell. You have to work to get ahead." His voice rose enthusiastically. "I like it! It's a place where things happen. Everyone is in a hurry. Everyone is going somewhere!"

"But…where?"

"That I don't know yet." He laughed. "I haven't even spent the night here. I don't know everything." His voice grew more serious. "You know what? I saw a policeman in a uniform with big brass buttons and no one was scared of him. He stood there and people bumped into him, just like everyone else."

"Yussel," Minna said slowly, "there's one thing I don't understand. Where are the Americans?"

"We're the Americans now."

Pearl looked dubious. "I'm not an American."

"You're here, aren't you?" Yussel proclaimed.

As they sat talking, a delicious aroma wafted into the room from the kitchen. The chicken was cooking in Mama's pot. They could hear her bustling around and in the background and Tata reading aloud in Hebrew.

Minna smiled, comforted by the familiar sounds. "I'm glad we're here," she said. "I'm going to be a real American!"

Cousin Avraim came by just in time for dinner. Although there were no extra chairs for the table, Mama solved the problem by serving everyone and eating standing, leaning against the sink.

Cousin Avraim didn't seem to notice. After his first taste of Mama's chicken, he sighed. "At last, I eat like home. That's the one thing I miss. I live alone and eating out …well, it's not a *haimisher* meal."

Minna looked at him and thought, it doesn't seem to have hurt you. She remembered how scrawny he had been in *der alter heym.*

"Of course," Cousin Avraim continued, "I'm lucky I can live alone. When I first came, I boarded with three other men. The *baleboosteh* whose house it was, she yelled at me for every drop of water I used."

His expression changed and he leaned forward over the table, wiping his mouth with the back of his hand. "So, we'll talk about business," he said portentously. "I'll tell you my plans."

They waited.

"You don't want *tzedakah*, something for nothing?"

They shook their heads emphatically.

"Nu, I didn't think so. That's why I helped you to come. So, you're here. Your apartment is nine dollars a month. For working in the store, Cousin Ruchel, I'll pay you $3.50 a week after I've taken out a dollar every time to pay back the tickets. Yussel, I'm gonna give you a *pekl* and you can sell my goods door to door. I'll share the profits with you. If you're lucky, you'll earn about $3.50 a week. Out of that I'll take a dollar for the tickets and a dollar for my profits. The same for you, Dovidl. This means you will earn seven dollars a week by the time you're done. Within little more than a year, you'll have paid me back and meanwhile, you can live quite well. Food, by the month, should cost you about sixteen dollars so you'll have, altogether, three dollars for extras after you pay the rent." He spread his hands and looked around the table complacently. It was clear he felt generous. "So, what do you think?" he asked.

Tata looked dubious. "To take a *pekl* and sell your goods, that means what?"

"You carry the goods and ring doorbells. Maybe the lady wants to sew a dress or maybe she needs matches or shoelaces or threads. You develop a list of customers, and you get what they need. You can even become their exclusive peddler."

"Selling? I should ask people to buy like a *schnorrer*?"

Mama interrupted quickly. "And what do you sell in your fine store?" she asked placatingly.

"After I get my ladies, I can choose what I think they'll like?" Yussel chimed in.

Distracted, Cousin Avraim answered their questions. 'To tell you the truth, Cousin Ruchel, I sell mainly piece goods in the store. But I'd like to add trimmings. That's why I want your help. I remember your stall ..."

Mama's eyes lit up. "I can build a business for you. Like locusts, they'll come."

Cousin Avraim beamed. "As for you, Yussel," he continued, "In time, you'll buy what your ladies want. You don't have to stay here, either. You can travel a little, look for customers." His eyes sparkled. "Once you learn the language, there's no reason you can't have American ladies as your customers!"

He turned to Tata. "As for you, Cousin Dovidl ..."

Mama interrupted again. "You'll pardon me, I haven't told you about your sister. You know she had a boy and he's named Shemuel?"

"No! They had a boy! After three girls … Tell me about the rest of the family."

"They all greet you. And I brought you from *der alter heym*, letters and a gift from your Mama. Wait, I'll go get them." Mama went into the front room where she and Tata would sleep and rummaged amongst the luggage.

While she was gone, Minna touched Cousin Avraim's sleeve. "What will I do, Cousin Avraim? I'd like to help in the store, too."

Cousin Avraim shook his head. "You and your sister, Pearl, will have to go to school. That's the law for *Amerikane kinder.*"

"But I could help you after school," Minna begged. "I used to help Mama in the stall all the time."

Mama returned to the room, carrying a package and some letters. Holding them to her chest, she joined in the conversation. "Naturally, the girls will come and help after school. They always help me," she declared boldly.

Pearl started to speak. Minna poked her. She knew it had been Chava who had helped Mama at the stall. But, Minna already feared Tata would be a disappointment to Cousin Avraim. She couldn't imagine him ringing doorbells. Mama, she knew, must agree, or she wouldn't lie to Cousin Avraim about them.

"The little ones, what can they do?" Cousin Avraim asked skeptically.

"You'll be surprised," Mama replied. "They'll keep the stock tidy, run errands … Minna is good with the customers. You'll see, between the two of them, it'll be like having an extra person. Now, let me give you your letters."

Cousin Avraim spent the rest of the evening reading his letters, exclaiming about the gift his mama had sent him, and asking for news of home. It seemed that he had forgotten about questioning Tata, but when he was ready to leave, it became obvious that he had missed nothing. After saying an affectionate goodbye to Mama, Yussel, Minna, and Pearl, he looked pointedly at Tata and said loudly, "I'll see you at my store tomorrow—all of you!"

When the door shut behind him, Mama hurried Minna, Pearl, and Yussel off to bed, saying, "It's been a long day in a new land. Tonight, I'll clean up. *Schlaft, mein kinder*, and dream of the promised land."

The three filed off into the tiny bedroom. Mama shut the kitchen door behind them.

"She's going to talk to Tata," Minna whispered.

She wanted to stay up and listen, but she was so sleepy, she barely had time to talk to Chava and Bubbe. She said the words in her head. 'We're here,' she thought. 'So, this is America. It's not as different as I imagined it would be. Everyone speaks Yiddish. There's no gold in the streets. At least, not in New York City. I'll help Mama and I'll learn English. I wish my dress looked more like Debbie's.' A wave of longing for Chava swept over her. Chava, she knew, would have discussed Debbie and her dress with her until she got tired of the subject. Pearl was too little and Mama, she knew, had no sympathy for such subjects. 'I wish more than anything else that you were here with us, Chava,' she concluded.

From the other room, she could hear Mama's voice raised in anger. Her last thought before falling asleep was one of apprehension. If Tata refused to peddle for Cousin Avraim, what would happen? He couldn't send them back, could he? Minna vowed to work as hard as she could to make up for Tata.

Much later that night, Minna woke with a start. Her body was covered in sweat. She had a familiar nightmare, the same one she had often had since Chava's death. The men…Chava…and instead of Pearl, herself hiding in the rain barrel, watching… waiting …helpless…paralyzed and silent as she watched her sister being violated and killed.

I'm here, in America, she thought, wiping away her tears. You'll be with me always, Chava. Finally, she closed her eyes and fell back to sleep.

CHAPTER 5

The next morning when Minna awoke, she thought she was in her old room at home. Clutching the familiar featherbed, she looked around lazily. She felt Pearl lying next to her and she heard Yussel behind the curtain.

The curtain...Then she remembered. They were in America. She propped her head in her hands. Already, the boat seemed far away, something that had happened in another lifetime.

Timorously, she opened the door and stepped into the kitchen. Mama was already at the stove, preparing breakfast. She nodded at Minna. "You and I, we're the first ones up. Go out to the hall and wash up. Then I have something to tell you."

Minna tiptoed into the hall so as not to wake Tata, still asleep in the front room. The apartment next door was silent. Minna was relieved. She wasn't quite ready to see Debbie again.

When she came back, she sat at the table and watched Mama heating up the big pot.

"What's in there?" she asked.

"Water," Mama replied. "We're going to get ourselves clean before we do anything else."

Minna was very interested in finding out what Mama wanted to tell her. It wasn't often that Mama spoke in that heavy yet playful manner, and when she did, it was usually to announce a pleasant surprise.

"Is that what you were going to tell me about?" Minna asked.

"No, I talked to Mrs. Perlman early this morning before she went out and she told me where your school is. It's on the way to Cousin Avraim's store, so we'll pass it this morning. Then, tomorrow, you will start.

"But…they'll all speak English there. How will I be able to learn anything?"

"You'll speak English, that's all!" Mama snapped. She turned to face Minna. "Why else did we come here, but that my children can have a different life? You'll learn English, and you'll teach it to Tata, Yussel, and me. Now here, take this cloth and the bowl of water and go to your side of the bedroom to wash yourself. Wake Pearl when you're done and let her have a turn."

Minna took the bowl of water, but she paused before opening the door to the little room. "If you care so much about us, why did you blame Pearl for Chava's death?" she blurted, before she had time to plan what she was going to say.

"What do you mean, blame Pearl? How could I blame Pearl?" Mama advanced, hands on hips, staring balefully at Minna.

"Don't you remember?" Minna persisted bravely. 'You shook her and said it was her fault."

"When?" Mama asked pugnaciously. "When did I do such a thing?"

"Right after we found Chava. Don't you remember?"

Mama bowed her head in thought. "I don't remember," she said slowly. "I don't want to remember. Such a time… May the Lord bless Chava."

"Pearl still thinks you blame her."

"I don't," Mama said defensively. 'Of course, I don't. How could I? I, too, had to watch my sister being… How could I blame her? Tell her, Minna, that I don't."

"But, you're the one to tell her, Mama," Minna pleaded.

Mama shook her head. "I won't …"

The bedroom door opened suddenly and Yussel came staggering out, rubbing his eyes.

Mama turned to him. "It's your first day in America." she announced. "Today, we visit Cousin Avraim's store."

"Tata?" Yussel asked nervously.

"Tata will come," Mama said firmly.

After Yussel had disappeared in the direction of the hall, Minna lingered, hoping to continue the conversation with Mama. She knew she would never have the courage to bring it up another time.

Mama had turned to the stove and was busily stirring breakfast in the small pot. Her back looked so unyielding that Minna was almost afraid to speak. Only the thought of Pearl gave her courage.

"Mama," she began timidly.

Mama swung around abruptly. "Silence, child! I don't remember, but if I did say something, surely Pearl is old enough to understand I didn't mean it. I refuse to dwell on such memories. Not now. There's too much else to think about. It's on my shoulders that this family rests. It's I who will make sure we don't starve in the streets."

Minna waited.

Mama made shooing motions with her hands. "Go, I said! Wash yourself! Soon, it will be time to leave."

Minna took the bowl into the bedroom and began to give herself a sponge bath. Sadly, she looked at Pearl. I'll make it up to her, she thought. I'll fix it.

Within an hour, the whole family was assembled. They were dressed in their best, as seemed appropriate for their first visit to Cousin Avraim's shop. Tata looked grim, but everyone else was eager to leave the apartment and explore their new surroundings.

Mama adjusted her kerchief and took the key. "I'll lock the door," she decided. "In this country, you have to lock the door." She turned the key and they went down the stairs.

After they closed the front door, Minna stood for a moment on the stoop. She felt a slight breeze. Even so early in the morning, there were already a few people sitting on the steps. They looked up curiously as the family passed by.

Next door, Minna noticed a very pretty lady dressed in a silk wrapper standing alone on the stoop, leaning against her front door. She was blonde, with brilliant coloring. As they drew closer, Minna saw she wore paint on her face. Behind her, a lamp with a red shade glimmered in the first floor window. The lady smiled at them.

Minna smiled back, but Mama marched by, her head in the air. "*Vilde chaya*," she muttered and made the sign to keep the devil away.

Minna looked back at the woman curiously. She associated Mama's reaction with Mrs. Perlman's whispered complaints about their neighbors, but she couldn't make more sense out of it.

Mama grabbed her hand and hurried her forward.

Before Minna could ask any questions, she was distracted by the sights and sounds of the street. Peddlers were already setting up their pushcarts. Several called to them, "I need a first. Who will be my first today?"

Mama ignored them as she plunged ahead, trying to remember the directions that Cousin Avraim and Mrs. Perlman had given her.

They turned a corner and passed an imposing brick building. Children of all ages were filing in through two large doors, the boys on one side and the girls on the other.

Minna stared.

"That's it." Mama said. "That's your school. You'll start tomorrow. Mrs. Perlman said Debbie will take you."

Minna stopped. The building seemed almost as big as the one on Ellis Island. It was far too grand to be a school, bigger than any building in the *shtetl.* And there were so many children…

Pearl held her hand tightly. "That's a school?" she asked unbelievingly. "We're going there?"

"It's just a big building," Minna replied valiantly. "Look at all the other children going in."

"They'll all speak English," Pearl quavered. "We won't know anyone."

"We'll know each other." Minna tried to smile. Looking at the other girls, she saw that most of them were dressed like Debbie. She decided she would shorten her dress so it would resemble the others.

By this time, Mama was far ahead. Minna ran to catch up, pulling Pearl with her. Mama hurried on, past the peddlers, the women selling roasted corn from vats set on ancient baby carriages, the vinegar barrels containing luscious green pickles, and the soda water stand on the corner with a portable marble counter and jars of rich preserves to add to the seltzer. The rest of the family followed in Mama's wake, casting hungry glances at the array of delicacies displayed along their way.

Finally, they stopped in front of a small shop on Grand Street. They paused to read the sign that said AVRAIM GOLDBERG, PROP. As they eyed the bolts of fabric tossed at random in the window, they were addressed by a shabby man who stood waiting in front of a fabric-filled cart outside the shop.

Leaning toward Mama, he spoke confidently. "So, you're looking at my goods. The finest quality in New York!" He picked up a bolt and thrust it in Mama's face. Waving it enthusiastically, he cried, "This piece I wouldn't sell to just anyone. Straight from Paris it is, I swear to you! And Mr. Goldberg's prices! You won't believe them!"

Mama, taken aback, did not reply.

He continued. "You're looking to make a new dress, an *Amerikaner* dress." He eyed Mama hopefully. "Or perhaps a dress for the beautiful young girl." He smiled at Minna. "Step inside and see. Choose from…"

Mama recovered herself. At home, she was the "puller", cajoling customers to her stall. Here, she was to learn, even the poorest business had a "puller" whose sole job was to entice the public through the doorway.

With dignity, Mama said to the man, "I'm here to see Avraim Goldberg. I am his Cousin Ruchel Ruben and this is my family."

The old man beamed. "From *der alter heym*! He's waiting for you." He bowed slightly. "My name is Benny Herschel."

Mama nodded, and followed him into the shop.

When all six—the family and Benny Herschel—were inside the shop, there was barely room to move. Small crowded tables, placed carelessly around the room, were heaped with fabric of many patterns and colors. Several naked light bulbs created pools of light, illuminating the precariously balanced bolts of material.

Standing in the back was Cousin Avraim, smiling broadly. 'This is my store," he said proudly. "As you can see, we sell the finest quality goods."

Mama cleared her throat, hesitated, and was silent. She inched her way around the shop, picking up a bolt of fabric here, touching another there. Standing in the center of the room, she examined the perimeters of the shop.

Finally, she smiled. "Such goods you have! It will be a pleasure to work here."

Cousin Avraim inclined his head, as if to say, 'Of course, what else did you expect?'

He turned to Yussel and Tata. "Now for your *pekls*. Here's what they look like." He reached behind a counter and with difficulty, held up a basket. The pots and pans attached to it clanked as he lifted it. Setting it on the counter, he beckoned to Yussel.

Cousin Avraim strapped the *pekl* onto Yussel's back and added a smaller one to his front, explaining, "This is a balancer, so you can stand up straight."

Although Yussel was bent almost double with the weight of the two baskets and their contents, he smiled gamely and tried to walk. He tottered and grabbed hold of the counter. "Maybe I'd better start a little lighter," he gasped. "Just till I get used to it."

Cousin Avraim frowned.

Yussel slipped the basket off his shoulders. "What's inside?" he asked.

Minna hunched her shoulders sympathetically. She realized that everyone, except Tata, was becoming an expert at distracting Cousin Avraim.

Cousin Avraim swept the fabric over to one side of a table and set the basket upon it. One by one, he drew out its contents. They watched, wide-eyed, as many lengths of fabric emerged, thread, needles, oilcloth, candles, matches, and other odds and ends. From the smaller basket, he pulled out patterns, buttons, a modest amount of trimmings, and some bottles of varying size containing oddly colored liquids.

He held up one of the bottles. "Patent medicines," he explained, "and potions. Something new I'm trying. This is how I began," he continued, "with a *pekl* and now…" He spread his arms to encompass the glories of his shop. "You see, Yussel. I wasn't much older than you and I carried even more. Soon you'll be able to manage."

Yussel nodded. "I'll do my best," he promised. "First, I have to learn what I'm selling so I can call it out. And how much it costs, too." He picked up a bolt of cloth and looked at Cousin Avraim inquiringly. "What's this?" he asked.

Mama stepped forward. "That's gingham." She fingered it. "It's the best weight, good for aprons, summer dresses…"

"The style nowadays is for shirtwaists," Cousin Avraim said importantly. "We've been selling this for skirts. You'll see, Cousin Ruchel."

Mama subsided.

"What's the price of everything?" Yussel asked.

"I'll tell you. Once you know how much everything costs me, we'll see how well you can do," said Cousin Avraim.

Tata watched, with a dismayed expression. Experimentally, he lifted the now empty larger pekl and held it in his hand, shaking his head.

Cousin Avraim clapped him on the shoulder. "Don't worry,

Cousin Dovidl. It's like a game, to see how much you can sell."

Yussel's eyes brightened. Tata frowned, but catching Mama's eye, said nothing.

Minna took Pearl by the hand and led her to the nearest table. They began stacking the bolts of fabric in neat piles. Cousin Avraim watched approvingly. Then he, Yussel, and an obviously reluctant Tata retired to a corner in the back of the shop with the baskets and the merchandise. Benny Herschel went back to the front to perform his function as a puller. Mama paced the narrow aisles, examining the merchandise and muttering to herself.

The door to the shop opened and a woman peered in. Benny now stood behind her, so she had no choice but to go farther into the shop. Mama, seeing that Cousin Avraim was still busy in the back, stepped forward.

"Good day, Missis," she said. "Are you looking to make a skirt or a dress?"

The woman, plump and well dressed, wore no *shaitel* or scarf over her intricately pinned hair. She stroked a curl coquettishly. "I'm thinking of a nice shirtwaist, something pretty, but sturdy. Of course," she added hurriedly, "I can't spend very much."

"We have just what you're looking for," Mama said, smiling.

Minna, who knew that Mama, just like herself, had learned about shirtwaists only a few minutes ago, was amazed at her temerity. Mama can sell anything, she thought proudly, as she watched her rummage through bolts of material.

Cousin Avraim stepped forward.

Mama gestured at him. "This is Mr. Goldberg, the owner. He'd like to show you personally," she said smoothly.

She watched intently as Cousin Avraim went from one table to another, selecting bolts of fabric. Clearing one table by shoving the merchandise to one side, he laid down the ones he had chosen. One by one, he picked them up and extolled their virtues. This one was his finest imported cotton, this one was guaranteed to last for years, this one was pre-embroidered, this one had a slight touch of color, this a genteel print …

The woman took a picture from her pocketbook and held it up nervously. 'This is the shirtwaist I'm making," she said, eyeing the assortment in front of her with trepidation.

Cousin Avraim examined the picture carefully. "An elegant style," he approved. "If I may suggest, this is what they're wearing uptown." He unwound a bold of sheer lawn and held it to her face. Narrowing his eyes, he said slowly, "It's perfect for you. The slight touch of blue makes your eyes shine like the sky." From his pocket, he whipped out a small mirror and held it up. 'See how it looks, my dear."

The woman nodded complacently. 'How much a yard?" she asked.

Cousin Avraim quoted a price.

She shook her head. "For that, I could make a whole dress! You think maybe I live on Fifth Avenue?" She offered him half the amount.

Cousin Avraim looked at her sorrowfully. 'You want I should give it away? You want me to starve? For that, I won't even get my cost!" He mentioned another price.

She countered.

He replied, his eyes sparkling and his hands flung out dramatically.

She shook her head firmly and turned as if to leave the shop. He remained silent until she actually had her hand upon the door. Then he called after her, "Better I should kill myself, but I can't resist. Your friends will want to copy your pattern, it'll look so beautiful on you, and they'll come to me to buy the fabric." He paused.

Gratified, she nodded in agreement.

"I'll give you a special price, but you can't tell anyone. It's just for you, you understand." He named an amount that was slightly higher than her original figure.

She came back to the table. Telling him how much fabric she needed, she watched while he cut the bolt. She paid him and left, taking the newspaper-wrapped parcel with her. Cousin Avraim ushered her to the door, saying, "Wear it well!" as she left.

Once she was out of earshot, he turned to Mama with a triumphant smile. "I paid only half of that. It's a good price. She doesn't know, she thinks she got a bargain, so she'll come back again. That's the way we do business here."

Tata and Yussel soon left, hunched over with the weight of their *pekls*. Although Yussel could barely walk, he was excited about starting. Tata, Minna noticed, managed to disassociate himself from the whole affair. The baskets looked as incongruous on him as a wooden leg. The effect was heightened by his gloomy expression.

By lunchtime, Mama was already selling. She had the girls unroll the fabrics to show them to the customers and, although she had to ask Cousin Avraim his prices, she bargained with as much gusto as he did. Listening, Minna thought, as she had before at Mama's stall, it was a little like lying, except everyone understood the process. Most of the customers, she decided, would feel cheated if the transaction were less of a battle.

Cousin Avraim nodded approvingly as he watched Mama selling. "It was a good idea, I had, to help you come," he said. Turning to the girls, he gave them ten cents and explained what it was worth. "Go out in the street and bring back lunch for us. Today we'll celebrate with pickles and cheese."

Realizing this was a test, Minna took the ten cents and hurried out with Pearl. By comparing prices and bargaining, she was able to buy bread, cheese, fruit, and two large pickles to be shared. Pearl carried some of the food and watched in amazement as Minna bargained with the lady who sold the pickles.

When they left, she nudged Minna. "You're just like Mama. How did you know the lady wouldn't be insulted when you started to walk away?"

"I didn't," Minna admitted. "But I did know that Cousin Avraim would be angry if I didn't get enough food, so I had to. Look, we even have a penny left to give back to him."

As they headed back to the store, Minna looked carefully at the buildings they passed to make sure they were going the way she had memorized. She was so busy looking at them, she didn't watch where she was going. With a thud, she bumped into a boy her own age.

"You almost made me drop the pickles!" Minna began, when she saw it was Yankel.

"Yankel!" she cried. "It's good to see you!"

He was just as happy to see them. He tweaked Pearl's hair and smiled at Minna. "Not so bad, this country, is it?"

"You like your uncle? He's glad to have you?"

"Of course, I do, and he is," Yankel replied nonchalantly. "I'm already working for him. I delivered for him. Now I'm on my way back."

"We're bringing lunch to Cousin Avraim and Mama. Come with us."

Yankel shook his head. "I can't. I have to get back. My uncle is waiting for me," he said with an air of importance.

Minna told him where they lived and he promised to come soon and visit. As he left, he called back over his shoulder, "I feel like a real *Amerikaner* already!"

A man in a nearby stall laughed and yelled after him, "Pretty quick work for a greenhorn!"

Minna beamed as they returned to the store. She was happy to know that Yankel was all right and they would see him soon. She was even more pleased when Cousin Avraim commended her for the lavish lunch, saying, "Like mother, like daughter," and let her keep the penny to buy something sweet to share with Pearl.

For Minna and Pearl, who were permitted to go outside and explore, the afternoon went quickly. For Mama, it was long. She stretched her back and sighed when it was finally time to leave the store. Cousin Avraim advanced one week's salary so she could buy food to fix supper.

Mama looked worried, Minna noticed, even though she bargained for their food with gusto. She knew what was on Mama's mind. What if Yussel had been unable to manage the weight of his *pekl* and sold nothing? What if Tata refused to go tomorrow? What would Cousin Avraim do?

Minna quickened her steps as they approached the apartment. She still hoped to shorten her dress for school tomorrow. She knew Mama wouldn't help her, so she had to get started as soon as she could.

As they ascended the stairs, they saw Debbie coming by, carrying her baby sister. "Be ready at eight tomorrow," she said. "We want to get to school in plenty of time so you can get registered."

Minna nodded, although she didn't know what getting registered mean. After all, she thought, excusing herself, I've never been to a real school before.

Back in the apartment, Minna was amazed at homelike it seemed, despite the lack of furniture. The red tablecloth added a warm touch to the sparse kitchen. In the bedroom, the featherbed on the floor looked inviting, but she didn't sit down. Instead, she helped Mama prepare dinner.

When the food was cooking, Minna asked Mama for a needle and thread. "I want to shorten my dress," she explained, "so I'll look more like the other girls."

Mama shook her head. "The dress is fine the way it is," she said impatiently.

Minna shook her head. "You saw Debbie. I want to look like her. With a shorter dress, it's a start."

Mama shrugged. "As long as you do it yourself." She stared at the front door, awaiting Tata and Yussel's return.

Minna changed to her old dress and, having pinned the other one to the right length, began to tack up the hem. She made the stitches as tiny as possible, but she sewed too rapidly for it to be as neat as her usual work. Pearl, who was an excellent seamstress, helped and, in what seemed like no time at all, they met each other's stitches. Pearl's dress was the right length, so they left it alone.

"Soon," Minna said to Pearl, "I'm going to make a pretty pinafore and get some ribbons for my hair."

"Me too," Pearl agreed loyally.

When Minna and Pearl went back into the kitchen, Mama was sitting at the table, her head in her arms, fast asleep. Minna stirred the supper and tiptoed into the front room with Pearl. The two of them sat on Mama's featherbed and watched the front door.

Finally, they heard a knock. They ran to open the door. It was Yussel. He looked exhausted, but triumphant. He held himself stiffly as if his shoulders were sore, but he smiled as he held out his hands to the girls.

"Did I have a day!" he exclaimed. "Imagine this—the baskets were so heavy I thought I would fall flat on my face. Finally, I came to the place where Uncle Avraim said I should start. I was afraid to go in, so I stood outside for a long time. Then, I thought, if I don't try, I might as well give up right away, so I knocked on the door. When the lady opened the door, I whispered, 'Perhaps you'd like to buy something?' She said, 'Speak up, my boy. I don't hear too well.' I had to yell and that broke the ice. She said I reminded her of her own son. He owns a store in the Bronx. She invited me in and gave me some tea. I showed her everything I had. She bought a lot for a good price and I felt so proud of myself! After that, I didn't have any trouble. If they slammed the door in my face, I went away, but once I was in, I was in, and I sold something. Cousin Avraim said, 'At this rate, you'll be making twice what we planned.' He said it's good I look so young because people feel sorry for me. Also, he said I shouldn't try to sell the medicines anymore. 'Who's going to believe a boychick about medicines?' he said. That'll lighten up my load a lot."

Mama appeared in the doorway to the kitchen. 'So, my scholar is a success. Come, I'll rub your shoulders with oil."

Yussel sat at the kitchen table like a king while Mama massaged his shoulders. "As for me," she said, "I can see many ways to fix up that store. I'll organize the fabric, we can sell patterns and notions. With Cousin Avraim, I'll go slowly with my ideas, of course. Today, I had a lady who wanted to make an apron and I convinced her to make dresses for her whole family!" As Mama chattered, she continued to look at the door anxiously.

"I saw Yankel today," Minna told Yussel and Mama. "He's running errands for his uncle and he said this country's not bad! He's coming to visit us soon."

"We passed our school again on the way home," Pearl mentioned.

There was another knock at the door. Mama ran ahead to open it. Tata stumbled in, his face gray and his eyes bleak.

"I can't do this," he shouted, even before he was all the way in. "You said, woman, I would have a study where I could read and pray. Lines, you said, there'd be lines waiting to see me. Instead, I've come to this—I beg, like a schnorrer, beg strangers to buy goods for money. The doors slammed in my face! The insults I received! From your Cousin Avraim, more insults! Woe is me to have a wife who forces me to grovel for pennies."

Mama flared up. "To grovel for pennies is to feed your family. Today, we have all worked, Pearl and Minna, too. I said to you that for the first year …"

“So that *gruber jung*, your cousin, can sneer at me when I return with a full pack? It's for this I have studied Torah all these years?"

"That *gruber jung* will show us the way to a better life. I can do well in the store and Yussel has worked to prove himself today. Even the girls… What will you do, my *mann*, sit and *doven* while your family struggles? In the old country …"

"In the old country? Already, it's the old country? After a day and a half, this is now your home?"

Painfully, Yussel stood up. "Cousin Avraim said I was as successful as two men today. Maybe Tata won't have to work for him. He can look for pupils. One of my customers told me that they still want their children to learn Torah, and they'll pay."

Mama patted Yussel on the back. "Just thirteen, and already, a Solomon. Let's eat and we'll talk more." She walked heavily into the kitchen, followed by Minna and Pearl.

Tata prayed so long before dinner, it seemed they would never get to taste the food. Minna thought he sounded as if he was complaining to God.

After dinner, as they sat at the table, Mama said, "I have a suggestion. Why don't you, Dovidl, stay home for the next few days and see if you can find some pupils. Maybe there is a Yeshiva where you could teach. You must ask the people in the street. I'll ask Mrs. Perlman, too. We won't tell Cousin Avraim anything till it's settled. We'll just say you're ill from the trip."

"If I could teach, it would be better," Tata said, relieved.

"We have to pay our debt to Cousin Avraim as soon as we can," Mama insisted. "Only then will our lives be better. If you can earn a few dollars a week so we can still give Cousin Avraim a dollar to pay back, or if Yussel can earn more… If the girls come in and help every afternoon, they should be paid, *nu*? Perhaps it will work out," she concluded.

"It must work out," Tata stated. He stomped into the front room and opened his books. His back to the rest of the family, he began to read.

Minna looked down at her plate, squeezing her eyes to stop the tears. It isn't fair, she thought. We all work hard. Why should Tata be different?

Mama, as if aware of her criticism, spoke firmly. "In *der alter heym*, it was an honor for me, the daughter of a shopkeeper, to marry a man as learned as your father. I promised myself when we married that I would keep him free from care so he could follow the Word of God. Sometimes it is hard. Sometimes I forget…but it is his right. None of us must ever forget that." She stood up and began to clear the dishes.

In their bedroom that night, Yussel and the two girls talked it over. "It is his right," Yussel agreed. "That's the way it was at home. Why should he have to change his whole life? He didn't even want to come. I would have lived like that, too, if we'd stayed there."

"Are you sorry we didn't?" Minna asked.

"I like to study," Yussel admitted, "but I like to sell better. No,

I'm not sorry. At home, I wouldn't have had such choices."

"I still don't think it's fair," Minna persisted. "When I marry, it'll be to a man who works for his family, not talks to God."

"Maybe his prayers help us," Pearl suggested.

"That may be true," Yussel agreed. "It certainly can't hurt." Changing the subject, he looked at Pearl "So, the two of you are going to the *Amerikaner* school tomorrow?"

"Oh, Yussel," Pearl cried. "You saw our school. It looks like a palace…or a prison…"

Minna laughed. "It makes a big difference which one!"

"What you have to do is to learn for me, too," Yussel urged. "When you come home, you can give me lessons. Today, someone told me there's a school at night. Once I get used to the *pekl* and I'm not so tired when I come home, I can try that. We have to learn English now, or we'll never get ahead."

Minna put her arms around Yussel. "Every night, I'll teach you everything I know, Yussel. I'll listen extra hard so I'll learn it the right way."

Pearl nodded her head vigorously. "I, too."

When they lay in bed, Minna spoke to Chava in her thoughts. 'If you were here, you'd be more help to Mama than I am. I'll try to take your place, but I miss you, big sister.'

Bubbe replied, 'Take her place, little Minna? No one expects you do more than your best. I'll be watching to help.'

Minna fell asleep, anticipating and dreading the day to come. Instead of her usual nightmare about Chava's death, she dreamt she was being chased by an ugly man dressed in red, white, and blue. He ran after her with a stick, shouting, "Speak English! Speak English!"

CHAPTER 6

Minna awoke with a start the next day, nudged Pearl, and hurriedly slipped her dress over her head. After she had pulled her lisle stockings as tight as she could so they wouldn't wrinkle, she tried to look at her reflection in the tiny mirror she had hung on the wall. She could only see herself in segments, so couldn't even imagine the final effect. She hoped shortening her dress had been the right thing to do.

In the kitchen, Mama flourished a bright red ribbon, which she tied at the end of Minna's single braid. She held up a blue one for Pearl and tied that, too. Stepping back, she narrowed her eyes and looked at her daughters. "You look like real *Amerikaners*!" she smiled.

Tata and Yussel had already left. Pearl and Minna ate a quick breakfast and waited outside at their door for Debbie.

"You shortened your dress," she said to Minna approvingly when she came out. She smiled.

"But where's your lunch? You have to bring lunch to school."

Tears began to fill Pearl's eyes.

Minna said quickly, "I forgot. Wait a minute and I'll get it."

She ran back into the apartment. "Mama!" she called. "I have to bring lunch to school."

She was about to leave. "I can't stop," she said hurriedly. "I'll be late for Cousin Avraim. Look in the kitchen, Minna."

Minna ran into the kitchen, but she saw nothing she could take. Conscious of Debbie waiting and afraid of being late, she shook her head and hurried out, locking the door behind her with the key Mama had given her.

"We won't have lunch today," she explained. "Maybe we can go by the store at lunchtime instead."

Debbie shook her head. "You can have some of mine, then, each of you." She ran back into her apartment and came out with a few extra pieces of fruit, which she thrust into her lunch pail.

The three girls hurried down the stairs. "You'll have to start out with the babies," Debbie warned. "But if you learn English quickly, they'll skip you. I skipped three times last year," she added proudly.

"Skip?" asked Pearl.

"That means they put you ahead," Debbie explained. "My teacher, Miss Kelly, says I'll be skipped again soon, but I don't want to be. I love Miss Kelly. She's perfect. I want to stay with her forever. Her shirtwaist is white as fresh snow, her red hair is shiny, even her shoes look new. When she speaks, her voice is soft. I'm going to be just like her when I grow up."

"Will Miss Kelly be my teacher, too?" Minna asked, thinking it would be wonderful to have such a paragon as her teacher. She had imagined all the teachers would be fierce old men, like Tata and the others at the Yeshiva .

"That's up to the principal. He's the head of the whole school. You have to see him first—or Miss Quinn, his secretary. They decide where you go."

"How will they decide?" Pearl asked nervously.

"By whether you speak English or not. The whole school's in English, of course," Debbie replied impatiently.

"Oh," said Pearl humbly.

Minna's heart sank. "Do they slap you if you don't understand?"

"Sometimes."

Minna and Pearl were silent the rest of the way to school, each thinking their own fearful thoughts. When they stood in front of the big brick building, Minna hesitated.

Debbie pulled at her arm. "Come on, come on! I'll be late!"

Minna hung back. 'Help me, Bubbe,' she thought. 'This palace is not for me. They'll laugh because I don't understand and my teacher will be a terrible old man, not that nice Miss Kelly.'

'Maybe so,' Bubbe reminded her, 'but if you're afraid, no one in your whole family will learn. Pearl will go home with you. Yussel, who has to work instead of studying, will never learn to speak English. You're lucky to have a chance, little Minna, and you think of running away?'

Minna squared her shoulders and followed Debbie inside the building. Pearl held her hand tightly. More children than either of them had ever seen in one place streamed through the wide corridors. Each of them seemed to have a destination. No one looked up or noticed the two of them as they trailed hesitantly behind Debbie.

Finally, she pointed to the end of long crowded corridor. "Go straight ahead and you'll see a big brown door at the end of the hall. Knock and go right in. I can't wait because the bell is going to ring and Miss Kelly will have a mad on me."

As she finished speaking, a clamoring bell rang overhead. Within seconds, all the children in the corridor had disappeared into different doors along its sides. Only Minna and Pearl remained in the now empty hallway.

Slowly, the two girls walked toward the large brown door. The closer they approached, the larger and more intimidating it became. Pearl squeezed Minna's hand so hard it hurt. They stood outside the door as Minna gathered enough courage to knock. Just as she lifted her hand, the door swung open.

A tall, thin woman with gleaming spectacles stared down at them. She said something in English which they couldn't understand. Shrugging, she gestured for them to follow her through the doorway.

Minna and Pearl walked behind her into a large office furnished with several chairs and a big wooden desk. To the side of the desk was another door. The woman pointed at the chairs and went back the way she had come, through the door into the hall.

The girls sat gingerly on the edge of the hard wooden chairs, staring around the room. Was this the way the inside of a school looked? Where were the other students, Minna wondered.

Finally, noticing how desperate Pearl looked, she tried to make a joke. "Don't worry, if this is school, it's not so bad. All we do is sit in chairs!"

The door to the hallway opened again and the woman returned, followed by a girl several years older than Minna. "My name's Ruth," the girl said. "Miss Quinn asked me to come and translate so she can write down your names. Then I'll take you to your class."

Minna nodded. "I'm Minna Ruben and this is my sister, Pearl."

Ruth told Miss Quinn the names.

"How old are you?" Miss Quinn asked them through Ruth.

"I'm ten and Pearl is eight."

"Do you speak any English?"

Despite her lessons on the boat, Minna shook her head. If speaking meant communicating, she knew nothing.

"What's your address?'

Minna told her.

Miss Quinn wrote everything that Ruth told her in a large ledger. Then she thought for a minute, said a few words to Ruth, and pointed to the door.

Maybe Miss Quinn has decided to send us home, Minna thought. Maybe she said to Ruth, 'Send them back. They don't belong.'

Ruth, as if reading her thoughts, explained, "Miss Quinn has decided that you should go together to the beginning class. Since neither of you know any English, it's a good way to start. Being together will make it easier. Come with me and I'll take you there."

Relieved, Minna followed her. Pearl smiled up at her, happy they were not to be separated. They hurried after Ruth, down the long corridor, and around the corner. She stopped in front of a door.

Looking down at them, Ruth smiled reassuringly. 'Don't worry," she consoled. "Soon you'll be able to speak for yourselves.'

Ruth knocked on the door. Without waiting for an answer, she opened it and stepped inside. Minna and Pearl followed.

Although Minna felt too shy to look around carefully, she was conscious of rows and rows of small desks. A raised podium with a single large desk on it was placed in front of the room. Standing behind it was the teacher. She wore a navy blue skirt and jacket over a crisp white shirtwaist. When she smiled at the girls, Minna thought she looked friendly. Then she turned to Ruth and said something to her.

"Go and sit at the back," Ruth told them.

Hesitantly, Minna and Pearl walked to the back of the classroom and sat at two empty desks next to each other. As they passed the other students, Minna noticed that only a few were her age. Most were Pearl's.

The teacher continued the lesson she had been teaching. Pointing to her head, she said, "Head." The students repeated the word after her, pointing to their own heads. Then she wrote the word on the blackboard. As the children copied it down in their notebooks, she walked down the aisles. All forty students sat up as straight as they could.

Stopping at one small girl's desk, she patted the child's head. "What is this?" she asked.

"Head," the girl repeated.

The teacher smiled.

Minna relaxed. She could repeat words as well as the next person.

The teacher pointed to the little girl again and said "Girl."

Again, the whole class repeated the word after her. Minna and Pearl spoke as loudly as the others did. The teacher smiled approvingly at them.

She pointed at herself and said, "Miss Wright." Gesturing with her hand for the rest of the class to remain silent, she looked at the two girls expectantly.

"Miss Wright," Minna said.

Pearl repeated it after her.

Miss Wright pointed to the two girls. "What is your name?" she asked in English. Her gestures were so vivid and the questioning tone in her voice was so obvious that Minna was able to reply without hesitation.

"Minna Ruben." She pointed to herself. "Pearl Ruben," she added, pointing to Pearl. Pearl nodded, reassured by the sound of her own name.

Miss Wright went back to her desk and picked up a smaller ledger like Miss Quinn's. She wrote in it, saying aloud, "Minna Ruben. Pearl Ruben."

The girls beamed. Even though Miss Wright pronounced their name in a strange way, they could understand her. They can't send us home now, Minna thought. We're in the book.

Minna listened carefully all morning. Enthusiastically, she repeated every word after Miss Wright. Soon, she had memorized more than thirty words. She repeated them over and over under her breath so she'd be able to repeat them to Yussel and Mama later.

She noticed that most of the other children had blue lined notebooks and pencils. That's what we need, she thought. Then I could be sure of remembering everything for Yussel and I could practice my writing, too. She wondered how much it would cost to buy one for each of them.

At lunchtime, she and Pearl followed the rest of the class. They looked around the lunchroom for Debbie, but they didn't see her. They had no choice but to take a seat and watch everyone else eat. Both understood they would not be allowed to leave and visit Mama at the store. For one thing, Minna thought, we'd never be able to explain where we were going. Finally, someone offered them a bit of apple, another a scrap of cheese, and another a bite of bread. Still hungry, they filed back to their classroom, more concerned about what was going to happen next than their missed meal.

Every time Minna heard one of the school bells ring, she flinched. It was so loud! It seemed she'd never be able to ignore the sound the way everyone else did. The other girls told her that each bell meant the beginning of another class. The older children, they explained, often had more than one teacher during the day. Minna shuddered. Miss Wright was all right, but she didn't want to take a chance with anyone else.

In the afternoon, their teacher showed both girls how to write their names. They practiced on a slate, copying it over and over again, until their scrawl looked something like Miss Wright's example at the top. They continued to repeat words with her along with the rest of the class.

When school was over, Minna felt slightly faint, a combination of hunger, relief, and excitement. They had been sitting still for too long, even though Miss Wright had done calisthenics with the class. She and Pearl skipped all the way to the store. Minna hummed happily. I can write my own name in English, she thought. I know lots of words now. Soon, I'll speak like a regular *Amerikaner.* As they approached the shop, Minna repeated the words she had already learned.

At the door, Benny Herschel stood sentinel, guarding the table of goods and "pulling" more customers into the shop. When he saw them he beamed.

"So, *nu*, how was your first day of school?"

"It was fine!" Minna crowed.

"I can write my name in English!" Pearl added.

Benny Herschel looked impressed. As they went by, he made a mock bow, as if to say, "The Queens of Sheba are passing by."

Mama came to the doorway as soon as they entered the shop.

"So, now you both speak English?"

"Not yet, Mama. But we can write our names and say a few words."

"Tonight, you'll tell them to Yussel and me. Now, quickly, straighten up the tables. Then I'll give you money for dinner. You can get some bones from the butcher and some vegetables to make a good soup."

Minna looked around for Cousin Avraim, but he wasn't there.

Mama, noticing her gaze, smiled proudly. "See," she boasted. "Already, he trusts me with the shop."

The two girls hurried through their work, straightening the bolts of fabric and putting them in neat rows. As she worked, Minna chanted the new words she had learned under her breath in a low monotone.

Mama helped them, smiling as she saw order emerge. 'It's still not really organized," she sighed. "They should be by color, or weight, or price, or ..." She shrugged. 'First, I'll have to convince Cousin Avraim. Then I'll be able to make a few changes."

When they were done, she counted out some money, handed it to Minna, and told her exactly what to buy and how to prepare it. "I won't be home till after eight," she explained. "Unless we get dinner started ahead of time, we'll eat too late."

Minna nodded reassuringly to Mama, but she felt a heavy weight on her shoulders. Suppose she spent the money foolishly, or ruined the dinner. In *der alter heym*, Mama had always helped her cook. 'Help me, Chava,' she thought. 'Show me how to go on.'

A customer came into the shop, demanding Mama's full attention. She waved at Minna, telling her to leave. When Minna seemed frozen to the spot, she motioned fiercely.

Pearl patted her on the shoulder and whispered, "Don't worry. Look how well we did yesterday."

Mama glared at them impatiently and they hurried out.

It took Minna a long time to finish shopping. She and Pearl visited what seemed to be every pushcart on Hester Street, seeking the best bargains. When they finally trudged up the stairs to their apartment, they were confident they had made no mistakes.

With Pearl's help, Minna started the meal. Only after everything was bubbling on the stove did she feel she could sit down at the kitchen table and try to put her thoughts in order.

The first problem was, how was she to get a notebook for each of them? There were a few pennies left over from the food money. Perhaps Mama would let them buy notebooks, especially because its purpose was to help her and Yussel. If not, maybe Tata had notebooks they could use. Minna sighed. She really wanted one with blue lines like the other girls.

There was a knock at the door. Pearl ran to open it. Debbie entered, holding her baby sister in her arms and a small brother by the hand. "So," she smiled, "how did you like school?"

"I have a really nice teacher," Minna answered. Her name is Miss Wright. I've already learned some English."

"She *is* nice. So that's why I didn't see you at lunchtime. The younger classes eat earlier. You must have been hungry."

Minna smiled. "I was, at first, but I hardly thought of it later. I've been busy. I had to start supper …" she began proudly.

"Well, make sure you bring something for tomorrow," Debbie interrupted.

"I already planned it," Minna replied. "But …"

"But what?"

"Where can I get two notebooks and pencils?" she blurted.

"You can buy them on the street. It's only two cents. Come on, I'll show you where."

"I…can't…"

"Well, you each have to have a notebook. Everyone has one." Debbie frowned. "I have four cents saved for myself. Mama said I earned it and I was going to buy some candy. I'll lend it to you instead so you can buy two notebooks. If you bargain, since it's the end of the day, maybe you can get two for one. Come on!"

Minna hugged Debbie. "Thanks!" she exclaimed. "I'll pay you back as soon as I earn the money. Mama said maybe they'll pay me at the store. If not, I'll find a way. Or maybe, Mama will give it to me." She said the last sentence dubiously, her voice dropping. After checking the pot to make sure it wouldn't burn, she gave it a quick stir, and hurried out of the apartment with Pearl, Debbie, and the two infants.

Debbie stopped next door to get her money. Then. still carrying her baby sister, she ran down the stairs, calling "Let's go!"

That night, Minna and Pearl proudly showed the rest of the family their notebooks. Each had written their name carefully across the top, just like the other girls in their class. Tata scrutinized the writing carefully, running his finger over the elongated scrawl. Mama gave Minna two cents to pay Debbie back, for they had gotten a bargain—two for one.

"Next time," she warned, "you'll have to earn the money yourself."

Yussel had again sold more than Cousin Avraim had expected. Even though his shoulders hurt, he was happy. He entertained the family with an imitation of one of his customers, a Mrs. Schine, who demanded, according to Yussel, "A bloomer for the window sill." Yussel described his embarrassment when she understood what he thought and the circuitous route it took before he realized that she wanted to buy a flower in a pot, not underwear. 'So,' I wanted to say, 'I'm not a farmer,' but instead, he concluded, "I promised to bring her one tomorrow."

Tata listened cheerfully. He had found a job at a nearby Yeshiva. His pay was only $3 a week, but Mama felt they could manage on the extra Yussel would be making and the small amount she hoped Cousin Avraim would pay the girls for helping in the afternoon.

After dinner, the whole family except Tata sat at the table imitating Minna and Pearl as they said "head," "girl," and the other words they had learned.

Yussel smiled. "America is truly a wonderful land! Four of us can go to school for the price of two! It's a real bargain!"

They went off to bed laughing. It seemed impossible, Minna thought, they had only been here for three days.

In bed, her arms around Pearl, she spoke to Bubbe and Chava in her thoughts, telling them what she had learned and how much she admired Miss Wright. 'She looks so tidy,' Minna explained. 'Even her fingernails are spotless. Tomorrow, I'll scrub my face and clean my nails before school. Tomorrow, I'll be able to write everything down!' Smiling, she fell asleep.

In the days that followed, Minna devoted herself to watching Miss Wright. She scrutinized her every action, convinced she'd understand how to be an American by some kind of magic. She learned that Miss Wright's lunch was dainty and insubstantial, a small sandwich with the crusts scrupulously removed and an apple cut in quarters, all delicately wrapped in a soft white napkin. She hardly ever gestured with her hands when she spoke unless she was showing something to the class. Her voice was low and even; she had two ways of smiling—one just barely turning up her mouth and the other, when she was more pleased, with her eyes, too.

Every evening, Minna practiced saying the English words she learned over and over again. When she told them to Mama and Yussel after dinner, she tried to speak like Miss Wright, keeping her voice modulated and her hands in her lap. Invariably, someone complained that she wasn't speaking loudly enough.

One important step, she decided, was to make herself a pinafore. If she had a pinafore, in crisp blue and white gingham, she would look more American. It was the way the other girls dressed. There wasn't much she could do about Chava's dress, even though it was too hot for this time of year. Everyone called it Indian summer and said it would get colder, but she had her doubts.

She had seen a bolt of material she liked in Cousin Avraim's shop when she was helping Mama, but she didn't dare ask about it. Noticing how Pearl took her shoes off as soon as she got home, methodically stuffing the toes with wet newspapers to stretch them, Minna had asked Mama to get new ones for her sister.

Mama had replied sternly, "It's enough we have a roof over our heads and food on the table. The shoes will have to wait."

Minna knew that Mama wasn't angry, but it was hard to remember when she spoke that way. Pearl, despite Minna's efforts to tell her what Mama had said about the night of Chava's death, refused to listen. She put her hands over her ears when Chava's name was mentioned. Around Mama, she was timid and uncomplaining.

I have to earn some money, Minna thought. I could get Pearl some shoes and the material for my pinafore. She already gave Mama the money she earned in the store. She knew it was needed to pay the rent and buy food.

Debbie, she noticed, earned spending money by helping her mother with the sewing. Minna spent as much time as she could at Debbie's while dinner was cooking, watching her work the sewing machine. She could, she learned, rent one for two dollars a month, but it might as well be a hundred, she thought, for all the chance I have of that happening.

When she was at the Perlman's, she often spoke to Irving, their student boarder. He seemed to enjoy helping her practice her English.

One day, he confessed, "I have a little brother at home just your age. When I become a lawyer, I'm going to send for him to come to America."

When Minna told Irving about her need to earn money, he mused, "The problem is, you don't have very much free time. You'd have to do it at home, so you can watch supper." He shook his head. "Let me think on it. Maybe I'll come up with an idea."

Minna didn't like to keep asking him, but she began to feel very discouraged. She had to come up with some way to get some *gelt*. One afternoon, as she was studying the new words she'd learned and practicing her writing, she heard a knock at the front door.

Pearl was in the bedroom, so Minna called out, "Who is it?"

"It's me, Yankel!" was the answer.

"Yankel!" She ran to the door and flung it open. She marveled at the vision she saw. Yankel wore knickers, bright suspenders, and sported a dashing cap upon his head.

"Where'd you get the new clothes?"

"I earned the money," Yussel said proudly. "Uncle doesn't mind what I do when I'm not running errands for him. Some days are slow and I have time. So, I've started junking."

"Junking? What's that?"

"You must have noticed one thing about this *cockamamy* country. There's so much of everything. Even the poorest *schlimazl* has furniture. You've seen what there is on the streets…exotic fruits I've never seen before…clothing for a king or a beggar…shiny pots and pans…They even sell rags. And what they throw out! They throw out what we'd starve for months to buy in *der alter heym*."

"So?"

"So, I collect what people throw out. I look at the junkyards, garbage on the street, even the railroad station. I collect it and the junkman pays me for what I find. Once, I even found a broken watch! For rags, I get two cents a pound, for papers, one cent for ten pounds, and for metals, even more. I've bought myself a little wagon and whenever I can, I go junking."

"Sometimes, I even go uptown," he continued. "You should see what rich people throw away! It's worth more money and I hardly have to lift a finger."

He smiled at her. "I'm saving some *gelt*, so I can send for my sisters. I want them to be able to go to school when they come. I can't, because I have to work for my uncle. He says, 'What do I need with school?'"

"You can come here and learn English," Minna offered. "Every night after dinner, Pearl and I teach Mama and Yussel everything we've learned in school that day. Yussel says it's four for the price of two. Why not five?"

Yankel beamed. "I'll come. If my uncle doesn't need me, that is. How about I take you with me one afternoon to go junking?"

Minna's face lit up. "Oh Yankel, I've been trying to figure out how to earn some money."

Yankel interrupted her. He lowered his voice. "You know, I do talk to my mama just like you said. It helps me."

Minna nodded. "I'm glad. Have you heard from your tata yet?"

"No, not yet. He must be still on the boat or making his way home."

"What's your uncle like?"

"He's very busy. I hardly ever see him. He sends me around to deliver messages for him and his friends. At night, he doesn't come home till late, but he gives me food and a place to stay. He has two rooms, all to himself."

"He must be rich."

"I guess so. I don't know… At least he never hits me or yells at me. He has a way of looking, though…I do exactly what he says every time."

Minna shivered. "I guess it's good. You're here! That's the main thing."

"You're right. I have to go now and deliver a message. Shall I come tonight for the English?"

"Oh yes! I'll see you after dinner." Minna wanted to ask him to eat with them, but didn't dare issue an invitation until she had asked Mama.

As she stirred the dinner, she thought about junking. I'll do it, she thought. She called Pearl.

Pearl stumbled out of the bedroom, rubbing her eyes. "I fell asleep," she explained sheepishly.

"Yankel was here and he told me about a way to earn money for your new shoes and a pinafore for me. It's called junking and he's going to take me along."

After Minna had explained, Pearl was enthusiastic. "One day, I'll prepare dinner and you can go junking," she promised. "I like to cook." She smiled. "What if you find a gold ring, Minna, so we can be rich?"

Minna gave Pearl a hug. "I'll do my best, believe me. Who knows? I know the first thing I'll get is a new pair of shoes for you."

Pearl beamed.

That night, Yankel came after dinner to practice his English. Mama and Yussel were delighted to see him. Even Tata inclined his head and asked him if he had heard from his father.

The English lesson was more fun than usual with Yankel there. When it was time for him to leave, Minna walked him to the door. "Can we go junking tomorrow?" she asked.

"I'll try," Yankel replied. "I'll come by here if I can and we'll go out together. Bring a sack to hold what you find."

As she folded a sack, Minna felt rich already. A whole sack full of stuff, all for nothing, and all worth *gelt.* In her mind, Pearl's shoes were as good as bought and her pinafore was already being cut.

The next day, Minna rushed home after helping Mama and doing the shopping. When she ran up the stoop and opened the front door, she found Yankel sitting inside.

"It's about time! I've been waiting for you."

Minna quickly went over the dinner preparations with Pearl, ran upstairs, got her sack, and hurried out the door with Yankel.

"I have a new place to go," he told her. 'That's why I brought a sack, instead of my wagon. It's uptown, off Fifth Avenue behind B. Altman's. They have big bins where they get rid of their garbage. Sometimes, there's no one watching, so I hope we'll be lucky."

"On Fifth Avenue? B. Altman's?"

"It's a big store uptown," Yankel said importantly. 'We'll take the subway."

"I don't have any money. If I have to pay money to get money, what's the good?"

"Don't worry. We can slip under the turnstile. I do it all the time."

When they left the subway uptown, Minna felt as if she has entered another world. She looked around in astonishment.

"We're going to 34th Street and Fifth Avenue," Yankel told her. "That's a few more blocks." Although he walked with a confident swagger, Minna could tell he felt as out of place as she did. He even lowered his voice when he spoke.

She felt very uncomfortable. Fifth Avenue was wider than any street she'd ever seen. The sidewalks were broad, too. Although there were many people walking, it wasn't crowded like Hester Street or Orchard Street. There were no stalls or pushcarts. None of the people called to each other loudly or "pulled" in front of the stores. Instead, they spoke English in low tones and walked sedately.

Minna felt she really was in America. So this is what it's like, she thought. This is the way I'll be. Wide-eyed, she absorbed everything.

Suddenly, she stopped short. There, in front of her eyes, was the largest glass window she had ever seen. Inside the window was a woman dressed in an elegant dress. Minna stepped closer to the glass and peered at her intently, wondering how she had gotten inside the glass and if she was paid to remain perfectly still. Then, she looked more carefully. The woman was only a giant doll! She continued to stare, fascinated.

She noticed someone else reflected in the widow. It looked like…it was a girl. Minna touched her hair and so did the reflection. It's me, Minna realized. Next to her reflection, she could see Yankel.

This was the first time she had ever seen so much of herself at once. In *der alter heym*, she had only the small square that now hung in her bedroom or the river. At the river, her reflection had wavered, trembling in the fast-moving current.

As she continued to stare, ignoring Yankel's tugs at her arm, Minna saw someone else reflected in the glass. It was a girl her own age. She looked as perfect as the woman in the window. Minna turned her head quickly to see if it was only another doll. Instead, she saw a real girl with shining golden hair, unlike anyone she had ever seen before.

The girl pulled away from the woman she was with and looked back at Minna. From her elegant black patent leather shoes to the bright blue satin bow in her hair, she was … Minna groped for the right word. The one that came to her mind was "rich-looking", but somehow, that didn't encompass the quality of this girl.

Minna turned back to the window, Yankel quite forgotten. In the reflection, she could see both the girl and herself. I look like a crow in my black dress, she thought.

The girl's lips parted.

Minna leaned forward.

The woman put her hand on the girl's shoulder. "Come, Susannah, we'll be late for your fitting."

Without a protest, the girl followed the woman. Minna turned to watch them enter the store. As the door closed, the girl turned and looked once more at Minna. Her expression was serious. Then she was gone.

Yankel pulled harder at Minna's hand. "Come on, Minna. Let's go to the back. Hurry! I'll get into trouble with my uncle if I'm gone too long."

Obediently, Minna followed him. As she walked, she tried to imagine what it was like inside the grand store. She wondered what the girl, Susannah, was doing now.

"Susannah," Minna whispered to herself. "Susannah."

"I have so much to learn," she mused.

Yankel looked at her curiously. "We all do," he agreed.

"Someday," Minna said, her hand on Yankel's arm, "I'll go inside that store and I'll…"

Yankel pointed ahead. There, in the back of the store, were many large bins. The guard, sitting inside a small windowed office, had tipped his chair back and was fast asleep.

I'll think about it later, Minna decided, as she followed Yankel, holding her sack firmly in one hand.

Yankel, his fingers at his lips, positioned her on the far side of a bin, away from the guard. Quickly, he scaled the bin and jumped inside. Minna held up her sack and he tossed in pieces of fabric, scraps of wood, metal rods, and even a chipped cup.

Becoming impatient with this passive role, Minna hoisted herself to the top of the bin and looked in. She watched Yankel. Then, she, too, jumped in and began scrabbling in the rubbish. Luckily, it had been separated, as it had to be by law, so it was only "dry" garbage.

Digging through a pile of papers, Minna suddenly felt something hard. Triumphantly, she pulled it out, crying, "Look, Yankel!"

"Shh! Shh!"

Minna held up a silver locket on a chain. Clutching it tightly in one hand, she continued to paw through the rubbish.

Yankel held up his hand.

Minna stopped.

They could hear the footsteps coming towards them. They both ducked down. The footsteps passed.

Hastily, the two of them filled their sacks. Then Yankel peered over the edge of the bin. He jumped down, motioning to Minna to follow him. Hurriedly, they ran around the block towards the subway.

Neither said a word until they were sitting down in the train. Then Yussel said, "Let me see what you found."

Minna held up the locket. Shaped in the form of a heart, it hung from a silver chain. As she held it, turning it in the palm of her hand, she must have pressed a tiny latch, for the locket flew open. Inside was a lock of golden hair. It was exactly the color of Susannah's.

"That will be worth a lot," Yankel told her. "It looks like real silver."

Minna closed the locket, unfastened the clasp, and put it around her neck. I'll keep it to remember, she thought, curving her hand protectively over the heart.

Minna was silent the rest of the way home. When they left the subway, she followed Yussel to the junk dealer. She watched as he bargained and gratefully took the five cents she had earned.

Yankel took her aside. "Are you sure you don't want to sell the locket?" he asked. "I have a friend in the jewelry business. I know he'll give you a good price."

Minna shook her head. "I want to keep it."

"Thanks, for taking me with you," she continued dreamily. "I'll see you soon." She turned and hurried towards home.

Yankel looked after her, shrugged, and went in the opposite direction to find his uncle.

For the next few weeks, Minna went out by herself and with Yankel to collect junk. They didn't go uptown again. The public dump on the East River was easier to get to and more lucrative. The locket was the single most valuable thing she found, but in a few weeks, she had earned enough to pay for Pearl's shoes.

When she showed Mama the money and told her how she had earned it, Mama reached out a hand to take it, saying, "This is very good, Minna. We can use this to pay back Cousin Avraim faster."

Minna pulled her hand away. "I earned it for Pearl's shoes, Mama. I want to make myself a pinafore, too." She looked at her pleadingly. She knew that no matter what she said, Mama would make up her own mind.

Mama hesitated. Then she held out her hand again. "That money belongs to the family. I'll decide where it goes."

Desperately, Minna stepped back. "I worked very hard for this," she said tearfully. "If I spend my extra time earning money, I should be allowed to keep it. That's fair! Pearl helped me, too, by making dinner." Minna's voice rose. "Did you see Pearl trying to stretch her shoes? She can barely walk!"

Mama advanced towards Minna, in a fury. "In America, who's the boss—the mother or the child? Give me the money."

Minna shook her head and stood her ground. "I won't!"

Pearl, who had been a frightened spectator, turned and ran to their room. Minna heard the slam of the bedroom door as if it were far away.

Yussel, hearing the commotion, came into the kitchen from the front room. "What's the matter?" he asked.

"I earned this money going junking," Minna yelled, brandishing it in front of Mama. "I told you about that, Yussel. It's to buy shoes for Pearl and a pinafore for me. Now, Mama says I can't keep it. I earned it on my own, so it's my right. I *will* keep it!"

"Do I keep mine?" Yussel asked sadly.

Minna stopped. She thought of how hard Yussel worked. He never took anything for himself. Tears filled her eyes. "Maybe you're right," she mumbled. She started to hand the money to Mama.

She stopped. "But Pearl needs shoes. I can wait for the pinafore, but Pearl can hardly walk in those old things."

Yussel looked at Mama. "Pearl does need new shoes. Why not use this money to buy them, since Minna worked so hard for her sister?"

Mama shook her head. "I don't mind that. I just… What a child has is the parents'. That's the way it has always been."

Not in America, Minna thought, but she said nothing. She already knew some girls in school who earned money and hid it from their families. One of them said to her, "I know they would take it all, but I'm the one who got it. I do my share. If I want to buy something for myself, I'm going to!" Minna had thought nothing could excuse lying, but now she wasn't so sure.

Yussel seemed to know what she was thinking. "I think," he said to Mama, "Minna and I should be allowed to save a small part of what we earn. It took Minna weeks to earn that little amount. Meanwhile, she worked at the store, cooked dinner or showed Pearl how, did her schoolwork, and helped you in the house. She's going to need things for school and if she can earn the money herself, so much the better."

"I suppose so," Mama agreed grudgingly.

Minna smiled thankfully at Yussel.

"Thank you, Mama,"' she said dutifully.

She hurried into the bedroom to tell Pearl it was all right. "We'll shop for your shoes tomorrow," she promised.

Mama, as usual, behaved enigmatically. The next day at the store, she approached Minna. "So you want a pinafore like the other girls?"

Minna hung her head. "Yes," she whispered. "But I don't know how much Pearl's shoes will cost and they come first."

"If you have money left, tell me how much and I'll talk to Cousin Avraim about it. Have you picked a fabric yet?"

Minna brightened. Reaching across the table, she held up a bolt of the small-squared blue and white checked gingham she preferred.

Mama fingered it and nodded. "That's a good choice. You know how much? You have a pattern?"

Minna shook her head. "I'm going to look at Debbie's and ask her mother. Then I'll make my own pattern so I'll know how much I need."

"When you decide, I'll talk to Cousin Avraim," Mama repeated.

Minna wanted to hug her, but she felt too awkward.

"Thanks, Mama," she said.

Mama turned away.

Minna ran after her. Pulling the locket out from her dress, she showed it to her. "I found this, too. I haven't shown it to anyone except Pearl. I'm going to keep it."

Mama bent over and gently opened the locket. "Such a beautiful color," she said, touching the lock of hair. She closed it and held it in her hand. "Once," she said softly, "I had such a locket. It was given to me." She stood awhile in thought. Then, she patted Minna on the shoulder. "Wear it well." Again, she turned away.

Minna looked after her in amazement. She had felt she had to tell Mama about the locket, but she hadn't expected that kind of a response. She shook her head. I'll never understand her, she thought. Not in a million years.

Minna told no one about the girl, Susannah, except Bubbe. When she tried to explain her feelings, Bubbe said gently, 'Don't try to explain, Minna. Who can explain a dream?'

When Minna persisted, trying to talk herself out of the fascination she felt for Susannah and her life as she imagined it, Bubbe continued, 'Keep your dream. Dreams are good company, for they bring hope.'

Minna realized Bubbe was right. She had changed since she had seen Susannah. She watched Miss Wright even more intently and practiced her English more often.

Someday, she promised herself every night before she fell asleep, I'll go to that big store and I'll walk in like a princess …

CHAPTER 7

After much bargaining, Minna was able to get a pair of shoes for Pearl at a very good price. She had plenty left over for the fabric. When Mama told Cousin Avraim why Minna wanted the gingham, he gave her the material for half price, saying, "After all, blood is thicker than water." He even threw in the thread, so Minna was able to make the pinafore for practically nothing.

Now that it was no longer a secret, Minna talked openly about her junk collecting at the dinner table. Yankel, who often came to dinner before his English lessons, joined her in a joking competition. Yussel always had a funny story about his ladies, and Mama described the changes she was making in Cousin Avraim's store with great enthusiasm.

Even Pearl began to lose her shyness as she became friendly with some of the girls her own age in Miss Wright's class. Occasionally, she chimed in with an admiring word about her teacher, for she worshipped her, if possible, even more than Minna did.

Only Tata was silent. Every night, it seemed as if the prayers he said before dinner took longer. The minute he finished eating he escaped from the table and went to the front room to bury his head in his books. Most of the time, he acted as if he was alone in the apartment. Once a week, he handed Momma his salary in an angry ceremony.

After the first rebuffs, Mama no longer made an effort to include him in their dinner conversations. Minna wondered what she was thinking, but Mama hid her feelings.

In the past, Minna remembered, Tata had been pre-occupied, too. Yet a pretense had been made. Decisions had been referred to him and his opinion sought. His invariable "no" was usually changed to a "yes" by Mama, who cajoled, nagged, and even yelled when necessary, just as she had done about the move to America.

Here, it was different. No one made even a pretense of deferring to Tata. Mama, with Yussel, made every decision with no show of consultation.

It came to a head one night at dinner. They had all been talking. Mama, by sheer volume, wrested the floor from Yussel.

"So, I told Cousin Avraim, if we want the business to grow, there's only one way we can…"

Tata stood up. Leaning over the table, he yelled, "Woman, who are you? Your children are Godless. My son, he studies Hebrew no more. Instead, he learns English and begs at doors. My daughter scrabbles in the garbage to earn a penny. And I—I spend my days teaching children for money—children who have no respect for me or the old knowledge. At home, I had *koved.* The highest came to speak to me and ask my advice. Here, I live with *goyishe* children and I walk the streets as low as the poorest *schnorrer.* This is a land from Hell you've brought us to!"

They all fell silent Mama bit her lip and looked away.

Finally Yussel said, "I'm sorry about the Hebrew, Tata. I have to learn English so I can get ahead." Noting Tata's darkening expression, he hurried on. "It's not for me, it's for all of us. After I work and have my English lesson, I'm tired. Too tired to study my Hebrew…"

"Too tired for the Holy word! So, that's what it has come to. You, who were to be a seeker of wisdom!"

Mama stood up, too. "This is a New World," she remonstrated. "We must learn new ways."

"I have no need to learn new ways! This is not my country, it's yours," Tata yelled angrily. He hit the table with his hand. "I want to go back where we belong."

Mama shook her head instantly, without even a pretense of considering his words. "Go back? Go back to where we can be killed, where our children haven't a chance? Go back so you can sit amongst your books when the Cossacks come?" She paused, shocked by her own words.

"Go back," she continued, her voice shaking, "so my only son can be taken into the Tsar's army for the rest of his life? I will never return. We're doing well here. We have a future. Someday, Yussel and I will have our own store. Minna and Pearl will speak English like ladies and, if they're lucky, they'll marry well and their children will be birth-Americans."

"What matters the riches of the world if you lose your God?" Tata said coldly. "I see my wife and my children becoming heathens in the sight of the Lord. You no longer keep the commandments in your heart. Do you honor me, your husband? Does Yussel go to *shul*? And my daughters, why must they go to an American school? What will they learn that will help them find a husband? Better, they, too, should work so their father can live as he should."

Minna looked at Tata in horror. Not go to school? Not learn English? Not become an American?

"In America," she quavered, amazed at her own courage, "girls choose their own husbands. I'm going to be a school teacher like Miss Wright, so I have to study."

Mama shook her head at Minna. "It's not you who makes the decisions for this family," she said to Tata. "It is I, and Yussel. He works hard. It's his *gelt* that's supporting us most of all. He's no longer a child." She turned to him. "Do you want to return to *der alter heym*?"

Tata hit the table again. "You ask him? I am the head of this family."

"In America, it's different…" Mama began.

Yussel interrupted her. "I'm sorry, Tata," he said humbly. "No matter what, I can't return to *der alter heym*. My home is here, now. Even if you all go back, I'll stay. Here I have a chance for life. I can hold my head up when I walk on the streets."

Tata reached out and grabbed Yussel's jacket. "Yes, you are an *Amerikaner*. Next, you'll take off your *yarmulke*, shave your *payos*. You'll look like Cousin Avraim, like a *goy*. You already think like him. My son is no longer a Jew!"

Yussel wrenched away from Tata's hand and stood up. He was six inches taller than his father. Looking down on him, he yelled, "I don't want to be the kind of Jew you are!"

Tata looked at Mama in disbelief. "May God strike him dead! A son to talk that way to a father! It says in the Book …"

Mama leaned forward. "Since we were chosen for each other, I have fulfilled the commandments," she stated proudly. "I have treated you with respect. I have provided food and shelter for our family. But here, in America, it is the men who work, not the women. Cousin Avraim says …"

"I don't care what he says! What is he, but a shopkeeper, may he choke on his own goods!" Tata's eyes dropped and he sat down suddenly. "Where am I in this New World? What is my part here?" he mumbled. "For me, there is only one thing—to grow in the eyes of the Lord— and only one way to do that. I must study and learn His laws."

Mama moved behind Tata and patted his shoulder. "I understand what you are saying. But, my *mann*, it's different here."

Tata looked up. "No one asks you to understand. You're only a woman. It is I who understand and you who must follow. We must return to a holier land, to *der alter heym*, where we will keep God's commandments as we always did, where our lives will follow the old, true patterns."

Mama shook her head. "Those patterns are broken. We have a new way to live. You don't need to change. Change is not given to all of us. Remain as you are. We'll earn the *gelt* to support you. But," her voice rose, "you cannot tell us we are wrong. Not here! You have no right!"

"I can't tell my wife, my possession, that she is wrong? I can't chastise my son, direct my daughters? Woman, it is my duty from God to live as my father and my father's father lived. This *trayf* country has stolen my rights. Here, I am not as I should be." He stood up again. "Hear this! I will return to my home, with or without the rest of you!" Tata stamped into the next room.

Mama followed him, her hands clenched tightly together. The others remained at the table and stared helplessly around the room. Finally, Minna and Pearl stood up and started to clear. As they washed the dishes, they could hear Mama and Tata yelling in the next room. The three of them began to talk softly amongst themselves, as much to drown out the loud voices from the next room as to share their feelings.

"I'll never go back," Yussel vowed. "I have a chance here. Someday, I'll own a store. When I have a family, they'll be safe from the likes of the Tsar. I'll try not to abandon all of the old ways, but there's more to life. Here, I'm a *mensch*. Here, I hold my head high."

Minna nodded. "Here, I can become a teacher. I have a choice in my life. I don't have to wait for the *shadchen* to pick a husband. I'll stay with you, Yussel."

"I will, too,' Pearl agreed shyly. "When I think of *der alter heym*, I think of Chava," she added simply.

Minna reached out to hug her. It was a good sign that her sister had mentioned Chava, she thought. She usually acted as if she had never existed. Of them all, she had been the most affected by what had happened.

They finished the dishes in silence. Then they walked through the front room to the outside door, their eyes carefully averted from Mama and Tata. Outside, they sat upon the stoop in silence, looking anxiously back up the stairs.

Finally, Minna said, 'Let's practice our English."

Half-heartedly, Yussel repeated words after Minna and Pearl. When it became too dark to see each other's faces, they reluctantly went back up the stairs to the apartment.

Tiptoeing through the darkened front room, they entered the kitchen. Mama sat at the table, her head bowed. When she heard them, she looked up.

She shook her head. "We'll stay, but he may go."

Without speaking, they filed off to bed.

That night, Minna had a long conversation with Bubbe. 'Am I wrong,' she asked, 'to want to change my own life? How am I hurting Tata? Must I live like a cow, to be traded for a husband?'

But Bubbe said, 'You can learn the new ways in a new country, little Minna, but that doesn't mean you should banish the old. I understand you, and I understand your Tata, too. I am only a woman, but I, too, believe in the Holy Scriptures and I say, why did the Lord take us from Egypt if our lives were never to change? The new has merit, but so does the old. Both are to be kept.'

Minna shook her head. She didn't understand how she could keep both. I am for the new, she thought defiantly. The old brings death and sorrow.

It was a long time before she fell asleep. She awoke several times during the night with her old nightmares, until, finally, she lay in bed, her eyes open.

The next morning, Tata had already left for work by the time Minna went into the kitchen. Mama's face was so drawn no one dared ask her any questions.

She ignored their anxious looks and merely said, as she always did, "I'll see you tonight, God willing."

All day, Minna worried about what was going to happen. Would Tata return to *der alter heym*? Would Mama stay here in the New World or would they, in the end, have to return—all of them? Mentally, she added up her earnings over and over, each time realizing they were not enough to support herself and Pearl.

Of course, if Mama wasn't here, I could work in the shop, she thought. I could go to school at night the way Irving's friend does. One minute, she'd think she could manage. The next, she'd decide that no matter what Yussel did, she'd have to leave.

In class, she watched Miss Wright, wishing she could ask her advice. She shook her head. How could she, with her dainty bread and low voice, possibly understand or help? For the first time since she started school, Minna paid less than full attention to her studies.

Miss Wright must have noticed, for when Minna and Pearl were leaving for lunch, she called Minna to her desk. "I hope to skip you soon," she said. "You must keep up with your work."

Normally, Minna would have been thrilled to be addressed privately by Miss Wright and dismayed by the thought of leaving her for another teacher, but today, she felt nothing. The day passed far too slowly. It was the longest she had ever spent. It seemed as if the dismissal bell would never ring. Despite everything, Minna carefully added the new words they learned to her notebook. There might still be a reason to practice their English. She forced herself to repeat the words so as to fix their sound in her mind, but all she could think about was Tata and what he would do.

When the bell finally did ring, the two girls hurried out of school. On the way to the shop, Minna noticed that Pearl looked more upset than she did. She stopped and pulled her sister down on the curb next to her.

"Don't worry," she soothed. "We'll figure something out."

"All I can think of is the graveyard." Pearl shuddered. "That's the only thing I want to see, but I don't want to either. I'm afraid, Minna."

That reminded Minna. "Pearl," she said, "you spoke of Chava last night. I've been trying to tell you what Mama said to me. She doesn't even remember what she said the night Chava died. She said that if she said anything, she certainly didn't mean it and I should tell you."

Pearl's eyes filled with tears. "If she didn't mean it, why can't she tell me herself?"

"I think," Minna said slowly, "she doesn't ever want to think of that time again."

"But she said it was my fault ..."

"You know Mama. When she gets upset, she blames everyone."

There was a pause. They both thought of the way Mama was.

"Maybe so," Pearl agreed. "Still, I was there. I watched and ..."

Minna reached out and shook Pearl. She was so worried about Tata, that for once she allowed herself to feel exasperated by Pearl's inability to stop blaming herself. "I tell you," she hissed, "it's not your fault. If I had been there, I couldn't have done anything except get myself killed, too. How would that have helped? You know," she continued in a calmer voice, "Mama had to watch her sister..." She looked at Pearl. "She probably felt just as bad as you do, Pearl."

Pearl looked back at Minna. "You really don't think it was my fault," she said thankfully.

"I've said it before. I've said it lots of times."

"Yes," Pearl said, half laughing and half crying, "but you never shook me before. Now I know you really do believe it!"

Minna couldn't stop herself. She too began to laugh and cry.

Pearl patted her hand. "It will be all right."

"It may not," Minna replied darkly. 'What will we do if Tata and Mama go home?"

"We'll stay," Pearl said blithely.

Minna looked at her. "You know what, I've been thinking about it all day. We have to make our own plans, the same way I did about junking. It's up to us."

"Of course. I always thought so."

Minna was surprised. It wasn't like Pearl to be so confident.

"I knew you'd have a plan," she explained. "We'll be able to do it once you figure it out."

"You're right! We'll stay here no matter what. We'll be able to work it out somehow. If Yussel stays too..."

"If Yussel stays too," Pearl echoed.

Minna retreated to her own thoughts and Pearl waited patiently. Finally, they stood up and continued on their way to the store.

When they arrived, Benny Herschel, as usual, had a warm greeting for them. Sensing Minna's discomfort, he patted her shoulder, wordlessly reassuring. Minna smiled weakly at him and rushed inside to see Mama.

She was helping a customer. Engrossed in the sale, she hardly looked up as they stepped in front of her. Minna gestured to Pearl and they began stacking the fabric and straightening the tables.

When the customer left, Minna looked at Mama hopefully, but she turned her head away and became busy counting the stock. Each time Minna approached her, she walked to the other side of the store.

Finally, as they were leaving to purchase dinner, Minna could no longer bear it. "Is Tata…" she began.

Mama shook her head briskly. 'We'll talk about it tonight. Go now!"

"But…"

Mama cuffed her lightly on the ear. "Go now, I say!"

The two girls hurried out. Mechanically, they bought chicken bones for tonight's soup, bargained with the lady at the vegetable stall, and trudged back to the apartment. After they started dinner, they wandered aimlessly around the front room. Minna didn't have the heart to go junking today.

Finally she turned to Pearl. "I don't care. I'm going to do my homework. You do yours, too. Then we'll see."

Dreading the waiting, they each took as long as possible with their homework. Just as they were finished, there was a knock at the door. Pearl looked fearfully at Minna. She opened it reluctantly, afraid it might be Tata. It was too early for Yussel.

Irving, the student from next door, smiled at her. "I haven't seen you for a long time. I've been worried about you. What have you been up to?"

"I've been junking," she explained. "Remember, I said I had to earn money."

"That's why I came over. I found a way for you to earn some *gelt*. You can make artificial flowers in the evenings. They'll pay you three cents every time you finish a gross, which usually takes an hour. What you have to do is to put the yellow centers in them. If you both can do it, you can earn six cents a night or even twelve cents if you work two hours. It's not so hard if you don't have to do it all day. I have a friend whose sister your age does it."

Minna brightened. Between junking and the flowers, she and Pearl could earn enough to provide some of the food for the two of them. If Yussel stayed too or if Cousin Avraim paid them more for their work in the store…

“You see, Pearl," she smiled. "We will be able to manage. If Yussel stays…"

"What do you mean?" Irving asked.

Minna was silent, unwilling to answer.

Finally Pearl said, "Tata wants to go back to *der alter heym*."

"I'm not surprised," Irving said. "It's hard to be a scholar in this country. That's why I decided to become a lawyer, instead."

His matter-of-fact attitude was reassuring.

"We're afraid we'll have to go back with him," Minna explained.

'If your Mama doesn't go back, you'll stay with her. She seems to like it here. It's she and Yussel who are supporting the family. My professor says this is a land for the strong. Your Tata's never been happy here."

"We don't know what Mama's going to do," Pearl said miserably.

There was another knock at the door. Minna opened it. Yussel stood outside.

He sighed. "I couldn't work any more. I was so worried."

Irving tactfully said his farewells, promising to tell Minna where she could pick up the flowers. She nodded her thanks.

As soon as the door closed, she turned to Yussel. "I've figured out how to earn more money," she said. "If Mama goes back, with what you earn and some from me, we could stay. At least, I think so. Pearl and I want to."

"It depends on how hard we can all work. You might not be allowed to stay if Mama goes. You're only ten, you know."

"I'm almost eleven," Minna insisted. "I can earn my way. I know I can."

"I think there are laws about children," Yussel said vaguely. "Mama will probably stay, anyway," he continued. "No matter what Tata does, I don't think she'll go back."

"But if Tata…”

"I don't care if he does go back," Yussel said angrily. "At home, he was a good father, but here, he only makes trouble. I'll never forgive him for Chava. I've decided to follow the new ways. If he's too old or too afraid to try, he shouldn't stay here, that's all!"

Minna tried not to show how shocked she was by Yussel's words. Although she agreed with him, it was frightening to hear it said aloud. Pearl sat stiffly, her hands clenched in her lap.

There was another knock at the door. It was early for Mama to come home. Besides, she and Minna had the only two keys. Hesitantly, Pearl opened the door.

Tata walked in. His face set, he walked by his children as if they weren't there and began to collect his belongings. Methodically, he packed his books in the wicker trunk.

They watched him, unable to say a word.

When he had finished, he faced them. "I'm leaving. I'm joining a group of *landsmen* who are travelling to the West to start a farm. They need me and my books. There, I will be useful. I'll be respected." He turned to Yussel. "You will come, too. It's your only chance to leave this corrupt place. Your duty is to me, your father."

"If I come," Yussel said slowly, "Mama and the girls will starve. They need the *gelt* I earn."

"Your mother will manage," Tata said coldly. "She needs no one, cares for no one."

Minna stepped forward to defend Mama, but Pearl pulled her back.

"I want to stay here," Yussel said, his voice shaking. "I like peddling."

Tata shook his head. "So says the *Amerikane kinder* to his father. So America teaches her children." Bitterly, he brushed by the girls and continued to collect his belongings.

"I'm sorry, Tata," Yussel pleaded. "I'm a man now. I must make up my own mind."

"And your debt to me, your father? That is as nothing to you?" Tata's voice softened. "All the years we've studied together… You remember those years?"

Yussel nodded.

"Come with me, my son. Together, we'll continue our work. The Lord God above will see and He will…"

Yussel reached out and touched Tata's sleeve. "I must stay here," he said desperately. "Can't you understand? When you were young…"

"When I was young, I did as my father asked," Tata replied angrily. "I married your mother, a black day it was. I became a scholar. He was proud of me, always."

There were tears in Yussel's eyes. "Can't I be different from you? Can't I choose my own path? All roads lead to God. "

Tata reached out and slapped Yussel across the face. "How dare you even speak of the Lord, your God?"

Yussel put his hand to his cheek. As he spoke, he rubbed it absently. "Since Chava died," he said angrily, "I have thought long and hard about your way. It is not mine. You chose to protect dead words while Chava was attacked. I went with you, but never again! What are books? I choose life first. I choose life!"

Tata turned his back on Yussel, closed the trunk, managed to hoist it upon his shoulder, and walk out the door. Grimly, he passed Pearl and Minna without a word.

The door shut with a bang that seemed to echo through their hearts. The three children stood looking after their father. They heard his footsteps slowly fading into silence.

"He never even said goodbye to me," Minna whispered.

Yussel rubbed his cheek. "He said goodbye to me."

Pearl ran and got a rag which she soaked in cold water. She handed it to Yussel.

"Thanks," he said, patting his cheek with it.

They looked at each other, wondering what to say to Mama when she came home. Minna wished she could run away or hide instead of having to describe the way Tata had acted. What words could she use?

"Mama?" Yussel asked. "What will she say?"

They remained in the darkened room for what seemed like hours. Minna forgot all about cooking. Only when she smelled something scorching did she jump up and run into the kitchen. She turned the gas off. No one would want to eat tonight, anyhow.

Finally, the doorknob turned and Mama came in. She looked around the room and saw that Tata's things were gone.

Nodding bitterly, she said, "So he's gone."

Yussel stepped forward.

"Yes," he agreed. "He's joining a group of *landsmen* who are going to farm in the West."

Mama nodded again. "He told me he would go." For a long moment, she stood without moving, her eyes closed.

Then she shrugged. "We'll manage, God willing." She sniffed. "What's that I smell?" She hurried into the kitchen. "The soup is spoiled, Minna. Come, I'll show you how to fix it."

She bustled around, adding this and that to the soup until its smell became savory. As they set the table, the two girls eyed Mama covertly. She seemed all right. They relaxed a little.

At dinner, Yussel took Tata's place. Gravely, he said the prayer and took the first spoonful of soup.

The meal was silent. Once Mama said, looking at Minna, "In America, you will choose your own husband."

Later, she said, "We can take two boarders in the front room. If we offer breakfast and do laundry, we can charge a dollar a week. For dinner they'll pay separately. That way, we'll be able to manage."

'Where will you sleep, Mama?" Pearl asked.

"In the kitchen. I can set up a bed there." she pointed to a small alcove in a corner of the kitchen. "I'll put up a curtain."

"I can sleep in the kitchen," Yussel offered. "You can have my bed in the girl's room.

Mama nodded. "That will be better. You're a good son."

Minna began to feel that they would manage very well without Tata. She thought Yussel and Pearl felt the same way. It was hard to tell just how Mama felt. She didn't seem distraught the way she had been when Chava died.

That night, Bubbe said, 'It's a bad sign when families separate. Yet I never liked him, my *aidem.* Nor has he been good to my Ruchel. She, too, had dreams. Just like you, Minna. There was never a chance for her to make them come true.'

Minna lay awake for a long time, trying to picture her mother as a separate person, a woman who had dreams, who had suffered, who perhaps wished to love. She remembered how Mama's voice had softened when she had shown her the silver locket.

She stroked it. When I get older, she decided, I'll make my own life. No one will force me to live the way they want me to. No one will make choices for me.

As she lay awake in bed, Minna could hear stifled sounds coming from the bed behind the curtain. Finally, she whispered, "Is that you, Yussel?"

The sounds continued.

Sitting up in bed, she stuck her head around the makeshift curtain. Yussel lay upon his bed, his head buried in his pillow, his body shaking.

Minna touched her brother's shoulder.

Yussel muttered, "He's still my Tata, and now, he's gone."

"I'm glad he's gone."

Yussel sat up. 'When he was teaching me, he was truly happy. His face softened. He would smile sometimes. He was proud of me."

Minna was confused. It was easier to hate Tata.

"It wasn't his fault," Yussel explained. "The Torah, that's all he knows. He and Mama married because it was arranged. He always wanted to be a rabbi, you know. There was never enough money for him to go to the right *yeshiva*. He would have been a good rabbi."

"I don't think so. He never cared about people. In *der alter heym*, the rabbi cared about all of us. When I was sick that time..."

"Now I'm the man. But, am I really a man yet?"

In the darkness, their whispers assumed an unearthly quality. It was as if each was alone, talking aloud to the black night. It was easier to speak from the heart.

"Mama is strong," Minna said, to comfort Yussel. "And we're here. You're not alone."

"Sometimes, I'm afraid," he said hesitantly.

"I am, too," Minna agreed. "I think even Mama is sometimes. We all are."

"Tata was afraid all the time." Yussel kept his voice steady with an effort. "Suppose I'm like him."

Minna reached out and gripped Yussel's hand as hard as she could. "You're not! You're not!" she insisted. "You have us, you know. We won't let you!""

Yussel tried to smile. She could sense it in the darkness. "You'll be like Mama when you grow up."

"No, I won't," Minna replied angrily. "I'll be like me, only me."

Yussel chuckled and brushed the top of her hair with his hand, a trick that used to make Chava furious.

Minna was flattered. "Good night, Yussel," she said softly.

She lay down in her bed again. As she closed her eyes, she heard Yussel say, "You'd better watch out, my ladies. Tomorrow, I'll sell you everything— even the shirt off my back —and you'll buy!"

Minna smiled to herself. We'll manage, she thought. We really will.

CHAPTER 8

For a year and a half, they heard nothing from Tata. As time passed, he was rarely mentioned. It was as if he had been forgotten. No one spoke of missing him. When she did think of him, Minna pictured him huddled in a dim corner in a strange house poring over his books. She couldn't imagine him living on a farm or working outdoors.

To her surprise, she did often dream about him, or about another father with his face. In her sleep, he was a different Tata, loving and helping her. Sometimes his face changed and he looked like the principal at school or Benny Herschel, who had become a good friend.

The family was prosperous and busy. Minna had skipped several grades, Yussel had become a customer's peddler with an ever-growing list of steady clients, and Mama had almost doubled Cousin Avraim's business. Pearl, an excellent cook, assumed full responsibility for their meals. She also acted as liaison with the two boarders who now shared the front room, Sarah Rabinowitz and Bessie Shostakoff.

Now that Pearl could take over the household after school, Minna was free to find other work. She was finally able to rent a sewing machine with her junking and artificial flower money. Every afternoon during the week and all day over the weekends, she sewed shirtwaists, which she sold to a jobber. The money she earned, added to Yussel's increased profits, the boarders' rent, and the extra that Cousin Avraim gave Mama now that she had repaid his loan for the tickets, was more than enough for the family's needs. Mama was able to save several dollars a month, which she carefully hoarded towards her dream, her own fine dress-goods store.

Minna hurried home from school one day in January. She had many shirtwaists to finish by the end of the week. As she passed the house next door, Rosie stuck her head out of her first floor window.

Rosie, of the blonde hair and the red light in her window, was as much disdained by Mama now as she had been on their first day in New York. Yet Minna found her friendly and warm. They exchanged words through the window every afternoon. When the weather was nice, sometimes they even chatted briefly on the stoop. By now, Minna knew what her profession was. Yet she found it hard to believe. Rosie was so smiling, pretty, and clean. She didn't seem like a bad woman.

"Can you come in, Minna?" Rosie called down to her. "I need some help. It's just for a moment."

Minna hesitated. If Mama found out, she'd be in trouble. On the other hand, she wanted to go. She was curious about Rosie's rooms. The way she imagined them, they were draped with satins and red velvet. Nervously, she ascended the stairs to the building entrance.

Rosie waited in the doorway, wearing a cotton wrapper. Her face was bare of rouge. "I want to write a letter to my mother at home in Yiddish. I thought you could help me. I'm not so good at writing."

Minna smiled. "I'll try," she offered. "I write mostly in English now."

Rosie ushered her into a well-furnished front room with an over-stuffed divan, tufted chairs, and even a few pictures on the wall. The primary color, Minna noticed, was blue, not red. The effect was elegant, not at all the way she had pictured it. Through the open doorway, Minna could see a large bed covered with a shiny satin throw. She averted her eyes.

Rosie sat down on one of the plump chairs and gestured to Minna to sit on the other. She handed her a crumpled piece of paper.

"I've already tried to write it, but I'm sure there are too many mistakes," she explained. "The whole village will read what I write.

My mother is so proud of me, she shows everyone. Usually I ask my friend, Mr. Dussel, to help me, but he's away for a few months."

Minna took the letter and read it aloud: "To my dear Mama, I hope you are warm this winter with the new quilt I sent you the money to buy. Here, in New York, it is cold, but since the store I work in is well-heated, I am warm all day."

Minna looked at Rosie questioningly.

Rosie blushed. "She thinks I work at a Fifth Avenue store."

Minna continued reading: "I have been very well. I am not married yet because in this country, a girl can make her own way without a husband. There is a young doctor who has been calling on me. I am sending you some money I have saved from my salary. This is for you to use and not to give to Father. I miss you very much and think often of *der alter heym* and the songs you used to sing to me before bedtime. Your Daughter, Rosie."

Minna read it over again to herself. "It's a good letter," she said. Tactfully, she pointed out a few minor spelling errors.

Rosie sighed. "The way I learned, I'm never sure."

Minna looked at her questioningly.

"I was only thirteen when I came here, all by myself. My father sent me away because there were too many girls at home. I know he was paid for me. I was supposed to work in the Bronx at a Mrs. Fein's. She's the wife of a *landsman* my father knew and they arranged it.

"They cheated me, those *gonifs*. I worked like a slave, day and night, and they never paid me. This went on and on. When I complained, they said, 'So *nu*, go back on the boat.' What could I do? I stayed there for more than a year. Finally, I left. Then I was out on the streets…"

She tossed her head. "That's another story. The thing of it is, I've learned to read and write since I was here. People help me," she added vaguely.

Minna's mouth opened. "All alone," she gasped. She couldn't imagine being without Yussel, Pearl, and Mama. "So, that's why…"

"When my English gets better," Rosie continued briskly, "I really am going to work in a Fifth Avenue store."

"I could help you practice," Minna offered impulsively. "You could come and talk to me while I'm sewing. I'll teach you what I know." As soon as she made the offer, she realized it was impossible. Mama would never allow Rosie to come to their apartment.

Rosie laughed quickly. "Oh no," she shrugged. "I don't have the time now. But it's a good offer. Thanks."

Minna looked at her. It was hard to tell if she was afraid of Mama or if she really didn't have the time. As Minna regarded her unadorned face, she realized Rosie must be about the same age Chava would be if she were still alive. She usually wore so much rouge on her cheeks and lips, it was hard to tell how old she was.

"You look pretty this way," Minna said shyly.

"They expect the rouge," Rosie answered. "That's the way they want me to look."

"Say," she continued, "I know a friend of yours."

"Who?"

"A boy. His name is Yankel."

"Yankel? How do you know him?"

"He brings me messages sometimes. He's a good kid—and some go-getter!"

Minna frowned. She sensed Rosie was talking about a different Yankel, the "bad" Yankel, the one Mama scolded and Yussel shook his head over.

Rosie shook her head. "Your Mama sure doesn't like me, does she? Every time she passes, she puts her nose up in the air as if she smelled something bad."

Minna stared at the floor.

Rosie patted her on the shoulder. "Well, never mind. Thanks, kid. You really helped me."

"Your letter was almost perfect," Minna replied. "You didn't need me at all."

As Minna hurried down the front steps, she saw the red light glimmering in the winter gloom. It looks inviting, she thought, and then blushed, recalling what the red light meant. It was impossible to reconcile her pleasant impression of Rosie with what she knew about her way of life. It was so unpleasant. One man is bad enough, Minna thought. She closed her eyes, remembering how Chava had looked, lying on the floor…

Automatically, Minna paused at the mailbox inside the doorway. She always looked, even though they very rarely received any mail. Occasionally, there was a letter from a distant relative in *der alter heym*. Today, she saw a large white envelope sticking out of the mailbox.

Minna picked it up. It was addressed to Mama. She turned the letter over to see the name of the sender on the back. It was from Tata!

All the way up the stairs, Minna held the letter gingerly, as if it might scorch her fingers. A letter from Tata! Does he want to come home, she wondered. If he did, how would she feel about it?

Minna shook her head. If he came home, their lives would change again. The *boarderkeh*, Bessie and Sarah, would have to go to make room for him. Less money could be saved for Mama's store. It would begin again, the complaints and the bitterness.

As she sat down in the kitchen at the sewing machine, Minna glanced anxiously at the family's newest possession,, a small tin alarm clock. She knew Mama wouldn't be home for several hours. Pearl, at least, would be coming any minute with the food she had purchased for dinner. She could tell her about the letter, but it was Mama who would read it.

By the time Pearl arrived, Minna had decided that Tata was writing to say that he wasn't coming home any more. She was surprised to feel a slight tinge of regret. Even though he walked out and left us, she thought, it's not easy to lose someone who had been a big part of your life. Even if it was a bad part. So what, she thought angrily. He doesn't care what's happening to us.

Pearl immediately noticed the letter, resting next to the sewing machine table in the kitchen. She picked it up, read the return address, and set it down. "I hope I never see him again. Bessie says only a coward would run away."

Annoyed that Pearl had discussed family matters with one of the boarders, Minna snapped, "Bessie says? What does she know of Tata? She never even met him."

"She knows. In her own life, her father came to America and left her with her mother in *der alter heym*. They had to track him down with the Rothschild Agency to make him send tickets. Then, when they got here, he divorced her mother. She's never seen him again."

"That's too bad," Minna concurred absently, inserting a basted seam tautly in the machine. She scowled at her sister. "It's Bessie this, and Bessie that with you," she exploded. "Can't you make up your own mind?"

Pearl turned her back and began to prepare dinner.

Six months ago, Minna knew, she'd have burst into tears and run from the room.

"It's not me you're angry at, Minna." Pearl said quietly. "It's the letter."

Minna took her feet off the pedals of the sewing machine and looked at Pearl. "You're right," she said at last. "I'm sorry."

"I do worry about Bessie, though," she added. "You seem to believe everything she says without even asking any questions. She has some strange ideas. She belongs to the Bund, and now she's talking about a Union. She's always going to meetings."

"I don't think her ideas are strange," Pearl replied stoutly. "If the Bund and the Union will help to make our lives better, I believe in them, too."

"But, Pearl, what does it have to do with us? We don't work in a factory. The only boss we answer to is Cousin Avraim and he's family."

Pearl came closer. "Don't you see? We'll have to work for someone else when we get older. Maybe it'll be in a factory. Who knows? If conditions are better by then, and it's because of people like Bessie and what they believe, we should be glad."

Minna considered Pearl's words. I should talk to Bessie myself, she decided. Glancing at the tin clock, she returned to her sewing.

"You wouldn't have to do piece work like this at home if the bosses didn't have control. In the factory, it's even worse, Bessie says. Instead of getting paid by the day, they get paid by what they get done. Whoever gets the least done, gets fired. So, they don't work together, they work against each other. That's what the boss wants," Pearl concluded.

Minna shouted over the noise of the machine. "That does make sense. But Pearl, if I couldn't work at home like this, I couldn't work at all and we'd probably have to move. So, what's right?"

Pearl shook her head. "I don't know. Bessie will have an answer. You should talk to her."

"I will," Minna promised. For a moment, she had forgotten Tata's letter.

Pearl went back to the stove to continue preparing tonight's meal.

The letter seemed to weigh less on Pearl, Minna thought. She, more than any of them, seemed to accept Tata's absence easily.

As the hours passed, neither Minna nor Pearl mentioned Tata's letter. Minna felt a heavy weight pressing against her. I'm sinking, she thought. If Tata comes back, what then? What will happen?

The first one to arrive home was Yussel. By now, he had his own key, for he sometimes came home in the middle of the day to pick up new supplies or to have lunch. His footsteps were heavy.

When Minna saw his grim face, she thought, maybe he already knows about the letter, but he didn't even notice it. He set down the small front basket and lowered his *pekl* onto the floor. Taking off his coat, he began to unpack, slamming the merchandise down on the floor.

"What's the matter, Yussel?" Minna asked.

"It's like *der alter heym*!" he stormed. "Today I was stoned by the Irish and a cop just watched. Then he told me I'd have to pay an extra dollar to buy tickets for the Policeman's Ball. I already give two dollars a month so they won't get me for loitering. You know, I've been selling by the factory at lunchtime."

"Did they hurt you—the Irish?" asked Pearl.

"No, they were only kids," Yussel sneered. At fifteen, everyone younger was a kid to him. "They couldn't hurt me. But I like to look good for my ladies, so I had to stop and clean myself off. Then the cop comes along… What does he think—-I'm made of money?"

"Can't you just ignore him? Bessie says it's against the law for him to make you pay. She says you could bring a case."

Yussel looked at Pearl in amazement. "What are you—a *farposhket farbrente*? I should go out and hire a shyster on top of everything else? What's he going to do, anyway? Tammany runs the graft. You think the judges don't get their cut?"

"Bessie says someone has to take a stand …"

Minna poured Yussel a glass of tea. "Here. Sit down and put your feet up. It'll make you feel better." She dropped the shirtwaist she had been sewing over Tata's letter, hoping to hide it until Yussel had rested for a few minutes.

It was too late. He had seen it. "What's that?" he asked.

"Oh, just a letter," Minna replied casually.

"Just a letter? We get so many letters here? Who's it from?" Yussel reached over to pick it up.

"It's from Tata," Minna explained quietly. "For Mama. I don't know what it says."

Yussel picked up the letter and examined it. "It's from

Galveston. What kind of a place is that? Galveston, Texas, it says."

He examined the letter painstakingly, turning it from side to side and peering at it as if he could see through the envelope and read its contents. Finally, he put it back on the table and looked at the clock.

"Mama should be here soon." He leaned back and sipped his tea.

The two boarders arrived before Mama. They worked at the same factory, so their schedule was identical. At home, they spent their time differently. Bessie sat in the front room reading and Sarah came into the kitchen to talk with the family.

Today, they both came into the kitchen. Minna looked up from her sewing.

Bessie sat down at the kitchen table. Her blue eyes, the most vital looking part of her pale, thin face framed with two wings of curly black hair, glistened as she spoke. "Today was the worst yet!" she exclaimed. "The boss refused to pay us till tomorrow. Said he'd give it to us in the morning. If he thinks he can get away with that…" Her voice throbbed.

"He did say, first thing in the morning," Sarah said mildly.

Bessie jumped up and stomped out of the room. At the outside door, she turned and yelled, "It's you who allows the exploitation of the masses!" Slamming the door, she ran down the steps.

Pearl made a slight movement as if to follow her. Minna shook her head.

"She's right," Sarah said apologetically. "It isn't fair. But what's the point of making a big fuss when it won't make any difference? We'll get it tomorrow. We always do." Her glossy brown hair framed a soft, round face. Despite her demure clothing, her ample curves were obvious.

"You're right and you're wrong," Yussel said judiciously. "If no one makes a fuss, nothing will happen. On the other hand, the one who starts it will suffer. She'll probably lose her job." He laughed. "What I want to know is, why does Bessie always sound as if she's yelling from a street corner?"

"You're right. The last girl who complained was fired."

As he talked to Sarah, Yussel seemed to have forgotten Tata's letter, yet when Mama finally came home, he jumped up. Minna stood next to him.

Mama, sensing that something was wrong, looked around the

room anxiously. She relaxed slightly when she saw her children standing there, all in good health. Then she noticed the letter on the table.

"A letter!" she cried. "A letter from *der alter heym*!"

Reluctantly, Yussel handed it to her.

Noting his anxiety, Mama eyed the letter apprehensively. She turned it over to read the return address. "From Tata?" she whispered to herself.

Sarah retired to the front room, closing the door behind her to give the family some privacy. Without a word, Mama took the letter into the small bedroom, shutting the door firmly behind her. Yussel, Pearl, and Minna waited in the kitchen, staring at the closed door. Pearl held Minna's hand as tightly as she would have last year.

Finally, Mama came out and stood by the edge of the table, gripping the top tightly She cleared her throat. "Tata wants a divorce. He says he is going back to *der alter heym* from Galveston. The rabbi on the commune will give him a *get* if I write a letter saying I agree." Her face was white. She sat down abruptly.

Minna went to get a cup of tea for her. Yussel sat by her and Pearl hovered between them.

"What do you think?" Yussel asked anxiously.

"We've been married almost twenty years."

"He's made up his mind?" Minna asked.

"He says that if I join him, we can stay married." Mama twisted the letter in her hands.

"I won't go back!" Pearl cried.

"What do you want to do, Mama?" Yussel asked.

"I didn't think it would go this far. I thought he would return. To be a woman alone…" She gazed at her family, clustered around her. "I'm not alone," she said decisively. "I have my family."

"He has none," Yussel stated. "He's no longer my father. I'll never forgive him."

"We never even said goodbye to him," Pearl added.

"I don't need him. I won't miss him," Minna said stoutly.

"It wasn't always so," Mama said softly. "Do you remember, when you were small, how he carved you each a small wooden animal? And you, Yussel, do you remember how you studied together?"

"And you, Mama," Minna asked bravely. "What memories do you have?"

Mama shook her head. "What good are memories? Will they put food on the table and a roof over our heads?" Her voice rose. "I spit on memories!" She stood up. "Get me a pen and paper, Minna. I'll write the letter. You'll help me if I need it, Yussel?"

Sitting at the table, Mama painstakingly copied the words Tata had written in the letter, the words that made her divorce legal. Yussel compared her copy to the original and nodded.

"Now, I'll write more," Mama said. "I'll tell him what I think." With many pauses and licking of the pen, she added ten more lines. She signed her name and placed the letter in an envelope without letting anyone see what she had written.

"Go!" she commanded Yussel. "Take it to be mailed right now."

Yussel took it, slipped on his coat, and hurried out the door to buy a stamp.

Mama remained at the table sipping her tea. Looking upwards, she agonized, "Tell me, was I wrong to come? Should we have stayed there, to be killed? I ask you, look at us now. Yussel works hard. He's already a success. Minna, she reads and writes like a professor. And Pearl, she's becoming a young lady. I don't worry they'll have to hide in a water barrel, my children."

Minna was about to reply, when Mama continued. "I'm a mother. You made me a mother, oh Lord. So, it's my duty to care for my *kinder*. If I find joy in this New World, is that a curse?"

Realizing that Mama was not addressing them, the two girls were silent.

"We eat meat almost every day," Mama went on. "People call me Mrs. instead of Ruchel. I have a chance to make something of myself. Someday, I'll even have a store. So I say, if he's afraid, let him go home and be killed. Let him face the Cossacks, hide from the peasants. Let him be the one."

Minna remembered Bubbe saying, long ago, that Mama had her dreams. Now she knew it was true. She glanced at Pearl and patted her shoulder reassuringly. Then she took her by the hand and tiptoed into the bedroom so Mama could be alone.

Unseeing, Mama put her head down, resting it upon her arms. Her shoulders were slumped and her head buried in her arms. The only sound Minna and Pearl could hear from the bedroom was the ticking of the alarm clock.

They sat on their bed, trying not to listen.

"You know, Mama's not so old," Minna whispered to Pearl.

"What do you mean?"

"I mean, she's not just our Mama..."

Pearl was confused. "Of course, she is."

"I mean..." Minna groped for words. She touched the bump the silver locket made under her dress. "I mean, she was young once, too."

"Of course," Pearl agreed, too readily.

Minna gave up. "All the same," she said firmly, "My life will be different."

When Yussel returned, the two girls rejoined Mama in the kitchen. She had recovered herself and was busily stirring the dinner.

She looked up. Facing them, she stated, "Let us not talk of this again. Life will go on."

Turning back to the stove, she commented, "You did a good job with dinner, Pearl."

Bessie gave me the recipe," Pearl replied. "It's a way her mother used to cook."

"That *farbrente*! She has a mother?"

Pearl stared at her mother reproachfully.

At dinner, the family spoke little. Sarah and Bessie, who paid for their share, ate heartily. As usual, Bessie did not apologize to Sarah for storming out. Instead, she was extra pleasant to everyone.

After the dishes were washed, Minna laid her schoolbooks upon the table. Pearl sat across from her and opened hers. Yet both stared at the pages unseeingly and looked secretly at Mama.

English lessons were now a thing of the past. Minna was busier and Yussel had already learned enough to transact business. He hoped to attend an evening class at the Educational Alliance soon. Mama had also learned enough words to get along, although she still relied upon the girls to read communications in English and to deal with officials. She complained that she was too tired at night to do more.

Yankel visited the family only rarely these days. He already spoke English as well as Minna and Pearl. "On the streets," he explained, "I either speak English or I give up!"

Nowadays, Mama often criticized him. Yussel disagreed with almost every thing he said. Only Minna remained loyal, defending him.

This evening, he made a surprise visit. He said hello to Mama and dropped a gift on the table as he always did. This time, it was a brand new copper pot. "For you," he offered, bowing slightly to Mama.

She picked it up and examined it suspiciously. "Where did you get such a thing?"

"I bought it."

"But…a pot like this! It must have cost a lot. So much money for you to waste."

Minna interrupted. "Thank you, Yankel," she said pointedly.

"Of course, I thank you." Mama flushed. "But Yankel, I worry. Where do you get the *gelt* to buy such a thing? This is finer than any pot I've ever had."

Yankel shrugged. "That's my problem."

He cleared his throat. "Call me Jake. Everyone calls me that now."

"So, now you're changing your name! You run around on the streets, up to God knows what, and now you're going to be Jake! You throw away money as if it grows on trees. What would your father have said, God rest his soul?"

Yankel looked away.

Mama shook her head. "I worry about you. There's no one else to worry, Yankel."

Yankel frowned. "I'm all right. I'm with my uncle."

He turned to Yussel. "So, how's the rag business? Still *shlepping* up and down stairs to get a few dollars?"

"It's an honest living," Yussel replied angrily. "At least I don't hang around with *shtarkes*!"

Yankel shrugged. "I can't complain. I'm not doing so badly."

"Your uncle!" Mama cried. "Everyone knows your uncle. I say, turn your back on him. He's no friend for you. Instead …" Mama swallowed. "Instead, I invite you to come and live with us."

Minna was shocked. Mama must really be worried about Yankel to make such an invitation. Especially after the way she had acted at Ellis Island.

Yankel looked at Mama in surprise. "There was a time I would have said yes, with tears in my eyes. Now, it's too late. I like living with my uncle. I can do what I want and go where I want as long as I do his errands. Otherwise, if I earn any money, I get to keep it. When he's in a good mood, he takes me to the ball game or buys me a present. When he's in a bad mood..." Yankel shrugged. "When he's in a bad mood, I just don't go home. That's all."

He put his thumbs in the lapels of his thick wool tweed coat. "You like my coat? You think it's nice? My uncle gave it to me."

Reluctantly, Yussel stroked the rich fabric of Yankel's new coat. "It *is* a nice coat," he admitted. "I'll give you that. But, where did it come from? From someone's back, that's where! I heard your uncle hired out his *shtarkes* last year at the baker's strike to help the scabs beat down the workers."

"So what?" Yankel sneered. "He's a big man, my uncle. If he wants to earn a few dollars, so what! Who cares about a few bakers?"

Pearl stood up. Minna, guessing she was going to parrot Bessie's ringing phrases, spoke quickly. "Do you want to go for a walk?" she asked Yankel.

Yussel shook his head. "I say, no. I say, don't go for a walk with such a person, who sneers at the poor."

Yankel flushed. "I didn't mean to sneer at the poor." He spoke slowly. "I was angry and..." His voice trailed off. "I still think my uncle is right. He is my uncle. He's been good to me."

There was still something sad in Yankel's eyes. There always had been. Minna sighed.

Yussel frowned. "I can't blame you for sticking up for your uncle, but..."

Yankel interrupted. "I know you mean well, both of you," he said, looking at Mama and Yussel, "but I have to live my own life."

He turned to Minna. "I'll go with you for that walk," he offered.

Hurriedly, before Yussel could say anything, Minna grabbed her coat and rushed out the door. All the way down the stairs, Minna thought about what she wanted to say to Yankel. She was so busy rehearsing it, she didn't even notice his quizzical looks.

When they reached the street, they sat on the stoop.

"Do you really want me to call you Jake?"

"Please. Everyone else does. It's a real American name. When I say Yankel, everyone knows I'm a greenhorn. Believe me, the kind of people I meet, I don't need that."

"I'll try to remember," Minna promised.

She looked at him intently. "Listen, Yankel—I mean Jake—what are you doing with your uncle? Why is everyone making such a fuss? When Yussel talked about *shtarkes*..."

"I want to explain it to you," he said earnestly. "Your Mama and Yussel just can't see it my way. They make me so mad, nagging all the time. But, Minna, if you could understand…"

She waited.

"Since my Tata died on the ship, my uncle's the only one I have here. I know my sisters won't be able to come over for a long time because I have to be able to make a home for them. They can't stay with him. So, I have to get a lot of *gelt* for them. My uncle, he's good to me. I earn a lot of *gelt* every day, so I say, why not? If he hadn't taken me in the first place…"

"If I could earn a lot of *gelt* every day, maybe I'd say 'Why not?' too. But the question is, what do you have to do to get it?"

"I know Tata wouldn't approve. But this is a different place than *der alter heym.* What was wrong there, is…different…here."

Minna looked at him questioningly.

"Well, one thing I do is hang around outside saloons. Sometimes I wait for my uncle. Sometimes I deliver a message for him. If a man comes out and he's really *shikker*, staggering around, and his money falls out of his pocket and I pick it up, that's all right, isn't it? It's like I found it."

Minna said nothing.

"Well, to be honest, sometimes I even take the money out of his pockets if he's lying in the street. I only do that if he's *shikker.* I figure, if he's stupid enough to drink too much, he doesn't deserve to keep his wallet?" Despite his attempt to sound definite, Jake's voice rose as if he was asking a question.

Minna answered slowly. "That is stealing, Jake," she said uncomfortably. "How is it not?"

"I didn't pick his pockets when he was walking around, like some friends of mine do. I didn't hurt him, or knock him down. I just took what was lying there, waiting for me."

"Oh, Jake," Minna sighed.

"But, I need it," He continued desperately. "Sure, my uncle is good to me when he remembers. Some days, he just doesn't come home. For all I know, he could have moved away, or got arrested. He doesn't think much about me. Suppose he never comes back. What would I do then?"

"You'd come live with us, the way Mama said. You could come right now."

Minna held out her hand, as if to pull Jake back into the

apartment.

"Your Mama wouldn't take me before, at Ellis Island, when I really needed help. Now I can manage on my own. I won't go. I don't need her, or anyone else."

He tried to smile at Minna. "I'm going to stop, for sure, when I have enough money hidden away. When my sisters are here… Besides Minna, it's so easy this way. Yussel works all day to earn a few dollars. I can earn as much in a few minutes and I hardly have to lift a finger. Why shouldn't I?"

"But, Jake, you know it's wrong…"

"In *der alter heym*, it was wrong. Here, it's different. Everyone I know, except your family, does the same thing. The cop wants a pay-off, Tammany wants a pay-off… That's the way they do it in America. That's what I see."

"You could get arrested," Minna said anxiously. "You could get sent to jail. Then what?"

"I'm very careful. They'll never catch me. All my uncle's friends look out for me. They know everyone, even the Mayor! They'll never let me get arrested."

Minna searched desperately for the right words. "But, maybe, the drunk man worked very hard for his money. Maybe he goes home and his children are starving because of you. You took the bread from their mouths. How does that make you feel?"

"If he has all those little children starving, why is he getting *shikker* at the saloon? It's his fault, not mine."

Minna rubbed her eyes. She knew Jake was wrong. She also knew she was the only one he could talk to about this. She had to say the right words.

"Do you still talk to your mama?" she asked softly.

He hung his head. "No."

"Why not?"

"Because she'd say what you're saying now," he burst out. "I know it! But, Minna, I don't have a choice."

"Of course, you have a choice. All of us have choices. I know that. Tata made a choice when he left. He's going back to *der alter heym*, you know. He asked Mama for a divorce today. So, that's his choice. It doesn't mean it's right. You have to pick the right one. I think you've…"

Jake stood up, interrupting her. "For me, this is the right choice. For now, it is."

Minna looked up at him. "It's never right to do the wrong thing! Never!"

Jake turned and slowly walked away.

Minna called after him, "Wait! Come back, Jake!"

He stopped.

"You're still my friend. I think, no, I *know* you're wrong. But, remember when you took me junking? Remember the boat?

"I remember."

"If I'm your friend, I have to try to help you. I have to."

"I don't need help—yours or anyone else's. I'm doing just fine all by myself," he yelled. "I'm going to be rich. I'll be a big man, like my uncle. I don't need your help, Minna!"

Minna couldn't think of anything to say.

He turned and strode down the street. His step looked jaunty, but as he disappeared from view, Minna could only think of how small he looked. She felt tears forming in her eyes.

She huddled against the step, trying to put the events of the day in some sort of perspective. Tata was gone. Yankel was Jake now and he was gone, too.

Minna did something she hadn't done for a long time. She raised her head to the sky and cried, "Help me, Bubbe. Everything is different, everything is upside down here."

'It wasn't hard in *der alter heym*? You didn't have problems there? You're almost twelve, Minna, no longer a child. Be strong, and make yourself a life here. This is where you are.'

By the time Minna opened the apartment door, Bessie and Sarah were asleep in the front room. She tiptoed into the kitchen, only to find Yussel waiting up for her.

She tried to move past him into the bedroom. "Good night, Yussel," she said.

"Sit down. I want to talk to you."

Minna shook her head. "There's already been too much talking. I want to go to bed."

She turned to him, with the intention of saying "good night" again but he looked so weary and disheartened, she pulled out a chair and sat next to him. "I had to talk to Jake," she explained. "I couldn't just let him go."

Yussel shrugged. "I wasn't thinking about that. Today has been a day of such *tsouris*. I don't know… Am I coming or am I going? What if Tata's right?"

"Tata is not right. I know that."

Yussel shook his head. "You make it sound so simple. What did Yankel say, anyway?"

"Jake. I'm going to call him Jake now. He…he wants to be a big man, like his uncle."

"When I look at him," Yussel sighed, "with his new coat and his fancy clothes, when I see the presents he brings, I wonder. I work so hard… For pennies, I work."

"But…" Minna sought for words. "You have a plan. You and Mama are going to open your own store. Jake says he's doing it to bring his sisters over, but I think he'll just put it off and put it off. He keeps saying he needs more money. The thing is, how will he know when he has enough?" She paused. "That's what I should have said to him. I should have asked him, 'Jake, when will you have enough?'"

"It's true. I know you're right. But it seems as if we'll never be able to save enough. Sometimes, I'd like to run away, too, like Tata. I'd go to look for Ephraim, that's what I'd do."

"You had a terrible day, today. Between the Irish, Tata's letter and the cop… Jake was right. Everyone is on the take, here."

Yussel shook his head impatiently. "It isn't that. It doesn't have to be like that. I laugh at Pearl when she tells me what Bessie says, but it's true. I can still hold my head up here."

"We have a chance here," Minna mused. "One of the girls in my class, her family is moving to the Bronx. She says they'll have four rooms and no boarders. Maybe after you and Mama open your store, we can move, too. We could live in a place where everyone speaks English."

"In that case, I'd better keep learning! But Minna," he continued, "what do you think about Tata?"

"I'm glad he's leaving," she said angrily. "If he doesn't want to stay, then good riddance!"

Yussel hesitated. "I agree. But…now we have a father who's not a father. What is he then?"

"To you, he may have been a father. To me, he just slapped and yelled. Well, I guess he did teach me to read and write. That's something."

"So, are you only angry, or are you sad, too?"

Minna pondered. "I guess I'm so sad, I'm mad. You know what I mean?"

They looked at each other.

"That's how I feel, too." Yussel smiled at her.

Minna smiled back. Imitating the old straw seller from *der alter heym*, she shrugged. "So, life is *meshugge*. What else is new?"

Yussel laughed.

As they stood up, he reached out to her and gave her a rare hug. Minna hugged him back and tiptoed into the bedroom, trying not to waken Mama or Pearl.

The next day was a special one for Minna. Her new teacher, Miss Israel, had planned a spelling bee. The first and second winners in each class would appear on the stage of the auditorium for another competition. The winner of *that* contest would be named the best speller in the whole seventh grade. The prize was a leather-bound dictionary.

Minna was determined to win. She never stopped practicing. When she had time, she went to the Public Library and scanned the big dictionary there. She constantly begged Debbie, Irving, and Pearl to test her on the list of words Miss Israel had given the class.

Minna admired Miss Israel so much. She was different from the other teachers. She'd been a greenhorn, too. She told the class all about how she'd saved pennies so she'd have enough money to go to college. She said anyone could do it if they worked hard enough.

Minna dressed, craning her head sideways to see herself in the small mirror hanging on the wall. As always, she saw only small squares reflected as she twisted around. Her white shirtwaist was freshly washed and pressed. It almost sparkled, or it would have, if it hadn't been so old. Her serge skirt was drab, but her high-buttoned shoes were as new looking as spit and polish could make them.

Minna hesitated for a moment. Then she pulled out her silver locket so it hung just below the collar of her shirtwaist. Looking at as much as she could see in the mirror, she thought hopefully, maybe I look as nice as Susannah, the girl I saw at B. Altman's. At least, as nice as Susannah would look if she had to wear an old shirtwaist and a shiny skirt.

She went into the kitchen to ask Mama for two new ribbons for her braids. When she saw Mama's stiff back, she knew this was not a good time. Without saying a word, she went back into the bedroom and found the two old ribbons she had pressed a few days ago just in case.

As she was tying them onto her braids, Pearl came back from the bathroom. "Here, I'll help," she offered.

After she had tied the ribbons, she stepped back and scrutinized Minna. "You look so pretty. I just know you're going to win. A girl in my class says everyone thinks you're the best speller."

"Don't say. It'll be a *kineahora*."

Pearl nodded and compressed her lips.

By the time Minna entered the kitchen, Mama and Yussel were ready to leave. Today was the day Cousin Avraim took inventory, so they had to be at the store early.

Yussel smiled at her. "What's this I see? A princess has come! Good luck in the contest, Minna."

Although she had spoken of nothing else for days, Minna could tell that Mama had forgotten all about it. Her face was pale and there were dark circles under her eyes. She looked as if she had been up all night. She must have been thinking about Tata, Minna thought.

"You look nice," Mama said vaguely, as she hurried out the door.

Pearl patted Minna's arm. "Don't worry. She'll be pleased if you win."

Minna looked down at the spelling list. "I *will* win," she promised herself.

The spelling bee was in the afternoon. All morning, Minna studied her list surreptitiously. At lunchtime, she practiced with one of the other girls. The two of them gabbled the letters aloud as they munched on apples and cheese.

Finally, it was time for the contest to begin.

Miss Israel stood in front of the class. "Close your books, everyone. Stand up, stretch, and take a deep breath. That's good. Now, we're going to have the spelling bee. We'll divide into two teams. If anyone misses a word, they'll have to sit down. Finally, there'll be only two spellers left—the two best in the whole class!"

Minna took her place in line. Debbie, who was in her class this term, stood on one side and Abe, a short, be-spectacled boy, on the other with her.

Miss Israel began with easy words. Nevertheless, some of Minna's classmates sat down at their first try. As the words became harder, more people were eliminated. Finally, there were only six children left. On their side, Abe and Minna were the only two still standing. On the other side, there were four.

Miss Israel pointed to the other team "We'll have to say that they are the best spellers."

Half the class cheered and the other half booed.

"Now," Miss Israel continued, "we'll make one line."

Abe and Minna crossed the room and joined the others. They waited anxiously for the next word. Minna narrowed her eyes, concentrating as hard as she could. If the person next to her missed a word, she'd have to spell it. In the beginning, some words had gone through four or five people.

Miss Israel smiled kindly as she asked the words. "Suggestion…meaningful… religious…"

By the time it was Minna's turn, there were only four people left.

"Continental," Miss Israel said.

"Con-tin-en-tal," Minna repeated. "C-o-n-t-i-n-e-n-t-a-l."

"That's right." Miss Israel nodded approvingly and went to the next person.

Finally, there were only two people still standing, Minna and Abe. The class was silent as they waited for the next word.

It was Abe's turn.

"Principal. The principal of this school is Mr. Shayne."

Oh no! Minna knew there were two kinds of principals, one spelled with an a-l and one with an l-e. Which was which? She watched Abe anxiously. If he didn't get it right, she'd know it was the other and would be able to spell it easily.

Abe waited, his forehead furrowed. Minna knew he was as unsure as she was. Which was which?

Finally, he spelled, "P-r-i-n-c-i-p-l-e."

"Wrong. Minna, it's your turn."

The class waited with bated breath. If they both got it wrong, no one would win. Or maybe Miss Israel would give them each a new word.

Minna took a deep breath. She was sure she was right, but it seemed too easy. Nervously, she tossed her braids over her shoulder, touched her locket for luck, and plunged in.

"P-r-i-n-c-i-p-a-l."

Miss Israel beamed. "You're right, Minna! You're the best speller in the class!"

Minna was so happy she actually felt dizzy. In America, I'm the best speller in my class, she exulted. An odd thought crept into her mind...Tata would be pleased. She banished it and flew back to her seat, as light as air.

"The next spelling bee, with the first and second best spellers of every class, will be held in the auditorium in a few weeks. Let's all help Minna and Abe prepare so our class can win, " Miss Israel said, walking back to her desk.

Minna blushed proudly. Everyone helping her!

"Settle down now, class. We'll go over our arithmetic until the bell rings." Miss Israel took out the green arithmetic book.

Minna opened hers automatically. What would it be like to stand in front of the whole school, she wondered, as she pretended to do the problem on the page.

"Let's study together," Abe whispered. "We don't want the other classes to win, do we?"

Minna nodded. It's true, she thought, there's more than me. The whole class wants to win.

Every day after that, Abe and Minna ate lunch together. As they ate, they practiced their spelling until Minna felt as if she were swimming in a sea of words and letters. Miss Israel helped by giving them more lists to learn.

At home, Minna practiced while she was sewing, at the dinner table (when the rest of her family permitted it) and whenever Pearl had a free moment to go over the words with her. Irving, the boarder next door, was almost as enthusiastic as she. Patiently, he helped her as often as he could.

By the time the day of the big match arrived, everyone in the family was sick and tired of the whole thing.

"I'm glad it'll be over," Yussel joked. "All I can say is, you'd better win, after all this!"

Catching Minna's apprehensive expression, he added, "Don't worry. I know you're the best speller whoever wins."

Mama warned, "If you don't win, Minna, it's not the end of the world."

Minna, who was already very nervous, couldn't tell if Mama was honestly afraid she might lose or was trying to ward off a *kineahora.* Either way, she began to worry more.

In class that morning, Miss Israel drew her aside. "Don't worry so much, Minna. I know you'll do well. The thing is, whether you win or lose, it's still an achievement to be the best speller in this class."

Her words made Minna uneasy. "Do you think I won't win?" she blurted.

"No, of course not. You have a good chance. But so do the others. They've worked hard, too. I don't want you to be too disappointed if someone else is the winner."

Minna frowned. Disappointed? It would be the end if she lost.

Miss Israel leaned towards her. "I want you to think about this. There are eight other children in the finals. Suppose each one feels just as you do. There will still be only one winner. You'll try your hardest. But if you lose, be a good sport. Just promise yourself you'll do better next time and be glad for the one who won."

Minna thought about it. A good sport? If she didn't win, she knew she'd never be happy again. Wait for next time… Who knew when that would be.

"Do you understand what I'm saying?" Miss Israel asked.

"I understand you. It just doesn't make sense."

"What do you mean?"

"Well…I want to win. If I want to win, how can I be glad if I lose? I'll just be mad, that's all."

"Angry at whom?"

"Angry with myself, of course. It'll be my fault if I don't win."

"So you won't be angry at the winner?"

"No, of course not. It's not their fault I didn't win. I won't be happy, but I can't blame them."

"And if Abe wins?"

"I'll feel the same except he's the one I want to win if I don't. So, for him, I'll be happy."

This chat was making Minna more nervous than before. Miss Israel, sensing her unease, turned away to attend to the rest of the class.

As they were waiting in line to go to the auditorium, Minna whispered to Abe, "If I don't win, I'm for you. Good luck!"

"Me, too," he whispered back.

Minna hoped she was being a "good sport."

In the auditorium, the eight finalists lined up on the stage. Minna imagined she could feel the stage tremble beneath her feet from the noise of the whole school clapping as her name was called. She clenched her hands and vowed to do her best.

The principal, Mr. Shayne, was to read the words. As they

waited for him to begin, each child stood as straight as possible, head slightly cocked to hear the words.

The first was directed to Abe. "Independence," he said.

Abe smiled. "I-n-d-e-p-e-n-d-e-n-c-e."

Mr. Shayne nodded and went on. Soon it was Minna's turn.

"Principle. I believe in certain principles," he said.

Minna knew Abe was smiling. "P-r-i-n-c-i-p-l-e."

Mr. Shayne continued. The words grew more difficult. Some Minna had never heard of—words like "conscienceless," "determinism," and "maneuverable." Finally a word came along that was so strange Minna couldn't even begin to imagine what it meant. The word was "fricassee."

Two more children were knocked out of the match with that. Now there was only Minna, Abe, and a tall boy from Mr. Dempsey's class.

Minna repeated the word over and over to herself. She tried to sound out the syllables as she had been taught, but it was nearly impossible to determine exactly what the syllables were. This time, it was her turn first, before Abe.

Minna frowned as she tried to think of all possible combinations. Remembering how the other two had spelled it, she took a deep breath and said, "F-r-i-c-a-s-s-e."

Mr. Shayne shook his head and turned to Abe, repeating, "Fricassee."

Abe swallowed.

Minna couldn't believe she had lost. It was so quick. After all that work, to lose, just like that. She watched Abe. At least, she thought, if he wins, our class is the best.

Abe spelled it wrong, too, adding an extra "c."

The audience was silent. They waited expectantly as Mr. Shayne turned to the last boy.

He gulped. Methodically, he recited the letters.

Minna looked anxiously at Mr. Shayne. She could tell from his expression that it was still not right.

There was a long pause. Finally, Mr. Shayne said, "No one has spelled the word right. The correct spelling is f-r-i-c-a-s-s-e-e." He thought for a moment. "The only solution is to start again with all the children who missed that word."

Minna was dazed. So it wasn't all over. She had another chance. She tried to concentrate, but all she could think of was the word they had missed. Suddenly, long before she was ready, it was her turn again. There were four students standing. She was to have a new word.

“Spell 'geographical'."

Minna smiled. That was easy.

Abe braced himself for his turn.

“Spell 'inexactitude'." Mr. Shayne continued inexorably.

Abe stumbled. He spelled the word incorrectly.

Minna smiled commiseratingly at him, but she barely had time to think when it was her turn again.

Finally, there were only two left - Minna and the tall boy. The word was "cylinder."

The boy went first. He spelled, "S-i-l-i-n-d-e-r."

Mr. Shayne shook his head and repeated the word for Minna. She hesitated. The silence seemed to go on forever as she repeated the word to herself.

Finally, she spelled slowly, "C-y-l-i-n-d-e-r."

Mr. Shayne sighed in relief. "You're right!" he exclaimed. He turned to the audience. "Minna Ruben is the best speller and champion of the whole seventh grade. Now, I will present her with this leather dictionary so she can look up any word in the English language." He handed it to Minna. "Keep it for the rest of your life." He smiled at her. "You should be very proud of yourself, my dear."

In a daze, Minna shook Mr. Shayne's hand, heard the applause rising from the audience, saw Miss Israel smiling at her from her seat in front, and turned to Abe, who beamed.

"I'm glad you won. At least, our class is better than Miss Dempsey's."

"You can use my dictionary sometimes," Minna offered, fondling the soft leather cover. Inside was a bookplate that said, "This book is the prize given to the best speller in the seventh grade. January 30, 1907."

Mr. Shayne reached out for the book. "If you give it back to me, I'll have your name inscribed on the cover."

Minna didn't know what inscribed meant, but she knew she didn't want to give the book back. Holding it tightly, she said bravely, "Thank you, Mr. Shayne, but I'd rather not."

He looked surprised, but he withdrew his hand.

That evening, with everyone sitting around the table, Minna

brought out her prize for the whole family to admire. It was the most beautiful book anyone had ever owned.

"Another scholar in the family," Mama said proudly.

"May I use your dictionary when I start taking classes?" Yussel asked.

Pearl touched the cover gingerly with her forefinger, tracing the raised gold letters that spelled out the title. She opened it and looked inside at the plate. "You have to keep this forever," she said.

"I will," Minna vowed.

That night, she wrapped the dictionary in a clean rag and set it carefully on the small shelf that Yussel had constructed above the bed she shared with Pearl. Touching the book one last time before shutting her eyes, she thought, I don't know if I'm a good sport or not, but I wanted to win and I did!

CHAPTER 9

For the next two months, the family worked as hard as ever. Since no one heard from Tata, they assumed he had already returned to *der alter heym*. One day, they expected, they'd hear indirectly about his arrival, perhaps in a rare letter from home, or mentioned by a newly arrived *landsman*, or in great detail from Cousin Avraim. His mother was a good correspondent and a noted gossip.

When Mama told Cousin Avraim about her dream of opening her own shop, he suggested advancing the money in exchange for a principal interest. Mama and Yussel discussed this offer for many nights. Without Cousin Avraim's help, they would have to wait many years. On the other hand, as Mama said, "If it's not our store, why bother? I can continue to work for Cousin Avraim anyway."

Finally, she confronted him. "Cousin," she said, "I thank you. This is a generous offer, but Yussel and I agree. We want to be the bosses if it's our business. If you would loan us the money or advance it to us for an interest in the profits, we'd be glad. If not, *nu*, we'll wait."

Cousin Avraim, taken aback, said he'd need time to consider.

Meanwhile, Mama, Yussel, and Minna continued to save money. Each week, they added a little to their hoard under the floorboards. Mama re-doubled her efforts in the store to impress Cousin Avraim with her abilities. Yussel, by this time, had so many customers he was able to hire an extra man to take over part of his route.

Minna found life damp and flat after the glory of the spelling bee. One afternoon, as she trudged through the dirty, slushy snow clogging Allen Street, she thought, I'm getting dingy, too. Every day, I do the same thing. It's go-to-school, come-home, work-on-my-sewing, have-dinner, study, go-to-sleep. On Saturdays and Sundays, it's even worse, especially now that we've stopped having a Sabbath meal. We say the prayers sometimes if we can, but Pearl's too worn out to fix anything special. Sunday, we catch up with household chores and rest as much as we can. Then it's Monday and it begins all over again. I can't bear it!

She approached her stoop with her head bent and her shoulders slumped. As she turned at the steps, Minna heard a voice calling her name. Surprised, she looked up.

Rosie leaned out of her window. "You look like you lost your best friend," she shouted. "Is the weather getting you down?"

"I guess so," Minna replied wearily.

"Come up and have a glass of tea with me," Rosie invited.

Minna hesitated. For the first time in days, she felt a slight spark of enthusiasm. Glancing around to make sure no one who would tell Mama could see her, she hurried up the steps, nearly smiling.

"Thanks! I'll come," she called.

Rosie waited, poised in the doorway of her apartment.

"Come in, come in," she beckoned.

It was warm and cozy inside. Minna noticed a new flowered rug, bright as a meadow.

She took off her coat and followed Rosie into the kitchen, where she was brewing tea. “I like your new rug. It looks like a garden."

“Me too. I just got it a few months ago. In the old country, only the *shayner Yids* would have one, and they’d hang it on their walls. Me, I walk on it!"

Taking Minna's arm, she urged her back into the front room. "Come sit and admire," she said. "I'll get the tea when it's ready."

After they were comfortable, she nodded. 'I've been hearing about you from your friend, Jake."

Minna leaned forward. She hadn't seen him since their argument. "How is he?" she asked eagerly.

"He's fine, as always," Rosie replied carelessly. "He helps me with my English, you know. His uncle is…an old friend."

"I haven't seen him for a long time,' Minna said sadly. "He was my first American friend. We came on the boat together."

"I know. He told me about it."

Minna felt uncomfortable. It bothered her that Jake was such good friends with Rosie. She shook her head. She was being foolish. She liked Rosie and she liked Jake. Why shouldn't they be friends?

"In *der alter heym*, I was like the two of you," Rosie sighed. "I had plans. I was going to be something…"

"You do have plans. To be a salesgirl on Fifth Avenue. You told me about it."

"It's too late now. My life is going to change very soon."

"What do you mean?" Minna asked anxiously. "Is something wrong?"

"I'm going to have a baby," Rosie said, shaking her head. "That's what's going to happen. I know one thing for sure, I'm not going to the old lady down the street. A friend of mine died that way. So, *nu*, I'll have the baby. It's all over for me."

Minna's eyes widened. A baby without a father! How would Rosie manage? Then she reminded herself. They had no father, either. But they had each other. To be all alone…with a baby…

"What will you do, Rosie?" she cried.

"I'm leaving here next week. I have a cousin in Detroit. What does he know? He thinks I work uptown. He's fixing me a match there."

"But…will you tell him, the new one, about the baby?"

"No, why should I? If we can arrange it soon enough, he never has to know. The baby will be born early, that's all."

"But, Rosie…" Minna's eyes filled with tears. "You're going to be married to a man you don't even know! This is America. You don't need to. And, then, you'll have to lie to him. Oh Rosie, isn't there anything else you can do?"

"I've thought and thought. There's no other answer for me. What can I do? I won't be able to work with a baby coming. And when I have a baby, what then? If I stay here, it would be impossible." Rosie began to cry. "If my mama knew! Oh, Minna, if my mama knew!"

Minna reached over and gripped Rosie's hands. "Don't cry, Rosie."

"I don't know why I'm telling you. You're only a kid. I probably shouldn't…" Rosie sobbed harder. Minna could barely understand her blurred words. "You're…the… only one I can…tell. I know so many men, but I don't have any girlfriends in this place." Rosie lifted her head. "You could be my sister. I had to tell someone before I left," she finished desperately.

"I had a sister your age," Minna whispered.

"You did?" Rosie tried to smile, but her tears kept falling. "What was her name?"

"Her name was Chava."

"What happened to her?"

"She was killed in *der alter heym.* A pogrom." As Minna said those words, she felt a sharp and unexpected pang of loss for Chava. With it came the guilty realization that she hadn't missed her in that way for a very long time. Forgive me, Chava, she thought. I don't forget you. It's just...sometimes...I don't think of you.

"O-o-o-oh." Rosie sobbed harder.

Minna went into the kitchen to prepare the tea. She came back into the front room with two steaming glasses, one of which she set down next to Rosie.

"Here," she offered. 'Drink some tea. It will make you feel better."

Obediently, Rosie took the glass. She looked at Minna over the rim, her eyes shy and hurt. "*Oyf kapores*! I didn't mean to make such a fuss. No shame for a *kurveh*, I guess."

Hearing Rosie call herself a prostitute made Minna angry. She jumped up. 'There must be something else you could do," she said desperately. "Maybe one of the men you know ..."

Rosie shook her head. "It's my risk," she said proudly, "not theirs. I wouldn't even tell them. Besides, it won't be so bad. I'll have my own little house and someone to take care of me. I always wanted a baby, anyway. And my husband, the baby's new father...I'll take care of him, too."

"You don't know who the real father is?" Minna asked timidly.

Rosie laughed. “How could I? But, as I always said, all my gentlemen are the finest. Maybe I'll know when she is born."

"She?"

"You don't think I'd have a boy, do you? Oh no, she'll be as pretty as pie. She'll go to school like the *Amerikane kinder*. She'll wear nice clothes and be good. That I'll take care of!"

She leaned towards Minna, again sitting across from her in one of the small chairs. "I just wanted someone to know. Until I saw you walking down the street, I didn't know it was going to be you. But ... you have a nice face. It makes people trust you. And you were sweet about my letter." Gently, she touched Minna's cheek with her finger. "Your Mama would kill me if she could hear. You shouldn't know from such things."

Minna frowned. "I know how babies are born. I know what happened to Chava, too. Now it's you who's in trouble. Men are the ones who cause all the problems."

Rosie held Minna's face between her hands and looked into her eyes. "Minna," she said seriously, "my life, it's my fault. No one made me do this. I've learned one thing—there are good men and bad men. You can find a good one. If I'm lucky, my new husband will be a good one, too."

"I hope so, Rosie. I hope so. Will you write me a letter and tell me what happens?"

Rosie shook her head. "You know, I'm not much for writing. Besides, when I leave, I'll want to leave."

"Just to tell me your baby's name and if she's a girl? I'll be thinking about you."

Rosie smiled. "If I write to anyone here, it'll be you. You're a good one to talk to."

She stood up. 'You'd best be going now. It's almost time for me to ..."

Minna jumped up and hurried toward the door. "I'll help you pack," she offered. "I'd like to."

Later, as she sat at her sewing machine, Minna thought about Rosie. It's a shame, she decided. She knew she'd soon be old enough to have her own babies. Debbie next door had told her all about it in detail. It sounded disgusting, but Debbie swore it wasn't.

"My Mama says it just means you're a woman. It's a way of knowing you're grown up. I'll be glad when it happens to me," she said proudly.

"But what does it feel like?" Minna asked. "How can I walk around with blood coming?"

"You wear rags and wash them out. No one can tell," Debbie assured her. "I don't think you even feel anything. Mama didn't say about that."

Minna, feeling this must be a mother/daughter subject, tried to ask Mama, but she turned bright red and walked away. "Time enough when it happens," she said over her shoulder.

Only in the bathroom did Minna have any real privacy. There she examined her body carefully, to see if her breasts were beginning to grow or if hair was appearing "down there." If I could hold it back, she thought, I would.

Although she had been telling Rosie the truth when she said she knew all about it, she couldn't imagine the actual process between men and women. Was it like the animals she had seen in *der alter heym* at nearby farms, grunting and groaning? Did it hurt? She wished she had asked Rosie. She knew she could trust her to tell the truth.

"There are good and bad men," Rosie had said. I guess that's true, Minna thought. She shook her head. The thing of it is, I know about too many of the bad kind. She touched her locket. Susannah will know only the good kind. She's so clean and pretty. They wouldn't dare… When I get older, I won't even look at the bad ones. She began to wonder exactly how to tell which was which.

The next week, Minna made sure to be home in time to say goodbye to Rosie. She was surprised to see Jake in front of the apartment, carrying her valises. He ducked his head and muttered "hello" to Minna, averting his face.

Rosie stood on the stoop. "I've sold all my furniture to another girl, so I have a nice little nest egg to bring to Detroit. That should sweeten the pot." She looked up at her window. Shaking her head, she swung around and hurried down the steps.

"Now for a new life!" she said.

Rosie bent over and kissed Jake on the cheek. She hugged Minna and stepped into the hackney. "Maybe I *will* write," she called as she disappeared inside.

Minna yelled after her. "Good luck!" She tried to imagine what Rosie must be feeling, going off to a strange city to marry a strange man. She shuddered.

Before she had a chance to walk away, Jake stepped in front of her. He looked at her without saying a word.

Minna hesitated. "How are you?" she asked finally. "Is everything all right?"

"Of course. Why not?" he replied flippantly.

She turned away.

He touched her arm. "Everything is fine. My uncle has given me real work instead of just errands."

Silently, Minna turned and faced Jake.

"I collect money for him. He really trusts me now, you see."

Minna nodded. She took a deep breath. "Jake," she began, "I was talking to Yussel and he said..."

Jake shook his head vigorously. "I don't want to know!" he shouted.

"But, Jake," Minna pleaded, "Please listen. If I'm your friend, I have to tell you what I think." She held out her hand. "I have to! I don't mean to nag ...."

"That's how it comes out," Jake cried. "Whenever I see you..."

"I can see how you feel," Minna said slowly. "I can see why it would seem that way. But...I can't just let you... I worry about it. What if you get caught?"

Jake leaned forward. "I have to do what's best for me and I gotta do it all the way. That's how I am. When you don't agree, it makes me worry, and that makes me mad."

He looked at her earnestly. "Even if I get caught, my uncle can get me off. And if he couldn't, I'll go to Hawthorne. It's just like a school, after all. It's only for Jews. They even make you learn Hebrew!"

Minna looked at him closely. He worries too, she realized.

She made up her mind. "Look," she offered. "I'll take an hour off from my sewing. Let's go for a walk, you and me, and we won't talk about it at all."

As they strolled down the street, Minna felt self-conscious. Every time she began to speak, she wondered how Jake would feel about what she said. Then she shrugged, thinking, this is silly. If I worry all the time, we can't talk at all.

She told Jake about the spelling bee and the money she was saving to go to college to learn how to be a teacher.

"That's what you say now," he laughed. "You'll just get married like everyone else."

"Rosie wasn't married."

"Poor Rosie. I liked her."

"She's not dead yet!"

Jake laughed. "You know what they say. Out of sight, out of mind!"

Minna was relieved to hear Jake use that tone about Rosie. At the same time, she felt impelled to come to her defense.

"You know why she's leaving?"

"Just that she's going to get married, that's all."

"Oh."

"She's my uncle's girl, sort of. He'll miss her."

"His girl? But… she saw so many men…I don't understand."

"That's the way it is with women like Rosie."

"It wasn't her fault." Minna defended her indignantly. 'She came here and she had no one and no money. "

"Everyone has a story. You wouldn't have done that, no matter what."

"No," Minna replied. "I wouldn't have. For one thing, the whole idea… I don't like the idea," she concluded weakly.

"Which idea?" Jake looked into her eyes.

"All those men. Any man, I guess."

"Any man?"

"After what happened to Chava, I hate men in that way!" Minna burst out.

Jake held her arm as they talked. "But, Minna, all men aren't like that. They were animals, those Russians! If you love someone and they love you, too …"

"But, who loves?" Minna asked. "My father left, Rosie has no one, and they hurt Chava… Tell me who loves like the stories?"

"In the nickelodeon…"

"Oh, Jake, you've been to the nickelodeon? I've never been."

"Come on, then. I'll treat you to a nickel's worth. Then we can talk about love."

They hurried down the street to a wooden storefront. Inside, there were two or three rows of slot machines, a few punching bags, and automatic scales. In the front, in a place of honor, were the nickelodeons, small machines with a slot for pennies. The room was filled with children.

In the back, a woman stood in front of a large curtain. At the side, a seedy looking man with a large black mustache watched everyone, his eyes moving slowly around the room.

Jake marched up to the woman. "How're you, Daisy?" he asked, handing her two nickels.

She smiled at him. "Go ahead. Go in. The show's about to start."

They filed in behind the curtain. A row of chairs faced a small screen. There were a few others seated in front of it. They sat silently, waiting for the show to start.

Suddenly, the lights went out and a picture appeared on the

screen. It said, "SHE DIDN'T KNOW". Then it showed a beautiful young girl walking through the streets of a city. Underneath, the subtitle said, "All alone in the world." In the background, Minna heard someone playing the piano. The music sounded desperate and frightened.

Minna sat without moving, entranced by the story. The heroine was approached by a white slaver, almost caught, and saved in the nick of time by the handsome hero. When the curtain was opened and the room was light again, she blinked, unable to believe the story was over. Like everyone else in the room, she clapped as hard as she could.

Reluctantly, she stood up.

"Oh, Jake" she sighed, her eyes bright.

"Pretty good, huh?"

As they walked out to the street, she sighed again. "That just proves what I was saying. You can't trust anyone."

"How about the hero? She could trust him."

"That's true."

"If you want it enough, you'll have a hero someday. You wouldn't be afraid of him, would you?"

"No…I guess not."

"Listen, Minna, some men are good and some are bad, just like women. Choose carefully, that's all. Don't be afraid. Remember on the boat, how brave you were."

Minna nodded.

"You don't want to be a coward."

Minna nodded again. 'That's what Rosie said—about some men being good and others being bad," she mused. "Maybe it's true."

Jake stopped in the middle of the sidewalk. "We're all just people—men and women. I think it must be nice to be in love. They write songs about it all the time."

"I suppose."

Jake looked around nervously. "I'd better go. My uncle, he'll be wondering where I am. Would you like to go to the picture show again?"

"Oh yes," Minna breathed.

"How about next week at three-thirty. I'll meet you here."

"I'd love to." Minna hesitated. "But, Jake, I don't have enough money…"

"I'll treat."

Minna frowned.

"I have plenty of money. It's more fun if we both go." Hurriedly, he turned to leave. "I'll see you then."

Minna thought about it on the way home. Was it wrong to let Jake spend money on her when she disapproved of the way he earned it? It probably was, she decided. On the other hand, she thought, if I see him, I can talk to him and try to change him. I've got to see the picture show, she swore. No matter what!

She thought about the heroine and the handsome hero. She shrugged. She'd never met anyone as handsome, as courtly, and as good. Of course, if someone like that came along, she know right off. She'd be sure to trust him. As for the other men, like Cousin Avraim, Tata, the ones she saw every day. Minna shrugged again. How was she to tell?

She decided to stop worrying about it. There was plenty of time. She wasn't even a woman yet.

Minna continued to go to the pictures with Jake once a week. All through the long dreary winter, it was the high point of her week. The women were so beautiful, the men were so handsome, and the villains so evil… She liked to imagine a life so well ordered that good and bad were immediately recognizable. She wished she were as rich as the heroine of "The Millionaire's Daughter", as beautiful as "The Girl of the Streets" and as brave as the teller in "The Great Bank Robbery."

She told no one else about her weekly jaunts with Jake. She knew that Mama and Yussel deeply disapproved of the way he lived. She justified her silence by thinking she wasn't hurting anyone. An hour a week is not so long. she said to herself.

Usually, she and Jake discussed the picture they saw afterwards. Then she'd tell him about her life, but he never said anything about his. At first, Minna asked him questions, but when she saw how uneasy that made him feel, she stopped. She lulled herself into thinking things must be getting better. At least, she thought, he's happy when we're together. Next time, she'd say to herself. Next time, we'll have to talk about Jake's uncle. But she always hated to break the mood.

One day in late March when the sun seemed brighter and the air indefinably sweeter, Minna rushed to meet Jake. As she stood outside the nickelodeon waiting for him, she looked at the streets. At least the snow was gone.

In the old country, she thought, I would be picking forget-me-nots and smelling the new spring grass. It seemed impossible to believe it was almost two years since Chava had been killed. Minna closed her eyes, trying to picture the familiar graveyard. She could see it as clear as the blue sky overhead, but it was too perfect, too complete, like a painting. She caught her breath, realizing she hadn't talked to Chava or Bubbe for a long time.

Soft as a whisper, she thought she heard Bubbe say, 'I'm with you all the time, Minna. You don't need to talk to me. That's not to say I wouldn't like it if you did.'

She opened her eyes and scanned the street. Jake still hadn't come. She looked at the clock in the window of the nickelodeon. It was a quarter to four.

Jake was never late. She gazed anxiously around the street again. Where was he? She began to worry.

She waited outside the nickelodeon until four fifteen before going home. On the way, she pictured Jake in jail, killed, or at Hawthorne, whatever that was. Jake said it was like a school. She'd have to find out more about it.

Meanwhile, there was one way she could try to find him. Tomorrow after school, she'd look for his Uncle Moishe and ask him. She'd have to be careful. She knew Jake wasn't supposed to spend time at the nickelodeon with her. She frowned. She'd say that her Mama had sent her because she hadn't seen him for a while.

Minna gasped at her own inventiveness. I'm planning to lie. She thought. She reassured herself weakly, I'm only lying so no one will be hurt.

All evening, she was pre-occupied. No one noticed. Mama and Yussel were deeply into their calculations about the shop they were planning to open. A small store had suddenly become vacant a few blocks away from Cousin Avraim's. They took out the money from under the floor and counted, then re-counted it, to see if they had enough.

"If Cousin Avraim decides to help, we'll have enough," Mama said finally. "I'll ask him tomorrow."

Pearl, as usual, spent all her time with Bessie after she had finished her homework. She sat, quiet as a mouse, while Bessie did her work for the Bund. Sometimes, she helped by doing her ironing and mending.

Minna reminded herself that she hadn't yet made an effort to talk to Bessie. She missed Pearl, who had been her shadow since Chava's death. Nowadays, she never left Bessie's side.

That night, as they lay in bed, Minna whispered to Pearl, "We never talk any more."

"You're so busy."

Minna peered at her in the dark, trying to read her expression.

"Besides," Pearl added, "I like spending time with Bessie. She's taught me so much."

Minna could tell Pearl was sincere. She felt rebuked. 'I'll do better,' she promised Bubbe. 'I said I'd take Chava's place and I will. After I find out about Jake…'

The next day, Minna ran over to Hester Street right after school. She asked a few shopkeepers where Jake's uncle lived. Most of them, she noticed, seemed reluctant to speak to her after she mentioned his name.

Minna entered his building and walked up one flight. So far, she thought, this doesn't look much better than ours. For such a big man, it's not so much.

She knocked on the door timidly.

It was flung open. A large, lean man looked at her. "And what can I do for you, my pretty?" he asked.

Minna gulped. "I'm looked for Jake's Uncle Moishe."

"That's me." He smiled and rocked back on his heels.

When he smiled, Minna noticed his eyes crinkled at the corners. He didn't look like an evil person.

"My name's Minna," she blurted.

"So this is Minna! I've heard all about you." He stepped into the hall, closing the door behind him. "What can I do for you?"

Minna pulled herself together. "My Mama sent me over to see how Jake is. We haven't seen him for a long time." She was so nervous she gabbled the words.

"He could be better," Uncle Moishe drawled. "He won't be around for six months."

"But, where is he? I've been so worried about him."

"The Gerry Society picked him up for not going to school. While they were at it, they found a few things in his pockets that didn't belong there. He's in a house of detention for six months."

Uncle Moishe said the words so calmly, it was hard for Minna to grasp their meaning.

"Hawthorne? Did he go to Hawthorne?"

"They were full up. He's upstate."

"But … he's in … prison?"

Uncle Moishe bent over and patted her head. "Don't you worry your little head. He's only there for six months. I've sent the word up. He'll do just fine. You don't see me worrying, do you?" He smiled expansively.

"But…he's in prison…" she repeated, bewildered.

"I said, don't worry," Uncle Moishe snapped. "He'll do just fine. He's a tough kid, our Jake." He felt behind him for the doorknob, turned and opened the door to his apartment. Before entering, he looked back at Minna. "Come and see me again, little girl, in about five years!" He laughed and shut the door in her face.

Minna almost knocked on the door again, but she paused, her fist still in the air. What was the point? There was nothing else to say. Jake in prison! She stumbled down the stairs, tears in her eyes.

I won't tell anyone else, she decided. She could just imagine what Yussel and Mama would say. If they knew… Jake in prison! It was too much for her to understand. She remembered Jake at Ellis Island, how determined he had been to be brave after his father was sent back. He's only twelve, she thought, and now, he's in prison.

All afternoon, as she sat sewing, Minna thought about Jake. One minute, she'd think, I should have asked for his address. I could write to him. The next, she'd decide, I'm glad I didn't. What could I say, anyway. Poor Jake. Poor Jake.

By the time Pearl arrived home, Minna felt sadder, but calmer. Resolutely, she banished all thoughts of Jake and smiled cheerfully at her sister. Today, she determined, I'll make a real effort to talk to Bessie. That, at least, I can do. She glanced upwards, as if at Chava.

When Bessie arrived after work, Minna put her sewing aside. She had almost completed her daily quota.

"How are you today?" she asked.

Bessie looked surprised. Minna usually ignored her.

"The usual," she answered. "But tonight, there's a meeting for the Bund. We have a speaker and Abe Cahan of *The Forward* is coming," she added importantly.

"What's he talking about?" Minna asked.

"The speaker? About the cause, naturally. He's come all the way from Poland and he's speaking in Yiddish."

Minna tried to look interested. "It sounds exciting."

"Why don't you come with me?" Bessie asked, her eyes gleaming. "Some day, you'll be working at a factory, too."

Minna thought for a moment. I can do my homework now, she decided, and then I'll have time. Out of the corner of her eye, she could see Pearl looking at her anxiously. "Maybe I can come," she said slowly.

Bessie nodded enthusiastically. "You won't be sorry," she exclaimed. "It's the right thing to do!"

Pearl smiled. "When I'm older, I'll come to all the meetings with you, Bessie."

That evening at dinner, Yussel and Mama were obviously bursting with a shared secret. Several times, Yussel started to say something and each time, Mama hushed him, saying, "Later. We'll tell them later."

Finally, Minna could bear it no longer. "What's later?" she asked. "Why won't you tell us now? Did Cousin Avraim say he'd help with the store?"

Mama smiled triumphantly. "Not only is he helping us, we take the lease to morrow! Tomorrow, we become owners!"

"I knew you'd do it!" Minna exclaimed.

"Can I sell in the store?" Pearl asked.

"I'm going to keep on with my ladies so Mama will need all the help she can get," Yussel said. He looked at Minna and Pearl.

"Of course, we will," they both said.

"May it be a *mitzvah*, your new shop," Sarah cried.

Bessie frowned. "I hate to say it, but you're owners now. In the class war…"

"*Nu*, we'll be your enemies," Mama said impatiently. "That doesn't mean we can't get along."

Bessie looked dubious, but said no more.

After dinner, Minna pulled Bessie into the front room to say, "I'm sorry, but I can't come tonight. Mama and Yussel will want to tell us all about their plans for the store. We'll be celebrating."

Bessie sniffed. "Just what I'd expect!"

Remembering Pearl, Minna controlled her temper. "Honestly, Bessie, don't you think we should try to get ahead? Why did we come to this country anyway?"

"I came because I wanted to be free," Bessie replied condescendingly.

"I know, of course," Minna agreed. "But part of that is making a better life for ourselves."

"Don't you see?" Bessie asked earnestly. "A better life has to be for everyone, not just the bosses. We all have to work together. What good is your store if there's others starving next door?"

"We can help them when we do well," Minna replied stoutly.

"Like *tzedakah*? The Yankee Jews—the Germans who spit on us and hand out pennies and lectures to change us so we'll be like them? No thanks! I don't need that kind of help!"

With an effort, Minna smiled. "It's not happening tomorrow, after all. We've a long way to go before we can hand out anything!"

"It's the idea. Why not work together for all, starting now? That's what I believe in."

"Not if it means staying here for the rest of my life!" Minna yelled, finally losing her temper.

"Already you give to the *pushke* in the kitchen for *landsmannschaft*, Yussel's *farband* from the old country. It's starting. Already you're talking charity."

"So, you think it's bad to help others?" Minna lowered voice to an angry whisper. Fortunately, there was enough noise coming from the kitchen so that no one could hear what they were saying. They're so happy, Minna thought. Why do they need to hear a fight?

"The only way to really help others is to change the conditions of their life by working for them—and yourself. Anything else is *tzedakah*—charity!" Bessie hissed.

Minna collected herself. "Listen, Bessie. Let's agree to disagree. It's not the end of the world if we think differently."

Bessie considered those words. Finally, she nodded. "For now, it's all right. But you'll see. Things will change. You'll be the capitalist and I'll be the proletariat. One day, it'll happen and then we won't be able to talk."

Minna laughed, relieved. "*Nu*, there's a long way to go before we're capitalists. Meanwhile, you're our *boarderkeh* and we live together."

"For now," Bessie stated darkly as she flung out of the apartment.

Minna looked after her, shrugged, and hurried into the kitchen to hear the plans for the new shop. As she entered, Sarah scurried by, retiring to her now empty room to give the family privacy.

Mama and Yussel sat at the table, poring over a sheet of paper. Pearl stood behind them, reading over their shoulders. They looked up as Minna entered.

"So, this is it," Yussel explained. "This is the rent, the cost of our initial stock, and the amount that Cousin Avraim is lending us." He pulled out another sheet of paper. "Here's what I earn, what you earn, Minna, and the *boarderkeh gelt* to make our budget for the week. We can manage without Mama's salary if we start earning money, or at least breaking even, quickly. We have to earn at least $15 a week by next month just to break even. What do you think, Minna?"

Minna looked at the two sheets of paper, nodding her head as she studied the figures. "You're only going to sell piece goods?"

"Piece goods and trimmings," Mama explained. "A few buttons in the beginning, some patterns… One thing, I thought I'd ask you, Minna, to make a few shirtwaists from the patterns. We'll put them in the window for people to see."

"That's a good idea!" Minna agreed enthusiastically. "We can offer to help them, too, if they have any sewing problems."

Mama smiled. "Maybe we should call it the Sewing Lecture Store. Everyone's always going to lectures around here."

Minna stared at Mama. She had stopped wearing her kerchief when Tata left. Tendrils of dark hair curled softly around her face, the rest wound in a dark bun at the back of her head. Her eyes sparkled and her cheeks had a slight tinge of color.

She looks young, Minna thought. Mama looks young! She remembered what Bubbe had said about Mama's dreams.

Spontaneously, she reached out and gave Mama and Yussel a hug.

"*Mazeltov!*" she cried. "We're becoming capitalists!"

To her astonishment, Mama actually hugged her back awkwardly. Yussel embraced her firmly. Pearl joined in.

"What are you going to call the store?" Pearl asked when everyone had settled down.

Mama shook her head. "I don't know. Ruben's?"

"There are too many Ruben's," Minna complained. "Can't we think of another name?"

Yussel frowned. "Ruben is our name. What else?"

"Does it have to be our name? What about Mama's idea? Why don't we really call it 'The Sewing Lecture Store'?"

Mama shook her head. "That was just a joke."

"But why not have an interesting name? It's more American."

"We're not American yet," Mama disagreed. "I think we should use our own name."

"Why don't we call it Chava's?" asked Pearl.

No one said anything.

"I agree," Minna exclaimed enthusiastically. "It will be as if she were still here with us."

Mama closed her eyes and looked down at the table.

Yussel thought it over. He looked at Mama. "What do you think?"

Mama kept her head down. Finally, after what seemed like a long time, she looked up, her eyes filled with tears. "I agree. We'll call it Chava's in her memory. It'll be a *broche* to bring us good luck." She turned to Minna and Pearl. "Tomorrow, we'll sign the lease. Then we'll clean the space and make it look like new. I'll need your help."

Minna spoke for both of them. "We'll come right after school. I've finished this lot of sewing and I can work extra hard over the weekend to keep up with the rest."

"I'll plan a dinner that'll cook quick," Pearl added.

Mama smiled and began to discuss the merchandise with Yussel. "I'll go to the Khazzer-Mark to buy the goods. Cousin Avraim will add some from his stock. The trimmings…"

The next day, the two girls met Mama at the store. They stopped in the middle of the street, dismayed. The shop was a tiny, filthy room, barely visible through the dirty front window. On either side were other piece goods shops.

As they opened the door, a bell tinkled overhead. Mama stood inside, surveying the room. By arrangement, the previous tenant had left tables and a counter.

"At last, you're here!" she said excitedly. "Look! There's a little room in the back, too." She flung open the door proudly, as if displaying the entrance to a castle. A very small closet gaped back at them. "All we need to do is to clean it up, and we've got a palace!"

Minna and Pearl tried to emulate her enthusiasm but they found the dirt and the limited space overwhelming.

Mama switched on the overhead light. "See, we have the electricity here. Once the window is clean, we'll hardly need it, but it's good to have for cloudy days." Quickly, she turned off the light.

Pointing at a pail filled with soapy water, she spoke firmly, "You two continue scrubbing this floor. I've already started. Then do the tables, the walls, the window," she ordered. "I'm going to see Cousin Avraim about the stock." She whirled out of the store and hurried down the street.

Minna and Pearl looked at each other.

"This isn't how I imagined it," Minna sighed.

"Maybe it'll look better when it's clean," Pearl said half-heartedly.

The two girls set to work. By the time Mama returned, the store was clean and they were filthy. Even the window shone. Now that it was clean, Minna thought as she stepped back to look, it did let in a lot of light.

Mama checked all the corners. The girls held their breaths. Finally, she nodded. "You did a good job. Now we're going to paint the walls."

"Paint the walls? We're going to paint?" Pearl gasped. "Where did you get the paint?"

"Cousin Avraim gave me some whitewash. This place is going to sparkle! You and I will paint, Pearl, and Minna, you stand on the table we'll bring outside and write a new sign the way you learned in school. With big letters, you'll write 'Chava's' in English and Yiddish. First, whitewash the old sign and then…" Proudly she went outside and came back in, flourishing a small can of black paint and a brush. "You'll write 'Chava's' in big letter so everyone will know this is our store."

Minna and Pearl lugged one of the tables outside. Quickly, Minna whitewashed the old sign. While she was waiting for it to dry, she practiced spacing the letters for the new sign on a sheet of paper from her school notebook. She showed the practice sign to Mama, who was enveloped in a large apron as she briskly spread the whitewash over the inside of the store.

Mama looked at it carefully. "That's good," she said.

By the end of the day, the shop looked like a different place. The white walls, still wet to the touch, made the space appear larger. The sign had dried quickly in the spring sun so that Minna could write her black letters on top of the white.

Exhausted, the three of them stepped outside to admire their work. The letters were a little crooked, but they *were* very big.

Through the sparkling glass windows, the shop looked fresh and inviting. They brought the table in and waited for Yussel.

"He'll be surprised to see how good it looks," Minna said.

Despite a long day and her hard work, Mama still had a lilt in her voice. "Tomorrow, I'll go to buy the goods and Benny Herschel will bring over the pieces from Cousin Avraim's shop. He said he'd come to see us today."

Yussel, Cousin Avraim, and Benny Herschel all arrived at the same time. Yussel beamed when he saw the sign and the white walls. "A regular emporium?" he exclaimed.

Cousin Avraim looked impressed, too.

Benny Herschel winked at Minna. "I can see I'll have to be a puller here so you can get ladies into your shop."

Mama smiled at him. "You're always welcome, Benny, but it's up to Cousin Avraim. Meanwhile, I'll do the job." She turned to Cousin Avraim. "If we could walk over to your shop for a moment, I could pick out a few pieces for Minna to use when she makes shirtwaists for the window."

"Shirtwaists for the window? They'll come looking for a shirtwaist, not your fabric!"

"We'll have a sign," Minna said quickly. "It'll say: 'You can make this shirtwaist. Buy your fabric here!'"

Cousin Avraim smiled. "Not bad. Not a bad idea at all. Maybe you'll make me one, too."

Minna nodded. "Let's go and pick out the fabric and the patterns now." She started out the door.

Mama took off her apron and hung it on one of the tables to dry. Carefully, she locked the door behind her and joined Minna. As they walked down the street, she and Yussel kept turning to admire their new store.

Minna chose enough different fabrics to make several shirtwaists. That night, she sat up late at the sewing machine, making small additions to the patterns so the waists would look more elegant. It was nearly 3 a.m. when she finished.

The rest of the family had long been fast asleep by the time she ironed and folded the waists neatly. Pearl slept with Mama and Yussel had used their bed so that Minna could work in the kitchen. Wearily, she laid her featherbed on the floor.

She was almost asleep when she remembered she hadn't yet written her sign. Jumping up, she set to work. Taking two pieces of notebook paper, she wrote out the words in careful script and Hebrew letters. "Buy Fabric To Make Your Own Waist", it said. She had made it as short as she could, Finally, she was done.

It was almost 4 a.m. by the time Minna fell back into bed. It seemed as if she had just put her head down on the pillow when it was time to get up and get ready for school. Sleepily, she rolled up her featherbed and straightened her clothes. She had been so tired the night before, she had fallen asleep in the same outfit she had worn during the day.

By the time she returned from the lavatory in the hall and went into her room to change, Mama and Yussel had already left, taking the shirtwaists and her sign with them. Only Pearl was waiting for her, holding out a piece of fruit and a chunk of bread for breakfast.

"I made you some lunch to take," she said. "Mama thought the shirtwaists were beautiful—and the sign, too. She says to come after school."

Minna nodded, too sleepy to talk.

Perhaps because she was so tired, the day passed more quickly than usual. When the last bell rang, she ran out to the front to meet Pearl, feeling suddenly invigorated.

When they arrived at the shop, the two girls stared in amazement. Mama had placed the shirtwaists and the sign in the window. Through the glass, they could see fabrics and trimmings stacked upon the tables and at the counter. There were two people in the shop—Mama and a customer.

They burst into the store, stopping short as Mama frowned at them. She held a piece of soft pink voile up to the face of her customer. "Look in the mirror," she suggested. "See how this shade compliments your pretty face."

The young woman posed in front of a small hand mirror.

"You like the waist in the window?"

She nodded.

"We have the pattern right here. It's so simple, a ten year old can make it. Then you can add extra touches if you want—embroidery or a little ribbon for the trim."

Minna nudged Pearl. It was like the old days, when Mama sold in the marketplace. She led the way to one of the tables and, with Pearl's help, began to straighten the bolts of fabric.

Finally the customer left, happily clutching a yard or two of the material, a pattern, thread, and ribbons for trim. "Be sure to come back and ask if you have any questions about the pattern," Mama called after her.

She grinned at the girls. "Already, five sales! I didn't even open the shop till twelve by the time I put all the goods out. We're going to be rich!" she almost danced over to the girls.

Minna was astounded. She had never seen Mama so exuberant.

"Look," Mama continued. "Look at our beautiful goods! The fabrics…see, here's the most delicate lawn…and this glorious red…and the ribbons…and the patterns…"

I can see why everyone buys from Mama, she thought. She's so enthusiastic, it would be hard not to. She glanced at the window. The whole point was to get ladies into the shop. Maybe she could make some skirts, too…

"They all come in because of the waists in the window," Mama said. "Once they're here, then I can sell them."

"I was just thinking about the window," Minna said. "What if I make a skirt, too?"

The bell over the door tinkled as another lady entered. Mama smiled at the girls, nodded "yes" to Minna, and approached the customer.

Pearl opened the door of the little closet. It was still empty except for a straw broom and the pail they had used yesterday. She shut it quickly.

Minna looked through the fabric, trying to choose a piece to make a skirt. Maybe the blue serge, with red braid trimming…or a soft lilac color in a lighter fabric. She waited patiently for Mama to help her decide as she riffled through the skirt patterns.

I wish the clothes were for me, she thought. When I get older, I'll wear soft lace shirtwaists and silk stockings. Her eyes narrowed as she tried to picture herself as a young lady.

Pearl poked her. "What are you thinking about?"

Minna laughed. "Just imagining I could make myself a dress, or at least, a new skirt. I hate this old serge one. It looks like a little old lady."

Pearl shrugged. As long as she was dressed the same way as most of her classmates and she had an occasional new ribbon for her braids, she didn't care.

Mama completed her sale and turned to the girls. "That makes six sales!" she cried triumphantly.

"What can we do to help?" Pearl asked.

Mama looked around. "Nothing really. I've fixed everything up. Today, it's still nice and neat."

Minna held up the pattern she'd chosen. "I thought I'd make the skirt from this. Can you help me choose a fabric?"

In the end, Mama agreed with the blue serge, but she suggested blue braid. "The red's a little too bright," she decided, looking at her selection critically. "I think this is perfect. It'll go with the two waists, too."

Minna wrapped the fabric in a piece of newspaper and looked questioningly at Mama.

"Why don't you go home now," she suggested. "The sooner we get the skirt in the window, the better off we'll be."

Although she was very tired, Minna felt proud to have contributed to the success of the store. Holding the package carefully, she left. Pearl stayed to help Mama in case too many customers came for her to handle alone. Minna could prepare the dinner tonight.

She decided to make it special to celebrate the opening of Chava's and the six customers. She shopped carefully, buying real chicken parts out of the money she was secretly saving for college. She even bought a small bottle of wine, something the family usually reserved for the High Holy Days and special festivities. For dessert, she stopped at the bakers, a rare treat.

That evening, the family and Sarah made many toasts as they sipped their small glasses of wine. Bessie had not returned for dinner, which meant there was more food and, Minna thought, a pleasanter celebration.

Flushed with success, Mama's eyes were bright. 'There were already twelve sales today. I've always wanted my own shop—a real shop, not a cart. She finished with a flourish. "Now I have it, and I know it will be a success!"

Yussel was already figuring out how soon he could stop peddling. "Or maybe I won't stop," he pondered. "I'll just hire more men. It depends on how much help we need in our shop."

Our shop… it had a good strong sound, Minna thought. When we move to the Bronx, I'll be a real American. We'll speak English every day and I'll go to college and…

She held up her glass. "To Mama's dream," she announced.

Mama blushed and raised her glass. "To my dream," she repeated.

"To all of our dreams," Yussel said.

"To America," Pearl added.

Solemnly, the whole table clinked their glasses in a final toast.

CHAPTER 10

Three years later, Minna sat cross-legged on the floor, her graduation dress spread out on her lap. Carefully, she picked at the basting with her needle, releasing the meticulous stitches and snipping them with her small scissors. The creamy lace she had chosen contrasted beautifully with Mama's most expensive voile, she thought.

After making clothes for Mama's window for so long as well as finishing piecework at home, Minna had become an expert seamstress. It was rare that she had a chance to make a fancy dress or, indeed, any dress for herself. She stroked the elbow-length sleeves tenderly, admiring the embroidered panels at their ends.

Enjoying the rare luxury of solitude, Minna looked up from her work and stared dreamily around the room. The shelf over her bed held all of fifteen books now, but the leather dictionary was still in the place of honor. Despite her care, its binding had become worn at the edges.

Above the books, Minna had stuck several photographs clipped from the daily papers. Each was a picture of a society lady in a different setting. Minna's lips curved as she tried to imagine herself watching the races at Saratoga, promenading at Newport, or dancing at the Grand Ballroom of the Waldorf Astoria.

The silver locket she had found with Jake so many years ago still dangled from her neck. She touched it for luck and bent over her sewing again. Soon Pearl would return. Then Mama, Yussel, Bessie, and Sarah would be coming home and her splendid privacy would disappear. Someday, she thought, I'll have a room of my own, a room just for myself.

Although at fifteen and a half she was the youngest girl in the class, Minna appeared older. Tall and slim, her long auburn hair and sparkling green eyes added a touch of bravura to what she still considered a very ordinary face. She held herself well, inspired by Miss Israel, still her favorite teacher.

Minna frowned, thinking of the conversation she had had yesterday. Mama had taken her into the bedroom and spoken to her sternly. "This talk of college," she had said. "Are we millionaires that we can think of such? I need you in the shop, especially now that we've moved to a new place. Am I *meshuggeneh* to hire a stranger when I have a grown daughter?" She had patted Minna's hand. "Don't worry, you're young. You'll get married soon enough."

Minna had answered fiercely. "I don't want to get married! I want to go to college and be a teacher—and I'll do it, too!"

Mama had pursed her lips. Shaking her head, she spoke forcefully as only she could do. "There's no more words. For the good of the family, you'll work in the shop."

There was nothing Minna could say. How could she go against the good of the family?

Perceiving her hopeless expression, Mama had relented slightly. "Wait," she suggested. "Work with me for now. Who knows, maybe we'll have enough money in a year or two to send you to college, or maybe I can pay you then and you could be saving."

It was obvious that Mama didn't take the topic seriously. She hated to spend money on anything that wasn't related to the store. She claimed she was working for everyone's benefit, but Minna had come to believe the store was more important to her than anything or anyone else.

We still don't live differently, she thought angrily. We still have the *boarderkeh*, we still share the bedroom, and we still save every penny for the store. Yussel has three men peddling for him now and Mama has a new shop in a better place, but nothing else has changed. Nothing at all!

She looked at her new dress. It had taken weeks of pleading for Mama to give her the material. In the end, it had been Yussel's support that had made the difference. If he hadn't spoken up for her, she'd have had no graduation dress at all.

A few years ago, Mama had discovered the small hoard of money Minna had been saving for college and had appropriated it "for the good of the family". After that, it was only by careful planning and small deceptions she was able to secrete a few pennies for books, papers, and minor luxuries, like the small bar of scented soap she kept hidden under her bed. She would not have had nearly enough left to buy material for a new dress on her own.

It was true, the shop did have its ups and downs. Some months, it did extremely well and more money could be added to the amount under the floorboards. Other times, it barely paid the rent. Mama had been able to afford the move to a larger location two months ago only by scrimping and saving. By *our* scrimping and saving, Minna thought angrily.

Having the boarders had helped, but it was becoming increasingly difficult to share the space with Bessie and Sarah. Minna thought it would be hard to share the space with anyone, not just those two.

She remembered the conversation at dinner last night. Bessie, who was now on the committee for the I.L.G.W.U., or International Ladies Garment Worker's Union, had become even more vehement in her opinions. The final blow was her statement at the table in support of Emma Goldman, the anarchist. This was too much for Mama, who usually listened to Bessie's statements with an air of weary tolerance. Last night, she lost her temper and accused her of being a *farpotshket farbrente*, a crazy firebrand.

Bessie had stalked from the table, threatening, as she often did, to move at the end of the month. Pearl, whose admiration for Bessie had waned as she had become more involved with friends from school, had remained in her seat instead of chasing after her. Maybe she really will leave, Minna thought hopefully.

Sarah was another problem. Her devotion to Yussel had become so obvious that even Mama noticed it. With a heavy hand, she teased him and made pointed remarks. Privately, she complained to Minna, "That girl, she wants a free ride, that's all. Now that Yussel's doing so well, he'll be able to pick and choose when the time comes."

Yussel's opinion was unknown. He was always pleasant to Sarah, but he never sought her out. Indeed, Minna thought, he never seemed to have time to do anything but work. He fell into bed exhausted each night and each morning, left the house before anyone was up. Like Mama, his horizons had grown smaller, bounded on one side by the shop and the other by the wholesale market. Rarely did his old sparkle appear.

If everything is going well enough for us to open a bigger shop, why can't we live another way, Minna wondered. Why can't we have chicken dinner more often, new clothes, no boarders? Why can't I be paid so I can start saving money for college? What's more important, the shop or us? In Minna's mind, the amount of money under the floorboards, the money that only Mama was allowed to count, became larger each time she thought about it.

She bent over her dress again, nipping the loose threads carefully. At least everyone will come to my graduation, she thought. She felt a pang of longing for Bubbe and Chava. She laid down the scissors for a moment, her eyes wide. Why, I'm older than Chava was, she realized. If we were in *der alter heym*, I would be visited by the *shadchen*. I'd be getting married. No wonder Mama…

She shook her head and bent over her work again. Not me, she thought. Not now. Someday, I'll meet the right man…a real gentleman… and he'll…

In the other room, a door slammed. It must be Pearl, Minna thought. She continued ripping, determined to finish removing the basting before she stopped.

When she noticed the unusual silence, she looked up and saw Pearl standing in the doorway, glaring at her.

"What's the matter?" Minna asked.

Pearl flung herself down on Mama's feather bed and buried her head in the pillow. She sobbed, her whole body shaking.

Minna set her dress down carefully and went over to Mama's bed. She sat down next to her sister and gently touched her shoulder.

Pearl rolled over. "It isn't fair! We work and work and what do we get? We still live the same way. Nothing changes. We'll never leave Allen Street. We'll never even have a parlor. All Mama cares about is the store. The store! The store! What about us?"

"What's the matter?" Minna repeated, concerned. Pearl rarely became angry or upset.

"There's a class picnic," Pearl sobbed, "and I can't go because we have to pay for the bus. And my friend, Rebecca, is moving to the Bronx. And…" Her sobs grew louder. "I have a hole in my stocking and I've already darned it three times. Someone made fun of me in school today for my hole. Nothing will ever change," she wailed.

Minna put her arm around Pearl and drew her up so she was sitting. "How much does the bus cost?" she asked.

"It's not that. It only costs ten cents and Mama will give it to me eventually. I just hate to keep asking her till she does."

Minna nodded. "I know what you mean. She always says 'no' first. But she usually comes around after a while."

"Rebecca's going to have a piano in the Bronx. She said she was glad to be moving. I won't visit her. It'll be like when I went to visit Sophy. I'll feel like I don't belong there. We'll never be friends again." She looked at Minna tearfully. "Will our lives ever change?"

Minna shook her head. "Not if it's up to Mama. Only the shop matters to her. You know she doesn't think of anything else. It's up to us, Pearl. We have to make our own plans. I'm still going to college, you know, no matter what Mama says. Someday, I swear I will."

Pearl stared at her. "How can you be so sure?"

"I don't know, but I'll find a way. I have to. Miss Israel says once you decide what's important, you have to work for it as hard as you're able. Since I have to help Mama in the store during the day, I'll sew at night and save money. I won't let Mama take it away from me this time. If I'm willing to work day and night, the money I earn will be mine!" she concluded defiantly, already imagining the battle that would ensue.

"But…I don't want to go to college! I only want to live in the Bronx. I want to buy a new pair of stockings instead of mending these again." She stuck out her leg and pointed at the hole with loathing. "I can't earn money. Mama takes it all. I have to be here to cook dinner every day anyhow."

"You could sew, too," Minna suggested. "After I graduate, I'll be working at the store, so you'll be alone in the house every afternoon. You can use my machine and…we won't even tell Mama," she finished bravely. "That way, you can for sure keep the money you earn. It won't be much, but if you keep saving, it'll add up."

Pearl considered Minna's suggestion. After a long moment, she said, "I could also leave school this year and get a job. Lots of the girls leave when they're fourteen. I could work at a factory."

Minna shook her head. "You know it's important to get a

diploma. With a diploma, you could even be a shop girl uptown. If you learned how, you could be a secretary. You wouldn't have to work in a factory. According to Bessie, that's no vacation."

"But…it will take so long." Pearl sighed. "I'll never be free. If I leave now…"

Minna glared at her. "You have to think of the future. Why do you think I want to go to college? I don't want to work in a factory all my life or marry some *schlimiel* and have six babies right off. My life is my life and I want it to be the way I decide. You have to do the same thing, Pearl. Mama's finally doing it for herself with the shop. If you go to the factory now, sure, it will be better for a little while. Actually," she paused, "it won't be anyway because even if she let you, Mama would take all your money. But if you could, and even if you could keep it, it would only be better for a short time. You'd be stuck. You'd live on Allen Street till you die. Is that what you want?"

"What about Rose Pastor Stokes? She married a millionaire!"

Minna turned away in disgust. "Oh well, if you're going to talk about Rose Pastor Stokes! There are so many millionaires out there waiting to find you, Pearl?" She took Pearl by the shoulders and forced her head up. "Don't you see? That's the difference between *der alter heym* and here. We have a choice! The *shadchen* isn't knocking at the door. It's up to us, not who we marry."

"It's easy for you to say," Pearl replied weakly. "You are so…definite. You always know what you want. I only know what I don't want."

"Then think of what you don't want," Minna snapped. "Think about it long and hard and do something about it. You can't sit around waiting for a millionaire to come along. Where are you going to meet him, anyway—on Hester Street? You'll be walking along and suddenly, Mr. Vanderbilt will bump into you and fall madly in love?"

"At the picture show, I saw…"

"At the picture show! I used to believe that stuff, but it's not true." Minna looked earnestly at Pearl. "If you want to marry a millionaire, then you'd better get ready to show yourself off when you meet him. Let's say he does notice you." Her voice dripped with sarcasm. "He says, 'I love you madly'. Then he brings you home to meet his mother, Mrs. Vanderbilt. She'll ask, 'and where did you go to school?' You'll have to reply. 'Why, dear Mrs.

Vanderbilt,' you'll say, 'I'm afraid I never finished high school.'

Pear nodded reluctantly. "I guess you're right. It's just…I'm not as patient as you are."

"Whatever we say about Mama, at least she's always agreed to let us finish school. Poor Yussel never had a chance. And look at Debbie!" Minna's voice rose. "That's right. Just look at Debbie. She went to the factory last year and she's already away in Denver with the Tailor's Disease. That's something to look forward to, isn't it?"

Although she blanched, Pearl refused to consider Debbie. "I could work at the factory during the day and go to school at night, the way Bessie does."

"You could, but would you? Look at Yussel. He said he was going to the Alliance, but he's so tired at night, he just falls asleep. And anyway, Bessie already finished high school, didn't she?"

"No, she never did. She says she doesn't care, either."

Suddenly, they heard a creaking sound as the front door opened and closed.

Pearl sat up abruptly and wiped her eyes. Minna straightened her collar and patted her on the back.

"Who can it be?" Pear wondered.

Minna jumped up and hurried into the kitchen. She looked into the front room. Head down, Yussel plodded towards her.

"Yussel," Minna cried, alarmed. "You're home early. Is anything wrong?"

Yussel shook his head. "No," he explained. "I was tired and, for once, I decided to come home and rest."

"Rest?" Minna repeated in astonishment.

Pearl stuck her head in the doorway, smoothing her hair with one hand.

'Why not?" Yussel asked defiantly. "The men are out peddling, I visited the market, and Mama's at the store. Why not?"

Minna shrugged. "Why not?" she responded, smiling. "Come, sit down, and I'll make you a glass of tea."

"I don't want a glass of tea," Yussel insisted. "I want to look at trees and sit on the grass the way we used to do in *der alter heym*."

"Sit on the grass here?" Pearl asked.

Minna frowned. "I know just how you feel! Why don't we…go to Central Park?" she continued bravely.

"Central Park? Go uptown to Central Park?" Pearl asked.

Yussel looked up, a gleam of interest in his eyes.

"Why not?" Minna said recklessly. 'It's time we took a little trip. If we leave now, we'll have time to walk around before it gets dark."

Yussel fished in his pocket. "I have the fare for all of us."

"The dinner?" Pearl asked. "What about the dinner?"

Minna thought rapidly. "We'll leave a note for Mama. You can just get it started and leave it in the pot to simmer. Come on, we deserve a vacation!"

Calling it a vacation made it seem more legitimate, she thought.

Yussel nodded. "Yes, we do deserve a vacation."

Hurriedly, Pearl put the dinner into the pot. Meanwhile, Minna wrote a note for Mama. When she finished, she read it aloud to the others. "We have gone out to do an errand. Back after dinner," it read.

"It's not an errand," Pearl objected.

"So, *nu*, I should say we're going to Central Park? She'll think we're *meshuggeneh*."

For the first time since his arrival that afternoon, Yussel smiled. "Central Park! I've never been there."

"So, I have? But I've read all about it!" Grabbing her straw hat, Minna stood at the door, ready to go. She looked back at her brother and sister.

Yussel's pale face was flushed with anticipation. Minna suddenly remembered his age. He was only three years older than she—not all grown up yet. Pearl expression was anxious. She's worried about Mama, Minna realized. She rushed them both out the door so quickly they had no time for second thoughts.

As they raced down the stairs, they pushed each other playfully. Suddenly, it seemed as if the years had dropped away and the three of them were children again.

Yussel's eyes were alight in the old way. "We sound like a troop of elephants," he laughed.

Holding hands, they hurried to the Second Avenue El.

As they waited, Minna took a deep breath. "We're free! We've been set free!" she exclaimed.

Yussel panted. "I haven't run for a long time. It feels so light without my pack." He pushed his hair back from his eyes and stood as straight as he could.

Pearl was still worried. "What if Mama…" she began.

Minna covered her ears with her hands. "No Mama right now. Don't forget, we're on vacation!"

Yussel nodded. Smiling at Pearl, he patted her shoulder.

During the long ride uptown and after they emerged at 57th Street and began to walk westward towards the park, their holiday mood was undimmed.

Pearl gaped at the large buildings and wide vistas as they headed cross-town. The streets were nearly empty compared to the lower East Side.

As she eyed the well-attired ladies and gentlemen who sauntered past, Minna was aware of her own shabbiness. She glanced at Yussel to see if he noticed too, but he seemed happy and oblivious.

They arrived at Fifth Avenue and began to walk north. Minna noticed a lady strolling towards them. She was dressed in the finest white lawn afternoon dress trimmed with openwork embroidery and lined with white silk. On her head she wore an exotic picture hat embellished with egret plumes. She was followed by a young man in livery carrying a small dog. She passed by the three Rubens with her head averted as if, Minna thought, we aren't here at all.

Pearl almost yelled, "Look, Minna. Did you see the tiny dog? When you're rich, even your dog doesn't have to walk!"

Although the woman turned and stared at them with disdain, Pearl's comment struck Minna as extremely funny. She began to laugh loudly. "Maybe he doesn't have any legs!" She laughed again.

Yussel joined in. "They say it's a dog's life," he chortled.

As they approached the entrance to Central Park, they stopped for a moment to admire an enormous marble building, embellished with creviced turrets and an elegant French roof. At the front of the building, separated by a street filled with auto-cabs, was a bronze and gilt statue of a man on horseback before a large fountain with several pools. The crystal clear water from the fountain dripped from a statue of a lovely woman holding a basket of fruit in her arms. On this hot summer day, the water looked cool and inviting. As they came closer, they could hear a delicate splashing sound.

Minna gazed at the fountain and the big marble building. "I didn't know they had palaces here," she whispered.

"I know what that is," Yussel explained. "It's the new Plaza Hotel. See the people come out of the doors and that man in uniform? He's the doorman and those are the guests."

"A hotel?" Minna's eyes grew round. "You mean anyone can stay there?"

"If they have the money."

"I'm going to stay there one day. I'll walk in like a lady and everyone will bow…"

Pearl laughed. "I wouldn't hold your breath, Minna. Meanwhile, let's cross over to the park, if your majesty agrees, of course."

Compared to the stiff formality of the Plaza Hotel and the graceful elegance of the fountain, Central Park was a welcome relief. Wordlessly, the three of them grabbed hands and ran down the shaded promenades. Finally, they stopped under a tall tree, panting and breathless. Yussel flung himself down on the grass and lay upon his back, looking up at the sky. The girls sat leaning against the tree trunk, Pearl settling herself daintily and Minna plopping down with abandon.

"Do you think it's like this in the Bronx?" Pearl asked. "It didn't seem that way when I visited Sophy that time."

"I don't think it's like this anywhere else in the world," Minna replied dreamily.

Yussel closed his eyes, enjoying the feel of the late afternoon sun on his face. He plucked a blade of grass and crumpled it in his fingers, holding it to his nose. Opening his eyes again, he extended his hand to Minna. "Smell the grass. I remember that green smell."

Obediently, Minna sniffed his hand. Pearl leaned over to do the same.

"It smells like spring in *der alter heym*," Minna said. "Remember the forget-me-nots growing wild near the graveyard? When they came up, I knew it was finally spring."

"I knew it was finally spring when I could take off my long underwear," Pearl said. "It's the same here."

Yussel's closed his eyes again. "I wonder what happened to Ephraim and his friends—the ones we met on the boat. They must have a big farm by now."

"Would you have gone with them if you could?" Minna dared to ask. "Are you sorry you didn't?"

"You mean, am I sorry now?"

Minna nodded. Noticing that Yussel's eyes were still closed, she spoke louder so he could hear her. "Yes."

"I'm not exactly sorry," he mused, "but sometimes I wonder what it would have been like. I miss the grass and the blue sky." He opened his eyes and looked up.

"But Yussel," Pearl said anxiously, "I thought you enjoyed peddling."

"What's to enjoy?" he asked. "It will be successful and we'll be comfortable, that's all. Mama is so proud of her new shop..."

"But Yussel, you work so hard," Minna pleaded. "If you are sorry..."

Yussel sat up. "I never said I was sorry," he replied brusquely. He picked a fat blade of grass. "Do you know how to make a whistle?" he asked. Holding the blade of grass between his two thumbs against his mouth, he blew, emitting a shrill whistle.

Pearl was entranced. "Show me how, Yussel. I want to do it, too."

Minna watched Yussel, noticing anew how thin and pale he was. His dark hair seemed limp and his forehead was already creased into a permanent anxious frown.

She burst out. "It's not fair!"

Yussel looked at her inquiringly.

'You work so hard," she continued lamely. "It's like...it's like you're the father in this family." She leaned forward. "I can help you. Once I graduate..."

"You're going to college someday," Yussel said firmly. "I promise, you'll have your chance."

"And you?" Minna asked. "When does your chance come?"

"When I own a big store on Fifth Avenue and I'm rolling in money, I'll buy a farm in the Catskills and raise cows," Yussel laughed.

"Mama will never let you stop working for the store," Minna said wisely. "She'll try to stop me from going to college, too. Ever since Tata left, she's only thought of one thing—it's that store!"

"I know it seems that way," Yussel responded, "but, did you ever think of why?"

Pearl put down the blade of grass she had been holding up to her mouth in a vain attempt to reproduce Yussel's whistle and leaned forward.

"I'll tell you why. If she hadn't been so determined, what would have happened to us? Cousin Avraim wouldn't have taken care of us. Don't you see—it's she who is the father, she who puts food in our bellies. So it's true, maybe she doesn't always remember to be a mother. At least it's thanks to her we're all still here. Who knows what happened to Tata in *der alter heym*!"

"He doesn't bother to write, that's all," Minna said bitterly.

"You'd think he'd want to know about us a little," Pearl commented.

"Maybe he's helping the Czar run the country," Minna said ironically, preferring to continue the conversation about Mama. "You mean," she continued, turning to Yussel again, "she's like that because…"

"Because she's afraid," Yussel said. "What if it was like when Tata left? What if we didn't have any money at all?"

Minna shook her head. "That's not it. She loves that shop more than anything."

"She loves the shop, too," Yussel explained. "It's being afraid and loving, both. It doesn't matter. If she weren't the way she is, you wouldn't be graduating in a few weeks, that I promise you."

"I guess you're right," Minna agreed reluctantly.

"Yes, but what's the point?" Pearl asked. "If we're doing a little better, why not enjoy it, that's what I say. I wish we had a parlor like Rebecca's going to have in the Bronx. She's getting a piano, too. I already told you, Minna. You know, when I asked Mama about a piano, she said, 'Music lessons yet! Every family in this building thinks they have another Rubenstein. Let's get rid of the boarders first and then we'll worry about a piano.' But that was a long time ago and nothing's changed."

"Do we have to keep the boarders?" Minna raised her voice. "Can't we use the front room for ourselves? We could put a screen up and you could have a real room, instead of the kitchen, to sleep in. We could even buy a horsehair sofa and a lamp to be pretty."

"I think Bessie actually might leave this time," Yussel pondered. "As for Sarah…"

Pearl and Minna exchanged glances at the mention of Sarah's name.

Yussel caught them at it and blushed. "She's a nice girl," he confided. "I like her. But that's all. I can't think of anything else. Not yet."

Both girls were flattered by Yussel's confidence.

"Once they go…" Minna began.

"We'll see. I agree with you. Yussel said. "Not about the piano and fancy furniture," he added hurriedly, "but I really don't see why we need boarders any more now that the store is bigger. If we continue to do as well as we've planned, we can manage living on our own."

A ball came flying through the air, bounced against the tree, and landed in Minna's lap. She stared at it in surprise.

Behind the nearest clump of bushes, a voice called out. "Oh, I missed! Now where did that ball go?"

A head poked around the edges of the bushes. A small boy a few years younger than Pearl dressed in a spotless white sailor suit smiled at them cheerfully. "Say, have you seen my ball? I missed it and they're waiting."

Minna held up the ball and tossed it over to him.

"Thanks. Thanks a lot," he called as he hurried back through the bushes.

The encounter made Minna feel as if she really did belong in Central Park.

"How do you think he keeps his suit so clean?" Pearl asked in awe.

"He doesn't," Yussel explained. "I'm sure he has many suits—and it isn't his Mama who washes them for him, either."

"I wish we had a ball," Pearl said.

"Next time, we'll bring one," Yussel promised, standing up. "Let's walk down the path," he added. "I want to see more of this park."

Following Yussel, Minna promised herself that she would help him as much as she could. I'll still go to college, she reassured herself, but for now, I'll devote myself to the store. Poor Yussel. It isn't fair…"

She ran to catch up. As she passed Yussel, she tagged him. "I got you!" she called and ran off.

Yussel and Pearl chased after her.

Minna ran so fast that she almost knocked into a large English perambulator pushed by a woman in a starched nurse's dress. Just in time, she stopped short, inches from the carriage.

The nurse glared at her and pushed past. "If you please," she sneered. Minna could hear her muttering under her breath as she disappeared down the path, "Young hooligans!"

Today that seemed amusing. "Come on, you bunch of hooligans," she yelled. "Last one to the next tree is a rotten egg!"

They pelted down the path, straight into the arms of a waiting policeman. He looked them up and down forbiddingly. "And where might you be going? Maybe there's a fire I haven't heard about..."

Yussel straightened, started to speak, stopped, and looked pleadingly at Minna. He knew she spoke English better than he did.

"I...I'm sorry, sir," Minna said timorously. "We didn't mean to..."

The police nodded, his shiny brass buttons winking in the sun. "No one ever does. I warrant they think this is a racetrack! Next time, slow down. There's no running on the paths."

Minna nodded in agreement, Yussel flushed, and Pearl looked at the ground.

The policeman patted Pearl's shoulder. "Now, don't look so worried. It's not the end of the world. Just slow down!"

Pearl gave him a radiant smile. As they continued sedately along the path, she said, "He's so much nicer than the policeman on Allen Street."

"Sure he is," Yussel agreed. "In Central Park, they have to be nice."

"Like on Fifth Avenue," Minna said.

They remained in the park for several hours, exploring as much of it as they could. As the day drew to a close and shadows began to cover the paths, they walked slowly to the exit. They said little as they returned to the Second Avenue El and stepped on the train.

It was only when they reached their own front door that Pearl exclaimed, "We never had any dinner!"

There was such a note of surprise in her voice that Minna and Yussel began to laugh, despite their fear of facing Mama. When they finally climbed the stairs to their apartment and opened the door, she was waiting in front of it, her arms akimbo.

"Where have you been—all of you?" she demanded. "What kind of an errand took you away for so long?"

Yussel smiled sheepishly. "I took the girls on a vacation. We went to Central Park."

"To Central Park? Uptown?" Mama glared at them. "I'm sitting here worrying and you were at the park? *Amerikane kinder*!" She sniffed and stomped into the kitchen.

Pearl ran after her. "We sat on the grass and walked under the trees. You would have liked it, too."

"Who's to say?" Mama stormed. "I don't have the time!"

"Oh, Mama," Minna pleaded. "It was only a few hours and it

did us good."

Mama shook her head. "Maybe it did you good, but it didn't do me good. How do you think I felt, coming home from the store to find no one here, no supper, and a *cockamamy* note. 'We have gone to do an errand.' What was I supposed to understand from that?"

"It's my fault," Yussel said. "I came home early and I just wanted to get away for a few hours." He smiled at Mama. "You'd like it there. Maybe we could go next Saturday, all of us."

"And bring a ball," Pearl reminded him.

Mama looked them up and down. "You haven't had dinner, have you?"

They shook their heads.

"Then come and sit down and tell me all about Central Park," she sighed. Gesturing at the table, which was set for them, she filled their plates from the pot on the stove.

She listened politely to their description of Central Park, but she shook her head when Yussel again suggested they go back on Saturday. "It's not for me," she said decisively. "I have the books to keep and the stocks to tidy, Sabbath or no!"

Their enthusiasm waned. They lapsed into silence.

As if she had been waiting for this moment, Mama continued talking. "Guess who came into the shop today?" she asked brightly.

"Cousin Avraim?" Pearl asked. "What did he think of it? Was that new wife of his with him?"

Mama shook her head. "He already came in this week. I told him, 'Don't bother to copy all my ideas. You're paid back and we're free and clear now!' He didn't like that, I can tell you! No, it wasn't him."

"So, who was it?" Minna asked impatiently. "Why does everything have to be a mystery?"

"Someone we haven't seen for many years. Someone we all know very well. He was very surprised to see me. Especially with his lady friend."

"His lady friend…" Minna pondered. It couldn't be Benny Herschel. He was too old. She knew what Mama's contemptuous tone meant. Who could it be?

"Someone we met on the boat," Mama hinted.

Minna caught her breath. "It wasn't…Jake?"

Mama nodded. "Dressed like a regular sport, he was. Such a tie like I've never seen and fancy shoes, too. His lady friend…"

"His lady friend?" Minna asked.

"That's what he called her." Mama shrugged. "All I know is she had the biggest hat and wore silk—pure silk—from her dress to her stockings. Jake was helping her choose some taffeta for an evening dress she was going to have made up. He called her Dolly, but he didn't dare introduce her to me. No better than she should be, that *goyishe kopf*. He did ask after all of you and said he would come and visit sometime."

"Did he look well?" Pearl asked.

"What's well? With his diamond ring flashing at me, how could I see his face?"

"His uncle runs a gang of *shtarkes*. Jake's supposedly the only one he trusts. I've seen him on the street," Yussel contributed.

Minna looked down at the table. Although she hadn't seen Jake since he left prison three years ago, she hadn't forgotten him or his uncle. At first, she had been sure he would come and see her as soon as he was freed. When he didn't, she had first thought he must be too ashamed and decided she'd visit him instead. Yet every time she set out, she turned back, embarrassed. Suppose he was still angry or worse, suppose he laughed at her.

As time passed, she had never stopped believing that one day she would see him again. She often pictured their reunion. Invariably, the climax consisted of his admiring gratitude. He'd look at her and say, 'You were right, Minna. All along, you were right. I've changed. I'm going to City College and all the while, I've thought of you and remembered what you said.' Then he'd step back and look at her. 'You've grown into a real beauty,' he'd say. At this point, Minna had to laugh at herself, but she continued to imagine the same scene in a thousand different ways.

"It's that uncle of his," she said angrily. "If we had taken him in the beginning…"

Yussel looked at her in surprise. "He likes the way he lives. He struts down the street as if he owns it. He always wanted to be a big shot."

"Who's this Dolly?" Pearl asked.

"They all have women," Yussel explained scornfully, "but those women, they don't get married."

"Oh." Pearl's eyes grew round.

"I think it's disgusting," Minna said.

That night she dreamed of Jake as she had many times before, but it was a different kind of dream. She pictured him walking by on the street with a buxom blonde on his arm. They were laughing and talking so gaily they never noticed her. She ran after them, calling out his name, but he didn't even look back. She watched as the two of them disappeared in the distance. When she awoke, there were tears in her eyes.

All during the next day, the dream burned in Minna's mind. In the midst of school, when she was sewing her graduation dress at home, and later, when she was studying, she found herself stopping at odd intervals and imagining Jake with his blonde, Dolly, who grew more voluptuous every time Minna pictured her.

This is ridiculous, she said to herself. I haven't seen him for three years. Why should I care what he does or who he does it with? Yet she couldn't stop thinking about him.

The night of Halley's Comet, when everyone was out in the streets, staring fearfully upward, Minna at first thought more of bumping into Jake than she did of the comet. It had been predicted that the world would end that very evening, but Miss Israel had laughed at the stories, so Minna was not really afraid. Only when some boys released a fiery red balloon, its flames shooting out from a rooftop on Grand Street, did she have a momentary doubt.

Along with what seemed like all of the lower East Side, Minna remained on the street, craning her neck to look at the sky until the comet's tail passed through the city skies at about three o'clock in the morning. For an hour, she watched in awe as it flew past.

Minna forgot Jake and even her family standing next to her. Compared to this amazing spectacle, her worries seemed petty and unimportant. What difference would it make if she worked in Mama's store or went to college? If Jake was her friend or not, how could it possibly matter? She vowed to concern herself with more important issues, the nature of which she hadn't yet discerned.

By the next morning, when she awoke, exhausted and ill prepared for school, Minna had forgotten her vows. Once again, she found herself thinking of Jake, agonizing over the faint hope of attending college, and persistently irritated by what she thought of as Mama's shop.

Minna was not the only one who was excited as her graduation day approached. Her feelings were infectious. Even Mama seemed to be looking forward to the great event.

The night before, she finally finished sewing her dress. She pressed it carefully, heating the irons on the old stove in the kitchen. When it was finished, she took it into her room and gingerly slipped it over her head. She peered at her reflection in the small mirror, even standing on the bed to see the hem. At last, she opened the bedroom door and stepped into the kitchen.

"Oh, Minna," Pearl sighed. "You look so…beautiful."

Mama, scouring the stove, turned and looked at Minna. Finally, she whispered, "Like Chava, may God rest her soul."

Yussel beamed.

Sarah, who was sitting at the table, peered at the dress. "It's just like a Fifth Avenue dress," she exclaimed and came closer. "Such tiny stitches! And the lace…it's so fine."

Even Bessie, who had already given her notice and planned to leave at the end of the month, looked up and nodded brusquely.

Minna was satisfied with the effect she had made. It was worth all the work. Gracefully, she pirouetted around the table and whisked back into the bedroom to take off the precious dress. Draping it in a sheet for protection, she hung it precariously on the single hook that was hers. Then she took out her old black kid shoes and began polishing them. I wish I had white, she thought. Then my outfit would be perfect.

She hadn't mentioned it to her family, but she hoped to graduate with honors. If she won the highest honors, she would even be presented with a bouquet. Although most girls would receive flowers—either a corsage or a nosegay—from friends and family, Minna expected nothing from hers. The custom was unfamiliar to them. She had decided not to mention it. It's enough, she thought, they're all coming and Mama gave me the fabric for my dress.

The next morning, when she awoke, Minna heard voices outside her door. Usually, it was quiet so early in the day. Mama and Yussel, who left first, always tiptoed so as not to disturb the others. Bessie and Sarah left next for the factory, and she and Pearl, rushing for school, had no time or inclination to do more than say "good morning" to each other.

Minna sat up in bed. She was surprised she felt just the same as she had the night before. She had expected to feel like a different person on her graduation day. Instead, it was the same as every other day, except...there were too many voices in the kitchen. She leaned forward, trying to hear exactly what they were saying, but all she could hear were vague whispers.

Then she heard Pearl say, "Shh! You'll wake her!"

Shyly, Minna walked over to the door and opened it. There, on the red checked tablecloth, was a small nosegay. Cascading from the flowers were soft pink ribbons, so pale in hue they were almost white.

Minna blushed and looked at her family, standing around the table. "How did you know?" she asked.

"You think no one ever graduated before?" Mama asked.

Next to the flowers was a small box. That, too, had a ribbon around it.

Minna looked questioningly at the others.

Yussel smiled. "Aren't you going to open your graduation present?"

"My graduation present?" Minna was dazed. "I didn't think…"

"We all chipped in," Pearl explained. "Even Cousin Avraim and Benny Herschel. Sarah and Bessie did too."

Minna sat down suddenly. Her eyes filled with tears.

Mama gave her a little push. "Go on. Open!"

Clumsily, Minna took the little box. Slowly she untied the ribbon and lifted the lid. Inside was a slim silver bracelet with a heart dangling from it. She touched it in awe.

"Look in the back!" Pearl urged.

Minna turned the silver heart over. There, inscribed on the back, was her name, the date, and in tiny script all around the edges of the heart, the initials of those who had given it to her. Wonderingly, she held it up.

"Put it on! Put it on!" Mama said impatiently.

Minna clasped it around her wrist and held up her hand. Twisting her arm this way and that, she admired the sparkle of the silver, the slight jangle of the heart against the chain.

She jumped up and hugged Mama, Yussel, and Pearl. "Thank you! Thank you! I'll wear it forever," she cried.

All through breakfast she admired her new bracelet. "It's the first piece of jewelry anyone ever gave me," she said to Pearl.

"You have the necklace," Pearl disagreed.

"Yes, but I found that myself. This is a gift. I never thought…"

"And why not?" Mama interrupted. "You didn't think we would know to give you a gift? When Pearl told us…"

Minna gave Pearl an extra hug.

Between bites, she bent over to sniff her nosegay as it lay on the table next to her plate. "These are the most beautiful flowers anyone ever had," she sighed.

"That was Yussel's idea," Pearl said.

Minna looked at Yussel, surprised.

"One of my ladies told me that most girls carry a bouquet," Yussel explained shyly. "So, I went to the flower lady on Hester Street and told her it was for a beautiful girl on her graduation. I don't think she thought I meant my sister!"

Minna leaned over and squeezed his hand. She gazed around the table and said softly, "I'll never forget this day as long as I live."

Mama looked at the clock in the kitchen. "You'd better hurry, " she said. "You don't want to be late for your graduation."

A face peeked into the doorway from the other room. "Happy graduation day, Minna," Sarah said. Bessie's face could be seen peering out from behind her.

Minna jumped up. Hugging Sarah and smiling at Bessie, she exclaimed, "Thank you both! This is the happiest day of my life. I'll wear my beautiful bracelet forever. See how it looks!" She waved her arm in the air so that the silver heart sparkled in the light.

"I can't wait to see how it looks with your dress," Sarah said.

Bessie smiled back at Minna. "I wish you well," she said, her voice serious.

Mama touched Minna on the shoulder. "Come," she insisted. "You must get your dress on."

Minna turned to Mama. "Thank you," she said.

Embarrassed, she shook her head. "You're the one who's graduating. Better we should say, 'Thanks to America!'"

Minna persisted. "We wouldn't be here if it wasn't for you."

Mama looked away for a moment. When she turned back, her face was somber. "Your sister Chava is here today. I can feel it. It might have been her."

Minna put her arms around Mama. "It's for her, too, Mama."

Mama hugged Minna briskly and stepped back. "Go!" she commanded. "Go get ready!"

Since everyone else had dressed earlier, Minna had the rare luxury of privacy. After going to the bathroom in the hall and washing her face with her precious bar of scented soap, she slowly put on her new corset and petticoats, savoring every moment. For the occasion, she even had a new pair of stockings, silk all the way up to her knees.

When she slipped the dress over her head, she hurried to the small mirror for reassurance. Perhaps she had been mistaken before and the dress really didn't look well. Maybe the place where she had ripped and re-sewn the lace showed.

She smiled at her face in the mirror. She looked just as she had yesterday. Holding up her bracelet so she could see how the silver looked against the lace-edged sleeves, she smiled again. Unbidden, the thought of Jake crossed her mind, but she pushed it away. Who cares, she thought happily. He can have his blondes!

Humming to herself, she fastened her dress. Then, with her comb and brush, she fixed her hair the new way she had practiced. The puffs she wore at the side were flattering, she thought, and made her look much older.

When she left the room, everyone was waiting for her. Mama looked sleek and dignified in her black bombazine, Yussel elegant in his suit from last year, and Pearl, as always, waif-like despite her freshly starched dress and bright red ribbons.

There was a moment of silence. Everyone stared at her.

"Your hair!" Pearl exclaimed. "It looks so grown-up."

Yussel handed Minna her bouquet with a flourish. "Not half as pretty as you," he said gallantly.

Mama nodded and twitched the skirt of Minna's dress to make sure it hung straight. "You'll do," she said firmly, flushing slightly.

Minna smiled from her heart. "I have the best family in the world." Linking arms with Pearl, she added, "Let's go! The Ruben family is on the march!"

When they arrived at the school, she showed them to their seats and hurried backstage to get in line for the procession. In her happy daze, the time passed so quickly it seemed only seconds before she was out in front of everyone, her name called as the graduating senior with the most honors.

When she accepted the bouquet of roses from the principal, Minna looked out at the audience. She thought she saw Mama's face. In the front row where the teachers sat, Miss Israel applauded with white-gloved hands.

Later, when she was called up to accept her diploma, Minna felt confused for the first time that day. This is the most important day of my life, she thought, but it doesn't seem real. It's another girl, standing in front of all the people and shaking the principal's hand.

It was only later, when all the ceremonies were over and she was again with her family that she felt she was herself, Minna Ruben, again. She accepted their good wishes, proudly introduced Miss Israel to Mama and Yussel, and congratulated her classmates.

That afternoon, Mama, Pearl, and Yussel went off to work. It had been tacitly agreed that Minna might have the afternoon off. Alone in the apartment, she sat in the kitchen, admiring her flowers. She had put the rich red roses from school in water and set them on the kitchen table. Later, she would press Yussel's small nosegay in her dictionary so she'd be able to keep it forever.

I suppose I should change, she thought, but she remained in the kitchen, enjoying being all dressed up. Today I'm beautiful and everything is perfect, she thought. Tomorrow, the real world will start.

Minna remembered what Miss Israel had said to her as a farewell. "You *must* go to college, Minna. Remember, decide what's important to you and then never forget it. If I can help you any time, come and see me. You will make a wonderful teacher."

Minna blushed, just thinking of Miss Israel's words.

I'll never give up, she thought. Some day, I'll dress in my best all the time and I'll have my own room. Young girls will look up to me and I'll help them, just the way Miss Israel helped me. Today, anything—no, everything—is possible.

CHAPTER 11

The next morning, as Minna readied herself for work, it was hard to remain optimistic. Casting a regretful glance at her graduation dress, again shrouded in the sheet, she put on her workday shirtwaist and dark skirt. Sighing, she pulled her hair back from her face the old way. Why bother, she thought, just to work in the store?

Listlessly, she glanced in the mirror. Catching sight of her new bracelet, she smiled reluctantly. Then, sitting down on the bed, she put her head in her hands.

"Help me, Bubbe," she mumbled. "I don't want to work in the shop. Not every day. How will I ever be able to change my life?"

She thought she could hear Bubbe saying, 'So *nu*, little Minna, so your life is not a fairy tale. You're grown up now. That means…'

She stood up impatiently. I won't listen, she thought. I know what she's going to say. It means…I have to accept responsibility. Well, I am, aren't I? I don't need to talk about it too!

She flounced out of the room into the kitchen, only to stop, surprised, when she saw Yussel was still there apparently waiting for her. She looked around. "Where's everyone else?" she asked.

"They've gone already. Pearl's helping Mama today."

Immediately, Minna felt guilty. She glanced at the clock. "It's seven thirty," she said hurriedly. "I didn't mean to oversleep."

"Mama's going through the stock this morning. I wanted to wait for you," Yussel said.

Minna smiled at him. It wasn't his fault she had to work at the store. "I'm glad you did. I don't feel enthusiastic this morning."

'That's what I figured."

Minna poured herself a cup of tea. Sitting down at the table, she held the glass between her hands. Its warmth, even on a hot day, was reassuring. As the steam rose and bathed her face, she bowed her head. "I want to be good," she murmured. "I want to do my part."

Yussel put his hand on her arm. "I know," he said.

Minna looked up.

'We're doing very well this month. With your help, we'll do even better. Soon we'll have enough money to hire an assistant or to pay you so you can save for college."

"Soon?"

"You're only fifteen and a half," Yussel replied gently.

Minna flushed. "I know. I know I'm being selfish. But Miss Israel said I have to remember what's important. If I forget, I'm afraid it won't happen, not ever. I have to go to college so I can learn to be like the others, those people we saw on Fifth Avenue, the people I read about in the newspapers—the real Americans."

"Is that what you want?"

She shrugged. "I know I don't want to live here on Allen Street all my life. I don't want to get married soon and have a pack of kids. I don't want to wear old clothes and worry about everything I buy."

As she saw the expression on Yussel's face, she added hastily, "It's not you or the others. I love you, of course I do, but I have to find a different life for myself. I've wanted that since the very beginning, when we first came to this country. Don't you want a different life, too?"

Yussel frowned. "I'm already having a different kind of life than I would have had. I can remember what it was like in *der alter heym*. I would still be studying in the *shul*. If I was lucky, I'd marry a rich girl and her family would support us. Here, at least I'm on my own. There's no one looking over my shoulder. Some day, if I want to enough and I work hard, I can even have a farm for fun. A farm for fun! Minna, I'm never afraid here. Sure, we don't have enough money and I worry about it all the time, but it's different. I don't have to cut off my leg like Mordecai to get out of the Czar's army or hide in the night from a pogrom. People tip their hats to me when I walk by."

Minna sat quietly, absorbing Yussel's words.

Finally, she replied. "Maybe it's because I was younger than you when we left, or because I went to school here, but I want more than that. I want to be a real American. I want to live where they speak English all the time, where people don't know from *der alter heym*, where people just think—oh, there's an interesting girl—and that's all."

Yussel looked at her dubiously. "Is that possible?" he asked. "The thing that makes you an interesting girl is everything about you, especially that you came here when you were ten."

Minna shook her head. "I want to be like the girls I read about. I want to be like Susannah!"

"But you're not and you never will be. It's only a dream. Don't you see?"

Minna gulped her tea and stood up. "No, I don't see. I can be any way I want to be. This is America. That's why we're here. I need a chance, that's all!"

Yussel pushed his chair back. "You have to make your own chance. No one can give it to you."

"I will. I will."

They walked out in silence.

As they approached the store, Minna stopped and looked earnestly at Yussel. 'That's how I feel," she said. "I can't change it. But for now, I'll work like the dickens in the shop to help the family, and myself, too."

Yussel hugged her lightly. "I can't ask for anything more."

As they entered the shop, Minna heard Mama's voice as it rang out from the small back room. "Take these out, Pearl, now that we've marked them. When Minna comes, she can help you arrange the tables."

Pearl staggered out of the stockroom, the top of her head barely visible above the bolts of cloth she carried. She rushed towards a partially empty table, bending backwards so the top bolts wouldn't fall to the floor.

Minna hurried over and took the top half of her stack, saying, "I'm here. I'm here. Where shall I start?"

Mama emerged from the stockroom just as Minna set down the fabric "Let's begin with the sale items. All the winter goods are reduced now. I thought we'd clear one table and put up a sign…" She gestured vaguely at the overcrowded tables and sighed. "No matter how hard I try, I can't keep this shop neat. Ever since we doubled our stock, it's impossible."

Minna looked around. All the extra space they had gained in the move had disappeared. Customers were forced to wind their way through tables of fabrics, each on piled high with goods. Even the trimmings, Mama's pride and joy, were half obscured by scraps of fabric and extra wheels of ribbon.

Minna thought for am moment. "I have an idea. What if we put the tables end to end around the edge of the shop?" She gestured with her hands. "Then, in the middle, we can put four together to make one big one. The trimmings can be in one corner and patterns in another. Do you see what I mean?"

Mama shook her head.

"It'll be good. I know it'll be good." In her enthusiasm, Minna forgot her reluctance to come to work. "Then, what we need are signs telling what's on every table—or the price," she continued. She closed her eyes for a minute. "I can see it so clearly." She marched over to a table and began pulling at it.

"Leave it!" Mama snapped, shaking her head. "I want you to help me, not change everything! Now you and Pearl clear a space there." She pointed at a table. "Put all the woolens on one side and…"

Shrugging, Minna followed Mama's commands. By nine o'clock, when the store was officially open, she and Pearl had finished putting out the sale goods and straightening the regular stock. It still looked like a mess, Minna thought, but she didn't dare say anything. While they waited for customers to come, she and Pearl tidied the notions, rewinding ribbons that had snarled and removing the scraps of fabric that had been tossed on top of them.

As the day progressed, Minna took care of several customers. Copying Mama's technique, she had sold a fat lady bright poplin for a wrapper, soft white lawn to a young girl, shiny red ribbons to her little sister, and advised a woman on the best way to complete the shirtwaist she had already started. Yussel was at the market and Pearl left in the afternoon to shop and prepare dinner.

As she worked, Minna sighed often. The shop seemed dark and dreary. She caught glimpses of the street out the big front window as she did her job. Never had the people hurrying by, the vendors calling their wares, the snatches of conversation that wafted in on the hot summer breeze seemed so enticing.

She gritted her teeth, determined to be a model assistant and utter no word of complaint. It's just as dark as this in school, she reminded herself, and I didn't mind that.

Mama, her lips set, seemed oblivious to Minna's feelings. That only made them more acute. When she did speak, it was only to issue commands or criticize.

Finally, during a lull, Minna turned to Mama. "If I draw you a picture of how I think it could look, would you at least glance at it?"

Mama glared a Minna. "Since when are you such an expert?" she asked angrily. "It's I who built this shop, I who have made it grow. Now you come in and after one day, you think you can tell me how to run it! Why should I listen?"

"But, Mama…" Minna began.

Just then, the little bell on the door rang and two customers came in. Minna hurried over to one and Mama to the other.

The bell kept ringing. It was not until several hours had passed that the shop was empty again. Minna pursed her lips and began restacking the bolts of fabric, trying to keep them in some kind of tenuous order.

Mama, fabric in her arms, brushed by her. "You are a good seller," she said grudgingly.

"Thank you, Mama," Minna said without looking up. She felt rather than saw Mama's expression of annoyance, but she continued stacking the fabrics without turning her head.

Finally, telling her to watch for customers, Mama stalked out to make a delivery. Alone in the shop, Minna leaned against a table, hating the shop, hating herself, and most of all, hating Mama.

In the momentary quiet, she thought she could hear Bubbe saying, 'So this is how you're a grownup. I'm ashamed of you, Minna. You think you're too fancy to help your Mama? You think you know better? A few years of school and you're ready to be the boss? Good work!'

Minna clapped her hands over her ears. It wasn't that, she thought. I really could make this a better shop. If we had an empty table to show the goods so we could unroll them for the ladies, and little signs so they could find what they're looking for right off, and…

'How do you think your Mama feels?' Bubbe's stern voice seemed to thunder in Minna's ears. 'She works and works and along comes a fifteen-year-old girl who says 'I know better.' Upsetting her. Is that helping Yussel? I'm ashamed of you.'

Minna put her head down on her arms, shutting out the shop, Bubbe, and Mama. Closing her eyes, she imagined she was far away. Maybe, in college…

In the midst of her dream, she heard the tinkle of the bell. She looked up.

An older woman marched in, pushing a girl about three years younger than Minna in front of her. "For the child," she declared. "She grows so fast. Already, she needs another new dress. Let me see the most practical fabric you have in a dark color, so it won't show the dirt."

The girl hung her head.

"With all I have to do, I have to make dresses, too?" the woman grumbled. "It's not enough, at my age, to cook and clean and sew on the machines for my daughter and her family. No, I have to make dresses, too. She wants something pretty, she says." She gave the girl a little push. "Pretty is for rich people, that's what I say!"

Minna smiled at the girl sympathetically. The dress she wore was far too tight across the middle and too short in length. By no stretch of the imagination could it be called pretty. Automatically, she pulled out serviceable serge. "This will be hot in the summer," she warned.

"So, she'll be a little hot." The woman shrugged. "What I want to know is, how long will it last? I can't be making dresses left and right for this child. She's not even of my blood. That *momzer*, my daughter's husband, he left her with us when he ran away. Soon, she'll be able to pay her way, but for now…"

Defiantly, Minna held up a bolt of gaily printed calico. "This costs much less than the serge," she said, "and it won't show the dirt, either."

The girl looked at it longingly.

"Too bright," the woman criticized. "She should dress like a princess while I work my fingers to the bone?"

The girl put her hands up to her face, obviously holding back tears.

Minna thought rapidly. Calculating in her head, she made an offer. "For the same price as the serge, I'll make a dress for her out of this calico." There would still be a profit, for the calico was much cheaper than the serge—particularly this bolt, which had come in a very low price.

"Probably stolen," Mama had sniffed.

Minna knew it would only take her a few hours or so to run up a simple dress. Judging by what the girl was wearing, there would be no embellishments expected.

Taken aback, the woman looked at her suspiciously. "What's in it for you? Why should you make Irene a dress? This must be damaged goods."

"We're trying to move our stock and particularly, the calico," Minna said quickly.

Just then, Mama came in. She strode over to Minna, stood next to her, and looked at the woman inquiringly.

'So, here's your boss," the woman said. "Let's see if she likes your idea."

She told Mama of Minna's suggestion. Mama, obviously taken by surprise, looked at the girl, at Minna, and at the woman. Finally, she spoke. "This is my daughter. Whatever she says is fine with me."

Minna had been sure Mama would be angry. Instead, she had defended her! She breathed a sigh of relief. She wanted to say "Thank you!" but instead, she composed herself and waited for the woman's reply.

"I'll take the serge," she said in a nasty tone. "Fancy dressmakers I don't need! I'll make her clothes myself."

As Minna measured out the serge, she caught a glimpse of the girl's face. She saw a tear fall. She shook her head and looked away. There was nothing she could do.

After the woman had gone, clutching the blue serge and pushing the girl ahead of her, Minna turned to Mama. "I'm sorry," she apologized. "It's just that I felt sorry for the girl. Besides, we would still have made a profit."

Mama, her head on one side, looked at Minna with narrowed eyes. "It's not such a bad idea," she said. "We could bring your sewing machine down here and you could make up simple dresses for extra. It would help to sell the fabric, too," she mused.

"You think it's a good idea?" Minna asked incredulously. "I thought you didn't want to hear any new ideas."

Mama patted her shoulder. "All in time," she said. "On your first day, you can't change the world. Even Moses didn't lead the Jews to the Holy Land in one day!"

"You're not angry with me?"

"I was angry. Then I remembered the first time I went to help Bubbe at her stall after I was grown up. I thought she was so old-fashioned. I wanted to change everything! By the second day, I wasn't so sure and after a week, I thought, I'd better wait and see."

Minna felt ashamed. "I'm sorry, Mama. I didn't mean to be bossy. Maybe in a few months, we can talk about changing things again." She smiled at Mama.

Mama smiled back. "Maybe so," she agreed. "The sewing idea is a good one, anyway."

By the time she and Mama closed the shop that evening, Minna was already feeling better than she had that morning. She planned where she would put the sewing machine and composed a sign to put in the window.

It was only as they were turning the corner to their apartment that Minna remembered something. "If I bring my sewing machine to the store, I'll have to stay late to do my own work. I've planned to earn some money for college by sewing shirtwaists at night."

Mama was silent.

Minna looked at her anxiously. "It won't interfere with the shop. I'll only work at night. It's just that if I don't start, I'll never have enough money."

Mama was still silent.

In desperation, Minna clutched her arm. "Don't you see?" she demanded. "Miss Israel said I always have to remember what's important. It's important that I go to college so I can be a teacher. That's what I want." Her voice wavered.

Mama stopped in the middle of the street and looked at her. "You want it that much?" she asked.

"I want it more than anything. I know I have to earn the money myself," she added hastily.

Mama shook her head. "College, yet! You're the first one in our family who's finished high school and now you want to go to college!"

"I said I'll pay for it myself. I'll work hard at the store, but at night, it's my time and I choose to earn money for myself. If I was working in a factory…"

"Yes?" Mama asked ominously.

Minna gulped and continued. "If I was working in a factory, I could earn something from my wages even after I paid for my rent and food at home."

Mama glared at her. "It's true, if you were working in a factory, you'd have wages. But they'd come to us, your family. Does Yussel keep anything for himself? Do I?"

"No," Minna replied slowly. "But, the store is for you and Yussel. It helps us all now, but when Pearl and I marry or leave, you'll still have the store. Don't you see, I don't want the store! I want something else for my life."

"In *der alter heym*…" Mama began.

"But this isn't *der alter heym*! This is here, America in the year 1910." Minna paused for a moment and then continued earnestly. "Don't you see, Mama? When Tata left us, we had to make our own way. You did it, you and Yussel. Pearl and I helped as much as we could. In *der alter heym*, could you have opened your own shop and moved to a larger one so soon?"

Mama shook her head.

Heartened, Minna continued. "In *der alter heym*, could I have graduated from high school? Could I have even gone to school? By now, the *shadchen* would be coming if we were lucky. Think of Chava." Minna stopped, aghast. She put her hand over her mouth. "I'm sorry, Mama. I didn't mean to…"

Mama looked down at the curb, oblivious of the people brushing by her.

After what seemed like an eternity to Minna, she lifted her head and looked up at the sky. "Chava," she repeated. Then, turning to her daughter, she looked her full in the face. "It *is* different here. You're right about that. For the rest, I'll have to think about it."

Minna nodded happily. Mama would think about it! That was something. Without daring to say another word, she quietly followed Mama up the stairs and into the apartment.

At the dinner table that evening, Mama insisted on telling everyone about Minna's idea to sew dresses for the ladies.

Yussel looked worried. "Suppose they want Minna to make a fancy dress with many fittings. Then it's not worth it for us."

"That's true," Mama agreed, rubbing her chin.

"Why don't you pick out two or three easy patterns and only offer those?" Pearl suggested. 'Charge a set price and allow one measurement and fitting."

"We're not in the dressmaking business," Mama said, changing sides. "This is *farposhket*!"

Minna had been sitting quietly, listening to everyone. Suddenly, she had an idea.

"I know what!" she exclaimed. "Instead of making dresses for the ladies, let's have a sewing clinic."

"A sewing clinic?" Mama asked.

'Yes. Like the doctor has. But this will be for sewing and I'll be the doctor. The ladies can come in and get help. I'll make all the newest patterns and put them in the window. We'll have a card saying, 'Sewing Expert Inside. All Questions Answered Free of Charge.'"

"Free of charge?" Mama asked.

"Well, the ladies who do sew, they'll come into the store if they have a question. The others will come in to learn. Once they come in, if we can't sell them fabrics, trimmings, and patterns, we might as well close up!"

Yussel was intrigued. "We can certainly try it. It won't cost us anything except the samples Minna will make up—and we can always sell the dresses she's made if it doesn't work."

"I don't know…" Mama said dubiously.

"Why not?" Minna asked. "As Yussel said, there's nothing to lose. It's my time and I don't mind. Don't worry, Mama, I'll have time to do everything else, too."

Mama finally agreed. Within a few weeks, Minna was teaching a regular sewing class twice a week. As she had predicted, the number of customers who came to the shop increased. Most of them now bought trimmings as well as fabric.

Minna kept her machine at the store, working on clothes for the window in her spare time. At night, after supper, she returned to the shop to sew shirtwaists on consignment. She kept the money she earned and Mama, by her avoidance of the subject, tacitly agreed.

It was slow work. Each dollar she earned meant hours of fatigue the next day. She often fell asleep at her machine, only to wake, startled, early in the morning. Then she'd jump up, run back home, change, and return to the store to work.

One night, as she was sitting and sewing, the single electric light over her head illuminating her work, she heard a tapping at the door. She hesitated, stopped pushing the treadle with her feet and looked around. The tapping continued.

She knew that everyone in the family had a key. There was no reason for any of them to be tapping at the door. There had been a series of thefts and vandalism in the adjoining shops. She glanced at the lock, glad she had pushed the bar home, and bent over her work again, determined to ignore the sound.

The knocking grew louder. Through the hum of the machine, Minna thought she could hear a voice, but she couldn't tell what it was saying. She stopped pedaling and tiptoed to the door.

"Minna!" she heard. "I know you're there. I saw you through the window. Let me in! For God's sake, let me in!"

The voice sounded familiar, but she wasn't sure.

"Who is it?"

"It's me, Jake. Let me in! Hurry!"

Minna opened the door a crack and peeked through it.

It was Jake, still recognizable after three years. Panting and disheveled, he looked like a beggar in wrinkled old clothes. In one hand, he carried a billy.

Minna stared at him. Then she saw that his forehead was bleeding. Quickly, she opened the door all the way.

"What's the matter?" she asked, forgetting the three years, his stay in prison, and Dolly. All she could see standing before her was a young boy, alone and determined not to show he was afraid.

"I got into a fight," Jake said, stepping into the shop and hurriedly closing the door. "The police are after me."

There wasn't time to think it through. She pointed at the back room. "Go in there," she said.

Jake stumbled, caught at one of the tables, righted himself, and barely managed to get into the storeroom and close the door before there was another knock at the door.

Minna looked back to make sure the storeroom door was closed. Then she called out, "Who's there?"

"It's the police," was the answer.

Straightening her dress and composing her face, she opened the door. "What's the trouble?" she asked.

"I'm looking for someone. Did you let anyone in?" The policeman stared around the shop.

She blushed. Without even considering what she would say, she let the words tumble out. "I'm here all alone, working," she lied, gesturing at the sewing machine. "I wouldn't dare let anyone in." She thought quickly. "I did hear someone running down the street, though."

The policeman looked her up and down.

Minna blushed again.

Satisfied, he nodded. "Thanks," he called as he hurried down the street.

She closed the door behind him and thought, I lied. I lied for Jake. She hung her head. This meeting was not going the way she had imagined it would. Reluctantly, she turned towards the closed door in the back of the shop.

The door opened and Jake peered out, his finger to his lips. He looked at her questioningly.

She shrugged. "I told him I heard someone running down the street," she whispered.

He looked relieved.

"What kind of a fight?" she asked. "What were you doing? Why was the policeman after you?"

He shook his head. "You don't really want to know, do you?"

She thought for a moment. "No, I don't. I guess I already know. Those burglaries down the street…"

He shook his head. "We were protecting the stores," he insisted. "That's why we were watching them. Cheeks Benny and his gang came by and they're the ones who…"

"You were protecting the stores?" she interrupted. "I don't understand."

"Well, they pay us to protect them," he said sheepishly. "See, it's Uncle Moishe's idea. He's my rabbi—like my teacher. We go to the stores and tell them all the things that could happen. Then they pay us to protect them so they don't happen. We're like policemen."

She looked at him. "Sure, I've heard about that. Someone came to Mama and she refused to pay. She said we wouldn't need protection if it weren't for them. Oh Jake, how can you?"

"If there's one thing I learned, it's every man for himself. If I don't do it, someone else will." He shrugged and stared at Minna. "You look good."

She didn't know what to do. In her dreams, she had planned to blush modestly and say lightly, "It *has* been a long time." Instead, she just stood there, staring back at him awkwardly.

He looks good, too, she thought, admiring him, wanting to stroke the dark curly hair falling over his face. Then she noticed the bruise on his forehead and thought, this is *meshuggeneh*. His rabbi is Uncle Moishe? He's a crook, that's all. She sighed.

She hurried over to her sewing machine and grabbed the bottle of tap water she had brought in case she became thirsty. Tearing a scrap of old material, she dipped it into the water and gestured to Jake to bend over. Gently, focusing only on his forehead, she dabbed at the bruise to wash the blood away.

When she had finished, she began to turn away. Jake held her arm. "I've wanted to see you," he said.

Minna looked at the floor. She wanted to say, well then, why didn't you? You could have come to see me if you'd really wanted to. She pursed her lips and said nothing.

"I've never forgotten you," he said. "I keep track. I know you graduated with honors. I hear about you from Benny Herschel."

Minna gazed into Jake's eyes and quickly bent her head again.

He continued, "I never came to see you because…after I got out, my life was so different. You wouldn't have understood. And your Mama. I know what she would have said. But I never forgot you." He looked away. Then he let go of her arm and started for the door. "I guess I'd better go now," he mumbled.

Numbly, she watched him leave. Finally, when he put his hand on the doorknob, she called his name.

He turned.

"I thought of you, too," she said. "I even went to see your uncle once when you were…away."

"I know. He told me. He said you were the prettiest little thing he ever saw. He still asks me about you once in a while."

She blushed.

He looked at her. "Don't you see? If I stay, we'll have a fight. I know what you'll say. Someday, when I'm rich, it'll be different. I'll have a big house and…"

"I don't care if you have twenty big houses!" she said indignantly. "I don't care about any of that and you know it. But…the way you live, you could go back…there." She gestured, unable to say the word, "prison".

He shook his head. "I'll never. They won't get me again. I'm not afraid of them!"

"Then why were you running?" Minna persisted. "If you weren't afraid of them, why did you knock on my door?"

"Maybe I just wanted to knock on your door, that's all."

She had to smile. "You could have knocked on my door any

time. You didn't have to get into a fight and come in the middle of the night! You know it."

He smiled back. "I haven't seen you in so long and here we are, just like it always was…"

She nodded.

The single light bulb created dark shadows in the corners of the shop. Only the sewing machine was bathed in light, its dark metal glimmering stolidly. As Jake stepped towards Minna, she thought he grew bigger, almost menacing.

She shrank and backed away as he came closer. Every detail in his face was clear and sharp. She thought, I can see him now, this moment, more clearly than I've ever seen anything before.

His eyes, she noticed, were warm and inviting. They seemed to beckon. Mesmerized, she took one step forward.

He stopped. The two of them gazed at each other for a long moment. This time, it was he who moved away.

'I…I think I'd better go," he said loudly. He looked into her eyes, hesitated, and then turned towards the door. "I'll see you again," he said, without looking back. Shutting the door firmly, he stepped into the street.

Minna stood in the middle of the room, trying to make sense of what had just happened. Jake came and then he left, she thought. He was running from the police. He said I looked pretty. He said, "I'll see you again." before he left.

She looked curiously around the room. Except for the small bloody scrap of material, all was as it had been before. It might have been a dream. She bent over and picked up the bloodstained scrap. She cradled it in her hand. Rolling it between her fingers, she touched it to her lips.

Suddenly, she couldn't bear the silence of the shop. She covered the sewing machine, shut the light, and left, still holding the scrap of material drenched in Jake's blood. She locked the door behind her and walked away, automatically heading for home. As she walked, she absently caressed her arm where Jake had held it.

The next night, Minna dressed carefully before returning to the shop after dinner. Surreptitiously, she combed her hair and pinched her cheeks to add a bit of color.

"You certainly look cheerful tonight," Pearl commented as she left.

Minna blushed and hurried out the door.

She did little work. Often she stopped pedaling to listen, thinking she heard a tap at the door. Most of the time, she stared off into the distance remembering the night before.

At least he hasn't forgotten me, she thought. Even if he is…a gangster, he hasn't forgotten me. Then she'd remember how he had to hide from the police. Angrily, she'd bend over her sewing. Turning a seam or setting a sleeve, she'd think of Dolly and stop. She'd pause and begin sewing again. What does it all mean, she wondered, rubbing her eyes.

Finally, she fell asleep, hunched over her sewing machine. In the morning, when she awoke, she looked around the shop in surprise. So I'm here, she thought, and he didn't come after all. Grimly, she decided to forget Jake, yet at the same time, she touched her arm where he had held her.

As the days passed and Jake did not reappear, Minna stopped fussing with her appearance in the evenings. He didn't mean any of it, she decided. He's with Dolly, stealing and fighting. He never remembered me at all.

She slept badly and ate lightly at dinner. Finally even Mama noticed. Assuming it was because she was working so hard for college, she asked kindly, "How much have you saved so far, Minna?"

"Fifteen dollars," Minna replied, conscious of how rare it was for Mama to bring up the subject. "It's a beginning, that's all. If I go to college here in New York, it costs nothing, but I have to pay my room and board here and for my books. I can work summers and at night, but I need to have more saved."

"So you could still help out in the shop, then," Mama said pensively.

"Oh yes. Whenever I didn't have classes, I'd work in the shop. And summers…I could work all summer." She paused. "Except, I'd have to make money over the summers to pay for my room and board."

Mama frowned. "We have so many new customers now. Soon, God willing, we might…just might…be able to manage." She shook her head. "I'll think on it."

Minna felt heartened. She resolved to work even harder. Yussel winked at her and Pearl kicked her under the table.

With Bessie finally gone, it was just a family dinner. Sarah had long since been accepted by everyone except Mama. She was so quiet, it was easy to forget she was there. Tonight she said timidly, "I saw Bessie today. She's working hard with the Union. She says safety conditions are so bad everywhere, there'll be a tragedy."

"Everything's a tragedy for her," Mama sniffed.

"I don't know," Sarah said. "Where I work, we were talking about it. If anything happened there…"

"What could happen?" Minna asked. "So far, there hasn't been a problem."

Sarah turned red, as she always did when defending her own point of view. "You don't work there," she said firmly, "so you can't possibly know."

"*Nu*, you're right," Pearl agreed.

"Thanks be to God, we don't have to," Mama said. "Those *gonifs* pay nothing! Look at Debbie. Consumption she has. Her mama said it came from the factory. Now she's away in Colorado. Who knows when she'll be back."

Minna shivered, thinking of Debbie. Although they had stopped being real friends when Debbie had quit school and gone to work in the factory, she had never forgotten her kindness in the beginning. She hated to think of her, lying still in a hospital bed."

"Are you going back to work tonight?" Yussel asked.

She had planned to stay home, but inspired by Mama's interest, decided to go back. "As soon as dinner is over, I'll go."

"I'll walk you over," Yussel offered. "I feel like a little fresh air."

On the way to the shop, he said, "You know, they came to see Mama again, those *gonifs*! It's Cheeks Benny. He demanded protection money. He said we might have a fire or a robbery if we don't pay. Mama got angry. You know how she gets. She told him, 'We left the old country because of *shtarkes* like you. I'll tell the police!' she yelled. He just laughed."

"Do you think…" Minna began.

"I don't know. I'm worried. It's just as well you'll be in the shop tonight. They always wait till everyone goes. Just make sure you keep the door locked, though."

"Did Mama tell the police?"

'She said she might tomorrow. The thing is, maybe they have to get paid too. Stay and we'll be all right."

"Couldn't we talk to Jake? Maybe his gang could…"

"To Jake? Why should he help us? Besides, maybe he's in it with Cheeks Benny. Who knows how those *gonifs* work!"

Minna shook her head. "I think he'd help."

"Jake? After all these years? If we go to him, we can't go to the police. We'd probably have to pay him, too. I don't know…"

They reached the shop. Yussel went in first, turned on the light, and looked around. "I could stay with you?"

Although she no longer expected Jake to come, she still preferred to be alone. "No, I'll be fine," she assured Yussel. "Go home. I'll lock up very carefully. Don't worry. I promise I won't open the door, even for Elijah!"

As she said this, she thought, if Jake comes, maybe I *would* open the door. Then she remembered all the nights she had waited in vain. I won't, she decided. No matter what, I won't open the door for him. Why should I? Let him tap-tap and I'll pretend I don't hear. She sighed, knowing there would be no tap-tap.

After Yussel left, she settled down to her sewing. Tonight, the silence seemed ominous. As she sewed, she sang softly to herself in an attempt to banish her fear.

When she heard a tapping at the door, she jumped away from her machine. Startled, she checked to make sure she had fastened the bolt. As she watched, the handle turned.

She picked up a bolt of fabric and held it over her head, ready to swing it against anyone who was able to force the lock. Luckily, it held.

"It's me," she heard. "It's me, Jake. Won't you let me in, Minna?"

Her heart beat faster. Jake! He had come! She remembered how many nights she had waited. Undecided, she stood in the center of the room, frowning at the floor.

The gently knocking continued. "I've been away," Jake said. "This is the first night I've been home."

Refusing to think any more, Minna put the bolt of fabric down and opened the door slightly.

Jake stood there, smiling at her. "I went away," he repeated. "Uncle sent me upstate. But I wasn't going to come, anyway."

She kept her hand on the door, ready to shut it.

"I thought…I thought…this is bad for you, I thought," he said awkwardly.

She shook her head. "Can't I decide what's good and what's bad for me?" she asked, opening the door all the way.

He came in. "I wanted to come," he continued. "All the time I was away, I thought of you."

"I thought of you, too."

"I don't know anyone else like you."

"What about Dolly?" Minna blurted. She held her hand to her lips, shocked by her own words.

"Dolly?" he asked in a surprised tone. "She's my uncle's friend."

Minna sighed. "Mama said she was your friend."

"Well, she is my friend, but she's uncle's really. He likes me to take her around sometimes." As he spoke, he edged closer to her.

"I thought…" Minna began. She looked into Jake's eyes. I'm drowning, she thought and stepped back.

He held out a small box. "This is for you."

She took it. Her hands were trembling. She tried to collect herself. It's because it's night, she thought. That's all it is. It's because it's dark and we're here alone. She moved towards the light. Pulling at the ribbon, she opened the box. Inside, she saw a small assortment of fancy chocolates.

"I thought you'd like these."

"They're beautiful." She smiled and held the box out to him. "Here, let's both have one."

Eating a chocolate and watching Jake eat his, she began to feel more comfortable. She leaned against the counter and asked idly, 'What were you doing upstate?"

"Just something for my uncle." He dismissed the subject. "Tell me," he continued, "what's been happening? How are Yussel and Pearl?"

He's more comfortable too, she thought. "They're fine," she answered. "Yussel has three men working for him now. Pearl is doing well in school. We only have one boarder left. Soon, maybe she'll leave, too and we'll have a real parlor!"

"Where's your Tata?"

"You know he went back to *der alter heym*? We never heard from him again—and no one else has either. I guess I'm a bad daughter, but I don't care."

Jake nodded. "Guess who Uncle Moishe heard from the other day. Remember Rosie? She has two kids and is really happy. Her husband's a good man, she says."

"She was lucky," Minna said thoughtfully. "Your sisters, Jake? Have your sisters come here yet?"

His face clouded. "They're both dead, like my Tata. There was an epidemic. It was typhoid. So I never saw them again." He looked away.

"Oh, Jake. I'm sorry."

'I'm lucky to have Uncle Moishe. Otherwise, I'd really be alone in the world."

"But Jake, you have our family," Minna said, knowing it wasn't the same.

"Uncle Moishe, he's enough," he responded in a flat tone. He looked at the sewing machine. "Why are you here every night working so hard if everything's going so well? It doesn't make sense."

"I'm working for myself," she explained. "I'm saving money so I can go to college and become a teacher. Mama doesn't pay me, of course, and this is the only way I can earn a few dollars."

"College? You want to be a teacher? You know you'll get married long before that happens."

She shook her head. "I don't want to stay on Allen Street all my life. Once I get married, I know what that means. A passel of kids and work, work all the time to feed them. Not me! I've seen Mama's life. I'm going to be a regular American. I'm going to live somewhere where people speak English all the time, even on the streets."

Jake looked at her in amazement. "You have bigger plans than I do. All I want is to make enough money. You want to change everything!"

Minna nodded. "It's true. I want to make my own life. That's why we came here, isn't it?"

He reached for her hand. "Don't you see, Minna? That's all I want to do—make enough money, Why is it right for you and wrong for me?"

She tried to pull her hand away. "Because what I'm doing, I won't end up in jail, that's why!"

Jake refused to let go. "Listen, Minna. What other chance do I have? If Uncle Moishe hadn't taken me in, I would have been sent back. How could I have gone to school? I had to please him… Now I'm doing so well, why should I change my life? I'm not *meshuggeh.*"

She thought about it. When he was holding her hand, everything he said made sense. Yet she knew it was wrong. She knew what Yussel would say. She looked into Jake's eyes. "It's wrong, that's all. What else can I say. It's just...wrong."

He leaned towards her. "I see you haven't changed at all. In a way, I'm glad."

Minna swayed forward. Although he was only holding her hand, she felt as if he were pressing against her. As if from a distance, she felt rather than saw his lips approach hers. Her breath quickened and she gave herself up to his kiss.

When Jake lifted his lips from hers, she smiled up at him. I wasn't afraid at all, she thought, surprised.

"So that's what I was waiting for," she whispered dreamily.

He smiled back and moved away, reaching out to touch her hair. "You're so beautiful," he said.

She held out her hands. "For you, I am."

In the background, she heard a rattling noise. She tried to ignore it but as she moved her head to look, she saw the doorknob turning back and forth. Luckily, she had re-bolted the door after Jake had come in.

Jake heard it, too. He whirled around. "Who is it? Are you expecting anyone?"

Minna shook her head. "Maybe it's Cheeks Benny. He was after Mama to pay protection money. Yussel said they won't do anything if they know I'm here."

Squaring her shoulders, she walked to the door. "Who is it?" she asked, her voice quavering despite her attempt to keep it firm.

The doorknob stopped moving.

Jake hurried over to her and put his arm around her protectively.

"C'mon," she heard someone say. "Let's go. It's no good tonight."

Minna heard footsteps moving down the street, becoming fainter and then disappearing. She clutched at Jake's arm. "I forgot to tell you," she said. "Cheeks Benny spoke to Mama yesterday. She refused to pay anything. Maybe you can help."

"This is our territory," Jake said angrily. "He has no right to be here!" He paused. "Of course, I wouldn't ever ask your Mama for anything," he said quickly.

"You mean you do the same thing?" She shook her head. "Of course, you do. You even told me about it. How can you, Jake? People like us, we have to pay the police, pay gangsters... Where does it end? Mama works so hard. Should she throw it in the street for a bunch of *shtarkes*?"

Jake frowned. "I said I would never ask you for anything."

Minna stepped away. "It isn't right. You know it isn't right. It's like we're back in *der alter heym*, only it's you that's doing it. You're hurting your own kind, Jake. Don't you see?" She was almost sobbing. "How can you?"

Jake moved further away. "So, here we go." He pointed his finger at Minna. "If you know so much, why are you working all night to earn a few dollars? I can earn enough in one day to send three girls to Normal School! Who's right—you or me?"

"It isn't the money and you know it."

Jake interrupted. "I love you, Minna! I always have," he yelled. "What good is it? You want me to be like Yussel, the hero, scrounging every minute like a slave for pennies."

Minna stared at him, aghast. Tears welled up in her eyes. "Don't talk about Yussel!"

"Sure, I'm not fit to mention his name!" He stamped over to the door and waited on the threshold.

Minna held out her hand. "Jake," she whispered.

He turned and stood waiting, his arms crossed.

"Look, Jake," she said as calmly as she could although her voice shook. "I can't change the way I think. But…I…I…love you, too."

Jake shook his head. "When I talk to you, you make me feel ashamed and then I get angry," he mumbled.

"But Jake," Minna replied, "if you feel that way, maybe you're not happy about…"

He looked her straight in the eyes. "I never had a choice. Sometimes, I think about it. My life, it just happened. If it had been someone else, it could have happened to him just the same. But it's mine, my life. My uncle is my only family. Besides," he shrugged, "I like the way I live. It's only when I see you…"

"Maybe you better not see me then." Her voice was tight. "Maybe it's easier if we don't meet again."

"Maybe it is." Jake shook his head sadly.

Minna clenched her hands. She wanted to run to him, but she forced herself to remain still, holding her arms tight against her sides. I won't beg, I won't beg, she thought.

He reached out and touched her arm. He caressed it gently. "Goodbye, Minna," he said softly.

Minna looked down..

"I won't forget you," he promised.

Minna shivered. Shaking his hand off, she looked at him. "Goodbye," she said flatly. She pulled the door shut abruptly, locking it behind her.

She leaned her head against the wall, pressing it into the wood. Her face twisted as she fought tears. I might have known, she thought. I might have known…

Remembering Jake's kiss, she pressed her fist against her lips as hard as she could. Then, stamping her feet loudly, she marched over to the sewing machine. Grimly, she sat down and began to work the pedals with her feet, automatically feeding the material through.

She tried to picture herself finally finished with school, a teacher, but all she could think of was Jake. I'll meet him in the street, she thought. I'll turn away and he'll look after me and then… She shook her head angrily. "No," she said aloud. "No, I won't!"

She bent over the sewing machined and sobbed. I love him, she thought, and he loves me. But…but…but…what good is it? I hope he does go to jail, she thought furiously.

She hugged herself, rocking her upper body back and forth. That's it, she decided. I'll never do this again no matter what. I'll work, I'll save… I'll live in another world. I won't even remember tonight.

Grimacing, she began to pedal the machine again, her body bent over as she focused on her sewing. She sewed all night, stopping only to wipe her tears as they fell down her cheeks.

In the morning, as she bundled the work she had completed for the jobber, she looked at it curiously. She had earned five dollars in one night. She held up each piece, checking the seams. They were perfect.

Exhausted, Minna locked the door of the shop behind her and walked wearily home, planning to stop at the jobber to drop off her work on the way. It will be all right, she thought fiercely. It will be all right.

The next few days passed in a blur. Minna told her family that she was getting the grippe, so no one said anything about the way she looked and acted. Since she felt she could tell no one about Jake, she said very little although he was always on her mind. She did manage to pretend a kind of weak good humor for the customers.

She kept as busy as possible, for the worst times were after she crept into bed and turned out the light or when she had nothing particular to do. When she walked down the street, more than once she whirled around, sure he was right behind her only to discover there was no one there at all. Once she thought she saw the back of Jake's head and followed a stranger two blocks out of her way until she realized it wasn't him. Each time she did something like that, she stopped herself, saying out loud, "That's enough!" only to have it begin all over the next day or hour.

CHAPTER 12

Minna returned to the shop every night, not only to finish extra work, but to keep Cheeks Benny and his men away. Mama had refused to give in or talk to the police.

Minna had tried. "I'm sure it was him at the door," she said to Mama. "What will happen if I'm not there? Maybe you should pay him...or tell the police...or even talk to Jake. Maybe he could help."

Mama shook her head stubbornly. "The police!" she said angrily. "What will they do—sell me more tickets for the Policeman's Ball? Ask me right out for money? Cheat me? And Jake? I wouldn't trust him! You think I should pay for what should be mine. I have the right to lock my door at night and know that I'm safe from *gonifs*! In this country, it's not the *goyim* I fear, it's the Jews! We came to this country to run from our own kind?"

Yussel tried too. "It's just the way it is, Mama. We can't change it all by ourselves," he had said. "If we don't pay off, they'll burn down the shop and destroy our stock."

"It shouldn't be that way! I'll never pay!" Mama yelled.

Minna and Yussel talked privately. They agreed to take turns spending the night at the shop, at least for a while. They said nothing to Mama. She pretended not to notice what they were doing.

Minna took twice as much work from the jobber, determined now more than ever to save the money for college. She grew more and more weary. Her sewing suffered, too. Sometimes, it seemed as if she spent more time ripping out her mistakes than finishing her work.

One night, Minna fell into a deep sleep at the machine. She was so fatigued she heard nothing, even when the door was jimmied open and two men entered.

They saw her and drew back in dismay.

Minna slept on, sighing heavily.

The two men tiptoed around the shop, pouring kerosene on the fabric. Silently, one of them struck a match in the far corner. The other, covering her face with a piece of fabric, lifted her and carried her to the street.

Still half asleep, Minna struck our wildly as she felt herself being lifted. The fabric over her face was suffocating. Smelling the fire, she panicked, remembering Chava's death. For a moment she was back in the *shtetl.*

"Mama!" she called. "Help me, Mama!" Her voice was muffled behind the fabric. This is a nightmare, she prayed. It's only a nightmare. I'll wake up.

Suddenly she felt herself falling. She landed on the street with a thud.

A man's voice yelled, "Run! Run!"

She struggled frantically to be free of the fabric wrapped around her face. Clawing at it, she finally pulled it loose and flung it aside. There, right in front of her eyes, she saw the shop—Mama's dream. Flames shot out into the street, threatening the shops next door, too.

Minna's English disappeared. "*Gevalt*! *Gevalt*!" she screamed. "*Oy vay'z mir*!"

Struggling to stand, she stumbled and fell back onto the street. Her legs trembled and her eyes filled with tears, obscuring her vision. "Chava!" she sobbed.

Painfully, she rose to her feet and staggered towards the store. Wiping her face on her sleeve, she hesitated near the flaming doorway. As if from a distance, she could hear a woman screaming. She thought, why doesn't she stop? Screaming doesn't help. The screams rose louder.

She looked around to see who was making so much noise, but there was no other woman in the street. It's me, she thought. I'm the one who is screaming.

Squaring her shoulders, she walked as steadily as she could to the door of the shop. Hot air hit enveloped her. Smoke billowed out, forcing her to cough and choke. Involuntarily, she turned her head away.

Someone grabbed her from behind.

She flailed wildly. "Let me go!" she screamed. "Let me go!"

She was dragged away from the fire.

"It's too late," she heard a voice say. "You can't save anything. Come away. Come here where it's safer."

She slumped. Her head fell forward and her eyes closed.

"It's the smoke," someone said.

When she awoke, she was sitting propped up against the outside wall of the store across the street. Pearl sat next to her, holding her hand. "I had the most terrible dream," she began. Then she saw Pearl's expression.

Without looking away from Pearl's face, she put her hand down and touched the ground. It was damp and cold. She could feel the rounded edges of the cobblestones. Fearfully, she forced herself to look up.

She recognized the street in front of the store. Many people stood in front of her, blocking her view. She noticed the owners of several neighboring shops. Then she heard the old woman who lived next door to the store sobbing loudly, despite attempts to soothe her.

Everyone was looking at something. Minna could tell from their stance. She leaned forward but she couldn't see past them. What were they looking at?

Slowly, with Pearl's help, Minna stood. Her stomach was heavy and her legs trembled. Holding Pearl's hand, she made her way through the crowd, which seemed to part before her.

Minna spoke to Bubbe in her head, repeating over and over, 'Help me, Bubbe. Help me. Make it not be true. Make it be a dream.'

She saw nothing yet. A woman touched her arm, but she felt nothing as she moved toward the shop. I'm still sleeping, she thought. It's a dream…just a dream…

Before she was ready, Minna found herself in front of the shop. It wasn't there. All that remained was a charred space. She gasped and looked around again. She could see only the street, and some fragments of cloth. The shop was gone.

There was Mama, supported by Yussel. Mama's hand was

outstretched, as if she were beseeching the ruins. Yussel's face was smudged with smoke and soot. His eyes were round with horror.

"All gone," she heard him say. "It's all gone."

Minna sank to her knees. I could have stopped it, she thought. If I hadn't fallen asleep…if Jake had…if I had asked him… Jake could have stopped it.

Somehow, she stumbled over to Mama and Yussel. She touched Yussel's shoulder gently. It was my fault, she thought again. Yussel looked up.

"Minna!" he cried. "Thanks be to God, you're all right."

Minna burst into tears. "I'm sorry," she sobbed. She looked at Mama, pleadingly, but Mama never looked up. Her face was white. Her hand curved. Wearily, she flattened it and let it fall to her side.

"Sorry?" Yussel said. "Why should you be sorry? You could have been killed. I should have been there."

He looked at Mama.

Slowly she lifted her head. "It was the will of God," she mumbled. "I was too proud …Tata said I was a proud woman." She clenched her hands.

Minna looked at her, aghast. She touched her cheek. "It's all right, Mama," she said. "We'll save money again and someday…"

Mama pushed her hand away. "We'll never! I know that now. Never!" she repeated in a despairing monotone.

Supporting their Mama, her three children guided her silently towards their apartment. They had never seen her give up. It felt like the end of the world.

At the apartment, Minna helped Mama undress while Pearl prepared a glass of tea. The two girls brought her tea in bed. She accepted it without a word, finished it, and lay back, her eyes closing slowly.

Minna and Pearl returned to the kitchen, where they joined Yussel and Sarah, who had been awakened by the commotion. The four of them sat in silence around the table, sipping hot tea.

Finally, Yussel said, "I can still sell to my ladies. I have some stock out with the men and I'll be able to get some credit for myself. The men will have to go, I'm afraid. I can't supply them without the shop. I can't make enough for us to live on, not right away."

"We can get another boarder," Pearl suggested.

Minna stared off into the distance. "I'll get a job at a factory," she offered. "With my wages, another boarder, and Yussel's business, we should be able to…"

"I want to work at the factory, too," Pearl insisted. "You know I've wanted to for a long time, but Mama wouldn't let me."

"We can manage," Yussel said. "You have to finish school, Pearl. Maybe Mama will…"

"She'll feel better in the morning," Sarah said.

Minna shook her head. "I don't know. I've never seen Mama like this. She's never given up before, no matter what." She felt her eyes closing, despite her sorrow. Painfully, she tried to keep them open.

As if from far away, she heard Sarah say, "It's the shock."

Yussel, patting her drooping head, said, "Let's all go to bed now. In the morning, it's another day."

The two girls slept in each others arms that night. Minna woke frequently, reliving the old nightmare about Chava. Each time she was sure she could save her sister if she could just find her and run to her, yet she was paralyzed, her legs too heavy to move.

Finally, early in the morning, she curled away from Pearl and lay still, her eyes wide open. Mama still breathed evenly and Pearl was fast asleep. Yussel was in the kitchen, so there was no place for her to go.

As she lay there, she thought about last night. If I hadn't fallen asleep, she thought. If Jake had come…if he had protected us… Why should he, she asked herself. It's his business, selling protection, isn't it? She tried to imagine what it would be like, working in the factory. No school, she thought. Not for years and years.

Mama stirred. Minna looked over at her bed. If Mama's…different, what will we do?

Mama opened her eyes and stared up at the ceiling. Without looking at the girls or even seeming to be aware of them, she sat up and covered her face with her hands. Silently, she rocked back and forth.

"*Gottenyu!*" she murmured. "*Gottenyu!*"

Minna sat up and crawled over to Mama. Timidly, she knelt next to her. "It's all right, Mama," she soothed. "We'll manage."

Mama took her hands away from her face and stared at Minna angrily. "We'll manage? How will we manage? Everything's lost! Everything!"

"What about insurance?" Minna asked. "We can get our money back, can't we?"

"We have none. They won't sell to Jews," Mama snapped. "They'll say we hired a mechanic to set the fire, like Mr. Solomon down the block. So we have nothing! Nothing!" she wailed.

"So *nu*, we'll begin again," Minna replied valiantly.

The tears slid down Mama's cheeks unheeded as she stared vacantly ahead. "I work and I work," she said, "so the *gazlen untervelt mentsh* can take it away. Jews against Jews! That's how it works in this golden country!"

Intuitively, Minna knew that Mama's anger was better than her tears. "So, we'll get back at them. We'll tell about Cheeks Benny and…"

"You'll tell?" Mama demanded angrily. "You'll tell who? The police, maybe? They'll laugh in our faces. We'd have to pay them, too." He anger subsided. "It's no use," she muttered, putting her hands over her face again.

Minna heard a tap at the door. "Come in!" she called.

Yussel stuck his head in. "I went down there this morning. It's true, there's nothing left. Nothing at all. I thought we could ask Cousin Avraim…"

Mama looked up. "I won't ask him. To go like a *schnorrer* to beg from him! He's done enough. Besides, a baby is coming to them. He can't help us."

"Then we must help ourselves," Pearl said firmly. "We made up a plan last night, Mama. We'll work and we'll save and we'll do it again, you'll see."

Mama shook her head violently. "Never again! God has spoken to me and shamed me for my pride." She held out her hands. "I'll work. We'll all work and we won't starve. We'll live, but…" She opened her hands helplessly. "We'll live," she repeated.

Her voice gentle, as if talking to a child, Minna said, "Here's what we thought, Mama. We'll go to work at the factory, Pearl and I." She looked apologetically at Pearl. "We'll take another boarder. Yussel can continue with his peddling. The men will have some stock to give back to him and he has a good name. He'll be able to borrow for more."

"And me?" Mama asked accusingly. "What am I to do in your big plan?"

Minna looked down at the floor.

"You can stay home and keep the house," Yussel suggested. "If we're all working, we'll need someone to take care of things and the boarders."

Mama shook her head. "The fault is mine. I refused to pay the *shtarkes*. I'll work in the factory, too. Pearl can continue school and take care of the house. I'll work at the factory," she repeated leadenly.

Minna and Yussel looked at each other. He shook his head slightly.

"Let's get up," he said. "I'll make some tea and we'll have some breakfast."

After she was dressed, Mama came into the kitchen. Sarah had left long ago so it was just the family, sitting grimly around the table, sipping their hot tea and eating the thick pieces of challah Yussel had brought back with him yesterday on his way home.

With a determined look, Minna stood up and went to the kitchen cupboard. She opened it and took out the jar of precious honey saved for special occasions. Brandishing it, she said, "We might as well have this now. If we ever needed a taste of sweetness, it's this morning." Defiantly, she spread it on her bread.

Mama watched her listlessly.

Yussel nodded. "You're right." He took some and passed it to Pearl.

Mama hit the table with her hand. "Our life has fallen and we eat honey?" Burying her head in her arms, she began to sob bitterly.

As they heard her hard dry sobs, the three children looked at her and at each other, aghast. Finally, Pearl leaned over and put her hand on Mama's shoulder.

Mama shrugged it off fiercely. "What good is it?" she asked. She lifted her head and looked off into the distance. "We'll manage," she said coldly. "We'll survive. But more…I want no more than that!"

Minna stood up. "I won't give up!" she stormed. "We did it once and we can do it again. We have a place to live and…and…honey for breakfast." She reached over and shook Mama's shoulder. "How can you give up? It's you who's been the strength of this family. If you give up, it will be harder, but we'll do it anyway. Are you afraid?"

Mama's eyes glazed with shock. She touched her shoulder,

absently rubbing it where Minna had grabbed her.

Yussel leaned forward. "We're all upset. Let's…"

"Let's not!" Minna yelled. "So our chance is gone for now. So we're back where we started. It's not the end of the world. When we first came, we had nothing," she continued earnestly. "Yet we managed." She lowered her voice. "Don't you see, Mama? If you give up now, you're a quitter. You might as well go back to the old country with Tata."

Mama shook her head. "Go back?" she repeated. "Go back to *der alter heym*?"

Minna held her breath.

"Is that what you want to do, Mama?" Pearl asked. "Should we go back?"

Minna opened her mouth to object. Then, catching sight of Yussel shaking his head, she closed it again and waited anxiously for Mama's reply.

Slowly, she straightened. Looking at each of their faces for a long moment, she extended a hand. "Pass me the honey, please," she said. Delicately, she spread it on her challah.

As she took a bite, Yussel, Pearl, and Minna let out their breaths in a soft sigh of relief.

Now we can plan, Minna thought. Now it will be all right.

Their first visitor was Bessie. "You'll be looking for another boarder," she said brusquely. "I don't like my new place anyhow…"

Mama didn't even look up. The rest of the family gazed at Bessie, dumfounded.

"Best to be with friends in time of trouble," she said awkwardly.

Minna jumped up. "You're right. Thanks, Bessie, thanks."

Bessie flushed and dipped her head. "I'll see you tonight then." She rushed out.

"She's a good friend," Minna commented, surprised.

"Such a good friend! Now she comes, like a vulture," Mama muttered.

"It wasn't like that," Minna replied, sitting down again. "You know it wasn't. She's just…she can't say what she feels, that's all."

Yussel nodded in agreement. Pearl watched Mama, who bowed her head again, losing the slight animation she had displayed.

The next visitor was Cousin Avraim. With him was his young wife, Annie, her belly distended and her gait hesitant. The baby, they knew, was due momentarily.

Minna stood and pushed her chair towards Annie. "Sit," she offered. "Rest yourself."

Annie smiled her thanks and lowered herself carefully into it. Avraim stood behind her.

"A tragedy!" he exclaimed. "Just when things seemed to be going so well, too."

Mama nodded.

"We've both lost," he continued. "I, for my loan towards your new shop and you, of course…so here it is…the good and the bad… Perhaps if you had been more patient…"

They sat silently.

"I'll forgive my debt," he said expansively, gesturing with his hands. "It is wiped out, forgotten. I know you'll start again some day. With the baby coming, I can't…"

"Thank you, Cousin Avraim, for forgetting the debt," Yussel said solemnly. "I'll be peddling again. Perhaps you could extend me credit for a week so I can fill up my pack… If there was enough for the men, too, I could keep them on, too."

Cousin Avraim looked down at his wife. Slowly, he shook his head. "I can extend you credit, Yussel, for a week. You have a list of ladies. But for your men—what do I know of your men? Business is slow for me. With the baby coming…"

"For me, I thank you," Yussel said gratefully. "I know I'll have to begin again. If you can't spare it for the men, at least I'll have a start. My men… Well, they'll have to find their own way."

"Perhaps you need help in the shop?" Minna asked timidly.

Mama looked up.

He shook his head. "I need no help now. I've already hired. Who could tell? I can't afford to add another person."

Mama looked away.

"We're moving," Cousin Avraim said proudly. "We're moving to the Bronx. For my child, I must have clean air." He patted Annie's stomach. "As soon as the baby is born, we're leaving."

Annie smiled.

Minna fought back tears.

"Are we not still your family?" Mama asked. "We sit in desolation and you talk of the Bronx!"

"I have my own family now," Cousin Avraim said, his hand on Annie's shoulder. "Before, when you were riding high, you didn't need my advice. It was only the money. It's always the money with you. Well, now the money is for my own. Yussel, I'll help you. You've always been good to me."

Minna sighed, remembering how Mama had scorned Cousin Avraim's advice about the new shop and refused to share her ideas. "You're right," she agreed. "Annie and your child should be your first care. You're kind to forget the debt."

Mama looked up "It's true," she said tonelessly. "You are right. It is I who has been wrong."

"You'll find your way, Cousin Ruchel. You always have," Cousin Avraim replied kindly. "You'll come to see me at the shop?" he continued, looking at Yussel.

"I'll come this afternoon," Yussel replied.

Cousin Avraim helped Annie up. At the door, he turned back to look at the family. "I am sorry," he said. "God willing, there will be another Chava's".

The family said nothing after he left.

Finally, Pearl said, surprised, "He was angry at us."

"It's me," Mama admitted. "I was too proud. He's right in what he said. It's my fault."

"There is no fault," Yussel pleaded. "Of what good is it to talk of fault when our shop is rubble in the street? We didn't start the fire. None of us did."

"I'd like to kill those *shtarkes*!" Minna cried. "If I knew where to go, I'd set their homes on fire with a smile. See how they'd like that!"

"I agree!" Pearl said emphatically.

'What good?" Mama asked. "If it wasn't those *gonifs*, it would have been something else. It was meant to happen, all of it…the fire…the failure…"

Minna looked anxiously at Yussel. "How can you say that, Mama? It's because of you we did so well. Now it's because of you we failed? That's not true."

Yussel nodded. "She's right, Mama. Why must you take the blame?"

"I know what's right," Mama replied. "If I had gone back to Russia with Dovidl…"

"If…if…if… That's not what happened. Ifs don't matter!" Yussel insisted.

"If you had gone to Russia, we'd be there, too," Pearl said. "I'd rather be here with no money than back in *der alter heym.*"

"That's true," Mama mused. "But still, I…"

"Still, nothing," Minna said firmly. "There is no fault. If any, it is mine for falling asleep so the men could come in."

"Or mine, for breathing," Yussel snapped. "We're wasting our time with these foolish words. Instead, we have to decide what to do."

They all turned to Mama, but she was oblivious, staring off into the distance.

Reluctantly, Yussel turned to Minna. "What do you think?"

Minna sighed. "It's not a question of think," she said angrily. "I know what to do. It's easy to know." She sighed again and continued grimly. "Mama and I will get a job at a factory. Maybe Sarah can help us find work. Pearl has only this year left to finish, if she works hard and skips a few grades. We can start saving money again. I think everything we had was spent on the new shop. I don't know what's under the floorboards in the box." She looked at Yussel. "It's the only way, don't you agree?"

He nodded.

"Why should I stay in school?" Pearl asked. "If I went to work, too, we could start saving money sooner. You know we could."

"Then why don't we just go back to *der alter heym*?" Minna flashed. "Yussel got cheated, but you're going to finish school just like I did." She slammed her hand down on the table. "You have to!"

Pearl sobbed. "You're treating me like a baby. I want to do my part too."

"It's your part right now to finish school," Minna insisted. "Otherwise, it'll be all for nothing. Don't worry, there'll be plenty of 'doing your part' afterwards." She looked at Yussel. "I'm right, aren't I?"

He cleared his throat. "If I can get the business going with my ladies and you and Mama can bring in ten or twelve dollars a week between you, and we add in the boarders, we can start saving again. It'll be a little bit at a time…just like we did before."

They looked at Mama.

"We can begin again," Minna said softly. "We'll have the shop again, Mama, you'll see."

Mama shook her head. "Never again! I'll work. I'm good for working, but that's all." She bent her head, cradling it in her arms.

Her voice was muffled, but heard clearly by the others. "That I should work in a factory!" she wailed.

They looked at each other in stunned silence.

Finally, Pearl said, "Don't cry, Mama. It'll be all right, you'll see."

Minna went to the stove and prepared a steaming glass of tea, which she held poised in front of Mama. Yussel, a look of anguish on his face, bent his head and stared at the floor.

Mama wiped her eyes with her hands and tried to smile. "Don't worry, *kindele*," she said in a broken voice. "Don't worry. We won't starve."

Reassured, Yussel and Pearl smiled back at her. Only Minna hesitated. For the first time, she realized how much they had all depended upon Mama's strength to make their way. It was always Mama, Minna thought, who pushed and shoved and forced them to move forward. But now… She eyed Mama dubiously.

Mama shook her head sadly. "We'll manage," she repeated. "We won't starve."

We'll have to do more than just manage, Minna thought. We'll have a shop again and we'll live as we've dreamt of living. If it's up to me, we'll do it, she promised herself.

"You'll see, Mama," she said aloud. "All will be well." She looked at Pearl and Yussel. "We'll do it!" she said fiercely. "It will happen. I'll start right now. I can do piece work until we get a job at the factory." She stood up. "I'll go and fetch it." Then she stopped. "But…I have no machine. The machine must have burned, too."

"The machine is gone," Yussel said. "We'll owe for the rent money, too."

Minna sank back into her seat. "How could I forget? My machine is gone. Without a machine…" Her words trailed off.

Pearl leaned forward. "We can start with paper flowers," she suggested. "I can do them in the afternoons. That will help."

Suddenly, there was a knock at the door.

"Come in," Yussel called.

It was Mr. Nussbaum, the landlord's agent. He sidled in, his gray beard more unkempt than usual. "If I might be excused," he began.

"Yes?" Mama glared at him.

"The rent, you know, is due. So sorry to disturb you at such a time, but Mr. Goldfarb, the owner, he told me to come and..."

Minna had always thought him a pathetic little man. Now he seemed menacing.

"The rent is not due until next week," Mama replied. "Don't worry, you'll be paid."

"I hear what you say. I know what you say. I believe you. But does Mr. Goldfarb?"

"We have always paid right on the dot," Yussel stated firmly. "We'll pay this time as well."

"But..."

"You can't force us to leave until next week," Minna said. "It's against the law." She stood up and led him out the door. "Don't worry, Mr. Nussbaum. You'll be paid next week when it's time. We have the money saved," she lied.

He shrugged. "I beg your pardon for such questions at a time like this, but Mr. Goldfarb insists. I'll lose my job if I don't collect."

Minna forced herself to smile at him. "Don't worry," she repeated. "We have the money."

When she had closed the door behind him, she was shaking. "They're like vultures. They circle, waiting..."

Mama stood up. "How much do we have under the floor?"

Without a word, they took out the box, set it upon the table, and opened it. Rapidly, Yussel counted the change and smoothed out the single wrinkled dollar bill. Mutely, they watched him.

"There's just about half the rent money," he said finally. "When the girls pay us their rent, we'll have enough for this month."

"But food? What will we eat?" Pearl asked.

"I have a little saved for college," Minna offered. "That will help." Reluctantly, she ran to get her college money and handed it to Yussel. In this emergency, she couldn't hesitate. It came to a little more than twenty dollars.

He added it up. "That's better," he said. His voice was relieved. He handed it back to Minna. "We should keep this as an emergency fund. It's extra. Let's try not to spend it unless we really have to."

Minna took it back. "If we don't use it tonight, we won't have anything to eat. You should keep it in with the rest."

Yussel shook his head. "We're lucky to have it. If anything else happens... anything else at all..."

Minna understood. It would be better for them not to rely upon the small amount she had saved. They should begin earning money immediately.

Mama sat up straighter. "We'll begin today with the flowers," she said decisively. "Minna, go to the flower ladies now and bring some home. Now is when it starts! Not a bite will I eat until we have begun to earn some money."

Minna ran to the door. The flower ladies always waited near the piecework men. Thanks to Irving, she and Pearl knew how to make the most complicated flowers. It was tedious time-consuming work, hard on the eyes and fingers, but it was a way to earn some money quickly.

On her way back, her arms laden with bundles of materials to make flowers, Minna, her face set, pushed her way through crowds of people. Several times, she was stopped by friends who had heard about the fire. She listened to each, as they expressed their sympathy. Then, saying an almost brusque "thank you", she hurried on.

Finally, as she reached her block and could see the stoop ahead of her, she stopped for a moment, leaning against a building. Wearily, she adjusted the bundles Head bowed, she squeezed her eyes shut to stop the tears. Straightening her shoulders, she marched briskly towards the apartment.

At the steps, she hesitated. There, seated on the ledge, was Jake. She shivered, suddenly ice cold despite the pleasant fall air.

Jake jumped up, blocking her way.

Minna stared at him.

"I heard about what happened," he said, extending his hands. "I'm so sorry, Minna. What can I do to help?"

A taste of bile rose in her throat. She was unable to speak. Shaking her head, she tried to pass him by.

He stopped her. "Won't you talk to me?" he asked. "I've come to help."

She gazed at him, memorizing the texture of his overcoat, the softness of his dark eyes, the lock of hair falling over his forehead. She reached out a hand and jerked it back.

'It's too late to help now," she said. "Why don't you talk to your friend Cheeks Benny and ask him to help?"

"He's not my friend and you know it."

"You're the same," she yelled. "You do the same thing. Tell me, how is it different?"

"I want to help you," he insisted.

"Sure, if it's me, you want to help. What about the others, the ones you sell protection to? Do you burn down their stores?"

He looked confused.

'Don't you see?" She lowered her voice. "You're no different. This time, it's us. Next time, it's someone else. I could have been killed! Mama has given up!" She began to sob. All the tears she had been holding back gushed forth. Dropping the bundles, she put her hands over her face and turned her back on Jake.

She felt his hand on her shoulder. Twisting away, she faced him again. "It could have been you," she sobbed. "It could have been you!"

He frowned. "But it wasn't me. I'd never hurt you, Minna."

"Don't you see, Jake? It's the same thing." She shook his arm. "Can you not see?"

He shook his head. "I don't see," he whispered. "I take care of my own. I would never…"

Minna bent over angrily and picked up her bundles. "There's no difference," she said wearily "You're the same, you and Cheeks Benny!" She pushed by Jake. At the top of the stairs, she turned back to him. "May you both rot in hell!" she screamed. Turning her back, she opened the door and went inside.

She was still trembling when she reached her floor. She paused outside the door to collect herself and to wipe her eyes. Help me, Bubbe, she thought. Help me to be strong and brave.

She opened the door. Mama, Pearl, and Yussel were still sitting around the kitchen table. "I'm back," she said, forcing a smile. She put the bundles on the table. "Here are our flowers. Pearl and I will show you how to do it, Mama. If we can finish this load by tonight, we can earn a few dollars for food."

Pearl began to clear the table so they could work. Mama straightened her back and pushed up her sleeves.

Yussel stood up. "I'd better check on my peddlers and see what stock they have left. Mine burned up in the shop. Then I'll go see Cousin Avraim."

Minna set the bundle she was unrolling aside and hugged Yussel with all her might. "Don't worry," she said. "It will be all right."

He hugged her back and went to get his jacket. Mama watched him without saying a word.

"Off I go!" he said, attempting to sound jaunty.

Minna smiled weakly and leaned over the bundles. "*Nu*, so now we make flowers. Flowers for the hats of rich ladies."

The day passed slowly. Even with their best efforts, the flowers took a long time to make. By the late afternoon, Minna's fingers were aching and her movements clumsy. She glanced at Mama and Pearl. Mama was winding the stems as carefully as she had in the beginning. Pearl, too, seemed indefatigable as she twisted the paper. Shamed, Minna bent over her work.

"We only have one more pile," Pearl said. "We're almost done."

Mama didn't look up. Meticulously, she wound green paper around a wired stem, her shoulders bent as she hunched over her work.

Minna smiled at Pearl. "Let's finish," she said.

She promised herself a cup of hot tea when they were all done. There was enough in the larder to make a supper of sorts, she thought. Tomorrow, they would have to shop.

The first person to return was Sarah. She arrived just as they were packing the finished flowers into bundles. She looked surprised when she saw what they were doing, but she said nothing.

Minna gathered the bundles and set them by the front door to return first thing in the morning. Without a word, Sarah helped her. Then she gestured at the bundles. "*Nu*?" she asked.

Minna shrugged. "It's work, isn't it? I was planning to ask you about working in your factory. Is there someone I could see? Mama and I…"

Sarah smiled. "I thought myself that you might be interested. So, today I spoke to my boss, Mr. Feigen, and he said for you to come and see him. You might have to sweeten him to get the job…"

"Pay him something you mean? Until we get jobs, how can we pay anything?"

Sarah looked doubtful. "Everyone does. It's worth it because otherwise he won't hire you. Maybe you could suggest a small gift from your first salary. There are so many girls who want a job… You'll have to show him how well you can sew, you know."

"That's no problem. Mama and I can do that."

They went back into the kitchen.

"Sarah has already spoken to Mr. Feigen at the Triangle Shirtwaist Factory. We can go in tomorrow, Mama," she said triumphantly.

Mama was still slumped over the table. Slowly, she looked up. "I thank you, Sarah," she said gravely. "We just go in and see this Mr. Feigen? Is he the boss?"

"He's the boss of my section. The way it's run, every section has a boss and every section makes a different part of a shirtwaist. Then Mr. Feigen puts our section's work together with the others. He's the one who pays us."

"So I don't make a whole shirtwaist by myself?" Minna asked.

"Oh, no, Minna," Sarah replied, shocked. "you do the sleeve, the seaming, the lace, or the collar. There's basters, too. That's what a factory is."

"We have to give this Feigen something to get the job," Minna said.

"To do that job, we have to pay, too?" Mama asked, flexing her tired fingers. "I guess if we have to, we have to."

"We could suggest giving him a gift out of my first salary," Minna continued.

"We're very busy now," Sarah said. "Last year, there weren't any lay-offs at all. Everyone's buying shirtwaists. Maybe you won't have to pay him. Maybe he needs good workers so much, he'll be glad," she concluded doubtfully.

"I want to work in the factory, too," Pearl said. "Why can't I…"

"Wait till Mama and I get jobs before you start agitating," Minna said. "First of all, we have to meet this Feigen. If we can sweeten him, and if we're very lucky," she finished sarcastically, "we get to work like slaves!"

Catching sight of Sarah's expression, Minna blushed. "I'm sorry," she said quickly. "It's just such a change for us, that's all."

Sarah nodded understandingly.

"Let's start dinner." Minna sighed. "We can talk while Pearl and I are putting things together. Sit down, Sarah, while I see what we have. Yussel will be home soon."

Mama looked up. "We have nothing."

Minna opened the cupboard and began pulling out the odds and ends that were left. "We have flour, water, a few potatoes, and…"

"Like *der alter heym*," Mama said bitterly. "I'll contrive. I always have." She stood up.

"At least we won't starve," Minna said.

The front door opened and Bessie entered. She held something behind her back. Glancing at the bits of food arrayed on the table, she smiled. "I brought a housewarming gift, since I'm coming back." With a flourish, she set a fresh loaf of bread, a parcel of chicken bones, a carrot, an onion, and some celery upon the table. "I thought a nice soup…"

"Oh, Bessie," Minna cried, near tears.

"Thanks, Bessie," Pearl said. "Thanks."

Sarah smiled at her friend warmly.

Mama was nonplused. Finally, she mumbled, "Thanks," and began assembling the ingredients for soup. Taking out a sharp knife, she began to clean the carrots and celery, cutting them into small pieces.

Minna sank down at the table again. "This has been a *gevaldikeh* day," she said to Bessie. "We finished the flowers, though. Tomorrow, Mama and I are going to the Triangle Shirtwaist Factory to find work."

"I went past Chava's on the way home," Sarah said. "There's nothing left. People were talking. They said that Cheeks Benny…"

Minna's cheeks flushed. "It *was* Cheeks Benny. He and his kind live off our blood. I say, bad luck to them! Someday, he'll suffer in hell!"

"You're going to work at the Triangle Factory?" Bessie asked. "I left them. The working conditions are terrible there. After the strike in 1909, they did nothing. To work there is asking for trouble."

"How about where you are now, Bessie? Is it a big factory? Could you speak to your manager about us?" Minna asked.

Bessie thought for a moment. 'No, it's tiny. There's no room for anyone else now. Triangle is one of the biggest. That's why they can get away with their exploitation of the workers."

"Come on, Bessie," it's not that bad," Sarah said. "We have our own Union from the company. The pay is about the same as everywhere else…and I haven't been laid off for a whole year."

"We struck for a 52-hour work-week, four paid holidays, and the right to negotiate wages through the Union. We got *bobkes*! Nothing, they gave us! At least, some of the smaller factories, like the one I work at, recognize the Union. A company Union is to laugh and you know it! Then I ask you, what about safety? At

Triangle, the conditions are *geferlech*, I'm warning you."

"If we don't have work," Mama snapped, "we'll have no life."

"It's true," Minna said. "We have to take what we can get. It's not easy to find work. If Sarah has an in with the boss, it'll help."

"You probably have to buy him off, too. To get a job, you have to pay? That's not fair," Bessie countered.

"*Nu*, what's fair?" Mama asked. "What in my life has been fair?"

Minna glanced at Pearl. Mama sounded so…angry. She sighed. It'll be better when we're working, she thought hopefully.

An hour later, a warm, revitalizing odor permeated the apartment as soup simmered on the stove. The four girls sat around the kitchen table talking quietly. Mama had retired to the bedroom. For the first time all day, Minna allowed herself to relax a little.

"So, is it all women at the machines?" she asked Sarah just as the front door opened.

"Yussel!" Pearl cried, jumping up. "How did it go?"

Yussel paused in the doorway to the kitchen, smiling weakly at the four faces turned towards him. With a gasp of relief, he lowered his pack from his shoulders. "Where's Mama?" he asked.

"She's resting," Minna said.

Yussel raised his eyebrows questioningly.

"*Nu*, it's all right," Minna said in answer to his unspoken question. "We worked all day on the flowers."

For answer, Yussel held out his pack, showing them with his hands that it was only slightly emptier than when he had begun the day. "It's hard work," he said, shaking his head. "What I don't have, they want; what I have, they don't need. I made a little to add to the rent money, but not as much as I had hoped. My ladies want me to be jolly. It was hard today. They all wanted to talk about the fire…"

Minna led him to the table. "Sit," she ordered. "Soon we'll eat. Tomorrow's another day."

Yussel put his pack in the corner of the kitchen, shrugged off his coat, and sat down gratefully. "In a few days, I'll have enough to buy some better goods. Cousin Avraim gave me only what he had left over and my men…their bags were almost empty, so I got nothing but *shmatte* from them. Cousin Avraim said I can pay him back in a couple of weeks." He rubbed his shoulders. "I've gotten soft, working in the store."

"We made a few dollars today," Pearl said proudly.

"Tomorrow, Mama and I are going to talk to Mr. Feigen, Sarah's boss at the Triangle Shirtwaist Factory," Minna added.

"Bessie brought us a present, too." Pearl gestured at the pot on the stove.

With an effort, Yussel smiled again. "We have good friends." He looked at the bedroom door.

"She must be sleeping," Minna said quickly. "I thought I'd wake her when you came home."

"Let her sleep," Yussel said. "I'll tell you about Mrs. Wasserman. She's my favorite lady. Her daughter's getting married and she talks about the new son-in-law. You should hear what she says about the poor *schliemiel*! First of all…"

The bedroom door opened with a creaking noise. "Is that Yussel back?" Mama peered around the doorway.

"It's me, Mama," Yussel said, half rising in his chair.

"I'm coming," Mama said. "Just a minute."

The five of them sat patiently, waiting for her.

"So *nu*, how did it go?" she asked, smoothing her hair as she walked over to the table and stood next to Yussel.

"It went well," he said. "My ladies were glad to see me back. In no time, we'll be able to pay Cousin Avraim."

Pearl looked at him in surprise until Minna nudged her.

Mama sighed in relief. "*Gott tsu danken*!" She pulled up a chair. As she was about to sit down, she noticed Yussel's pack in the corner. She walked over to it. "Your pack is still so full!" she exclaimed.

"I stopped and bought some more already," he said quickly, "so my ladies shouldn't be disappointed."

Mama smiled, the first real smile Minna had seen her make since the morning began. So now we're lying to her, she thought. Now we're protecting her. She felt both proud and frightened. It's up to us, she reminded herself. Yussel knows. I'll talk to Pearl tomorrow.

Despite the grim day, dinner was more comforting than Minna had expected. Everyone automatically slipped into their old roles—Bessie the provocateur sure to arouse Mama's scorn, Sarah watching Yussel worshipfully, Pearl and Minna squabbling amiably over a certain teacher whom Minna disliked and Pearl adored.

There were strange silences when realization would seep in, followed by determined conversations on other subjects. Yet, Minna thought, it was almost like any evening in the past. Except for Yussel. He tried to smile, but he was more silent than usual, staring off into space.

When Mama asked him what was the matter, he replied, "I'm thinking about my ladies and what they need."

Although Mama was satisfied with this answer, Minna frowned. I'll talk to him later, she decided.

As soon as dinner was finished, she hurried Mama off to bed, saying, "We have to impress Mr. Feigen tomorrow. You'd better get a good night's sleep."

Pearl could barely keep her eyes open. Soon, she too joined Mama.

Tactfully, Sarah shepherded Bessie into the other room after offering to help clean up, saying, "I want you to help me with one of my dresses, Bessie. If you could pin up the hem…"

At last, Minna and Yussel were alone in the kitchen. "What's the matter?" she asked him. "There's something wrong."

Yussel shook his head. "No, no. Everything's fine. Business will pick up, I know it will."

"Come on, Yussel. Tell me," Minna demanded.

"It's Mama," he blurted. "Did you hear me? I lied to her. I'm protecting her!"

"I know, Minna agreed. "I thought the same thing. But, maybe, when we start working…"

"I think…I think I'm going to be a peddler all my life. I think… Oh Minna, it's so dark. Remember the day we spent in Central Park? I want to see the sun, God's trees, smell the green grass. Before, I thought, someday, maybe someday… I used to think about owning a farm… Now I see my life will be spent here, in the cold streets."

"I won't give up!" Minna said. "We did it once, so why can't we do it again? So, I'll wait a while. Someday, I swear it, I'll be a teacher and the rest of my dream will come true.

"But, if Mama doesn't…"

"Then we'll get her settled. Pearl will work. I'll go to night school. You'll have your farm."

"By the time I'm sixty!," Yussel repeated bitterly. "It's a foolish dream, I know, but can I give it up?"

"Give it up?" Minna asked in amazement. "Now's the time to give nothing up. Now's the time we need our dreams. Mama has lost her dream, that's what's the matter with her. I won't! I won't ever!"

"Do you really think…"

"Yes, I do. I know it."

They sat quietly.

"I hate Tata," Yussel said suddenly. "If he were here, it would be his job to worry, not mine alone. If he was a real father…"

"If he was here, we'd have another mouth to feed. He'd sit with his books like a king. He wouldn't lift a finger!"

"It's true, " Yussel agreed. "It isn't fair! It isn't fair!"

"Who said life was fair?" Minna said lightly. "Someday, they'll be looking at us in our carriage and they'll say, 'Life isn't fair' about us."

"It's true," Yussel continued. "We're not starving yet and we have a roof over our heads."

Perversely, as Yussel began to feel better, Minna began to feel worse. "For now," she said darkly.

Yussel looked at her in surprise.

"Suppose I don't get a job tomorrow," Minna worried. "Suppose we don't have any money coming in. Will I sit in this room making paper flowers for the rest of my life?"

"About the job. Sarah told me you have to give the boss a little money."

"Well, we can't. So I'll just have to…I don't know."

"Minna, take a few dollars from your money. It'll be worth it if you and Mama get jobs."

"A few dollars? Do you think that'll be enough? Who knows what the boss expects?"

"It will have to be.

"Yes, it will have to be," Minna agreed solemnly.

They looked at each other.

"We've said enough," Yussel said.

"I agree. Wish me a *broche*—we should celebrate tomorrow night."

Yussel hugged her. "Sleep well," he said.

"You, too."

In bed next to Pearl, Minna stayed awake for hours. First she planned what to wear tomorrow. Then she rehearsed how she would try to avoid giving Mr. Feigen any of their hard-earned money.

As she closed her eyes at last, she thought she heard Bubbe say, 'Now it's you, Minna. Now you're the one. You must care for the family. You have the strength, thanks be to God, and your Mama is tired. You must be the Mama now until…'

As she fell asleep, Mina wondered, until when? Until I am old and gray? Until I have my own children? Until I become a teacher?

As had happened to her the night before, Minna woke up several times dreaming of the fire. Sweating, she relived it all until she finally fell back to sleep.

CHAPTER 13

She awoke, not refreshed, but ready to begin work at the factory. As ready as I'll ever be, she thought wryly. Pasting a smile on her face, she shook Mama gently to awaken her.

"It's time to get up!" she said as cheerfully as she could.

Mama opened her eyes. "*Oy vey'z mir,*" she moaned. "Today it's the factory." She sat up in bed.

Minna wrapped her robe around her and went to the hall to use the toilet, worrying about the day and how Mama would act. She'll never get a job if she acts that way, she thought. No one will hire her.

By the time she hurried back, Mama was waiting at the front door of the apartment. Silently, she passed Minna and went into the hall.

Minna had already decided what to wear. If I can look like a factory girl that's half the battle, she thought. As Mama came back into the bedroom, she was still leaning over the small mirror, putting up her hair. "This will make me look older," she explained

Mama slipped her serge dress over her head and, as usual, took off her nightgown underneath, her arms flailing. "For the factory, it matters?" she asked, her voice muffled under the dress.

"If we look like factory workers, maybe it'll help, Mama."

Mama sniffed, but Minna noticed that she, too, took special care with her hair, glaring at herself in the mirror as she arranged the long coils. After she had finished, the two of them left the bedroom together. Sarah, Bessie, and Pearl were already in the kitchen.

"Good morning," Bessie said.

"What's good about it?" Mama asked angrily. "To go off to the factory makes a good start for the day?"

Pearl looked at the floor.

"It won't be so bad," Minna said weakly. "You'll see. Besides, it'll only be for a while till we can save up."

Sarah smiled. "I'll like having you there, Minna. We can have lunch together."

"Lunch? I have to bring lunch? What shall I fix for us?"

"We have some cheese and a little challah left," Mama said. "We'll make a nice lunch."

Minna remembered her first day at school, when she and Pearl had nothing to eat. At least today I'll be prepared, she thought.

"Bring a small scissor, each of you," Sarah said. "If you don't, Mr. Feigen will charge you to use one of his."

Minna wrapped two lunches in newspaper and went into the bedroom to collect her scissors. She glanced in the mirror again on her way out. I look all right, she decided. Pausing for a moment, she set her face into an expression of calm assurance. "I want to work for Triangle," she practiced.

She had to smile at herself as she turned away and walked over to the door. She stuck her head out. "I'll get your scissors for you, Mama," she offered.

"In the sewing box," she replied as she sipped her glass of hot tea.

Minna pulled Mama's sewing box out from under her bed and rubbed her hand over the carved wooden top. She could still remember the time that Mama first taught her to sew and how later, she had helped her make a new dress. She closed her eyes and there was Bubbe bending critically over her work. 'Those stitches!' she had said. 'You're not sewing for an elephant. The stitches are supposed to be hidden, not seen—like your heart, little Minna.'

She smiled and went back into the kitchen. Handing Mama her scissors, she poured herself a cup of tea and sat down at the table.

Sarah looked at her apologetically. "We should leave in a minute or two. We want to get there early to talk to Mr. Feigen."

Mama stood up abruptly. "I'm ready now."

Minna gulped down the rest of her tea and stood up, too.

Bessie extended her hand. "Good luck today, although working there is no luck. But for your sake, I hope you get the job."

"I'll tell you tonight." Minna grasped her hand.

Pearl hugged Minna. "I wish it was me," she whispered. "I want to know all about it."

Finally, Mama and Minna followed Sarah out of the apartment. Mama, pulling her cloak on as they went down the stairs, frowned and walked heavily. Despite her fears about the factory, Minna felt an unexpected anticipation. At least, she thought, I'll be doing something to help.

Halfway down, she remembered the paper flowers. "The flowers!" she exclaimed. "I can drop them off on the way. I'll hurry."

She ran back up the stairs and picked up the bundles, holding them carefully so as not to squash the delicate paper blossoms. Staggering, she hurried down the stairs, stopping at the landing to readjust them.

At the bottom, Mama was waiting for her with her arms outstretched. "I'll take some," she said.

The flower lady was waiting for them on the stoop outside her building. Before accepting the flowers, she opened each bundle and inspected its contents. "You do good work," she said grudgingly. "Come back tonight for more."

Minna nodded, thinking they could always come back if they didn't get jobs at the factory. Even if they did, Pearl could do some in the afternoon.

The woman counted out a dollar and twelve cents, which she handed to Mama. Minna smiled. "That's something for the rent," she said. "At least it's a start."

Mama looked at the money. Her fist closed over it, Carefully, she put it into her pocketbook. She rubbed her fingers gently. "For three of us, working all day, it's not so good."

"You'll do much better at the factory between the two of you," Sarah said. "Of course, they'll only pay you a learner's rate at first…"

"A learner's rate?" Minna asked indignantly. "I've been sewing all my life and so has Mama."

"That's the way it works when you start out," Sarah explained. "They charge you for everything, whatever they can get away with."

Mama stared straight ahead, scarcely looking at where she was going. As Minna watched, she nervously touched the pocket where she had put her scissors. "How do the machines work with electricity?" she asked.

Why Mama's worried, Minna realized. She's worried about doing the job.

"There's a belt," Sarah said. "It carries the power to all the machines. You'll see. It makes the work easier. Your feet don't get so tired and it goes much faster."

"Oh." Mama touched her scissors again.

"Don't worry, Mama," Minna said. "We'll do a good job. I'm sure of it."

"And why shouldn't we?" Mama replied angrily. She quickened her steps.

Minna looked at Sarah and shrugged.

It was a long walk to Washington Square Place where the factory was. Minna felt her feet dragging after six or seven blocks, but Mama never slowed down.

Although it was early in the morning, the streets were beginning to come alive. Stall owners were setting up for the day and shopkeepers were opening doors and turning on lights. By the time they reached their destination, the sidewalk was crowded.

Out of the corner of her eyes, Minna evaluated the other young girls headed for work. I'll do all right, she assured herself. She averted her gaze from the men who brushed by her on either side. Covertly, she watched Sarah, who seemed oblivious.

Sensing her discomfort, Sarah patted her arm. "Don't worry, Minna. You'll do just fine. I hope Mr. Feigen is in a good mood today," she added. "Remember, just say 'yes' to whatever he says. He's the boss."

While Minna was mulling this over, they arrived at the corner of Washington Place and Greene Street. Sarah pointed up. "It's this building here. The factory is on the top three floors. We'll be on the ninth. See, it's there." She pointed to the windows.

Mama stopped, too and looked up. "How high is the building?" she asked.

"The Asch Building is ten stories," Sarah replied. "See—on one side is the college, N.Y.U. and on the other, over there to the north, is Fifth Avenue."

Mama squared her shoulders. 'So, why are we wasting time? Let's go in." She moved forward.

Minna hesitated. "It's so high up."

"You don't even know it when you're inside," Sarah reassured her. "Believe me, once you're sitting at your machine, you don't even see the windows. You could just as well be in a basement."

They entered the lobby of the building. Without hesitation, Sarah moved towards the elevators, calling greetings to others as she brushed by them. Minna and Mama followed her.

They all waited for the elevator. When they stepped in, the operator, a young boy, smiled at Sarah. "Good morning. You're in early this morning."

"Hi, Sammy," she replied. "Is Mr. Feigen in yet?"

"Just went up. Brought some friends, I see."

"Mrs. Ruben, Minna, this is Sammy." Sarah gestured at the elevator boy.

"Good luck!" He brought the elevator to a stop on the eighth floor. "No, don't get off here," he said to Minna, noticing her instinctive move towards the door. "This is for the cutters. You want the ninth for Mr. Feigen."

At the ninth floor, he opened the door with a flourish.

"Thanks," Minna called as they stepped into a large room.

She noticed rows of tables with one wide aisle at the end. Most of the wooden chairs at the machines were still empty as the girls were just beginning to file in. Each, she saw, would face two others diagonally across from her.

"But, how do you get in there?" she asked in amazement.

"You have to walk along that aisle at the end of the machines and then to your machine. It's the only way to get by. I'll show you later. First, we'd better speak to Mr. Feigen." Sarah looked around the room.

At the table closest to the elevator, a short, squat man with steel-rimmed glasses was bent over a machine. "Just replace the belt!" he yelled at the boy who stood next to him. "You know how to do it. Hurry! The girls will be here any minute!"

Sarah walked over to him. Shyly, she waited for him to turn and notice her. As he straightened, she leaned toward him. "Mr. Feigen, here are the two new workers I mentioned to you," she said.

Mr. Feigen looked at Minna and Mama, his lips pursed as he examined them from head to toe. "*Nu*, you think you can work the machines? You've sewn before? You think you're good enough to work here?" He shot out the questions in a loud voice, speaking so rapidly Minna had trouble understanding him.

She cleared her throat and replied, "We can sew."

He looked at Mama. "And you?"

Mama nodded, too. "I can sew," she said firmly. "We can do your work."

He thought for a moment. "Work is hard to find," he hinted. "I turn five girls away every day."

Minna reached into her pocketbook and took out three dollars of the money she had brought from the emergency fund. Awkwardly, she held it out to Mr. Feigen. "I know we can do this job," she assured him.

He looked at the money critically and said, "You're lucky. I need someone right now, so I'll give you both a trial." He began to talk even more quickly than before. "You're both learners, so you'll get paid accordingly. The rate is per shirtwaist. Keep up with the rest of the girls, do your quota, and you can each earn five dollars a week. Hours are eight to six, Monday through Saturday, and time off for lunch." He continued reciting as he reached out and took the money from Minna, scarcely looking at it as he pocketed it. "Charge for electricity, lockers, rent for chairs." Noticing Minna's look of surprise, he added, "This is a business, what do you think? Don't forget, you get paid by the piece, so don't stop to rest. You're not sitting at home like a lady. This is a factory!"

He led them over to a table. "I'll put you next to Sarah," he said to Minna. "And you…" he looked at Mama and thought for a minute. "I'll put you next to Mrs. Levy. She'll tell you how to get on. You'll both be sewing side seams. They're already basted for you." He pointed at another machine against the wall two tables over. "That's for you, Missis. Mrs. Levy is on your right."

He started to walk away, but then he turned back. "Say, what's your name, anyway?" he asked.

"Minna. Minna Ruben. This is my mother."

He nodded and walked quickly away, followed by the young boy who had fixed the broken machine. "We'll check this one, too. It was running slow yesterday. The girl said it was the machine. We'll see…"

Minna and Mama looked at Sarah in confusion.

"Don't worry," she soothed. "Come on, let's find Mrs. Cichetti. She's in charge of lockers and she'll get a key for each of you. Then I'll show you what you have to do. It all depends upon how many you can sew, but since you're new, he'll keep checking you both all day to make sure you're doing it the right way."

Stunned, Minna followed Sarah as she went back towards the elevators, turning into a small room nearby. What if I can't do it, she worried. Sewing seams will be easy, but how fast do I have to go? She looked back. Mama was still standing by the machines as if paralyzed.

"Come on, Mama," Minna called. "Let's put our cloaks away. "Then Sarah can show us what we have to do."

Mama shook her head mournfully and followed Minna. "So, what is this, a prison?" she muttered as she came closer.

"Don't worry, we'll get used to it." Minna patted Mama's arm. "It was like this the first day of school, too."

As they were talking, more women and girls entered the room. They headed directly for the cloakroom, shouting greetings to each other.

"Such a time I had with David!" Minna heard one of them say. Someone else answered with a giggle.

A round, cheerful woman, her hair pulled tightly back from her face in an intricate bun, stood by the door to the cloakroom.

"Mrs. Cichetti," Sarah greeted her. "This is Minna and her mama, Mrs. Ruben. Mr. Feigen just hired them, so they need lockers."

"Glad to meet you." Mrs. Cichetti smiled warmly. To Minna's surprise, she spoke English well, although her accent was different from Mama's.

"Here," she continued. "Leave your cloaks here for now and at lunchtime, I'll give you locker keys."

Mama frowned. Minna could tell that she didn't want to leave her cloak.

"Don't worry," Mrs. Cichetti laughed. "Your cloaks will be right here, believe me. On your first day, you don't want to be late."

Minna slipped off her cloak. "Thanks." She laid it upon the table. "I'll keep my pocketbook," she whispered to Mama.

Reluctantly, Mama took off her cloak and set it on top of Minna's. As they headed back into the workroom to wait for Sarah, who was putting her cloak in her locker, Mama kept looking back at the table to make sure hers was still there.

"My machine faces the door," Minna said. "I'll watch out for your cloak." She stifled her feeling of impatience. It's hard for Mama, she reminded herself.

By now, girls were moving between the tables towards their machines. Behind them, boys were laying piles of unfinished shirtwaists into the wicker baskets that sat next to each chair.

"That's the work we're supposed to do," Sarah explained. "We don't measure time by hours here, we measure it by the number of shirtwaists we complete." She strode over to her machine, followed by Minna and her mother. Picking up one of the shirtwaists, she pointed out the seams to be sewn. "After you get done, you drop it in the trench in front of your machine," she continued.

"The electricity, how does it work?" Mama asked nervously.

"You just use the treadle the way you always have. To go faster, push it harder. You know what I mean."

Mama looked relieved. "Oh." As Minna sat down, she followed Sarah to the machine Mr. Feigen had pointed out as hers.

Sarah waited with her for a moment. Then she pointed at a tall, thin woman with a serious face standing by the cloakroom. Unsmiling, she came towards them. "That's Mrs. Levy," she said. "She'll tell you how to go on."

Mama nodded and began examining her machine.

Sarah hurried back to Minna. "I like to get started as soon as I can. The more I do, the better off I am at the end of the week. Usually I can just barely finish the quota. They keep raising it..." She rummaged in her basket. "The electricity will come on in a minute."

Minna looked at her machine. Then she picked up one of the shirtwaists from her basket and held it up to the light. I can do this, she thought. If Sarah can do it, then I can, too. She turned her head. With a sigh of relief, she saw Mama talking earnestly to Mrs. Levy.

The noise became louder as the girls moved into their seats. The lights flickered for a moment and now, in addition to the hum of voices and rattling of chairs, a whirring noise was added to the cacophony. This grew louder as each girl started her machine. Minna had to stop herself from putting her hands to her ears. Yet the other girls seemed unaware of the noise as they bent over their machines and began sewing.

On Minna's other side, a plump dark-haired girl slid into her seat. She smiled briefly at Minna and reached into her basket, taking out the first shirtwaist to be sewn.

For a moment, Minna was afraid. Hemmed in, surrounded by

noise and people, she felt trapped. She looked around the room. Someone across from her sang softly to herself as she sewed. At the end of the row, she could hear another girl reciting the multiplication table over and over again. She leaned forward, trying to see her face.

Sarah nudged her. "What are you waiting for?" she hissed. "Mr. Feigen, he'll be watching you."

Minna started nervously and took out her first shirtwaist. She inserted it into the machine and carefully touched her foot to the pedal. The machine surged forward with a power she wasn't expecting. Surprised, she raised her foot. "It goes so fast!" she exclaimed.

"That's the electricity. Keep your foot light at first."

Minna barely touched the pedal as she pulled the shirtwaist through to complete the seam. It's not bad, she thought. It's better than my old machine. As she turned the shirtwaist around to do the other side, she was relieved. She glanced up to smile triumphantly at Sarah, only to discover that her friend had already finished her first shirtwaist and was well into her second.

Grimly, Minna bent over her work, determined not to fall behind. As the morning progressed, she dared to operate the machine faster, increasing her tempo slowly and lifting her foot often as she accustomed herself to the electric power. Mr. Feigen stood over her shoulder several times during the morning, watching her work. As she finished a piece, he plucked it out of the trench and examined it carefully, pulling at the seams to make sure they were firm. Minna didn't even look up. Instead, she bent over her work, frowning in concentration. She'd win the race.

When the lunch bell rang, she slumped over her machine, exhausted. As all the girls stopped their machines, the mechanical whirring ceased and the noise of human voices rose. Shyly, Minna looked around, for the first time eyeing the others in the room.

"Hurry!" Sarah urged. "We have only half an hour for lunch."

Minna pulled the newspaper-wrapped bread and cheese out of her pocketbook. Holding it in her hand, she stood up. "I'd better see how Mama's doing," she told Sarah.

Girls had pushed their chairs out and were leaning back, unwrapping sandwiches, bits of cheese, an apple, a piece of salami, whatever they had brought. Minna found it hard to walk down the crowded aisles to reach Mama. She could see her holding her food, her face pale.

Finally, she made her way down the narrow aisle, across the wider central aisle at the end of the room, and to her right down another narrow aisle to Mama's machine. "Is it all right, Mama?" she asked, when she stood in front of her.

Mama nodded.

Mrs. Levy smiled at Minna. "She's doing very well. Mr. Feigen is pleased."

Minna smiled back. She remained standing uncomfortably, poised over Mama, who did not lift her head. "Well," she said finally, "I'd better go back so I can take care of getting our locker keys."

"I'll walk with you," Mrs. Levy offered, standing up. "It gets to my bones, just sitting."

As they walked away from Mama, Mrs. Levy touched Minna's arm. "Don't worry. It's often like this the first day. It'll be different tomorrow. Your Mama's doing just fine."

Minna looked at Mrs. Levy. "Thank you for telling me. It's hard for her. She's not used to…"

"So who's used to it? At night, I wake up and all I hear is the machines. But, *nu*, I can't complain. Before, I worked at home with no electric. Fifteen hours a day and I earned half of what I get here. She'll get used to it, your Mama."

"Thank you," Minna repeated.

Mrs. Levy patted her on the shoulder and turned to go back to her machine. Minna hurried to the cloakroom.

Mrs. Cichetti was waiting for her. "Here." She held out two keys. "I've put both cloaks in lockers. "Yours is over there," she gestured to the left, 'and your Mama's is five down. See—there's the number on the key."

"Thanks."

Minna put the two keys in her pocket and rushed back to her own machine, imagining she could hear a clock ticking. As she slid into her seat, Sarah looked at her questioningly.

"She's doing the work," Minna said. "It's just that she didn't speak to me."

"Eat while we talk," Sarah urged. "Don't worry. It's hard at first." She smiled. "On nice days, we go out on the roof. Then it's a mess, with everyone trying to find a space to sit down.. So, Minna, how many shirtwaists have you got to do? I've finished half my quota."

"I don't know," Minna replied, with her mouth full. "Shall I count?"

'I'll count for you." Sarah bent over Minna's basket. Rapidly, she thumbed through the pile of shirtwaists. When she was finished, she looked up, surprised. "That's very good. You're only one behind me. For the first day, that's really good!"

Minna sighed. Chewing her challah, she felt stifled suddenly by Sarah, by the girl next to her, by the sea of faces surrounding her. She closed her eyes for a moment, willing the noise to go away.

"It's all right," Sarah said awkwardly. "You'll get used to it, Minna."

Minna sighed again. "I suppose I will."

But, she thought to herself, I don't want to get used to it. There's still hours left. Is this going to be the story of my days? Sitting here forever, listening to the whirr of a machine, feeding the material in, pulling it out?

She picked up one of the shirtwaists and for the first time, looked at it as more than just a task to be completed. Of sheer lawn with a multitude of tucks and pleats on the front of the bodice, it would be very pretty when it was finished.

I would wear this myself, Minna realized. I might buy it if I had enough money. Soon, girls all around this city, even all over this country, will be wearing this exact shirtwaist and others I have sewn. Do they know how we make them, she wondered. Do they know we are girls too?

Just as Minna finished her bread, the lights blinked for a second and the noise of the giant axles running under the table to power the machines began again. A bell rang as the girls began to sew.

By the end of the day, Minna felt slightly dizzy when she stood up. She had managed to finish her quota, but only by maintaining an unyielding concentration, grimly blocking out the clatter of the machines and the distracting sounds of other voices.

Mr. Feigen suddenly appeared in front of her. "You're doing the job, for now. I'll keep you as a learner for a few weeks to make sure you can keep it up. Your mother, too."

Minna stared at him wordlessly. Afraid to disagree, she bowed her head. His job, she now understood, was to have his section complete a certain number of shirtwaists so he could hand his daily quota to the factory owner.

As he walked away, she turned to Sarah. "Why am I a learner if I'm doing the job?"

Sarah shrugged. 'That's the way it is. He gets to pay you less, that's all."

Minna stood up straighter. "It's not fair," she protested. "If I'm doing the job…"

"But you have the job," the girl on the other side of her said. "Mr. Feigen, he's the one who gave it to you—right? So he's the one who decides. What are you going to do? My name's Rosa," she added as an afterthought.

'I'm Minna." She eyed Rosa, noticing she wore a crucifix around her neck. Otherwise, she didn't look different from any other girl Minna knew. Yet she found it hard to avoid looking at the cross.

"It'll be easier tomorrow," Rosa said as she bustled past towards the cloakroom.

Tomorrow, Minna thought. Everyone says tomorrow. She looked for Mama, peering through the pushing crowds of women and girls, all trying to reach the wider aisles at the end of each row of tables.

"Mama!" she called. "Mama!"

"I'll meet you outside," she yelled to Sarah and began to push her way to Mama's chair. It took her a long time because she was going in the opposite direction from the others. Finally, she reached Mama's machine, only to find the chair empty. Sighing, she turned and began to push in the other direction, back to the cloakroom. She could feel herself sweating, so she stopped for a second to calm herself.

By the time she emerged from the main aisle, the large workroom was almost empty. Now she could see Mama waiting anxiously near the door.

"Mama!" Minna called. "I have the locker key."

Mama looked up. For a brief moment, Minna saw her as a stranger. She observed a short, stocky woman with a strong neck and a grim expression on her careworn face. There was a streak of gray in her hair, she noticed. She couldn't remember seeing it before the fire.

"I'm here!" she called again.

When she reached Mama, she stuck her hand into her pocket and extended a key. "I don't know which is which. One is yours and one is mine. Come with me—we'll find our lockers."

Mama followed her silently.

Minna carefully matched the number painted on the door of the locker with the one on her key. She inserted it and opened the door. Inside, Mama's cloak hung upon a hook.

Mama took the key from her, removed her cloak, and relocked the door. As she wrapped it around her, she patted it in relief, smoothing it carefully to make sure it hadn't been damaged.

Then she followed Minna to the other locker and waited while she found her cloak. The two of them went downstairs in the almost empty elevator, meeting Sarah, who was waiting for them on the ground floor.

On the way home, Mama lagged behind. Unlike the way it had been in the morning, it was Minna and Sarah who had to slow their steps so she could keep up.

After walking for a few minutes, Minna felt refreshed. She stretched her arms. "Whew! It's good to feel the fresh air! Take a deep breath," she said to Mama. "You'll feel better."

Mama trudged onwards, barely looking up.

"Mama? Are you all right, Mama?" Minna asked.

"All right? So what's to be all right? I can still hear the machines in my ears."

Minna looked at Sarah helplessly and continued. "Everyone says we'll get used to it. It'll be better tomorrow," she said weakly.

Mama looked up, her eyes black with anger. "You can get used to anything! That I know." Her gaze caught Minna's. "And you? You did the work?"

Minna nodded.

"You're a good girl, Minna." Mama patted her brusquely and continued walking.

Minna flushed. "Thanks, Mama," she said. "We'll manage, won't we? We can do it."

Sarah, who had slowed her pace so she was abreast of Mama and Minna, added "It really does get better, Mrs. Ruben. My first day, I thought I would die. I certainly didn't finish my quota, the way Minna did."

"I finished, too," Mama said proudly. "That at least I can do."

Minna shook her head. Mama was still blaming herself, she realized. She hesitated, trying to think of what to say. Finally, she decided to wait. Tomorrow, she thought, it will be better. Timidly, she put her arm through Mama's so they could walk together.

Without saying another word, Mama continued forward. Minna noticed that she leaned harder on her arm as the blocks passed. Although she wanted to run ahead, breathing in great gulps of revivifying fresh air, she slowed her pace. Sarah walked slightly ahead.

Mama stopped at the front stoop. "Now it's the stairs," she complained.

"We're almost there," Minna soothed. "They'll be waiting for us, to hear what happened."

Mama took her arm from Minna's, stood up straight, and with an obvious effort, started up the stairs. At the landing outside their apartment, she paused. Head up, she opened the door. "We're home," she called.

A savory smell of soup rose from the kitchen. Pearl rushed to the front door. "How was it? I knew you had gotten the job when you didn't come home. You look tired, Mama. Come, have a glass of tea. You'll feel better." She led the way into the kitchen.

Mama said wearily, "In a minute, Pearl." She went into the bedroom and shut the door behind her.

Minna sank down at the table. Stretching her arms out, she sighed. "I'll have the tea, Pearl."

Pearl stared after Mama. Then she brought Minna a glass of tea and sat down next to her.

"Sarah!" Minna called. "Do you want a glass of tea?"

"Not now," Sarah answered from the front room. "I'll wait for dinner."

"So?" Pearl asked. "How did it go?"

"Well, we got the job and we finished out quota, both of us," Minna replied wearily. "Mama's just tired. It's hard work. And it's so noisy and close in the factory. So loud… The machines, Pearl, they're electric! I'm almost glad I lost my old one. If I could get an electric machine, I could make clothes one, two, three. That's if I could face a machine at night after working all day."

"But…what was it like?" Pearl repeated impatiently.

"You'll visit me and you'll see," Minna replied. "Oh, the flowers. I meant to pick up some for you to do in the afternoon tomorrow."

"I did it," Pearl said proudly. "I went myself after school. See how many I've done already!" She pointed to a sack in the corner.

"Oh, Pearl! But your homework? You still have to do your homework."

"Don't worry, Minna. I'm almost finished with it. Don't worry." Pearl beamed.

The door from the front room, which Sarah had tactfully closed, burst open and Yussel strode in. Although he was very pale, he had a triumphant expression on his face. "It was better today." He smiled as he set down his pack. "I can do it again. It will just take time. So *nu*, you got the job, Minna?" He sat down at the table.

'We both did."

"Where's Mama? Is she…"

"She did fine," Minna reassured him. "We both did. She's just…resting. It's a long day when you're not used to it. But Yussel, we both did our quota. I had to give Mr. Feigen three dollars and he's only paying me a learner's wages for a few weeks, but he said we could end up earning as much as five dollars a week each. We'll have enough for the rent. And Pearl's already made some more paper flowers."

Yussel smiled at Pearl approvingly. "That's good." He turned back to Minna. "If you finished your quota, why is he paying you a learner's rate?" he asked.

"Rosa said—she's the girl next to me—she's Italian—she said that's what they do. Sarah said we can't argue. I agree it isn't fair, but…"

The door opened and Bessie came in with Sarah. "So, how did it go?" she asked.

"It was all right. But, Bessie, we did our quota and they're only paying us a learner's wages for a few weeks."

Bessie's eyes sparkled. "So, they save a few pennies on your heads! That's what they do, those *gonifs*! What I was saying about the Union…"

Mama stuck her head out from the bedroom. 'There'll be no talk about the Union. We're lucky to get any job. We can't afford to take any chances."

"Mama!" Yussel stood up. 'How did it go for you today?"

"I did the work," Mama snapped. "What more is there?"

There was a pause. No one could think of anything to say.

Finally, Minna said, "It was thanks to Sarah. That's how we got the jobs. She helped me a lot, too. Oh Yussel, the electric machines! They go so quick!"

"Not so quick they don't keep piling on the work," Bessie commented.

"Well, the more I do, the more I earn. Right, Sarah?"

Sarah frowned. "It's not so simple. It's more what you don't get done, they pay you less. If you really can't keep up, they find someone else to do the job. See, if you do too many, everyone else looks bad. At first, Rosa, the girl next to you, she was much faster than anyone else. None of us would talk to her because they kept raising the quotas. She didn't understand."

"But…" Pearl's voice rose. "Don't you want to do as much as you can to earn more *gelt*?"

"If you do, the rest suffer." Sarah sighed. "To keep up is enough at Triangle."

Minna looked at Bessie questioningly.

"That's why the Union…" she began.

"To keep up is enough," Mama said firmly. "Jobs don't grow on trees. We already paid Mr. Feigen three dollars." She sat down at the table. "Pearl, the soup smells good. Let's have dinner." As Pearl went to get the bowls and put the soup pot upon the table, Mama turned to Yussel. "And you, my son, how were your ladies today?

Minna looked intently at Bessie, signifying that they would talk later. Then she stood to help Pearl, bringing the bread to the table with a knife so chunks could be cut.

After dinner, Mama went right to bed, saying, "It was a long day. I must sleep."

As Pearl cleared, Yussel, Bessie, and Minna sat around the table, speaking in low voices so as not to disturb Mama.

"What did you mean, Bessie?" Minna asked.

"Don't you see? They set worker against worker. At Triangle, the conditions are so bad that many of the girls work together, as Sarah said, so the quota won't be increased. That's actually the beginnings of a Union. A Union is only a group of workers banding together against the bosses. When they strike, they're saying, 'If you don't make it better, we can't work for you.' What's bad about that?"

"Last time they went on strike, they got nothing! *Bupkes*!" Sarah exclaimed. "Then they couldn't come back, some of them. The bosses fired them and hired other girls. How did that make their lives better?"

"Some of the bosses listened," Bessie said patiently. "My boss—he's still a *gonif*—but he changed a little. Next time, he'll change more. Don't you see? There's more of us than there are of them. If we all band together like Clara Lemlich said, then someday our voices will be heard."

"It's your first day on the job and you're already worrying about the Union?" Yussel asked Minna. "Wait and see how it goes. Give it time."

"It's because of being called a 'learner'," Minna explained. "It's not fair if I can do the work."

"We need the money," Yussel said. "Now's not the time to worry about Unions. Let's get on our feet first and then, if you want to…"

Sarah nodded. "I agree."

'You make me so mad! A Union is not a toy to pick up and put down. You have to believe in what's right and fair!" Bessie stomped out of the room.

Minna ran after her. "I see what you're saying, Bessie, but I have just started. Yussel's right. I can't afford to lose this job. Not now. We can talk about this again?"

Bessie turned her back on Minna. "It makes me furious! To me, it's as clear as crystal. We'll talk later if you want." She picked up her cloak. 'I have a meeting tonight, anyway." She walked briskly to the front door.

Slowly, Minna came back into the kitchen. Sarah, Yussel, and Pearl looked at her questioningly.

"I said we could talk more about it another time. You're right, Yussel. It *is* my first day."

Yussel smiled. 'Did I tell you about Mrs. Goldberg, one of my ladies? What she said today! When I rang her bell, she…" Yussel began.

Soon afterwards, Pearl spread her books out on the table to finish her homework, Yussel began to talk quietly to Sarah, and Minna discovered her head was drooping and her eyes closing.

"It's been a long day," she yawned. "I'll join Mama." She smiled at Sarah. "I'll see you tomorrow. And thanks!" Giving Pearl and Yussel a hug each, she went out into the hall to use the toilet before bedtime.

By the time she had returned to the bedroom, hung her skirt and shirtwaist on the hook on the wall, and snuggled under the feather bed, she no longer felt sleepy. She thought she could still hear the whirring of the machines, loud in the tiny bedroom. She remembered what Mrs. Levy had said. That Rosa, she thought. She does look like a nice girl even if she wears a cross. I wonder who was saying the multiplication table…

At least, I did it. As long as I don't have to spend the rest of my life doing it. Maybe I can bring a book tomorrow. Some of the girls were reading at lunchtime and in the morning before the machines were turned on. To her surprise, Minna found she was looking forward to the next day just a little. I'll get to know some of the other girls and…

'Bubbe,' she asked, 'why is Mama so different?' There was no answer. After all, she reminded herself, Bubbe had never worked in a factory. She doesn't know…

She fell asleep trying to explain her feelings to Bubbe, forgetting, as she finally closed her eyes, that for once, she had received no answer.

CHAPTER 14

By the time two weeks has passed, Minna and Mama felt more comfortable at the factory. They received two week's salary and Mr. Feigen said they would have to be learners for only another week because they had done so well. Their combined wages with Yussel's peddling money, Pearl's flower money, and the boarders meant they had enough to pay the rent and replenish the larder.

"Next week, when you're no longer 'learners', you'll earn more. We'll be able to put something aside after we buy food and save for the rent," Yussel figured.

Mama nodded. Although she was no longer as fatigued by the work, she hadn't yet recovered her old spirit. She did her share but was content to leave all the planning in Yussel's hands. She did talk to Mrs. Levy at lunchtime, Minna noticed.

Now that she had begun to feel more comfortable about completing her work, Minna looked around and observed the other girls. Slowly, she began to recognize their faces.

Anna, who sat across from her, was the most beautiful girl she had ever seen. With her Roman nose, long golden-brown locks, and soft blue eyes, she looked like a film star, Minna thought. Her shirtwaist was always the crispest and her hat, the most graceful. Every evening, she watched Anna set it upon her head in front of the tiny mirror in the cloakroom. Seemingly oblivious of the others waiting to use the looking glass, she stared at her own reflection, completely absorbed in the placement of a curl or the tilt of her hat brim.

Whenever Minna looked up from her work, she saw Anna's face across the work trench. Occasionally, the two of them exchanged smiles or quick comments.

Finally, one day at lunchtime, Anna walked around the trough so she was standing in front of Minna and Sarah. "I'm Anna," she said to Minna after nodding at Sarah. "You're new here, aren't you?"

Feeling shy, Minna bobbed her head to say yes.

"I'm glad to meet you," Anna smiled.

'I am, too," Minna replied timidly.

'I've been working here four years, since I was fourteen," Anna said. "I guess Sarah already said it's not too bad once you get used to it.

"It's easier than it was at the beginning," Minna said. "You've been working since you were fourteen?"

"I had to," Anna replied simply. "But I've been saving. A little, anyway. It's hard. Every time I pass a shop, I'm tempted. Didn't you used to work in a shop? I thought I saw you once in the window."

"It was our shop. Chava's, it was called," Minna said proudly. "My Mama started it. I made the clothes in the window and sold to the ladies."

Anna shrugged. "I don't like to sew that much when I'm home. Besides, I don't have a machine. But I have friends who do. Ben, he's my fellow, he likes me to look good."

"I don't see how you could look bad," Minna blurted.

Anna smiled. "Where do you live?"

"On Allen Street. Where Sarah lives."

"Oh. Well, we could walk home together one night if you want to. I live around the corner."

"I'd like that." Minna smiled.

Sarah said nothing.

Later, when Anna had returned to her machine, Minna asked Sarah if she liked Anna.

"I guess I like her. I don't know her very well. She's pleasant enough to everyone. And the boys, they follow her like bees to honey, but I've never really talked to her. The way she looks…"

"But she doesn't put on airs."

"No," Sarah replied dubiously. "I guess she doesn't. I just keep thinking she will."

"I know what you mean," Minna said slowly, "but that isn't really fair, is it?"

The lights flickered and the power went on. As she bent over her sewing, Minna found herself thinking about Anna. She looks like a Fifth Avenue lady, Minna thought, yet here she is, working right across from me.

Rosa, sitting next to Minna, managed to make a joke about almost every situation. Her eyes sparkled and her mouth curved as she tossed out laughing comments about everyone and everything. She came from a large family, Minna learned, and all of them were working to help Tony, the youngest boy.

Rosa described the situation to Minna. "He's smart, you see, and he should get ahead. We each put by a little something for him every week so he can go to college. Mama says he'll be the making of our family. The priests say he should go into the church, but I think he'll be a lawyer."

"How old is he?"

"He's only twelve, but everyone can tell he's the smartest. Giuseppe, my big brother, watches him like a hawk. Every night, he makes sure he does his homework. Mamma Mia! How that boy studies!"

"But…what about you?"

"Me? Oh, I never liked school anyway. One day, I'll get married and have my own family. My sister Angelica, she already has three. Such bambinos!"

The girl who repeated the multiplication tables every day was named Hilla, Minna discovered. Serious and bespectacled, she had big plans. "I'm doing this just for now," she informed Minna almost as soon as they began to talk. 'I'm going to make something of myself. I go to night school at the Educational Alliance. It's true I never had a chance," she continued angrily. "I've always had to work. It's my brothers who have had the chances. But, just wait. I'll do it if it takes me a million years!"

There were so many others. Some were older women, censorious of the young or faded to gray wisps, performing their daily work like automatons, barely speaking to anyone. When they left the factory in the evening, their shoulders were bowed and their faces stoic.

Then there was Mrs. Levy, kind and warm to all. Nothing seemed to disturb her calm placidity. Without her, Minna would have despaired for Mama. Despite the half-hearted attempts she made to be cheerful for Yussel and Pearl, she was grimly suffering. It was Mrs. Levy who reassured Minna. "It takes time, my dear," she'd say. "When I first came here..." She never finished that sentence.

Sammy, the elevator operator, was always friendly. He greeted Minna with a smile at the beginning of every day and waved goodnight cheerfully at the end.

Mr. Feigen continued to hover over Minna and Mama for a few days until he was sure they could accomplish the work. Then he treated them like the others, "my girls" he called them, regardless of age. With neither a pleasant nor an unpleasant word, he collected their work, sent it off to be finished, and hurried it to the tenth floor where it was checked, sorted, and prepared for shipping.

The boys...there was Ike, the youngest, who slipped in behind the girls to repair a broken belt, replacing the connection between the sewing machine and the receiving axle that gave it electric power. Abe, younger than Pearl, refilled the girls' baskets and picked up the finished work. Gino emptied the wooden oil shells, mounted above the girls' knees to catch the machine drippings. His job was never-ending. Minna often checked her shell nervously, sure the oil would spill over and stain her skirt. They called themselves men even if they were only thirteen or fourteen. Some, like Isidore, were working as a temporary measure, vowing to save enough money to continue their studies.

The cutters, most skilled of all the workers, were usually older. They seemed more relaxed when seen in their enclave on the eighth floor. They knew they could find work elsewhere if they had to. A good cutter, Minna learned, was worth his weight in gold, saving his employer much *gelt* as he laid out the patterns in the most economical way.

One of the cutters, Mr. Steinberg, was a jovial man of about sixty. The deep smile wrinkles around his eyes and mouth and his short gray-and-white beard made him appear approachable. He was Minna's favorite of all the men she noticed on the eighth floor. He called hello to each of the girls by name and always had a cheery word to offer.

Once, at lunchtime, when Minna decided to dash outside for a quick turn around the block, they met in the elevator. He asked if he could join her. When he did, she was surprised at how fast he walked. She almost had to trot to keep up.

"So, you've joined the Triangle band," he said.

She nodded, thinking to herself, I hope I won't be here for long.

"I thought that, too," he said, seeming to read her mind. "When I came from *der alter heym* and began cutting, I thought, I'll find real work, the work God chose for me. But it never happened. So here I am, twenty years later, still cutting." He laughed. "It's not so bad. It's a life, after all."

"What was the other, the real work?" Minna asked.

"I'm a poet," he replied. "Still am a poet in the evenings. But who can live on pennies? My son, he's a doctor and my daughter, she's still in school. It's for the young we must work. And you, my dear? You are young, too."

"We had a shop," she explained. "It burned. So now…now we'll begin again. I won't be here in twenty years! I promise it!"

"You have plans, then?"

"Oh yes. Everyone here has plans," she said bitterly.

He nodded. "It's true. The only crime is to give them up. Don't you know that? God means us to have dreams as much as He means for us to follow His commandments."

She looked at him in surprise. "You think God wants us to be happy then?"

He smiled. "There is joy in following God's will. If He hadn't wished us to find joy in life, why did He create a world of beauty and love?"

"Beauty and love!" Minna sniffed. "I don't see much beauty around here!" She waved her hand scornfully at the dirty streets.

He touched her arm. "My daughter's not much older than you, my dear. If I may take the liberty… Open your eyes, that's what I say. There's beauty all around—in the reflection of a newly washed window, in a child's face in an alley, even in the sorrow of a new widow. Beauty is not always happy, but it's always there."

"In loss, there's no beauty," Minna objected.

"But don't you see, my dear, loss means that there was something once. If once it was part of your life, then perhaps, if you believe, it will come to you again." He looked down at her, his eyes gentle. "In the end, what is there but life? It's all we have. We don't believe in heaven. Now, is the Lord God so terrifying that He created man only to suffer? I don't believe that. I can't."

She was silent, pondering his words.

They had circled the block. As they reached the door of the Asch Building, Mr. Steinberg patted Minna's arm again. "We'll talk more another time," he said.

"Will you show me your poems?" she asked.

"Someday," he answered. He smiled back at her as he strode ahead to join his fellow cutters, also returning to work.

Minna thought often about their conversation in the next few days. Unconsciously, she began to look for the beautiful in her life. She found that if she allowed herself to be open, once in a while she would see something that was sharply and unexpectedly beautiful. Often, it was as simple as the things Mr. Steinberg had described—the rainbow reflected in an oil slick on the street, the look in Yussel's eyes as he bent over Mama, and even the pungent odor of fresh onion as she chopped it for soup.

There were men who patted her arm in a different way. Minna avoided them if she could, but sometimes, in the crowded elevator, she had no choice but to be pushed next to one of them. She learned to surround herself with other girls whenever possible, especially when she saw a certain group of young Italian men. One of them, named Marco, wouldn't leave her alone. If he wasn't pressing up closer to her in the elevator, he was nudging her as they passed in the lobby or saying things in Italian to his friends when they met on the street. He made her so uncomfortable she never looked him in the face, preferring to walk by as if he didn't exist.

The Sunday after she had worked two weeks, Minna remained in bed until almost eight o'clock, lying back against her pillow luxuriously. When I'm rich, she thought, I'll never get up before eight o'clock.

By the time she emerged from her room fully dressed, it was nine fifteen. The rest of her family greeted her with smiles. (It had long been understood that no words were spoken to anyone in the morning en route to the bathroom in the hall.) Even Mama seemed more cheerful than usual.

"I'm off soon," Yussel said. "I just waited to say 'good morning' to our sleeping beauty!"

Minna ducked her head sheepishly. "Once a week…"

"I've been up for hours!" Pearl teased.

"If you can sleep, it's good," Mama volunteered. "I still hear the machines at night."

Minna sat down at the table. "Where are Sarah and Bessie?"

"They're in the other room," Yussel answered. "Bessie said something about a meeting. Sarah... Sarah's going to come with me when I go buying. She says she wants to pick out some fabric for herself."

Minna restrained herself although it was difficult to repress a knowing smile. She could not refrain from exchanging a glance with Pearl. Mama looked up, frowned, and remained silent.

"Let's go somewhere today," Pearl suggested. "Let's walk down by the river. The leaves are turning and I've seen only one tree, the one by the school."

"I think I'll clean the stove today," Mama declared. "It must be taken apart and scoured. I haven't had time..."

"Do you want me to help you?" Minna asked reluctantly.

"No. I want to do it myself. I'll feel good when my stove is clean."

"Then let's go for a walk, Pearl. Let's take lunch and have a picnic."

Pearl beamed. "We can look for pretty leaves on the ground. My teacher showed me how to press them."

After breakfast, Minna and Pearl prepared a small lunch to take with them on their walk. As they left, Mama called after them, "Be back in plenty of time! We'll have dinner from a clean stove tonight."

They strolled down the street towards the river. Minna felt happier than she had in a long time. "Mama sounded like she used to, don't you think?" she asked Pearl.

Pearl looked at her in surprise. "She sounds...like Mama," she replied nonchalantly.

Minna realized that Pearl hadn't seen Mama as she was at the factory—silent, grim, and, Minna thought, stoic like some of the other women. Deciding not to worry her sister, she changed the subject. "Did I tell you about Mr. Steinberg?"

"Did you tell me about Mr. Steinberg! That's all we've heard for the last week. My teacher says his poems are in *The Forward* sometimes. He's a well known worker-poet."

"I already knew that. He said he was a poet."

There was a pause for a moment and then Pearl asked eagerly, as if she had been waiting for the last two weeks to find out the answer. "So, what's it really like at the factory?"

"I already told you. It's not so bad. It's not as bad as I thought it would be now that I'm getting to know some of the people. But it's no fun, I can tell you. The noise, there's always the noise. I'm sitting there, staring at my machine and rushing because if I don't get done, I don't get paid. I can't stop no matter what, so I just keep sewing and sewing. The building could fall down and I'd still be bent over my machine."

Pearl laughed. "I can just picture you, sitting in the middle of the street sewing, with the building in pieces around you!"

"It's not so funny when you're in the middle of it. I think about it a lot. Suppose I'm still there in a year or two years. Some people study during lunch, but I have to walk around a little or my back hurts at night. Others study at night or go to classes, but, Pearl, I'm so tired when I get home. Not tired exactly. I want to run and jump and say, 'I'm free for now.' But even at night, how can I concentrate on reading when all I can see are seams? Then I think, if I don't keep up, I'll never..." She turned to Pearl. "You know what it is? I'm afraid. I don't think I will ever leave the factory."

Pearl stopped. "You're going to follow your dreams, Minna. I know you will!"

Minna shook her head. "I wish I was so sure."

"You want to so much. You're the one who said you had to decide what was important and work for it."

"Sometimes, it's hard to say, harder to remember, when you're in the middle of it. What about you, Pearl? What are your dreams?"

"I don't love school the way you did, Minna. I just want to go to work. I'd rather. It isn't just because I want to help. It's what I want."

Minna shook her head. "Finish first. After so many years at school, it's foolish not to go to the end. If you skip again, you can graduate by the end of the school year. Then you can come to work with me. Believe me, you won't always be so anxious to do it."

'I know it's what I want. Could I come by after school one day and see what it's like?" Pearl asked.

"Not yet. Wait till...well, till I feel more comfortable there." Minna said, hoping that Pearl would forget about it. "So, tell me what's going on at school? We never have time to talk any more."

As Pearl talked about her schoolmates and her favorite teachers,

Minna listened avidly. It seemed only yesterday, she thought, that she had been in the same place learning the same things.

"Oh, Miss Israel asked about you," Pearl remembered. "I told her about the fire and she said you should come and see her when you can. Maybe she can help you."

"How can she help?" Minna asked unhappily. 'She can't pay for my college. I have to work at the factory and that's all. There's no point in seeing her."

"She said to come," Pearl repeated.

'I will, I will," Minna said, knowing she wouldn't. Why make myself feel worse about the path I have to take, she thought. Better to accept my life for now, or at least, not talk to someone like Miss Israel about it."

Later, she interrupted Pearl in the middle of a story about a boy named Mo. 'You know, Mr. Steinberg said there's beauty everywhere. Did I tell you that?"

"Several times."

"Well, just look. There's the park ahead of us. It's beautiful and it's right in the middle of the city."

They stopped and admired the green grass, the trees, now turning gold and red, and the river in the distance.

"Life can't be all bad when there's a park," Minna said.

Pearl skipped a few steps. "That's what I say. Life's not bad!"

They wandered through the park, stopping to watch the East River as it wound its way towards the ocean.

As they leaned over the parapet, Minna exclaimed, "See, even the river sparkles today!"

Then she stiffened. In the distance, walking towards them, she could see a group of young men. Fearful that it might be Marco and his friends, she looked around nervously. She was able to relax only when she saw other people near them.

"What's the matter, Minna?"

"I...got worried for a minute. There's a boy at work. His name is Marco and he's Italian. Anyway, he's always...you know...bothering me. He talks in Italian and I can't understand what he's saying to his friends. Then they laugh. I hate it!"

"He probably likes you," Pearl said wisely.

"Well, that's no way to show it!" Minna stamped her foot on the pavement. "If you like someone, you don't go bothering them all the time and touching them! I know that." She sighed, remembering Jake. She shook her head. "I don't know, Pearl. It seems like you can't trust anyone."

"Do you really think that?"

Minna considered. "I don't know. Sometimes I do."

"I think you can trust most people," Pearl replied in a serious tone. "At least, you have to give them a chance. Sid, he's my friend—he sits next to me in three classes because of our last names—he says it's not any easier to be a boy than a girl."

"That's not true and you know it! Men get everything. They run the world. We have to pick up the pieces afterwards."

"You sound like a suffragette."

"No, I wouldn't make a fuss the way they do. But it isn't fair. What's so hard for men? They're the kings!"

"Sid says it's not so easy to be the king. Honestly, that's what he said. His mama expects him to be perfect all the time. He has to do well in school, be brave, earn money, be successful. He has a lot to worry about. So does Yussel, now that I think about it."

"Oh well…Yussel… He's the exception."

"No, I don't think so. There are lots of men like Yussel. I know it," Pearl insisted. "What about Mr. Steinberg?"

"He's different. But he's old."

"I bet he was always like that if he's a poet."

"Well, maybe you're right. I just…"

"Yes?"

"I don't know what to think any more."

"Well, as long as you admit it!" Pearl touched Minna on the shoulder. "See if you can catch me!" she yelled as she began to run.

Minna didn't hesitate. She ran as hard as she could but Pearl stayed maddeningly in front of her. It felt marvelous to run without restraint. The wind blew against her face and her hair escaped from its tidy bun as she sprinted along.

Passing an elderly couple strolling along the promenade, she noticed they stared after her. "A great big girl like that, running!" she heard the woman say.

"What's wrong with running?" she called back over her shoulder.

Finally, she caught up with Pearl and tapped her on the shoulder. "You were saying…" she panted.

Pearl, her cheeks rosy and her eyes sparkling, said nothing, but poked Minna playfully in the stomach. "Slowpoke!" she gasped at last.

"I caught you, didn't I?"

"That's because I let you, silly!"

They continued their walk, strolling sedately as they searched for the perfect park bench to sit on for lunch. Most of them were already occupied, or in the shade, or too far from the river.

"We can't have lunch just anywhere," Minna said. "We have to find the best spot."

"When we do, let's pretend we're at a restaurant where you can order whatever you want to eat. A restaurant with tables and a waiter."

"A restaurant?"

"Yes. Someone in school was saying their whole family went to a real restaurant. They could order anything they chose and the waiter had to bring it to them. Let's pretend we're ordering our lunch."

Just then, Minna saw it, the perfect bench. It was sunny, not too far from the path, and it faced the river. Best of all, it was empty. Hurrying ahead, she sat down quickly and spread her skirt. When Pearl joined her, she said, "Spread your skirt and put our lunches down. That way, no one else will come."

Pearl did as she asked and turned to Minna. "I think I'll have some challah and cheese for lunch. Perhaps I might have an apple for dessert. How about you?"

"That sounds like a good choice. Waiter!" Minna beckoned to an imaginary man. "Please bring our food right away!" she commanded.

Pearl laughed. "Do you think we'll ever go to a restaurant?"

"Maybe someday," Minna said doubtfully. "It probably costs too much money."

As they ate their lunches, Minna and Pearl watched people walk by. Minna eyed an older couple. Dressed in what looked like their Sunday best, they sauntered by. The woman leaned on the man's arm and listened as he named the different kinds of trees they passed.

"That's nice," Pearl commented, startling Minna.

"What's nice?"

"See, that couple. They probably come out for a walk once a week. I think they work hard the rest of the time, but they don't forget to come out for a stroll. See how she leans on him?"

Minna shook her head. "I don't think that's nice at all. What's so nice that their best idea of fun is to go for a walk on Sunday. I'm not going to live like that!"

"What do you mean?"

"I'm not going to live like that, that's what I mean. There may be beauty in everything, but there's more away from here. I know it." She fingered her locket. "There are other ways to live.'

'Other ways? You mean, like the *goyim*?" Pearl's voice rose.

"Like…I don't know…Like rich people live."

"Compared to *der alter heym*, we're rich right now," Pearl said seriously. "Even without the store, we have enough to eat. I remember what it was like back there. We have new clothes and no one comes banging on the door. We'll have more, too. I know we will someday."

"The way we're going? From the factory?" Minna's eyes filled with tears. "I don't know, Pearl. When I talk to Mr. Steinberg, I feel like I'm blind not to see what's around me. Then, sometimes, I can't help it, I feel so…angry. I don't know what I want!"

"I do," Pearl mused. "I want to meet a prince and we'll get married and live happily every after."

"And if he works at the factory or sells on the street?"

"I don't care. I guess he'll still be a prince, won't he? He'll be my prince. Sure, sometimes, I wish he'd be rich. Like Rose Pastor Stokes. Remember, we read about her. But then I think, you can be rich and still not be happy. I read a story the other day…"

"You and your stories! I'm sure it's easier to be happy when you're rich. Just think, whatever you want, you can have. You wake up one morning and say, 'I think I'd like cake for breakfast' and you can have it. Or you say, 'I'm going to the Plaza Hotel tonight' and you can. You eat in restaurants whenever you want and you're never tired because you can stay in bed all day if you feel like it. You even throw out your old clothes every year and buy all new ones!" Minna had to laugh at her last statement. "I guess no one does that…"

'We're not doing so badly," Pearl repeated.

"Oh no? Look at Mama. All her life, it has been work and more work. Finally, she gets a little ahead and we have the store. Then what happens? It burns down. Look at Yussel. He never had a chance to go to school or have fun. From the moment we landed here, he's had to be the man. Even when Tata was here. If we were rich, we could just sit around in our house and laugh, no matter what happened."

'Well, we're not," Pearl said impatiently. "So what's the point of thinking about it. Saving pennies, it'll take till you're a hundred to have anything."

"I don't know. It won't be easy, but I'll do it. We'll all live on Easy Street. Wait and see!"

'Not me!" Pearl laughed. "My prince and I, we'll be on Allen Street. You'll come to visit us and bring gifts for our children and they'll say 'There's our rich Aunt Minna,' and be very nice to you."

Minna laughed too. Then she shook her head and sighed. She couldn't help thinking of Jake. Decisively, she jumped up, collected the paper she'd wrapped her lunch in, carefully strewed the crumbs for the squirrels, and dumped the rest into the trashcan.

"Let's walk some more," she suggested to Pearl. "Let's walk all the way to the end of the park."

By the time they returned home, it was late in the afternoon. As they ascended the stairs, they smelled a delicious odor pervading the hallway. They quickened their steps, looking at each other in wild surmise.

"Chicken?" Pearl whispered.

Minna shrugged and opened the door. The smell grew stronger.

"It is chicken!" Pearl danced into the kitchen.

Mama, Yussel, and Sarah were seated around the table. On the stove simmered a pot of... Pearl lifted the lid. "It's a whole chicken!" she exclaimed.

"Cousin Avraim brought it," Yussel explained, smiling. "They had the baby. It was a boy, thanks be to God, and he was celebrating."

Even Mama seemed more content than she had been in days, Minna noticed. "We'll eat well tonight," she said complacently. "From a clean stove, too."

'We're just waiting for you two and Bessie," Yussel said. "Then we'll have a feast. Sarah added some raisins and sugar and we had some flour. We even have dessert tonight!"

Pearl looked at Minna, as if to say, see, it's not so bad, but Minna, didn't notice. Taking her cue from the others, she began to smile broadly. Grabbing Pearl's hands, she danced her around the table.

'You see," Pearl whispered. "It's not so bad, is it?"

"For now, I agree," Minna said. "Tomorrow, who knows how I'll feel? Who cares!" Panting she dropped into a chair.

CHAPTER 15

When they left for the factory the next morning, Minna still felt traces of last night's exhilaration. Even Mama, she noticed, was more like her old self than she had been since the fire.

In no time at all, they arrived at the Asch Building. As Minna exchanged jokes with Sammy at the elevator, she was surprised to realize she was looking forward to the day. She thought about it. It wasn't the work. It was the people she wanted to see.

"Sometimes, I watch Anna while I'm at my machine," she whispered to Sarah. "She's so beautiful." What would it be like, she wondered, to look that way? It would affect every moment, from the first second of waking to the last moment before sleep. Even when Anna frowned over her work, she was enchanting.

Rosa hurried to her seat.

"You're late," Minna commented.

"I know. Guiseppe got into trouble over the weekend." Rosa pulled out her chair, sat down, and reached into her basket for her work.

"What's the matter?" Minna asked, shaking out her first shirtwaist.

"I can't say. But he's really in trouble. What will we do without Guiseppe at home?"

"But…where's he going?"

"Away. We don't know where. Just away." Rosa's eyes filled with tears. "Papa says he has to go."

Minna inserted her fabric in the machine and began to sew. It was hard to talk while working, but she had to start or she'd fall behind. 'What happened?" she asked, speaking loudly enough to be heard over the noise of the machines.

Rosa looked up, embarrassed. She immediately bent over her sewing again. "Shh. Everyone will hear you," she hissed. "We can talk later."

Minna wondered about Guiseppe while she sewed. What could he have done that was so terrible? As the morning passed, Jake again crept into her thoughts. As usual, she tried to avoid thinking of him.

Instead, she made herself remember her conversation with Mr. Steinberg. Could life really be beautiful when you worked in the factory? Could her days be that way? Why, she asked, did some people have such *tsouris* in their lives and others seemingly none at all? Were some meant to have lives filled with beauty and others with ugliness? Her thoughts wandered off into a glorious day dream about how it would be if she was rich, with a room of her own, new clothes whenever she wanted, a chance to eat in restaurants… As she mused, she sewed automatically.

At lunchtime, she turned to Rosa. "Let's go outside to eat," she suggested.

"No, I can't," Rosa replied. "There's someone I have to talk to. Someone who might help." Frantically she pushed her chair aside and hurried down the aisles. She was soon lost to view in a crowd of people.

Minna looked around for Sarah, but she had already left to eat with her special friend on the tenth floor. Sarah had introduced her, but she couldn't remember her name.

Shrugging, she grabbed her lunch and hurried to the cloakroom to get her cloak. I need some fresh air, she thought. I'll eat while I walk.

She was pleased to see Mr. Steinberg at the door downstairs. When he saw her, his eyes lit up. "Here comes my walking companion," he said, smiling.

She smiled back happily.

"I've been thinking about what you said," she began shyly, as they went out of the building.

"Yes…" he encouraged.

"Well, if we are meant to be happy and live in beauty, why are some of us poor and unhappy and others rich and surrounded by luxury and beauty?"

Mr. Steinberg chuckled as they rounded the corner. "That's a good question. Shall I tell you what I think?"

Her mouth full, as she munched her apple, Minna nodded.

"I think…I take my own life in my hands and make of it what I will. It's not for me to look at my neighbor's garden, but to cultivate my own."

"But…" Minna began.

He chuckled again. "It's true, it's human nature to look across the way. Isn't it so? Sometimes, it seems as if all the sunshine falls on my neighbor's garden and none on mine. Yet I notice, my neighbor, he has so many flowers. He doesn't cherish them—each one—as I do mine. When one grows on my stony soil, I am happy and proud for days. I often go to admire it. I even tell strangers that I meet, 'Do you know I have a flower in my garden?' I get so much more pleasure from my one flower than my neighbor does from his full garden."

Noticing that Minna was frowning, he continued, looking earnestly down at her.

"Many philosophers have said this in many different ways, my dear. Cultivate your own garden. The miracle of Creation is that the Lord God, He gave us each the seeds and the will to persevere. Then we have to choose. As to why some of us have a sunny strip and others are surrounded by shade and rocks, I don't know. Maybe it's because He craves beauty and He gives the strongest of us a greater challenge. What can be harder than to create beauty in a desert?"

She hesitated. Finally, she burst out, "I should be glad I am poor and have to work in a factory? I should be glad I can't go to college? It's wrong! You're wrong!"

Mr. Steinberg shook his head. "What I tell you is my way, not yours." He continued gently. "It is the way I live my life."

She shook her head, stopping to face him. "I'd like to believe that, too. But when I see what happens, it's not right. It isn't fair!"

"What will you do about it?" Mr. Steinberg asked.

"I'll work harder so I can have what I want, so Mama can have another store, Yussel, his farm, and Pearl, enough money to marry her prince. I'll change the unfairness."

Mr. Steinberg nodded. "Don't you see, you *are* cultivating your garden. I never said we should be content with misery and poverty, only that we should work to better them." His voice grew firm. "What we shouldn't do is to waste time with jealousy and envy. Who cares if the neighbor has more flowers? Plant your own and worry about them. That's what I say."

"Like when you keep writing poems," she said timidly. "You could have said, 'I want to be a rich man and do nothing but write poems. If I can't do that, I won't even try.' Instead, you keep creating your own beauty."

"You're right, Minna. You must do the same for yourself. Continue along the path you believe is right for you. Sometimes I think, I'm too tired. Work is too hard. Why should I sit and write something that no one will read? But I persevere and now my poems are printed and everyone can read them."

"When I talk to you, it seems so clear. Then I go home and think about it, and I have more questions."

Minna gazed at Mr. Steinberg so earnestly, she didn't watch where she was going. Carelessly, she bumped into a young girl, knocking parcels out of her arms. "Oh, I'm sorry," she said, stooping to pick up the packages. The girl frowned at her and hurried away.

'You bumped into her because you weren't looking where you were going, right?"

She nodded.

"You weren't looking where you were going because you were thinking your own thoughts. You could have passed a dying man and you wouldn't have noticed."

She nodded again.

"Well, I think our gardens are all around us. We can't afford to concentrate only upon ourselves. To make a garden is to create a thing of beauty, but if we hurt others along the way, we no longer have beauty. Do you understand?"

She blushed. "I should have looked where I was going."

"You should always look where you're going, my dear." Mr. Steinberg held the door of the Asch Building open for her.

In the lobby, Minna gave Mr. Steinberg a warm handclasp. "Thanks," she said "I'll think about what you said." Abashed by her spontaneous rush of affection and admiration, she hurried to the elevator without looking back.

It was strange to return to the crowded room filled with the sounds of women's voices. It was so different from the imaginary garden Minna was trying picture. Where are my flowers, Minna wondered. Will they ever bloom?

As she neared her seat, she noticed Rosa, sitting hunched over her machine, her head in her hands. Glancing at the big clock on the wall, Minna saw she still had a few minutes. She walked briskly to her seat.

'So, tell me," she asked, leaning over Rosa. "Why does your brother have to go away?"

Rosa buried her head in her arms and mumbled something, but Minna was unable to hear what she was saying. She leaned closer.

"I can't hear you," she said.

"He did something very bad and Papa said he must go away. I love him so much. He's always taken care of me. What will it be like without him? Where will he go? Poor 'Seppe."

"If he goes out west, he can get a farm and…"

"I told him that, but he said, 'What do I know from farms? I'm a city boy.' I think he's going to Chicago. He'll get into trouble there, too. I know he will. He thinks it isn't fair when he looks in the shop windows. He wants us all to have what's there. So he…"

"Oh."

"He's going to meet me after work to say goodbye. Papa won't ever let him come home again. He won't be able to write either, because Papa said… Mama cries all the time. We won't know what's happening to him."

"I have an idea, Rosa. Why doesn't he write to me? I mean, write to me at my house and I'll give you the letters," Minna suggested impulsively. Once she had said it, she worried. What would her family think? Receiving letters from a strange man! Worst of all, Guiseppe was a strange man in disgrace with his family. Too bad, she decided. If they don't like it, I'll still do it. If it was Yussel, I'd want someone to help me. I can do this for Rosa.

Rosa smiled tremulously. "Oh, Minna, thank you. Come with me after work and give him your address. That was the worst, thinking I would never be able to hear from him."

The lights flickered and Minna just had time to say "yes" when the whirr of the machinery signified that it was time to begin work again. As she sewed, she rehearsed what she would say to Mama, who would think it strange she didn't walk home with her and Sarah.

When the day was over, Minna whispered to Rosa, "I'll meet

you in the cloakroom. I have to tell Mama I'm meeting you."

"Don't tell anyone about 'Seppe," Rosa pleaded. "I'm not supposed to."

"I won't," Minna promised. She hadn't planned to tell Mama the whole story anyway.

She waited by Mama's aisle for her to come out.

"Don't wait for me, Mama," she said as soon as she could. "I'll catch up with you. I have to talk to my friend, Rosa, for a minute." Without giving Mama a chance to reply, she hurried to the cloakroom, gathered up her cloak, and joined Rosa, who was anxiously waiting at the door to the elevator.

"Hurry," Rosa urged. "He can't wait long. I think he's going to take a train. I gave him a few dollars and so did my sister."

Nervously, Minna followed Rosa as she left the Asch Building and walked around the corner. There, leaning against a lamppost, was a young man about Yussel's age. He had a suitcase tucked beneath his feet. He peered around anxiously, awaiting their arrival.

"Rosa!" he called, when he saw them. "Hurry!"

Rosa raced down the block to where he was standing. "This is Minna," she panted. "She says you can write to her and she'll give me the letters."

"Of course, I won't open them," Minna assured him.

"I thank you," he said with dignity.

Minna gave him her name and address. He repeated it a few times to make sure he'd remember it.

"I'll write it down when I get on the train," he said. He turned to his sister. "Rosa, won't you come with me to the station and take the bus back? Then we'll have time to talk."

Rosa nodded. "Of course, I'll come, 'Seppe."

Minna began to turn away.

Guiseppe grabbed her arm. 'Thank you again," he said. It was the first time she had a chance to really look at him. She had been too nervous before and too worried about whether he had her correct address. Involuntarily, she smiled. He was tall and lean. His dark eyes were already slightly crinkled at the corners as if he preferred to smile most of the time.

Minna looked up at him, blushed, and turned away again. "Good luck!" she called over her shoulder. "I'll see you tomorrow, Rosa."

Walking briskly to catch up with Mama and Sarah, she allowed her thoughts to wander. He was handsome, 'Seppe. He looked like a bit of a rogue, too. It was too bad he was leaving… Minna blushed again, shocked at her own thoughts. He was a Catholic. There was no possibility…

She tried to imagine what it would be like if Yussel were forced to leave. How could they live without him? Of course, Rosa had a Papa. That made a big difference.

Catching sight of Mama and Sarah just ahead, she ran after them, clattering down the street. "You see," she gasped, "I told you it would only take a minute."

"What did Rosa want?" Mama asked.

"Oh, nothing. She wanted to show me a pattern," Minna replied, having already decided that she'd tell only Pearl what had happened. Pearl, always first at home, could look out for the letter so Mama wouldn't see it.

Mama looked at her sharply, but said nothing. They walked the rest of the way in silence.

That night, Minna had much to think about. She had already told Pearl what had happened and had been heartened by her ready sympathy.

"You were right," she had said. "What if it was Yussel?"

Reluctantly, she realized she had to tell Yussel, too. She couldn't keep that kind of secret from him. He won't tell anyone, she thought, excusing herself for breaking the promise she had made to Rosa again. I'll feel better if he knows.

After dinner, she suggested that Yussel come for a walk with her. It was either that or waiting till Pearl finished her homework and Mama was in bed so they could have the kitchen to themselves. Yussel refused at first, but catching a glimpse of her expression, changed his mind. "I'd like a little walk without my pack," he laughed.

As they walked down the stoop to the street, Minna said, "We don't have to go far. I just want to tell you something that happened today and ask you what you think."

She told him about Rosa, Guiseppe, and her own offer. She concluded by saying, "I hope you don't think it's wrong. I don't even know Rosa's family but I do know Rosa. He was so young, Yussel. He looked about your age. It's not so much that he's going off on his own. Lots of people do that. It's that he can't see his family or even write to them. If I can fix it so Rosa gets his letters…"

"You were right, Minna. It's a good thought. Even if they are different, they're still people."

"When I see Rosa's cross," Minna began, "I feel… Well, I guess I feel a little uneasy. But when I talk to Rosa, I see she's just the same as me. What do you think?"

"I don't know, Minna. One of my customers is Irish, but she's just as nice as the other ladies."

"In America, we're all supposed to be the same," Minna said dubiously. "But those boys who beat you up when we first came—do you remember? They call us names sometimes—the others. In school, I've heard them."

Yussel shook his head. "I don't know the answer. Except, I do know the only way is to try to take everyone separately, as a person. It's not always easy…"

"Sometimes I feel I can't trust anyone," Minna mused, thinking of Jake. "Other times, it seems as if people are really good. Did I tell you what Mr. Steinberg said?"

Yussel laughed. "You certainly did! All through dinner, you did. If he wasn't old enough to be your father, I'd worry."

Minna blushed, thinking of Jake and her momentary feelings toward Guiseppe. "Mr. Steinberg? It's not that way at all. It's just that he's so wise. I wish I knew his daughter. I think about his words so often. I wish…I wish I had a father like that."

"I wish I did, too." With a visible effort, Yussel changed the subject. "Mama seems better these days, don't you think?"

"I guess so. She's more cheerful at home for sure. But she was always the one to push ahead, to find the way. Now she seems content to let us make all the decisions."

"I think she's tired, tired of being the Mama and the Tata. Now we're old enough to take charge and that's what she wants," Yussel said.

They turned back towards the apartment. "I don't understand how she can simply give up," Minna said half-angrily. "She's still the mother, isn't she?"

"Think of it," Yussel replied. "All her life, she's been trying to do what's best for us and for herself. Tata never helped. Finally, her dream came true. Then, suddenly, in one moment, it was gone, as if it had never been. How can she start all over again?"

"You mean, her dream failed and now she has none?"

"That's one way of saying it. She's not so young any more, you know."

"I won't give up! Never! Even if I live to be a hundred," Minna exclaimed. "It makes me angry that she…"

"I'm not angry. It's our turn now."

"You speak as if she's old. Mama's not so old."

"Look at her, Minna. Look at her face. Look at how she walks, like an old woman. She never did before."

"I will, but I don't want to know if she is…like that. I don't want to think of Mama as…old."

Yussel shook his head. "I know. It's hard."

They didn't speak again until they were almost at the stoop. Minna turned to Yussel. "And you, Yussel? How is it going?"

"I have to walk farther every day. There are too many peddlers. Now, some of my customers are uptown Jews—the Germans. The way they live, Minna. You would be shocked! They act as if I'm a *schnorrer*. Oh, don't worry, they buy. They buy! But when I speak Yiddish, they say they don't understand. They look at me as if I'm a greenhorn. They make me feel ashamed and then I have to say to myself, 'So *nu*, you came here too, once, and you didn't speak English so well either.'"

"One of the girls was telling that she goes to classes at the Alliance. It's run by them, the Germans, and it's as if everything we have, everything we've brought, is all wrong, she says. They want us to learn new ways—their ways. You think they'd help their own kind."

"They don't want to see us as their own kind. They want to be *Amerikaner* all the way."

"If I got here first, I'd help others when they came," Minna said firmly.

"You think you would, but are you sure? What if you were afraid you'd lose what you'd got, that real *Amerikaners* would think you were less good? It's not so simple."

"You're too understanding. I don't want to make excuses for them. It makes me mad!"

'Sometimes, I feel angry, too, but what's the point? I have to get along with my ladies. If I try to understand them, it's easier."

Minna reached out and hugged Yussel. "You're so good. When I heard about Guiseppe, I thought, what if it was Yussel? What if he left us? We couldn't manage without you. I couldn't manage without you. That's why I have to help Rosa."

Yussel hugged her back without saying a word. As they walked up the steps, Minna, following him, noticed how bowed his shoulders were, as if he still carried a heavy pack.

Minna watched Mama surreptitiously over the next few days. It was true. She did walk like an old woman. Her dark eyes were dull, and when she spoke, there was no vitality in her voice. Yet she didn't seem unhappy. She wasn't as angry as she had been. Yussel's right, Minna decided. It's up to us now.

Rosa said little the next few days. When Minna asked her if Guiseppe had gotten off all right, she nodded. "It's hard to talk about it," she said. "Mama's not well and Papa's still angry…" She sewed furiously, exceeding her quota until one of the older women pointed it our to her

Minna looked for Mr. Steinberg at lunchtime every day, but he didn't appear. She felt shy about asking the other cutters, so she continued to wait in the lobby before her walk, hoping he would show up.

One day, Anna caught up with her on the street. "Where do you run to at lunch every day? Are you meeting someone?"

Minna blushed. "Oh no. I just like to take a walk." Thinking Anna might laugh at her, she did not mention Mr. Steinberg.

"I'll come with you, then," Anna said.

Minna looked at her sidewise. Anna wanted to walk with her! "Sure," she managed to say.

"Do you have a fellow?" Anna asked.

"No."

"I don't either."

"What about…you said that Ben was your fellow."

"He's gone. He went out west to find work. I won't see him for a long time. He writes, but I'm not much for letters." She straightened her collar and fluffed her hair. "I'm going to find a new fellow. I'm attending a dance tomorrow night. Would you like to come?"

"A dance?" She was astounded. Mama had always said the dance halls were bad places. 'Someone will take you away and do bad things,' she had warned. Sarah and Bessie didn't go to dances.

Anna noticed her expression. "I know, I know. They say it's a bad place to go, but this hall is all right. It's called the Palais de Danse. Mrs. Fine, who runs it, she's my friend. Besides, I'm not going to work all day and stay home all night." She flung her arms open. "I want to see life! I want to have fun! I'm young. Now's the time. Don't you ever feel that way?"

Minna thought about it. "I don't know," she said slowly. "I've never had time to think of…fun." She remembered when Jake had taken her to the nickelodeon and how she had waited eagerly every week for the day when she would meet him. "My Mama says…"

"I know what your Mama says. My mama used to say it to me, too. But now I live alone and I do what I want. I met Ben at a dance, so if I go, I will meet someone else."

Minna thought of a problem. "But I don't know how to dance."

Anna smiled. Minna thought her smile was like an angel's. "I'll show you. Come to my room tonight and you'll learn. Then we can go tomorrow."

Minna thought about it. What would Mama say? What would Yussel say? She looked down at her hands. I *do* work all day. Why shouldn't I have some fun? In the back of her mind, she thought maybe Jake would find out she had been to a dance hall. That would show him, she thought obscurely.

"You said you live near. I'll come over after dinner if you tell me where."

Anna smiled. "I'm so glad." She gave Minna her address and turned back into the building. 'It's too cold out here," she said. "My coat, it isn't so warm but," she smoothed its blue velvet collar, "isn't it pretty? Ben gave it to me before he left." She smiled, showing her dimples, and ran inside.

Minna looked after her, automatically continuing to walk. To go a dance hall! She wondered what it would be like. Would there be rows of men staring at the women, choosing this one or that? What if no one picks me, she worried. Then she considered something else. What should she wear? What did you wear to a dance hall?

That evening, at dinnertime, she told her family she was going to visit her friend Anna one street over.

"Anna?" asked Sarah, her eyes wide.

"Who's Anna?" Mama asked.

"She sits across from me at work," Minna replied. "She invited me to come visit." Her expression was so unyielding no one dared say another word as she went to get her cloak. "I'll be back soon," she said casually.

She noticed Yussel looking after her with a worried expression on his face, but she paid no attention and hurried down the stairs.

It was cold outside. She crossed her arms in front of her body to keep the wind from blowing through her cloak. As she rushed along the darkened street, she thought about how different it would be at this time of night in the warm weather. The stoops would be filled with people. She'd hear a thousand hellos from friends mingled with catcalls from some of the young men when she strolled by.

Anna's room was two flights up. The building was dingy, with the same cooking smells and loud voices seeping under the doors as her own building. She knocked on Anna's door.

She opened it immediately, saying, "Come in."

Dazzled by her, Minna hardly noticed the apartment at first. After she took her cloak off, she looked around. The room was tiny. It contained a bed, a bureau, and one chair. On the bureau sat a small gas ring and what was obviously the remains of Anna's supper.

"Sit here," Anna offered, gesturing grandly at the single chair. "I'll sit on the bed."

Minna noticed that Anna had laid a coverlet and several embroidered pillows on the bed in an attempt to make it look like a divan. Her clothes dangled from a series of hooks on the wall. Minna stared at them. There were so many.

Following the direction of her gaze, Anna smiled. "Aren't they pretty?" she asked. "I love clothes. Here, look at this." She held up a hand-embroidered white dress in the finest silk. "It took me six months to save up to buy the silk. I embroidered it myself."

Minna reached out to touch it. The stitchery and tiny tucks were intricate and painstaking. "How can you have the patience to make such tiny stitches! Where will you wear such a dress?"

Anna shrugged. "I haven't worn it yet, but I will. Maybe it'll be my wedding dress…or my shroud!" She laughed. "What do you think of my home?"

"It's very nice," Minna said politely. "You live all alone?"

"I've been here for a few months. I left home. My mother died last year and I've been waiting on my father ever since. I worked all day, came home, cleaned the house, made the dinner, gave him my salary—what he knew about, anyway—and then he decided it was time to get me married. He called the *shadchen.* The richest man he knew was a butcher in Brooklyn, a widower. I saw his picture and I thought of my sister, and how she was sold. I'm the youngest. So I said 'no.' My father, he said I had to. I wasn't going to, so one night, after he was asleep, I took my things and left. I knew Ben by then and he helped me find this room."

Minna stared at her, open-mouthed. "So you just walked away? Weren't you afraid to be on your own?"

Anna laughed. "At first, maybe a little. My father said *Kaddish* for me. My sister told me, that's how I found out. She said I could stay with her and help with the children, but I said 'no.' I'll have my own soon enough, but now's the time for fun. Now, while I'm young, I can take care of myself."

Minna tried to imagine what it would be like to be on her own, without a family. There'd be no one to care whether she came home or not. "What if you get sick?" she asked.

"I never get sick. I just don't." Anna jumped up. "Let's practice dancing. You have to know how to dance at the dance hall."

Anna stood in front of her. Placing one of Minna's hands on her shoulder and one on her waist, she began humming softly. As she moved, Minna was jerked off balance and almost fell back into the chair.

"No, silly. You have to follow me. See, I'm showing you with my hands and the way I move my body where I want you to go." She made exaggerated movements until she was sure Minna got the idea. Then she began humming again.

After awhile, Minna began to follow Anna with ease. The room was so small they could only dance in a tight circle. Anna explained that in the dance hall, there would be so many other people on the dance floor, it would be almost the same.

Flushed and happy, Minna sank back in the chair. "It's not so hard to dance!" she exclaimed.

"Of course not," Anna agreed. "Now, there's a couple of things to remember. Bring a handkerchief and put it under the man's hand on your back. If he sweats, you don't want to ruin your dress. It's best to say 'yes' to everyone who asks you, at least once. Mrs. Fine will introduce you in the beginning, but after that, it's up to you. Then if they want to walk you home, that's up to you, too."

Minna listened intently. "But what should I wear?"

"Well, this is what I wear." Anna pulled out a fancy shirtwaist and a serge skirt. "I dress it up with ribbons."

"But how do I deal with mashers…or worse? Mama says…"

"Just keep your eyes open and don't do anything foolish. You can judge people, can't you?"

Minna wasn't so sure, but she didn't want to disagree.

Noticing her worried expression, Anna spoke quickly. "I've never had any problems. Oh well, once I did. I met this fellow and he said I was so beautiful. He said he lived uptown and wanted me to come with him. I was tempted. He was a good-looking fellow, so who wouldn't be? But then I thought, if he lives uptown, what's he doing here? I said 'no' and he kept after me and after me. Finally, I told Mrs. Fine and she sent him on his way."

"You could be in pictures," Minna said.

"I've heard that before." She laughed. "But this is where I live. This is where I work. What do I know from the pictures? I only want to have a little fun."

'But if I looked like you…" Minna began.

"I'm happy here," Anna said. "I'll meet someone who's doing well for himself. I'll help him, we'll have a family. Maybe someday we'll move to the Bronx."

"Still, I think…"

"Meet me here tomorrow at the same time," Anna interrupted, changing the subject. "We'll walk over to Mrs. Fine's Palais de Danse together."

As if under a spell, Minna agreed. Then, glancing at the small clock on Anna's bureau, she jumped up. "I'd better go home now. It's late. They'll be wondering where I am."

On the way home, she thought about tomorrow evening. If it's the way Mama said it would be, I won't stay. I won't tell anyone what I'm doing so they won't worry. I deserve some fun, like Anna says. Who can it hurt, going to the dance hall just this once? All the same, she felt guilty. I'll tell them afterwards, that's what I'll do.

Unbidden, for the first time in a long time, she heard Bubbe's voice saying, 'Ah, don't you know, Minna, when you lie, you become a hostage to the devil. I warn you…' Minna squeezed her face, holding her eyes tightly shut for a moment. I won't listen! I won't listen! I'm old enough to do what I want and what I want is a little fun.

By the time Minna let herself into the apartment, everyone was asleep except for Yussel, who was drinking a glass of tea at the kitchen table. "So, you're back."

"Yes, I'm back. You didn't have to wait up for me," she said angrily.

"I waited up for you because I wanted to make sure you got home all right," he replied.

She looked at the floor. "I'm sorry, it's just that…I want to have some fun once in a while."

"Some fun?" He looked at her, astonished. "What do you mean—some fun?"

'You know, see my friends, go out a little. Not just work, work, come home, sleep, and work some more."

"Oh."

She felt called upon to explain further. 'You should see Anna. She's so beautiful."

"I heard, from Sarah. She lives with her family?"

"She lives alone in one room. She has the most gorgeous clothes, Yussel. You should see the dress she made. The embroidery she did!"

"So, next time, invite her here so we all can enjoy such beauty."

"I will," she said. Remembering tomorrow night, she added, "But I promised to go and see her again tomorrow. I'll ask her to come the next day.' She looked Yussel straight in the eyes, willing him to ask no further questions.

As if he sensed her mood, he paused, and then said, "Well, goodnight then."

"Good night, Yussel."

She lay in bed for a long time, tossing and turning. As she felt Pearl's warm body next to hers, she moved as far over to her corner of the bed as she could. This is wrong, she thought clearly. I shouldn't do this. Yet she knew she would. It was already settled and she no longer had any choice in the matter. After all, I said I'd go, she repeated to herself. I can't let Anna down. Just this once and then I won't do it again.

In the morning, Pearl had trouble rousing her. She walked slowly to the factory, politely ignoring Sarah's whispered questions about Anna. She excused herself, saying "I'm very tired this morning."

Mama was quiet as she always was these days. She doesn't care anyway, Minna thought.

When she slid into her seat, she looked over at Anna, who gave her a big smile.. "I'll see you tonight," she called.

Minna nodded and smiled back.

At lunchtime, the two girls walked together. Anna suggested she bring her good shirtwaist with her and change into it at her room. "That way no one has to know what you're doing. After all," she added, tossing her head, "what business is it of theirs?"

Minna said, "You're right," but when she said the words, she knew they weren't true. It was Yussel's business—and would be Mama's, too, if she cared. So what! She stamped her foot.

"I'll be there," she said several times.

CHAPTER 16

The day passed very slowly. Minna thought it would never be time to go home. At the dinner table, time seemed to stop. She tried to talk to everyone, but all she could think about was the moment of leaving. What would she say? How could she take her good shirtwaist with her? She'd pretend Anna was going to help her fix it. That's what she'd do. She noticed Yussel watching her intensely throughout the dinner.

After she had helped Pearl clean up, Minna said, "I'm going to Anna's again tonight. She's going to show me how to embroider my shirtwaist the way she did her dress."

Mama looked up. "Don't be back too late," she said carelessly.

Pearl was disappointed. "I wanted to talk to you about something," she said. "You spend more time with Anna, the beautiful Anna, than you do with your own family."

Minna forced a laugh. "It has been only two nights. That's not too much, is it?"

Yussel said nothing. Instead, he simply looked at her. "I'll walk you over," he offered.

She didn't know what to say. Finally, she replied, "No, you don't need to. I can go myself."

'But I want to. I'd like to get a little fresh air."

"You're treating me like a baby," Minna complained, raising her voice. "If I want to visit my friend, I can."

Mama looked up.

Minna cleared her throat and spoke softly. "I'm being silly.

Thanks, Yussel. I'd like some company."

As they walked out the door, Minna tried to think of a way to keep Yussel from meeting Anna. She was positive it would be a mistake. What if Anna said something about the dance?

"I don't think it's a good day to meet Anna. She's not expecting you. Yesterday, she was wearing a wrapper."

"I'll come up with you and you can ask her," Yussel replied patiently.

Minna stopped in the street and faced Yussel. "Are you afraid she's a bad friend? Why don't you trust me?"

"Should I trust you?"

She colored and hung her head. "No, you shouldn't," she gulped. "I'm going out with Anna."

"Going out with Anna?"

"Yes," Minna continued defiantly. "We're going to the Palais de Danse. That's Mrs. Fine's dance hall. She's a friend of Anna's."

"To a dance hall?"

"You don't have to repeat everything I say, Yussel. I think I deserve a little fun. That's what Anna says."

He frowned. "So you lied to me, you lied to Pearl, you lied to Mama. Is that the way you have fun?"

She began to cry. "But, could I have said, 'I'm going to a dance hall?' It would have been labeled a sin. I don't see why it's so bad. Anna says it's all right. She's gone lots of times. That's how she met her fellow, Ben."

Yussel said nothing.

"I'm sixteen now. I never do something…something for myself."

His eyes narrowed. "I suppose everyone else does."

"Well, nothing's happened to Anna. I'm not a baby. I can take care of myself. It will be all right!"

"Lying is not taking care of yourself!" He raised his voice. "Since when is life supposed to be fun? Tell me where the fun is, Minna. Carrying a pack all day, is that fun? Coming home too tired to do more than eat of sleep, is that fun? So we go for a walk in the park once in a while. What else is there? Maybe some day…"

"Sure, someday! By the time I'm a hundred years old, that's someday!" She sobbed harder.

He turned away. "I can't do this all alone," he muttered.

She looked up. "I know!" she cried. "It isn't fair. But I'm doing my part. If I have enough energy at the end of the day to go somewhere and do something, why can't I? Why can't I have friends and be like the other girls?"

She stopped and touched his shoulder. "Look, why can't we do things together? Come with me tonight. Or, if we don't go to the dance hall, there are free lectures. It's all right to go to a lecture, isn't it? There are classes and concerts. One of the girls was telling me about it. We can even go to the Alliance."

He turned. "At the end of the day, I don't want to do anything. I'm always worrying…"

"You wouldn't worry so much if you had something else on your mind, Yussel. Can't we at least try?"

He shrugged.

She looked at him earnestly. "Don't you see, Yussel? For me, there has to be something else. Maybe not the dance hall. But…something… There *has* to be." She gripped his arm.

'He sighed. "I…envy you, Minna. Since the store burned, I've felt hopeless. I used to think about working on a farm some day. I knew it was unlikely to happen, but I could see it. I could see it as clear as I can still see *der alter heym*. Then I'd get so angry at Tata. If he hadn't left… if he had taken care of his family…"

Minna hugged him. "Oh, Yussel." She remembered the resolutions she had made in the park, her determination to help Yussel so he wouldn't be alone. "Oh, Yussel," she repeated.

He tried to laugh. "It's not so bad."

"It is bad, and I'm making it worse. But, Yussel," she shook her head, "I am working and bringing home money. I do try to help you. You know I don't want to make it harder for you, but it's just not enough for me, this life. If I don't try to change it for myself, no one will."

"If you don't try to change it for yourself, no one will," Yussel repeated. "That's true, Minna. But is going to a dance hall the way to change it?"

She flushed. "Maybe not."

"Look, we both need some fresh air in our lives. Let's get a lecture schedule. That much I can do."

She smiled tremulously. "It'll be a start." Then she remembered. "But I can't just not go to Anna's. She's expecting me. What shall I say? It's not her fault."

"I'll go with you," he said. "I'll explain."

"Maybe she won't want to go alone. Maybe I've ruined her evening."

"I'll talk to her," he repeated. "If she's a friend, she'll understand."

They continued on their way. As they approached Anna's apartment, Minna began to feel very uncomfortable. Finally, she said, "Don't say anything, Yussel. Won't you wait downstairs and let me tell her? I'll be right down. If you come, it looks as if I can't make up my own mind."

"You'll come right down?"

"I promise."

He nodded his agreement.

As Minna entered Anna's building, she paused. What could she say? I won't lie again, she thought. I'll never lie again. I'll just have to say, 'I can't', that's all, and 'my brother's waiting downstairs.' She'll probably never talk to me again.

Her thoughts lingered for a moment on her vision of the dance hall. On herself, gracefully gliding around the room in the arms of a handsome man, smiling up at him. The music… She made herself stop. What do I think, I'll meet a millionaire? She walked firmly to Anna's door and knocked.

"It's me," she called. "It's Minna."

Anna flung the door open. "You're late! Come in and change so we can go."

Despite her preoccupation, Minna noticed how lovely Anna looked with her cheeks flushed and her soft shirtwaist clinging to her body. Her heart sank.

"Oh Anna. I can't go," she blurted. "See, I brought my blouse." She held it up. "I was going to go, but Yussel, my brother, he found out and he says…" She stopped.

"You can't go." Anna's face fell. "What does your brother say?"

"He says I can't go to a dance hall. I suppose he's right. Anyway, I have to… No, I want to do what he says. He works so hard…" She smiled weakly.

"So, we all work hard. Come anyway, Minna. You deserve a little fun."

"I can't. He's waiting for me downstairs. I can't."

"He's waiting for you downstairs? Your brother? I'd like to meet him and tell him a few things!"

"Oh no, I'd better just go." She turned to leave.

Anna's face brightened. "Look," she said, holding Minna's arm. "I'll walk down with you. I'm going to go anyway. You can at least introduce me to your brother. Maybe I can change his mind."

Minna shook her head sadly. "It's not his fault. I suppose he's right." Now that she was with Anna, visions of the dance hall beckoned again. "Of course, I want to see it…" Her voice firmed and she shook her head. "I can't, that's all."

Anna grabbed her coat with one hand and shut the door behind her with the other. "I'll just walk down with you," she said soothingly. "That's all. I won't say anything." Taking Minna's arm, she almost pushed her down the stairs.

Minna's mind raced. Suppose Yussel insulted Anna. Suppose Anna insulted Yussel. She dragged her feet and walked as slowly as she could.

"Don't worry." Anna squeezed her arm. "I won't make a problem. I understand. Why do you think I moved out of my house?"

They walked through the outside door and down the front steps of the apartment. Yussel was waiting there at the bottom, looking up at them. He smiled when he saw Minna.

"This is Anna," Minna said awkwardly when they were halfway down the steps. "She's going to go anyway, so we walked down together…" Her voice trailed off.

Yussel stared at Anna the way some of the men did at the factory. Minna followed his gaze. In her new coat with the velvet collar, her eyes sparkled. When she smiled at Yussel, her dimples flickered.

"My name's Anna Gold," she cooed, holding out her hand.

"Yussel Ruben." He clasped her hand for a moment. Reluctantly, he let it go. "I'm glad to meet you," he mumbled.

"I'm glad to meet the villain, too." Anna's laugh removed any sting from the words. "I'm sorry you don't think it would be good for Minna to come with me tonight. Mrs. Fine's dance hall is very safe and I don't like to go alone."

"Alone? You're going to go anyway?"

"Of course." Anna laughed again. "Unless you'd like to come, too."

Yussel almost nodded 'yes'. Recollecting himself, he shook his head. "We'll walk you there, won't we, Minna?"

Without waiting for an answer, he took Anna's arm. As she

showed him the way to go, Minna followed behind, gazing at Yussel in amazement.

"It's around the corner, this way," Anna said, looking back at Minna and winking.

She was dumfounded. Viewing Yussel's back as he leaned towards Anna, she thought about it. It was true, he wasn't bad looking. If his expression was careworn most of the time, it certainly wasn't now. As he glanced back to make sure Minna was following, she saw that his eyes glowed and his back was straight. She shook her head and smiled to herself.

All too soon, they arrived at the dance hall, which was on the ground floor of an empty building. The sounds of music drifted through the large glass windows onto the street. 'Palais de Danse' was written on a placard pinned on the door.

"Usually it's upstairs," Anna explained, "but Mrs. Fine is allowed to use this empty store front till it's occupied."

Minna looked through the window. Inside, she could see many people, some dancing and others sitting along the sides of the room. Faces were flushed and feet beat time to a waltz played on the piano by a young boy. As Minna continued to peer inside, she could see that the men, dressed in their best suits, were the same ones she saw in the streets and at the factory every day. Here and there, she could pick out a real sport, dressed to the nines in a fashionable jacket and spats. The women were neither plain nor beautiful, yet they looked happy as they whirled around the floor.

An older woman, standing near the door, looked up as they stood outside. When she saw Anna, she smiled and opened the door. "Come in, come in, my dear. Your admirers have been waiting for you. And your friends?"

"Thank you for walking me here," Anna said to Yussel. "I'm sorry you can't come, Minna. Won't you consider changing your mind? You can see, it's not so terrible." She looked up at Yussel. "I'd like it if you came."

He flushed.

Minna stepped forward. "Maybe we could just go in and look for a moment." The music was enticing. "What can happen to me if you're there, Yussel?"

He hesitated.

"It costs money to go in," Anna said. "Not for me, because I know Mrs. Fine."

Yussel shook his head. "We'll leave," he said. "Have a good time, Anna."

She looked disappointed. "I'm sorry. Maybe next time. I'll see you tomorrow, Minna." She swept inside, shutting the door behind her.

As Minna and Yussel watched through the window, they saw Anna taking off her coat and becoming almost immediately surrounded by a group of men. Smiling, she accepted the arm of one and began to dance. The sound of the music reverberated through the street as brother and sister turned silently away.

The street seemed darker than usual. In her mind's eye, Minna could still see Anna whirling away with the young man. She thought she could still hear the faint tinkle of the piano, fading as they walked on.

"It didn't look so bad," Minna said finally.

When Yussel didn't reply, she continued, "Anna taught me how to dance. Would you like me to teach you?"

"She already has a fellow?" he asked. "Was he there?"

"Ben was her fellow. Now he's gone away. She's beautiful, isn't she? At work, I can hardly stop looking at her."

"I'd like to learn how to dance," he said slowly.

She stopped. "It's like this. You hold me like this." She positioned his hands as Anna had put hers. "You show me what you want me to do with your hands and by moving your body. That's what Anna said. Of course, I never danced with a man. Then you keep time to the music, like this." Humming, she began to move, pulling Yussel along with her. "Except you lead me, not me you."

She kept humming. Stumbling slightly, Yussel began to take the lead. They both stopped suddenly.

"We're *meshuggeneh*, dancing in the streets," he said.

"It's not as nice as the Palais de Danse," Minna said wistfully.

"It didn't look so bad," Yussel said thoughtfully.

She held her breath.

'But we have no money to spend on such. We're barely managing to scrape by as it is, and we need to keep enough to put a little in the moneybox. To spend it on such foolishness!" He began to walk more quickly.

"Anna Gold," he mused, as they arrived at their stoop. "Where is she from in *de alter heym*? A *landsleiter*—from Russia as we are?"

"I don't know. You liked her, eh?"

"She is the most beautiful woman I've ever seen."

Piqued, even a little jealous, Minna realized it would be better not to tease Yussel. "Yes?" she said.

"She lives alone?" Yussel asked.

Minna nodded.

Yussel shook his head and almost bounded up the stairs to their apartment. Minna caught a glimpse of his expression as he rounded the corner at the first landing. His mouth was set and his eyes bleak.

When they entered the apartment, she was surprised to find Sarah, Bessie, and Pearl sitting around the kitchen table. Closing her eyes for a moment, she could almost hear the music from the Palais de Danse. Opening them, she saw their familiar faces. It was as if the evening had never happened. Yussel, she thought, might feel the same way, for he went to the stove and poured himself a glass of tea without saying a word. Sarah, Minna noticed, looked at him longingly. Bessie and Pearl were too deep in conversation to do more than smile at them as they walked in.

Yussel sat at the table sipping his glass of tea. Sarah watched him. "You didn't stay with Anna long," she said to Minna.

"No, Minna said, forgetting the lie about her shirtwaist. "She went to the dance hall."

"Maybe I can help you with your shirtwaist," Sarah said.

Yussel put down his glass of tea and stared off into the distance.

"Oh no, thanks," Minna tried to say casually. "I'll fix it another time."

She wanted to shake Yussel, to call his name, so he would come back to them. "Yussel," she called.

He looked up, his eyes dreamy.

"Oh, nothing" Minna said, looking away. It's Anna he's going to like, she thought. Out of everyone, he has to pick Anna? No matter how hard she tried, she couldn't imagine the two of them together.

She began to talk loudly. "We walked Anna over to the Palais de Danse. Then we came home," she said to Sarah.

Yussel looked up when he heard Anna's name.

It seemed so obvious to Minna. She was sure Sarah would notice. "What are you two talking about?" she asked Bessie and Pearl.

"Bessie brought home a lecture schedule from *The Forward.* We're looking through it" Pearl said.

"You did? Yussel and I were just talking about that, weren't we?"

Yussel looked up and nodded vaguely.

Minna wanted to shake him to make him pay attention. Instead, she stood behind Pearl and Bessie, reading over their shoulders. Slowly, Sarah joined her.

The schedule was full. Every day of the week, it seemed, there was another lecture. It was possible to learn about mesmerism, a trip to Paris, to hear new poems read by the poets who wrote them, to listen to music… Minna was astounded. Forgetting Yussel and Anna, she perused the program avidly.

"If I went to all these lectures, it would be like going to college!" she exclaimed.

Bessie shook her head. "They're interesting, but they never tell you quite enough. I always have so many questions they don't answer,

"So, *nu*, it would be good to have those kinds of questions for a change. Shall we all go? Which ones should we attend? We can't go to every one of them—there's too many."

Yussel remained wrapped in his thoughts while the four girls discussed their choice of lectures. It was finally decided that the three older girls would attend one at Cooper Union in a few days on the subject of Darwin.

Yussel looked up. "About Darwin? I don't think so. Not this week, anyway."

Sarah eyed him anxiously as she and Bessie said good night and retired to the front room. Pearl went to the toilet in the hall before going to bed, leaving just Minna and Yussel in the kitchen.

Minna tried to think of what to say to her brother. He was so preoccupied, no words came to her.

When Pearl came back, Yussel had not moved. He sat in the same position, his elbows resting on the table and his head in his hands. He said goodnight to Pearl in a soft voice.

Patting his shoulder, Minna said softly, "Goodnight, Yussel."

"Good night," he muttered and remained seated, his expression unchanging.

The next day at the factory, Minna watched Anna closely as she sat down. She thought she knew how Yussel felt. The question was, how did she feel?

"Did you have a good time last night?" she asked.

"Oh yes," Anna replied. "I'm sorry you couldn't come."

"I was, too. Yussel wanted to stay…"

Just then, the lights flickered and the machines were turned on. No more conversation was possible. Minna looked avidly at Anna all morning, trying to see a flaw in her beauty.

At lunchtime, she hurried over to her machine. What kind of a person was she? If she could make Yussel act the way he did…

Anna smiled at her. "I can't have lunch with you today, Minna. I met a fellow at the dance hall and he asked me to meet him a lunchtime. He works down the street."

"Oh, sure," Minna said. She wanted to ask about Yussel, but she clenched her teeth. She knew it would be a mistake. He would hate it.

As she walked slowly back to her own seat, planning to have lunch by her machine, Rosa looked up at her anxiously.

"I'm sorry, Rosa. I would have told you right away if I had received a letter. How's your mother doing?"

"She cries all the time, worrying about 'Seppe. It's been too long, she says, since we've heard from him. Maybe something happened. I miss him so much, Minna. It's all I think about lately."

Minna patted her hand. "I know. I'd feel the same way if it was Yussel."

"Even Papa's sorry now, I think. He doesn't say it, but I can tell. I hope I'll hear soon."

"I hope so, too." Minna consoled her. "Look, he's probably starting a new job and he's doing so well he just doesn't have time to write. I bet that's what it is."

Rosa shook her head. "He knows how much we're all worrying. He'd write."

Minna didn't know what to say. To change the subject, she asked, "Do you ever go to lectures?"

'Oh, no," Rosa replied. "I have to stay in at night."

"Oh. I'm going to my first one the day after tomorrow. It's about Darwin."

"We don't talk about him," Rosa said. "It's stupid to think we come from monkeys! Father Halloran says it's against God's will to blaspheme about Creation."

"I don't know much about it yet," Minna replied weakly.

"That's why I'm going to the lecture."

Rosa smiled. "It's okay for you. Mama would die if she even thought we were talking about it."

Minna munched her apple and Rosa nibbled on a chunk of cheese. Finally Minna said, "I hope I get a letter very soon."

"I do, too."

As she sewed the rest of the afternoon, Minna thought about their conversation. Rosa didn't look so different, but she lived by different rules. Imagine not being allowed to learn about Darwin—or anything else, for that matter! I wonder if Tata would have forbidden me to go to the lectures. He certainly wouldn't have wanted me to go to college. He seemed so far away from her life, as if he was a stranger. Perhaps, she thought, Mama feels the same way.

That evening, as they walked home, she stayed next to Mama. "The factory's not so bad if I don't have to do it the rest of my life," she said.

"No, it's not," Mama replied. "Not so good, either."

"We've already saved up some money..." Minna began.

"As long as we can live and have a little food on the table, I'm content," Mama said loudly. "As God is my witness, I'm content!"

Obviously trying to be companionable, she turned to Minna. "Did you have a nice time with your friend, Anna, last night?"

"Oh, yes," Minna stumbled.

Sarah came up and asked a question, allowing Minna to walk ahead by herself. She thought of Anna and wondered how Yussel would be tonight. She frowned as she pictured Anna running out to meet her new fellow. If only Yussel had never met her. It's my fault, she thought. If I hadn't wanted to go to the dance, it would never have happened.

Minna was prepared to meet the unfamiliar preoccupied Yussel of last night, so she was surprised to see his usual smile when he came in about an hour after they arrived home.

"Yussel!" She jumped up to greet him.

He slipped the pack off his shoulders. "I'm glad to be home," he said in his usual tone of voice. "How was the factory today?"

"As usual," Minna replied.

Before she had a chance to say anything else, Pearl interrupted. "Yussel, I need you to help me. I don't understand my arithmetic."

He rubbed his hands. "Nothing I'd like better."

Mama hovered over him, handing him a glass of tea and taking his jacket from him.

Minna looked around the table. Despite her fears, everything was the same as it always was. Nothing had changed. Yussel was still Yussel.

All through dinner, she continued to watch him. As usual, he regaled the table with the story of his ladies and their difficult demands. Laughing, he told about one uptown customer who wanted a ribbon for her dog. "It had to be just the right color," he explained. "We held it up to the creature to make sure it harmonized!"

Minna remembered the small dog they had seen the day they went to Central Park. "It's a dog's life!" she said, and joined in the laughter.

Sarah laughed, too, and seemed more at ease than she had yesterday. Even Mama seemed to be in one of her rare good moods.

I must have been crazy, Minna thought, making up a grand romance. Yussel is fine. Maybe he was tired yesterday, or he thinks she is beautiful. It doesn't mean his whole life is changed. Her thoughts veered to Jake. My life isn't changed either, she thought sadly, almost wishing it were.

"Do you think ladies really go into a decline?" she asked the table at large.

Everyone stared at her. She realized she had voiced her thoughts out loud. "It was in a book I read," she added hastily.

"For love?" Pearl asked.

Minna nodded.

"That's only in books," she said scornfully.

"Who has time to decline?" Bessie asked.

"Decline, I don't know," Sarah said. "But you can…it can…be part of your life. Love can be there every day, even if the person doesn't love you back."

There was silence. Sarah, embarrassed, looked around the table for support. "Don't you think so, Minna?"

Minna shook her head. "I don't think any one declines exactly…" she began.

"Foolish love is best forgotten," Yussel snapped.

Sarah blushed.

Mama looked up. "In America, they talk about love all the time.

The songs I hear, they're always about love. In *der alter heym*, we didn't worry about love. We did our duty to our children and our man, that's all."

"So, love is just for Americans?" Minna dared to ask.

Bessie laughed. "If they spent as much time worrying about the hungry as they do about love, this would be Utopia."

"I don't know. I think it's romantic," Minna said. "Maybe for some people, it's true."

"Not for me!" Yussel jumped up and began clearing the table. "There are more important things in life," he continued over his shoulder.

Mama nodded in agreement.

Minna stood up. Yussel sounded angry. I'll talk to him later, she thought as she handed him the dishes. But when she tried to, after everyone else was asleep, he shrugged and changed the subject. Finally, she went to bed, where she tossed and turned all night.

CHAPTER 17

The next day, Minna left for work early, before Mama and Sarah, hoping to have a chance to talk to Anna. She waited at the door for her to arrive. She finally saw her strolling along the street in animated conversation with a man. At the factory door, she looked up at him, her dimples flickering.

"I'll be by at lunchtime," he called as he left.

"Is that your new fellow?" Minna asked.

"He wants to be. But I got a letter from Ben. I'm not making up my mind in a hurry."

As they waited for the elevator, Minna spoke quietly, "I think my brother, Yussel, really liked you."

"I liked him, too," Anna said politely. "But let me tell you about Jerry, the man I was talking to. He's going into business for himself. He says he's been waiting for the right girl to come along. He'd want me to open the shop for him. It would be just the two of us—his family's not here. That's good, don't you think?" She looked at Minna brightly. "I don't want to have another Mama hanging over me. One was enough!" She laughed.

Minna forced herself to smile in agreement. Poor Yussel, she thought. It's no use.

"He took me dancing last night and out to a restaurant," Anna said proudly. She held out her arm. "Look! He gave me a bracelet. If he's giving me bracelets now, what will come later? Of course, I'd like him if he didn't give me anything," she added piously. 'But," she flashed, dancing to her seat, "It's nice when he does!"

Sorrowfully, Minna sat down at her machine. As they began to whir, she thought, at least Yussel knows. She's not for him. Anna began to seem less beautiful. Then, by accident, her gaze wandered in her direction for a moment and she was struck again by the perfection of her appearance. It was partly the way she held her head as if to say, I know my own value.

When everyone stopped for lunch, Minna hurried to get her cloak. She hoped to meet Mr. Steinberg. I can talk to him about this, she thought.

She peered around the lobby looking for him. He wasn't there. Glumly, she stepped out to the street and began to walk down the block. She had only gone a few steps where she was interrupted.

"Do you mind if I walk with you? Steinberg, the poet, asked me to look out for you."

She looked up, startled. She saw a tall, thin young man, his pallid face almost translucent in its whiteness. Yet, despite his slight stoop, he looked, she thought, like someone she'd want to know. Perhaps it was his eyes, which glowed with a rare intensity.

'My name's Saul," he said, ignoring her surprise as he held out his hand. "I work with Steinberg. He's been staying in to do extra work and he wanted me to tell you he hadn't forgotten you."

Despite her disappointment, Minna smiled, relieved to know that Mr. Steinberg was thinking of her. "It was good of him to remember me."

"He's like that."

"He's the wisest man I know!" Minna exclaimed. "When he tells me something, I go home and think about it over and over."

"He's a good man—and a good poet. Do you mind if I walk with you, Minna?"

She looked at him. He appeared harmless enough, except for those eyes. "All right," she said.

They walked for a little way until she asked shyly, "Are you a poet, too?"

"Not a poet, a writer. I met Mr. Steinberg at the paper and he got me this job until I can sell more of my work."

"What do you write?"

"Stories… articles… I write about this life we lead. I'd like to learn to write in English as well as Yiddish. There's something to be learned from the way we live that no one's told yet."

"The way we live? But all we want is to live the way real

Americans live. So what's to tell?"

Saul stopped. "What's to tell? There's a hundred stories on this street right now. See that man over there?"

She followed his gaze. She saw an old man in a shabby coat, its sleeves pulled down over his hands. The man staggered as he wavered down the street. Behind his unkempt beard, she saw his mouth moving. He was talking to himself.

"That old *schnorrer*? What kind of a story can you tell about him?"

"Well…" Saul pursed his lips, considering for a moment. "He is poor and old. He's alone, because he came to this country and left his family behind. He became very successful here. He came to owning a little business and he thought of getting married, not remembering his little wife Dora in *der alter heym* and his children, Jacob and Rachel. He looked around for a good wife. He had enough money to live in Brooklyn, you see, and soon, he would hire a man to run his shop for him. His wife in *der alter heym*, she was starving. Then his children died and his wife, she died, too, thinking he was dead or had forgotten them—which he had." He paused.

'So *nu*, he's a big success. Why is he walking the streets like a beggar?" she asked, fascinated in spite of herself.

"Well," he continued, his voice growing more serious, "he found a little wife. So young and plump. He wasn't so young any more now. He was making the arrangements when suddenly, clear as day, he saw the spirit of his real wife. She was thin and scrawny, her cheeks gray with pain. He couldn't go through with it. He thought, at least I'll send her some money so she can live. But when he wrote to the old address, his letter came back with a note from the village Rabbi. 'Now they're all dead,' the note said. 'May God be with her and your children.' The man felt so guilty, he neglected his business. Around every corner, he thought he saw his Dora staring at him reproachfully. You see his lips moving? He's talking to her, trying to explain why he didn't write or send her money."

Minna stared after the old beggar. "Really?"

Saul laughed. "I don't know from really. It could be."

She stared at him in amazement.

"Or maybe he's just come to this country. His son sent for him after many years. He is so happy his son finally sent for him, but when he arrives, he discovers that his son's wife doesn't keep a *kosher* home. His grandchildren don't know from the old ways and they laugh at him. He's given a little room in the apartment and soon he understands that he's to keep out of everyone's way. Sure, he sits down to dinner, but how can he eat if the food is *treyfe*? He's worked all his life—maybe he was jeweler—and now, what's to do? He sits in his room. He sits all day. He's afraid to come out. His son isn't home all day and he's so busy, he doesn't have time to worry about an old man. He thinks, 'I didn't have to send for him. I did right. I took care of him. Now it's my own family that's important.' He forgets when he was a boy, what the father did for him. He sacrificed so he could go to *shul* and later, he sent him to America. One day, the old man walks out of the apartment without telling anyone and he never goes back. 'A roof over my head is not a home,' he says to himself. He'd like to go back to *der alter heym*, but he has no money and besides, they're all dead back there. So he lives on the streets, I don't know how, but at least he's still free to make his own life."

"Which is true?" Minna asked.

"How do I know? Maybe neither." He shrugged.

Minna shook his arm. "You're making it all up. I thought…"

"I was just trying to show you that we are Americans, yes, but we are different. There are a thousand such stories to be written and they all happen here, in 1910, in New York City."

She swung around and looked after the old man again. She narrowed her eyes. "You're right. Either one could be true."

"Or half a dozen others."

"In Yiddish, I can see. But would anyone want to read such a story in English? What do they care about such stories?"

"They should care," he said seriously. "We're part of this country, too. In ten, twenty, thirty years, there won't be such stories about us. We'll all be real Americans then. Shouldn't we have a way to remember what it was like when we first came? And our children and our grandchildren—they should understand, too."

"I guess so," she replied dubiously. "I don't know. I want to be the same, not different. I hope my children," she blushed, "will be better. I want them to be real Americans. Don't you?"

"I wouldn't know, since I don't have any yet. But I hope they won't forget what there was in their parents to make them come here and how hard it was at first."

She looked away, embarrassed. This was a very personal conversation to be having with someone she had just met, a stranger, talking about children and grandchildren.

As if he sensed her feelings, Saul changed the subject. 'So, tell me about yourself, Minna. I've been talking about my ideas all the time. It's a habit I have."

Minna laughed, recovering her equilibrium. "If you know so much, why don't you tell me?"

'Well…" He looked her up and down. "I already know, because Steinberg told me, you don't want to work in a factory all your life. I'd know, anyway. You didn't look very happy when I first saw you walking by yourself. There's some problem… An affair of the heart? Let me think. If it was an affair of the heart, you'd be thinking of him right now, your prince. No, I think…"

He stopped as he saw her eyes fill with tears. "I'm sorry. I get to talking and I forget there's someone listening. I'm very sorry."

She shook her head. "It's not me, it's…someone I know. He likes a girl who will never like him. He's so good and for him to be suffering…"

"It makes you suffer, too. Is that it?"

She nodded. "It's so unfair!" she cried. "He should have his pick of anyone, but…he doesn't have any money and he doesn't know how to…show off. It isn't fair!"

'Who said life was fair?" he said softly. Touching Minna's arm, he added, "I don't think anyone really dies for love, do you? For a poet, it's not a bad thing. Helps the inspiration. For others, it can be only a dream. We don't get all our dreams in this life."

"I know that. It doesn't make it any better."

"This man you care about. Maybe you, yourself, wish to take the other girl's place?"

"Oh, no. He's my brother. I just want him to be happy. He works so hard. He's always worked so hard."

"Would he want you to worry about him like this?"

Her hand flew to her mouth. "He would hate that I even knew. And now I've told you. I don't even know you!"

"That's all right. I don't know him, so it's no problem. Besides, telling me is like…like telling yourself. That's what a writer does, he listens."

She still felt uncomfortable.

"You were going to talk to Steinberg about it, weren't you?

"Yes."

"Well, then."

'He could be my father. I don't mind talking to him. You're…well, you're young. It's different."

He sighed. "It's no different. We can be friends, too."

She still looked doubtful.

"I'd like to be your friend, Minna," he said seriously. "It's all right. I…I have a sweetheart. She writes to me. But I don't have a lot of friends."

She turned and looked him full in the face. "You have a sweetheart?" she asked, relieved.

"Yes."

"Then we can be friends." She smiled at him.

He smiled back.

Looking at him closely for the first time, Minna noticed that his whole expression changed when he smiled. She gave a little skip. Suddenly, she felt very happy.

"I'm going to a lecture tonight," she boasted.

"Oh? Which one?" he asked.

"At Cooper Union. It's about Darwin."

"Who's speaking?"

"I don't know. It's the first time I've ever gone. For me, it's very exciting."

"I remember, I felt the same way when I first started going to lectures. I thought, what a great country! For nothing, I can educate myself. Of course, it's not that easy. Popular culture…"

'What do you mean, popular culture? What's that?"

He shook his head. "I won't say anything else. You go to the lecture and see what you think. Tomorrow, at lunchtime, you'll tell me."

"All right."

They headed back to the Asch Building. As they turned the corner, Minna gasped. "I forgot to eat my lunch!"

"What a compliment! When I 'm a famous writer and everyone praises me, I'll say the best compliment I ever had was that I made Minna forget her lunch."

She laughed. "And you?" she asked, hurriedly unwrapping her bit of cheese. "What about your lunch?"

He shrugged. "I don't eat lunch."

"You don't eat lunch?" She paused in front of the doorway. She examined him, noticing again how thin and pale he was. Decisively, she broke her bit of cheese in half, tore her bread, and handed them to him. "Here, take this. I won't have time to eat it all, anyway."

He hesitated.

"Go on. I had a big breakfast."

"Thanks," he said finally. "I don't mind if I do." Hastily, he began to bite into the cheese.

"I'd give you half of my apple, too," Minna said, 'if I had a knife to cut it with."

"Oh, I'm not really hungry" Saul said, as he swallowed the cheese rapidly. "But thanks, Minna."

They stood next to each other in the elevator. As Saul got out on the eighth floor, he called, "Have a good time tonight! I'll see you tomorrow."

"I'll see you tomorrow," she called back.

Throughout the rest of the afternoon, she found herself remembering their conversation. It made her feel warm and comfortable. It's nice to have a new friend, she decided. Although she still found herself eyeing Anna, she seemed less important than she had before lunch.

As soon as the day was over, Minna grabbed Sarah's arm. "Let's hurry," she urged. "We're going to the lecture tonight."

"I wish Yussel would come," Sarah said.

"He'll come another time. I'm sure he will. I'll try to get him to come," she amended. "It'd be good for him."

Walking home, Minna almost bounced in her excitement.

"What are you so excited about?" Mama asked.

"Tonight's the lecture," Minna replied. "I told you about it last night. Maybe you'd like to come."

Mama shook her head. "I'm too tired. I need to sleep for tomorrow."

"I'll tell you all about it," Minna said. "We'll all learn!"

Mama smiled tolerantly. "I'm sure you will." She stretched her arms. "I'll be glad to get home."

As soon as dinner was over, Bessie, Minna, and Sarah got ready to go to Cooper Union. Yussel watched them. Thinking he might be regretting his decision to stay home, Minna asked him again if he'd like to join them.

"Not tonight," he said. "Maybe another time."

Sara brightened.

"I'll tell you all about it tomorrow, Pearl," Minna promised.

"I don't see why I can't go."

"Because you still have to go to school, that's why."

"When I graduate, I'm going to go to lectures every night!" Pearl stated defiantly.

"That's fine with me," Minna laughed.

At the lecture hall, Minna was amazed when she saw how many people were present. Safely ensconced in the middle of the auditorium, she watched as they pushed and shoved to find room. Many struggled to find a place to sit. The man sitting next to her held a notebook and a pencil in his lap.

Minna looked worriedly at Bessie. "Should I be writing down what they say?"

Bessie shook her head. "What you want to know, you'll remember."

A hush fell over the room as a youngish man ascended to the podium. He surveyed the audience for a moment and cleared his throat. To Minna's surprise, he spoke in Yiddish.

"Charles Darwin was born in 1809," he began.

Minna settled back to listen. As he continued, she heard references she didn't understand. Social Darwinism...Jack London...Malthus... She wished she had brought a notebook so she could write down the words and ideas that puzzled her.

When the lecture was finished, the audience began to buzz. The lecturer asked if there were any questions.

An angry looking older man stood up. "You blaspheme when you mention this man's name. The Bible tells us that the Lord created the earth and all upon it. In Genesis..."

The speaker interrupted. "Charles Darwin was a scientist. Matters of faith are another subject entirely. I cannot..."

The man began to yell. "You speak with the words of the devil! Darwin was a blasphemer. The Bible..."

The audience began to hiss. Those sitting next to the man pulled him back into his seat. "We come here to learn, not listen to the Bible," one man called.

Another voice erupted from the back. "You're saying you can't listen to the Bible and learn?"

A woman sitting near the girls yelled out, "It's the bosses who use the theory of natural selection. Is it right we should be trampled by the so-called fittest? I say…"

Suddenly the whole room was in an uproar. From every corner, men and women were standing up yelling at each other. Minna was shocked. She nudged Bessie. "Does this always happen?"

Bessie's eyes were gleaming. "Sometimes," she said. "Look! The speaker is leaving."

Minna looked up at the stage. She saw the speaker shrug his shoulders and leave. The commotion continued. Voices rose. She noticed that some people were standing and putting on their coats. Fascinated by the hubbub, she wanted to stay, but Sarah tugged at her hand.

'Let's go," she whispered.

Minna looked at Bessie.

"It's all right. They'll calm down soon," she said. "If you think this is strong, you should attend some of our Union meetings!"

"I still want to go," Sarah said.

Feeling uncomfortable between the two of them, Minna stood up. "I don't see anything to worry about, but if you want to go, we can, Sarah."

As they began to file towards the door, Bessie joined them. "I guess I'll come, too. What did you think of the lecture, Minna?"

Minna turned to answer her when they were outside. "I thought it was really interesting." The words, 'survival of the fittest', 'natural selection', 'descended from the apes' chased through her mind. "I certainly learned something. But there's more that I don't understand. Maybe you know who Malthus was. And Jack London? What does he have to do with it? I feel as if I came in at the end without knowing the beginning."

Bessie smiled. "That's one of the problems of these lectures. They never tell you enough. What you're supposed to do is go to the library and find out about Malthus and Social Darwinism. Well, not what you're supposed to do, but what you can do."

"Oh."

"Well, at least I know more than I did when I started," Sarah said. "That's all I expected."

"A friend of mine says that lectures are to pique your interest, that's all. To really learn, you have to do some work, not just sit and listen," Bessie continued.

"Oh," Minna repeated. She was quiet the rest of the way home thinking it.

As they arrived at the steps, she turned to Bessie and Sarah again. "Do you believe we come from monkeys?"

Sarah shrugged. "I don't care all that much. We're here, aren't we? Why does it matter?"

"I don't agree," Bessie said quickly. "It does make a difference. It makes what I do different, too, when I know about it."

Minna opened her arms. "I want to learn more! I want to know what makes a difference for me!"

Bessie patted her on the shoulder. "You will, Minna. If it's important to you, then you will."

They entered the apartment as quietly as they could. The door to the kitchen was open. Minna could see Yussel sitting at the table, staring into space. She went in.

"Oh Yussel, it was so exciting! I learned all about evolution." She said the unfamiliar word proudly. "After the lecture, there was a big ruckus with people disagreeing. You should come next time, you really should."

As if waking from a dream, he listened. "So now you know all about evolution?" he asked ironically. "A few hours, and you're an expert?"

She blushed. "Well, at least I know a little about it. That's more than I did before."

Sarah and Bessie stuck their heads in the doorway. "Good night, Minna. Good night, Yussel," they called.

"Let's go again next week," Minna said. "We'll look at the newspaper and decide which one."

They both nodded in agreement and shut the door behind them.

"Maybe you'll come with us next week, Yussel? At least, I have something different to think about for a change."

"Maybe I will. Good night, Minna. I'm falling asleep."

Turning his back on her, he began to make up the corner that was his bed.

"Good night, Yussel," she replied.

She thought her brain was stuffed so full of provocative thoughts she'd never be able to fall asleep but, to her surprise, she closed her eyes almost as soon as she crept into bed next to Pearl. The last thing she could remember was a mental picture of all the girls at the factory turning into apes as they sewed assiduously.

In the weeks that followed, Minna continued to attend one and sometimes two lectures a week on such widely varying subjects as Frank Lloyd Wright, the assassination of Stolypin, the art of Henri Matisse, and the life of Nobel prize winner, Marie Curie. Sometimes the other two girls went with her and sometimes she went alone. Yussel invariably refused to come.

After each lecture, she felt like an expert, at least until the next day, when she had lunch with Saul. She almost always discovered he already knew more about the subject than she did. Often, he suggested books for her to read. Partly because she knew that Saul would question her, she did her best to get to the library and take them out, but she didn't always have enough energy or time to read them.

Minna's friendship with Saul deepened every day. They talked about everything, from Tata and her dreams to his stories. The only thing he never mentioned was his sweetheart. When Minna asked, he said, "I don't like to talk about her. She's so far away, it makes me sad." She wondered, but was tactfully silent on the subject.

As a matter of course, she always saved half her lunch for him, saying she wasn't hungry. Each time, he refused it politely and then, upon her insistence, took it and ate rapidly as if he was starving. When Mr. Steinberg joined them, as he often did, Minna noticed that he, too, offered Saul some of his lunch.

Yet he continued to grow thinner every day. As the weather became colder, he began to cough frequently, excusing himself by saying, "It's just a cold. I have a cold every winter."

Although Minna looked for it every evening, no letter from Guiseppe arrived. She had long since told everyone except Mama about her arrangement, so there was no need to keep it a secret. Sadly, Rosa stopped looking at her expectantly every morning and did her work grimly, rarely smiling. Not matter what excuses Minna made for him, she refused to believe that 'Seppe would not have written if he could.

From what she said, the whole family, even her cherished brother, Tony, was affected by his absence. "He's not doing his schoolwork," she said. "I know he's making friends with the wrong boys. It's killing Mama."

Anna, on the other hand, bloomed. She was more radiant each day, displaying a new bracelet, a new shirtwaist, or a tiny silver mirror with pride. "He gave it to me last night," she'd say, referring to her new fellow.

Although Yussel was quieter than usual, Minna no longer worried about his feeling towards Anna. He never even mentioned her name after Minna told him about her new fellow. He spent more time with Sarah, too. She looked prettier than she ever had. In her quiet way, she blossomed. I was foolish to worry, Minna decided. No one falls in love just like that. It's only in a story that it happens.

There was already a small amount of money saved in the secret box under the floorboards. Although Mama never participated in the discussions about a new shop, she seemed relieved to know that they would not starve if business slowed at the factory and they were laid off for a season. Pearl continued to make flowers every afternoon, adding her wages to the small hoard.

Only Bessie remained aloof from the general feeling of well-being. She stopped asking Minna to attend Union meetings with her, but she became busier, often skipping dinner. Every day, she worked to enlist new members by buttonholing girls at factory doors.

Now that she had Saul and Mr. Steinberg to keep her company, the factory didn't seem so bad to Minna. As she tried her best to keep up with Saul's suggested readings, she felt reassured about her future. At least I'm learning, she thought. After we save enough money and have another shop, maybe I *will* be able to go to college. Although that time seemed far off, she was not as disheartened as she had been in the past. I won't forget, I can't forget, she reminded herself.

One evening, she sat sipping a cup of tea and casually leafing through the latest book of poetry Saul had suggested she read. Mama, as usual, had retired to the bedroom to put on her wrapper before dinner. Pearl bustled around, stirring the food on the stove and fixing the table.

"Guess what happened today?" she asked.

Minna looked up. "What?"

"I didn't tell you, but I've been doing extra work at school. Thanks to Miss Israel, I skipped twice. I'll graduate early this January. Then I can come and work in the factory with you."

Minna looked at her, surprised. "Really? Oh, Pearl, good for you! I'm so proud of you. If you can work in the factory, too, then we'll be able to save money that much faster. We can all take turns with dinner. Oh, Pearl, you've been working very hard, haven't you?"

Pearl shook her head. "You and Mama go out to work every day. All I do is sit here. I want to be like everyone else."

"You already are—making dinner, keeping the apartment, doing those flowers, and your homework. You've been doing a lot—and to skip two grades! You're the smart one in the family!"

Pearl blushed. "I don't care about that. I just want to go to work in the factory, too. I'll put my hair up and…"

She hugged Pearl. "You're already grown up, little sister. If you weren't, how could we all rely on you?"

Pearl blushed again.

Minna watched her as she hung her head. Pearl was really pretty. Suddenly, she seemed more like a contemporary and less like a little sister. Minna could imagine her at the factory, bent over her machine, making her own friends, choosing her own way.

"There are some fresh boys at the factory," she began.

"Oh, I can handle them!" Pearl banged the silver down on the table. "Don't worry about that!"

Minna laughed. "I bet you can handle them better than I can!"

"Are those Italians still bothering you?" Pearl asked.

"Once in a while. I just ignore them. Now that I have lunch with Saul every day, they leave me pretty much alone."

"Tell me more about Saul," Pearl said, sitting down next to her.

"Well, he's the nicest person I ever met, besides our family. Maybe because he's a writer, he seems to understand what I'm going to say before I say it, just like Mr. Steinberg. Of course, he's a lot younger."

"Is he handsome?"

"Handsome? I don't know," Minna mused. "I never think of him that way. He's tall with such eyes! They see everything. But handsome? I don't think he's what you'd call handsome."

"You said he had a sweetheart," Pearl hinted.

"Oh yes. He writes to her. She's away somewhere." Minna looked up. "I'll tell you what, I'll invite him here for dinner one night. Then everyone can meet him."

"I'd like that," Pearls said. "But Minna, don't you care that he has a sweetheart?"

"Care that he has a sweetheart?" Minna thought about it. "No, of course not. Not as long as he can be my friend."

"But…"

Suddenly, Minna realized why Pearl was asking so many questions. "I don't think of him that way," she said decisively. "Not at all. It would be very different if I did." She thought of Jake and shook her head. "I just like him, that's all."

"Oh."

She could tell that Pearl really didn't understand. "It's different when you love someone. You feel…different."

Pearl looked at her questioningly.

"I just know." Minna blushed. "Don't ask me how." Changing the subject, she asked. "Shall we tell everyone else about your skipping tonight? Let's make it a special occasion! Don't say anything till we're all sitting down at the table."

"All right," Pearl agreed.

Minna looked in her pocketbook. "I have another idea. I have a little change. Why don't I go and buy some oranges for dessert? Then you can tell us while we're peeling them at the table."

Without giving Pearl time to demur, she grabbed her cloak and ran out the door. As she hurried into the street, she stopped at the small row of mailboxes. She had forgotten to look and Pearl had long since given up. Peeking through the glass door of the box, she saw something white. A letter! Maybe it was from Guiseppe.

She opened the mailbox and sure enough, it was for her, written in a scrawly hand. On the back of the envelope, she could just make out the return address. It was from Guiseppe. She tucked the letter carefully away in her pocketbook. Rosa will be so happy, Minna thought, as she ran to the fruit seller down the street. I can't wait till tomorrow!

It seemed no time at all before she was back, proudly brandishing three oranges. "That's all I could afford. We can share, though, don't you think?" She asked Pearl.

"Of course." Pearl smiled.

Mama came out of the bedroom in her wrapper. "You two certainly look happy," she said suspiciously.

"It's a secret" Pearl said.

"You'll find out after dinner," Minna added, whisking the oranges away.

Mama looked worried.

"It's a happy secret," Minna said, determined to allow Pearl to make her triumphant announcement.

Mama nodded anxiously. "We haven't had any happy secrets lately."

"Well then, it's about time," Minna said impatiently.

Aware of the surprised expression on Pearl's face at her shortness with Mama, Minna felt impelled to make amends. "You'll see, Mama. It's good news," she placated. "Just wait and see."

The door burst open and Yussel strode in. "This was the best day ever," he crowed. "See my pack?" He held it up with one hand. "It's almost empty. If this keeps up, we'll add a pile to the store money.

Mama turned away, as she always did when the store was mentioned.

"The ladies were falling all over me today. 'And what have you got for me, Yussel?' 'How did you know that's exactly what I need to finish my dress?' 'I'll take two dozen extra pins today.' I could do nothing wrong!"

"Maybe it's because you're a master salesman," Pearl teased.

"Maybe I am," Yussel replied boisterously. "At this rate, I'll have my men back sooner than I thought."

Mama shook her head. "Thanks be, we have a roof over our heads and food on the table. We ask for nothing more."

Noticing Yussel's stricken expression, Minna interjected. "I ask for lots more, Mama. I know we'll have it! See if we don't!" She stood up and took the pack from Yussel. Dangling it in one hand with some difficulty—it wasn't *that* light—she marched all the way around the room, stopping as she reached Yussel. Bowing, she handed him his pack. "Your pack, Master. But wait, I think I want to buy everything else that's in it. I wouldn't want you to go home with old merchandise!"

Yussel's face cleared and he laughed. "I swear, it was almost like that today.:

Sarah peered through the doorway. "May we come in? Is dinner ready?"

"In a few minutes," Pearl said.

By the time Bessie raced in and they were all sitting down, even Mama was looking as if she might smile. Minna called Yussel 'Master' and bowed to him every time she spoke to him. His lofty acceptance of her obeisance made the other girls giggle.

After the dinner plates were cleared and everyone was about to get up, Minna said, "Wait. We have a surprise." With a gesture, she laid the three oranges on the table. "Tonight we have oranges for dessert in honor of Pearl."

"In honor of Pearl?" Yussel raised his eyebrows.

"Your sister, the genius! Pearl, tell what you did."

With everyone's eyes upon her, Pearl felt shy. "I skipped two grades so I can graduate in January. Then I can come and work at the factory with all of you." Because she was nervous, she spoke rapidly. It took a moment for the meaning of her words to sink in. Yussel was the first one to understand what she had said.

"You skipped two grades? That's wonderful!"

"With everything else you have to do, you can hardly study at all. You must be brilliant," Sarah added.

"That's good work," Bessie smiled.

Only Mama said nothing. "It's a *kineahora*," she said finally, sensing everyone's eyes upon her. 'We will be sorry to fly so high. God will be angry."

Pearl's eyes filled with tears. She looked desperately around the table.

Minna stood up. "Oh Mama, maybe you feel that way, but I don't. Neither does Pearl or Yussel. We have hopes for the future. For us, it's right to fly high."

Mama shook her head. "You work and you work…and then what happens? In a flash, it's all gone."

Yussel stood up, too. "It's all gone for now. That doesn't mean we can't try again. I'm proud of Pearl. With her help, we'll be that much closer to having another shop. If you don't want to be part of it, Mama, you don't have to be." His face was white.

Pearl began to sob. "I thought I had such good news but now, everyone is fighting. I'm sorry I worked so hard!"

Minna put her arms around Pearl. "You should never be sorry. We're all glad. I think you're wonderful. So does Yussel. If Mama can't, she can't. That's all."

Pearl sobbed harder. "Mama's always hated me since Chava's death. Nothing I do is right! I know it."

Mama stood up. "That's foolish talk. It's just…I worry about you, that you'll be disappointed, too. There's an evil spirit upon us and nothing we do will succeed. I know." Heavily, she pushed her chair back, stood up, and went into the bedroom.

Minna yelled after her. "You're wrong. If you don't want to help us, that's fine. But don't try to stop us, either. We're

Americans, and Americans don't give up."

Yussel stared after Mama for a long moment. Then he turned to Minna. "You're right. It's up to us to make the future." He hugged Pearl, who was still sobbing. "I'm proud of you, Pearl. Don't worry, the three of us will work together. Thanks to you, it will go much faster."

Pearl buried her head in Yussel's shoulder. "Why couldn't she just say, 'That's good'? She never thinks anything I do is good. She doesn't even notice."

"She doesn't notice any of us," Minna said. "It's not only you. It's like…like she's under a spell so all she sees are the bad things these days."

"When we have our shop, she'll feel differently. I'm sure she will," Yussel said.

"I don't care if she does or not!" Minna replied angrily. "I meant what I said to her. If she can't help us, at least she shouldn't hold us back."

"Calm down, Minna," Yussel said soothingly. "Remember, it's because of Mama we're here in America. She's done her part. Now it's up to us."

Minna shook her head.

Pearl looked up at Yussel. "Is that what you really think?"

"It is."

Minna remembered Sarah and Bessie. Glancing around the table, she saw they were no longer there. They had tactfully withdrawn to the front room.

Putting her hand on the table, she looked at Pearl and Yussel. "Let's make a pact. We'll keep trying and we won't give up. Someday, I'll go to school, Yussel will have his farm, and Pearl her handsome prince. We can do it if we work together, the three of us."

Yussel put his hand on top of Minna's. "I agree to the pact," he said seriously.

'I do, too." Pearl put her hand on top of theirs.

They looked at each other. Then Minna picked up an orange. "I say we celebrate the way we planned. Shall I call Bessie and Sarah?"

Pearl wiped her tears and nodded.

Yussel went to the door. "Aren't you going to have some orange?" he called.

The two girls came in hesitantly and sat at the table. Although the atmosphere was strained, there was at least the semblance of a celebration as they shared the juicy segments of the oranges.

"My teacher told me," Pearl began bravely, "that in California oranges grow on trees everywhere. You can just walk outside and pick your own orange whenever you want one."

"There's gold in the streets, too," Bessie said cynically.

"That's what they said about New York. I can remember my uncle telling me about it in *der alter heym*," Sarah said. "If it wasn't true here, why should it be true in California, unless it's a magic land?"

"Someday, I'll go to California," Minna said, "and I'll send everyone at this table a crate of oranges. I'll pick them myself from trees!"

They all laughed. A crate of oranges for one person was beyond imagining.

"Why not send us a little gold while you're at it?" Yussel quipped.

"Add some diamonds, and I'll not say no!" Pearl continued. "But truly, there are oranges growing in California. My teacher said so and she should know."

Minna remembered the letter she had received. They all knew about Rosa. "I got a letter from Guiseppe today for Rosa." She pulled it out. "He's in California. See the return address? I guess he didn't have time to pick any oranges yet. At least, not for us!"

"I guess not," said Pearl, her faith unshaken.

"Rosa will be so happy," Sarah commented. "She hasn't been herself at all."

"I hope the letter is good news," Yussel said, "so there's a reason for her to be happy."

CHAPTER 18

The next morning, Mama was her usual somber self. Unsmiling, she prepared for work. Pearl had already left for school and Minna decided to act as if nothing had happened.

"Let's go," she called to Sarah and Mama.

Sarah, aware of Minna's constraint, made a special effort to talk to Mama, who replied gruffly. Minna walked ahead picturing Rosa's expression when she handed her the letter.

As soon as she saw her, she waved the letter in the air. From across the room, Rosa's face lit up. She hurried over to Minna, meeting her in the aisle by their machines.

"It's from 'Seppe?" She asked.

"Yes! It came yesterday."

"Thank God! He must be all right." Taking the letter, she held it uncertainly for a moment, as if she could decipher its contents from the envelope. "I hope he's all right," she muttered. "He must be doing well…"

Minna led her back to her chair. "Why don't you open it and find out?" she asked, laughing.

Rosa hesitated, looking at the return address. "California? He's so far away! He'll never come back." She stroked the envelope, reluctant to open it.

Minna watched her sympathetically. "I'm sure it's good news," she said. "Open it now!"

"All right. I will." She slit the envelope open with the point of her scissors, being careful not to mar the return address.

Before she politely turned away, Minna saw that it was several pages long.

When the lights flickered, the signal that their machines were turned on, Rosa was still reading her letter. For once, it seemed as if she might fall behind. Minna worked as fast as she could, planning to do some of Rosa's work if it became necessary. When she finally looked over, she saw Rosa sewing frantically with a big smile lighting up her whole face. So, he's all right, she thought, and felt a gush of relief for Rosa's sake.

At lunchtime, before hurrying out to meet Saul, she questioned Rosa. "So?" she asked. "He's all right?"

"Guess what?" Rosa's lips trembled with happiness. "He's working on a farm. After all he said, he's working on a ranch—a tree ranch! What do you think they grow? Oranges, that's what. Oranges on trees."

Minna laughed. "So they do grow oranges in California."

"He says the sun always shines there. He really likes it. He's healthy and well. He's earning good money, too. He says he's saving it and if he can buy a couple of acres, maybe we can all go out." She frowned. "If Papa agrees, of course. Just wait till I show the letter to Mama! She'll feel happy again, I know she will." Rosa's eyes sparkled and her cheeks were flushed. "I'm going to go tell my friend he's all right."

As she pushed her way through the crowded aisle, she stopped and turned to Minna. "Thanks! It's thanks to you I feel happy."

Minna smiled back at her and hurried to meet Saul. She knew he was waiting for her at the door.

As she raced towards him, her scarf flying behind her, she saw he was coughing. Delicately, she hesitated, giving him a chance to recover before she approached. When she saw he had stopped, she hurried towards him.

"Guess what?" she asked. "Rosa's brother is in California and he's working on an orange tree ranch. There really are oranges growing there!"

Saul laughed. "I never doubted it! That's good news, Minna."

"We had oranges last night," Minna continued, "and Pearl said that in California, you just pick them off the trees in the street. We were laughing at her, but she was right. Guess what? She skipped two grades so she can graduate in January. Then she'll come and work here, too. That means we can save the money for our shop more quickly."

He beamed down at her, his eyes glowing. "That's really good news, Minna. With four of you of you working, you should be able to save a lot of money."

"I promised I would invite you to dinner," Minna said. "Everyone wants to meet you—well, Pearl does. I don't think Mama even notices."

"What do you mean?"

She told him about what had happened last night.

He thought it over. "I'm sorry, Minna. It's hard when the one person you rely on can't help you any more. I know that from my own life."

"You sound very…bitter?" she questioned.

"In my family, it was my older brother. He was the one who came to America first. He was going to send for the rest of us. How we scrimped and saved to find the fare for him! At first, he wrote often and seemed hopeful. 'Soon,' he'd say. 'Soon I'll be able to send for you, Saul. Then together, we'll get the whole family over.'"

He turned to Minna. "When I was growing up, my brother was like a prince to me. He was strong and handsome; I thought he was like God. He always took time with me, too. I believed in him. Well, to make a long story short, he stopped writing to us. When we sent him letters, they came back. We didn't hear from him again. At first, I feared something had happened to him. We all did. Then a cousin wrote to us and said he had seen him all dressed up with a blonde *shiksa* on his arm. So he must have decided his family wasn't important in his new life."

She responded to the pain in Saul's voice. "You don't know that," she said. "Maybe he couldn't write, or maybe your cousin saw someone else who just looked like your brother. You don't know for sure."

"Yes, I do. We scrimped and saved again so I could come here. At first, every time I turned a corner, I thought I'd see my brother's face. After a while, I gave up. I came to believe he was dead, that our cousin was mistaken. Then one day…"

She leaned closer to him. "Then one day?"

He continued. "One day, I saw him, all dressed up in a fine suit. I went to him. 'Isaac,' I called. 'It's me, Saul. I'm here!' At that moment, I swear to you, I forgot the past. I was just glad to see him, to know he wasn't dead. He looked me up and down. 'So, you got here, too, brother,' he said. 'I suppose you want money.'"

Minna gasped. "What did you say?"

"I didn't know what to say. A thousand thoughts went through my mind. I thought of my mother and father, suffering, hungry, saving every penny to pay for his fare and then for mine. I thought of my sisters. I looked at him and I said, 'I want nothing from you. To me, from this moment, you are dead.' I turned and walked away. I haven't seen him since."

"Oh Saul, I'm so sorry. What a terrible story. How could he act like that?" Tears came to her eyes.

"I don't know, Minna. I've made a million excuses for him, but in the end, there are none. I never told the family I'd seen him. Better they should think he's dead."

"So that's why you are always hungry," Minna said without thinking.

Saul looked away. "I'm saving every penny. Soon, I will have enough for them all to come here. Then my own life will begin." He coughed.

Minna patted his back. Unwrapping her lunch, she held out a few segments of orange she had saved from last night. "Here, suck on these. They'll make you feel better. I saved them just for you."

Saul coughed so hard he couldn't extend a hand to take the fruit. His shoulders shook and he bowed his head.

She waited patiently. When he finally stopped, she held out the pieces of orange. "Here," she repeated.

Ruefully, Saul accepted her offer. 'Thanks, Minna," he sighed. "When I'm a famous writer, I'll send you a bushel of oranges to make up for it!"

"Oh no. I already promised my family that I'd send them oranges. You can send me…let's see…" she smiled. "You can send me a crate full of books, that would be nice. I promise to read them all, every one."

He laughed. "I meant what I said—about saving money. But I hate for you to give me your lunch every day. It *is* every day, isn't it?"

She thought fast. "We always have a little extra. Besides, if I eat too much, I'll get as big as a barn. You wouldn't want to be responsible for that, would you?"

He shook his head. Then he looked down at her and shook it

again. "Somehow, I doubt that's a problem."

"It runs in the family," she said solemnly. "My cousin, in *der alter heym*, she was so fat they had to carry her around." She crossed her fingers behind her back.

Seeing her earnest face, Saul gave in. "Well then, all I can say is 'thanks.' Instead of books, I'll send you a giant turkey. How's that for a deal?"

They both laughed.

"I guess I shouldn't get angry at Mama," Minna mused. "Maybe she can't help it. If we always did rely on her, that's to her good. If now we can't, well, maybe that's the way it has to be. That's what Yussel says."

"I'd like to meet him."

"Then come to dinner next week," Minna invited. "You can meet everyone." Plus have a good dinner for a change, she thought.

They set a date and Minna began to plan what they would eat and how they would all be seated around the table. Maybe I can ask Bessie and Sarah to eat earlier, she thought. Or I can borrow a chair from the neighbors. If we squeeze, we can all fit around the table. Better that then to have Sarah and Bessie think they aren't welcome. We can save up and have a chicken. That would be nice…a whole chicken, and soup, and some fruit…

She worried about how to tell Mama and the others about her proposed guest. She's never had a guest before. Would they make too much out of it? Maybe Mama would refuse, saying it was a waste of money. She decided to mention it that very evening, just to get it over with.

It was with great trepidation that she broached the subject at dinner. She could think of no way to say it except baldly. "I've invited my friend, Saul, to dinner next week."

Conversation stopped. Except for Pearl, everyone was surprised.

"A dinner guest?" Mama asked. "Like the Astors, we should have a dinner party?"

"It's not a dinner party," Minna replied, as patiently as she could. "He's my friend and I want to invite him for dinner. He could do with a good meal."

"I'd like to meet him," Yussel said seriously. "He's been a good friend to you."

"How will we all sit?" Pearl asked.

"We don't have to come," Sarah offered. "We can eat earlier…"

"I'll probably have a meeting, anyway," Bessie chimed in.

"On no," Minna said. "I want you all to come. I'll borrow a chair from next door and there'll be room. It's only one more person. You'll like him."

"And what are to serve your famous guest?" Mama asked sarcastically.

"Pearl and I will decide everything, won't we?" She looked at Pearl.

Pearl nodded.

Minna leaned toward Mama. "In *der alter heym*, we had guests. Why is it so different here?"

"It was different there," Mama replied coldly.

"Why?"

'It was…different, that's all."

Minna shook her head. "We didn't have any more room and we had even less food. I don't see how it was different."

"Life was different there." Mama stood up and went into the bedroom.

Minna looked after her. When she glanced at Yussel, he shook his head.

"So, between the two of you, I assume we'll have a feast," he teased, changing the subject.

"Don't worry." Minna nudged Pearl. "We'll do it up the right way. I *was* planning a banquet, but I guess I'll have to compromise."

Everyone laughed.

By the time the great day arrived, even Minna was nervous, despite her protestations of calm. They had never had dinner guests, not since the first day when Cousin Avraim had joined them. She and Pearl had planned a delicious meal, based on the plump and inviting chicken they had purchased the night before. Minna had done her best to make the table look pretty, even buying a sprig of flowers for the kind of centerpiece an article in *The Forward* had suggested. She stood back and surveyed it. So the dishes didn't match the way they did in the picture she'd seen. It still looked pretty.

Mama, strangely enough, had spent extra time fussing in front of the mirror. When she came into the kitchen, she nodded approvingly at the table. Lifting the pot cover, she inspected the boiled chicken. Then she went back into the bedroom and from a box under her bed, brought out a lace doily for the center of the table. Carefully, she wiped the glass containing the flowers and set it back on top of the lace.

Then she surveyed the table and nodded. "Now it looks nice," she said.

Minna noticed there was a sparkle in her eyes, a sparkle she hadn't seen since the store burned down. Impulsively, she hugged Mama. "Thanks," she said. "Now it looks perfect!"

Yussel, entering in the middle of this, beamed. Pearl frowned worriedly as she checked the food. Finally, Sarah and Bessie sidled in.

"How pretty the table looks!" Sarah exclaimed.

'Well," said Minna uncomfortably, 'I don't know why we're all standing around like this. Let's sit." As everyone sat down, she watched them anxiously, afraid that the symmetry of the tale would be ruined. No one, she noticed pushed their chair in. They were afraid, too.

She jumped up when she heard the knock on the door. "There he is!" she exclaimed.

She hurried to answer it. In the front room, she hesitated. Why am I so nervous? She asked herself. It's only Saul. I must be nervous because everyone else is.

It's only Saul, she repeated to herself as she opened the door, half expecting to see someone else altogether—perhaps a dapper young man like those she had seen through the window at the Palais de Danse.

As soon as she saw Saul, the same Saul she saw every day at lunch, she knew it would be all right. He had made an effort, too. His collar was starched and his newly shined shoes gleamed. Holding out a small bouquet of flowers, he smiled. "For you," he said.

She took the flowers. "Thank you, Saul. Come in. Everyone's already in the kitchen." She gestured around the room. "This is Sarah and Bessie's room. We don't have a parlor."

Saul laughed. "I only have one room. To me, this looks like a palace."

Minna preceded him into the kitchen. Everyone looked up.

"Hello, Saul," Sarah said.

He smiled at her.

"Saul, this is my Mama."

He bowed slightly. "It's a pleasure to meet you, Mrs. Ruben."

With dignity, she bent her head,

"This is my brother, Yussel."

Yussel stood up and held out his hand. "I'm glad to meet you, Saul. I've heard a lot about you."

As Saul shook Yussel's hand, he nodded. "I have heard about you, too."

"This is my sister, Pearl."

Pearl dipped her head.

"And this is Bessie."

"Glad to meet you, Bessie." Saul hesitated until Minna gestured to the empty chair.

"Sit," she said. She realized she was still holding Saul's flowers. She held them up. "Look what Saul brought! I'll put them in water."

As she set them in a pitcher and removed her few sprigs so she could put his flowers on the table, everyone remained silent. She felt her stomach sink. This is going to be terrible, she thought. Why can't someone speak up? She looked desperately at Yussel.

"So, you work with Minna," he said heartily.

"I work at the factory," Saul said. "Actually, I'm a cutter. I learned in the old country."

"Where are you from?" Mama asked.

"From Riga before here."

Silence.

With a flourish, Pearl set the chicken on the table. In a separate bowl, she brought the vegetables. Somehow, she had even found an extra plate for the bread.

Saul looked at the feast. "That looks delicious! I haven't had a meal like this since I came here. It's just like what my Mama used to make."

Pearl beamed as she sat down.

"Saul writes stories," Minna said proudly as she gestured to everyone to help themselves. "That's what he's going to be, a writer."

Saul laughed. "That's what I hope." He looked around the table. "A wise man once said to me that everyone has a story in them and if they could write it, the rest of the world would want to read it.

What do you think?"

Pearl frowned. "A story is about things happening, about adventure and romance. Nothing ever happens here."

"Do you really think so?" Saul asked. He turned to Yussel. "What's your opinion?"

Yussel shrugged. "I don't know. It's not exciting to me because it's my life."

"That's just it," Saul replied. "We're the heroes and heroines of our own lives. If we could tell others what it's really like, they'd be interested. That's what I believe." He ducked his head. "Of course, I don't write about myself all the time, but pieces of myself are in everything that I write."

"What do you mean?" Minna asked, beginning to relax.

"Well, tonight's a story. Tonight, I'm learning, for the first time since I came to America, what it's like to be a guest. If I write a story where my hero is a guest, I'll know how to explain his feelings."

"A life is a life," Mama said impatiently "How can it be a story?"

Minna's heart sank again.

"But, don't you see?" Saul replied, undaunted. "Here we all are, sitting around a table in the year 1910 in New York City, America. How did we get here, each of us? How did we arrive at this point in time so we're all sitting here together?"

Mama looked puzzled.

"If we hadn't wanted a change, we wouldn't be here at all—we'd be back in *der alter heym*. Coming here was a brave thing to do. That's a hero—someone who has the courage to start again in a new place. Or a heroine." He smiled at the girls.

Yussel leaned forward. "That's interesting. I never think of a story as being about real people. What happens to people in a story isn't like what happens in our lives, it's exaggerated. Maybe, if you took some things out of everyone's life, it would be a story. But what happens every day, who cares except the person it's happening to?"

"It depends on how you tell it. I bet there's a story in what happened to everyone today." He looked at Pearl. "When you bought the chicken, what were you thinking?"

"I was thinking, Minna's friend is coming and I want to have a nice dinner," Pearl replied, blushing.

"What do you think was in the chicken lady's mind? Did she care, or has she sold so many chickens to people that she never wonders who's going to eat them?"

Pearl shrugged. "I never thought about it."

"But it's interesting," Saul said intensely.

"Will you have some more?" Pearl asked, noticing that he had finished what was on his plate.

"Thank you. I will." He held out his plate and let Pearl serve him.

"I hear stories every day," Bessie said. "When I talk to people about the Union, they tell me about their lives. Most of the stories make me sad, not happy. I wonder, where's the happy ending? Then I think, there aren't any."

"There can be, if you want it enough," Minna said stoutly.

Bessie shook her head. "Not for some."

"When you write the stories," Yussel began, "do you always have happy endings?"

"Oh no, life's not like that. But, you see, I can if I want to—if the characters want to. That's the good part of writing stories. They can come out the way you want."

"Life isn't that way," Mama said.

"Why can't it be?" Minna asked. "I know it's not easy but it can be done. I believe it!"

"Do you think if you wish for something hard enough, it will come true?" Sarah asked shyly.

"It depends on who you are and what you do to make it come true," Saul said. "What do you think, Yussel?"

Observing Saul with her family, Minna noticed, as she had on other occasions, how easily he drew others into conversation by asking questions. He does it with me, she thought, but here, he does it with everyone. Even Mama is part of it. She beamed at Saul and the others around the table. I'm glad I invited him. Surreptitiously, she added more food to his plate.

"I don't know," Yussel said. "Sometimes I think, yes, and sometimes, I think, no. There are other considerations…people to take care of, responsibilities…"

"But, don't you see?" Saul responded. "If you meet your responsibilities, that's part of you, too. There's a fulfillment in that."

Yussel was surprised. "I never thought of it that way."

"Saul keeps writing and studying even though he works all day," Minna volunteered.

"That's because it's important to me. If it wasn't, if something else were important, I'd do that. We all make choices. The problem comes when we don't realize that's what we're doing, when we fall into choices instead of making them."

"That's interesting," Bessie mused.

"God makes our choices for us. We can't escape," Mama stated.

Saul looked at her for a moment. "I'll tell you a story. I know a family that struggled to come here from *der alter heym.* Then, when they got here, there was nothing but tragedy. The father was unable to find the work he sought, the mother was ill, they lived like pigs in one tiny room. Despair fell over them. 'Why did we leave, why did we sacrifice for nothing?' the mother asked."

He looked around the table. Everyone was staring at him. Even Mama leaned forward slightly.

'Usually, it was the father who spoke words of hope, but this time, he couldn't. He looked at his children, thin and scrawny, at his wife, half dead yet unable to remain in bed because there was no one else to do her work. His oldest child, still too young to help, looked at him, her eyes large in her pinched face. 'Why did we leave, Tata?' she asked.

"The father was unable to answer. Like a criminal, he slunk out once more to find work. Yet all day, he thought, is it my fault that I have brought them here to suffer? If we had stayed, we might be better off. At least, we could have been helped by the rest of our family. Here we are alone.

"As he wandered about during the day, knocking on one door after another, he met a holy man from his village. The man, seeing his downcast face, said, 'What is the matter, Reb Joseph?' The father let out a cry of anguish, told him the litany of his complaints, and finished with, 'It is all my fault!' The holy man shook his head and said, 'It is the will of God.'

"The rest of that day, Joseph mulled over the holy man's words. 'It is the will of God…' He thought, when I go home tonight, I will be able to answer the child. I will say, 'It is the will of God.' He was relieved. How could it be his fault if it was the will of God?

"That night, when he arrived home, there was a letter waiting for him. He opened it and read it aloud to his family. From his dearest cousin, it told a story of woe. His favorite son had been inducted into the Tsar's army, his youngest daughter had died, there was no food because of the drought… As he read the letter aloud, he looked at his desperate family. Suddenly, they didn't seem so badly off after all. 'You see,' he said, chucking his oldest daughter under the chin, 'that's why we came. We came to find a better life for ourselves. And we will. One day, you, my daughter, will have silks and satins and you, my son,' he lifted the baby, 'will be free to choose your own path, not the Tsar's.' He smiled. With his resurgence of hope, the whole family took on new life.

"'It is because of you, Joseph, we believe.' His wife said. 'We follow your dream.' The father nodded, well pleased with his decision to come to America. I was right, he thought. In the back of his mind, he couldn't help but wonder. What about the Lord God? Is it not His will that brought me here? No, he thought. Today I am the author of my own story. Tomorrow, when things go ill, I can always blame Him!"

He looked around the table again. With a sigh, Mama leaned back in her chair, frowning. Their lips parted, the others waited for the rest of the story.

Finally, Minna leaned forward. 'So what happened?" she asked. "What happened to the family?"

The others looked at him.

Saul laughed. "What do you think happened?"

"I think the father found a job and the daughter did wear silks and satins," Pearl said.

"I think he found no job and family grew poorer and more desperate. Then one day, Joseph met a *landsleiter* and through him, he found a job and joined the Union. After that…" Bessie began.

"With you, everything's the Union," Yussel interrupted. "I think he found a job and he worked hard the rest of his life. If his daughter didn't wear silks and satins, at least his son wasn't inducted into the army. In the end, his grandchildren had all he ever desired for his family. An old man, he sat in the sun watching them play, remembering his life. All the struggle, he thought, it was worth it."

"I think…" Minna began, when Mama interrupted her.

'So, you are saying it is up to us?" she asked.

"I'm saying that I believe we make our own choices with the tools God has given us. The father could have stayed in *der alter heym*, but he was brave enough to take a chance. All we can do is to try and make our lives reflect our dreams. We don't always succeed, but it is the trying that's important."

Mama shook her head.

"I agree," Minna said loudly. "It's up to us to do the best for ourselves and the ones we love. Maybe God can help or hinder, but only we can choose."

Mama looked down at the table, the set of her shoulders expressing disagreement.

Minna noticed that Sarah had tears in her eyes. "It was brave to come here, wasn't it?" she murmured. "No matter how it comes out, it was brave."

Slowly, Yussel nodded in agreement.

Saul looked around the table with great interest. As each person spoke, he listened intently. Suddenly, without warning, he began to cough as he had that afternoon. His head bowed, he was racked by a paroxysm.

Conversation stopped, as everyone watched Saul helplessly.

Pushing his chair back, he left the table and went into the front room. From the kitchen, they could hear him hacking and gasping. Yussel started to get up, but Minna shook her head.

"It's the tailor's disease," Sarah whispered. Of common accord, they all turned to look at the *pushke*, the small collection box affixed to the counter where they donated money for *landsleiter* to go to Denver Tuberculosis Sanitarium.

Minna shook her head. 'Oh no, he's had a cold," she whispered. Speaking more loudly, she continued. "I wish I could write stories like Saul. Not about rich people, but about people like us and how we live."

"Why can't you?" Saul asked as he came back in the room and slid into his chair. "I'm sorry. I've had a cold for a few weeks." The set of his lips made it clear that no comments were to be made about his cough.

"I…I'm not a writer," Minna continued bravely. "I couldn't write a story."

"You could try," Saul said quietly.

Minna shook her head. "I'll leave that to you." She stood up to clear the table. She helped Pearl prepare the tea and set the fruit upon the table and she made sure to add a large spoonful of honey to Saul's tea.

Over dessert, Saul encouraged Yussel to describe some of his customers. His laughter was as light-hearted as everyone else's when Yussel imitated the most outrageous of them. At one point, he looked around the table and smiled broadly. "My stomach is filled and I have laughed. This is a new experience for me in New York City. To have both together is truly rare."

"Then you must come to dinner more often," Minna said impulsively. "It's been the same for us."

Later, thinking about it, she realized there was something about Saul that brought out the best in everyone. Yussel's stories were funnier, her thoughts more profound, and even Mama's sadness was mitigated by Saul's presence. It's because he listens so hard, Minna thought. He makes each of us feel important.

Although it was never actually discussed, Saul's weekly dinner with the family soon became accepted by everyone. Minna found she looked forward to those evenings all week long. Even Bessie, she noticed, was sure to stay in on Saul's night.

Minna continued to meet Saul for lunch. His cold became worse, yet he never complained. More and more often, she found herself watching helplessly as he coughed, holding a handkerchief up to his face. She dared not say anything to him, although she did ask Yussel about some of the patent medicines he sold to his ladies.

He shook his head. "I have nothing that will help."

Saul began to look more and more drawn. As the weather grew colder, he shivered in his light overcoat. Minna began to knit him a scarf in secret.

One day, she caught Mr. Steinberg alone. "I'm worried about Saul," she said. "He's not well and he gets thinner every time I see him."

Mr. Steinberg shook his head. "I know."

"Can't we do something? He works so hard. All day here and then, at night, studying and writing. If he could rest more… If he could go to a doctor…"

Mr. Steinberg shook his head again. "We can do nothing," he said wearily. "It's beyond our hands. The disease…"

'He has a cold, that's all. He'll be better soon," Minna almost shouted. "It's only a cold!"

Mr. Steinberg looked away. "Minna, you must know…"

"No! I don't know! I won't know!"

She walked away, refusing to listen any further. Yet despite herself, she monitored Saul more closely, counting to herself the times he coughed, eyeing the handkerchief he held to his face to see if there were any traces of blood.

If they never talked about his illness, the other subject they still never mentioned was his sweetheart. Minna found herself wondering more and more about her. Was she still in *der alter heym*? What did she look like? Yet she could not ask any questions. Saul had made it very clear that he did not want to speak of her. If she comes here, Minna worried, will she like me? What if she doesn't? Suppose Saul spends all his time with her, how would I feel? At night in bed, she often found these questions whirling around in her brain. Yet when she saw Saul, they seemed unimportant.

Minna and Anna continued to smile at each other across their machines. Although her beauty was in no way diminished, Minna no longer felt overwhelmed by it. She made sure to mention her occasionally at home, if only to say that she seemed very happy with her new fellow. Yussel listened in silence.

So, he thinks she's beautiful, Minna pondered. That doesn't mean it's a tragedy. I was foolish to make so much out of it.

Almost every week now, Minna had another letter to give Rosa, who smiled all the time now. "He says that he has saved more than he ever could here," she told Minna. "Mama says maybe we will all go to California. We're saving, too. Of course, we haven't told Papa yet. But the rest of us, we all know about 'Seppe."

As the days settled into a regular pattern, Minna found that although she thought often of future, she thought less of the particulars. "When I am a teacher" was the way she prefaced many of her thoughts, but she no longer planned how to accomplish her goal. Between Saul and her lectures, she felt she was, at least, learning something. It seemed impossible to pursue anything further.

Each week, the sum of money under the floorboards grew larger, yet the amount was still too small to be more than an emergency fund. I'll only get discouraged if I think of how far we have to go, Minna thought. Yussel must have decided the same thing, for he said little of the future, talking more about his every day business. When Pearl works, too, Minna reminded herself, it will go faster. To sit down and calculate when their goal could be reached had seemed futile, but with Pearl's salary added it would be different.

Mama's attitude added to her unwillingness to make concrete

plans. Although she seemed relieved when their savings were counted, she refused to see beyond the present. She never spoke of another shop or of the future, seemingly content to simply feel safe.

Only Saul continued to ask Minna about her plans. "You should find out about night school," he said one day. "You could start taking courses now. It may not be too expensive."

She shook her head. "I'll wait. I don't want to make plans I can't fulfill. Not yet. When we are closer to our goal with enough money for a new shop, I'll begin to plan."

Mr. Feigen raised the quotas almost every week. Minna found her work more difficult as she struggled to complete the requisite number of shirtwaists. Sometimes, she wondered about the big bosses, Mr. Harris and Mr. Blanck, who generally remained on the tenth floor. Did they know about the new quotas? Did they know how hard it was for the girls?

She mentioned this once to Bessie, who laughed at her. "Don't be foolish, Minna. They don't care from the girls. They tell Feigen what he has to have done and he does it. He's in the middle, too. But if Feigen and the others like him refused the owners and stuck up for their workers, it could be better."

As she sat sewing, concentrating on the seams she had yet to finish, Minna's thoughts usually wandered. The sewing had become so automatic that nothing interfered with her progress. Perhaps, she imagined, the big bosses would notice her and choose her to work upstairs. Other times, she remembered Bessie's words and found herself whipping her shirtwaists through angrily, thinking, it isn't fair! Yet the idea of pleasing her bosses and moving up was powerful. In reality, she received no encouragement from Mr. Feigen, who only noticed her when she fell behind or, more rarely, made an error in her sewing.

She often gazed at the other women sitting near her. Each one, she knew, had a story—the kind of story Saul told. He had taught her that much. I may not think about my story because I live it, she thought, but the girls who buy these shirtwaists, what would they think if they knew about our lives—we, who sew like the wind all day long, whose backs are bent, and whose eyesight is dimmed by our work? And there was the sound, the constant buzzing and whirring of the machines. Although she had become so accustomed to it that she hardly noticed it any more at the factory, it was later, at night, that it haunted her. Sometimes, she'd sit up abruptly in bed and look around wildly, her fingers automatically curved to push material through her machine.

At times like that, Minna vowed to herself that she would talk to Bessie and learn more about the Union. It's not right, she'd think. We work so hard for so little. Yet the next evening, when she was face to face with Bessie, she shrank from introducing the subject. Perhaps she was looking forward to a lecture, or waiting for Saul, or reading a new book. I'll wait, she'd decide, till I have more time to get really involved. I can't do it now.

She received little support from anyone else. In the factory, it was dangerous to talk about the Union. It was rumored that the bosses had spies who would report your name. Most of the women she worked with were afraid, like Mama.

When she had complained one day, Mama had replied, "What are you *meshuggeneh*? Now we have work, we're bringing home *gelt*, and you want we should lose it? Let the others, those who have nothing else to lose, no family to support, worry about injustice. For me, I work for food and a roof. As long as I get paid, I won't complain."

Saul, too, was curiously uninterested in talk about the Union or changing their working conditions. "You're right," he'd say to Bessie at the dinner table. "I'm glad you are working for us. But I don't have time. I go home and write my stories and hope for the future. That's all I can do."

"The intelligentsia!" Bessie would sneer, yet like the others, she found it impossible to be angry at Saul. He listened too hard and cared too much about each of them.

CHAPTER 19

More quickly than Minna would have believed possible, it was the week before Pearl's graduation. Recalling her own feelings on the same day, she had embroidered a hand-made shirtwaist as a gift for her. She had also gone to Mr. Feigen days in advance to ask for half the morning off for herself and Mama, swearing to make up the work by doing a little extra each day. He agreed reluctantly, but was pleased at the thought of hiring another hard-working Ruben and had already received the "honey" given to him to ensure her a job.

Pearl was walking on air. She seemed to have none of the regrets Minna had felt. On the day she went with Minna for her meeting with Mr. Feigen, she put her hair up and stood as straight and tall as she could.

"Soon I'll be working, too," she caroled as she skipped beside Minna. "You think he'll take me, don't you?"

Minna nodded bitterly. "He'll take you all right. He knows when he's found a good thing. But Pearl, this doesn't have to be your future. It's only a beginning. Some day…"

"Some day!" Pearl laughed. "I don't care about some day. I only care about now. Some day, I'll be an old lady."

Minna stared at her. She saw her cheeks, bright in the cold morning air, her shining hair, and her eyes afire with the excitement of this day, Pearl looked expectant and very young—younger than she could ever remember feeling. It was impossible to imagine her as an old lady. "Why, you really *are* happy to be working at the factory," she said.

"I told you, I am."

"I couldn't believe you. I thought you were making the best of it. When you see what it's like, Pearl, you might change your mind."

Pearl smiled. "I don't care what it's like. I just want to get started."

She watched Pearl carefully as they entered the ninth floor. Pearl was to go to school after they talked to Mr. Feigen, so they had arrived very early. The machines were still quiet. There was the usual bustle around the cloakroom and the sounds of female voices calling to each other across the room. Here and there, women sat at their machines, reading or chatting to the person next to them as they waited for the day to start.

Wide-eyed, Pearl gazed around the room. "So, those are the electric machines. That's what they look like. And in the middle, it's there you drop your finished shirtwaists. It's just the way you described it, Minna."

She blushed as Minna introduced her to Mrs. Cichetti.

"So, you'll be joining us, too. If you're like your sister, it's a good day!" she said heartily.

Minna hurried through the aisles after Mr. Feigen, pulling Pearl after her. "This is my sister, Pearl," she said breathlessly when she caught up with him. "You said you'd have a place for her next week after she graduates." Having given him the "honey", she felt no uncertainty about his response.

Mr. Feigen smiled at Minna and Pearl impartially. As his gaze fell upon Pearl, even he seemed to be affected by her enthusiasm. "So you're coming to work here," he said, almost warmly.

She nodded.

"See that you do as well as your mother and your sister." He said, turning away.

Minna showed Pearl her machine and where Mama sat. Then she gave her a push. "You'd better go or you'll be late for school."

"Can't I stay and see the machines go on?" Pearl asked.

"Go!" Minna urged, giving her a little push. "Soon enough, you'll *have* to stay."

"But I want to. I want to see what it's like."

"Do you know the way back to the door?" Minna asked, almost angrily.

Pearl nodded.

"Then go! Go back to school while you can!"

Pearl looked at her with a hurt expression. Silently, she turned to leave.

Minna ran after her. "I'm sorry, Pearl. I do think you should go. It makes me feel bad that all you have to look forward to is to work here." And worse than that, she thought, you are actually happy about it.

Pearl put her hand on Minna's arm. "I really do want to come here," she said softly. "I want to be grown up. To me, this is grown up. Maybe I'll be tired of it one day, or hate it the way you seem to, but for now, I'm glad to leave school. I'm not like you, Minna. This is what I want." She turned and ran towards the door without looking back.

All day, Minna thought of what Pearl had said. When she told Saul, he was unsurprised.

"Each of us wants something different for themselves," he said quietly. His voice was husky, as it often was these days. "Yussel wants his farm, your mother wants to be safe, and you want to change your life. Why should Pearl want the same thing you want?"

"It makes sense when you say it, but I still can't understand. Why should Pearl think it's a good thing to work in the factory? Why doesn't she want more out of life? She's smart in school…"

"Why? I don't know why. How can I tell who Pearl is? I can make up a story, but then it's my story, not hers. What I do know is that you have to accept what she wants and be glad for her."

"But…what will her life be like if she doesn't have any dreams?"

"Who's to say she doesn't have any dreams? They are different from yours, that's all. Listen to her—to her—not yourself. Then maybe you'll be able to understand. That's the most you can hope for."

"I do want her to be happy," Minna said weakly.

"In her own way?"

She was silent.

Saul began to cough and she forgot the conversation in her concern for him. When she was back at her machine, she thought, maybe Pearl is better off. Maybe her way is more real than my foolish dreams. But isn't it better to have dreams? Someday, I will live another life and I want Pearl to be part of it. As the machine whirred, she laughed out loud, causing Sarah and Rosa to look at her in surprise. I'll make her part of it whether she wants to or not, she decided, and laughed again at her foolishness.

That evening, Minna managed to get everyone except Pearl aside to discuss her graduation. "We'll have a special dinner that night after work to celebrate. Too bad, Pearl will have to prepare it because Mama and I will be at the factory. I've invited Saul to come, too. And for desert, I'll stop on the way home and buy something special—maybe even a cake! We've never bought a cake."

Mama offered a gift for Pearl, a brooch that had been given to her upon her marriage.

"I've never seen you wear this, Mama," Minna exclaimed.

"I used to wear it when you were much smaller. After Tata left, I put it aside for one of you."

Minna examined the brooch. It was beautiful. Garnished with little seed pearls, it glistened in the darkness of the bedroom. "Oh, Mama," she said. "Pearl will love this, especially because it was yours."

Mama turned away, saying, "That's as it should be."

Minna shrugged. It was no use expecting Mama to act a certain way. At least she did have a gift for Pearl. As for Yussel, Bessie, Sarah, and Saul, Minna left it up to them after mentioning the shirtwaist she was making.

Every night, she and Pearl sat and sewed together. Minna told her that the shirtwaist was for herself. She watched as Pearl created her graduation dress. Her head bent over her sewing, her face was unreadable. After her conversation with Saul, Minna wondered what she was thinking, but she found it hard to ask.

She chattered about her classmates and their plans. Twenty of them were graduating with her in the middle of the year. Most of them were going to work, too. A few were planning to marry. She spoke of them wistfully.

"You see," she said. "that's what I want, too. If I have to work, well, we all have to work. But I want to have a family, to care for them. All these years, when I've been the *balaboosteh*, I've thought, it will be different when I'm doing it for my husband and my children."

Minna felt a pang. "I'm sorry you've had to do it. It was the only way… It won't be so easy for us once you're working. We'll have to take turns cooking every night."

"I knew I had to. I never minded while I was doing it, but it's one of the reasons I'm so glad to be out working like everyone else."

Minna thought this over. "If that's how you feel, why do you look forward to doing it again with your own family?"

'That's different," Pearl explained. "Besides, I'm not getting married tomorrow. I have time to kick up my heels for a year or two before then." She giggled.

"Kick up your heels?"

"Well, why not? I'm grown up now, aren't I?"

Minna couldn't think of how to respond.

The night before her graduation, Pearl tried on her dress for Minna after everyone else was in bed. Mama slept so soundly, nothing would wake her.

In the dimness of their room, Minna looked at Pearl in admiration. "Oh, Pearl," she sighed. "You look so beautiful. The dress is perfect!"

Pearl smiled at her shyly. "Will you help me with my hair tomorrow? I want to put it up for my graduation and it still takes me so long."

"Of course."

In the candlelight, held discreetly so as not to wake Mama, the white graduation dress shimmered with a soft radiance. As the light flickered, it seemed to add a special glow to Pearl's face. Looking at her sister, Minna sighed, remembering her own feelings on a similar evening last year. Speechless, she leaned forward and kissed Pearl. "May your life be as you wish it to be," she whispered.

Pearl kissed her back and slipped the dress off over her head carefully. Handling it gingerly, she hung it on her hook and slid into bed next to Minna. As far as she could tell, Pearl fell asleep almost immediately. Minna lay awake for a long time, thinking of her own life, of Chava, and of Pearl, about to follow a new path in her life.

The next morning, Minna was awakened by Yussel hissing her name through the door. She crawled out of bed, being careful not to wake Pearl, who was still sleeping. As soon as she had made her toilet and slipped on her best dress in honor of the day, she went into the kitchen.

She stopped in front of the kitchen table. There, in the middle, was a bouquet. Next to it was a lavish breakfast consisting of special bread baked with raisins and sugar on the crust. In a place of honor, a brand new pot of honey sat waiting to be eaten.

She smiled at Yussel. "You did it again!" she cried. "It looks like…a restaurant!"

"I only brought the flowers," Yussel said. "Sarah brought the sweet bread. She had to leave for work, but she said she and Bessie will have another surprise at dinner time."

Minna heard a rustling in the bedroom. Hurrying to the door, she stood in front of Pearl. "Don't look," she commanded. "Not until you're all dressed and ready."

Obediently, Pearl closed her eyes as Minna led her through the kitchen to the toilet in the hall. On the way back into the bedroom she closed her eyes again. As they went into the bedroom, Mama came out. She wore her best black dress.

'We'll be out in a minute," Pearl said.

In the daylight, her dress now laid out on the bed looked even more beautiful than it had the night before.

Minna reached up onto her small shelf. "Here," she offered, extending the single pair of silk stockings she owned. "These are the ones I wore. You can have them for today."

"Oh Minna, thank you. I couldn't stand those old lisle ones under my new dress."

Slipping the dress over her head, Pearl waited for Minna to fasten the tiny buttons that ran up the back. Then, bending over, she looked at herself in the small mirror, twisting and turning her head. "How do I look?"

Minna stood back. "You look magnificent!" She took the hairbrush and began fixing Pearl's hair. Today, it seemed as if each strand had a life of its own, twisting and curling away from her busy fingers. "Hold still!" she said. "Your hair doesn't want to graduate!"

Pearl laughed.

Her reaction to the lavish breakfast and flowers was perfect. Hugging Yussel, she thanked him for the bouquet. "Just like Minna!" she said. Eyeing the sweet bread, she waited until everyone was seated before she cut the first slice. "I'll thank Sarah tonight," she said.

That reminded Minna. "I want you to buy a chicken tonight. We're going to have a feast! Unfortunately, you have to cook it—your own graduation dinner!"

Pearl smiled. "I don't mind. I'll do something special."

Mama stood up. "You did a good job with your dress. There's one thing missing."

Pearl looked down at herself nervously. "Missing? What's missing?"

Mama held out her closed hand. "This!" she cried, opening her fist.

Pearl looked at it. "A brooch! Oh, Mama, it's beautiful! Oh Mama!" She took the brooch and admired it in her open hand. "Look at the tiny pearls!" she exclaimed. "Oh, Mama!" Whirling, she ran into the bedroom. "I'll put it on right away."

When she came back out, she had pinned the brooch to the neck of her dress. Mama was right, Minna thought, surprised. It was the final touch Pearl needed.

As they exclaimed over the beauty of the brooch, Pearl looked shyly at Mama. "I've never seen this before," she said.

'It was a wedding present to me," Mama said. "I saved it for you, Pearl."

Pearl slid her fingers over the pin. Bending her head, she tried to see it, but it was pinned too high on her collar. "Your wedding present…for me… Thanks, Mama!"

Mama sat down abruptly, picked up her glass of tea and began to drink.

'I have something for you, too, but I'll give it to you tonight," Minna announced. "Isn't it time to go now?"

"The special assembly for us is at nine o'clock," Pearl said, looking at the clock on the wall. "Yes, we'd better go, right away." Her voice rose.

They rushed out of the house and raced towards the school, only to discover they were fifteen minutes early. Pearl left them to get in line with the other students who were receiving diplomas. It would be a small ceremony compared to the one in June.

"Who cares? What matters is, you've earned your diploma!" Minna had replied.

Now, sitting in the auditorium next to the other families, she felt a pang as she remembered her own graduation day. For a moment, she mourned her own unfulfilled dreams and regretted that Pearl's were so different. Yet as her sister walked across the stage, Minna saw her beaming, just the way she had. With a shrug, she smiled too, yielding to the happiness of the moment.

After the ceremony, Minna and Mama hurried to the factory and Yussel to work. First, they each congratulated Pearl in their own way. Her eyes sparkled and her cheeks were rosy as she accepted their good wishes.

Minna carried the image of Pearl beaming with her all day long. After spending the morning in school, the clatter of the factory seemed twice as noisy as ever, the chill of the badly heated room even more unpleasant than usual, and the weary sewing, exhausting. I have to go ahead with my plans starting next week, Minna decided. Otherwise, I *will* be here the rest of my life.

At lunchtime, it was a relief to escape from the factory and go out into the cold air. Saul wore his new scarf proudly, swearing it kept him warm as toast. Minna was dubious, but his cough did seem better when he was outdoors, so she said nothing about turning back despite Saul's occasional shivers.

'You're coming tonight," she reminded him.

"You've only told me about sixty times," he said. "How's Pearl? Did she like her graduation?"

"She did. You know what? Mama gave her a brooch, a wedding present I've never seen. Pearl really liked it. Why can't Mama ever show her feelings when we say something nice to her?"

"Some people can't. To some people, it's too difficult to accept the good because they always expect the worst."

With her mind on the evening ahead, Minna thought little of Saul's words at the time, but she found herself puzzling over them later as she sat at her machine. Did Mama only expect the worst these days? That hadn't been true in the past. It was Mama who decided to come to America. But was that because she had to escape a bad life or because she dreamt of a better future—or both? It was Mama who had started the store—but maybe that was simply a matter of survival. Too bad it was hopeless to talk to her about this. She couldn't even imagine broaching the subject.

That evening, Pearl had outdone herself preparing dinner. Yussel's flowers were set in a vase on top of Mama's doily so the table looked almost as colorful as a picture from a magazine, Minna thought. Just before they sat down, she whipped out the shirtwaist she had made for Pearl and presented it to her.

Pearl was in ecstasies. "Oh, Minna, I was jealous when you were making it. I never thought it would be for me. It's so elegant."

Minna beamed.

Sarah and Bessie stepped forward and handed Pearl a small gift wrapped in colored crepe paper.

"Oh, look!" Pearl cried. "It's wrapped up special. How pretty! I hate to open it.."

Sarah blushed.

Bessie said, "Open it! Open it!"

Pearl unwrapped the paper carefully, smoothing it out so she could save it. Inside, there was a small box. Holding her breath, she opened the lid. "Ooh!" Her eyes grew wide. "How did you know this was just what I wanted!" She hugged Sarah and Bessie. "It's perfect for tomorrow."

Minna looked over her shoulder. There, nestled in the box, was a tiny scissors, just the right size for clipping threads. It was shaped like a crane, the beak being the points.

Before Pearl had a chance to thank everyone all over again, Saul arrived. With a bow, he presented Pearl with his gift, a slim volume of sonnets by Shakespeare. "Look at the first page," he said.

Pearl flipped the book open. There, on the first page, was an inscription. It said: "To Pearl on the day of her graduation. May your life be like a poem. Your friend and well-wisher, Saul."

"Oh, Saul," Pearl sniffled. "I will always cherish this." She looked around the room. Flinging her arms wide, she extended them as if to embrace everyone. "I thank you all," she said seriously. "This is the best day of my whole life. I will never forget this moment." Overcome, she bowed her head, only to lift it almost instantly. "The chicken! If we don't eat it right now, it will be soup instead of a chicken." Rushing to the stove, she took the chicken out and began to set it on a plate to serve.

Gently, Minna pushed her aside. "At least tonight you can sit down like a queen and let me serve you."

Smiling, Pearl acquiesced. Leaning forward, she sniffed Yussel's flowers. "I'm so happy," she said.

The rest of the evening was glorious until the very end, when the three Ruben women had to sit down together and figure out how the cooking and housework would get done after tomorrow. Once Pearl was working, they would take turns and plan ahead. They worked out a schedule and hoped for the best.

Pearl settled into the daily routine at the factory with ease. Her machine was near Mama's, not Minna's, but she joined her sister and Saul for lunch every day. Together the two of them shared their food with him, tacitly ignored his coughs, and herded him inside when he seemed to be chilled.

One day, Pearl excused herself. "Anna invited me to lunch," she said proudly. "Her fellow can't come today."

Minna was surprised. "Anna?" she asked.

"Yes, isn't she beautiful?" Pearl asked.

"Yes, she is, but…"

"But what?"

Minna didn't know what to say. "Have a good time, I guess," was all she could think of.

At lunchtime, Anna was all she could talk about with Saul. "I told you how I almost went to the dance…Then there's Yussel and his feelings. Pearl's too young. Anna doesn't mean any harm, I 'm sure, but I don't think Pearl should be her friend."

"All you can do is tell her what happened to you. She doesn't know about that, right?"

"I can tell her. But suppose she still wants to be friends with Anna?"

"She has to decide that for herself. You know that." Saul said gently.

"Maybe I could talk to Anna…" she began.

"And say what? That you don't think she's a good friend for Pearl?"

She shook her head. "Of course, I wouldn't say that, but…"

"No matter how you put it, that's the way it would sound."

"I'll talk to Pearl tonight," Minna decided.

Saul touched her arm, a rare gesture. "There's something I've been wanting to tell you, Minna."

She looked at him.

"I think…" He began to cough violently.

Unable to ignore it as she had been doing, Minna put her arms around him and led him, head bowed, to a corner of the building more protected from the wind.

When he was no longer coughing, she moved away. Forgetting he had begun to say something, she leaned toward him and burst out, "I can't pretend not to see it any more. You must go to a doctor, Saul. This is more than a cold."

Saul bowed his head. "I know."

Minna looked at him.

"That's what I was starting to tell you. I couldn't make myself do it before. The Landsleiter Society is sending me to Denver. I'm leaving tomorrow." His expression was tragic.

Minna gulped. "You're leaving tomorrow? Why didn't you tell me?"

"I…couldn't. I…just couldn't. Who knows when I'll return or even if I will return?"

She grabbed his shoulder. "You will," she said fiercely. "If you want to, you'll return." She remembered Debbie from next door and how long she had been away. "You'll come back fat and healthy…" Her voice broke. "Oh, Saul." Her hands dropped to her sides.

"The doctor says it's not too late," he said bravely.

"Of course not." She forced herself to smile. "Think of all the time you'll have to write with no distractions. Finally, you'll have time."

Saul looked anguished. "Sure, I'll have time. And my family…they'll be waiting till I can earn more money. I haven't told them yet. I'm going to write them. Oh Minna, what can I say to them? It's all up to me and I'm failing too, just like my brother."

"Don't say that, Saul. It's not true and you know it. You can't help it if…" She choked, hardly knowing what she was saying. She couldn't imagine life without Saul. "It's you," she said suddenly. "It's you that's made the factory all right." She caught herself. "I'm glad you're going because they'll get you better." She gazed at him pleadingly.

"I'm going to try, Minna," he said intently. "I want to come back more than anything else in the world."

Minna remembered each person who had drifted away or been wrenched from her life. There were too many, she thought, too many such partings. How could she bear it here without Saul? She bent her head to hide her tears.

'I'll miss you," she whispered.

"I'll miss you, too. But we'll write to each other, won't we?"

"Oh yes," she replied. "But Saul, won't you come for dinner tonight to say goodbye to everyone?"

"I can't. I…just want to go. I'll write instead. I'll write letters to you."

"Do you need help in getting ready to go?"

"No. What have I got to pack? A few books, my papers…it's nothing. They'll bring me to the train tomorrow and…that's it."

"The doctor said…"

"He said if I'm lucky, I'll be as good as new."

She forced herself to smile. "So you just have to obey the doctors. I think it's secretly a vacation, that's what I think. All day, you'll be relaxing, looking at the mountains…" She stopped. "I'm glad they're sending you. I've been so worried."

He patted her arm. "I know."

"I'll think of you every day," she promised. "If wishes could make you better, you'd be better this minute!"

He patted her arm again.

Minna bestirred herself. "You're going and I'm fussing. It should be the other way around."

"I'll never forget you," Saul said somberly.

"Of course not," she said quickly. "How could you? You'll be reading my letters all the time and soon…" She took a deep breath. "Soon, you'll be back."

"I hope so." He looked over her shoulder. "I can see the others going in. We'd better start back."

At the door, Minna looked at him desperately. 'I'll miss you every day."

"I'll write to you as soon as I get there," Saul said.

She turned to go, her eyes filling with tears.

"Wait." He held her arm. "I want to tell you something else."

"What?"

"I want to tell you, I'll…I'll miss you, too." He shook his head. "Goodbye, Minna."

She leaned over and kissed his cheek. "Goodbye, Saul," she said and walked away. I won't cry, she thought. I won't cry. Saul would hate it if I cried. She bit her lip.

As she sat down at her machine, Sarah took one look at her face and whispered, "What's the matter, Minna? You look as if you're lost your best friend."

She put her hands against her eyes. "Nothing," she said. "Nothing."

Sarah persisted. "Can I do anything to help you?"

She shook her head. "I'll tell you tonight."

All afternoon, as the machines whirred, Minna thought about Saul. He is my best friend. What will I do without him? Suppose he never comes back? Suppose he…dies… As she sewed, tears fell upon the shirtwaist she was seaming.

She said nothing to anyone on the way home. Sarah and Mama were quiet. In the background, she could hear Pearl prattling about Anna and their lunch.

At the apartment, Minna hesitated. She knew there would be a long wait for dinner since it could be started only once that they had arrived home. "I think I'll go for a walk," she said finally. "I need more fresh air." Without waiting to see the reaction of the others, she hurried down to the street.

She walked unseeingly for what seemed like hours, jostled by men and women returning home from work. Finally, she stopped. Looking around for the first time, she noticed she was far from home in a strange neighborhood. The buildings looked sinister as they leaned over the now empty streets. She turned back.

I will miss him so much, she thought, but that doesn't matter. What matters is that he gets better. I don't think I would have wanted him for my sweetheart…at least, I don't think so…but I love him. And here I am, worrying about myself, when he has to go alone to the sanatorium…when he might be dying…

Finally, she began to sob, leaning her head against the side of a building. Her shoulders shook. Remembering where she was, she turned away and continued walking towards home, tears running down her face.

I'll never forget him, never, she promised fiercely. I'll write to him always. She shook her head. No, I'll write to him until he comes back. Someday, he will. If I write to him, it will be all right. I'll make it all right.

She wiped her eyes and slowly ascended the steps to their apartment. She slipped quietly in and stood for a moment in the empty front room before going into the kitchen.

Everyone was seated around the table. Obviously, they had all been waiting for her.

Mama looked at her. "We've been waiting for you to have dinner. If you want to go for a walk, you might…"

Yussel, noticing her red eyes, jumped up. "What's the matter, Minna?" he asked, interrupting Mama.

She shrugged off her cloak. Automatically, she hung it on the hook. "It's Saul. He's going to Denver tomorrow."

"He is going? I'm so glad," Yussel said. "Now he can get better."

Minna looked at him.

"It's good that he's going," Yussel said. "Don't you see? He's been wasting away in front of our eyes and no one dared say anything."

"You really are glad?"

"Many are cured," he said calmly. "It's better to try than to give up or pretend everything's all right."

Minna was taken aback. "I never thought of it as a good thing." She looked at the others.

"I agree," Bessie said. "It's the best thing. Some that the Union has sent have returned in good health."

Pearl's eyes filled with sympathetic tears. "No wonder you're so upset. How terrible! Poor Saul!"

Sarah spoke up. "Bessie and Yussel are right. This is a good thing, Minna. I know it doesn't seem that way right now, but…"

"When he comes back, you'll forget all this." Bessie said.

Minna looked at Mama, but she was silent. Finally, she murmured, "In *der alter heym*, your uncle had this disease. He died…"

"Saul won't!" Minna stormed. "He won't! I agree with you, Yussel. It *is* a good thing."

"He's leaving tomorrow?" Pearl asked.

"He didn't want to tell anyone," Minna explained. "But he said he'd write to all of you."

Mama stood up and brought the pot to the table so everyone could help themselves.

"You know many who have been cured?" Minna asked Bessie.

She nodded. "Don't worry, Minna," she said brusquely. "It doesn't help to worry. Better to think strong thoughts than to be afraid."

"You're right," she agreed. "It's just such a shock. I'll miss him so much.:

"We'll have lunch together every day," Pearl offered stoutly. "I'll keep you company."

Minna smiled weakly. "He said he'd write as soon as he gets there."

"He'll write wonderful letters," Sarah contributed. "You'd better practice, Minna."

She nodded.

"Yes," Pearl continued. "I'd be almost afraid to write to a writer!"

"You know he's not like that," Minna said. "I wish… You know what I wish? I wish I had a picture of Saul to keep—and one to give him, too."

"Foolishness!" Mama said. "To worry about writing to a dead man!"

Minna stared at her, shocked. "A dead man?" she repeated.

Everyone began to speak at once.

"You're wrong, Mrs. Ruben. Many have recovered," Bessie insisted.

"Mama!" Pearl gasped.

"No, Mama," Yussel said loudly. "In this country, they know how to make people well. Saul's going to the best hospital in the world. He's young. He'll get better. I'm sure he will."

Minna looked at Yussel gratefully.

Mama pushed her chair away from the table and stomped into the bedroom, closing the door behind her.

They all looked after her. No one spoke.

"I don't care," Yussel said. "She's wrong." He patted Minna's hand. "I know he'll get better."

"How can Mama say such a thing?" Pearl sobbed.

"For some people, it's hard to accept the good because they only expect the bad," Minna said finally, as if talking to herself. "Saul said that. Since the fire, that's how Mama has been, always seeing the bad. I don't think she was that way before, but I don't know…" She looked at Yussel.

"She got us here, didn't she? We can never forget that. So, maybe it's our turn to understand," he said.

Minna shook her head. "How can I forget she called Saul a dead man? How can I forgive her?" She put her head down on the table.

Bessie, who was sitting next to her, put her arm around her shoulders. "It doesn't matter what anyone else says." She soothed. "If you believe and Saul believes, that's what counts."

"If Saul believes…" Minna whispered. "I'll help make him believe when I write to him."

"I'll write to him, too," Bessie offered.

"We all will," Pearl agreed. "You'll just have to help me with my letters, Minna, so I don't make too many mistakes."

Minna looked around the table. "*Nu*, we'll all write to him." She looked down again. "How long do you think it will take for him to get better?"

Yussel frowned. "I don't know. But one of my ladies is a doctor's wife. I'll ask her."

"One of our men came back in a year," Bessie volunteered. "He looked plump and healthy, better than before."

"A year? That's not so long," Sarah said. "It's not long at all."

"It might be longer," Bessie added hurriedly. "I don't really know."

"It doesn't matter. As long as we know he's coming back," Pearl said stoutly.

"I wish I could see him again before he leaves," Minna said. "I was so shocked when he told me, maybe I didn't say the right thing."

"You care about him, don't you? Then you said the right thing because that's all you could say. If you seemed too sad, then when you write to him, you'll be more hopeful." Yussel smiled at her. "Don't worry. I have faith in Saul. He will understand."

Minna frowned, trying to remember exactly what she had said to him. "I told him he would return, that I was glad he was going because they would make him better."

"Then you were right," Sarah said.

Yussel stood up. "Let's begin by putting more money in the *pushke*. It'll help Saul." He went over to the box and put a few pennies in. Everyone followed his example.

"I know, I'll write to him tonight," Minna said. "I can find out the address of the sanatorium from the society that collects the *pushke* money. That way, he'll have a letter waiting for him when he arrives." She began to plan out what she would say. "I'll write to him after dinner," she said aloud. "It's something I can do right now, tonight."

Yussel nodded. "What a good idea, Minna!"

As soon as dinner was finished and the table cleared, Minna sat down with a piece of paper from her old school notebook. Pen in hand, she dipped it into the bottle of ink and held it poised over the paper. "I wish I had pretty paper to write on, like in the magazines," she said.

Pearl, who was sitting next to her, shook her head. "Saul won't care what kind of paper you use. He'll be glad to get your letter and you know it!"

Minna nodded and wrote, "Dear Saul." Then she paused. What

should she say? Suppose she said the wrong thing? Maybe it would be better to wait for Saul to write first.

"Don't be afraid. Just write!" Pearl urged.

"It's easy for you to say," Minna retorted. She put the pen to the paper and began to write rapidly. An hour later, she had written four pages.

Setting the pen down, she re-read what she had written. Pearl and Yussel watched her anxiously. Finally she nodded.

"I'll send this," she said. "Tomorrow, I'll find out where. I'll put his name and 'Please hold for arrival' on the envelope. That way, they'll save it for him if the letter gets there first." She folded the letter. "I'll have to buy an envelope tomorrow—and stamps. I'll do it at lunchtime." She swallowed, picturing lunch without Saul. "That will be a good time to mail the letter," she continued bravely.

"There's a little space at the bottom," Pearl observed. "Why don't you say that we all send our best wishes. We'll all miss him."

"Yes, say that," Yussel agreed.

Minna picked up the pen again and added a few more lines. Then she re-folded the letter.

"Thanks," she said to Yussel and Pearl. "I feel much better now. It's always best to do something. The hard part is sitting and waiting."

"Why are you thanking us? You wrote the letter," Yussel said.

"Because…because I wouldn't have written it if we hadn't talked. As for Mama, I will never forgive…"

Yussel put his finger to his lips. "Don't say it. Mama is…Mama…"

Minna disagreed. "I want to believe in Mama," she said, "but how can I when she…"

"Believe in yourself," Yussel stated. "It's the only safe way. Believe in yourself."

"Believe in myself? So if I don't expect from Mama, I can't be angry? But, she's Mama. How can I not expect?"

"You can't any more. There's good in the past for us to remember and be thankful for, isn't there, Pearl?" Yussel insisted.

"I suppose so," Pearl replied dubiously.

Minna was near tears again. Leaving the letter on the table, she excused herself and went to the toilet in the hall. Closing the door behind her, she put her face in her hands and cried quietly until she could cry no longer. Wiping her eyes, she walked back into the kitchen. Pearl had already gone to bed. Only Yussel was still up, spreading his quilt on the floor.

"Sometimes, it's too much," Minna sighed. "We deserve good news, but…when will it happen? We deserve it!"

Yussel turned his back to her. "I know," he said softly.

She touched his shoulder. "I'm glad you're my brother."

"I am, too."

"Good night, Yussel."

"Good night, Minna."

CHAPTER 20

Minna mailed her letter to Saul the next day. Then she waited. She checked the mailbox every day to no avail.

The factory was different without him. Every morning, when she awoke, she found herself dreading the day ahead. Although Pearl faithfully joined her at lunch, it wasn't the same. She stopped going to lectures, returned all her books to the library, and barely spoke to anyone. What was the point, she thought, of learning new things if she couldn't discuss them with Saul? At the dinner table, she ate too little and responded listlessly when the others tried to talk to her.

Even Mama noticed. In her own way, she tried to make things better by forcing food upon Minna, who was still angry about her attitude towards Saul's illness. She ignored Mama, often impolitely disregarding her suggestions.

Finally, Yussel invited her out for a walk. When she said no, he insisted.

"I'm surprised at you, Minna," he said as they strode briskly through the cold streets. "You're rude to Mama, Pearl says you hardly talk to her at lunchtime, you sit around like an old lady…it's not like you."

'She shrugged angrily. "I'm doing my work, aren't I? What's it to anyone else?"

Yussel stopped. "What's it to anyone else? Am I your brother? Is Pearl your sister?"

She flushed. "I just can't… Oh, Yussel, maybe Saul is dead.

Why hasn't he written?"

"So you agree with Mama," Yussel replied coldly.

"What do you mean, I agree with Mama?"

"You've given up right from the beginning, just like she did after the fire. I didn't think you were like that, Minna." Yussel shook his head.

"I've given up? Like Mama?" Minna walked more quickly, now almost running.

Yussel hurried to keep up with her. 'How are you living?" he asked breathlessly. "Like a hermit! The other day, Sarah asked you a question and you acted as if you didn't even hear her. How do you think she felt? And Pearl, she has lunch with you every day and you never say a word. That's wonderful, Minna. You're really thinking of others."

She stopped. "Oh, Yussel, I didn't mean… I wasn't thinking."

"Mama doesn't mean either. She's not thinking also. But you blame her."

"It's not the same."

"A disappointment, a sorrow, it's the same. Do you think Saul would be proud to know you now?"

After a long silence, Minna hung her head. "No," she whispered. "But I'm so worried about him." She looked up. "Everyone leaves," she sobbed. "When I love someone, then I lose them. Bubbe, Chava, Tata, Jake…" she stopped, her hand over her mouth.

"Jake?"

She blushed. "It doesn't matter. Whoever it is, they always leave."

"But, Minna, that's the way life is. We lose, we gain. You've still got to live your life. It's all we have. You're mourning for the people you love, Mama's mourning for a shop—maybe people she loves, too—but just like her, you're inflicting your feelings on everyone else. You, the one who's strong in our family!"

"I don't want to be the strong one," Minna sobbed. "I'm tired of being the strong one."

"It doesn't matter," he said. "That's the way you are…the way you've always been…" He paused and his voice rose. "Don't you see, you're leaving it all to me. I can't do it alone. Pearl's too young…she's not the strong one, anyway."

"You need me to help you?"

"I need you to stop mourning. I need you to be Minna again, the one who keeps us going."

"I keep you going?"

"Have you given up your dreams, Minna?"

She thought for a long time. "No." She shook her head.

"You're the one who has dreams, who dares to have dreams. When I think I can't sell another thing to my ladies, when I don't even want to look at them, I say to myself, Minna has dreams, Minna will find her way. It helps me so I don't give up."

She looked up at him through her tears. "You mean…"

"I mean, this is a family. All together, we can live. Apart and alone, we are nothing. I still hope Mama will come back to herself, but now, it's you, Minna, who's our inspiration and you're not trying at all."

"But…Saul…"

His voice softened. "I know how you feel about Saul. Maybe I even know how you feel about losing the people you love. But, Minna, that's only a part of your life. The rest of it is still going on. That's all we can do, isn't it—just go on together?"

She bowed her head.

"I think Saul will be all right," Yussel continued desperately. "But I don't know for sure. I do know if he were here, he'd agree with what I'm saying."

"You're right," Minna said slowly, looking up. "But, Yussel, how do I do it? How can I stop fearing Saul's dead, knowing Chava's dead, Bubbe's dead, that they are gone forever, both of them?"

"You can't stop fearing. But you have to think of the others around you here and now. They're not dead, they're alive, and they need you, Minna. I need you."

She buried her head in Yussel's shoulder. The hard wool of his coat was scratchy against her face as she cried.

"I'm sorry, Yussel," she said in a muffled voice. "I've been so selfish. I didn't mean to…"

"It's hard when you love someone."

"I love Saul, but I don't *love* him—not that way," she said. "It's just…this was the final straw. It seems as if nothing will turn out the way I want it to."

"I know," he replied sadly.

"Oh, Yussel, its been hard on you. And Pearl—how could I be

so unthinking? I'm sorry. I'm so sorry." She buried her head harder against the rough wool.

He patted her on the shoulder and stepped away. "Look up, Minna. It's all right. Everyone understands."

"They shouldn't have to understand. You're right. I've been just like Mama. I didn't think… Saul would hate it if he could see me. He'd understand. He always understands, but he'd hate it. I'm sorry, Yussel."

"If being sorry makes you cry more, that's no good." He smiled and put his arm around her. "I know how you feel, Minna, but it doesn't help. Believe me, I know."

"I want to help you, Yussel, just the way you always help me. Can't I?"

He shook his head. "You can help me by being yourself again. That will help us all. And don't be so angry at Mama. Maybe now you can understand better how she feels."

"How did you get to be so wise?" Minna asked.

"I…watch people," he explained. "So, maybe, it's easier for me to understand them. But, Minna, I have the same feelings. Sometimes, I snap at my ladies or act like I'm not there at dinnertime. It's the same."

"I guess so. But I haven't helped you the way you're helped me."

"Usually you do. I rely on you, Minna."

"That makes me feel good. Most of the time, I like to be called on. Just sometimes, I wish…I wish I didn't have to be, you know?"

He nodded. "I know."

They turned and headed back to the apartment. Minna took a deep breath and began to walk more briskly, her head up. Yussel looked at her, smiled, and joined her.

At the door, Minna stopped. "All right," she said. "Let's take the money out from the floor and count it. We haven't done that for a week. Let's see how we're doing!"

Yussel smiled again. "Just what I was thinking," he said.

Everyone looked up as they came into the kitchen. Even Mama, Minna noticed, looked anxious. Minna smiled and said, "We're going to count the money. Yussel and I have decided it's time."

With great ceremony, the box was lifted from under the floorboards and opened. Yussel counted rapidly, separating the change. Sarah and Bessie, who were privy to the family's secrets, watched him just as anxiously as Pearl and Mama.

While he was counting, Minna leaned over to Pearl. She spoke softly. "I haven't been very good company for the last few weeks, have I, Pearl? I'm sorry."

Pearl gazed into Minna's eyes. "It's all right now?" she asked.

Minna sighed. "It's not all right. How can it be until I hear from Saul? But it's better."

Pearl smiled.

Yussel cleared his throat. "We've already saved twenty dollars. That's with Pearl working only three weeks. At this rate, I'll be ready to hire a man soon. After we have a few men, like before, we'll be earning enough to think about opening another shop."

Mama stared at the money. "We have to save it, to be safe," she said.

Minna leaned forward. "We will, Mama," she said, surprised at her own patience. "Don't worry. But when we have enough, then we can have another shop like before. I'll run it if you don't want to."

Mama frowned. "You'll run it?"

"Yes, Mama."

"If we ever have another shop—and I don't see how we can—but if we ever do, I'm the one who'll run it!"

Minna exchanged glances with Yussel. "All right, Mama," she said meekly.

Sarah and Bessie, who had been watching quietly, stood up. "I have a meeting," Bessie said apologetically. "I'm glad all is well," she added, looking at Minna.

"I have a lecture to go to," Sarah said, smiling broadly. "Do any of you want to come?"

"Maybe tomorrow," Pearl said. "I'm sleepy tonight. I want to go to bed early."

After the girls had gone, Minna helped Yussel put the money back under the floor. "I'm going to write another letter to Saul," she said. "Maybe he didn't get my first one."

"Tell him I hope he's getting better," Mama offered as she went into the bedroom.

Minna looked after Mama in surprise. "I will, Mama, I will," she called. Spreading the paper out on the kitchen table, she opened the inkwell, dipped her pen, and began to write.

Pearl went into the bedroom to fetch her sewing.

Companionably, she sat next to Minna, knotting and re-knotting the embroidery on the new collar she was making for an old shirtwaist. Yussel sat across from them, pencil in hand, figuring his profits from the day's sales.

"When we're rich, we'll still sit like this, won't we?" Minna asked.

"Of course, we will," Yussel said.

"Not like this," Pearl disagreed. "No, we'll sit like royalty. There will be someone else to do all the work for us. We'll sit and watch them, that's all."

"But, still together," Minna laughed. She squirmed on the hard kitchen chair. "We'll have velvet cushions, too."

"What do you mean, velvet cushions?" Yussel looked at her quizzically. 'You're not thinking big enough. We'll have velvet chairs!"

They laughed with him and returned to their work. Life's not so bad, Minna thought as she held her pen in the air.

The next day, she set off for work more cheerfully. If she wasn't enthusiastic, at least she wasn't filled with dread. I think I'll look for Mr. Steinberg today, she decided. It would be good to talk to him—and Pearl would like it, too.

As she sat down at her machine, she gave Rosa a big smile.

She looked startled. "I swear, Minna, this is the first time you're smiled in weeks!"

She hung her head. "I'm sorry. I feel better today. How's 'Seppe? What's the latest news?"

"Well…" Rosa leaned forward. "Mama told Papa about the letters last night and you know what? He said he was glad. He said you were a good friend, but he guesses that his own son can write to his own house from now on. I never thought Papa would say that. Neither did Mama."

Minna beamed. "That's great news! So I won't get any more mysterious letters?"

"Not after the next one, anyway."

The lights flickered and everyone bent over their machines. As she sewed, Minna thought, I'll hear from Saul soon. I know I will. Until I do, I won't give up. I'll never give up again! She smiled to herself. I probably will, she qualified, but at least next time, I'll try to realize what I'm doing.

At lunchtime, she and Pearl looked for Mr. Steinberg. They saw him standing with a group of other men near the outside door. Minna walked boldly over to him. "Will you come for a walk with us, Mr. Steinberg?" she asked.

His friends exchanged a glance. "You'd better go, Steinberg," one of them said. "If two pretty ladies were asking me, I'd be out the door already!"

Minna and Pearl blushed, but they stood their ground.

Mr. Steinberg twinkled. "How can I refuse such an enticing invitation? If you'll excuse me, gentlemen…" With a bow, he gestured toward the doorway.

Once they were outside, he spoke first. "I'm glad to see you, Minna. And you too, Pearl. I've been worried about you, Minna. Since Saul left, I haven't seen you."

"Have you heard from him, Mr. Steinberg?" Minna asked.

"Not yet, but it usually takes a while for them to get settled in. My nephew went there, too, you know. When he came back, he was as good as new!"

Minna sighed in relief. "So, you're not worried?"

"Put it this way. I'm less worried now that they're taking care of him than I was when he was coughing his heart out here. If anyone can help, they can in Denver."

"That's what I think, too," Pearl said.

Mr. Steinberg looked inquiringly at Minna.

"I guess I feel the same way, she replied slowly. "Yes, I do," she added firmly.

He looked at her sharply for a moment and nodded to himself. "How do you like being a factory girl, young lady?" he asked, turning to Pearl.

"I like it!" Pearl said. "It's better than staying home or going to school."

He laughed. "An interesting commentary on the factory system—better than staying home or going to school. I don't know if everyone would agree with you."

"I don't," Minna said baldly. "I'd much rather be in school."

"Work is what you have to do. If you're still enjoying it, Pearl, I'm glad for you. Soon enough, I'm afraid you may begin to feel differently." He sighed.

"Soon enough," Pearl replied, "things will change. Minna says if we all work hard, we can save. Then we'll be able to open a shop again. I wouldn't mind working in a shop till…"

"Till what?"

She blushed. "Well…I don't know."

"Till you get married, that's what you mean," Minna teased.

"You, Minna, you're planning to be a bachelor lady? Maybe you're a suffragette," Mr. Steinberg commented, trying to look shocked.

Minna shrugged. "I don't know much about it, but if it means I can be as free as a man, I wouldn't mind."

Pearl gasped. "You never said that before!"

"I never thought of it before. What's your opinion, Mr. Steinberg?"

"My daughter says I'm old-fashioned, but I think a woman's first joy should be her family. After that, if she has time, she should do what she wants. If she has to work anyway, she ought to get paid the same as a man. That's only fair. As for voting, I don't know. Most women don't have time to learn enough to decide."

"They could if they tried," Minna insisted.

"That's just what my daughter says!"

"I wonder what Saul would think," Minna mused.

"Ask him the next time you write."

Minna found it reassuring to note that Mr. Steinberg took her correspondence with Saul for granted. Maybe there'll be a letter waiting for me when I get home today, she thought.

"Minna says you write poetry, Mr. Steinberg," Pearl said timorously.

"I do my best. To write a poem is to distill beauty from life. If it is a good poem, you can share your vision with others."

"May I read some of your poems?" Pearl asked.

"I am in *The Forward* now and then. If you keep your eyes open, you'll find one."

"We both will." Minna resolved to buy the paper more often.

"I don't like to write. I want to be and do, not sit around writing all the time," Pearl said.

"Then for you, your life is your poem," Mr. Steinberg said lightly.

"That's just Saul said he wished for me in the book he gave me for graduation!" Pearl exclaimed.

"And you, Minna? How do you feel about writing?"

"I don't know," she said slowly. "Sometimes I think I would like to write stories, but I never do. I like writing to Saul, though.

Sometimes," she looked at Mr. Steinberg shyly, "I imagine my own life as a story I am writing. When I lie in bed a night, I try to think how to tell it. Most of the time, though, I'm too busy worrying to think about it."

"You should keep a journal. That's a good way to begin."

"I know. Saul said that, too. But there's too much else on my mind."

Pearl smiled. "When I was little, in *der alter heym*, you used to tell me stories, Minna. Do you remember?"

Minna nodded. "It seems so long ago." She looked at Pearl. "Now you're all grown up."

Pearl ducked her head.

"So old you both are," Mr. Steinberg commented. "Ancient, I'd say."

They all laughed.

As they waited for the elevator after returning Mr. Steinberg to his cronies, Pearl whispered to Minna, "I really like him. He's like Saul—truly interested in everyone else."

"I know." Without thinking, Minna continued. "I wish we had a Tata like that, don't you?"

Pearl looked surprised. "I wasn't thinking of Tata, but you're right. I never think of him. It's been so long since he's gone."

"I know."

Sitting at her machine, Minna's wondered—what would it have been like if Tata had stayed? She shook her head. The way he was, it would have been worse. But what if they had a Tata like Mr. Steinberg, who cared about them and worked hard to make their lives better? She shook her head again. We don't, she mused, so what's the use of thinking about it? He would have sat there with his old books while we worked all the time.

I won't get married, she decided. Then I won't have to worry about anyone else and no one will tell me what to do. When we have the store again and things are going well, I'll do what I want. Maybe, someday I'll get married, but not until I really want to. She thought of Jake and grimaced. I'll meet someone who truly will be a prince and then I'll be glad to share my days with him. We'll work together…

She laughed out loud. Leaping from never marrying to imagining my prince in two seconds! I guess I'm not really a new woman, she thought. She glanced over at Anna, who hummed to herself as she sewed. Anna—and Pearl, too—they don't have dreams by themselves. It all depends upon the right man, their prince. Suppose he doesn't come along? Then what will they do?

She noticed the sparkle of a shiny new ring on Anna's finger. Tomorrow, she decided, we'll have lunch with her, Pearl and I. If she's free, that is. It's not her fault, the way she looks. She means well, as long as she doesn't make Pearl want to be like her. A warning voice in her mind said, maybe Pearl is like her already. Maybe she's that way all by herself. She stifled the thought.

After work, Minna walked home briskly, slightly ahead of Pearl, Sarah, and Mama. She remembered a game from her childhood and tried not to step on any of the cracks in the sidewalk. If I don't step on a crack, she thought, there will be a letter from Saul. Then everything will be all right.

When she arrived home, she raced to the mailbox. Peering through the glass window, she saw that it was empty. Head down, she waited for the others to catch up.

"No letter?" Pearl asked. "I can tell from the way you're standing."

"Maybe tomorrow," Sarah said, as she always did. "Don't give up!"

Surprisingly, Mama echoed her words. "Maybe tomorrow."

Minna smiled weakly although she felt like crying. "I'll get one soon," she said, and ran up the stairs, hoping to be alone for a moment.

By the time she took off her cloak, the others had caught up with her. Unless she went out for a walk or locked herself in the toilet, there was no place she could go to be alone.

When I get rich, Minna planned, I'll have a big house with lots of rooms. There'll be a room just for sitting. I'll have my own bedroom, too. When I feel like being by myself, I'll just shut the door and no one will come in. Then I'll be able to keep a journal. I'll have plenty of time to write in it.

She remembered a book of poetry Saul had lent her and forgotten to take back when he left. Taking it from her shelf in the bedroom, she brought it into the kitchen and sat down at the table.

As soon as she opened the first page, Yussel came in. She sighed and closed the book. "Did it go well today?" she asked, making an effort to sound cheerful.

Although Minna still saw Mr. Steinberg sometimes at lunch, she began eating with the other girls, especially as the weather grew colder. They remained inside, leaning on their machines or perched against the table nearby. Anna, very pleased to join them when "her fellow was busy", introduced several others to the group. Sarah usually came, too. Less frequently, Rosa sat with them instead of the other Italian girls.

Pearl seemed content to sit and giggle with Anna and her friends, Lily and Hannah. Yet she never suggested joining them in the evenings, although Minna had worried that she might. Their conversation, she thought scornfully, had two topics: men and beauty. The latter seemed to be the most popular...what to wear... how to fix one's hair...whether it was really evil to add a touch of rouge... Despite her best intentions, Minna found she couldn't help but participate, even to the extent of experimenting with new hairstyles in front of the mirror at home.

One day, when she was angry at herself for listening with such avid interest to frivolities, she walked away a little. As she stepped away, she bumped carelessly into another girl, facing sideways in her seat as she ate her lunch.

"I'm sorry," Minna said. "I wasn't looking where I was going. Did you spill anything?"

"No. It's all right."

Minna looked down at her. "My name's Minna," she said. "You must be new."

"I'm Erma. I just started yesterday."

"I've been here for a couple of months," Minna said. "Actually, it's been about six months," she finished with a note of surprise. "I didn't realize is was so long. Anyway, it gets easier to keep up—until they raise the quota again."

"I know. I used to work down the street, but business was bad and they had to let most of us go, so I came here. I was lucky," she continued soberly. "Most of the girls couldn't find another place. My cousin works here, though, and he helped me. He told me about you."

"He did? Who's your cousin?"

"Sammy, at the elevator. He said I should come and say 'hello', but I didn't want to bother you. Your group seem to be having so much fun at lunch," she said wistfully.

"Well then, come and sit with us." Minna almost propelled Erma out of her chair. She introduced her to the other girls, who looked up, smiled, and continued their conversation.

Erma glanced at Minna, saying, "I don't fuss that much with my clothes."

Minna was not surprised to hear it. Although her shirtwaist was nice enough, it was coming untucked at the waist. Her skirt was slightly shabby and her hair fastened insecurely. She smiled.

"My friend, the *Amerikaner*, she says it's silly. She says, 'Why should women have to fuss more than men? It isn't fair!' She has beautiful clothes, though." Erma said.

"You have a friend who's an *Amerikaner*? A real *Amerikaner*?"

"I do," Erma said proudly.

Minna tried to imagine what it would be like to have a friend who was a real American. "Where does she live?"

"Uptown."

Minna examined Erma more carefully. She didn't look any different from the other girls. Yet there must be something special about her if she had a friend from uptown. "How did you meet?" she asked.

"I go to the Alliance to take classes and she was there, helping the teacher. We got to talking. We go out for coffee sometimes."

"I've been there for a few lectures, but I've never taken any classes. I was told they looked down on us. My friend, Saul said…"

Erma interrupted. "I know, everyone says that. But I say, I want to be an American, why shouldn't I change? Whoever wants to help me, I don't care. My friend, she says, 'The important thing is to grow.'"

"Oh," Minna said, with a dubious expression.

"Why don't you try coming with me one time? You can meet Priscilla—that's my friend—and see what it's like there. I'm taking an art class. There are some very good painters in my class."

"I don't know."

"They like us to bring friends. Why don't you come tonight? I can meet you there at eight."

She hesitated. She hadn't gone out at all since Saul left. Yet she'd never met a real *Amerikaner* of her own age. She fingered her locket and pictured Susannah, the girl she had seen so long ago with Jake. "Yes, I'll come," she said, surprising herself.

"Good."

The lights flickered and they all hurried back to their machines.

"I'll see you at eight then, just inside the main door," Erma called as she pulled her chair out so she could sit straight and face her machine.

Minna nodded and began to sew.

That evening, disappointed again when she received no letter from Saul, Minna hurried out to meet Erma. Everyone at the table had had something to say when they found out where she was going.

'You're not going to like it," Bessie said. "They'll laugh at you unless you do everything the way they want you to."

"I thought Erma looked kind of…messy," was Pearl's comment.

Even Mama added her two cents. "Going here, going there. You never stay home, Minna." That was so patently untrue, she didn't even bother to reply.

Sarah looked as if she was going to offer to come along but before she had a chance to say anything, Yussel smiled at her and asked if she would help him go through his stock.

As Minna was leaving, he walked her to the door. "Have a good time," he said. "It will do you good to go out for a change."

"Thanks, Yussel," she said, touching his hand.

At the Alliance, Minna waited for Erma to come. Because she had worried about being late, she was ten minutes early. While she waited, she amused herself by watching the others as they passed her in the large hallway.

She saw girls and young men of her own age as well as older ones. Everyone seemed friendly, yet intent, hurrying past her as if they had no time to spare. As she gazed at them, she noticed one thing. They all seemed alive, vital in a way that was different from most people she passed on the street or saw at the factory. They look, she thought, as if they know a secret.

The ten minutes passed so quickly Minna was surprised when Erma touched her arm "Here I am!" she said. "I'm sorry if you were waiting."

"Oh, I didn't mind." Minna smiled at Erma. "It's interesting to see the people."

"I know, but we'd better hurry now. I don't want to be late."

Minna followed Erma through long corridors and twisting halls to an unadorned door on the ground floor. Before they entered, Erma turned to her. "I'll show you what it's like and introduce you. If the teacher says it's okay, you can stay. If not, you can wait in the reading room upstairs by the entrance. You'll like it there."

Minna nodded.

Erma pushed the door open and entered a large room. In the front, an older man was arranging a group of objects on a table. Positioned in front of the table were a number of easels, each bearing a clean white sheet of paper backed by a piece of cardboard. Students, talking noisily to each other, stood by each easel. They waved at Erma as she marched by, leading Minna to the front of the room.

"Mr. Einstein," she began.

He looked up. "Just a minute, Erma." He stepped back to get a better view of his arrangement. Narrowing his eyes, he moved forward again and deftly moved several of the objects. Minna saw a vase, some fruit, and a stack of plates topped by a sharp knife.

Nodding at the final result, he looked at Erma. "Yes?"

"This is my friend, Minna. She'd like to come and watch."

"We can do better than that," Mr. Einstein said. "Moses Soyer can't come tonight, so she can use his easel. We're working in charcoal today."

Minna was aghast. "But…I've never…"

The teacher hurried to a cupboard in the back corner of the room and dashed back. Thrusting a smock at her, he said, "Here. You can wear this. Charcoal's on the easel."

Before Minna knew what was happening, she was standing in front of an easel across the room from Erma. A large piece of charcoal rested on the small tray. Automatically, she picked it up. Behind her, she could hear the rustle of long strokes upon the paper. She lifted the charcoal and held it poised in the air in front of the paper. The paper looked so white. She hesitated.

She heard a voice behind her. "He did the same thing to me when I first came. What you're supposed to do is to make a picture of the things on the table."

She turned and looked at the man behind her gratefully. His smock was covered in paint. Above the rainbow of colors, a pale face emerged, almost shocking in its absence of hue.

"But…I don't know how to draw," Minna protested. "I only came to keep Erma company."

"That's all right. The only way you'll find out how good you are is to try. See," He held up the charcoal. "It's soft so you can draw broad lines or thin lines. You can smear it, too." He looked at the still life and drew a few lines on his paper. Then he smiled at her. "The thing is, there's no right way. There's only your way—and that's what counts."

Slightly reassured, Minna looked at the still life again.

Just as she was about to touch her charcoal to the paper, Mr. Einstein came over to her. "The classic problem of the beginning artist," he said. "How to start. Minna's going at it the right way. First you must observe, feel the objects. Sense the curves, the palpable the energy of the fruit, the dangerous sharpness of the knife. Acknowledge your feelings and try to suggest them on the paper."

Minna blushed. She wanted to say, I wasn't acknowledging anything. I was simply too scared to start.

Mr. Einstein walked away to look at someone else's work.

Valiantly, Minna touched her charcoal to the paper, trying to copy the roundness of the apple she saw. In a way, she thought, it's like Mr. Steinberg, seeing the beauty in our lives. I just have to look.

By the time the class was over, an hour and a half later, Minna had become completely absorbed in her drawing. She discovered that by smudging the charcoal, she could almost erase her previous lines. Stepping back, she looked at what she had drawn. Now that she saw it clearly, she sighed in dismay. It didn't look like the objects on the table at all. She peered at it more closely. Where were the rounded edges of the fruit, the sharp angles of the knife? She remembered how carefully she had drawn them, over and over.

Mr. Einstein came to look at her work.

She smiled at him weakly.

"It's a start," he said. "Take this home and look at it some more. Think of what you were trying to draw and how it emerged." He looked at her kindly. "It *is* a start," he added.

She followed the example of the others and carefully rolled up her sketch. Wiping her hands on her smock, she returned it to Mr. Einstein and walked over to Erma. She looked at her drawing.

"Why, Erma," she said in surprise, "that's really good."

In Erma's picture, she could see the fruit and the other objects clearly. They sat upon the table, outlined with a clean purity.

Erma shook her head. "Oh, I can make it look like whatever I'm copying, but there's something missing. See, what he said, Mr. Einstein, about the roundness of the fruit, the feeling it gives you.

That's the hardest part to show."

"I don't know," Minna said, shaking her head. "Mine didn't look anything at all." She unrolled her picture to show it to Erma.

She laughed. "Drawing is like everything else. You have to practice. I bet this is the first picture you've ever drawn, right?" Ignoring her smudged hands, she pushed back the lock of hair that kept straggling over her eyes, leaving a trail of charcoal on her forehead. "I've always liked to draw, so I had lots of practice at home." Taking off her smock, she rolled up her drawing, stuffed the smock into the large bag she carried, and led the way towards the door.

"Is there somewhere we can wash our hands?" Minna asked, holding hers up. "They're black!"

Erma looked surprised. "Sure. Follow me. I guess I could use a little wash-up, too."

As they washed their hands in a small washroom, Minna wondered if they were going to meet Erma's *Amerikaner* friend. It seemed as if Erma had forgotten about it and she didn't like to remind her.

After they had dried their hands, Erma bustled out, pulling Minna with her. "I'm meeting Priscilla at the cafe on the corner. That's where we always meet. We'll have a glass of tea and sit, just *schmooze* for a little."

Wide-eyed, Minna followed her. At the café! She had often passed the cafés. At all hours of the evening, they were crowded with men and women talking loudly, wedged up against the tiny tables. She had often wondered what they found to talk about so intently, their voices echoing and their gestures vehement.

At the café, a small shabby room on the ground floor of a narrow building, Erma walked in as relaxed as if she were entering her own home. She waved at various groups of people and headed towards a small table in the back corner of the room. "This is my table," she said. "We'll need an extra chair." She took one from the nearest empty table. "Priscilla will be here soon. She has to put her classroom in order to help the teacher."

Minna sat down, her back against the wall. Her position afforded her a perfect view of the others in the café. The women, she noticed, were very serious looking. They leaned across the table, thrusting their faces forward to speak intensely to their companions. The men looked even more forceful, their eyes burning as they pursued an argument or extended a finger to make a point. At the table nearest them, two older men sat poring over a chessboard and stroking their beards as they pondered.

A waiter came over. "The usual, Erma?" he asked.

Minna stared at him. She remembered how she and Pearl had pretended to be at a restaurant in the park. She was tempted to ask for the most extravagant thing she could think of. Then, realizing it would be expensive, she hesitated.

"Yes," Erma replied. "Would you like something, Minna?"

"Not yet," she replied.

After the waiter left, she whispered to Erma, "How much does a glass of tea cost?"

Erma looked at her with understanding. "It's a dime with a piece of cake."

Minna decided that if she *had* to buy something, maybe she could manage a cup of tea and a piece of cake this one time. "Do you come here every night?" she asked. "They seem to know you very well."

"I come here a lot. Whenever I'm at the Alliance, this is where I end up. This café is mostly for students. There are others. The Café Royal is where al the actors and writers go. The Monopole on Second Avenue and Ninth Street is for the radicals. Supposedly, Trotsky was there once."

Minna looked around the room. "Do you know everyone who's here?"

"Not everyone, but most of them. They let you sit all night once you order." She stood up and waved. "Here comes Priscilla now."

Minna stared at the girl who was approaching the table. She was dressed with simple elegance, her dark hair framing a slim, aristocratic face. Despite the richness of her clothing, her coat hung upon her in a slightly crooked fashion, as if she had literally thrown it on. Her large brown eyes twinkled when she saw Erma.

"Here I am!" she exclaimed as she sat down. "Who's this?"

"This is my friend, Minna Ruben," Erma replied.

Minna smiled.

"I'm glad to meet you," Priscilla said, holding out her hand.

Surprised, Minna shook it. "Glad to meet you," she repeated.

"What a day!" Priscilla continued. "I haven't stopped since this afternoon. I help teach English," she explained, looking at Minna.

"How are you?" she asked Erma without a pause.

"As usual," Erma replied.

"And you, Minna? Do you work with Erma?"

The question was asked with such sincere interest that Minna had no hesitation in replying. "I work at Triangle," she said. Then, excitement overcoming her shyness, she burst out, "I went with Erma to an art class tonight!"

"Oh yes, the charcoal." Priscilla nodded. "I can always tell when Erma has been working with charcoal." She pointed to Erma's forehead. Reaching into her pocket, she brought out a delicate lace handkerchief. 'Here," she said, holding it out to Erma. "Wipe the charcoal off your forehead!"

Erma accepted the handkerchief. She dabbed briskly at her forehead. When she handed back the handkerchief, Minna was aghast to see that it was covered in big black smudges. Without looking at it, Priscilla stuffed it back into her pocket.

"Did you like the class?" she asked Minna.

"Yes, I did! I don't think I'm an artist, but it's fun to try. It's the same as Mr. Steinberg, what the teacher said."

"Mr. Steinberg?"

"The poet. I know him from the factory." She hesitated. Seeing that both girls were looking at her with interest, she continued. "He says there's beauty in all parts of life, from the rainbows in a puddle to the sorrow in a widow's face. He says we should notice, we should stop when we see beauty and pay attention. Isn't that the same as what Mr. Einstein says?" She looked at Erma.

Erma smiled. Minna caught her exchanging glances with Priscilla, as if to say, 'See, my friend is very interesting.' She began to relax.

Slipping off her coat, Priscilla leaned forward. Minna noticed that she wore an exquisite cameo at her throat. Small gold earrings dangled from her ears.

"That's why I like to come here!" Priscilla exclaimed. "Everyone has ideas. At home, if there's an idea, they beat it over the head and chase it away."

Erma smiled as if she had heard this before.

"I went to a meeting last night," Priscilla continued. "I told you about my friends." She turned to Minna. "My friends, Erma knows, believe women should have the same rights as men. They think it's not fair that women can't vote."

"You say it as if you don't believe the same thing," Erma said. "You know you're a suffragette."

Minna said nothing. She was a little frightened by the word and unwilling to join Erma in teasing Priscilla. She sat quietly and listened to them.

"I don't use the word, my dear! The parents would disown me. But..." She lowered her voice. "I went to an evening three days ago and I told a few other girls what I believe in. They said they'd come the next time we have a big meeting. That's the only way to change people's minds—to help them to see for themselves. Don't you agree, Minna?"

"I guess so," she said doubtfully. "Sometimes, they don't want to listen, though." She thought of Mama with Bessie. "You can't make a person listen if they don't want to."

"That's true," Priscilla agreed. "But you can show them by your own example."

The waiter arrived with a glass of tea for Erma. He looked at Priscilla and Minna. "Ladies?" he asked.

Minna shook her head.

Priscilla ordered the same as Erma—a glass of tea and a piece of cake. "Are you sure you don't want anything, Minna?" she asked.

"Not tonight," Minna said, thinking, ten cents is a lot of money.

As if reading her mind, Priscilla looked at the waiter. "Bring an extra glass of tea," she said, "and an extra cake. I feel hungry tonight."

Minna shook her head, but the waiter didn't notice and left the table.

"I don't think..." she began.

"You'll have a sip of the tea and I'll have both pieces of cake," Priscilla said. "I honestly didn't have time for supper tonight."

'You have to order to stay," Erma explained.

Minna was embarrassed, but she couldn't think of how to leave now that the waiter had accepted their order. "I didn't bring very much money," she said finally.

"Don't worry, Minna," Priscilla urged. "I want you to stay. It's only a few cents for the tea alone."

Erma leaned forward. "You know, that makes sense. I always thought you had to order both."

Minna sensed that wasn't true, but there was nothing she could do. They *were* trying to make her feel comfortable.

Priscilla leaned forward. "It's simple. I have too much money, more than I could ever spend. For me to buy a glass of tea and a piece of cake is nothing. For you, it's not so easy. Does that mean we can't sit and talk together? Erma understands."

Minna looked at Erma.

"It's all right, Minna. Really it is. I felt the same way at first, but now I see that Priscilla is right. Why should we sit outside in the cold when we can sit here in comfort? If Priscilla truly doesn't mind…"

Minna shook her head.

Priscilla looked into her eyes earnestly. "The only time I feel alive is when I'm working or visiting down here. It's different at home. And the money means nothing to me. For a glass of tea and a piece of cake, we can sit for hours."

Minna still felt uncomfortable, but she shrugged in agreement. She didn't see what else she could do. She resolved to talk to Erma about it later.

Relieved, Priscilla smiled.

"I'll explain further," she continued. "It's always best to be honest. My grandfather made a lot of money by exploiting others. In a way, I started working at the Alliance to make amends for what he did. Then I found I liked it better here than I do at home. I'm thinking of moving downtown and doing settlement work next year. Here, I can be myself. At home, I am the peculiar one, not interested in marriage or teas or dances."

Minna laughed in amazement. "You have everything we work so hard to get, yet you wish you were like us!"

"At home, it's all been decided a long time ago. There's a right way and a wrong way for everything. Here, it's still being decided. People are growing and hoping. At home, all we do is worry about losing what we already have."

Minna frowned. "I can't imagine…"

"I know," Erma interrupted. "I can't either. All I want is a room of my own and time, time to do what I want to do. It seems so simple, yet I don't have it. Priscilla has it all, yet it's still not enough. Maybe no one is ever truly happy."

"To be happy is to be content. How many do you know who are content with their lives?" Priscilla asked.

Minna thought about it.

"I don't know anyone who doesn't wish for something different."

"There, you see!" Priscilla cried triumphantly. "Most people I know don't wish for anything. It makes them dead in a way."

Minna tried to imagine what it would be like to wish for nothing, but it was impossible. "If they wish for nothing, they must enjoy what they have." she said, after thinking about it for a few minutes.

"How can you notice what you've had all your life? It's meaningless because it's taken for granted."

Minna looked at Erma, frowning. There was something familiar in what Priscilla had just said. She tried to remember what it was. "I know!" she said finally. "It's like Mr. Steinberg's garden. It's just what he said." She repeated his words to them.

"I wish I could meet him," Priscilla sighed.

"His poems are in *The Forward*."

"What good is that to me? I can't read Yiddish."

As they sat and talked, sipping their tea and eating cake, Minna realized she liked Priscilla. It was easy to see she was unhappy in her life and seeking something different. Erma, she noticed, was completely at ease with her friend.

Finally, Priscilla looked down at her waist where she wore a small watch pinned to her belt. "It's late! I must fly or I won't be allowed in!" She gestured to the waiter, paid him, smiled at Minna and Erma, and began to put her cloak on. "I really enjoyed meeting you, Minna," she said. "I hope we'll meet again soon." To Erma, she said, "I'll see you next week."

"Yes, I'll see you then," Erma agreed.

"Thank you for the tea and cake," Minna called after her as she hurried out.

She stood up. "Which way are you going?" she asked Erma. "I live on Allen Street."

'We can walk together for a little while," Erma replied.

As they hurried down the icy streets, Erma said, "Did you like my friend?"

"Oh, yes. I don't understand, though. Why should she come down here? I know what she said, but I can't believe it. Can you?"

"The way she lives, there are too many rules. When she comes down here, she feels free. That's what she says. I only meet her here, so I don't know exactly where she lives or what her home is like. She's still my friend, though."

"Did she mean it when she said they wouldn't let her in? How could they not let their daughter in?"

"I don't know if she means it or not."

"I never sat down with an *Amerikaner* before," Minna said.

"Neither did I till I met Priscilla. I think she's different from the others, don't you?"

"I don't know. How could I know?"

They walked slowly.

"Do you always go to the café?" Minna asked.

"Since I met Priscilla, I do. Before, I went to classes and then straight home. But when she offered to treat and explained it the way she did to you, I felt all right."

"Isn't it strange?" Minna blurted. "I'd like to change my life to be more like hers and she wants to be like us."

"I know. She told me once that her family came over on the Mayflower. That makes them real Americans. If I was a real American, I think I'd just sit back and smile at the world. But I guess it doesn't work that way."

"What's your dream?" Minna asked.

"I don't plan to stay at the factory forever, that's for sure! Beyond that, I don't know. I keep taking classes and I hope, one day I'll take the right class and I'll know, just like that!"

"I'm going to be a teacher. As soon as we save enough money for another store—ours burned down—then I can start working towards college."

Erma was impressed. "You know what you want. I only know I want to change, but that's not enough."

"You could be an artist," Minna suggested. "Your drawing was good."

'I don't know. No one in our family has ever been an artist. Besides, I just draw for fun. I always have."

"If I could draw the way you can…"

"Come to the class again next week and you can practice," Erma laughed.

"Maybe I will."

After they said good night, each to go in a different direction, Minna thought about the evening. It was the first time in many days she hadn't worried about Saul. She clutched her rolled up drawing. And Priscilla! No matter what she said, Minna couldn't imagine that her own life was more interesting than hers.

For her, it's interesting… What did she say? She called it vital and alive, but for me, it's a question of a roof over our heads and food on the table. No matter how much Priscilla tries to pretend she lives down here, it won't be the same for her. And the other way round for me. Will I ever be able to forget that food on the table is a blessing not to be taken for granted? I hope it does become easy to take things for granted once you have them long enough.

The streets were cold and deserted. Minna walked quickly, peering through the dark to avoid the icy patches. When she arrived home, she hurried up the steps, anxious to snuggle under her quilt in the warm bed. She tiptoed through the darkened front room and past Yussel, who was already fast asleep in the kitchen.

She left her drawing on the kitchen table, still rolled up. I'll look at it in the morning, she thought. Maybe it will look better then. She undressed and curled up next to Pearl.

The next morning, despite her late night, Minna woke up early enough to spend a moment with Yussel before he left. Timidly, she unrolled her drawing, hoping that it would look better than it had the night before.

"Look, Yussel," she said, as she laid it out on the table. "Last night I went to a drawing class and I did a still life." She looked down at it dubiously. "I guess it doesn't look like much."

Yussel peered at the sketch. "Of course, it does," he said valiantly. He looked more closely. "Exactly what is it supposed to be?"

She quickly rolled it up again. "Never mind! Anyway, it was fun to do it. I met Erma's *Amerikaner* friend. Her name is Priscilla. We sat in a café!"

He frowned.

"It was just students from the Alliance. Erma and Priscilla and I sat together." She added quickly, "We had a glass of tea."

Yussel looked at her piercingly.

"Can you imagine, Yussel? Priscilla's family came over on the Mayflower. She lives uptown and she'd rather live the way we do. Isn't that strange? I never met a real *Amerikaner* to talk to before. She's different…but she's the same. She helps to teach at the Alliance. Maybe you could come and meet her, too, next week at the café."

Yussel looked relieved. "Maybe I will. I'd be interested to meet someone like that." He stood up. "I have to hurry now. I'll see you tonight."

"Have a good day," Minna called after him. She stuck the sketch in a corner of the kitchen and went into the bedroom to get dressed. She decided not to show it to anyone else.

At lunch that day, she and Erma sat together, a little bit away from the other girls. Minna was curious to find out more about her. "Do you live with your family?" she asked.

Erma shook her head. "I live with my married sister. The rest of my family is in *der alter heym*. They didn't want to come here. My sister came first and then I came four years ago to help watch the children. Now she stays home and I work."

"What about her husband?"

"He works, too. He's studying to be a lawyer. He was born in this country," she said proudly. "His family has a hotel in New Jersey. Well, it's actually more of a boarding house. He's Hungarian. He works all day and goes to school at night, but when he's a lawyer, it'll be different."

"Don't you miss your mama?" Minna asked.

"At first, I did. Now my sister is more like a mama, but it's better, because she's not so bossy. As long as I do my part, she doesn't worry about me." Erma flicked back her hair. "And you?"

"I live with my Mama, my brother, Yussel, and my sister, Pearl. You met her. We had a store—I guess I told you—but it burned down."

They continued to talk. Minna found herself telling Erma about Saul. It was the first time she had talked about him to anyone outside the family except Mr. Steinberg.

"So, you're waiting for a letter," Erma said. "That must be awful, just waiting. Can't you write him?"

"I already have, twice," Minna sighed.

"I'm sure it takes time to get settled there," Erma said hopefully. "Don't worry. It won't make anything better if you do. You said Mr. Steinberg didn't seem worried."

"But I am worried about him and…I really miss him. We saw each other every day. He's my best friend."

"Just a friend?"

"Yes, just a friend. Love is different."

Erma looked at her inquiringly, but Minna shook her head and changed the subject by asking Erma about Priscilla. Together, they puzzled over her.

"Anyway," Minna said finally, "I don't think she'd like it if she had to live the way we do. She has a choice. She can always go uptown. To her, it may seem exciting but for me, it's my life."

"I think she means what she says," Erma said slowly.

"Oh, I'm sure she does. But there is a difference between choosing and having to do something. We *have* to work here. She can pretend, but she doesn't *have* to. She's visiting, but we live here."

Erma frowned. "You make it sound as if she's…I don't know…playing a game."

"I don't think she means to. I think she's honest. But…" Minna shook her head. "Anyway, I really liked her. I'd like to meet her again."

Erma's face cleared. "Why don't you come to class with me next week? Then you can see her afterwards."

Minna smiled. "I'd like that."

The lights flickered and they both went back to work.

That evening, when Minna arrived home, she glanced at the mailbox, expecting to find it empty as usual. To her surprise, there was a letter in the box. Fumbling, she pulled out her key and opened it. Holding up the envelope, she looked immediately at the return address. It came from Denver.

"I have a letter from Saul!" she called to the others who had preceded her up the stairs. "I have a letter!"

They waited for her.

She hurried up, fondling her letter. "It feels very thin," she said.

As soon as they stepped into the apartment, she rushed into the bedroom and opened the letter, carefully using her scissors to slit the top. She pulled out one sheet and read it quickly. It said, in a very elaborate and curlicued script:

Dear Minna,

One of the nurses is writing this for me. I just wanted to let you know that I arrived safely. They say I should do nothing for a little while, not even read or write. The trip was tiring, but I'm beginning to feel a little better. Please keep writing to me. I wait for your letters.

Saul

She read the letter several times, trying to glean more information from it. At least, he arrived in one piece, she thought.

She looked at it again. After all her waiting, she hated to receive a note from a stranger. She couldn't help but wonder what the nurse looked like. Poor Saul, she thought finally. He must be really sick not to be able to read or write. I'll send him a letter tonight.

She left the bedroom carrying the letter. As she stepped into the kitchen, everyone looked at her anxiously.

"It's from his nurse," she said, holding it up. "Here, read it."

Pearl took the letter and read it aloud. When she finished, no one spoke.

Finally Sarah said, "Poor Saul, if he can't even write."

Mama bowed her head.

"It says he's getting a little better," Pearl quavered.

"I'm going to write to him right now," Minna said. "At least he can read my letters." Then she had a terrible thought. "Maybe the nurse reads them to him. I'm not writing for a nurse to read!"

"What difference, as long as he knows we're thinking about him?" Pearl said. Gulping, she added, "I'll write to him, too."

"I'll add a note at the bottom of yours, if I may," Sarah said.

Mama went into the bedroom, muttering to herself.

By the time Yussel walked in, Minna was in the middle of her letter and Pearl was getting ready to hand hers over to Sarah for a post script. Without saying anything, Minna handed Yussel the note from Saul's nurse.

He read it quickly, paused, and read it again. "It does say he's getting a little better," he said finally.

"We're writing to him," Pearl said.

"I'll write to him, too," Yussel said decisively.

"We can send it all in one envelope," Minna suggested, looking off into the distance as she decided what to say next. Just writing Saul about Priscilla helped her to understand her own feelings. I wonder what he'll say, she thought.

"If you're feeling better, tell me what you think about Priscilla," she added to the letter. "Your opinion will help me. If we can't talk in person, we can by mail." She continued by promising to write to him every week whether he replied or not.

By the time she and everyone else had finished their portions of the letter, it was late for dinner. Minna gathered up the letters, folded them together, and inserted them into an envelope.

"I'll buy a stamp tomorrow," she explained. "I feel sorry for the nurse if she has to read this! She'll never be able to decipher my handwriting or read Yussel's. Who's to say she speaks Yiddish, anyway! Sarah, your handwriting's clear as a bell, but so tiny. I would have been willing to give you an extra page. Pearl, you're the only one of us who writes just like the penmanship books we studied."

"I hope Saul will be well enough to read this himself," Yussel said.

"I'm sure he will," Sarah chimed in. "After all, he won't get it tomorrow. By the time it gets there… He's resting up now. Maybe he'll be much better."

"I hope he will," Minna said. In her pleasure at writing the letter, she had almost forgotten to worry about Saul. "I'm sure he'll be better," she added hopefully.

Mama came back into the kitchen as Minna spoke. Although she said nothing, her expression was forbidding. Minna pretended not to notice.

CHAPTER 21

The next day, Minna hurried out of the workroom at lunchtime and went to look for Mr. Steinberg. Next time, she thought, I'll invite Erma to meet him. Today, she wanted to see him alone.

Fortunately, he was in the lobby, talking with his friends from the eighth floor. As soon as he saw Minna step out of the elevator, he hurried over to her.

She beamed.

His friends smiled. "Off with your young lady again, Steinberg?" one of them called.

Minna blushed.

"I'm glad I saw you," he said to Minna as they went outside. "I've been thinking about you."

"I have, too. About you, I mean."

'Have you heard from Saul?"

'I got a letter yesterday, but it was written by his nurse. He says he's not allowed to read or write for now. The trip was tiring, but he's feeling a little better." She looked anxiously at Mr. Steinberg.

"It sounds as if he's in good hands. The trip must have been difficult."

"I can't imagine Saul just lying there, not reading or writing. Probably, he can't even talk very much. That's too bad. He likes to *schmooze*."

"In the end, it may be good for him," Mr. Steinberg replied pensively. "How many of us have the leisure to let the world go by and look within? Saul has always absorbed so much. Maybe his writing will be all the richer from this time."

"Do you really think so?"

"I'm sure of it. At least we know they're taking care of him."

"I said I would write to him every week whether he replied or not—and I will. But, maybe I shouldn't tell him what's happening here so much. I mean, if you think it's good for him to be away from the world, maybe…"

"That much being away, he wouldn't like!" Mr. Steinberg patted her shoulder. "Don't worry, Minna. All we can do is to think about him and write him. He'll do the rest with the help of his doctors."

"I hope so."

"I'm sure of it. I'll write to him, too—maybe not every week, but as often as I can. It will be good for him to know he's not forgotten."

"How could I ever forget Saul? I think of him every day. But…things happen. I feel bad if I'm interested in anything else when he's so sick. I should think about him all the time."

"Do you really think Saul would like that? Not Saul! Besides, if you do nothing but think of him all the time, what will you have to write him about?" he stopped and looked earnestly at her. "Life. It's the one thing that must continue. Let yourself grow and change so when Saul comes back, you'll have more to share with him. Seek the honey of your days. You remember what we said about gardens?"

"Oh, yes."

"What happens to a garden when it is neglected? It becomes full of weeds and the flowers and fruits die. If you thought only of Saul every minute, you'd be allowing your own garden to wither. You know Saul wouldn't want that."

She thought about it. "I feel bad," she said at last, "because it seems so unfair that he should be lying there and I should be here, seeing and doing."

"It's hard to see why God has allowed this to happen, but he has. All you can do is to remember Saul, write to him, and include him in your life as much as you can without closing your own doors. Do you know what I mean?"

She nodded.

"Never in a thousand years would Saul expect you to suffer for him. Each must live their own life and make their own beauty."

"You always make me feel better," she said shyly. "You're so wise."

"Not so wise. I've lived longer, that's all."

She smiled and shook her head. "Your daughter is lucky," she said.

He laughed. "Believe me, she doesn't always think so. She has her own ideas, too. That's the way it should be, even though I don't always agree with what she says."

She looked at him, surprised.

Seeing the expression in her eyes, he laughed again. "Truly, Minna. There are no angels or devils. We are all, every one of us, part angel and part devil. You and I, we meet, we talk, and it's easy for my angel to shine out. At home, if I am tired, or the dinner is burnt, or we have bad news, the devil appears. I am just a man, neither perfect nor imperfect."

Minna said nothing.

"Believe me, it's true, Minna. Now, tell me what has been happening to you," he continued. "I see your eyes are alive and there's a lilt in your voice.

"Nothing much. It's just I went to an art class at the Alliance and I met a real *Amerikaner*. She said she liked it better here than uptown. She wanted to live down here because…" She frowned, trying to remember Priscilla's exact words. "Because, she can be herself. She says something like this, 'People are hoping and growing, making their own rules. At home, it's all been decided ahead of time.'" She looked at Mr. Steinberg. "But I don't understand. We're all of us, at least I am, trying to be real *Amerikaners*. And she's trying to be like me? It doesn't make sense."

"Our dreams are not always what we think they are. Perhaps she looks at you and others like you and to her, it seems romantic—the same way you think it would be romantic to live the way she does. She forgets that you *have* to go to work, that there are days when you may be ill, or tired, or unhappy, but still, you must come and sit at the machines. You forget there may be parts of her life that are not pleasant, even though she is a real American, even though she may have—although you didn't say it—nice clothes and much *gelt*."

"You're right. It's true. I've been thinking about it. How would it not be good to have everything I've always wanted? That's what we're all working for, isn't it?"

"We're all working for something. For everyone, it's different.

But maybe the important part is the working, not the getting. Maybe some day, when you live on Fifth Avenue, you'll look back and wish you could be here again, just as you are now."

She shook her head. "I'll never think that! I'll just be glad I live there. I'm positive."

He shrugged. "There's no way to know. If someday you have all that you wish, think back upon this conversation and see if I'm right."

"I'll come and tell you," she laughed. "But…"

"Don't you see? We, all of us, look around and wonder if there's another way to live. At first, there seem to be many choices, each better than our own. Then, as we grow, we learn to choose. Your friend, the *Amerikaner*, if she looked hard enough, she'd find a way to be herself, in her own life. Just as you can find a way to be a real *Amerikaner* even if you live here and work at Triangle."

She hesitated. "You mean, it's all in me?"

"That's exactly what I mean."

"But if I lived somewhere else and I wore silk dresses, I'd be different."

"You'd look different, but you'd still be Minna."

She shook her head. "I don't know."

They had returned to the steps.

"I'd like a chance to find out, anyway!" she concluded.

"I hope you will."

At the door, he paused. "Did you write to Saul about this?"

She nodded.

"That's good. I'll be interested in what he says."

They parted at the doorway before Minna had a chance to thank Mr. Steinberg. All afternoon, as she worked at her machine, she thought about what he had said. No matter how hard she tried, she couldn't agree with him. It seemed so clear that there were better lives, better paths than hers. It's up to me to find them, she reminded herself.

For the rest of the week, Minna waited eagerly for Tuesday, the day of Erma's art class at the Alliance. The two girls had lunch together every day. Sometimes, they were joined by Pearl, but most often, they ate alone. At first, they talked mostly about Priscilla, but as time went on, Minna found that Erma had an interesting opinion on almost every subject. While not a scholar or as well read as Saul, she had no hesitation in expressing her own point of view.

Mr. Steinberg, who seemed to like her as much as Minna did when they spent a lunch together, said, "You have an inquiring mind, Erma."

She had blushed and laughed. "If that means I ask lots of questions and I don't mind saying what I think, it's true. How else can I learn?"

Later, Minna had asked her, "You don't mind admitting you don't know something, do you?"

"Of course not," she had replied. "A fool who is afraid to ask remains a fool. My *Zayde* in *der alter heym* used to say that."

"But," Mina had continued, "if I ask too many questions, people will think I'm ignorant."

"It you are ignorant, what's wrong with appearing that way?" Erma had responded.

Minna thought about this conversation later. She realized that the thing she admired most in Erma was that she never seemed to be afraid. She reconsidered. It wasn't that she wasn't afraid, it was that she never seemed to worry about her own role. She just went ahead and did what she thought she should do, regardless of how it might look to others. Take Priscilla, for example. Minna knew she would have been too uncomfortable to talk to her if Erma hadn't already known her. And to go to a café! Yet Erma seemed to take it for granted. She remembered what Mr. Steinberg had said about choices and ways to live. It wouldn't be so bad, she decided, if I was a little more like Erma.

On Tuesday, before the art class, Erma came to their house for dinner. Unlike Saul, she made no apparent effort to get dressed up. At first, Mama, Yussel, and Bessie looked at her curiously. Minna knew they were observing her untidy hair, her less than neat appearance.

As the dinner progressed, her genuine interest in the others, amplified by her warm eyes, won them over. Although she made no special effort to be the center of attention or to talk about herself, when she spoke, everyone listened. When she actually dared to disagree with Mama about the Union, concurring with Bessie's position, Mama rebutted her calmly, without the anger she had shown to Bessie on the same subject.

After dinner, Minna and Erma hurried to slip on their cloaks. To her chagrin, Yussel had long since shown Minna's masterpiece to everyone else, so there were many laughing comments about her artistic aspirations.

Minna had to laugh with them. "A genius, I'm not! But I like to try and see things the way the professor says." She turned to Erma. "Suppose the one who was sick comes back? There won't be any room for me in the class."

"Don't worry," Erma reassured her. "We'll make room." She looked at the others. "You shouldn't laugh. Who knows—maybe Minna will start a whole new style of art!" As she spoke, she buttoned her cloak.

"You may be a great artist, but first you have to learn how to button up!" Mama shook her head.

Erma looked down. She had put the buttons in the wrong buttonholes. Ruefully, she buttoned her cloak the right way. "One day, I'll forget my head!" She smiled at Mama. "Thanks, Mrs. Ruben. Thanks so much for dinner. It was delicious!"

Minna looked at Yussel inquiringly. Last week, he had suggested he might come with them. He shook his head. "Have a good time," he called after them as they shut the door behind them.

"I like your family," Erma said to Minna as they hurried down the stairs. "They laugh, something my sister doesn't do too often."

"It's because of you."

Erma looked surprised. "Are you saying I'm funny? I don't think so! I never tell jokes like the men at the factory. Or are you saying I'm so odd they laugh at me?"

"Oh no, I didn't mean that." Minna struggled for words. "I think it's because of the way you see things. It's a little different and it seems funny, in a good way."

"That's all right then," Erma said, reassured. "My sister says I'm *meshuggeneh* sometimes, but I don't mind that. Bessie certainly is serious, isn't she? Do you agree with what she says?"

They were hit by a blast of cold wind as they stepped outside. Minna pulled up her hood and put her hands in her pockets. Erma followed her example. Heads down, the walked towards the Alliance.

"I think she's right," Minna answered after a pause while they became accustomed to the cold. "I agree with what she says. It's just that I'm not ready to do anything about it. Then I feel guilty, because if I really do agree, I should help her."

"I know what you mean. Why don't we go to one of her meetings and see what they say? We won't have to join unless we want to."

"Maybe. Since she lives with us, I might not be able to make my own choices once I start. Or, at least, Bessie won't let it go."

"That's true. She *is* very committed."

"I don't think she talks about anything else."

Erma chuckled. "Maybe she likes waving a red flag in your Mama's face. She's almost like those bull fighters you read about, dancing around her." She paused. "I didn't mean to suggest that your Mama's like a bull, Minna. I'm sorry. I always speak before I think."

Minna had to laugh. The way Mama and Bessie sparred, it was like a bullfight. Somehow, despite Mama's greater authority, Bessie usually seemed in charge of their encounters.

"You're right," she mused. "Sometimes Mama plunges ahead without thinking. Bessie certainly brings out the worst in her. You said almost the same things to her and it didn't seem to bother her at all."

"They both probably enjoy a little fireworks once in a while," Erma suggested.

"Maybe they do," said Minna agreed.

When they arrived at the class, Minna was delighted to discover that someone else was absent so she'd have an easel to use. Mr. Einstein greeted her warmly and when she said apologetically, "I know I'm not a great artist, but I want to try to understand how you see things," he seemed very flattered.

Today's exercise was to draw another still life in charcoal. This one consisted of a statue surrounded by several small objects.

"I want you to try and express the curves you see. Look here, and there," Mr. Einstein explained, pointing at different angles of the statue, "and the detail—here and here," nodding at the small objects. "Contrast the two. Choose a focal point and…"

Minna listened carefully. Today she brought her own smock—an old shirt of Yussel's. She looked at the still life Mr. Einstein had arranged, trying to see the lines he had suggested the class should note. Finally, without too much hesitation, she touched her charcoal to the paper.

This time, her easel was next to Erma's, so she found herself glancing over at her work often. With broad sweeping strokes, she reconstructed the statue and the more detailed smaller objects. She stepped back and looked at what she had done, sighing loudly.

Mr. Einstein hurried over to look.

"It's boring, isn't it?" Erma asked.

"Perhaps it is a little too literal," he agreed. "Your details are magnificent, yet…"

"Yet…" Erma repeated.

"Yet I still don't know your point of view. As the artist, you must have a point of view. In Paris, they talk of nothing else."

Minna looked at her work dubiously. She was sure she had a point of view, but neither that nor the real objects were recognizable. Angrily, she lifted her hand to smudge the entire picture.

From behind, someone grabbed her arm to stop her. "I know exactly how you feel," an amused voice commented, "but it's the only way to learn."

Surprised, she spun around, only to find herself looking up at the same man who had spoken to her last week.

"Now," Erma smiled, "don't be bossy." She came over and looked at Minna's drawing. Narrowing her eyes, she stepped back and looked at it again. "Well, it's interesting," she said weakly.

"I know what I see and what I want to draw, but I can't seem to make the two things come together," Minna complained.

"Let's see yours, Harry." Erma looked at the man for a moment and then walked around his easel to see what he had drawn. Minna followed her. When she saw his work, she stopped in amazement. It had all the detail of Erma's, but it had something else as well. Minna gazed at it for a long time. She stepped back and looked at Erma's sketch again, trying to compare the two.

"Oh, Harry," Erma said. "You've done it again."

Harry shrugged. "Done what?"

'You know." She frowned. "I could copy what you've done, but it's your point of view, not mine."

"Some of us are deep, some aren't. What can you do?" Harry spread his hands out. Then he smiled, lifting his brow sardonically.

Erma looked up at him in mock admiration. "I bet you say that to all the girls," she murmured.

Minna was stunned. Erma, flirting with a man, was a stranger to her.

As if sensing her thoughts, Erma turned to Minna. "What do you think?" she asked. She waited patiently for an answer as Minna tried to organize her thoughts.

"I see what you're saying, Erma." She turned to Harry. "But I don't see how you did it."

He shrugged again.

Just then, Mr. Einstein came over and joined the little group around Harry's easel. When he saw Harry's drawing, he, too, stepped back to look at it. He moved closer to the easel and picking up the charcoal, added one line. 'What do you think?" he asked Harry. "Do you see how that accentuates the curve just there?"

Harry looked at his drawing, scrutinizing it from every angle. Finally, he nodded. "You're right. I'll remember that for next time."

Glancing at Minna's work, the professor smiled and said, "Keep trying."

She sighed. Then she brightened. I'm glad I did it anyway, she thought.

As she began to roll her drawing, she noticed that Erma lingered by Harry's easel. She spoke to him in a low voice as he rolled his picture. Minna saw him shake his head and Erma, crestfallen, return to her easel to roll her own work.

While they were washing their hands, Erma said, "I asked him to join us at the café. He always says no, but I keep asking. He's so talented, Minna. Someday, I guarantee, we'll hear his name. he'll be famous. I'd like Priscilla to meet him. Maybe she'd help him if she saw how good he is."

"Why won't he come?" Minna asked as she dried her hands.

"He says he hasn't time to waste at cafes and he doesn't want to meet a girl who's going slumming, anyway. It makes me mad because Priscilla isn't. I know she isn't."

"I don't think she's going slumming," Minna agreed, "but I also don't think she's very realistic."

"That's one thing. It's another to be laughing at us or staring as if we're animals in the zoo. Harry is saying she's like that and he won't listen when I tell him it isn't true."

Erma seemed so upset that it worried Minna. "Have you known him for a long time?" she asked hesitantly.

"Since I started with this class." She looked up at Minna, letting the towel drop. "Oh, don't be silly," she said, flushing. "I just want to help a good artist, that's all."

Minna nodded knowingly.

"No, really," Erma said, looking her straight in the eye.

"I believe you! I believe you!" Minna laughed.

This time, as they entered the café, Minna felt more comfortable. Confidently, she followed Erma to "their" table. When the waiter came, she ordered a glass of tea with no cake, having ascertained from Mr. Steinberg that it was perfectly acceptable and cost much less. She settled back in her chair and gazed around the room like an old habitué.

"By the way," Erma said, leaning forward. "I really like your brother, Yussel. When he talks about his ladies, he's so funny. Are he and Sarah…?" She let her voice dwindle off tactfully.

Naturally, Minna knew exactly what she meant. "Not really. I don't think Yussel's ready to settle down with anyone." Although she trusted Erma, she could not reveal anything about Yussel and Anna—if there was anything to be told. It was Yussel's secret, not to be shared. Besides, she thought hopefully, I probably made it all up.

"I know exactly how he feels," Erma said. " When I look at my sister and see how she's tied down with the children, I think—not me! It's already the children's lives that are important, not hers. Then I remember, in *der alter heym*, I'd already be an old maid."

"Not in America," Minna said stoutly. "Here, you can get married whenever you want after you meet the right person. I'm not ready to have a family yet either. Besides…" she paused, thinking of Jake.

"Besides what?"

Just as Minna was thinking of how to answer, she saw Priscilla coming towards them. "Here she is!" she cried, glad of the distraction.

Erma looked up and joined Minna. smiling and waving. Priscilla smiled back half-heartedly. As she came closer to the table, they could see that she didn't look well. There were faint circles under her eyes and her mouth curved downwards, as if she had forgotten how to smile.

They looked at her with concern as she slid into her seat and beckoned to the waiter. "If I don't have a glass of tea, I'll die," she said.

"What's the matter?" Erma asked. "You don't look well."

"Problems at home." Priscilla sighed.

Erma patted her hand and Minna gazed at her sympathetically.

Priscilla slipped off her glove and extended her left hand. "This is the problem," she said, looking down at the diamond ring glittering on the fourth finger of her left hand. "I'm engaged."

"Engaged! You're going to be married?" Minna asked, amazed. "But…I thought you wanted to move here and…"

Erma said nothing, simply looking at Priscilla as if willing her to talk.

"I'm going to be married in a few months," Priscilla said heavily. "It's all arranged. Our families have known each other for years. My father says it's the right thing. My mother is planning my wedding."

"And he?" Erma asked quietly. "What's his name?"

"His name is Jack. Oh, I like him. I've known him since we were children. But…" She put her hands over her eyes. "I don't want to get married. Not now. I'm not ready."

"Can't you just refuse?" Minna asked. "It's up to you, isn't it?"

Priscilla shook her head. "My father says if I say no to Jack, he won't support me any more. I'd have to leave home. How could I manage?"

"But I thought…" Minna began, confused.

"You said…" Erma began.

"Oh, saying is one thing," Priscilla said bitterly. "I could *say* it. But how could I come and live here and never go home again? Live in a tiny room, work at the factory…I couldn't!" She looked down at the table. "I have no choice. It's quite clear. He doesn't want me to work down here anymore, either—Jack, that is."

Minna shook her head, not knowing what to say.

Erma leaned forward. "We could help you, Priscilla. You don't have to marry a man you don't love. It will be for the rest of your life. Forever. You always said you wanted to make your own rules."

'I know." Priscilla sounded hopeless. "Now I'll be just like my mother and all the other ladies I know. I'll go to tea parties, have babies, shop…I won't be different any more."

Erma persisted. "But you don't have to, Priscilla. You can make your own decision."

"You don't understand. How can you imagine what it's like for me? It's so different."

"Is it so different?" Minna asked. "My friend, Anna, she left home because she refused to marry the man her father chose for her. She manages. She works hard, she has a nice room, she goes to dances."

Priscilla had looked up as Minna was speaking. Now she turned away. "For her, it's different. You don't know… Why, no one would ever speak to me again if I left home to come and live here."

"Her father said Kaddish for her," Minna continued. "That means she's dead to him."

Erma had drawn back. "Then you didn't mean everything you used to say, about envying us and wishing you could live the way we do?"

Priscilla looked at the two girls pleadingly. "Of course, I meant it. When I said it, I meant it. But to give up everything! How could I? You wouldn't if you were in my place, would you?"

"I'd give up everything before I'd marry a man I didn't love," Erma stated.

Minna nodded in agreement.

'But what do you have to give up?" Priscilla asked. Her words lay across the table, palpable and heavy, their meaning accentuated by the silence of the two girls.

She continued frantically. "To sit in a coffee house and talk is one thing. To live like a slave is another. Look at my hands!" She held them out. "The hardest work I've ever done is to wash out a teacup or help clean the classrooms here. Can I suddenly teach them to earn me a living? I'm fit for nothing except the life they're planned for me." Her voice rose. "My rules are what I've always had. I can't change them in the middle."

The two girls said nothing.

'We are what we are," Priscilla continued more quietly. "I've thought of being someone else, but when I come right down to it, I know…"

"You know you don't have enough courage," Erma said coldly.

Priscilla did not respond. Finally she spoke. "Yes," she said, "I don't have enough courage to change my life. I am a good little sheep." She looked at Erma apologetically. "I'm sorry."

'It's not to me you should be sorry," she replied sternly. "It's to yourself, if you choose the wrong path."

Despite everything she had said, Minna couldn't help but feel sorry for Priscilla. "Maybe for you, this is the right path," she said. "You're the only one who can choose."

'Choose? Paths?" Priscilla laughed bitterly. "I do what I am told. Coming down here, knowing you, that was my revolt. Now it's over." She stood up. "I won't see you again." As she pulled on her gloves, she looked at Erma. "We could have been friends if…"

"If things were different?" Erma asked.

Priscilla nodded. She stood up and walked away from the table without looking back.

The two girls looked at each other. Minna saw tears in Erma's eyes.

"Oh, Erma," she soothed, "you must feel…"

"I feel like a fool!" Erma said angrily. "Harry was right."

"She said she meant what she said. I think she did, when she was saying it."

"Good for her! I don't want to be anyone's rebellion!"

Minna said nothing.

"I thought she was my friend. I honestly thought she was. But I was only a new toy for her." She looked down at the table. "I was so proud of having a real *Amerikaner* for a friend and she wasn't. Not at all."

"But," Minna said slowly, "don't you see, you always thought of her as your *Amerikaner* friend. You never forgot the differences between you. If you didn't, how can you blame her?"

"I do blame her. I'll never trust another *Amerikaner* to be my friend. I wouldn't have said goodbye so meekly. And I would…I would have made choices, not given up."

"That's the difference. We make choices all the time. For you, coming here was one of them. To her it's like the end of the world to even imagine changing the patterns of her life."

"I guess I feel sorry for her…"

"So do I," Minna agreed automatically. Then she thought about it. "I really do, you know. I'm afraid of lots of things, but I'm not afraid of earning my own way. I don't need anyone else to do that for me."

"You're right," Erma said slowly. "I really do feel sorry for her, not just because I'm angry. If being a real *Amerikaner* means you have to do what your family says all the time and you're afraid not to, then I'd rather be me. No one's going to pick out a husband for me!"

"Me, neither. And no husband's going to tell me what I can do and what I can't do, as long as it doesn't interfere with him. It was a pretty ring, though," Minna added wistfully.

"So what! Rings, shmings—it's who gives it to you that counts.

You know what, Minna? I'd rather be me a million times than someone like Priscilla."

"I would, too," Minna agreed. "But, Erma, do you really think we can never be friends with an *Amerikaner*?"

"I don't know. I haven't met any other to know. They're not lining up to meet me, that's for sure. I won't be so ready to trust any of them another time!"

Minna sipped her tea, even though it was now ice cold.

"I thought we were the same—just two girls. I really did." Erma wiped her eyes and sat up straighter. "I should have known we were too different. Look, you and I meet and you invite me home. I'd have invited you too except my sister doesn't like guests. I've known Priscilla for a while and never once did I think of seeing her outside of this café. Her life is a mystery to me. Mine is less to her because I told her all about it. Now I see that she always kept everything separate."

Minna was more shaken than she appeared. If Priscilla's life was no better than hers—maybe even worse—what about her plans for the future? Did she still want to become a real *Amerikaner*? "You think it's better to stick to our own kind?" she asked.

"Right now, I do. I guess I might feel differently after I think about it some more. But I won't be a curiosity for someone else! That I know." Erma shook her head violently.

The busy waiter finally came to the table with Priscilla's glass of tea. Erma shook her head. "She's gone. She couldn't stay."

The water shrugged and brought the tea to another table. Then he came back. "Anything else for you, ladies?"

Minna shook her head.

"I think we're ready to go, don't you, Minna?" Erma said, standing up.

Minna stood up, too.

They paid the check and went outside. The cold air was refreshing.

"I'm glad to get outside," Erma said. "The cold feels good."

"I'm sorry, Erma," Minna said. "Is there anything I can do? I know you've been disappointed…"

"I'm glad you were with me, that's all. Imagine if I had been alone when she told me!"

They walked in silence until they separated and went in different directions.

"I'll see you tomorrow," Erma said, and hurried off.

Minna looked after her. She knew Erma was still upset, but what could she do about it? I'm upset, too, she thought, but more because what happened changes my picture of the world, not because I thought Priscilla was my friend. I wonder what Saul would say if he was here.

As she continued home, she was conscious of a rare feeling of anticipation. I am lucky, she reminded herself, to have a family waiting for me. She hurried her steps.

When she arrived home, Yussel was still up, sitting at the kitchen table and staring pensively off into the distance.

She smiled as she took off her coat. "I'm glad to see you," she said.

Yussel started as though he hadn't heard her come in. Then he smiled back.

"Where were you, Yussel? A million miles away, I guess."

Yussel shrugged and changed the subject. "Did you have a good time in class? Let's see your drawing."

Minna realized she was still carrying her drawing, although she had forgotten it was in her hands. Automatically, she started to open it. Then she shook her head and crumpled it up.

"You don't want to see it. It's really terrible, even worse than last week. An artist, I'm not." She looked down at the table. "I saw Priscilla," she began.

"Priscilla?"

"Erma's *Amerikaner* friend. She came to the café."

Yussel tried to appear interested although he did stand up and start to walk towards his bedding preparatory to laying it out for the night. Turning his head, he smiled at Minna encouragingly. "Tell me about it while I fix my bed."

She shook her head. "She's not Erma's friend, not really. She's getting married even though she's not in love. She told us she won't come downtown any more. Erma was very upset. It was like…"

Yussel paused, turned, and came back to the table. He sat down and asked, "Like what?"

"Like she was just playing a game, knowing us and coming to the Alliance," she blurted.

He frowned. "What do you mean?"

'She always said she was going live downtown, that she envied our freedom. But she was afraid to lose what she had. I told her about Anna. You know, she ran away from her father because he was going to make her marry someone and he said Kaddish. But she wasn't afraid and she manages."

"Anna manages…" he said in a questioning tone.

Minna, surprised, gazed at him.

He nodded slightly and gestured for her to continue.

She hurried on. "She said she didn't know how to earn a living and she couldn't bear it if her family and friends wouldn't talk to her. That's not what she said before. Oh, Yussel!" She put her head in her hands. "If she's not happy and free, and she has everything, then who is? Is anyone? What am I working for if it's no good anyway?"

He shook his head. "What are you saying, Minna? What's everything? Sure, *gelt* is a nice thing, so is living uptown, but is it everything? Think about it!"

She said nothing.

"Do you really think that you'll be a different person if you live somewhere else? You're still you, no matter how you live or where you live, So, if you're not happy to start with, nothing is going to make any difference. Even if you buy a new dress every day, you'll still be Minna."

"But…it would be so much easier to be happy if I could," she replied weakly.

"Maybe. It didn't seem to work for her."

She stood up. "So what are you saying to me? Must I be content to stay here all my life?"

"Not if you don't want to. We all have to believe in something. But there's no magic. You don't become a different person just because you live somewhere else. It's the becoming, the making it happen, that changes you." He stood up, too.

She faced him angrily. "It will be different, I know it will. I'll be different too. I don't care about Priscilla or what you say or Mr. Steinberg, either! When I live on Fifth Avenue, I'll be…" Her eyes grew misty. "I'll be a …real *Amerikaner*, a princess." She touched Yussel's arm

He shook his head and turned away. As he bent over his bedding, he looked back at her. "It's not going to happen tomorrow, so why worry? Wait and see how you feel when the time comes."

"I don't need to wait. I know!" Minna turned her back on Yussel and went into the bedroom. She undressed and curled up next to Pearl, imagining what it would be like, living in a big apartment, having a closetful of clothes, and eating whatever she wanted. As she closed her eyes, she smiled, thinking about having chicken every day.

Although Erma tried to be cheerful in the days that followed, she remained depressed. No matter what Minna, she couldn't help her. In desperation, she even asked Mr. Steinberg for his advice.

"An *Amerikaner* is just a person," he said. "If this girl betrayed Erma, or if she thinks she did, it's not because she's an *Amerikaner.*

"That changes it a little, but it won't make Erma feel any better. She had a friend who wasn't a real friend."

He shook his head. "In life, we all experience betrayals," he commiserated. "To make a rule from any one is like eating an unripe fruit and deciding that all fruits are sour."

When Minna repeated his words to Erma, she replied, "He's right, I guess, but I don't feel what he says—I can only think it. And," she added bitterly, "Since I don't have any other *Amerikaner* friends to compare, it's hard not to blame them all."

CHAPTER 22

A few days later, another letter from Saul finally arrived. It was only half a page and his handwriting straggled over the paper, but he had written it himself.

It said:

Dear Minna:

I lie in bed staring out the window at the desert. Except for my nurses and the doctor, I see no one, although they say that soon I'll be able to join the others. This gives me more time to think about your letters, about you and your family. I wish I could write half the things I think, but it would be far too much.

The doctors say that with time and rest, I should get better. It's strange, but I don't mind being still. In the quiet that surrounds me, it is a great adventure to sit up, take a pen, and write to you.

Don't worry. I will take care of myself. The next letter will be more interesting, I hope. Please keep writing. I miss you.

Your friend, Saul

Minna pored over the letter for hours after she received it, interpreting it first one way and another. Eagerly, she showed it to the others, asking for their opinion.

"It doesn't sound like Saul," Pearl said doubtfully.

Her words made Minna speak out positively about his health. "The doctors say he'll get better. That's good news. He's writing his own letters now, which is a big improvement."

Yet when Yussel took a determinedly optimistic point of view, Minna felt impelled to take the other side. "His writing's so weak," she complained. "Look how faint it is! He must be really sick to get so tired after sitting up for just a little while."

Finally, she arrived at a state of cautious optimism, believing that he would get better but that his progress would be slow. She sat down and wrote him a long letter, telling him all about Priscilla's defection and, for the first time, believing her own words when she mentioned his return as if it was assured. Maybe, she thought hopefully, he'll feel well enough to write me a long letter next time.

It seemed like no time at all till the day of the next art class arrived. Minna asked Erma if she was planning to attend.

"Not this week," she said. "I don't want to go back to the Alliance just now and I'm needed at home. But you go, Minna."

She thought about it. "I'll skip it, too," she decided. "Instead, if you can get away, why don't you come home with me for dinner tonight? It won't be anything special, but everyone will enjoy seeing you."

Erma considered. "I'd like to see your family again," she mused. "It would be good for me. I'm not feeling very patient these days and the children know it." She brightened. "Yes! I'd love to come. I'll go home first to tell my sister and then I'll come over."

Minna hurried home after work to start dinner and get the kitchen ready to receive a guest. Mama, Pearl, and Sarah lagged behind, although they had all expressed pleasure in having Erma to dinner. Mama, of course, had merely nodded, but she took that as a positive sign since she had not made an unpleasant comment.

When Erma arrived, the table was set, dinner was simmering on the stove, and everyone had been reminded of Priscilla's change of heart and Erma's feeling about it. "Don't say anything," Minna had concluded for the third time, after telling them the story.

Erma arrive smiling. "It is so nice to be here," she said. "I haven't been anywhere but the factory and home for a whole week. My littlest niece is sick—oh, not very—and she's uncomfortable, so she cries all the time. Everything's a mess because my sister tends to her all day. I'll take over tonight when I get home. She'll probably be up all night again."

Minna commiserated and ushered her into the kitchen, where everyone was waiting. Bessie, believing Erma might be a kindred spirit, greeted her heartily. Even Mama had a smile.

Throughout the dinner, Yussel kept the whole table amused

with imitations of his ladies. Finally, he concluded by saying, "If you could see how they look when they're trying to decide!"

Minna nodded. "You're right. I remember when we had the store and I made a few things to order. The expression on their faces at the first fitting!"

"You'd be just the same," Pearl said. "I've seen you in front of the mirror…"

Minna blushed.

Erma laughed. "Once I thought I'd slip a note into the cuff of one of my shirtwaists. Wouldn't that be a surprise for the girl who bought it? I never did, of course. Still…I think about it."

'What would you say?" Sarah asked.

"Oh, something like, 'This shirtwaist was made by a sixteen-year-old girl just like you except she works in a factory ten hours a day.'"

"It's not such a bad idea to do something like that," Bessie commented. "Why, some girls at Vassar Collage supported our strike last year. They say we're all sisters."

"Some sisters, rich and poor!" Erma said bitterly. "Women and slaves is more like it,"

Pearl spoke bravely. "You can't blame the other girls if they don't live the way we do. It's not their fault. It's the way they were born."

"But why should some people have everything just because of the family they were born into? It's not fair!" Minna said angrily.

"I agree!" Erma's eyes flashed.

"It may not be fair, but it is the way it is. Anger doesn't change anything," Yussel intervened. "Instead of being angry, change your life. That's the way to begin, if that's what you want. Besides, Minna, our cousins in *der alter heym* could say it about us—it's not fair that they are afraid and we aren't. Not of the same things, anyway."

"That's different," Minna replied hastily. "They could have taken the chance to come here. No one stopped them."

"No one's stopping you either," Yussel said. "You always talk about changing your life. So, do it, but don't waste your energy on anger, that's all."

Minna looked around the table. Everyone was following the conversation with great interest except Mama, whose face was cold and closed. She spoke to Erma urgently. "How do you feel? Don't you think we should make something of ourselves and show them all?"

Yussel answered, raising his voice. "If anger's your reason for getting ahead, it will stop you in the end. Anger is no reason to work for a lifetime."

"I asked Erma."

"She cleared her throat. "I am angry just now. I guess you all know why. But it doesn't make me want to do anything. As a matter of fact, it makes me do less because I feel like I haven't got a chance."

Yussel looked at Minna triumphantly.

Pearl shrugged. "Anger, shmanger! What's the difference? The point is to live your life, that's all. Your life is here, Minna, so you might as well enjoy it. If you're always looking somewhere else, it won't be real."

"It's as God wills," Mama recited.

"And God wills we do for ourselves," Minna concluded. "So, for me, I'm right. It isn't so much anger, anyway. It's more that I don't want to be passed over by them."

"Who's this 'them' anyway? I do believe we're all sisters. We need the help of others. They have much to give. It's the only way that things will change for us," Bessie retorted.

"We might need their help, but we have to do for ourselves. too. That's the main thing," Minna insisted.

"No one said we shouldn't do for ourselves," Bessie retorted. "The point is, if they want to help us with money, I'm not going to say no. Except for an accident of birth, they could be living here, too, working for nothing and getting paid less than men."

"I don't trust any uptown ladies, not now. But if they want to give money for a cause, I say, 'Take it!'" Erma proclaimed.

"If I work hard, it's my children who will be real Americans. They'll live in the Bronx and their children won't even know what it was like for us," Pearl said earnestly.

"I don't want to wait for my children to change things," Minna insisted. "Why can't I? Why can't all of us?"

"Maybe we don't want to as much as you do, Minna," Sarah said.

Yussel nodded.

Minna thought for a moment. "That's true. You have to want to. And I do!"

"All I can say is, 'Good luck!" Yussel said wearily. "What's important to you, you have to do. But not with anger."

Minna nodded slowly. "Maybe not with anger. Maybe it's because of the kind of person someone is, that's all. Like I am."

Bessie shook her head. "If you care about your own kind, you have to care about others, too. We're all people, aren't we?"

"But Minna cares about herself, not about her 'own kind'. She wants to make a life for herself," Erma said pensively.

"You think there's something wrong with that?" Minna asked. "I'm not running away. I'm here, doing the best I can for my family."

"Of course, it's not bad," Yussel soothed. "As long as you meet your responsibilities first. Then it's all right."

"Well, thanks a lot!" Minna snapped.

"You have to listen to your dreams," Pearl mused. "Just as I have to listen to mine and Yussel to his."

The omission of Mama's name was unnoticed by all.

Minna smiled. "That's all I was saying. Except, maybe, you're right about anger, Yussel."

'I know you're right," Erma said, "but I know one thing and feel another. I hope that will change in time, when I've forgotten what happened."

Mama stood up and began to clear the table. The others disregarded her movements and continued the conversation.

"Where do you think we'll be in five—no, ten—years from now?" Minna asked.

"I'll be married. My husband will have a little store and I'll stay home and take care of my babies." Pearl blushed.

"I hope the same," Sarah said, carefully looking away from Yussel.

"I'll be celebrating the triumph of the Union. It will have grown stronger and bigger. The bosses will listen and no one else will have to work the way we do," Bessie said.

"I don't know." Erma pondered. "I can't say. I won't be living with my sister, though, or working in the factory. That I know. And you, Minna?"

"Yussel, you speak first."

"We'll have a store again and…" His face grew red. "I don't know. Maybe I'll have a family, too."

"And your farm in the Catskills?" Minna persisted.

"I don't know. I hope…well, we all have hopes."

"As for me," Minna tried to speak with assurance, "I'll be a school teacher by then." She looked around the table. "Surely, by then, I will, don't you think? I'll go to work, but it'll the kind of work I like. I'll live in a little room all my own and…"

Mama interrupted. "Foolish dreams! In ten years, God willing, we'll still be here. This is where we belong."

Minna shook her head and started to speak. Then she stopped herself. What was the point of arguing with Mama? Instead, she laughed. "We'll see in ten years, won't we? Till then, who knows? Not me or you or anyone."

Erma nodded. "Now is what's important. It becomes ten years soon enough, I guess. So we shouldn't cheat ourselves of every day by always waiting for another time." She looked at Minna. "Do you know what I mean?"

"But if we forget, if we don't keep our hopes in front of us, nothing will change, not ever. That's why I think…"

Yussel interrupted Minna. "Patience is a good quality. I wish I had more. But I will try to live each day more than I have been doing. It seems as if I never have time to think. I get so tired at night…"

"Dreams and real life. How to make the two become one—that's what we have to learn," Erma murmured.

"Just do the best we can, that's all," Minna said firmly, standing up to help Mama with the dishes. She resolved to talk to Mr. Steinberg about this tomorrow. It was confusing. Was she being selfish to want what she wanted? She shook her head. As long as I do what's right for the family, I can think what I choose. Still, it seemed disloyal to want to live differently.

The rest of the evening, Minna found herself mulling over the quandary. Perhaps because she felt guilty, she was more affectionate than usual to everyone, even giving Mama a quick kiss goodnight. At least, she thought, I'll be glad for what I have now.

The next morning, Minna awoke reluctantly. Spring will never come, she thought. Here it is March 25th and it's till cold and damp. "It doesn't come here, anyway," she said out loud.

Pearl looked over at her. "What?" she asked.

Minna blushed. "Oh, nothing." She tried to recapture her thoughts of the night before, but instead of feeling even slightly contented with what she did have, she could only think of what she didn't have.

Later, as they hurried through the busy streets, she began to list everything she wanted. My own room, she thought, some green grass…to see the sky at night…to be a teacher, an American teacher…new clothes… She looked back at Pearl, Mama, and Sarah, who were lagging behind. I want everything for them, too, she reminded herself guiltily. A nice place for us to live…

"Wait up!" Pearl called. "What's your hurry, Minna?"

She waited for them to catch up.

"What's your hurry?" Pearl repeated. "You want to get in early and surprise the boss? Or maybe you want to see Sammy, the elevator boy? I know, you love it so much at Triangle you just can't wait to get started!"

Minna had to smile.

As Pearl continued to look at her with an air of innocent inquiry, she began to laugh. "Sorry," she said, wrapping her cloak around herself more tightly. "I guess I woke up on the wrong side of the bed."

"Since we sleep in the same bed, that must mean that I slept on the right side," Pearl said triumphantly.

Sarah giggled. "I always get up from the same side of the bed, so I could never understand why sometimes it's the right side and other times, the wrong side. It doesn't make sense."

Minna and Pearl began to laugh. After a minute, Sarah joined in.

"I have a suggestion. Get up on the other side tomorrow," Minna said, "and see what happens. Then you'll know for sure what's the good side and bad side."

"Who knows," Pearl continued. "Maybe you're been getting up on the wrong side all these years. Maybe to morrow, you'll find *gelt* in the street or you'll meet a millionaire and he'll whisk you off to Fifth Avenue!"

"We'll take notes tomorrow," Minna continued enthusiastically. "We'll all try getting up on the other side of the bed and see what happens!"

Mama shook her head and walked away from them, which only made them laugh harder. Sammy, the elevator boy, stared at them.

"I never saw anyone so happy to get to work!" he said.

This made them giggle all the more.

After they had put their cloaks away, the three of them stood together near their machines, talking and laughing. More of the girls came over and joined them. Each one was told about the experiment for tomorrow.

"Now, remember, keep notes!" Minna called over her shoulder as she sat down at her machine. "Tomorrow's going to be a lucky day for us all."

"It'll be better than today, anyway! At least on Sunday, we can stay home," Sarah said in a low voice.

Just before Anna bent over her machine, she called across to Minna. "I heard what you're planning. What if that's the wrong side of the bed? Then there'll be a problem!"

Minna shrugged. "In science, you have to try," she called, suppressing another giggle. She could hear Sarah chuckling quietly next to her.

All through the morning, she thought about the right side and the wrong side of the bed. Although she knew it wasn't true, she couldn't help but wish that suddenly, tomorrow, when she got out of bed on the other side, everything would change. We'll have our store again, she thought dreamily, and I'll be able to go to school…

At lunchtime, she tried to tell Erma why it suddenly seemed so important to get up on the other side of the bed. "I know it's silly," she began.

Erma nodded vehemently. "It *is* silly. It's like believing in magic, Minna. You don't really…"

"Not really, I suppose. Still, wouldn't it be grand if such a simple thing changed everything? Like…like…"

"Like magic," Erma concluded tartly. "Since when do you think that way, Minna?"

She flushed. "I guess I'd rather believe in magic than in nothing." She went on to tell Erma how disheartened she had felt this morning.

Erma patted her on the shoulder. "I know just how you feel," she said. "It's because of Priscilla, isn't it?"

"That, and Saul." She looked at her, dismayed. "Sometimes, I don't think anything will ever change. I'll be an old *bubbe* still working here at Triangle." She looked off into the distance. "I'll say to my children, 'Once I had dreams, too.' and they'll look at me in surprise."

Erma laughed. "You really are down, aren't you? That's how I felt yesterday. Today…who knows? It's a different day. Something might happen to change everything. I did decide, I'm going to class next week. Do you want to come?"

Minna frowned. "I don't know. An artist, I'm not." She smiled weakly. "I'll think about it anyway. I wouldn't mind seeing Harry, that's true." She looked at Erma, her brows raised.

Erma gave her a push. "Oh, Minna!" she blushed.

When the lights flickered, Minna hurried back to her machine. On the way, she leaned over Pearl and touched her shoulder. "Let's go somewhere tomorrow," she whispered. "Somewhere special. All of us."

Pearl looked back at Minna. "I'd like that," she replied. "How else am I going to meet my right-side-of-the-bed millionaire?"

Minna laughed.

As she sat at her machine for the next few hours, she tried to picture what it would be like to be Priscilla. Was Mr. Steinberg right? Did new clothes and a fancy house really make no difference? Would Priscilla still be Priscilla if she had grown up here on the lower East Side? She had to smile to herself. In the first place, she thought, her name certainly would not be Priscilla. She glanced down at her basket. She was finishing her last shirtwaist of the day. Soon the bell would ring and her work would be done. Automatically, she pushed the cloth through the machine, already planning what she would suggest to the family for tomorrow's outing.

She had just finished the final seam when she saw Anne, the forelady, dropping her pay envelope on the worktable next to her. She took it, folded it up, and put it in her pocketbook. Smiling happily, she thought of how much she could afford to put in the hiding place under the floorboards.

The bell rang and the machines stopped. Officially, the day was over. With a sigh of relief, Minna jumped up and hurried towards the cloakroom. She knew from bitter experience that if she didn't hurry, she'd have to wait before she could leave the narrow corridor behind her chair. At this time of day, everyone pushed and shoved, wanting to be the first to leave the factory behind.

"I'll meet you downstairs," she called back to Pearl and Sarah as she rushed by, knowing she'd much rather wait outside than in a mob.

Used to Minna's ways, the two girls nodded and stood up slowly. They didn't see any reason to be the first out."

As Pearl had said a few days ago, "The way you run out, Minna, you'd think there was a fire. What's the point? You'll have to wait for us anyway, so you might as well take it easy."

She had laughed. "I'll take it easy away from the machines, thank you!"

By the time Minna reached the cloakroom, there were already many girls putting on their cloaks, peering into the mirror to set their hats straight, and calling out to each other. She ducked under the arm of one, slid past another, excused herself loudly, and finally arrived at her locker. As she opened it and took out her cloak, she heard a scream.

She looked up, clutching her cloak to her. Everyone in the crowded room looked up as well, turning in the direction of the scream. "Fire!" someone in the large room shrieked. "Fire!"

Minna dropped her cloak and looked around. Without realizing it, she let out a low moan. The girls behind her began to push frantically towards the elevator. Others shrieked and yelled. Minna heard a confused babble of voices in Italian, Yiddish, and English. A girl standing next to her fainted. Minna caught her and eased her to the floor.

Pushed by those behind her, forced towards the door, she stepped on the very girl she had just lowered to the floor. Tears streamed from her eyes. I'll die, she thought. Like Chava, I'll die. I wasn't meant to…

Without volition, her limbs seemingly frozen, she allowed herself to be pushed here and there by others. Suddenly, as clearly as if Bubbe was standing right next to her, she heard a voice in her ears. 'Go to the stairs,' the voice said. 'Minna, little one, don't be afraid. Be brave. Go to the stairs!'

She clenched her teeth and thrust herself forward, aiming for the door into the corridor. As people flowed by, she saw familiar faces, distorted by fear. Near the door, she saw Anna, one hand firmly on her hat and the other extended.

She turned left and began to make her way toward the Greene Street stairs. They were farther away than the others, but so many people were crowded together near the closer ones, she was afraid she would never get through.

The stairs…the stairs… The words reverberated in her mind. She shoved her way past the…was that the fire escape? She looked at it. Two girls were hammering at the steel shutters that kept that exit closed. Frantically, they banged at the rusted steel pin that kept them locked.

She pushed on towards the stairs. Looking back for a moment, she saw women standing on tables, trying to jump or crawl across the room and reach a doorway. Others, apparently frozen in place, huddled over their machines. Determinedly, she moved forward, thinking only of the words in her ears—the stairs…the stairs…

When she reached them, she opened the door. She immediately jumped back. Tongues of fire were lapping towards the ninth floor from the eighth. She hesitated, looking back into the room towards the fire escape and the elevator on the Washington Square side of the building. It was impossible to get there.

Instead, she turned back towards the fire escape, now open and blocked by many screaming girls. Every step seemed to take an hour. It was as if her feet were fixed to the floor. All she could hear was the high pitched nightmarish screaming echoing all around her, yet she had never felt so alone.

"Help me, Bubbe," she muttered continuously under her breath. "Help me."

When she finally reached the fire escape, she had to wait her turn to climb onto it. It was filled with panic-stricken girls moving slowly down the iron steps. At last it was her turn. Just as she was about to step out onto it, she heard a loud, wrenching noise. Looking ahead, she saw the fire escape swing out and collapse. The girls who were already on it fell to the street like paper dolls, their bodies twisting as they hurtled through the air.

Almost forced forward into the now empty space by those behind her, Minna braced herself against the shutters and pushed back. "It's collapsed!" she yelled. "It's no good!"

There was so much noise, no one could hear her except those standing right next to her. The girl directly behind her recoiled and repeated her words. There was a slight movement away from the fire escape.

Minna pushed her way back towards the stairs, thinking, in a strange calm way, how foolish of me. I should have gone into the fire in the first place. Without understanding why she was doing it, she picked up a bolt of white lawn lying on the edge of a table.

As she approached the stairs again, with the flame shooting upwards, she began to wind the material around her body. As she struggled to put it around her, she was suddenly doused with a bucket of water. She looked up in shock. Did anyone think this fire could be extinguished so easily?

Ducking her head, now wrapped in the sodden lawn, she forced herself to enter the stairwell, run through the flames and up to the roof. At least I'll be out in the air, she thought. As she ran up the stairs, she unwound the flaming lawn, leaving it trailing behind her. The stairs were almost empty because of the encroaching flames.

By the time she reached the roof, the sheer fabric was gone, all burned away except for a small bit tucked under her chin. She let the scrap drop by lifting her chin. She felt a sharp pain, but in the frenzy of the moment, she ignored it.

Gulping the cold air, she hurried to the edge of the roof. Looking down at Greene Street, she gasped. Below, she saw flaming objects falling to the ground…large objects, with skirts flying… She screamed. It was the girls, jumping from window ledges. Even though she was high up at the top of the building, she could hear a series of thuds as each body hit the pavement. Far, far below, she could see people scurrying to and fro. In the distance, she saw a fire engine approaching.

As she watched, she was hit with a burst of hot air. The flames from the tenth floor were coming higher and higher towards the roof, seeming to reach for her. Hypnotized, she leaned forward.

Suddenly someone grabbed her by the waist. "Watch out!" a man called. "Come to the other side. There's a ladder. We've put up a ladder!"

She followed blindly. She awaited her turn to climb on the ladder to the next building. The man helped her. She filed through two lines of young men, all urging her forward. As she reached the ladder, she stopped.

"Pearl!" she yelled. "*Mein Gott*! Mama!" She turned to go back down the stairs. "How could I forget?" she screamed.

As she tried to go back, the men continued to push her towards the ladder. "This way," they insisted. "Climb up the ladder to the NYU building. You'll be safe."

She balked. "It's my mother and my sister," she cried. "I have to go back and help them. Let me go!"

They refused to let her turn back. "It's too late," one of them said. "You can't get back through the stairs now."

"They'll die! I have to save them," she wailed. Suddenly, it seemed as if everyone in her way was an enemy. She flailed out, trying to get back to the stairs, when she slipped and fell. As she felt herself falling onto the roof, she suddenly felt dizzy. Overcome by the smoke and heat, she fainted.

The man who had propelled her towards the ladder, lifted her in his arms. Twining her hair over one arm so she couldn't fall, he began ascending, first one ladder to the height of the NYU roof and then another, across the air space between the two buildings. She remained unconscious, opening her eyes only after she was propped against a table in an NYU classroom.

Her gaze flew around the room. "Where am I?" she murmured. "I…" Then, remembering the fire, she forced herself to stand up. Knowing that she *had* to touch the ground and breath fresh air, she followed another girl to the elevator.

Going down, she was mute. Her throat hurt. She fingered the skin under her chin and felt a sharp pain.. It must have been the fire, she thought, almost absently. Only later did she discover it was the one burn she had sustained, where she had anchored the flaming lawn under her chin.

At the bottom, Minna hurried outside and around the corner to the front of the Asch Building. Although she had no cloak and her clothing was torn, she did not feel the chill. She didn't even notice how people stepped back as she hurried past, allowing her to move through the crowds easily. One old woman actually touched her, as if for luck. She was oblivious. All she could think about was going back inside to look for Pearl and Mama.

As she approached the building, she saw she wouldn't be able to get close. Police blockaded the sidewalk, already littered with bodies. Firemen climbed their ladders, yet they could only reach the seventh floor. Above, men and women leaned out of window ledges, poised as if waiting for the right moment. Then they jumped. Some calmly and some with abandon, they flew through the air.

Minna gazed at the sidewalk along the side of the building. Bodies lay askew, their limbs bent and their heads crooked. The gutters, she noticed, were streaming with water from the fireman's hoses. But the water was red, the color of blood… Maybe she thought, the water was always red when there was a fire.

She looked up. There, standing on the window sill, she saw Anna. Minna almost thought she could see her familiar smile as she surveyed the street below, pausing as if she were looking into the mirror. With a graceful movement of her arm, she unpinned her hat and sent it flying to the crowds below. Then she dropped her pocketbook. Finally, holding her skirts daintily at her sides, she stepped off the ledge as gracefully as if she were about to dance. Almost languidly, she fell through the air until she reached the bottom with a thud. Minna turned away.

She felt an arm around her. "Are you hurt? Come with me," the woman said.

Minna pushed her away. She knew she had to stand and watch until the very end. Down the street, she could hear someone screaming, "Dead! All dead!" All around her, she heard sobs and shouts. She continued to watch the roof.

So, Anna's gone, she thought. That was Anna. Then Pearl will be all right. That made sense. They couldn't both die. She felt a momentary pang as if she had consigned Anna to death, but she reminded herself, I only saw her jump. I didn't push her. It's not my fault.

She thought about going home. Pearl was probably waiting for her there. And Mama… she'd be there, too.

She almost turned to leave, but she couldn't stop watching the roof. More bodies fell through the air. Like flowers, blowing in the wind, the skirts of the young girls belled out. Only at the end, as they hit the ground, were they revealed as distorted and human… dead.

She stared upwards. Some of the dresses looked familiar. Some of the faces… Dispassionately, she waited, wondering when it would be over. It seemed unreal, a kind of spectacle. She shivered, beginning to feel the cold. I'll stay to the end, she thought. Then I'll find Pearl and Mama and we'll go home. Almost impatiently, she watched and waited.

A man came by and offered her a glass of milk. "For shock," she heard him say. She took it thankfully.

Next to her, a small dark woman dressed in black keened as she watched the helpless victims fall to the ground. "Rosa," she called. "Where are you, my Rosa?"

Minna almost reached out to her. Could that be Rosa's mother? It's all right, she wanted to say. Rosa told me about 'Seppe. I'm waiting for my family, too. Soon, we'll all go home…

The woman began to sob.

Minna turned away.

Now she was shivering so hard she could barely stand upright. I was stupid to leave my cloak in there, she thought. I could at least have brought my cloak with me. I hope Pearl and Mama are smarter than I am.

Suddenly she felt something warm over her shoulders. She looked back. It was Jake, putting his coat over her, his face drawn. She didn't question his presence. It seemed right.

"I'm just waiting for Mama and Pearl," she said calmly. "Then we can all go home."

He looked at her. Were those tears in his eyes? "I heard about…" he began.

Minna shook her head violently. "I'm just waiting for Mama and Pearl." She repeated more loudly.

He was silent. Then he took her arm. "Let's go home," he said. "We'll meet them there. I know Yussel will be waiting…"

She thought about it. "They are probably worrying about me." She started to follow him. Then she stopped. "They may be still coming out. Maybe we should…" She looked at the building expectantly.

He turned her gently away. "Come with me," he begged. "You're burned under your chin, you're shivering. You don't want to get sick…"

Listening to his soothing voice, Minna allowed herself to be led away, although she kept looking back. Stumbling and leaning on Jake's arm, she walked towards home.

Jake kept on talking, looking at her anxiously, but Minna remained oblivious of the stares of those she passed on the street. She didn't seem to hear the wailing and commotion behind her.

When they were nearly halfway home, Yussel came running towards them. Like Minna, he accepted Jake's presence without thought.

"Thank God! Thank God!" he cried. "When I heard about the fire, I thought…" he put his arms around Minna, his eyes filling with tears. "Thanks be to God!"

Minna hugged him back and patted his shoulder. "Don't worry," she said softly. "It's all right. They'll be waiting for us at home."

Yussel looked at Jake, who shook his head.

"They got out ahead of me. I'm sure they did. They were closer to the elevator, you see. Then they decided not to wait because it's so cold." She shivered. "They knew I'd be all right." She shivered again.

"How did you get out?" Yussel asked.

"I climbed on a ladder from the roof," she said dreamily. "Young men from NYU helped me. I saw Anna," she continued. "She took off her hat before she floated away, floated…" She opened her eyes wide. "Oh my God, Yussel! Where are Mama and Pearl? I haven't seen them. We must go back."

"I'll go back," Yussel said. "I'll find them. Don't worry. You go home now with Jake and take care of your burn. Get under the quilt and get all warmed up. I'll be back before you know it." He hesitated. "You saw Anna?"

"I saw her fall to the ground," Minna said.

He ran off. Minna stared after him.

"He's right," Jake said. "He's the one to find them. We'll go home now."

She thought it over and nodded. "Yussel will find them …" she repeated. As they trudged along, each step became more difficult. It seemed as if they'd never stop walking.

Finally, they approached the entrance to the apartment. She turned to Jake and whispered, "It's like Chava. They're gone. I know they're gone. If I had looked for them, maybe…" She closed her eyes. "It's like before. This time, there's no one left except Yussel and me." Minna clung to Jake. "Why wasn't it me?" she asked desperately. "Why am I always the one left?"

Jake half carried her inside and up the stairs. Pushing her into the bedroom, he commanded. "Take off your wet clothes now. Put on the warmest thing you can find and wrap yourself in the quilt. I'll make you some tea."

She followed his instructions automatically, dropping her damp and smoke stained clothing on the floor. She put on her flannel dressing gown and wrapped the quilt around herself. In the kitchen, she could hear the reassuring gurgle of the teapot.

Slowly she left the bedroom and stood in the kitchen doorway watching Jake as he looked for a glass for the tea. "I guess they didn't get here yet," she began bravely, but her voice shook. Sitting down at the table, she put her head in her hands and began to sob, kneading her head over and over again.

Jake handed her a steaming glass of tea. Then he sat down next to her and put is arm around her. "Drink this," he said. "It's good for you. Then lean against me." Clumsily, he patted her shoulder.

"Don't cry, Minna. Wait and see," he mumbled. "Maybe they'll come in the door and everything will be…"

She shook her head. "I know they won't," she said leadenly. "I know they won't come home again. I know…" She began to sob again, her head buried against Jake.

Suddenly, she pulled her head back. "I don't believe it!" she yelled. "I won't believe it! Never! How could they not be here—Mama and Pearl? It's not…" She stopped. "Yussel will find them. I'm sure he will. If it's up to him, everything will be all right." She jumped up. "They'll be cold when they come home. I should fix some soup. That would be good." The quilt still wrapped around her, Minna began to rustle in the larder. Jake watched her helplessly.

She picked up a pot, put it down. Then she looked at Jake and shook her head. Silently, she sat down at the table again. "I'll wait," she said, her hands over her eyes and her body still shivering.

She remained in that position, almost unmoving, for two hours. As she stared at the kitchen door, she willed Pearl and Mama to come through it with Yussel. Clenching her fingers into fists, her legs tensed, she was ready to jump up when they appeared. Jake said nothing. He merely put his hand over Minna's and waited with her.

Finally, she heard a noise at the outside door. She stood up, her body trembling from the long wait. She watched the doorway anxiously…staring…listening…waiting…her whole being focused on the entrance to the kitchen.

She heard slow, dragging steps as Yussel appeared in the doorway. He walked heavily toward them, his head hanging and his shoulders drooping. "I looked everywhere," he said in a broken voice, "but I couldn't find them. They could be wandering around on the way home…"

Wearily, Minna shook her head.

"We have to go back. There's a place we can go to see if…" He swallowed. "To see if their bodies are there." He finished.

Minna nodded. "We'll go. I have to get dressed first." Trembling, she went into the bedroom and flung on some clothes. She took as many shawls as she could find to keep herself warm for she no longer had a cloak.

By the time she came out, Jake had joined Yussel by the door. "I'll come, too," he said.

They left the apartment together. Silently, the three of them made their way to the Mercer Street Police Station. There, along with many others, they were told to go to Misery Lane, the 26th Street pier. "They'll be laid out there, my dears," a ruddy Irish policeman said to the crowd.

They moved as in a procession, the women wailing, the men crying silently. No words were said, yet there was a kinship between sufferers. Once, the woman ahead of Minna stumbled and instantly, three men were at her side to help her forward.

As they approached the pier, they saw long lines of people seeking admission, with heads bowed and faces covered with scarves and shawls. The line was silent except for the sounds of weeping. Occasionally, a nurse or a policeman would come by and question those on line.

"Who are ye lookin' for?" a policeman asked the three of them.

"My Mama and my sister," Minna replied.

"Mrs. Ruchel Ruben and Pearl Ruben," Jake said.

"And Sarah Rabinowitz," Yussel added.

The policeman nodded and moved on.

Minna kept watching for him, thinking he would come back when he had information for them, but he never did. Later, she realized that he only asked to check their right to stand on line. Some, it seemed, had come out of curiosity and were willing to wait on line to gratify it.

As morning began to approach, others joined the mourners. Street peddlers held up trinkets and scraps of cloth. "Get your souvenirs of the great fire! Buy a dead girl's ring! Buy a piece of a dead girl's dress!"

Minna stared at the vendors, her mouth open. She felt a kind of rage she had never felt before. She looked the closest peddler in the eye as he approached. "You're making money out of dead bodies! A curse on you!" she hissed fiercely. She began to step out of line. She felt she had to hit, smash, grab away the bits of cloth and trinkets.

Yussel and Jake grabbed her arms.

She glared at them. "Don't you see what they're doing? How can they? They could be selling Mama's…" She choked.

Jake shook his head. "Wait, Minna. You're right, but wait. That's not what is important."

Feeling that if she hurt one of the peddlers, it would ensure

Pearl and Mama's survival, she struggled against Jake's arm.

Yussel spoke tearfully. "He's right, Minna. What's important is not this. What's important is…" His voice broke.

She subsided.

They inched closer to the piers. As the hours passed, exhausted women walked up and down the lines to keep warm, wringing their hands and calling the name of the one they feared to see inside. Minna shivered and wrapped her shawls closer around her. Yussel stared at the ground, his lips pinched and his face grim. Jake waited in silence, his presence strangely reassuring.

As they reached the head of the line, Minna became more and more apprehensive. What if she did find Pearl and Mama? What then? All she could think of was Chava and the shroud Mama had made.

Finally, it was their turn to enter. Shrinking, they came into a large open room. They joined a group of about twenty, guided by several policemen. The first thing that Minna noticed was the grisly dampness and cold. It pervaded her body and heart with a deathly hopelessness.

The overhead arc lights glowed dimly, creating more shadows than light. Policemen standing by the bodies swung lanterns to help illuminate the corpses so the mourners could identify their loved ones. Minna heard screams of grief from those ahead of her as they recognized a mother, a daughter, or a father.

All the coffins were laid upon the floor. Some of them had small yellow cards tacked to them. Those, they were told, meant that the body had already been identified.

The three of them made slow progress as they stopped and bent over every unidentified female body. The ghastly flickering light as the lanterns swung back and forth added to their feelings of terror and anguish.

Yussel stopped short and bowed over a coffin. "It's Sarah," he said, his eyes filling with tears. "There's Sarah. *Gottenyu*, it's Sarah!" He reached out a hand as if to smooth her hair, held it in the air for a moment, and let it fall back to his side. "Goodbye," he said.

Minna bent over and looked. She must have jumped and landed upon her side, for her face was still recognizable, although her dress was torn and shredded. As Yussel spoke to the policeman, giving him Sarah's name and address, Minna walked on with Jake, her legs trembling. She believed she was scarcely looking at the bodies as she bent over them, yet had she been asked to describe each one, she could have done so. She wanted to close her eyes so she need not look at all, but she knew she had to find Mama and Pearl.

All at once, she let out a shriek. "It's Pearl! There, see... It's my baby sister lying there." She bent over the coffin and smoothed Pearl's hair. Her face, too, was relatively unmarked. It seemed, for a moment, to feel warm as if she was still alive. Minna looked again. Maybe there was a mistake... "Pearl!" she called. "I'm here, Pearl!"

Yussel came to her. With Jake, he held Minna's arms, yet he, too, reached out to touch his sister.

Holding onto both sides of the coffin and staring into it, Minna memorized Pearl's face. "I'm sorry, Pearl," she mumbled. "If I had looked for you..." She stroked Pearl's cheek.

As the policeman approached, she gave him Pearl's name. Yussel and Jake said nothing.

Somberly, they moved on, still looking for Mama. Without comment, Minna passed the bodies of many she knew and had worked with. Only when she saw Erma's body did she stop for a moment, motioning to Yussel. He came to her side and peered down. When he recognized Erma, he gasped.

By the time they had almost reached the end of the room, Minna feared the horror of it would overwhelm her. Where was Mama? They had to find her. She pushed her way forward. Although she had been gazing at more and more ghastly sights, she couldn't help but hope that by some miracle Mama had escaped.

Finally, at the very end of the room, Minna came upon a very small table guarded by a policeman. Upon it, pieces of jewelry.had been placed. She stopped and looked at the policeman.

Responding to her look, he explained. "These are from the ones who were so badly burned nothing remains. This is the only means of identification right here."

Minna and Yussel scanned the table. Suddenly, Yussel wailed. Holding up a small gold wedding band, he cried, "I think... it's Mama's! I know it is."

The policeman held his lantern over the ring so that Minna could see the inscription on the inside. Her voice trembling, she read the initials out loud. It was Mama's. Mutely, she looked up at the policeman.

"This lady was found at her machine. She burned just sitting there, God save her soul. She never moved." He shook his head. "See, it's as if she didn't even try, because those next to her, they at least got up. Their chairs were empty."

Minna held the ring tightly in one hand. With the other, she gripped Yussel's arm. The two of them stood for so long in silence that Jake apologetically began to spell out Mama's name for the policeman.

Then he looked at Minna and Yussel. "We have to get permits from the cops," he said. "If we go to the office outside, we can receive permission to take the bodies for burial."

Minna and Yussel followed Jake out of the pier and towards the small office. By an act of will, Minna stopped thinking of anything, anything at all. Instead she concentrated on Yussel. "It's all right," she murmured, hardly knowing what she was saying. "It's all right."

As they walked, her legs felt stiff and unreal. She looked down at her hands and saw they were trembling. Still, she kept repeating, "It's all right. It's all right," in a flat voice.

In the office, she let Yussel and Jake do the talking. Although her eyes were open, she saw nothing of the room or the policemen. All she could picture was the flames shooting higher and higher and Mama, sitting at her machine, unmoving. Mama… Minna stifled a sob. She didn't even try, she repeated to herself. She didn't even try.

Jake came home with them. He helped Yussel carry Minna up the stairs when she seemed unable to move any further. After she was settled, he turned to leave.

"Thank you, Jake," Yussel said, shaking his hand.

Jake swallowed. "I won't see you for a few weeks. I have to go away. I have to! Tell Minna."

Numbly, Yussel nodded.

Lying upon her bed, Minna was afraid to close her eyes. When she did, she saw flames, confusion, death…and Chava. Although she was exhausted, she forced herself to stay awake, lying stiffly in the now too-big bed. So now, she thought angrily, you've got what you wanted. You said you wanted a room to yourself. She shook her fist at the sky. "Thank You, God," she whispered bitterly. "Thank You for listening to my prayers!"

Finally, despite all her attempts to stay awake, she fell asleep. Although she was periodically disturbed by nightmares, disturbing pictures of Mama, Pearl, and Sarah waving at her as they were burning in the fire, when she awoke in the morning she forgot for a moment what had happened.

She looked around for Pearl, remembered, and burst into tears, the feeling of loss as fresh and new as it had been the night before. Hearing a noise in the kitchen, she went to the doorway.

Yussel was at the table. Bessie sat next time, patting his shoulder. She looked up as she heard Minna. Wordlessly, she held out her hands in a gesture of sympathy.

She exchanged looks with Bessie and sank down next to Yussel. She put her hand over his. After what seemed like a long time, he looked at her and nodded.

She nodded back. Listlessly, she sat at the table, accepting the glass of tea Bessie thrust at her. There was nothing she could say.

Finally, Yussel broke the silence. "I have arranged for the burial," he said. "Sarah's, too, She had no family here."

Minna looked at him.

"There's a meeting on Wednesday to remember those who are lost," Bessie said. "It's for all, by the Union. Abe Cahan will be there."

Minna was quiet. Finally, she looked at Bessie. "The doors were jammed! And I saw the fire escape collapse! Even if Mama had tried…" she gulped, and continued, "had tried to get out, she wouldn't have been able to. I was lucky."

"They say 146 were killed in the fire. Some men, but mostly girls and women from the ninth floor. The tenth floor—the bosses—they got out mostly," Bessie said.

"The eighth?" Minna asked, thinking of Mr. Steinberg.

Bessie shook her head. "I don't know."

"I feel…" Minna began. "I feel…" She looked at Yussel beseechingly. "I should have found them, shouldn't I? I should have gotten them out."

Yussel stood up abruptly and leaned towards her. "Don't say that!" he shouted angrily. "Then…you'd be gone, too. You did all you could, Minna, and I never want to hear anything else." He waited for her answer, looming over her.

She finally nodded. "You're right, Yussel," she replied. To herself, she thought, I should have found them. If I had found them and led them to the roof, they'd be here now.' Yussel, satisfied, sat down again.

CHAPTER 23

The next days passed excruciatingly slowly. Minna viewed the world through a veil. Although she made the right gestures, said the expected thing, and carefully read the newspaper to see who the other survivors were, none of it had any meaning for her. Mechanically, she ate, tried to sleep, and stared through unseeing eyes, her shoulders slumped and her movements lethargic.

Every moment of every day, she missed Mama and Pearl. At night, she missed her sister's soft body next to hers in the bed. During the day, she missed talking to her. Many times, she found herself beginning to say something to her—or to Mama—only to stop, in anguish, when she realized abruptly they were gone.

Bessie had suggested they utilize the services of the Hebrew Free Burial Society for Sarah and Pearl. For Mama, there was nothing left to bury. Pearl and Sarah were buried at the same time—Pearl in her graduation dress. Many attended—the neighbors, Cousin Avraim, Pearl's classmates, and even Miss Israel. Afterwards, they came back to the house to offer their condolences.

She and Yussel had decided not to sit *Shiva.* So much had changed since their arrival in America. The old rituals no longer seemed part of their lives.

Minna, alone upon a mountain peak, looking numbly down at herself and the others, responded appropriately to everyone and felt nothing. When Yussel told her what Jake had said about going away, she simply nodded. It didn't seem very important. In later days, she found she remembered nothing of the funeral or the day immediately following. Nothing, that is, except a pillow, a handkerchief, a sleeve wet with tears.

From what she could learn, it seemed that no one would be blamed for the deaths, or, more accurately, everyone would be blamed. Minna read a statement by Lilian Wald, the beloved nurse of the East Side, which said, "The crux of the situation is that there is not direct responsibility. Divided, always, divided. The responsibility rests nowhere!" The Building Inspectors blamed the Fire Inspectors and the Fire Inspectors blamed city policies, which gave them little funding for staff. The factory owners, Harris and Blanck, were accused of locking one of the exit doors, preventing the escape of many of the girls.

On Wednesday, Minna and Yussel attended a meeting at Grand Central Palace held by ILGWU Local 25. The large room was filled with survivors, relatives of Triangle employees, and others who cared about their plight.

Minna felt the tension in the hall around her. Poised uneasily on the edge of her chair, she looked around, hoping to see friends who had survived. Mr. Steinberg's name had not yet appeared upon the list of those who had been killed. Although it was unlikely he had been saved, she couldn't help hoping. Most of the deaths were from her floor, not his.

Yussel held her hand. As she looked at the audience, she was overwhelmed by its size. Memories of the fire crowded upon her. She pictured flames suddenly beginning to rise here, in this room. She saw madness, people screaming, pushing, and yelling. She gripped Yussel's arm so tightly he almost jerked it away in pain. When he realized she was afraid, his put his other hand on top of hers. The warmth of his grasp helped to reassure her.

She listened to the speakers, from Abe Cahan, the editor of *The Forward* to the others. Their words were interrupted by hysteria and sobs. She became more and more agitated until finally, she could bear it no longer.

She jumped up and stood upon her chair. "I was there," she said. "I know what happened. The rest is just words. Now they come forward, the rich and the powerful, and they try to make amends. I say, it's too late. I say, we are the only ones who can be trusted to make changes. We are the ones who have died because of this fire. We are the ones who will die from consumption or malnutrition or overwork. We are the ones who have to make the important changes." Unable to finish, she burst into tears. As she hid her face in her hands, she heard a noise that sounded as if thousands of pages were turning at once. She looked up. The audience was applauding. Abashed, she sat down abruptly.

After the meeting, others sought her out. The first to reach her was Bessie, who put her arms around her and squeezed her shoulders approvingly, stating, "That was well said."

Minna shook her head. "I wasn't trying to speak well. It's only…I feel so impatient with all this. Meanwhile," she said, her eyes filling with tears, "they lie dead and buried. So many of them…"

All at once, she saw a familiar face coming through the crowd. She gasped. It was Mr. Steinberg. He hurried towards her, his arms outstretched.

"Oh, you're alive," she sighed, hugging him. "You're alive!" With a pang, she thought of those who were no longer here. "They're all gone," she sobbed against his shoulder.

After a time, she stepped back. "This is Mr. Steinberg, Yussel," she explained. "He's alive, thanks be to God."

Yussel nodded.

"That was good, what you said," Mr. Steinberg said earnestly. "I'm angry, too, although I'll try to overcome it." He thrust a piece of paper at Minna. "See, I've written a poem about the fire. Here's a copy." He pressed her hand and disappeared.

Minna clutched the poem tightly and turned to Yussel and Bessie. "Can we leave, please?" The feeling of suffocation came back as they pushed their way to the door.

Once they were outside, she looked up at Yussel. "Do you think I'm going to be afraid the rest of my life? While we were there, especially at the end when everyone was pushing and shoving, I felt trapped and helpless. I felt that way here again. It was all I could do to stop from screaming."

Yussel clenched his hands, but tried to smile reassuringly. "I think it will be get better. It will just take you some time."

Bessie excused herself. "There are a few people here that I have to see," she said as she plunged back inside. They hurried home.

Only when they were once again sitting at the kitchen table did Minna pull out Mr. Steinberg's poem. Carefully, she smoothed it out in front of her and read it aloud so Yussel could hear, too:

Remembrance

The young girls, like flowers,
In a desert garden,
The mothers and the fathers,
The young men, like warriors,
In a forgotten battle,
I saw them all.
I wept for every one.
Blood in the streets,
Red flames in the sky,
And falling, falling,
The bodies to the ground.
I mourn their lives,
I mourn their deaths.
For each who died,
We'll sing sad songs.
Yet let us mourn,
Those who remain.
They, too, suffer.
Hungry and afraid,
They are the exploited,
Victims in a cruel world.
They, too, will come to die,
Like angels in the streets.

After reading the poem, Minna closed her eyes for a moment. "I mourn," she said. "I mourn for Momma and Pearl and Sarah and Anna and Erma and all the rest. I mourn for us, too, Yussel. What will we do now? Where will we go?"

"I'll keep on peddling." Yussel said. "We can find a smaller place to live and…"

"Is that what you want to do?"

He hesitated. "What else can I do?" he asked at last. "We must live."

Minna thought for a moment. "I don't know, Yussel, but I think we have to make new choices, now that it's only the two of us."

There was a long pause. Finally she continued. "We can talk of this tomorrow. Soon the money under the floor will run out and we'll have to decide. We can't stay here unless we get more boarders…"

He shook his head. "You're right. We'll talk of this tomorrow."

The next morning, when Minna awoke, she heard a noise in the kitchen. She hurried out of bed to see what was happening. Standing in the doorway, she saw Yussel cutting a fresh loaf of bread. When he looked up, she tried to smile.

As she dressed, she took especial pains to look tidy. By the time she came back into the kitchen, she felt a little better than she had the day before, although her eyes filed with tears when she saw the empty chairs around the table.

She sat next to Yussel. "What shall we do?" she mused. "We can go on as we are, but is that what we really want?"

"If I could," Yussel said, "you know I wish we could have a little farm of our own."

"And I wish to go to school and become a teacher. I wish to never enter the door of a factory again. I wish to leave this apartment of death." She gulped back a sob.

"Unfortunately, we're not millionaires," Yussel said in his first attempt at humor since the fire.

"I want to leave!" Minna burst out. "This is a place of sorrow now. I want to go somewhere else to live. To a farm, maybe, or another city, or…I don't know…" She sipped her tea pensively.

There was an unexpected knock on the front door. Minna started. She looked at the kitchen clock. It was nine o'clock. "Who can it be?" she wondered. "Everyone is working."

Yussel went to the door. Minna didn't even turn her head to see who was there until she heard a strange note in his voice as he called her name. She turned around.

He was followed into the kitchen by an unknown woman. Dressed primly yet luxuriously, in some indefinable way she reminded Minna of Priscilla.

The woman extended her hand. "My name is Mrs. Peabody," she said. "I'm with the Red Cross Emergency Relief Committee. It's my job to see those who have been in the fire as well as the families of those who are gone. You must be Minna Ruben."

She stood up and nodded, overwhelmed.

"And you are?" She looked at Yussel.

"That's my brother, Yussel," Minna said.

Mrs. Peabody squeezed her hand. "I'm so sorry, my dear. You have been through so much and lost so much. You both have."

She looked around the room. "May I sit down?"

Numbly, Minna gestured to one of the empty chairs.

They sat around the table. Mrs. Peabody leaned forward, facing the two of them. "We have raised a tremendous amount of money to help the victims of this tragedy. In some cases, like yours, two members of a family have been killed. In others, children are left with no one to take care of them. We want to offer money to all who can use it, not because it will 'pay' for what happened, but because it's the only way caring people can be helpful to strangers." She paused, as if expecting an interruption and then continued. "Some of those I have seen are bitter and say they do not want help, they do not need help. It's up to you. All I can say is that we want to make the lives of the survivors a little easier for a while. If some one wishes to make a new start, perhaps we can make it possible. There may be other alternatives besides working at a factory again or even going back to Triangle, if it ever re-opens." She leaned back to await their response.

Minna looked at Yussel. He cleared his throat.

"I don't want charity," he said gruffly.

"I don't think of this as charity," Mrs. Peabody said. "You have not asked for it. No one has. The money has just come pouring in from so many different people—the rich, the poor, small children, even the Vaudeville Theatre has had a benefit performance. For once, we see the best part of human nature."

Yussel sank back, frowning.

Mrs. Peabody looked at Minna sympathetically. "If you could do anything you'd want to do, my dear, what would it be? Perhaps a small store… We have arranged for one widow to buy a small store or…?" She looked at Minna questioningly.

"I want to be a teacher," she said. "I want to go to college."

Mrs. Peabody looked surprised.

"She will, too," Yussel said, responding to her expression. "She won honors in high school. Minna will make a good teacher some day."

"And you?" Mrs. Peabody asked Yussel.

He was silent.

"He wants to be a farmer—to work on a farm," Minna said.

"What are your plans?" Mrs. Peabody asked them both.

Minna's eyes filled with tears. "I don't know," she sobbed, embarrassed to be crying in front of a stranger, but unable to stop.

Yussel put his arms around her and stared at Mrs. Peabody angrily, as if accusing her of making his sister cry.

"I don't mean to upset you," Mrs. Peabody said gently, "but life does go on. I know you must have been worrying. The question is, can I help? What if I can help you to find a small farm or a group of farmers? She smiled at Yussel. "And if I can find a college that will take you on scholarship—or we can help you…" She nodded at Minna. "Perhaps then you could both make a new start."

Despite herself, Minna's eyes widened. "You could do all that?"

Yussel frowned.

Mrs. Peabody stood up. "Why don't the two of you talk about this? If I may, I'll return in a few hours and we can see what you decide. Meanwhile, I'll meet with some people I know." She smiled. "Don't bother to show me out. I know where the front door is."

When she reached it, she turned back. "This is help out of caring, not charity. That's how I think of it." She opened the door and hurried out.

In the kitchen, Minna looked at Yussel. "If you think this is wrong…"she began.

"We are not beggars," he said stubbornly. "Mama and Pearl didn't die so we'd have money by them. It doesn't feel right."

She looked at him. "What is right? Is it right that you and I should go on slaving for the rest of our lives, our hopes growing fainter each year? If Mama and Pearl's lives mean anything, they could mean that we will follow our dreams. To me…" she paused. "To me, it would be as if they followed their dreams, too. If we grub away forever, it will all have been for nothing—our coming here, the store, the work, the dreams. Can't you see that?" she asked fiercely.

He shook his head. "I still don't think it's right."

"I don't know if it's right or not," Minna said. "I just know that if I have a chance to escape, I'll take it! I can't bear it here any more." She covered her face with her hands and sobbed loudly. "All I see are the dead," she cried. "In my sleep and in the daylight, I see them all around me. I can't bear it, Yussel. If I could get away…"

"But, Minna," he said leaning closer to her, "if it's wrong? Would you still want to take the money?"

"I don't believe it's wrong," she insisted. "You heard what she said. She said it was a gift of love and caring. Well, I hope I'm not too proud to accept a gift!"

She stood up and began to pace the floor. She stopped abruptly in front of Yussel. "If they got all this money from people wanting to give it, what are they going to do with it if no one takes any of it? They can't return it."

He stood up. "You can do what you want. I don't think it's right to take money from strangers. I would rather live here all my life as a peddler than have a farm someone bought for me. Can't you understand?"

She shook her head. "No, I can't. How can you say no when all your dreams may be given to you?"

He sat down again. "I don't know. You seem so sure this is the right thing to do. But…"

"We could agree to pay them back," she pleaded. "Of course, if I did get a scholarship, I wouldn't pay the college back. Why can't this be like a scholarship for you? Maybe someday, we'll be in a position to give money to help someone else. Maybe that's the way we'll pay back." She sat down again. "If you had enough money to help people, wouldn't you want them to take it and be glad?"

"I don't know, Minna. Shouldn't we stay together now that it's just…the two of us?"

She looked squarely at him. "Now that we're the only ones left? That's what you mean. Maybe we should, but we have different dreams. We can write to each other and visit. I don't know, Yussel. I don't know what is right. I guess…if you can do what you've always wanted to do and I can do what I've always wanted to do, it *is* right. I'm not sure, but that's what I think." She grabbed his hands. "Oh, if we could both get away from here, Yussel. If only we could."

They sat in silence, looking at each other. She dropped her eyes first.

If I could talk to Bubbe, what would she say, she wondered. I like to think she'd agree and say, 'Go ahead, Minna.' but I don't know. She shook her head defiantly. I don't care! This is right. If it's right to want, then it's right to take a chance even if it means accepting a gift, even if it means being separated from Yussel. If out of agony, good can come, it has to be right.

She said the words out loud. "If out of this horror, good can come, should we say no? Would Mama or Pearl have wanted us to say no? The store was Mama's dream, not mine or yours."

Yussel grabbed his coat and hat. "I need to think by myself," he said. 'I'll go for a walk. I'll be back soon."

She watched him leave. Once she was alone, she called out in her thoughts, Bubbe, tell me. Am I wrong to want? Would I be wrong to allow my dreams to come true? She held her breath.

There was a long pause. Then she was sure she could hear Bubbe saying, 'My little Minna. Now you and Yussel are the only left of my blood. When I was a girl and my Tata found a kopeck by the roadside, first he made sure it belonged to no one else. Then he'd say, 'Praise God! We are lucky today!' and use the money to buy something for us. Nothing can bring your Mama or Pearl back to you. They are with me now. So I say, yes, take the money. Make something of yourself for them and always, keep the memory of those who are no more.'

Minna remembered the story of the kopeck. For days after Bubbe had told her about it, she had walked with her head down, looking at the ground, hoping to find a kopeck for herself. Now, she concluded, I have found my kopeck. I won't leave it to lie by the roadside for someone else to take.

She waited anxiously for Yussel's return. What would happen if he disagreed with her? In the end, Minna didn't think she'd be able to go against him. To stop from thinking about it, she began to scrub the stove, finding relief in the work. She remembered the Sunday when Mama had cleaned it with such pride. She rubbed each grease spot thoroughly until it disappeared, willing her tears to disappear as well.

When Minna heard Yussel at the door, she put down her cleaning rag and the bar of brown soap. Slowly, she turned to face him, her expression anxious.

He came into the kitchen, took of his hat and coat, and looked earnestly at Minna. "I've thought about it," he said hesitantly. "The thoughts are chasing through my brain like smoke from the chimney on a windy day. I have decided."

Minna felt her heart drop. It didn't sound as if he was going to agree. She gripped the edge of the table.

He smiled. "What I will do is this. I will accept the help. If it's money, I'll pay it back when I can. You can do as you choose."

She sighed in relief. "Now we'll wait for Ms. Peabody to come back and see what our fate will be," she said excitedly, forgetting

Mama and Pearl for just a moment. Catching Yussel's surprised look, she flushed. "I can never forget," she said seriously. "Mama and Pearl are part of me, the way Chava and Bubbe are. But…" She hesitated. "Life is life, isn't it? It has to go on."

He nodded.

When Mrs. Peabody came back, the two of them ushered her back into the kitchen. Sensing the difference in their attitudes, she asked, "So you've decided to accept our offering of help?"

They both nodded.

"I'll have to get more information." She looked at Yussel. "I'll need to see if you know enough to run your own farm." To Minna, she said, "I'd like to talk to your teachers to get an idea of the kind of work you can do. I've made a few inquiries myself. It looks as if we will be able to help you find what you want, both of you."

"If it's money," Yussel said, "I'd like to tell you that I plan to pay you back as soon as I can."

"That's not necessary," she said, "but if you want to, your money can go to the American Red Cross and be used to help someone else. So that will be good."

Yussel was relieved.

"Of course, you know you will both have to work hard. We are only helping you get a start. Past that, it's up to you."

Minna couldn't help herself. To her own surprise, she said, "Now, everyone wants to help. Before, no one cared. My Mama and my sister, they'd be here now if anyone had cared." She was abashed by her own words, but she couldn't apologize.

Mrs. Peabody stared at her, obviously surprised by her words.

Minna feared she had lost her chance for a new life. I'm still glad I said it, she thought. I believe it, so why shouldn't I say it?

"It's hard, I know," Mrs. Peabody finally said sympathetically. "If others had paid attention to the plight of your mother and sister and those like them, there would have been no tragedy. It's too late to help them," she said regretfully, "but it's not too late to help those who remain."

Minna nodded. "I know it's not your fault, Mrs. Peabody, but…"

"But there are many who have done nothing. It's true. Still, does that mean you should be angry about their help now that they finally do offer it? It is, at least, better than not caring at all."

Yussel showed that he agreed and finally, so did Minna.

That evening, when Bessie returned home, they had much to tell her. Minna, and then Yussel, explained about Mrs. Peabody. "She'll be back in a few days after she looks into everything. That's what she said," Minna concluded.

"It's a chance you should take," Bessie said immediately. "It's a chance they owe us for our suffering, don't you see?"

"I don't think anyone owes us anything," Yussel insisted.

Bessie shook her head. "We're the exploited. We're slaves of the system. They should make up for that. When the Union comes to power…"

"Yes, you always say that. When the Union comes to power… What will happen then?" Minna asked.

"I don't know. But I'm sure it will be good. There's been so much interest shown since the fire. The Union grows stronger every day. That reminds me. I wanted to ask you something, Minna. Would you speak at a meeting tomorrow? It's for a memorial. You were so good the other night."

Minna looked at her in surprise, thought for a moment, and shook her head. "I'm not a speaker," she said. "That night, I just couldn't help myself. If I have to plan to speak ahead of time, I'll be too nervous!"

Bessie was disappointed. "It would be so effective," she coaxed. "You, being a survivor. Just say the same thing you said before."

"I don't even know what I said before, so how can I say it again? I will come to the meeting, though."

"But…" Bessie began. Then glimpsing the expression on Yussel's face, she hesitated and said, "That would be nice, Minna."

"The Union is growing stronger because of this, then?" Yussel asked.

"The support is amazing. You have no idea how many have now become involved. Some say, 'Too little, too late.' I say, 'Any help is good help. Only the rich can afford to be bitter.' Do you know that some of the people helping us are Andrew Carnegie. Mrs. J.P. Morgan, and Mrs. Belmont? Rabbi Wise said, 'The disaster was not the deed of God but the greed of man.' Morris Rosenfeld, the worker poet, had his poem printed on the whole front page of *The Forward*. Did you see it?"

They shook their heads.

"I'll get you a copy so you can read it for yourselves."

That reminded Minna, "I have a poem from Mr. Steinberg. He

writes for *The Forward*, too. Do you want to see it?"

"Sure," Bessie said.

Minna ran into the bedroom and found her copy of the poem, which she handed to Bessie. She and Yussel watched her as she read it.

She looked up with tears in her eyes. "This is beautiful. May I take it? Perhaps someone can read it at the next meeting."

Minna thought for a moment. She didn't want to give Mr. Steinberg's poem away. What if he didn't approve? On the other hand, she remembered him saying how he felt when others read his poems. Yes, she thought, he would be glad.

"Let me copy it. Then I'll give you the copy," she agreed.

While she was copying the poem at the table, Bessie and Yussel spoke in low voices. Minna, wholly concentrated upon her writing, paid no attention to what they were saying. Just when she had finished, she heard a knock at the door.

"It must be Cousin Avraim," Yussel said as he stood up.

Cousin Avraim had been very faithful, visiting the apartment every night to pay his respects even though they were not sitting Shiva as he thought they should. Tonight, he had brought his wife and their son with him, followed by Benny Herschel.

As soon as he saw Minna, Benny hurried over to her. Holding both her hands, he looked into her eyes. "I've known you so long and now, to have this happen. Your mother, a woman in the prime of her life and your sister, a bud beginning to open. I'm so sorry, my dear."

Minna bowed her head. She felt a touch of shame. How could she be planning a new life on the ashes of the old? Had she forgotten about Mama and Pearl so soon, despite her brave words to Yussel?

"Thank you," she replied meekly. "It has been hard."

Cousin Avraim came closer, his wife two steps behind him. "You needn't worry about the future, Cousin Minna," he said heartily. "There will always be a place for you in the store. We'll get you a sewing machine and you can run classes and sell, just like you did for your Mama."

Minna wanted to yell at Cousin Avraim and say, why didn't you let Mama come and work for you before, when we lost the store? Then she wouldn't have had to work at Triangle at all. You just want me because I'll be cheaper than someone who's not family.

But she held her tongue, forcing herself to think of it differently. At least he does want to help me, she thought. If it's too late, it's not his fault. He is trying to help in his own way.

"Thank you," she said softly, determined not to tell about Mrs. Peabody until it was all settled. She peered around Cousin Avraim at his wife. "And how is your son?" she asked.

As the reply was given in detail, she allowed her thoughts to wander. What would it be like if she and Yussel left to go to a new place, either together or separately? Maybe there was a place where everyone spoke English and the fields were green… She looked over at Yussel. She could tell he felt uncomfortable. Excusing herself, she hurried over to him.

He looked up at her gratefully. He, too, she realized, didn't want to talk about the future until all their plans were definite.

At that moment, Minna made up her mind. With or without Mrs. Peabody, we will help ourselves, she decided. We'll leave New York and go somewhere else, some new place where there's a patch of sky, where we can breathe, where the world doesn't know from Yiddish. Somewhere, she sighed, where there are no ghosts. Either way, she knew they would say farewell to this place. Wishing she could tell Yussel about her decision, she squeezed his hand and waited for their guests to leave.

Before bedtime, Minna told Yussel her thoughts. He shrugged, as if to say 'of course.' It was clear that once he accepted Mrs. Peabody's offer, he had decided to go forward with his life.

The days dragged on. Minna still awoke screaming several times a night. She felt her sleep would never be peaceful again. She had attended several other meetings with Bessie and each time, without planning it in advance, she stood and spoke. She was always greeted with applause. Afterwards, her indignation grew stronger and her sleep more uneasy as she relived the horror of the fire.

Mrs. Peabody stopped by almost every day, but as yet there had been no definite word on the future. Although Yussel agreed with Minna about leaving New York, he finally said, "I will go back to peddling on Monday. Whatever we decide, whatever happens, we need money right now. You, too…"he began delicately.

She agreed. "You're right. We have to make some decisions but first of all, we need *gelt.* We have to decide about the apartment, too. If we stay for a while, we'll have to get more boarders."

"We can manage if we both work for now," he said. "Mrs.

Peabody says we'll know in a day or two. Let's wait on her about the apartment. I have faith in her, don't you?"

"She means to do well by us," Minna said dubiously. "It's hard to believe in it, though. I'll go to Cousin Avraim on Monday. I can't go back to a factory. Not now."

He nodded.

It would be good, Minna thought, to be occupied. The days seemed so long. Mama and Pearl were always on her mind. Everything in the apartment reminded her of them. The others, Erma, Anna, Mrs. Cichetti, Erma's cousin, Sammy, who had so bravely kept the elevators running… They, too, were often in her thoughts.

Her world, she realized, had become too circumscribed. It contained so little…just Yussel, Bessie, and her meetings…the anger that welled up in her heart when she remembered the fire…the loneliness from which there was no relief…and worst of all, the bitter emptiness of each slow moment…

In all this time, Jake did not return. Minna remembered his presence on the afternoon of the fire only vaguely. She recalled that he had come to Misery Lane with them, but she couldn't remember his departure. Where was he, she wondered. It had been reassuring to have him there, yet… She shook her head. She didn't want to think about him now.

When she finally asked Yussel about him, he shrugged. "He's a friend. That much he has proved. How much of a friend, how reliable he is, I don't know."

With that, Minna was content. If I'm turning my back on Allen Street, she thought, I'm turning my back on Jake, too. Still, she was glad he had come to her when she needed him.

As for the others she might be leaving behind, she knew she'd miss Bessie and Mr. Steinberg, but since she wouldn't be working near him, she might never see him again anyway. Maybe I could write to him, she thought vaguely. As for Bessie, she knew if she couldn't share her interest in the Union, her friend would always be disappointed in her. Cousin Avraim, Benny Herschel, the neighbors, they were people she saw only rarely. Since Debbie had been in the sanitarium, she had hardly ever stopped to visit her family. She feared it made them sadder to see her.

The sanitarium…that reminded Minna of Saul. If he had read about the fire in the paper, he would be beside himself. On the other hand, if he had read about the fire, why hadn't she received a letter? She decided to wait to write to him. Just now, she felt, it was too close, too hard to put words on paper.

The trouble is, she thought, everything seems far away to me except the fire. Even Yussel. I know I love him, but I can accept living apart from him. I thought I loved Jake, but I'm glad he's not here. The pain is too great to think of anyone except Mama and Pearl.

She listened to Mrs. Peabody as they planned her future. She reproached herself for feeling even a modicum of excitement when it was decided she would attend a small mid-western coeducational university called Oberlin. There she would live in a boarding house and work as a helper to the owner while she completed her studies.

Although Mrs. Peabody had arranged a full academic scholarship for four years, it did not include room, board, or spending money. She had been apologetic to Minna, saying, "We can pay your fare out west and for the first year, I can give you a small sum to pay for clothing and books. After that, you'll have to earn money over the summers and on the side. Your work for Mrs. Boone at the boarding house is in exchange for room and board. It's going to be difficult, Minna, but it's the best we can do."

"The best you can do! In a million years, I could never do so well!"

An accusing internal voice said to her: So, you're happy. You haven't got a care in the world, have you? You've got what you wanted. Too bad Mama and Pearl aren't here, but you don't really care.

She stifled the thought and forced herself to listen to Yussel's plans with a clear heart. It had been arranged that he would receive a lump sum of money, but he had decided to work in a communal farm for a year or two to familiarize himself with the necessary skills before he used it. The commune he had chosen was similar to the one he had heard about on the boat so long ago. His eyes lit up when he described it to Minna.

Once everything had been decided, Minna found she began to think of her life as divided in two, a drama with two acts. First, there was the family. Then a curtain fell and everything was different. When it rose again, she stood upon the stage alone, facing the audience through a gauzy curtain. On her own, trembling and afraid, she prepared to face a new world.

She did what she had to. Anesthetized, she went through Mama and Pearl's things to clear the apartment. There was little to keep. A few books, the brooch Mama had given Pearl, and the shirtwaist she had made for her graduation were put aside, as well as the few papers Mama had kept in the box under her bed. Yussel kept the brass candlesticks, the big pot, and Mama's lace doilies for his new home in the West.

When Minna asked Mrs. Peabody when they would begin their new lives, she had looked worried. "That's a problem," she had said. "I'm afraid you can't start college until September. It isn't like high school when you can come any time. They don't skip or allow you to start in the middle. It's still March. The question is, what will you do till then? Your brother can go now to start his life upon the farm or he can wait. That's up to him."

Minna was taken aback. March, April, May, June, July, August… That's six months before I can begin. Six months, to stay here." Her face fell.

The voice inside her sneered: Can't wait, can you. Enjoy the blood *gelt*! She forced herself to ignore it.

"Of course, we'll stay together," Yussel said.

She had disagreed. "No. I want you to get started. No more peddling. No more Allen Street."

He had even raised his voice to object. "You can't stay alone, Minna. I won't let you! It's my responsibility."

"You're not Tata!" she had snapped. Immediately rueful, she extended her hand to him. "I'm sorry. I just don't see why we both have to wait. I won't stay here, either. I'll rent a room or…"

Mrs. Peabody interrupted. "I may have a solution," she offered. "Let me talk to some people and I'll tell you about it tomorrow."

The next day, she suggested that Minna live with an acquaintance of hers, a Mrs. Young, who lived uptown on Fifth Avenue. "She told me she needs a seamstress. If you can make other clothes as beautiful as the shirtwaist you showed me, the one you made for your sister, she'll have plenty of work for you to do. There are two girls just out in her house and money is no object. This way, you can earn something before you go off to school and you'll have a place to stay. What do you think?"

She hesitated. "I won't be a servant, will I?" she asked. "I don't want to be a maid. My friend told me how she was treated when she was a servant."

Mrs. Peabody cleared her throat. "You'll be a seamstress. All you have to do is to sew, nothing else. If that's being a servant, then…"

"A seamstress," Minna mused. "I can do that. Yes, I will! Thank you, Mrs. Peabody."

Although Yussel protested, she convinced him that this was the best course. In the end, he admitted he was glad to leave New York and start a new life. "Here," he said, "I remember. Every minute, I remember. There, everything will be new. I can begin again. I only wish you would come with me, Minna. Together, we could…"

She was glad to find Yussel agreeing to the plan. "Someday," she promised, "when you have your farm and I'm a teacher, we'll live together. I'll teach and you'll grow tomatoes or cows and…" Unable to continue, she put her hands over her eyes.

He held her shoulder gently. "I will always come to you if you need me," he swore.

Finally, far too soon, the two of them stood on the platform at the station. Yussel's train was to leave in ten minutes. They looked at each other, bewildered.

"I can't believe…" Minna began.

"I can't either," Yussel agreed.

Suddenly, she felt very much alone. "You'll write me, won't you?" she asked Yussel desperately. "You'll take care and…"

He put his finger to her lips. "Shh. We can still change our minds. We can stay together instead of parting."

She was tempted. Then she shook her head fiercely. "Don't be silly!" She forced herself to smile. "You know we'll be together soon enough. You have to get your farm first and I, my education. Such a good strong plan has to succeed! If we give up now, we'll never leave Allen Street."

He gave her a tight hug. "I'm worried. Maybe we decided too fast. Since we made this plan and now, there wasn't enough time. All of a sudden, here we are, and we're separating. But only we two are left. I'm not ready. Should we…"

The train whistle blew.

"I don't want to leave you," he cried, torn between his fear of missing the train and the thought of Minna, remaining mournfully alone on the train platform.

"It's the right thing to do," she insisted. "We've already talked about it a million times. You know this is right. I'll earn *gelt* for school and you can begin your future. It's about time for you to plan your future, my dear brother. Six months will pass in no time at all, and then I'll be starting my future, too."

Reluctantly, he boarded the train. "It's happening too soon," he muttered. Then, louder, he urged, "Take care, Minna. Remember…don't be foolish…and…" He kept talking, even though his back was to her as he ascended the steps into the train.

At the top of the steps, he turned around to face Minna. "Remember when we left *der alter heym*?" he called. "Remember the family always!"

"I'll never forget," she called back.

As the train left the station, she stared after Yussel, who was waving furiously at her. He was standing straighter, she thought, than he had in years. Despite his nervousness, his sorrow, and his unwillingness to leave her, she had noticed alertness in his eyes, an almost-twinkle, the kind of gleam she had thought would never appear again. He was only, she realized anew, a little older than she was. Now he could become a young man again. For the first time in many years, he had only himself to worry about and his own yearnings to fulfill.

Minna watched the train until it disappeared from view. Then squaring her shoulders, she went back to the apartment to pick up her possessions so she could bring them to Mrs. Young's.

All she had was an address on upper Fifth Avenue. When she had shown it to Bessie, her friend had sniffed. "It's no boarding house, that's for sure! Not with that address! You'd better be careful, Minna, with those people," she had added suspiciously.

That had almost been enough to stop Yussel from leaving. Minna had had to reassure him over and over again that it would be all right, that Mrs. Peabody had said this or that about Mrs. Young, none of which was true.

Now, as she slung her bundle, wrapped in a strong linen sheet, over her shoulder, she looked around the apartment for the last time. She was taking very little. She had sold the few bits of furniture she owned to the landlord who planned to offer them to the new tenants and she had given Bessie the clothing she couldn't use to be given to needy Union members. The extra feather bed she had offered to Bessie as a gift.

Although her belongings were bulky, they were not too heavy. Indeed, as she looked at the apartment and her bundle, she realized she was bringing very little from her old life to what she now considered her new life. That's good, she thought stoutly. I'll start with little and earn the rest.

Standing in the doorway, her eyes filling with tears, she whispered, "Farewell, Mama. Farewell, Pearl. You will come with me, but I won't see you in life again. Whatever happens, you know it will be for you, too." Resolutely, she shut the door behind her. Mournfully, yet with measured steps, she began her journey away from Allen Street.

CHAPTER 24

By the time Minna arrived at Fifth Avenue, she was tired and disheveled. Clutching her belongings on the Elevated and walking through the streets with them while trying to keep her shawls wrapped around herself for warmth was exhausting. In her pocketbook, which she gripped tightly, she had five dollars, half of what was left from the floorboard money. She had insisted that Yussel take the other five for his trip as he had already put all of his newly acquired money in a bank.

As she walked up Fifth Avenue, she noted the house numbers. To her eyes, the mansions became larger and more lavish with every step. Already apprehensive, she grew more nervous as the numbers climbed. Suppose she had to live in a palace? Would she know how to act? She squeezed the handles of her pocketbook anxiously. Would they laugh at her?

She gulped as she arrived at the right number. She stood before a large, imposing mansion near 74th Street. It was even bigger than she had feared. A tall, sharply pointed iron fence surrounded the property. Through the bars, she saw a well-manicured garden overlooked by imposing casement windows.

She followed the fence to the front entrance. Bravely, she forced herself to walk up the wide, curving portico to the front door. She hesitated, reached out her hand, and pulled the brass bell to announce her presence.

To her surprise, the door opened immediately. There must be someone just waiting by the door for the bell to ring, she thought.

A stout man in a formal black suit stared down at her haughtily.

"Mrs. Peabody told me to come here," she began. "My name is Minna Ruben and..."

The tall man pointed away from the door. "To the back!" he sniffed. "Go to the servant's entrance around the corner." He slammed the door in her face.

She stood in front of the door for a moment, nonplused. Automatically, she repeated his words. "To the servant's entrance...around the corner..." Near tears, she shook her head. What kind of house was this to have two doors? I'm not a servant, she reminded herself. I won't...

Aware of how heavy her bundle was and how exhausted she had become, she hoisted her belongings onto her shoulder and sought the right entrance. She was so tired and frightened, there seemed little else she could do. "I'll leave in the morning," she muttered to herself.

Staggering with weariness, she followed the fence until she came to a half flight of stairs leading down to an unimposing door below the street level. This time, she had to wait quite a while for someone to answer the bell. Finally, the door was flung open. A small, round young girl, dressed in black and sporting a large white apron, smiled at her cheerfully.

"And what do you want?" she asked.

She stammered. "He told me to come round here," she said, gesturing back towards the front door.

The girl cocked her head. "You're expected?" she asked.

She nodded.

"Then you'd best wait inside. Mr. Bates will see to you."

Thankfully, she stepped inside. There she halted, still grasping her belongings and gasped in amazement. She was in the most beautiful room she had ever seen. It seemed to be a kitchen, but was so brightly furnished she was sure it must be the most important room in the whole house. Even though it was bigger than their whole apartment on Allen Street, it was warm and inviting.

In its center was a clean wooden table, large enough to seat twelve. Upon the table, a bowl of roses nodded. Each place was set with a red placemat and napkin. This must be where the family has dinner, she thought, relieved to find that although the mansion was so large, it was still cozy.

Savory smells arose from the stove, tended by a plump middle-aged woman wearing a flowered dress and a starched white apron. "Sal, Come here and stir the sauce," she commanded the girl who had opened the door.

"Yes, Ma'am," Sal replied and scurried over to the stove. She had to push a small stool over to the range so she could reach the top of the pot. Standing upon it, she stirred busily with a large wooden spoon.

The older woman looked at Minna. "And who might you be?" she asked.

This made her feel slightly less afraid. At least someone wanted to know her name and took the time to talk to her.

"Minna Ruben," she said shyly. "Mrs. Peabody sent me here to sew."

"Ah, so you'll be the one. Escaped from that dreadful fire, did you?" She led Minna over to the table. "Sit down," she said warmly. "Would you care for a cup of tea? It's raw out there!"

She sat down gratefully. The young girl stared at her, open-mouthed.

"My name's Mrs. Brown," the cook explained. "That there's Sal. Mr. Bates is the butler. There are two others of us here—Mrs. Young's personal maid, Helene, and Millie, the parlor maid. The chauffeur, of course, doesn't live in the house. He eats at home with his wife. They're over the garage."

Minna nodded, although she barely comprehended a word of what Mrs. Brown had said. She spoke clearly enough. But what was a personal maid? She thought she could remember a book she'd read once that mentioned a butler, but she couldn't recall exactly what he did. He must be important, she thought, for both Sal and Mrs. Brown said he would talk to her. He must be the one who was in charge.

Just as Mrs. Brown was about to hand her a cup of tea, Mr. Bates came into the kitchen. Minna, who was fascinated by the thought of having tea in a cup instead of a glass, such a pretty cup, decorated with painted pink flowers, didn't notice his presence at first. Alerted by the reaction of Mrs. Brown, who simpered and returned to the stove, she looked up to see him standing over her.

"Now, what's this?" he asked.

Afraid to say anything, Minna stared at him mutely.

"She's Minna Ruben, come to sew. You know, from the fire.

Mrs. Peabody sent her." Mrs. Brown spoke from her position at the stove.

Mr. Bates smiled at Minna briefly. Then he spoke to Sal. "Come here, girl. Take Minna to her room. It's the single next to you and Millie."

Minna picked up her belongings again, shifting their weight uneasily. Hesitantly, she followed Sal, who went through a small door in the corner of the kitchen and up a narrow winding staircase. Straining to keep up, she hurried up two flights of stairs and down a long corridor.

At last, Sal stopped and pointed at a door. "That's your room. You're next to me and Millie. We all live up here except for Mr. Bates. He has a room downstairs."

Minna was too confused to respond. She looked at what would be her room for the next six months if she decided to stay. It was small and dark, but the furnishings were more luxurious than anything she had ever seen. There was a bureau, a wardrobe, and even a hard wooden chair for her to sit on. The bed had a rounded wooden headboard and footboard painted blue, the same color as the rag rug on the floor. There was even a picture on the wall.

She looked at Sal. For a moment, she feared there might have been a mistake, but she could tell from Sal's expression that it was indeed her room. If I'm a servant, she thought, and this is how they live, maybe it's not so bad.

Sal stood in the doorway. "I'd best be going back. Mrs. Brown is that strict! I'll see you later, Miss."

By the time Minna looked up to reply, Sal was gone. She called me 'Miss', she thought. Automatically, she unpacked her few possessions and put them away. She set her books on top of the bureau and placed her featherbed on the bed. Despite the fancy headboard and footboard, it began to look more familiar with her quilt on top of it. Gingerly, she sat down on it, bouncing slightly as she tested its softness. She had never slept on a bed set up from the floor like this before.

Closing her eyes, she tried to imagine what the rest of the house looked like if this was only her room. She dozed for a moment, awoke with a start, and jumped up. Closing her eyes had been a mistake.

I'd better get freshened up and go back downstairs, she thought. Someone might want to see me. Maybe they'll want me to start sewing right away. A fine thing, indeed, to fall asleep before I even get started!

Out in the hall, she found the bathroom, washed up, combed her hair, and straightened her dress. Then she slowly retraced her steps through the narrow hallway and down the twisting stairs to the kitchen.

At the doorway, she stopped and stared into the room, abashed. Five people were seated at the table, including two girls she hadn't met. She paused, not quite sure what to do.

Mrs. Brown gestured to a chair next to hers. "Sit down, Minna. We're having dinner now."

As she slid into her seat, Mrs. Brown continued. "This is Helene," she said, nodding toward a plump girl on Minna's other side, "and this is Millie," smiling at the brunette seated next to Sal. "Now we're all here! What will you have, my dear?"

Minna looked first at Helene and Millie and then at the table. Her eyes widened. It was laden with food. Everything was set out in matching decorated plates and bowls. She had never seen so much food at the same time before. She saw potatoes, meat, vegetables, soft white bread, butter, relish, and a large pitcher of milk.

Mrs. Brown waited for her answer.

Not knowing what to say, she paused. She couldn't believe she could have whatever she wanted.

Mrs. Brown waited, smiling kindly.

Finally, in desperation, she said, "Everything."

Mrs. Brown was surprised but she beamed at Minna. "So you think it looks good, eh?" She filled her plate with huge portions.

She gulped. She didn't think she could eat so much. "Not too much," she protested weakly.

The portions became generous rather than gargantuan. Mrs. Brown handed her a heaping plate.

Carefully, eyeing the others to make sure she was eating properly, Minna started her dinner. Slowly, conversation between the others, which had ceased when she entered the kitchen, began again. She was too conscious of her manners, too worried about the amount of food on her plate, and too afraid everyone was staring at her to pay attention to what anyone was saying. Gradually, as she ate, she became more comfortable. She *was* hungry. She'd had no breakfast in her hurry to go to the train with

Yussel.

Helene, sitting next to her, leaned over. "I read about the fire. It must have been terrible."

Minna nodded, unwilling to talk about it. She sensed that Helene's interest reflected curiosity, not concern.

"I'm glad you're here, anyway. We need a seamstress," Helene continued. "I've had to do all the mending and that's not my job. Have you seen the sewing room?"

She shook her head.

"You do talk, don't you?" Helene asked sarcastically.

Thinking of Erma and imagining how she would have behaved in a similar situation, Minna decided she'd say what she thought. "What would you say if you were me?" she asked.

Helene looked at her in surprise. So did the others, who were now listening avidly.

"Have you ever lived in a big house before?" Mr. Bates boomed.

She shook her head. "No, I haven't!" she said, as clearly as she could. To her embarrassment, she almost yelled the words.

"You don't have to yell!" said Mr. Bates, smiling.

She blushed.

"You'll meet with the Mistress after dinner. She'll show you the sewing room and explain what she wants done. Meals you'll have down here with us. Since you're only temporary, I don't know what rules… You should ask the Mistress about days off and evenings."

Minna had stopped concentrating upon his words as soon as he said, "You'll meet the Mistress after lunch."

"You mean Mrs. Young?"

'That's right. There's young Miss Serena and her cousin, Miss Agnes, too. They're both out this year. I know they'll have a lot of work for you."

Helene nodded. "The way they treat their dresses, we've been needing someone for the last six months! It's a thankless job, Minna, keeping Miss Serena looking elegant."

Minna cleared her throat again, recalling especially what Erma had said about asking questions. "What do you mean, they're out?" she asked Helene softly, hoping that no one else would hear her.

"They've come out. They've made their debuts," Helene replied impatiently.

"Oh," Minna replied, still not understanding.

Mrs. Brown took pity upon her obvious lack of comprehension. "They've been introduced to society, that's what. So now, they go out to parties every night until they're married."

"Oh." Minna still didn't understand, but she was unwilling to ask any more questions. Introduced to society! She imagined a young girl sitting on an ornate throne while many lavishly dressed peopled filed past, bowing and nodding.

Suddenly, she heard a loud bell ring. Nervously, she started and looked around. There, high up on the wall, was a large box with a bell attached to it. As Minna watched, fascinated, a red tag bobbed up and down as the bell rang. The tag had letters on it, spelling 'Sewing Room.'

'That's for you, Minna. That's the Mistress. She's ready to see you," Mr. Bates said.

She looked at her plate, still filled with food.

"Hurry, girl," Mr. Bates said as he stood up. "We don't want to keep her waiting."

She stood and followed him out of the room. They went up one flight of stairs and emerged into a wide hallway. Hurrying to keep up with him, she barely had time to notice the rooms glimpsed through half-open doors, the soft carpeting on the floors, or the many pictures on the walls.

Mr. Bates sailed ahead. Minna had to scamper to keep pace. When he finally stopped in front of a door at the very end of the hall, she almost cannoned into him. Jerking to a halt, she peered at him anxiously. Then she realized they had arrived at their destination. Ineffectually, she patted her hair and straightened her shirtwaist.

Mr. Bates gestured for her to enter the room. She went in slowly, not sure what to expect. If Mrs. Young were like Mrs. Peabody, there would be no problem. If she was unpleasant…

"Minna Ruben, Ma'am," Mr. Bates announced.

Startled at hearing her name, she turned to look at him. He frowned. Following the direction of his gaze, she turned again to find herself facing an elegant blonde woman.

"Thank you, Bates. That will be all," Mrs. Young said casually. Without a pause, as if his presence or absence was completely immaterial, she smiled at Minna. "Sit down, my dear," she invited, pointing at a wooden chair. She remained standing.

Minna sat and waited for her to continue.

"I was so sorry to hear of your terrible experience in that dreadful fire. As I was saying to my ladies' group, the least we can do is to lend our support. Of course, when my dear friend, Maria Peabody, asked if I could help..." She paused. "I understand you're met Mrs. Peabody?"

Minna nodded.

"You'll be seeing her again, I'm sure. You must remember to tell her how pleased I am to help out." She continued in a more business-like tone. "I trust you have recovered completely from the tragedy."

Without waiting for her to answer, Mrs. Young hurried on. "This, you see, is our sewing room. We have the newest home electric machine, good light, and a table for you to work on."

Minna looked around the room and saw everything Mrs. Young had mentioned. In addition, there was a wardrobe, a pressing iron on a small stove, what looked like an ornate screen folded back in the corner, and a large mirror on a stand.

"I have been assured you are an excellent seamstress. The kind of work I require is not factory work. I demand the utmost care and precision in mending as well as alterations. When it comes to making new garments...well, we'll have to see."

Minna nodded. For good luck, she had changed into the shirtwaist she had made for Pearl. "I made this," she said, pointing to it. "All the detailing is by hand."

"You'll call me Ma'am," Mrs. Johnson said sternly. She came closer, allowing Minna to smell a delightful scent of roses and to examine her tightly coiffed hair. She was dressed exquisitely. Every detail, Minna thought, is perfect, yet she is handsome rather than beautiful.

Mrs. Young stood tall and straight, accentuating the softness of her muslin and lace lingerie dress with its high waist and rich embroidery. "It is beautiful work, indeed. If you can do as well for me, your time here will not be wasted. Your pay, of course, will be commensurate with the work you do."

Although Minna wasn't quite sure what she meant, she bowed her head in agreement.

"We'll start today, shall we?" She smiled. "There are some alterations that must be done for my daughter, Miss Serena. She'll be here in a moment and you can begin. Remember, I expect the best workmanship at all times, whether it shows or not."

Minna inspected the machine. It was very similar to the one she used at work, so she'd have no problem with it. Next to it was a large sewing box on a wicker stand. She looked through its contents, took out a pincushion stuck through with pins, and waited for Serena to appear.

"Your family?" Mrs. Johnson asked carelessly.

"My brother's farming out West," she replied. With a pang, she realized what the words meant. I'm here, she thought. Servant or no servant, I have to stay for six months, so I'd better make the best of it. Otherwise, Mrs. Peabody might decide not to give me the money for Oberlin. She lowered her eyes.

She heard a rustling noise and looked up to see a figure in the doorway. She was never to forget her first sight of Serena. She looks like a princess, like my princess in that long ago picture, she thought, admiring her golden hair, her delicately flushed cheeks, and her limpid green eyes. She couldn't help but compare her looks to Anna's, although they were as different as night and day. Anna had been day, radiant, alive, and bursting with vitality. Serena, equally beautiful, was night, mysterious and fragile. Her slight figure seemed precious and rare; she looked as if she might disappear any moment in a gossamer cloud.

"Here I am, Mama," she said in a soft whispery voice that suited her ethereal looks perfectly. "Helene is bringing the dresses that need to be fixed."

For the first time, Mrs. Young smiled warmly. "That's good, dear." Reaching out, she gently smoothed Serena's soft curls. "You needn't have hurried."

Minna heard more rustling. Helene hurried in, her arms full of dresses. Minna helped her to lay them carefully upon the sewing table. Making sure that no one else could see, Helene winked at her.

"This is Minna," Mrs. Young said to her daughter. "She'll fix your dresses if you show her what's wrong with each one."

Serena picked up the first dress and showed the hem to Minna. "See," she said. "I stepped through the hem here and ripped the flounce. Can you fix it?"

Minna could hardly speak, but even though she was nervous, she did know about sewing. Mechanically, she examined the tear. "I can fix it," she said. "If I take a little from here and a little from there…"

"I don't care how you do it," Serena said pettishly. "Just as long as you can fix it so it doesn't show."

Smiling proudly at her daughter, Mrs. Young left the room, motioning Helene to follow.

Miss Serena smiled at Minna as soon as they were gone. The smile changed her expression, making it warmer and more friendly. "I'm glad to meet you," she said. "Did you really work in a factory and did it really get burned in a fire? My mother won't let me read about such things."

Minna nodded.

"How old are you?" she asked.

"I'm seventeen," Minna said.

"So am I."

Minna sighed. How different their lives were!

Oblivious, Serena continued to point out the repairs on all of her dresses. Finally, as they reached the bottom of the pile, she held up an elaborate ball gown in off white with a pink overskirt. The layers of tulle, the dainty rosebuds knotting the waist, the delicate gauzy sleeves… Minna blinked. It was the most beautiful dress she had ever seen.

"This needs to be taken in at the bust. It's too big here." Serena pointed at the shoulders. "And here." She pointed at the side seams. "I had to have Helene tack it the last time I wore it. The waist could be let out a little, too."

Minna examined the dress. "If you could try it on," she suggested, "I can pin it."

"Of course." Serena stuck her head out the door and called, "Helene! Helene!"

Minna was surprised. Couldn't she try on the dress by herself? She was about to say something when she stopped herself. Nothing was as it seemed. Both Serena and her mother were different from anyone she had ever met. How could she tell what they were thinking or how they should act? In any case, it was obvious no one wanted to hear her opinion.

Helene bustled in. As soon as Serena explained, she unfolded the ornate screen Minna had noticed before. She went behind it with Serena and helped her to remove her dress. Then she brought the ball gown and helped her put it on.

When Serena stepped out from behind the screen, Minna gasped. In the dress, she looked flawless, as exquisite as a creature from a fairy tale. Noticing her reaction, Serena smiled complacently.

Awkwardly, Minna pinned the dress to suit the slim contours of Serena's body. When she had finished, she examined it from all angles. "How does that feel?" she asked worriedly.

Serena moved her shoulders and peered into the large mirror. It was clear that she considered this a serious matter. Finally, she said,. "That's good."

She returned behind the screen so that Helene could help her remove the dress and assist her in putting her own back on. When she stepped out, she smiled coolly at Minna and said, "I hope you can do this quickly. I need these three for tomorrow morning." She pointed at three of the dresses.

Minna nodded. "I'll do them." She wondered just how many dresses Serena could wear in one day. After seeing all the tears she had to mend, she also wondered how anyone could be so careless, especially when the clothes were so beautiful.

Serena and Helene left the room hurriedly, leaving Minna alone with the dresses. For a moment, she looked around the room, disconcerted. It was too quiet without the clatter of machines and the noise of voices.

The first thing, she decided, was to get her own thimble and Mama's scissors. To make sure there was nothing else she needed, Minna re-checked the sewing box. There were needles and threads of every color. She picked out a spool to match the first dress she planned to fix.

Then she tiptoed into the hall. She finally found the back stairs at the other end of the corridor, ran up to her room, and grabbed her thimble and Mama's scissors. She hurried because she didn't want anyone to come to the sewing room to look for her and find her gone.

She worked on Serena's dresses all afternoon. As she finished each one, she hung it carefully in the wardrobe. At last, they were all mended.

She had seen no one for what seemed like hours. Although she heard the noises of the household faintly in the distance, they seemed far away and remote. To reassure herself, she thought of Yussel and tried to imagine how far he had gone and what he was doing on the train.

Just as she had decided to go back upstairs to her room, Sal came running in. "It's time for supper," she said. "They're out tonight—the family, I mean. So we can eat earlier than usual."

Minna stood and stretched. She was pleased to see Sal. At least she had not been forgotten. As she followed her downstairs, she thought, I haven't cried all afternoon. It's as if Allen Street is another world, as if it all happened to another girl.

She felt slightly more relaxed at supper than she had at dinner. For one thing, she had completed her work speedily and proficiently. For another, she was glad of company after spending the whole afternoon alone.

The food served for supper was even more elaborate than the dinner menu. It was, Minna learned, the meal that would have been served to the family in their dining room if they hadn't gone out at the last minute. She wondered how the Youngs could afford to feed so many people, but decided it was just the way things were done on Fifth Avenue.

"Did you finish your work?" Helene asked her.

"I finished what was wanted for tomorrow," Minna answered. "I said I would. But…I don't understand. How can she wear three dresses in one morning? Why does she need all of them?"

"She doesn't!" Helene sniffed. "Her highness just wants to have a choice. Every day, it's two or three dresses on the floor. How do you think they get so ripped?"

Minna was shocked. She remembered Anna, carefully hanging her white dress in a place of honor, the sheet she had put around her own graduation dress, the care with which she sponged her clothes to keep them clean. In a flash, Minna saw that was the main difference between the way Serena lived and the way she lived. For Serena, everything was replaceable.

She remembered Mr. Steinberg's story of the garden and the flowers. So, she thought, my one is more important to me than her many. She sensed that this would be important to remember in the days to come but before she had time to ponder over it, Mr. Bates spoke to her.

"Did you straighten your days off, my girl?" he asked.

"I forgot," she replied, hanging her head.

He frowned. "In that case, you'll keep the same schedule as Helene. That's no callers, every other Thursday, and half a day Sunday."

Minna didn't understand exactly what that meant, but she

decided to ask Helene later. She also meant to ask her what "commensurate with your work" meant. How much was she going to get paid?

"Could you tell me something about the family, Mr. Bates?" she asked timidly.

He smiled. "She's a Winter. You know what that means. He's a railroad baron. He travels."

Minna nodded as if she understood. She knew she was being cowardly not to ask more questions, but it was implied so strongly that she *would* understand, she couldn't bear to admit her ignorance. "Serena's so beautiful," she sighed.

"That's Miss Serena to you, my girl," Mr. Bates said sharply.

"They say she's going to marry a Duke," Millie giggled.

"A Duke?" Minna's eyes grew wide.

"That's enough!" Mr. Bates snapped. Ostentatiously, he turned to talk to Mrs. Brown, ignoring the others at the table. They sat silently as if they were listening, but Helene smiled at Minna knowingly, as if to say, 'I'll tell you more later.'

After dinner, Minna started to clear the table, but Mrs. Brown shook her head. "That's Sal's job."

"I don't mind helping," Minna insisted.

Helene poked her fiercely. Minna subsided. That must be another one of the strange Fifth Avenue rules, she thought. She did understand she would be scorned if she did help Sal. Poor girl! Minna watched her pityingly. What with serving and clearing, she hardly had a chance to eat her own supper.

Helene excused herself. Millie and Minna joined her and headed upstairs to their rooms. When they reached the top of the second flight of stairs, Helene asked, "Would you like to come to my room?"

"Yes, thank you," Minna said.

She noticed that Millie hung back until Helene expressly asked her to join them. As they filed into Helene's room, which was about the same size as Minna's, Helene offered her the single chair. She leaned back against her bed and Millie perched uncomfortably on its edge.

Minna looked around the room. On the dresser, she noticed an ivory-backed vanity set with a comb, brush, mirror, and hairpin jar.

"The Mistress gave these to me," Helene said nonchalantly.

"She must be very generous," Minna responded.

"To me, she is," Helene boasted.

Helene is the right person for me to talk to about my salary, Minna thought. Mrs. Young must be very fond of her to give her such a nice present. "I'm only here till September…" she began."

The other two girls nodded.

"Mrs. Peabody said I'd get well paid, but Mrs. Young said she would pay me 'commensurate with my work'. What does that mean? I'd like to know what I'll be earning. I need the money for next year."

Helene and Millie laughed. "Well, if that doesn't take the cake!" Helene said. "Trust her to try to get something for nothing. I wouldn't do another stitch until you find out what she's going to pay you!"

Minna was surprised. "But I thought you said she's so generous."

Helene shook her head. "Not really. She only gives me what she doesn't want any more. What else can she do with it—throw it out? She even tried to pay me less one year, showing me a list of the 'gifts' she'd given me, but I soon put a stop to that. 'Forget your gifts, Madam,' I said. 'I'd rather be paid!'"

"I had to serve yesterday," Millie volunteered. "I heard her boasting about taking you in to the other ladies. She acted like it was all her idea, except she couldn't bear not to mention Mrs. Peabody, because everyone knows how important she is. Anyway, they all said how kind-hearted and generous she is."

Helene sniffed.

"But she is," Minna protested. "If I didn't stay here, I'd have to live in a tiny room alone. I'd work in my uncle's store, following his orders every minute."

"Mrs. Young doesn't do anything for nothing," Helene insisted. "Believe me, I know. Its taken me three years to really understand her. She pays me well enough, though, and if Miss Serena does marry a Duke…no one else knows how to fix her hair as well as I do. No one else knows the secrets of her boudoir…"

"Does she paint?" Millie gasped.

"The Mistress? That's nothing any more. Everyone paints. It's more than that."

Minna noticed the look of avid curiosity in Millie's eyes and quickly intervened. "But how should I ask her. I mean…"

"The next time you see her, you could ask her what she meant by what she said or you could just ask right out about your salary. It's your right to get paid for what you do."

"I know, but I'm living here and I get food. I don't even know how much to ask for, but I have to earn money for college. That's where I'm going in September," she said proudly.

Helene ignored her words. As Minna came to know her better, she understood that she rarely heard what displeased her or made her jealous.

Millie, on the other hand, was impressed. "College! You're going to college?"

"I'm going to be a teacher."

Millie sighed enviously.

Helene sniffed. "An old maid teacher! What's so good about that?"

Minna was about to defend herself when she realized it would be smarter not to. "Tell me about Miss Serena and this Duke she's going to marry," she coaxed, changing the subject.

Helene leaned forward. It was obvious that she loved imparting news. 'Everyone knows about it. It's what her mother has planned for years. I don't know which Duke yet. Miss Serena has her own ideas, too. Just wait and see! It'll come out the way the Mistress has planned. Her schemes always do."

"What about her cousin, the one who's coming out with her? I haven't seen her yet."

"You mean Agnes? She's nice enough, but she can't hold a candle to Miss Serena. She's only here to keep her company, anyway."

Minna noticed that no one called Agnes 'Miss'. It was very complicated. There seemed to be a secret code governing all aspects of behavior here. Why am I 'Miss' to Sal and Agnes is not 'Miss' to Helene, she wondered sleepily. The long day had begun to catch up to her. She yawned widely.

Noticing Helene's displeased expression, she apologized. "I beg your pardon," she said. "It's just that I'm very tired. I was up quite early this morning."

Helene nodded graciously. "Of course."

Millie jumped up a second after Minna. Following in her wake, she went into the hall.

"Breakfast's at seven!" Helene called.

"I'll wake you if you want me to," Millie offered.

Minna smiled at them both. "Thank you," she said impartially. She went into her own room and closed the door firmly behind her.

After undressing and taking care of her toilet, Minna slid into the bed. She was glad for the extra warmth of her own feather bed. She snuggled against the mattress, reveling in its unaccustomed softness. Automatically, she found herself reaching out for Pearl, just as she done every night since the fire.

For the first time since she had arrived, she felt profoundly sorrowful. Her aloneness, the grandness of her room, even the empty feel of the bed alerted her to the strangeness of her new position and reminded her of her loss. I wish Yussel were here, she thought.

She closed her eyes, too tired to think any more. "Good night, Mama, goodnight, Pearl, goodnight, Chava, good night Bubbe," she whispered. "I hope you are all altogether."

Her last thought was for Yussel. 'I wish you well, big brother," she murmured to herself.

CHAPTER 25

The next day, Minna continued to work on Miss Serena's dresses. She had decided to wait a little before saying anything to Mrs. Young about her salary. If I show her I can do good work, she decided, it won't hurt. She'll have a chance to see how much I'm worth.

As she sat sewing, she heard a tapping at the door. She looked up and saw a girl about her own age looking at her inquisitively.

"Hello," the girls said. "My name's Agnes. You must be Minna."

She smiled.

"When you finish my cousin's dresses, I have a few things I'd like you to mend," she said timidly. "If you have time, that is."

Minna looked at her. Short and slight, with long dark hair and deep brown eyes, she appeared insignificant compared to Miss Serena. Her dress was entirely the wrong shape and color for her. The frills, very suitable for her cousin, made her look washed out.

"Of course," Minna said politely. "I'm here to do everyone's sewing."

"Thanks. When should I…"

"Why don't you bring it to me tomorrow. I'll get to it as soon as possible."

Later in the day, Mrs. Young appeared. She looked around the room inquisitively. "You've been doing…?" she asked languidly.

Minna opened the wardrobe. "I've finished all these. Miss Serena wanted these three by this morning, but she hasn't come by to get them, so here they are." She went on to point out the exact work she had done on each dress.

Mrs. Young was impressed. "That's very good. You're quite skilled. I'll give you some of my things to do, too. You're very fast, aren't you?"

Minna, emboldened, decided now was the time to mention her salary. "I was wondering…" she began tentatively.

Mrs. Young looked at her in surprise, as if to say, 'You were wondering…how dare you!'

Minna persisted.

"I was wondering exactly what my wages will be. You said it was commensurate with my work. Well, here you can see some of the work I am able to do. I can also make clothing for you and your family while I'm here. Perhaps, if some of your friends need sewing, too…"

Mrs. Young said nothing.

"I have to save money, you see," Minna continued desperately. "I'll need it when I leave in September."

Mrs. Young frowned. "Maria Peabody did say something about college… Let me think…"

Minna waited.

"Of course, you do have room and board…" Mrs. Young mused.

She remained silent.

'How would you live if you didn't stay here?" Mrs. Young asked, obviously expecting her to have no answer.

Luckily, she had thought about this. "I would work for my cousin in his store and sew for others at night. There's a friend I could share a room with." She answered honestly, thinking of Bessie. Almost instantly, she realized she had unknowingly been very clever. She had made Mrs. Young realize she was not completely dependent upon her.

"I had thought of giving you a gift when you left…"

"Oh no, Ma'am," Minna exclaimed, shocked. "I need to get paid every week, the way I did at the factory. I have to know what I can plan on." She stood up, gripping her scissors. "I'm sorry, Mrs. Young, but I have to be able to plan. Mrs. Peabody said…"

"I'm trying to do a charitable action," Mrs. Young retorted, her voice sharpening.

Minna's eyes flashed, "I'm not looking for charity. I'm looking to earn a living. I know I can do it downtown. If you would like me to leave, I'll be glad to go."

"In that case," Mrs. Young began, her voice rising. She stopped herself abruptly and continued in calmer tones. "I've already told everyone you're staying here…your work is good…" She frowned at Minna. "Let me think about it and tell you later."

She had to agree, although she would have preferred to have it settled.

Later that morning, when Mrs. Young sent Mr. Bates to invite Minna downstairs to meet the ladies, she hesitated. I'm not a curiosity, she thought. She only wants to show me off so she can prove how generous she is and they only want to see me because of the fire. Ready to refuse, she reconsidered. Maybe Mrs. Peabody will be there, she thought, and I can ask her about my wages.

She followed Mr. Bates down the front stairs, which she hadn't seen before. Gliding down the highly polished wooden steps, she clutched the ornate banister to keep from slipping. She couldn't imagine what it would be like to use such stairs all the time, descending like a queen.

Mr. Bates led her to what he called the South Parlor. At the doorway, he gave her a little push, as if to say, 'Go in! Go in!'

Too surprised to be nervous, she entered the room with a start. She saw a group of well-dressed ladies staring at her as if she had come from a zoo.

"This is Minna," Mrs. Young announced. "She's staying with me for a few months to recover from the fire. Maria Peabody and I thought it would be a good idea."

Not knowing what else to do, Minna bowed her head uncomfortably. She was aware that Mrs. Young had made it sound as if she was a guest. She wanted to correct that impression, but she didn't know how.

"Were you in the fire?" a lady asked.

"Yes, I was." Her expression was so outraged, no one dared to ask her anything else.

There was an uncomfortable pause.

Finally, Mrs. Young said, "You may go now."

"She hasn't quite recovered, poor dear," Mina could hear her saying as she left the room.

On the way back to the sewing room, she fumed. What does she think I am, a stick of wood? I'm not her slave!

She shut the door firmly behind her, not sure if it was allowed, but not caring if it wasn't. Yussel was right, she thought. We don't need charity! If that's what they think this is, we don't need them! Only two things stopped her from leaving. One was her recollection of how careful Mrs. Peabody had been not to call this charity. The other was the thought of working for Cousin Avraim and sharing a room with Bessie. I will if I have to, Minna decided, but meanwhile, I'll do the best I can here.

That night, she sat silently through dinner and went to bed right afterwards, politely refusing Helene's invitation to 'come and visit.' As she lay in bed, she fingered the silver locket she always wore. If this is what it's like, she thought, I don't know if it's worth it.

A wave of homesickness swept over her. She missed Mama, Pearl and Yussel, but to her astonishment, she also missed Allen Street, its hustle and bustle, the sound of many voices calling out, the joking and bargaining. She could imagine Yussel laughing at how she felt. 'You who said you want to live where they don't speak Yiddish, now you miss the sound of it?' he'd say. She could clearly picture his expression.

I don't belong here, she sighed. I've made a mistake. I'm better off where it feels like home. She paused. But where was her home now that Yussel was gone? She no longer had a home.

Make the best of it, she said to herself fiercely. Here you are, where you always wanted to be, and you're afraid. You always said you wanted to be alone. Now you are. So act like a grownup, act like Mama did when she decided to take us all to America. Don't be a baby!

Bewildered, she closed her eyes. "Help me, Bubbe," she whispered. "Help me, please."

She was relieved to hear the familiar voice. She had feared that this place was so alien, Bubbe would never be able to find her.

'This is a step, little Minna. Think of a baby, wobbling and falling. New steps are never easy, but soon, you will look back on this as a beginning. Remember, wherever you go, my little one, we are all with you. You are not alone. We take these steps with you.'

The next day, Minna worked hard all morning, hoping Mrs. Young would reappear so they could finish their conversation. Her solitude was interrupted only by Helene, who collected Serena's mended clothing with a smile. As she hurried out the door, she whispered to Minna, "She's in a bad mood today!"

Just before lunch, Agnes came into the room, carrying a dress. When she saw Minna sewing busily, she started to turn away. "I guess you're too busy…" she began.

Minna was tempted to take out her worries by being short with the girl, for she felt Agnes would accept any treatment uncomplainingly. She opened her mouth to say, 'I am' unpleasantly, but she stopped herself. This girl's situation didn't seem to be much better than her own. True, she had a nice roof over her head and good food to eat, but she didn't seem to feel very comfortable about it. Apparently she had no ability to stick up for herself.

Minna stood up. "Why don't you show me what needs to be done?" she offered, extending a hand for the dress.

Agnes pointed at the armhole. "See, this is where it came apart. I do most of my own sewing, but it's really ripped and I don't know how to go on with it."

Minna nodded and then looked at her curiously. "Did you choose this dress for yourself?"

"Oh no, it's Serena's from last year. It was altered to fit me. Why do you ask?"

She smiled. "It doesn't look like…"

Agnes shook her head. "You mean it's not my style. I know, but I don't have any choice."

Minna nodded sympathetically, thinking, even if I do end up leaving, I can certainly do one nice thing before I go. Why not?

"I'll fix it," she offered. "If the lace came off here, and bows here…I think you'd look well in a simpler dress. I could change it for you. I'd like to."

Agnes frowned doubtfully. "I don't know. They might think I'm not grateful. I mean, they gave it to me like this."

Minna laughed. "No one will notice," she promised, sure that Mrs. Johnson and Miss Serena were too self-involved to pay attention to anyone else.

Agnes thought for a moment. Finally, she nodded "Do it! If you ruin the dress, I'll be in trouble, but…you're sure you really can do it?" She gazed at Minna trustingly.

Minna smiled. "I'm sure. Come back this afternoon," she suggested. "I'll be done with Miss Serena's ball gown by then and you can try the dress on for me. I'll work on it as soon as I can."

Agnes smiled back tentatively. "Thank you! I'll come."

Minna remembered her first day in the shop and girl who had

wanted to buy pretty material and had been thwarted by her unpleasant relative. It's for you I'm doing this, she thought. Maybe by now, you can choose your own fabric.

She hurried through dinner and raced back upstairs to finish Serena's ball gown. She found she was looking forward to fixing Agnes' dress. She'll look so much better, Minna thought.

By the time Agnes returned, Minna had already transformed her dress. In fixing the sleeves, she had narrowed them; in removing the lace from the neckline, she had lowered it; eliminating the ribbons from the bodice, she had added tiny tucks to make it fit more closely; at the hem, she had replaced some of the ruching to create a smoother, more flowing look. The result was a simpler, more form-fitting and up-to-the-minute dress.

Agnes had a worried expression on her face when she looked at it. "It looks so plain. I don't know…"

Minna thrust it at her. "Try it on," she suggested, too pleased with her results to be polite. "Go behind the screen and try it on!"

Agnes was surprised, but she followed her instructions meekly. When she came out from behind the screen and looked in the large mirror, she smiled at her reflection in surprise. "It makes me look much taller," she said, looking delightedly at Minna. "It's more the style, too. Thank you! Thank you so much!"

"It looks very nice. Now if you were to wear your hair like this…" She held Agnes' hair up over he head. "You see, it makes your face stand out."

Embarrassed, Agnes looked away from the mirror. "I'll wear the dress tonight," she promised. "I'll do my hair that way, too." She hurried behind the screen. "If I don't rush, I'll be late. Serena doesn't like to be kept waiting and I have to…" Her voice was muffled under her dress. She hurried out from behind the screen hugging the dress to her and rushed out of the sewing room.

The next day, Minna brought a book to the sewing room. She had finished Miss Serena's ball gown and there was nothing else for her to do until she was brought more work. Besides, she thought, I might not stay anyway. It all depends upon Mrs. Young.

Almost as soon as she sat down and opened her book, Agnes came dashing in, her cheeks flushed and her eyes bright. "The dress was a success! Everyone said how well I looked. I danced all the dances. I felt so pretty!"

Minna beamed. "Why don't you let me fix your other dresses,

too?" she asked. "Right now, I have some time."

"Oh, would you?" Agnes breathed.

There was something child-like about her, Minna thought. She wanted to give her a shake and tell her to grow up! "Of course," she said soothingly. "Bring them in a few at a time and I'll see what I can do."

Before she could say another word, Agnes hurried away to get a few more dresses. It's as if she's afraid I'll change my mind if she doesn't respond right away, Minna thought indignantly. There's such a thing as being too meek.

As Agnes raced back, she almost bumped into Mrs. Young, who was about to enter the sewing room. She stopped short, a guilty expression upon her face.

"You're using Minna's services, Agnes?" Mrs. Young inquired.

"I've finished Miss Serena's work," Minna said quickly. "I offered to do a little mending for Miss Agnes."

Agnes looked at her gratefully and smiled nervously.

"Certainly, you may leave your things here in case Minna has time," Mrs. Young agreed. "However, I have some work for her to do first."

Minna nodded at Agnes, who dropped her dresses on the table and scurried out of the room as quickly as she could.

She looked at Mrs. Young. "I've fixed Miss Serena's ball gown," she said, opening the wardrobe and taking it out. "I hope you're pleased with the work."

Mrs. Young examined the dress. It was impossible to see where the original tear had been.

'That's very good" she said. "Helene will bring you my dresses, too." She turned to leave the room.

Minna stepped forward. "Have you thought about our conversation, Mrs. Young?" she asked awkwardly. She didn't know exactly how to word it, but she was determined to settle the question of her pay.

"What conversation was that?" Mrs. Young asked carelessly.

In a strange way, this reassured Minna. She was sure Mrs. Young couldn't really have forgotten it altogether. That meant she had taken the time to think about it. "The one about how much you will pay me each week," she said politely.

"Oh, that one. Well, I have thought about it…"

Minna waited.

"What did you earn at the factory?" she asked.

"I usually earned five dollars a week, depending upon the amount of work I had to do."

"Very well, then. I'll pay you three dollars a week as long as you're here, on the condition that your work continues to be good."

Three dollars a week! Minna's mind raced. She'd be able to save a substantial amount at that rate. If she spent nothing, she's have almost seventy-two dollars by the time she left for school. And if she could find extra sewing work from the kitchen…

"That will be just fine," she said enthusiastically. Then, remembering how difficult it had been to get Mrs. Young to offer anything, she added more coldly, "I should be able to manage with that."

Mrs. Young shrugged, as if to say, I don't really care whether you can or not, and left the room.

She had already disappeared when Minna realized she had forgotten to ask her about days off and such like. I won't ask, she decided. As long as I do my work, no one can complain. If they do, I'll say I didn't know. I'm not a servant—not really. I won't even ask permission, I'll take a walk every evening. The days are getting longer. I need some fresh air.

The rest of the day, Minna worked busily upon Mrs. Young's dresses. As she worked, she planned how she would re-do the ones Agnes had brought. She smiled when she pictured the change her work would make in Agnes' appearance.

Now that the question of her wages had been resolved, Minna felt she could afford to relax a little. It was time to get to know the others in the house. She began at dinner by asking Mrs. Brown how she had become such a good cook.

Mrs. Brown was flattered. She beamed and told the story of herself as a young girl, the daughter of a farmer from New England and how she had "helped out" as a hired girl until she began to work for a wealthy family in Boston. They arranged for her to assist their cook. It was then she discovered she had a gift. "That," she said, "was that."

The others at the table listened open-mouthed. It was the first time they had heard the story.

"You discovered you had a skill. That's what made all the difference," Minna said.

Mrs. Brown agreed. "Just like you, my girl. I hear you're quite good at sewing."

Minna frowned. "I don't want to do it the rest of my life," she said. "I might have a skill but it's because I *had* to learn it. I never had a choice. What I really want is to learn how to be a teacher. When I go to school in the fall, that's what I'm going to study."

She looked around the table. This was a good opportunity to ask for extra work. "I do have some free time in the evening. I'd be glad to do mending or altering or new patterns for everyone here. You can be sure I'll do a good job. I know you'll be pleased with the results. My rates will be reasonable, too. If any of you or your friends have work for me, please let me know."

"Exactly how much will you charge?" Helene asked.

She hesitated. As much as I can, she thought. "I don't know exactly. Not much. It depends upon the job."

Mr. Bates changed the subject, so Minna had no idea if any of the others were interested. She had decided she would find the time to do as much extra work as she could manage. She'd end up with much more than the three dollars a week promised by Mrs. Johnson.

After dinner, Minna excused herself, ran upstairs, and picked up her warmest shawl. She hurried back through the kitchen to the back door, her only way out of the house.

Mr. Bates, still sitting at the table sipping his coffee, called out sharply, "And where do you think you're going, my girl?"

"Just out for a walk," Minna replied. "If I don't get some fresh air every day, I'll turn into a ghost!"

He looked dubious. "The rules are…"

"Mrs. Young said nothing to me," Minna explained promptly, having rehearsed her answer beforehand. "As long as I get my work done, my evenings should be my own. Besides, all I want is a little fresh air."

She left quickly before he could say another word. She was determined not to be cowed. After all, I'm not a slave, she thought angrily.

Once she was outside, standing in the street, she hesitated. It was the first time since her arrival that she had left the house. It was also the first time she felt truly alone, for even at night she knew the other girls and Mrs. Brown slept just down the hall.

Thoughts of Mama, Pearl, and Yussel overwhelmed her. As she

looked down the unfamiliar street with its imposing homes well separated by grass and entryways, she felt a pang of homesickness once more for the tiny crowded buildings of Allen Street, the stoop sitters, the pushing crowds, and the familiar-looking faces.

Again, she wondered, what am I doing here? This isn't where I belong. Then she remembered her conclusions of the other night. With Yussel far away, I don't belong there, either. I don't belong anywhere any more.

She began to walk briskly. Listen to you, she taunted herself. You're afraid again. You work and you plan and you're afraid to stretch out your hands and take what you've gained. Homesick? After all the years you wanted to leave there. That's crazy!

Suddenly, clear as a bell, she heard Bubbe's voice. 'Listen to me, my child. You and Yussel are the only two left. I say, remain faithful to the old and reach out for the new. If you don't, you might just as well stayed in *der alter heym.* All the suffering, the deaths, would be for nothing. You and Yussel are our hope, our survivors. For all of us, for Chava, your Mama, Pearl…we're all watching and protecting you.

She began to walk more slowly, thinking of Bubbe's words. She knew it was up to her. She was the only woman left. If she was afraid…

In her thoughts, Bubbe's words rang out in the darkened street. 'Of course, you are afraid. We have all been afraid in our lives. Courage means moving on even when you are trembling inside, like your Mama did when your Tata left, like Pearl did when she learned to forget Chava's death, like we all have done. Each of us has a story, you know, for each of us has endured.'

She sighed. 'I'll try, Bubbe,' she promised and continued her walk. For the first time in several days, she began to think of her friends. I'll go and see Bessie, she planned. Maybe I can find Mr. Steinberg. For a minute, she thought of Jake. Automatically, she stopped herself. Then she shook her head. He was kind. I'll write to him. Maybe if I see him…

The only one she hadn't thought of was Saul. When she realized this, she tried to understand why she hadn't written to him since the fire. I don't want to explain everything, she thought uncomfortably. He wasn't here…he can't know what it was like… It was easier with strangers or friends who already knew about it. To explain it all, to understand my own feelings by writing to Saul,

I'd have to live through it again…

Besides, why hasn't Saul written to me, she wondered. He must know what happened. Although she knew logically that it might not be his fault, she could not forget that her closest friend had not shared her grief. Even Jake, she thought, was there when I needed him.

She stopped for a moment and stood still, frowning. I'm not being fair, she thought. He could be really ill. Maybe he *can't* write, she worried. He could be… She shuddered. I'll write to him tomorrow, she promised herself.

She continued her walk, trying to put the events of the last few days in perspective. When she was in that house, its presence was so overwhelming, it was difficult to step away. Out here, I can try to understand it all, she thought, laughing to herself at the difficulty of the task. At least, for tonight, I know the house isn't the whole world. She sighed.

When she finally returned, she felt refreshed in body and spirit. As she opened the kitchen door, she was surprised to see Mr. Bates sitting at the kitchen table waiting for her. Remembering how rudely she had hurried out, she was abashed.

"I'm sorry…" she began.

Mr. Bates, noting the color in her face and brightness in her eyes, simply nodded. "I had to wait up to lock the door," he said.

She flushed. "I'm sorry," she repeated. "What shall I do? I have to walk out… get some fresh air…be on my own… I have to be away for a little each day. I must."

He looked at his watch. "It's not very late," he said. "I'm usually up anyway." He tapped his pipe. "We can work something out. Just be sure you tell me when you're leaving so I can wait for you. Otherwise, you'll be locked out."

"Thank you, Mr. Bates," she said as she turned to go up to her room.

Later, as she lay in bed, she thought over the events of the day. "I love you, Bubbe," she whispered as she closed her eyes.

The next evening, Minna forced herself to sit down and write to Saul. It was difficult. She found she could only write a few short sentences about the fire and its immediate aftermath. The rest of the letter was about her Fifth Avenue life. Reading it over, she found it so strange, she added a postscript saying, "I can't write about the fire, dear Saul. Not yet."

She sent it off unhappily, for she felt it was not the kind of letter she wanted to write, but she knew it was the best she could do. As she mailed it, she repeated, almost as a prayer, "He will write back. He will write back."

She sent a letter off to Bessie, too, telling her she'd come by on Sunday.. She knew, from what Bessie had told her, that the Union had grown stronger because of what had happened. "We'll make a difference now. I know we will," she had said triumphantly. Then, her expression stricken, she had whispered, 'But the dead…146 of us dead… What does it cost to make people listen?"

The meeting she was planning to go to later on Sunday afternoon was a Union meeting. Minna knew that Bessie hoped she'd say something as she had before. She promised herself she would not, but she knew that if the spirit moved her, she'd be unable to sit still and say nothing.

When Sunday arrived, Minna hurried out of bed. She had made many plans for the day. Right after breakfast, she'd go downtown. Before the meeting, she wanted to walk around the old neighborhood.

She dressed carefully, taking an extra shawl against the possibility of rain. As she fixed her hair, she wondered what her day would be like. Although she hadn't even been away for a week, it seemed far longer. Perhaps, she thought, I was already away after the fire came, leaving Yussel and me alone.

Minna slipped out unnoticed as soon as she finished her breakfast. Everyone else was rushing to get ready for church. She walked briskly to the Elevated. How odd, she thought. All my life I couldn't wait to leave home and now, after one week, I'm hurrying back. She quickened her steps.

When she descended from the Elevated, she felt impelled to visit the Asch Building. She didn't know why it was so important, but it was the first thing she had to see. With trepidation, she walked towards it, her pace slowing as she came closer.

Her first glimpse of it surprised her. It was hard to believe it had been the scene of such horror. The top three floors did look scorched, but from the outside, there was no way to tell how much damage had been done. Inside, she knew there must be parts that were gutted.

She walked all the way around the building. The fire escape dangled against its side, crazily twisted in mid-air. As she stared at it, she could still hear the screams, the flat thuds, and see the gutters running with blood. She put her hands to her face.

She squeezed her eyes shut, trying to erase the memories that assailed her. Her shoulders rigid, she turned away. I won't come here again, she decided. I will remember, but not here. I'll remember in my own way.

Slowly, her head bent to hide her tears, Minna walked to Allen Street, where Bessie had taken a new room. The way was so familiar, she could almost hear Mama and Sarah talking and Pearl giggling as they hurried home after a long day. It was early enough on a Sunday so the streets were almost empty, which added to her eerie sense of being followed by ghosts.

Outside Bessie's building, she hesitated. It was too early, she thought. Just as she was deciding to go around the block a few times, she heard a voice from across the street.

"Minna! Minna!" the voice called.

She turned.

It was Jake. He came towards her. "I spoke to Bessie and she told me you were coming this morning. I've been waiting. I wanted to see you."

She smiled at him. After all that had happened, it was no longer awkward to speak to him or be with him.

"I was going to write to you," she said. "I wanted to thank you."

He shook his head. "No need, and you know it. I couldn't come to you before. I had to go away for a little… As soon as I could, I went over to your apartment and I discovered you were gone! I didn't know where you were. If I hadn't seen Bessie and asked her… Anyway, here I am."

Minna held out her hand. "I'm glad. It was good that you were with us when…when…"

He nodded. "I'm happy I could be. We may not always agree, but…"

She smiled. "But we're always friends, aren't we?" As she said it, she realized it was true. Maybe that's all we are now, she thought.

He looked startled. Then he nodded. "Yes, we are friends. You are my first American friend."

She put her arm in his. "Let's walk," she suggested. "I can go up and see Bessie later."

As they strolled, she told him about college and about the

Young house on Fifth Avenue. "They even have a butler!" she concluded. "His name is Mr. Bates and he can be very pleasant sometimes."

"You shouldn't be working as a servant," Jake said angrily. "I could give you *gelt* and…"

She hushed him. "If I'm a servant, which I don't admit, then I'm a superior one. I get paid plenty and all I have to do is sew. That's what I did before, and I didn't get paid as much when you add in my room and board."

"You still have to do what they say, don't you?"

"No more than I did at Triangle. The big difference is that I live there—and I don't mind that, or not so much, anyway."

She turned to face him. "See, it's worth it. I'll have saved more than seventy dollars by the time I leave if I'm careful. Even more, if I can get outside work, too. I won't have to start at Oberlin with nothing."

"I have plenty. I could lend you…"

She shook her head. "How could I accept it? You know I couldn't!"

"We're friends, so you could."

"Look," she said earnestly, "if I'm ever in need, I'll come to you. For now, I'll take what Mrs. Peabody can arrange, even if I have to put up with Mrs. Young."

He accepted her words and changed the subject. "Have you heard from Yussel yet?"

"Not yet," she replied. "I don't expect to until he's settled. He said he wouldn't write until he gets where he's going." She looked at Jake. "What have you been doing?"

He frowned. "The usual. Nothing much." He shrugged. "You know."

She looked away.

"I'm not much of a one for writing," he apologized. "But I want to hear from you when you go away."

Minna stared hard at him and, for the first time in years, evaluated what she saw. He was still handsome, but the vitality of his too-sharp face contrasted strongly with the style of his clothing. Although he was quite dapper, his outfit was too old, and too luxurious for his age. There was something slightly tawdry about his appearance.

Actually, she reminded herself, I haven't seen him as a stranger since we met on the boat. He looks, she decided, disreputable. The old Jake, her sympathetic memory of a lost small boy abandoned at Ellis Island, was gone forever. He was grown up now. They were both different. She sighed deeply, nearly weeping.

"What's the matter?" he asked, alarmed. He patted her shoulder.

"I'll write to you, Jake," she promised, knowing she would and knowing at the same time that at last, her dreams about him were over. "We'll always be friends," she repeated, wishing with all her heart for it to be true.

Jake, recognizing the intensity of her feelings yet unable to understand them, looked at her anxiously. "Is everything all right, Minna?" he asked.

She smiled widely at him, knowing she was at last free of an old ache. "Give me your address so I can write. At least once, I'll write. After that, if I don't hear from you, it's goodbye, Charlie!" She laughed to show she was teasing. "You can certainly write a few words to say that you're well, can't you?"

He shook his head. "I guess I can try. You won't forget me, will you, Minna?"

"I won't forget anyone," she said seriously. "My life is all of this, all it has been. I can see that now. If I do change things for myself, it will come with me wherever I go."

"You sound as if you're not coming back," he said slowly.

"Of course, I'm coming back to visit. But…no…I'm not coming back, Jake. There's no one here anymore." She caught herself. "I mean, the family…"

He spoke with dignity. "I understand what you're saying. I also understand why you say it. But, we're still friends."

"We're always friends," she agreed. "If you write back to me, I'll talk your ears off in my letters. I'll never forget you," she repeated.

There was a long silence.

Finally, he took out a pieced of paper and a pencil. "Here," he said. "I'll write down my address." Lips pursed, he slowly wrote it out.

Minna took it and put it in her pocketbook. "You'll hear from me," she promised. "But I'm not leaving till September. I'll be here for a while."

He shook his head. "I won't be. I have to leave town now."

She wondered if he was in trouble or if he thought it would be better if they didn't meet, but she asked no questions. Instead, she smiled at him once more. "I'm sorry I won't see you. I still remember the nickelodeon years ago."

He laughed. "You really believed everything you saw on the screen, didn't you?"

She blushed. "Of course not!"

He laughed again.

"Well, maybe a little."

Jake left her as they approached Bessie's building. He held her hand tightly, bent over, and kissed her on the cheek. "Goodbye, Minna," he said softly.

Her hand flew to her cheek and, for a moment, she remembered the way it had been. Then she reached out with her other hand and touched Jake on his cheek. "Goodbye, Jake," she replied.

As she watched him walk away, his head bent, she sighed. In the end, I'm glad I loved him, she thought. Now I feel cold without a secret to keep me warm. Slowly, she turned and climbed up the stoop to the entrance of Bessie's building.

To her surprise and delight, the first thing that Bessie did was to hand her a letter. "Do you remember that you asked me to see if you got any mail at your old address? Well, I checked the other day and I found this."

Minna took it eagerly. It was from Saul! The address looked as if it had been scrawled, unlike Saul's usually neat handwriting. For once, she didn't stop to savor her prize. She tore the envelope open and began to read.

The letter said, in a barely decipherable handwriting:

My Dearest Minna,

I have just heard today about the terrible tragedy. The nurses have been keeping the news from us. I am writing to you because I know you must be all right. You must be. I couldn't bear it if…but I won't think that.

We have had no casualty lists. They keep the New York papers from us. Any excitement is supposed to make us worse. Of course, so many of us have family and friends who may have been affected, it's a hundred times worse not to know.

Three of you were working there. I pray that you are all well. Please write immediately and let me know what has happened. I think of you and miss you.

Saul

Minna held the letter to her. He's all right, she thought. She realized how frightened she had been when she thought that he, too, might be dead. Thank God, she said to herself, over and over.

I'm so glad I wrote to him, she thought. Tonight, I'll write again. Now that he knows, now that I'm sure he's all right, it will be easier.

Later, at Bessie's meeting, Minna did speak out. As before, she was applauded and as before, she said, "It's not me you're applauding. It's the memory of those who died, of those who needn't have died."

Bessie walked her back to the Elevated and they embraced as she left. Minna promised to come back again soon. "Maybe we could do something else besides going to a meeting?" she asked hopefully.

Bessie was shocked. "I like going to meetings," she protested.

Minna laughed. "That's no surprise to me! I just thought that for once…" When she realized she was upsetting Bessie, she shook her head. "I was just teasing, Bessie. I know the meetings are important."

On the way home, she thought about it. The meetings were important. Now, more than ever, the Union was growing in membership and power. But was it so important that nothing else should exist? To Bessie, it was.

She realized it would be too easy for her to get caught up in the Union and Union affairs. Especially now, she thought. The Union could become my new family, my reason for living. But if that happens, she warned herself, I'll end up not going to school. I'll end up just like Bessie, spending every moment working for the cause. As a teacher, I can help others in another way. She vowed to remember that the next time Bessie asked her to speak at a meeting.

She had been disappointed that she hadn't seen Mr. Steinberg. I hope he's all right, she thought. She had no way to get in touch with him except through the factory. In any case, it would have been presumptuous to go to his home.

It was still early when Minna arrived at the kitchen door. Trying the knob, she discovered that it was locked. Softly, she knocked.

Mr. Bates opened the door almost immediately. He stared down at her. "And where have you been?" he asked.

"I had the day off," she replied. "I went to see my friends. Mrs. Young never said I couldn't."

He retreated in the face of her indignation. As she hurried past him, she was stopped by Mrs. Brown.

"Would you like some tea, Minna?" she asked.

Minna smiled at her gratefully. "Thank you, Ma'am. I would, very much."

She sat at the kitchen table with Mr. Bates and Mrs. Brown. Mr. Bates leaned back in his chair and read his paper. Mrs. Brown offered Minna teacakes and tiny sandwiches. Minna asked her how she had spent her day.

"I went to church and then I went to visit my niece and her baby. It was a good day," she replied contentedly.

"So was mine," Minna agreed. "I wish it wasn't over."

Mrs. Brown nodded in agreement, Mr. Bates rustled his paper, and Minna sipped her tea from a flowered cup. For a moment, it was as if Miss Serena, Mrs. Young, and the others didn't really exist. Here, at the table, she felt as if she was almost part of a family group.

Helping herself to a teacake, she leaned back in her chair. "It's nice here, too," she said sleepily.

CHAPTER 26

As the days passed, Minna found herself doing more work for Agnes. For her own reasons, the girl chose to spend time with her each day. At first, she assumed it was a demonstration of gratitude for the wonders she had wrought with her clothing. Later, she realized it was the only place Agnes truly felt comfortable in her cousin's house.

In the beginning, she sat quietly, content to sit and watch Minna work. As she became more comfortable, words gushed from her mouth. It was, Minna thought, as if she had stored up all her thoughts and, at last, believed she had found a safe audience. It was quite clear that Agnes considered her only a listener. She was not invited to reciprocate.

Simply by sitting quietly, Minna learned all about the Young family. Mrs. Young was indeed a Winter. Apparently, that was an important name in New York society. Mr. Young, Agnes explained, was a "jumped-up railroad baron."

"He's got the money," she continued, "but the family took a long time to decide he was good enough for a Winter."

Agnes herself came from a subsidiary branch of the family. "We're poor, but proud," she said. "Not too proud, or I wouldn't be here. It's good for me and good for Serena. I give her an unexceptional companion that she needn't be polite to, and she gives me a chance to come out and wear her old dresses." Agnes sighed. "It's not fun being an object of charity."

Minna wanted to agree strongly, but she contented herself with nodding. She knew if she said anything, the flow of words would stop. She felt a nebulous kinship with the speaker although her concept of charity and Agnes' were very different. Dependence, she thought, was never acceptable.

"She's going to marry a Duke, at least," Agnes continued. "We're to go abroad this fall. Aunt Bella has big plans. It's the thing to do. It's one of the reasons why Mrs. Peabody's approval is so important to her. Her daughter married a Lord somebody and she can give us introductions to British society. Besides, she's the queen of New York society. What she says, goes."

Minna began to understand a few things that had puzzled her. Now she could see why Mrs. Peabody called Mrs. Young an acquaintance and Mrs. Young called her a "dear friend". That was the reason she was here. She laughed, finding it amusing that she was a link between two grand dames of high society.

Agnes, startled by her laughter, sat up. "I should go," she began.

"Miss Serena is so beautiful," Minna murmured, changing the subject quickly.

"I know. If it was me…"

Agnes, Minna learned, saw her fate inextricably bound up with her cousin Serena's. "If she marries a Duke or a prince, maybe at the same time…" she hinted.

When Minna suggested she might make her own plans, she was taken aback. "What plans?" she had asked. "What could I do but live with my family? To live here is better than at home. It's more comfortable, for one thing."

Thinking it over later, Minna was astounded. She's like Priscilla, she thought. Even thought they're surrounded by luxury, those girls are like prisoners. They're more childlike than I ever was. Maybe Mr. Steinberg was right. I'd certainly rather be me than be a Young or a Winter if the only future they can imagine is marriage. Imagine having no plans!

When she mentioned this to Helene, she replied, "Of course, Minna. Naturally, they're looking to get married. So am I! Do you think I'd still be here if I didn't have to work? Not me! I'd be sitting in the parlor receiving callers."

"But Helene," Minna had objected, "when you get married, you'll end up depending on your husband, the way you talk. Suppose he doesn't treat you well, or he dies, or…"

"I'd better pick carefully, that's all," Helene had replied pertly.

Minna knew she had several beaux, including a New York City policeman, who begged to see her on Sundays, but she hadn't realized how much Helene focused on them. She thought of Bessie, of the intense women she had seen at the café near the Alliance, of Emma Goldman and what she had heard about her. She knew there was more than one path to choose, but she was sure she wanted to make her own life, not depend upon some man. She could never forget what happened to Mama.

It's easy for you to say when you haven't met the man yet, her inner voice warned her. It would never have worked with Jake, but if you meet someone else and he offers… He better be perfect, she decided. I demand absolute perfection! The subject struck her as so silly, she giggled aloud, causing Helene once again to look at her strangely.

At first, she saw Miss Serena and Mrs. Young, only occasionally when they had to be fitted or they demanded the return of alterations and repairs that had already been begun. Most of the time, if fittings were not necessary, Helene was sent to bring dresses to Minna and to retrieve them. Since she always had plenty of work, Minna assumed that Mrs. Young was satisfied with her skills.

Then one day, she simply appeared. Narrowing her eyes as she looked at Minna, she nodded once, as if her mind was already made up and addressed her. "For our trip to Europe, we'll need a great many new things. I'll buy the finest silk, lace, and batiste. Then we'll decide on the styles and you can make Miss Serena's lingerie. You can copy what we already have, can't you?

"Of course." Minna sighed as she thought of how time-consuming this work would be. Everything, she knew, would have to be sewn by hand. A fashionable lady's lingerie had to be luxurious and delicate.

She finished the work she was doing for Helene and Mrs. Brown hurriedly, assuming she would have neither the time nor the inclination for extra work while she was doing so much fine sewing. She had saved a lot of money already. Instead of making herself several new outfits for school, she had finally decided it would be wiser to hold the money in reserve for the future. I'll see what I need when I get there, she thought.

Most of Miss Serena's other clothing was to be purchased

abroad. "We'll shop in Paris," she heard Mrs. Young promise her daughter.

As she stitched the lingerie and lacy undergarments, Minna dreamed about what it would be like to visit Paris, London, Rome, Vienna, and all the other cities that were to be part of the girls' itinerary. Agnes called it the "Grand Tour".

"It's meant to be cultural, but it won't really be," she had said cheerfully. "Mostly, we're there to find husbands."

"Don't you mind being on display like that?" Minna had asked.

"I wouldn't mind if I was as beautiful as Serena," Agnes had replied. "Then I'd be the one to have most of the suitors…"

Minna realized that for Agnes, Serena's beauty excused and permitted everything. Although she was often brusque and unpleasant, Agnes overlooked her actions. Beauty, to her, was the final perquisite of privilege.

She shook her head. She remembered how she had felt about Anna in the beginning. It is hard, she knew, to see great beauty and treat it normally. It was such a gift. But, she recalled, as she had come to know Anna better, she had been more easily able to see her in perspective. Her beauty was only part of her, just as Minna's hair or her eyes were part of her. I'm glad I'm not ugly, she thought, but I'm glad I'm not beautiful. It's not easy.

Her thoughts wandered to Mr. Steinberg, as they often did. His words seemed more true as she learned more about the Youngs and the way they lived. There was much to envy, but more to repudiate. Riches couldn't solve personal problems or erase pettiness and condescension. As for Agnes, money could never make up for the way she allowed herself to be treated. If it were me, she vowed, I'd leave!

Mostly she was glad she had taken this job. I'm learning about another way to live, she thought, I'm getting paid for it, and best of all, I'm not all alone in the old apartment. There, Mama and Pearl were everywhere and nowhere. Every moment I was wounded again by the realization they are gone forever. Here, they seem almost part of another life. Sometimes, I can even believe for a moment they are still at home, waiting for me.

She wrote to Saul every week and he replied as often. She could tell from the tenor of his letters he was feeling a little better. He had even confessed, in one of them, that he had made up his sweetheart so Minna would feel more comfortable with him.

Although she hadn't actively doubted her existence, she wasn't completely surprised. Even if we are just friends, she decided, I would have been more jealous if I truly believed he had another girl.

Saul wrote about the fire as he tried to come to grips with the tragedy. Sometimes she found what he said to be helpful, although she didn't choose to reply in kind. She was unable to write anything about it to him.

He was also fascinated by her stories of the Young household. "*It's a saga,*" he had written. "*I didn't know the goyim had such stories!*" His letters were a solace, for she had no close friend in the Young house. She could confide in him and share her hopes and fears for the future.

When she finally received a letter from Yussel, she felt a burst of pure joy. She laughed and smiled without a sense of shame or apologies to the dead. The ugly voice that continued to castigate her for her 'selfishness' disappeared temporarily. She carried the letter around with her for days, reading parts of it over and over again.

Yussel wrote from Petaluma, California. She pronounced the strange name carefully, trying to get a sense of the place from the sound of its odd syllables. Yussel worked for a chicken farmer, which was not exactly what he planned. Yet he was enthusiastic about the area, its fertility, and its climate.

"*Everyone says,*" he wrote, "*that I should look further south when I decide to start my own farm—if it's not a chicken farm, that is. Here, the world lives, breathes, and thinks chicken. Some say it's best to start with hens and sell eggs. Others think it's best to sell the chickens themselves. Then there's all the theories about chicken houses and chicken diseases. I've seen men come to blows about such questions!*"

He described the family he lived with enthusiastically. "*My boss,*" he said, "*came here himself only eight years ago and already, he's a success. I am not the only one who works for him. It's not easy, the chores, but the family is* ***heimish****. There's a daughter your age who helps me pack the eggs for the market.*"

For Yussel, Minna knew, it had been good to get away. He said nothing in his letter about Mama and Pearl. Instead, he described his living conditions and the people he met.

She found it romantic to think she had a brother who lived in Petaluma, California. She tried to picture the daughter Yussel had mentioned—the one her age—and wondered if she was pretty and lively. In her return letter, she asked more questions about the farm than Yussel could possibly answer. At the same time, she told him about her life. On the subject of the mysterious daughter, she was discreet, simply asking casually what her name was.

As the month of May approached and the weather outdoors became more inviting, Minna began to take a piece of fruit and a bit of cheese outside for the mid-day dinner instead of sitting in the kitchen. At first, Mr. Bates objected, but, as usual, he shrugged his shoulders when Minna insisted. Although he was pleasant to her, she realized that he saw her as only a temporary responsibility, so he could be more lenient with her than with the other girls.

She often walked across the street to Central Park. There, she ate her dinner sitting upon a park bench, enjoying the sight of the trees and the sounds of the birds. Sometimes, the benches were occupied by nursemaids or governesses and their charges. They spoke only to each other, ignoring Minna. She found them intimidating in their stiffly starched uniforms.

One day, a gentleman came and sat down next to her. She moved as far towards the other end of the bench as she could and stared straight ahead, lest she be seen as encouraging him. When he said nothing, she peeked in his direction.

He was a well-dressed man of about fifty. With his arms crossed and his eyes half-closed, he stared straight ahead. He had an unpleasant expression on his face, but he certainly didn't seem interested in her. She relaxed, giving herself up to the enjoyment of the sun and trees. Mentally, she composed an addition to her most recent letter to Yussel.

Suddenly, without warning, as often happened, she thought of Mama and Pearl. She had learned it was sometimes dangerous to let her thoughts wander, for that was where they usually landed. Her hand flew to her mouth and her eyes filled with tears. Sighing, she put down the apple she was eating and stared off into the distance.

She was so self-involved, she forgot about the unknown gentleman sharing her bench. It wasn't until he cleared his throat that she remembered he was there. She averted her head, trying to hide the tears.

"What's the matter, young lady?" he asked.

She shook her head.

"Don't worry," he said lightly. "I only asked because I don't like to see tears when the sun is shining."

She looked at him. The unpleasant expression was gone and he was smiling at her, his eyes seeming as guileless as a child's. If she hadn't seen his first expression, she would have trusted him implicitly. Instead, she looked down at her lap dubiously.

"It's not a day for tears," the man repeated. "It's a day to forget your problems. For me, it's a day to remember the past."

Surprised, she looked at him. "I don't want to remember the past," she blurted.

"A pretty young girl like you—what kind of a past can you have? It should be honey and roses."

She was infuriated by his assumption she had nothing to cry about even though she understood it was well meant. "You don't know," she said despairingly.

"Perhaps I don't," he said quietly. "We carry our own baggage."

Determined not to talk about herself, she looked away.

'Why don't you tell me?" the man asked gently. "We'll never meet again and I guarantee to listen. It might do you good to talk about it."

"No one here understands," she said. "No one wants to know what it was really like. Mrs. Young, she just want to show me off as a charity and Helene is merely polite. As for the rest, they don't care at all."

The man looked startled when she mentioned Mrs. Young. He leaned forward. "Mrs. Young?" he asked.

"She's the lady I work for till September. She thinks she's being charitable but truly, she just wants to impress everyone with her charity," she said bitterly. She thought for a moment. "That's not true. She's not a bad person. It's just that I'm not real for her."

"Is that why you're crying?"

"Oh no," she responded, shocked. "That doesn't matter. I'll be leaving soon enough. It's…it's…" Her eyes filled with tears again.

He said nothing, but looked very interested.

"It's Mama and Pearl," she sobbed, saying their names out loud to another person for the first time after leaving Allen Street. She buried her head in her hands and cried, surprised at the violence of her tears and relieved as they flowed. She realized she hadn't allowed herself to cry since the day Yussel had left.

When the paroxysm had passed, she looked back at where the

man had been, expecting him to have moved on, but he was still there, looking at her sympathetically.

"I'm all alone," she whispered. "Yussel's in Petaluma and I'm all alone. I'm the only woman left in my family."

He started to extend a hand to her, thought better of it, and continued looking at her.

His silence forced her to speak. "They all died in the fire," she explained brokenly. "Mama and Pearl and Erma and Anna—they all died. It was my fault. I could have saved them, I know I could have."

"How could you have saved them?"

"If I'd thought about them, if I hadn't been so frightened that I ran away. Then I tried to go back inside…Pearl jumped, you know," she whispered. "She jumped to the pavement and Mama…she just sat there at the machine. Why do you think she didn't get up and try to leave? Maybe she was thinking of Chava, too."

"Chava?"

"That's my other sister. She died in a night of fear in *der alter heym*." She stopped, confused. Why was she saying all this to a stranger?

"It's all right," he said reassuringly. "I won't tell anyone. It will do you good to talk."

For half an hour, Minna spoke to the man on the park bench. He said little, but listened intently. His expression was so interested and concerned, she felt it was all right to tell him. It made her feel better, too. To no one else could she have spoken so freely. It would have been too hard to do it with Yussel—too upsetting for both of them. Bessie was not the kind of person with whom she could share such feelings. Afterwards, having said all that was on her mind, she sat quietly, feeling freer than she had in a long time.

The man looked at her. "I know the fire you are talking about. There's nothing you could have done—nothing. Believe me, I know. I've been in a kind of fire myself. There's no time to think or plan. You just go here and there and if you're lucky, you find a way out."

She gazed back at him. "That's just how it was," she said. "I didn't think anyone could understand."

"You are not at fault," he repeated firmly. "Believe me, if your Mama and Pearl were here, they'd be the first to agree."

She nodded. She would still feel responsible, but, as she gradually absorbed his words, she knew the pangs would be less strong. He understood. He knew what it was like to be in a fire.

"That helps," she said.

"When you lose someone you love," he continued, "you must accept the loss and go on. You'll see their face a thousand times, but you will know, more and more as time passes, they are no longer here. So you go on and make another life." He shrugged. "That's all."

She wished she could give him some kind of solace, for she heard the pain in his voice. As she watched him, he shrugged again and forced a laugh. "This is history. It's foolish to think of it now. As for you, young lady…"

She looked at him confidingly.

"As for you, young lady, you must have faith in yourself. I can tell you are the kind of person who will follow her dreams. I can see," he continued softly, "that your Mama and your sister would be proud of you."

She bowed her head for a long time, thinking of what he had said. Entirely self-absorbed, she didn't notice when he slid off his end of the bench and strode down the path. When she finally did look up, she was shocked to find him gone. "And I never said 'Thank you'. " She murmured.

In the days that followed, she often looked for the man she termed "the old gentleman" although he wasn't *that* old, but he never reappeared. She made up stories about him, about the loved one he lost, about the reason that he would be sitting on a park bench in the middle of the day. She often recalled their conversation and pondered over his words. She hoped the intensity of her loss would wane although there were still many times each day when it seemed brand new, as if it had just happened.

For the first time, she spoke of the day of the fire in a letter to Saul. It was difficult to write, but she felt better after she had finished. Unable to bear re-reading it, she put it in an envelope and sent it off. If I can write about it, it's better, she thought. She knew Saul would be glad she could.

A few weeks later, as Minna was sewing fine lace on a cambric petticoat for Miss Serena, she heard a knock on the open door of the sewing room. She looked up to see Mrs. Peabody smiling at her. "May I come in?" she asked.

Minna jumped up. She had begun to consider Mrs. Peabody an old friend. "I'm so glad to see you," she cried.

"I'm sorry I didn't come sooner. I've been at Newport. I haven't forgotten you, Minna. I hope every thing is going well?"

She hesitated. She only had three more months. It didn't seem worthwhile to make a fuss because she didn't like Mrs. Young or Miss Serena. Everyone else had been kind to her and the pay was good. She nodded. "Everything is fine."

Mrs. Peabody came closer. "I understand Mrs. Young is pleased with you. I thought she would be."

At first, Minna was surprised. Then she thought about it. What else could Mrs. Young say under the circumstances? And she had done her work well.

"I wanted to ask you…" she began hesitantly.

"Yes?"

"I've saved some money. I was wondering if I should get some new clothes for school. I don't know what the other girls will wear. Then, I think, maybe it would be better to save the money."

Mrs. Peabody thought about it. "You should save the money," she said firmly. "I have another idea. You make over clothes, don't you?"

"Of course," Minna said, wondering how that could possibly help her. She had nothing that was good enough to be made over. It would be a miracle if her wardrobe lasted another six months.

'The reason I ask is that there are some clothes…" Mrs. Peabody looked embarrassed. "They're not really hand-me-downs. You see, my daughter has just gotten married and she has so many new things now… I'd like for you to have them."

Minna thought about it. What did she care if they were hand-me-downs or not? If she could fix them, they'd be hers, wouldn't they? Besides, she now understood how easily the rich bought everything. They probably did have a new wardrobe each year. What harm was there in taking the ones they no longer wanted?

"Thank you very much. I'd like that," she said.

"I'm sure Mrs. Young will allow you time to work on them."

Minna nodded, although she doubted it. I'll work on them at night, she decided. No one can complain about that.

"I'll send them over tomorrow. I'm so glad to think you will use them. As far as what the girls at Oberlin are wearing, I don't know. When I was growing up, few females went to college and my daughter, of course, didn't, so I don't really…"

"That's all right!" Minna exclaimed. "I'll figure out what to do with the clothes, don't worry!"

"Have you heard from your brother?" Mrs. Peabody asked.

"Oh yes!" She took the much-folded letter from her pocket. 'Look, see what he says. I'll read to you about the chicken farm." As she read out loud, Mrs. Peabody listened attentively.

"That's good, Minna," she said. "I'm happy he likes Petaluma."

She laughed. "Petaluma…I wonder what it's really like, with a *cockamamy* name like that." She put her hand over her mouth. "I don't mean to criticize…" she began.

Mrs. Peabody smiled and held out her hand. "I'm glad everything is all right. I'm going away again tomorrow, but I'll be back in plenty of time to meet with you again and help you start off. I'll let you know when to expect me."

Minna stared at her in amazement. They had been talking so nicely. Had Mrs. Peabody been offended by her use of the word '*cockamamy*"? She'd never understand these people. She shook Mrs. Peabody's hand and walked her to the door.

"Thank you for coming," she said politely. "Thank you for the clothes, too."

Mrs. Peabody seemed gratified. "You're more than welcome, Minna. It's a real pleasure to see you." She spoke so warmly that Minna was surprised again. She wanted to say, if it's such a pleasure, why are you running off, but she was silent.

"I'll see you at the end of the summer." Mrs. Peabody smiled and hurried out the door.

Minna stood looking after her.

Two minutes later, Mrs. Young came rushing in. "Has Maria Peabody been here?" she panted.

"Yes, Ma'am. She just left."

"She left? Oh, I had hoped…" Mrs. Young recovered herself. "Thank you, Minna," she said stiffly and left.

Later, Agnes told Minna what had happened. Mrs. Peabody, as the doyenne of old New York society, acted as a law unto herself. She had refused to let Mr. Bates announce her and had simply requested his escort to the sewing room in such a way that he couldn't deny her. She had spoken to Minna and left without even greeting Mrs. Young.

"I'll bet she was in a hurry," Agnes explained. "She's giving a huge party in Newport tomorrow night. We don't have a house there yet, so Mrs. Young was hoping to be invited as a houseguest, but it didn't work out. That's why she was so disappointed not to see her 'dear friend'. Although at this late date, she couldn't expect to be asked anyway."

Agnes continued by describing Newport and some of the people who lived there. The way she spoke, it sounded like a small kingdom of palaces and intrigues.

Now she could understand why Mrs. Peabody had been in such a hurry. As long as I remember I'm only a "case" to her, I can't complain, she thought. She's been very nice. She chastised herself. That I should expect more is asking too much. I should be grateful that she's helping me at all.

Although she persuaded herself that she had been unreasonable to be disappointed, her feeling of chagrin remained. It was not until much later, lying in bed at night, that she had an insight. It's not Mrs. Peabody, she thought, it's anyone. I don't have a mother or a sister, or even a friend who cares about the details of my life except Saul—and he's so far away. I miss that. Here, there's no one, for they all know I'll be leaving soon and Helene's too self-centered to care about anyone. Bessie cares, but she sees everything so differently. I have no one…I'm all alone…

Bubbe's voice was a strident interruption. 'So now you're going to feel sorry for yourself! You're not alone, Minna, for we are all part of you. If it's more friends you want, wait till you get to college. For now, be glad you're alive and that you're going to make your dream come true.'

At first, Minna was angry, but as she thought more deeply about Bubbe's words, she had to agree. I *am* lucky, she thought. At least, I'm here. At least, I have a life.

As she closed her eyes, she wondered what Mrs. Peabody's clothes would be like. If this is the daughter that married a Lord, they must be nice. She had to smile as she wondered what Mrs. Young would think about it.

The next day, Mrs. Peabody's footman delivered armloads of clothing to Minna in the sewing room. Fortunately, Mrs. Young and Miss Serena were out, so Minna was able to examine them at her leisure. She caressed the fabric and lace, unable to believe that such beautiful garments had been discarded by another girl. She immediately began planning how she would alter them to suit her needs.

She counted how many there were. I will have to buy a valise, she thought. I can't carry all these in a sheet. She was pleased to notice that Mrs. Peabody had included some accessories and undergarments, too.

Undaunted by the amount of work to be done, she put the dresses aside in a corner of the sewing room and continued working on Serena's lingerie. I'll have to stop doing extra work for Agnes, she decided. I'll use my extra time to do my own work. Almost everything she owns has already been altered anyway.

When Agnes came in that afternoon, she asked Minna about the clothing lying in the corner. "Mrs. Peabody gave them to me to make over for myself," she explained. "I'll do it in my spare time, of course."

Agnes was impressed. Without asking permission, she began to paw through the pile.

Minna wished she wouldn't, but didn't know how to say it.

Agnes held the dresses up, one by one, and exclaimed over each one. "These belonged to her daughter, Alice, didn't they?" she asked. Without waiting for an answer, she continued. "I know they did. I remember this one. She's married now. She married a Lord and she lives in England. But she was the best-dressed girl in New York when she was here. You're so lucky to have these. I wouldn't mind a few for myself!" She smiled covetously. "Look! They've hardly been worn. When you re-do them, no one will know where they came from."

Nervously, Minna changed the subject by asking Agnes to try on one of the dresses she had already altered for her. She resolved that in the future, she'd keep Mrs. Peabody's clothes in her bedroom. She didn't want anyone else envying her or possibly trying to take them away. She could handle Agnes, but if Miss Serena said anything… They are mine, she thought, and no one else will have them.

Agnes stood in front of the mirror admiring Minna's work. She had seemingly forgotten about Mrs. Peabody's dresses. "I ought to thank you for all you've done for me. It has made such a difference, the way I look now."

Minna thought, if you ought to thank me, why don't you? When we started this, you were so grateful. Now you take my work for granted. More than ever, she regretted that Agnes had seen the clothing Mrs. Peabody had given her.

Agnes continued. "You know, I met someone yesterday. A man. He talked to me instead of Serena, even though she was standing right there. Of course, he isn't one of our set. He lives out West. He's someone's cousin, I think. He was so interesting. He was telling me about the Indians he sees near his ranch. He has cattle, you see."

Despite her annoyance, Minna was interested. She smiled.

Agnes smiled back. "His name is Charles," she said slowly. "I've never met anyone I liked so much." Ignoring Minna, yet continuing to talk aloud, it was as if she was speaking to herself. "I wonder what it's like to live so far away from New York City. It sounds like a hard life…" She slipped the dress over her head, forgetting to go behind the screen. "We'll meet again tonight," she continued dreamily. "I'll see…"

She continued describing Charles. Listening to her, Minna could see that she didn't understand what it would be like to live in an unsettled territory out West. Mostly, she was simply delighted to be singled out over her cousin. Yet she did speak of him very warmly. Minna wondered what he was really like. If his choice is Agnes, she thought scornfully, he can't be very dashing.

As soon as Agnes left the sewing room, Minna made two trips upstairs carrying Mrs. Peabody's clothing. Laying the dresses carefully on her bed, she breathed a sigh of relief. Tonight, she'd find a way to store them. She shut the bedroom door behind her and dashed downstairs to finish her work.

Since her conversation with the old gentleman, she continued to eat her lunch outside every day. She didn't meet him again, but she did begin to speak to one of the nannies. Kathleen, it seemed, was not accepted by the others because she was Irish, not British. Although she and Minna chatted, it was tacitly understood by both that this was only a stopgap acquaintanceship till the other nannies accepted her.

Minna didn't mind, because she found it fascinating to learn about the way children grew up in the great houses on Fifth Avenue. They were pampered, yet isolated from the real world and their own families. At home, Minna thought, we couldn't be isolated because there wasn't enough room to keep us separate. I hated that, but this is no better.

One day when she was about to go out, she saw Miss Serena

crossing the street towards the entrance to the park. Seemingly oblivious of her presence, she brushed past her and hurried into the park. When Minna crossed and entered it, she was surprised to see her disappear around a corner.

She was almost tempted to follow her. By now, she knew it was "not done" for Miss Serena to be without her mother, Agnes, a beau, or even the chauffeur. Then she shrugged. It was no business of hers. She sat upon her usual bench and munched her fruit and cheese while inhaling the fresh smells of summer.

Just as she was about to return to the house, she saw Miss Serena, her head down and shoulders slumped, dragging her feet as she walked back towards the house. When she approached Minna's bench, she looked up for a moment, hesitated, and stopped.

"May I sit down?" she asked.

It was so strange to have Miss Serena asking for anything, Minna was speechless. Usually she demanded in a polite but too-firm voice. She nodded and patted the seat next to hers.

Serena sat. As she looked off into the distance, Minna thought she could see traces of tears in her eyes. Leaning towards her, she asked softly, "Is anything wrong?"

Miss Serena shook her head and seemed about to rise. Then she hesitated and turned to face Minna. " Yes, there is. You can help me. The way your life has been, you probably know more than I do. I'll ask you."

Minna disliked the comparison, but decided to hear what she had to say. She waited.

"The thing is…" Miss Serena hesitated. "I don't understand… What does happen between a man and a woman?" she asked, averting her eyes.

Minna glared at her indignantly. First of all, she resented Miss Serena's idea that she knew so much more about the subject because of the way she had lived. Secondly, she didn't know very much herself except what she remembered from the farms around *der alter heym* and what Rosie had told her. Last, it was not a topic she could find easy to talk about with anyone, especially Miss Serena.

As she was groping for a way to say all this, Miss Serena turned her body so she was facing the other way. "No one will tell me. Yet sometimes, they look at me so… men, I mean…and today, when I was alone with…someone…he…well, he frightened me."

Minna could understand being frightened. She remembered how she had felt when she first began to bleed. She had been so scared. What did it mean? Maybe she was going to die. When she told Mama in tears, Mama had slapped her across the face. "That's to remind you of the pain of being a woman," she had said, explaining that Bubbe had done the same thing to her. Afterwards, she had been helpful, but Minna was never able to forget that unexpected slap.

It wasn't until she found herself confiding in Miss Israel one day when she feared she had spotted her skirt that her attitude changed. Miss Israel had said, "This is not a disgusting thing, Minna. This means that now you are old enough to bear a child. What can be more beautiful than a woman with a child? You should be proud, not ashamed."

Then, when she had been with Jake… Minna remembered how she had felt. Warm…melting…yielding… She hadn't been frightened then. She had liked it.

"What did he do?" she asked.

"He put his arms around me and kissed me. But the way he kissed, I felt I would suffocate."

"If you felt that way, you don't love him, that's all."

"I thought I…cared. Then when he touched me, I felt so uncomfortable. He said I was cold."

Minna hesitated and then decided to help. "Once, I loved someone. When he kissed me, I was scared for a moment but then I was happy. Maybe this man's just the wrong one for you."

Miss Serena shook her head. "I've loved him all season. Everyone admires him. Maybe if I understood…"

Minna hedged. "Can't you ask your mother or Agnes?"

"Agnes knows nothing and my mother…how can I ask her? Anyway, if she knew I was seeing Stuart, she'd forbid me to leave the house. I'm to marry a Duke. It's all decided."

Minna shook her head. "All I know is that if you love someone and they love you, you like to kiss them. Then, at night, that's when babies are conceived. The man and the woman they…well, it must be like the animals at the farm. Anyway, I do know that if you love someone, it is good to kiss him and touch him. I know that." She looked earnestly at Miss Serena.

She shuddered. "I think it sounds disgusting. I don't like to be touched by anyone, particularly a man. Why can't I love someone another way?"

Minna shrugged. "That's just the way it is. I don't know why. I suppose so there'll be babies.."

Serena made an ugly face. "I won't ever...I just won't!"

Minna shook her head. "When you get married, every night... That's part of being married."

"I won't!" Miss Serena shook her head violently. "It's not for me. I won't allow it!" Abruptly, she stood up. Without looking at Minna, she hurried away.

Minna stared after her. As usual, she thought, I didn't really exist for her. She only talked to me because I don't matter. She could say *anything* to me...

She thought about Miss Serena's words. Maybe, she thought, that's another problem that comes with living on Fifth Avenue. Their lives are so removed from reality, they have no way to learn about anything. Then she laughed. If that was really true, there wouldn't be a single baby in the great houses!

Although she saw Miss Serena many times after that in the sewing room, they were never alone. Either Helene, Agnes, or her mother were with her. With neither look nor word did she refer to their meeting in the park. She remained, as always, beautiful, fragile, and remote.

Minna wondered. She kept her ears open for a mention of someone named Stuart, but heard nothing. She had decided not to ask Agnes for fear of betraying Miss Serena's secret. What will she do when she marries, Minna worried. A woman has to...

Agnes looked more rosy and contented than she had ever been. Although she was silent on the subject, it was obvious she was still seeing Charles, the man she had mentioned to Minna. She didn't visit the sewing room in her spare time any more. She was either with Miss Serena or running out to "do an errand".

CHAPTER 27

Minna worked hard on Mrs. Peabody's dresses. Every night, she sewed until she could scarcely keep her eyes open. Helene, who knew what she was doing, followed her progress enviously and occasionally kept her company.

Most of the time, she was left to her own thoughts. As she sewed, she tried to imagine herself wearing this dress or that dress at school. What would the other students be like? Would she find a friend?

She spent time gazing at herself in the mirror, trying to decide if she would fit in with them. Then she'd turn away in disgust, thinking, I must be crazy! I need an education—not friends!

After her talk with the old gentleman, she found herself thinking of Mama and Pearl frequently, yet it was more bearable than it had been. The evil accusing voice that had blamed her for their deaths disappeared. When something amusing or interesting happened and she found herself thinking, I'll have to tell Pearl, she still felt an intense sense of loss when she knew she couldn't do that. Tears came to her eyes, but the wrenching immediacy of grief happened less often. It was becoming a deeply sad memory instead of a tragedy that had just happened.

Yet, even as she began to accept Mama and Pearl's death, she continued to think bitterly about the fire. So many had died...Anna...Rosa...Erma...even her heroic cousin, Sammy... She missed Erma. She would have been the friend who could have commiserated and shared her feelings.

One evening, Minna slipped out, after telling Mr. Bates she was leaving. Thinking about Erma, she decided to visit the Alliance. She felt a need to see the art class again, to remember anew the time she had shared with her friend there.

Yet when she peeked in the doorway, it was all different. The professor was another man and the students were unfamiliar. Disappointed and relieved, she walked back towards the entrance of the building.

Just as she was about to leave, Minna saw Harry. Tears came to her eyes as she remembered how Erma had cared for him.

When he saw her, he stopped short, staring at her. "I remember you," he said. "You're Erma's friend, Minna."

Unable to speak, she simply nodded.

He shook his head. "It's strange. I didn't know her that well. We only saw each other in class. Yet I miss her. I find myself looking for her…" he stopped, embarrassed.

She looked up at him. "She cared a lot about you. She thought your work was important. She thought you'd be famous one day. I used to tease her and she'd blush when I mentioned your name." If Erma had been alive, Minna would never have been so indiscreet, but she was sure Erma would have wanted Harry to know this.

His eyes were damp. "I'm sorry I never went with her for coffee after class," he said softly.

He was carrying a large portfolio. To change the subject, she pointed at it. "You're still working, I see."

"Yes. Do you want to see what I've done?"

"I'd like to."

He led her to an empty classroom and laid the portfolio upon a desk. Carefully, he untied the strings that kept it closed and opened it, holding up a drawing done in ink.

Minna gasped. It was the fire! There was the Asch Building with people peering out of the windows, lining up at the ledges. No one was recognizable, for their faces were distorted in fear.

Her hands trembled as she looked at the next one. It was a girl falling through the air. Her face was unrecognizable. It might have been anyone Minna knew. Against a backdrop of flames, the body seemed to float, fragile and resigned, to a tragic death. Harry had skillfully contrasted her delicate appearance with the urgency and horror of her fall.

Minna thrust the drawings away and put her hands to her face.

Her mouth twisted as she tried to hold back her sobs.

"I'm so sorry, Minna," Harry said very apologetically, taking back the sketch. "These drawings were the only way I could stop thinking about the fire. So I had to do them although it was agonizing when I was sketching. Such a loss! I've stared at them so intently for so long that when I see them now I can almost leave my pain behind and concentrate on technique. I didn't think…I forgot… they would have such an impact on anyone else. I'm very sorry, Minna."

She took her hands away. "Doing them helped you to feel better?"

"Yes. It was a way of allowing my feelings to come out. It's also a way of showing people how it was so it won't happen again."

"Like Mr. Steinberg's poem," she mused.

"I don't know the poem," he said slowly, "but it's probably the same."

"I'd like to see the others," Minna choked. "Maybe it would help me, too."

"Another time." Harry began put them away. Then he pulled one out from the bottom of the pile. "Maybe you'd like to have this one," he offered, holding it up.

Minna looked at it. It was a picture of Erma at the easel, her hair disheveled, her head cocked, and her hand poised to work on her drawing. It had so much vitality, she had to smile, remembering. Yes, she thought, that's the way Erma was.

"But don't you want to keep this?" she asked, her hand already reaching out for the drawing.

"I have others. I have been thinking of her so much lately I did a whole series. You take it. I want you to have it."

She could only smile tearfully at Harry and clutch the drawing. "Thanks. I'll keep it always. If you like," she continued shyly, "I'll make you a copy of Mr. Steinberg's poem."

"I'd like that very much," he said heartily. "Very much," he repeated.

"You were right about Erma's friend, Priscilla," she continued irrelevantly. 'She was just playing a game. Erma said you were right."

"I'm sorry if it gave Erma pain."

"It did, but it wasn't your fault."

Harry took the drawing from her and rolled it. "And you?" he asked. "What's happening with you?"

"I lost my Mama and my sister in the fire, my brother, Yussel, is in California now, and I'm to go away to college in September," Minna said starkly.

He looked at her. "I didn't realize…"

She shook her head. "I wish I could write a poem or make a drawing. But, in time, it will be all right, I guess. Someday…it will be all right." As she said those words, she suddenly thought, yes, it *will* be all right. For the first time, she was sure. "It really will be," she repeated.

"You're a strong person. I can tell from your face."

She nodded.

"It's not easy…to be a strong person."

She nodded again.

"Would you like to have a cup of coffee with me?" He asked. "We can talk a little more."

She thought about it and finally nodded. "Yes, I would."

At the café, Minna was, at first, overwhelmed by her memory of the way it had been when she had come with Erma. She stared at the table that had been "theirs" and was relieved to see that the two chess players had moved over and were sitting there now. It seemed fitting.

Over coffee, she learned that Harry had had to leave his family to continue painting. It was against all orthodox belief to be an artist and his father, a rabbi, had disowned him. "But I couldn't give up," he said earnestly. "I don't have a choice. I *have* to be an artist. Someday, maybe they'll understand. That's what I hope."

She shook her head. "You have *chutzpah*," she said. "To leave everything to be an artist—it's romantic!"

"Believe me, it's not romantic when you have to work at a factory all day and paint at night. That's not romantic—it's grueling."

She frowned. "I can understand wanting something so much, but to hurt those who love you. That's hard."

"So, who said it was easy?"

She knew his flippancy hid his feelings, so she began to tell him about the Youngs to change the subject. He was fascinated.

"They live like kings," he mused, "but they're not happy."

"It's not enough to have 'things'," Minna said. "You have to have been without to appreciate them. Otherwise, it means nothing. It's like what Mr. Steinberg said." Suddenly she realized that it must be very late and Mr. Bates would be angry at her. He might even lock the door so she couldn't get in.

Standing up abruptly, she explained the situation to him. As she turned to leave, he stopped her. "Can we meet again?" he asked.

She thought for a moment. "I can't usually come out at night. It's hard… I can meet you on Sunday in the park along the river."

"Splendid! We'll go for a walk."

They arranged a meeting place and Minna hurried out. As she left, she heard Harry call after her, "Don't forget the poem."

When she returned to Fifth Avenue, Mr. Bates was waiting impatiently for her. As he let her in, he frowned, "This is the last time…"

"I'm so sorry. It won't happen again. Thank you for waiting for me," she said, smiling sweetly.

Clutching her picture, she hurried up to her room. There she unrolled it carefully and tucked the end of it into her mirror frame. It looked just like Erma. As she fell asleep, she said goodnight as usual to Mama, Pearl, Chava, and Bubbe. Looking at her mirror, she added, "Good night Erma," feeling almost as if she was sharing the room with her friend.

Minna copied Mr. Steinberg's poem for Harry so she could bring it with her on Sunday. She found she was looking forward to seeing him. It had been a long time since she had planned to meet any friend other than Bessie. It was not always fun to see her, for there was usually a meeting to attend. As for Saul, she had grown so used to writing him it was hard to recall what it had been like when she could see him every day.

As she headed for the park, she remembered with a sad smile how she, Yussel, and Pearl had gone on "vacation" in Central Park. Harry was already waiting for her when she arrived. A fresh breeze was blowing over the East River. He looked cool and relaxed as he leaned against the railing.

She smiled at him. As she came closer, she saw he carried a small sketchpad and a drawing pencil.

Gesturing at them, she laughed. "You're always ready," she said.

He flipped the pages. She saw heads, bodies, scenes…a panoply of life on the lower East Side. "I want to look through this," she said.

He closed the notebook. "Later, later. Let's walk."

As they strolled along the path enjoying the breeze, Minna noticed that Harry didn't just glance at the people they passed, he examined them. She was surprised to see that no one seemed to object, or even notice.

"If I wasn't with you," she asked, "would you be drawing every minute, even while you're walking?"

He smiled ruefully. "It's an obsession with me. No one knows what it's like downtown. No one sees it the way I can. All they have to do is look. I'd like to show others what my eye sees so that no one can ever forget, even in years to come when we're all living in the Bronx, or Brooklyn, or uptown, or Paris."

"Paris?"

"Someday, I'll go there when I sell some of my work. I hear there are prizes you can win. The thing is, my subjects are not what the judges want to see. They're not picturesque or romantic. They're just…life."

"Why do you want to go to Paris?"

"That's where everything starts. The new ideas. I hear about some of them. They all begin there. Honestly, did you ever hear of anyone who didn't want to go to Paris? Wouldn't you go if you could?"

"I don't know. Maybe someday. Serena's going to Paris," she mused. "She's not excited about anything but shopping. Of course, she's going to marry a Duke, not meet artists!"

Harry sighed. "She should take along an artist to chronicle her trip. That would solve my problem."

She laughed, finding it impossible to picture Harry and Serena in the same room.

When they reached an enticing spot in the shade, Harry stopped and suggested they sit on the bench. As they sat down, he took several newspaper wrapped parcels out of his pockets. "Care for something to eat?" He gestured grandly as he unwrapped each one.

There were two apples, some cheese, and half a loaf of bread. A feast! Minna laughed in surprise.

As they were eating, she gave Harry Mr. Steinberg's poem. While he read it, she flipped through his sketchbook. The faces he drew were somber and careworn, yet they had am certain energy despite their fatigue and anxiety. She was fascinated by his work. She turned the pages back and forth to see some of the sketches more than once. Then, realizing Harry had been quiet for a long time, she looked over at him. The poem was in his lap and his hand over his eyes.

She touched his arm. "I know," she said softly. "I felt the same way when I first read it."

Automatically, Harry reached for his notebook. As if unconscious of his own actions, he began to draw, his hand moving rapidly over the page. He bent his head as he became more and more engrossed in his work. Minna realized that he had forgotten she was there. She stared off into the distance, enjoying the brightness of the day, the crisp apple she munched, and the people as they strolled by.

After what seemed like a very long time, Harry put the pencil down, sat back and looked off into the distance. Minna put her hand on the drawing and asked softly, "May I look?"

When he didn't answer, she took the book and gazed at his work. At the first new sketch, she gasped. Somehow, Harry had drawn the same people she had grown up with, the same men and women with worn, often ugly faces, yet in the drawings, they looked like angels, Angels in the streets, she thought. It wasn't that they had wings, yet somehow, she knew they were more than individuals and the streets more than a grimy part of New York City. It was an angry picture, she thought. As she looked at it, she felt despair and anger.

He waited.

"Oh, Harry," she said, aware that he would be pleased that she was moved by his drawings but that it wasn't important to him either way. He would, in any case, keep sketching. That was what he did.

He took the book away from Minna and closed it firmly. "Shall we walk?" he suggested.

Minna tried to picture the paintings she saw every day at the Young's house. None of them looked anything like Harry's. None of them made her feel sorrow or anger. They were beautiful, she supposed, but it was a cold kind of beauty.

"You really can't paint the other way?" she asked.

"No, how can I? I can only paint as I see it. Otherwise, what's the point?"

By the time the afternoon was over, Minna had given Harry her address and taken his. She promised to write to him when she had an address at school. They agreed to meet again before she left, but

Minna could tell that Harry was itching to recapture his notebook and get back to work. It's the only thing that's important to him, she thought. Erma would have been disappointed. He's talented and sometimes charming, but he doesn't really look to women for...for... She couldn't think of exactly how to say it. For completion, she finally concluded. For him, everything comes second to his work.

As the summer progressed, Minna saw Harry occasionally. More often, she spent the day with Bessie. Each time she saw her, she learned new facts about the fire. Now the two owners, Isaac Harris and Max Blanck, were crying anti-semitism as the press accused them of locking the fire door, not providing fire exits, having no fire drills, and many other violations.

Bessie grew more and more indignant, but Minna sometimes wished she would never have to think of it again. Even if the owners got off scott free, which she couldn't believe possible, she vowed she would not get involved. It was true their punishment might deter others, as Bessie said, but instinctively, she knew it was dangerous for her to wish for revenge. It would be far too easy to become obsessed by such thoughts. As if anything could change what happened, she thought sadly.

When she asked Saul how he felt, he agreed with her. He wrote: *If you allow the fire to become the most important thing in your life—the fire and your revenge—then the burden is too great. The tragedy has happened. We must all try to change what caused it, but our lives, especially your life, must go on. You were a soldier in the forefront of the battle and you have survived. Now others must take up the cause.*

Besides, it seemed to be very difficult to fix responsibility. Some blamed the fire safety laws, saying that inspections were not made as often or as rigorously as they should be. Others said that the laws themselves were outmoded, dating from the use of such building space as storage rather than factories. Even the fire department came in for its share of the blame. Their ladders had reached only to the sixth floor, yet the fire station that first answered the alarm was considered the most modern in the city. The Mayor's office was blamed, too.

In all the time that Minna had been working for Mrs. Young, she had never seen Mr. Young. Apparently, he left the house early in the morning before anyone was up and returned home very late, regardless of his wife's dinner plans. Often he made extended business trips to his railroad lines, traveling in his own private car. When he was home, he spent his time in his upstairs study, a room that no one was allowed to enter, and his bedroom, barely appearing for meals.

Minna thought this strange but when she asked the others, they seemed to take it for granted. "After all," said Mrs. Brown, normally the most kindly of women, "he's where he is because of his railroads. He'd better make sure he keeps them running!"

When Minna protested, remembering it was he who paid all their salaries, she was surprised to find that the kitchen unanimously agreed with Mrs. Brown. Some, it seemed, were meant to toil and others to shine. Mrs. Young and Miss Serena were meant to shine because of the accident of Mrs. Young's birth.

This seemed patently unfair to Minna. She tried to make them understand by saying, 'You work hard, don't you? Would you like someone to live in luxury from your efforts and not even feel grateful?"

It was no use. To the others, Mr. Young's good fortune in marrying a former Miss Winter was so obvious, it need not even be mentioned. The other thing was that Mr. Young was so wealthy it was impossible for anyone, even Minna, who really tried, to feel a bond of sympathy with him.

Millie said, "He's hurt a lot of people, he has. If you read the papers, my friend told me, his foreman fired on the workers last year when they wanted to earn a living wage."

"What papers? Yellow journalism, I'll be bound," Mr. Bates sniffed.

To Minna, comfortable with the idea of the Union and the Bund, it was a revelation to see how closely most of the kitchen identified with the family rather than their fellow workers. There was no one she could talk to about this. Bessie, she knew, would say, 'Well, what did you expect? They're corrupted by their association with capitalists.' Even Millie, despite her expressed sympathies, took pride in Mrs. Young's social successes, listening enthralled as Helene read aloud every account of the family that appeared in the newspapers.

Despite Millie's accusations, Minna could not help but feel it was unfortunate for Mr. Young to be considered a non-person in his own home by his own servants. If Mrs. Young didn't foster this impression of him, she thought, no one else would. Of course, if he really did fire on his workers, he probably deserved everything bad. She decided to reserve judgment. Since it seemed unlikely she'd ever meet him, the issue was hardly a burning one.

One day at breakfast, when she was least expecting it, Minna received a package in the mail. She held it in her hands, feeling its weight. As usual, when she was worried or unsure, she tried to delay the moment of revelation.

Could it be from Yussel, she wondered. For one wild moment, she thought he was sending her oranges. She had to laugh. If that was oranges, they were tiny and they certainly didn't feel round!

Maybe it's from Saul, she thought. But she couldn't imagine how he could buy anything to send her a gift. What could it be?

Everyone at the table was waiting anxiously to see what she had received. Finally, Helene could stand it no longer. "For goodness sakes!" she exclaimed. "Open your package, Minna!"

Too preoccupied to respond, she continued to pat it. She even gave it a gentle shake to see if anything rattled. It feels like a book, she finally decided. Who could possibly be sending me a book? Maybe it *is* Saul, she mused.

Just as everyone in the room was about to explode, Minna slowly untied the string and carefully opened the brown wrapping paper. They all leaned forward.

She gasped. "It's my catalogue from Oberlin College!" She held it to her breast and looked around the room triumphantly. "It's my catalogue!" she cried.

She half-rose from her seat, wanting nothing more than to run upstairs, lock herself in her room, and pore over it. As she held it up, a letter fell out. She picked it up and began to read. They all watched her.

Finally, she looked up. "It says, 'Welcome to a new freshman.' It says I should think about my classes for next year."

She sat back in her chair, blissfully ignoring the rest of the food on her plate and the others at the table. She decided to put the catalogue in her room and save it until the evening. If I start looking at it now, she thought, I'll never get my work done and I won't read it carefully. It will be better to wait until I have more time. Conversation flowed around her, but she remained preoccupied for the rest of the meal although her eyes sparkled.

"She looks as if she just got a letter from her beau," Helene whispered enviously to Millie. "She's a million miles away."

"She looks so pretty when her eyes sparkle like that," Millie replied, ignoring Helene's disapproval.

All day, Minna thought about the catalogue waiting upstairs for her. It was a terrible temptation to picture the grayish book lying on her neatly made bed. There was nothing she wanted more than to run upstairs and begin reading. Instead, she persevered and did more work than usual.

Finally, at the end of the day, she finished her supper, excused herself from the table, and hurried upstairs. As she lay across her bed turning the pages of her precious catalogue, she smiled to herself in awe, tempted to pinch herself to make sure it wasn't just a dream.

She saw that the first day of school was Wednesday. September 20th. So soon! Minna wondered how long it would take her to get all the way out to Ohio. I hope Mrs. Peabody knows the right date, she thought anxiously.

She went on to read a description of the college. Determined to read the catalogue all the way through, skipping nothing for fear of missing an essential nugget of information, she was interested to learn that Oberlin was run on the Honor System. That meant, the book said, she would have to sign an honor pledge stating, "I have neither given nor received aid in this test" every time she took an exam. When everyone had signed the statement, the professors would leave the class alone to finish their work.

She was overwhelmed to know that the cost of tuition, gymnasium, laboratory fees, and books would come to $117 a year not including her room and board. She felt both humble and thankful for her scholarship. Those who were giving it to her had great faith in her abilities, she realized, promising to spend so much for the next four years. I'll deserve it, she vowed.

Mrs. Peabody had said her room and board were free in exchange for her work. I'll earn extra money by sewing during the year, she vowed. Of course, I'll work over the summer. She spared a moment to think about Mrs. Boone, the owner of the boarding house. I hope she's nice, Minna thought wishfully. Then she shrugged. Living here, she had learned that nice didn't matter. What was important was to for her do the work properly and to be treated fairly.

She stared off into the distance. Although she hadn't even read about her classes yet, Oberlin began to seem more real. She imagined herself living in that far away place. On the fold-our map, the campus looked very large.

Try as she could, she was unable to visualize the other students except as ideals—each as beautiful as Serena and as intelligent as…her favorite teacher, Miss Israel. I'm the one, she realized, who won't fit in. I'm the one who will be different.

She jumped up and looked again in the mirror. Examining her face carefully, she sought visible signs of difference. It's my hair, she thought. If I wore it another way… She held it away from her face and looked in the mirror again.

She shook her head. Since the other students at Oberlin were perfect, nothing about her would fit, from her background to her hair to her re-modeled clothes. As she turned back to the bed and picked up the catalogue again, she had to smile. She remembered Benny Herschel's favorite expression when faced with a potential problem: "No point in wading across the river till I'm standing on the bank."

Finally, she came to the section of the catalogue she had been eagerly anticipating, "The College of Arts and Sciences". She read descriptions of the faculty and the subjects she was supposed to take over the next four years. It was both frightening and exhilarating.

Luckily, she saw that registration for classes would occur after she arrived on the campus. Perhaps there would be someone there who could help her understand her choices. Otherwise it was too confusing.

In the back of the book, a list of students was printed. Looking at the freshmen, Minna checked to see if her name was there. Yes, it was! There it was: Ruben, Minna, New York City. Her address was Mrs. Young's. Minna laughed to think she had a Fifth Avenue address. She couldn't believe her name was listed with all the others.

She read the name of the each freshman, trying to imagine which would become her friends. Most of them, she noticed, had two first names. There was Agnes Louise, Helen Jane… Minna frowned. Why hadn't she thought to make up a middle name so she'd be like them? There was even a girl from Africa and others with foreign addresses.

By the time she fell asleep over the opened book, her thoughts were a happy daze. She tumbled into bed, said good night to her family and Erma, and closed her eyes as soon as her head touched` the pillow.

CHAPTER 28

In the weeks that followed, all she could think about was college, the classes she would take, and the other students. As time passed, she found she had almost memorized the names of the other freshmen as well as the various courses offered. At odd moments, these ran through her mind, almost like a litany or a prayer. The others commented on her absent-mindedness, but she barely noticed.

Anxiously, she awaited a visit from Mrs. Peabody, to find out when she was to leave. As the month of September approached, she began to worry. Could she have forgotten? Was she too busy at Newport to remember Minna?

Although she continued to see Bessie, she felt she had already said farewell and was merely waiting for the day when it was time to leave. She was careful not to talk too much about Oberlin to anyone in the kitchen for fear they'd be offended. It didn't seem possible that everyone would not be envious. Only to Yussel and Saul did she write her true feelings.

She had finally finished remodeling the clothes she had been given and she had almost completed enough elegant hand-stitched underclothing and sleepwear to last Miss Serena for years, when she realized she needed a trunk. As she examined her pile of dresses, skirts, and waists, she knew she couldn't simply tie them up in a sheet. Yet she didn't want to spend money needlessly.

One day at dinner, she mentioned her problem to Mrs. Brown. As she spoke, the rest of the table became quiet so everyone could hear what she was saying.

Mrs. Brown frowned as she considered the matter. Finally, she said, "Instead of buying a trunk, you could use a heavy box. My nephew, he's a carpenter. If you paid for the wood, maybe he'd do me a favor…"

Minna's eyes lit up. "Do you really think he would? That would be wonderful."

As she said that, she realized how worried she had been about the problem. She'd have to lug her books and her feather bed as well. If she had a box or trunk, it would be perfect. It was strange having no place, no home, to leave things behind. Never mind, she thought bravely. Oberlin will be my home from now on.

"Perhaps I can do even better," Mr. Bates offered. "The family has an old trunk in the cellar. I know for a fact it hasn't been used in years. It's completely empty. Maybe they would be willing to give it to you."

Minna flushed. "I couldn't ask…" she began.

"It's I who will ask," he said firmly. "It would be a liberty for you to say anything."

Fearing she was getting into deep water, Minna decided to remain silent. She allowed herself to say "Thank you" and bent over her food.

Afterwards, she puzzled over just what had been decided. Suppose the family said no or suppose the trunk was too old to use. Would it then be too late for Mrs. Brown's nephew to make the crate for her? There seemed to be no step she could take without offending someone, so she remained silent and continued to worry.

She had been seeing less and less of Agnes, especially now that her clothes no longer needed re-modeling. When they did pass in the hall, Minna noticed that she still seemed very happy. She must be in love, she thought. The trip to Europe was all set. What would Miss Serena do if Agnes decided not to come? It was clear that she was an essential although inconsequential part of Miss Serena's entourage.

One day, as Minna sat sewing and mulling over the trunk issue, Agnes stuck her head in the doorway. She asked if she could come in.

Minna was surprised. It was the first time she had ever asked permission. "Of course," she said.

Agnes stepped inside and looked at Minna pleadingly. There was obviously something she wanted to talk about. Minna composed her face into an expression of intense interest and waited

"We're in love," Agnes blurted. "We're really in love! He wants me to marry him and go back out West."

Minna smiled. "That's wonderful. You must be so happy."

Agnes' eyes filled with tears. "That's just it. I know my Aunt Bella will say no. She wants me to go to Europe with them."

"What will your parents say?" Minna asked.

"Oh, they like him. I don't think they'll mind. But if Aunt Bella disapproves, everyone in society will agree with her. We won't have a real wedding and when we come back to visit, people won't receive us."

Minna was astonished. "But, I don't understand. You're going to live out West anyway. What difference does it make what folks here think if your parents agree?"

"But…if I go to Europe, it's a great opportunity. Think of what I'll see! And if Serena does marry a Duke or a Prince…well, anything could happen."

Minna put down her sewing. "What do you mean, anything could happen?"

"Oh, I don't know," Agnes replied vaguely with an embarrassed look on her face.

Minna shook her head in amazement. "I don't understand you. If I was in love with someone, that would be the most important thing. You said you were in love with him, so why are you worrying about Dukes and Princesses?"

"But to live out West in a small town… It will be so different than it is here. Think of what I'd be giving up."

'Giving up?" Minna's astonishment led her to speak more freely than she had ever done with Agnes before. She remembered how the girl had been when she had first come, how she talked non-stop because no one else would listen. "I don't understand what you're giving up."

Agnes looked at the floor. "It's hard to explain," she began. "I guess you just can't see it."

"I guess not," Minna agreed impatiently. "What's more important than the man you love and want to marry? That is, if you really do."

"Of course, I do," Agnes said quickly. "It's just not that simple."

"I suppose it never is," Minna agreed, shaking her head and thinking of Priscilla.

Agnes hung her head. "I don't know what to do."

Minna stared at her. Suddenly she realized Agnes was enjoying the situation, reveling in her sorrow and the drama of it. She pursed her lips and shook her head, determined not to participate further.

As if sensing her feelings, Agnes hurried out of the room without another word and without looking back at Minna.

After she had left, Minna thought about what she had said in the conversation. Do I really believe that nothing is more important than the man you love, she asked herself. I didn't feel that way with Jake, thank goodness. But, her eyes grew dreamy, if I met the right man, the prince of princes, then anything he wanted me to do would be right, so I'd be glad to do it.

She frowned. There was something wrong with that analysis. Then she shrugged. Since I haven't met him, why worry? It's silly to think about it.

Long after Minna had stopped anticipating Mrs. Peabody's arrival and begun to worry about it, she came again. It was already the first week in September. Mrs. Young, Serena, and Agnes, if she decided to join them, were to leave for Europe very soon.

She was still anxiously awaiting word of the trunk from the cellar but otherwise, was all set to leave. At least, she admitted, as ready as I'll ever be.

On this visit, Mrs. Peabody was shown into the formal reception room, the Morning Room. Mr. Bates was sent upstairs to fetch Minna.

He arrived and announced portentously, "Mrs. Peabody to see you in the Morning Room."

Minna jumped up. "I'm so glad! I've been hoping she would come. Now I'll know when I'm leaving." She looked up at Mr. Bates pleadingly. "Have you heard anything about the trunk yet? I have to plan…"

He shook his head. "Don't worry, though," he said. "If you can't use that one, we'll find something for you."

She remembered to smile thankfully, but she was worried about his meaning. Find something? Did that mean a sheet or an old box or what? Then she mentally shook herself. That's what possessions do to you, she realized. I haven't stopped worrying about the trunk since I heard of it. It would be better if I didn't have the dresses.

She straightened her hair and walked sedately into the Morning Room. She had only peeked in before, so she had to make an effort not be overwhelmed by her surroundings. The ornately brocaded drapes, the lush oriental rug, and the heavy furniture made her feel undeserving. Sand floors, checked linoleum, and orange-crate furniture suited her more, she thought as she strode forward resolutely to stand in front of Mrs. Peabody.

She was welcomed by a big smile. "How are you, Minna? Are you ready to leave? School starts the 20th. However, I thought you might like to go a little earlier so you can get acquainted with Mrs. Boone and she can show you how to go on."

Responding to Mrs. Peabody's tone of efficiency, Minna nodded. "I'm ready," she said. "The only thing is—I'm waiting for a trunk. Otherwise, I've caught up with all my work and have altered all the dresses you gave me.. They are so beautiful, Mrs. Peabody. Thank you so much."

She smiled. "I'm glad they suited. What 's this about a trunk?"

She explained the situation.

Mrs. Peabody listened attentively. "Don't worry about it, Minna. I'm sure you'll work something out," she said reassuringly. "I'll plan to come and pick you up in a week. With the long train journey, you should get there at just the right time. Does that sound like a good arrangement?"

"Oh, yes," Minna agreed. Suddenly, she felt she had a million details to think of, a million things to plan. "Oh yes," she repeated in an abstracted voice.

Mrs. Peabody extended her hand.

Minna took it and shook it warmly.

"Then tomorrow week, nine in the morning," Mrs. Peabody said. "Make sure you're ready."

"Yes. Thank you!" Minna replied.

Mrs. Peabody smiled again. "I'll have money with me for next year and the address of the committee, so you'll be all set."

Before Minna had a chance to say anything else or even to tell her about the catalogue, she was gone. Looking at her retreating back, Minna wondered why she had seemed so warm and friendly on Allen Street and so different here. Maybe it's easier for someone like Mrs. Peabody to be friendly in a strange setting, she thought. If

I'm here, than it's like…like I'm a servant…or… Minna knew that such speculation was fruitless. Instead, she gave herself up to planning her departure. The first thing she resolved was to talk to Mr. Bates again and explain why she was worried.

At suppertime, she raised the issue. "So, you see, if I don't have something by next week—or sooner so I can pack—I won't be able to leave," she said earnestly. "I don't mean to keep bothering you, but…"

Mrs. Brown chimed in "My lands! How can you get ready to go if you can't pack? If you can let us know tomorrow, Mr. Bates, there's still time for my nephew to make the crate if necessary, but it'll be a close thing."

"You're really going!" Helene exclaimed, as if she had never believed it.

Mr. Bates, chastised, dipped his head momentarily. "You've right on your side," he said to Mrs. Brown. Turning to Minna, he added, "I'll do my best tomorrow. It's the Mistress who won't give me an answer."

"What is she like? Mrs. Peabody, I mean," Millie asked.

"She's…well…she's very pleasant," Minna said, thinking that's the truth. All I know about her is that she's very pleasant. Because I was frightened, I thought she'd be my friend. She helped me, but we're not friends.

"What was she wearing?" Helene asked.

Minna frowned. "Do you know, for once in my life, I didn't notice. I was so interested in what she was saying, I didn't even look."

Helene sighed.

The next day at dinnertime, Mr. Bates approached Minna, beaming. He reached into his pocket and took out a small key. "It's yours!" he said triumphantly. "They agreed. Sal will dust it off and I'll get it to your room this afternoon."

Minna was so relieved and happy, she turned bright red. "Oh, thank you so much!" she exclaimed. She would have given anything to go down to the cellar and look at the trunk, but "I can't wait to see it!" was the most she dared say.

Mr., Bates patted her on the shoulder. "You're welcome," he said.

She knew he didn't even consider that she would want to look at her new possession right away, so instead of saying anything she would regret, she began to mentally pack her new dresses. Just when she had gotten to the forest-green suit, she noticed that the rest of the table was very quiet. Startled, she looked up.

Everyone was staring at her. "I asked you if you know when your train leaves," Mr. Bates said sharply, obviously not for the first time.

'I'm so sorry." Minna blushed. "I was thinking of my new trunk and how I'd pack it."

Reluctantly, he smiled. Everyone joined him except Helene, who snickered.

"All I know is I'm leaving a week from today at nine in the morning. Mrs. Peabody is picking me up and taking me to the station."

Mr. Bates nodded and began to discuss the American railroad system. Minna, afraid to be caught out again, composed her face into an expression of intense interest and pretended she was listening.

That evening, when she returned to her room after finishing her day's work, the trunk was waiting. She looked at it in awe. It was a beautiful trunk. The outside was scratched and the inside faded, but what did that matter when it could be closed and locked with a key?

She tried the key a few times to make sure it worked. Then she leaned back on her bed and gazed at it admiringly. In her imagination, this was the first step towards her new life—the first real step. My own trunk, she thought. She could still remember the trip from Russia—Tata and his books in the straw box, the oddly shaped parcels they lugged with them. A trunk seemed so American. She wished Pearl could see it.

She bowed her head, feeling guilty for being so happy. She thought she could hear Bubbe saying, 'So, nu, little Minna. Life's for the living. Believe me, we're living on manna and honey where we are. Be happy. That's your lot in life.'

Bubbe was the only one she was able to talk to, but Minna could picture them all. There they were in a rich and beautiful place, like that old picture book. Pearl, Mama, Chava, and Bubbe, dressed in luxurious robes and dining on honey and white bread. She didn't know exactly what manna was, but she imagined it to be like white bread since it was always coupled with honey in her mind.

After dinner, Minna began packing the trunk. It was the first of many attempts, as she tried to fit everything in efficiently. In the days that followed, she took everything in and out at least thirty times. She discovered that if she managed carefully, she could fit it all. It only remained to tie her feather bed into a sheet and to make a small bundle to be carried with her in the train—changes of linen, a book to read, some sewing, and whatever else she thought she'd need en route. She remembered how Tata had hated to be separated from his books.

On Sunday afternoon, Minna went to visit Bessie for the last time before leaving. She was about to rush off to a meeting, but she paused when Minna began to say goodbye.

"I have to go to the meeting," she said. "They're depending upon me. But, Minna, I won't see you for so long."

"You've been a good friend," she replied. "I'll never forget you, Bessie."

Bessie flushed. "I won't forget you," she said softly. As if embarrassed, she raised her voice. "Don't forget the Union, either!" she said, half-laughing.

Minna knew she meant it. "I won't," she promised. "I'll write to you, too."

Bessie smiled. "That would be good. I'm not much for letters, but I'll try to get an answer back to you as soon as I can." She looked Minna straight in the eyes. "I won't forget anyone," she said. "I'll never forget them."

Minna wiped her eyes. She hugged Bessie warmly and then gestured with her hands as if to say, "Go! Go to your meeting!"

As she waved goodbye, she couldn't help but think of the other farewells, the ones she couldn't say to those she would never see again…Mama, Pearl, Erma, Anna, Rosa, and all the others…

Shaking her head, Minna hurried down the street towards the park. It was the one place here that had only happy memories. If only I could see Mr. Steinberg before I leave, she thought. If we could talk, I know it would help me.

At the park, she looked at the sluggish river, but she saw only the fire and its aftermath—the empty apartment, the mourners, and the survivors. Suddenly, in a moment of clarity, she knew, once and for all, she was not to feel guilty. The fire was so much a part of her, she could *never* forget it, just as she could never forget those who had died. Instead of feeling that I *have* to remember, she thought, I *know* that I will, always. Then I must be glad my life will go on. If I don't move forward, I might as well be with them now. When I achieve my dreams, I will keep Mama and Pearl with me forever. Like Bubbe, they will know.

She reached into her pocket book and pulled out Yussel's latest letter, already worn and creased from constant re-reading. Although she almost knew it by heart, she sat on a bench, laid it on her lap and read it again, skimming until she came to a certain part. It began: *When I talk to Becca or listen to the sound of cackling all day long, or visit town with some of the other fellows, I feel guilty. Should I be enjoying my life when Mama and Pearl are dead? Then I say to myself, 'How would it help them if I climbed into a dark corner and covered my head?' Mama always wanted me to get ahead. But, still, I feel guilty. It isn't fair, what happened. Do you know what I mean, Minna? Do you have the same feelings?*

She planned what she would say to Yussel when she wrote to him that night: *In answer to your question, I have felt the same way. But today, sitting in the park, I suddenly felt differently. I don't need to prove I'll miss Mama and Pearl. I'll miss them all my life. But, for their sakes, I must go on and have a life or it will be for nothing. Do you understand, Yussel? 'Life is,' Bubbe said once, and that's true. It would be as much of a crime as those devils, Harris and Blanck, if we didn't go forward. I truly believe that. I hope you agree with me, dear Yussel.*

Leaning back against the hard wooden slats of the bench, she closed her eyes. The sun felt good on her face. I'll get freckles, she thought, and laughed. "So what!" she said out loud. "What do I care!" For once, instead of trying to picture what Oberlin would be like or worrying about the train journey, Minna simply relaxed.

When she awoke two hours later, the sun was still shining. Her face felt hot. I guess I'll have a red face, not to mention freckles, she thought as she stretched. She touched her cheek gently. It felt warm. She slid down to the other end of the bench and felt a slight chill as the coolness of the shade covered her body. She was still stiff, so she stretched again, trying to be inconspicuous. A well-bred lady, she was sure, never stretches in public.

Just as she was nearly ready to stand up, she saw a familiar form walking towards her. It was Jake. She stood up too abruptly, almost falling with the sudden movement.

"Jake!" she called.

As he approached, she said, "I thought you were going to be away."

"I was, but I got back today and I had a feeling you'd be here. I don't know why I was so sure, but I came."

She patted the bench. "Here," she offered. "Sit down next to me."

With alacrity, he plumped himself down on the sunny side of the bench. "I was afraid you'd have gone by now," he said.

"Next week." Her eyes sparkled. "I even have a trunk, Jake. You should see! I look like a Vanderbilt with my trunk and my new clothes, the ones I made over!" She looked at him intently. "I'm so glad you came by. I wanted to tell someone, and Bessie, I know, wouldn't approve. Yussel's so far away…"

He laughed. "When is your train?"

"It leaves early in the morning on Wednesday. Oh, Jake, I've never been on a fancy American train before. What should I know to behave right?"

"It's nothing," he said nonchalantly. "You go to the dining car to eat or you can bring your own food. You have to pay at the dining car. If you're lucky, you'll have a berth, a little room with a bed in it. If not, you can sleep in your seat. All you have to do is to guard your ticket well."

She was relieved. "Is that all? It doesn't sound so different from the other train in *der alter heym*."

"Not so crowded and a dining car. And—a toilet right in the train."

She blushed.

"Where are you going again?" he asked.

"The train goes to Cleveland. Then I have to take an Electric Railway to Oberlin. They run every hour. Mrs. Peabody's picking me up at nine, so I guess the train leaves at about ten." She stood up. "Do you know, I fell asleep on this bench. Let's walk a little. How have you been, Jake?"

"Fine, just fine," he said hurriedly. "You're the one who's doing something exciting."

"It's true. I have never gone so far by myself before. Then, when I get there…" she hesitated.

"What is it?" Jake asked, looking at her tenderly.

"I hope Mrs. Boone is nice. That's the lady I'll be working for. I guess she will be. If you run a boarding house, you have to be nice, don't you, or else your guests will leave?" She knew her reasoning was weak. "I mean," she continued, "I hope she is nice, that's all."

"If she isn't, you write to me and I'll come and get you," he said.

She laughed. "Oh, of course, you'd come all the way out to Ohio! It's a nice offer, but…"

He stood up and moved so he was in front of her. He looked down at her face. "We *are* friends," he told her. "I know I said that. But still, I'd come to Ohio for you and it's not just because we're friends."

She blushed and hung her head.

"Thanks, Jake," she whispered. "You know I'd never…"

"It doesn't matter," he said firmly. "I would, anyway."

She stood, too and they began to walk. They continued along the path without speaking. At last, Minna felt she should say something. Uncomfortably, she began to describe the Young's house. "Can you imagine," she asked, "there's rooms I've never even been in? It's that big. And I've never even met Mr. Young. Maybe he doesn't exist at all!"

Jake laughed. "He exists. That's for sure. I've heard all about him. They call him the 'Old Man'. He fired on his workers last year when they went on strike."

She sighed. "I heard about it from Millie, but I wasn't sure it was true. I feel sorry for him."

"Sorry for him? Why? He has everything."

"Maybe so, but his whole family and the others, the kitchen family, they look down on him. Yet he pays the bills. It doesn't seem right, does it?"

"So what! He fired on his workers. I know it's true because I heard about it from someone who was there."

"If everyone says so, then he did. I'll never understand those people. Sometimes they seem like babies, yet they have so much power over the lives of others. How can that be?"

"Easy." Jake laughed bitterly. "Money is power. I know that."

"There's more…" she began, but she didn't know how to explain her feelings. "There's the way we live, too," she finished weakly, knowing that he wouldn't understand.

"Sure, a mansion on Fifth Avenue or a third floor walk-up for us.. You're right, it is the way we live!"

She struggle to make herself understood. "It's more than that. It's how you feel about the house on Fifth Avenue." She paused to collect her thoughts. "I guess what I'm trying to say is that having all that money doesn't automatically make you happy. Everyone in that house wants something they don't have. Mrs. Young wants to be recognized by Mrs. Peabody, Miss Serena wants to fall in love but she's afraid, and Agnes wants to stay with her fellow and also live like a princess in Europe. Mr. Young probably wants everyone in that house to respect him. I don't know. I used to think if you had enough money, you were bound to be happy. Now I see it's not that easy."

He shook his head. "You can say what you want, but when I have a million, I promise I'll enjoy life. Why not?"

She considered trying to make him understand, but realized it would be no use. Instead, she laughed and said, "Let me know how you feel when you're on Easy Street. Then we'll know who's right!"

"Don't worry. You'll know" Jake said meaningfully. He took out a big gold pocket watch. "It's late, Minna. I have leave," he said reluctantly, shaking his head at the watch.

She extended her hand. "Goodbye again, Jake. I'm glad we met."

"You'll write to me?" he asked.

"How about you write to me?" she countered.

He moved impatiently and glanced at his watch again. "I really have to leave," he said. "My uncle will be waiting. Write to me, Minna!" With that, he turned and ran off.

She stared after him in surprise. After all he'd said or hinted, it didn't seem like much of a farewell. How important his uncle's wishes were to him! She shook her head. I'm glad I didn't… Then she shook her head and concluded, I wouldn't have anyway.

The few remaining days passed slowly for her. With little to do, she offered to help Helene pack Miss Serena's clothes. As she followed instructions, using masses of tissue paper, she soon realized that what had seemed like riches to her was, indeed, the merest trifle of subsistence compared to Miss Serena's possessions.

Each evening, she went over the list of things in her trunk, sometimes trying to decide what she could leave behind. Better to go with less than more, she thought. The next moment, she felt the other way round.

During her last day, both Miss Serena and Agnes came to say goodbye. Neither referred to any previous conversations.

"I hope you have a very good trip," Minna said to them.

"I will," Serena said carelessly.

"I hope so," Agnes said hesitantly, blushing as she caught Minna's eyes.

So she's decided not to marry, Minna thought. What a mistake! She had already learned enough about the foreign marriage market to know that Princes and Dukes were not to be had for love alone. Without a rich father and a dowry, Agnes had no hope of marrying one of them.

"Good luck to you," they chimed. Serena handed Minna a delicate silk purse. "Thank you for all your help," she said offhandedly and turned to leave.

Minna took the purse. "Thank you," she called after them.

Agnes extended her hand. "Thank you," she offered and turned to leave abruptly.

Minna could not then or ever determine whether she was embarrassed at not having a small gift to offer or, if having revealed too much, she didn't want to talk to Minna again. In any case, for all my work, she thought, I receive nothing. It goes to show, it's not worth it to be nice to this kind.

Later, Mrs. Young came in and paid Minna her wages to date. "You've done a good job," she said grudgingly. "If you ever want to come back, let me know."

Minna thanked her smilingly, although she thought, what am I thanking her for? She's only paying me what I've earned. Even Miss Serena probably gave me a little extra. As for working for her, I'll never be a servant in a rich man's house again. I can always work in a factory if I have to. Her eyes clouded.

Mrs. Young, about to whisk out of the room, noticed Minna's expression. Hastily, she extended a small velvet box. "This is for you, too," she said. "I hope you will enjoy wearing it. Please tell Mrs. Peabody I have been most pleased to be of service and will be glad to do so again in the future."

Minna held the box awkwardly, not sure whether she was to open it in front of Mrs. Young or wait. Mrs. Young took the decision out of her hands by hurrying out the door.

Slowly, Minna opened the box, unable to guess what she would find. To her surprise, it was a lovely brooch—a bar pin with small gold scrolls at the edges. It would be perfect to wear with almost anything. She turned it over in her hand, admiring the sparkle of the gold. Despite her understanding of Mrs. Young's motives, especially her desire to appear generous to Mrs. Peabody, she couldn't help but think more kindly of her. The brooch was so pretty.

Then she opened the silk purse and then gasped in amazement. Miss Serena had given her three dollars! A week's wages as a gift! Rapidly, she figured. I'll have eighty-five dollars, she thought. The school says I should have fifty, so I'm well fixed. Now, if I can find some extra sewing in Ohio…

On the way down to supper, she hurried through the hall, thinking, this is almost the last time. After tomorrow, I will never walk down this hall again. She looked at the pictures on the walls, determined to remember everything. She was looking so hard, she didn't notice where she was going. To her surprise, she bumped into someone.

Blushing furiously, she looked up. "I'm so sorry," she began. Then she stopped in surprise. It was the old gentleman from the park. Her mouth dropped open.

"Wh—what are you doing here?" she blurted.

"I live here," he said calmly.

"But…"

"You're leaving today, aren't you?" he asked.

"Yes, I am. You know, I've looked for you again. What you said was very helpful," she began.

He gestured downward with his hands, as if to say, 'I don't want to hear that' so she subsided.

"I made sure to meet you," he continued. "I wanted to wish you good luck in your new life."

Minna smiled up at him. "Why, thank you. But…" She looked around nervously, sure that Mr. Bates would see her friend and tell him to leave.

He held out an envelope. "I want you to have this," he said. "And I want to thank you, too."

She looked at him in amazement. "Thank me? For what?"

"For listening to me," he said briefly. Then he hurried past her and down the stairs.

She looked after him. She still couldn't imagine who he was or how he had entered the house. Half fearfully, she remained in place, listening to his retreating footsteps. When Mr. Bates came up behind her, she jumped and looked nervously at the stairs. Luckily, the old gentleman had disappeared.

"Come to supper. Hurry along, girl," Mr. Bates said impatiently.

Flustered, Minna thrust the envelope the old gentleman had given her into her pocketbook and followed Mr. Bates. At the kitchen doorway, she stopped in amazement. Everyone was standing up and looking in her direction. She looked behind her to see if they were staring at someone else.

Mrs. Brown laughed. "It's for you, my dear," she said. "Did you think we wouldn't be saying farewell in the proper way?"

She flushed. She didn't know what to say.

Mr. Bates, as if reading her mind, ushered her into the seat of honor at the head of the table—his seat—with a smile. "Later, you'll have to say a word. For now, just enjoy yourself."

Minna felt strange being the center of attention at the table. She was served first every time and toasts were made with glasses of water. Mr. Bates didn't hold with wine with meals. Too Frenchified, he said, for the kitchen. The high point of the evening was a presentation by Mrs. Brown, from everyone, of a parting gift. This time, Minna knew she was to open the box right away.

Slowly, she tore off the wrapping paper to discover a beautiful dresser set in ivory, with her initials carved on the handles. Awestruck, she caressed the pieces. It included a comb, a brush, a mirror, and a little container for hairpins.

She looked around the table with tears in her eyes. "What can I say?" she asked. "It's the most beautiful thing I have ever seen. I'll think of you all, every day, when I use this elegant set." She paused. "I'll write to you, too," she promised.

Even Helene had tears in her eyes. Whether it was for sorrow at losing Minna or jealousy, she could not tell.

"Here's another present, for tomorrow," Mrs. Brown said, whisking a cloth off a large wicker hamper. "Food for the train." She opened the hamper to display a small traveling knife, fork and spoon, as well as a cup and plate. "I'll fill it full tomorrow morning, of that you can be sure," she promised.

Without even stopping to think about it, Minna jumped out of her seat and rushed over to Mrs. Brown. Giving her a big hug, she whispered, "Thank you. I'll never forget you!"

By the time Minna returned to her room, she was in a happy daze. Her trunk was packed, as it had been since the night before. All that remained was to fold her feather bed and tie it up in the sheet. She planned to take a small sack she had sewn on the train with her necessaries. The new dresser set would fit neatly into the trunk. She set it on the bed and ran her hand over the monogrammed handles. If I don't watch out, she thought, I'll turn into a lady before I learn how to do it! She used the brush, holding it gingerly for fear she'd damage it.

It was only after she'd already changed for bed that she remembered to go though her pocketbook to make sure it was all set for tomorrow. She would keep most of her money in a small bag she had sewn to her petticoat.

As she opened it and took out Mrs. Young's pay and Miss Serena's present, she remembered her meeting with the old gentleman. Slowly, she withdrew the envelope he had given her and opened it. Astonished, she stared at the bills inside, dropping the envelope in her surprise.

Her hands trembled as she counted the money over and over again. It was ten dollars! And she still didn't know her benefactor's name. Aimlessly, she picked up the envelope again.

A small card fell out. It said, "Good luck to Minna." She turned it over and then dropped it again. There, engraved on the card, was the name of her old gentleman. It was Mr. Young! She gasped. The old gentleman was Mr. Young! She sank back on the bed, trying to assemble her thoughts.

So that was Mr. Young. I won't think badly of him, no matter what, she vowed. He's been generous to me. She looked down at the money. In the secret pouch attached to her petticoat, she would be carrying more money than she had ever seen in her life, thanks to Mr. Young, Miss Serena, and her own hard work.

Now I won't have to worry, she thought. No matter what happens, I'll be able to find a place to stay and a bit of bread to eat. As she thought about that, she admitted to herself that despite her exhilaration, she was afraid. What if Mrs. Boone was unpleasant, or Mrs. Peabody didn't come tomorrow, or the scholarship didn't really work out, or…

She put her money away. Mr. Young's card she stowed carefully in her prized dictionary, always a favorite hiding place. Then she lay in bed, her eyes wide open trying to imagine the next few days. This room suddenly began to seem like a haven. It was almost tempting to think of staying on. She remembered her family, always with her, and sighed. Of course, she had to go forward. There were no two ways about it. Besides, she thought as she fell asleep, I don't want to return all my gifts!

The next morning, she was up and dressed long before it was time for breakfast. She wore her new pin—the one Mrs. Young had given her—and she had unpacked her trunk to use her new dresser set.

As she stripped her bed and folded the sheets at its foot, she touched her graduation bracelet nervously to give herself courage. Methodically, she folded her featherbed and wrapped it in the same sheet she had brought from the old apartment. Then she put her dresser set back in the trunk and locked it, adding the key to the muslin bag where she kept her money.

At breakfast, Minna eyed the basket Mrs. Brown had fixed for her with awe. There was so much food in there, it seemed she'd be eating for weeks, but when Mrs. Brown explained that she had to plan for breakfast, lunch, and dinner for several days, it didn't seem like *too* much.

"Eat from the top down," Mrs. Brown said. "That way, nothing will go bad."

Minna held the basket possessively. "It's the cleverest thing I've ever seen," she exclaimed. "The way you've planned it all out and the little knife, fork, and spoon. You've even put a napkin in."

Mrs. Brown was delighted by her enthusiasm. The others were interested, but the needs of their day had to be met. Their goodbyes were caring, but perfunctory.

After all, Minna thought, it's hard to sustain a long farewell when you're the one leaving. She suddenly understood why Saul had refused to let her go to the station to see him off. He had known it would be too hard.

Just as she was preparing to go upstairs and wait there for Mrs. Peabody to arrive, her chauffeur rang the service bell at the kitchen door. "I've come for your trunk," he announced.

In a flurry, Minna hurried up the back stairs ahead of him. She pointed out her trunk. As he took it, she grabbed her featherbed and her package for the train. The wonderful wicker basket was still in the kitchen.

By the time she arrived downstairs again, the chauffeur had come back in. "I'll take that," he said, reaching for her featherbed and the wicker basked. Minna scarcely had time to think about it before she was following him out the door.

As she passed through it, she looked back. Mr. Bates, Mrs. Brown, and the girls were posed in characteristic stances, all staring at her. Mrs. Brown was faintly tearful, yet exhilarated by this change from the usual routine. Mr. Bates looked warmly in her direction. Helene, as usual, looked faintly disapproving. Millie and Sal watched her leave open-mouthed.

She waved briskly and hurried out, afraid to keep the chauffeur and Mrs. Peabody waiting. Yet she was never to forget the picture of Mrs. Young's kitchen and the staff as they stood watching her leave.

Out in the street, she saw an impressively large motorcar. She had never driven in one and if so much else hadn't already happened, that alone would have been enough to thrill her.

Inside the car, she saw Mrs. Peabody waiting for her. The chauffeur, who had preceded Minna, held the door for her. She was about to step into the motorcar when she heard someone calling her name.

She spun around. It was Jake! Panting, he ran up to her. He held out his hand, thrusting a giant bouquet of flowers at her.

"I knew I'd make it!" he panted. "Have a good trip and be sure to write to me!"

Automatically, she accepted the flowers. Speechless, she watched Jake as he turned and left as rapidly as he had come. She held the flowers to her chest, smelling the fragrant roses. She felt like a heroine in one of the films she used to see with Jake. "Minna Begins her New Life" would be the subtitle, or maybe, "Minna Leaves Her Old Home". She had to smile to herself. As if the Young's mansion was her old home!

Stepping into the motorcar almost jauntily, she came face to face with Mrs. Peabody, who looked at her disapprovingly. "So your young man gives you flowers," she said.

"He's not my young man," Minna replied quickly. "He's my oldest friend in America. We came on the boat together."

Mrs. Peabody looked relieved. "I'm glad to hear it, I must say. After working so hard to get you the scholarship, it would be a shame to have you quit after a year or so."

"I won't," Minna promised. "I would never!"

Mrs. Peabody smiled. "Sit down, Minna," she commanded.

She sat gingerly on the edge of the sea, afraid she might be crowding Mrs. Peabody.

"Sit back! Sit back!"

She sat back, clutching the door nervously. She knew this

motorcar would go faster than anything she had ever experienced. It started with a jerk. She looked out the window fearfully as the streets began to whiz by.

As they passed people walking on the sidewalks, she thought, they don't know who I am. They see me and they think, there goes an heiress in a fancy motorcar. She smiled, taken with the absurdity of it. Saul will laugh when I describe how elegant I am in my next letter, she thought.

Graciously, she leaned further back in the seat. It seemed very fitting she should start her new life holding a bouquet of roses and riding in a motorcar. It won't always be like this, she thought, but whatever happens, I'm going to like it. I'm going to like it all, from start to finish.

The End

GLOSSARY

aidem—son-in-law
Amerikaner—American
Amerikane kinder—American children who refuse the ways of the old country
bissel—a small amount, a pinch
baleboosteh—excellent homemaker
boarderkeh—a female boarder
boychick—affectionate term for a young boy
broche—a blessing
bubbe—grandmother
challah—a special braided loaf of bread
Chutzpah—audacity, impudent daring
cockamamy—ridiculous
daven—recite Jewish prayers
der alter heym—the old home
der goldener medina—the golden land, America
dybbuk—evil spirit
eppes—something, a little, debatable
el mole rachamim—funeral prayer
farpotshket farbrente—mixed up firebrand
feh—expression of distate, disgust, or lack of interest
geferlech—terrible
gelt—money
get—divorce in Hebrew
gonif—crook
Gott tsu danken—we thank you, God
gottenyu—oh, dear God!
goy /goyim/goyishe—non-Jew
grauber jung—a crude fellow
haimisher—cozy, warm
kaddish—prayer for the dead as well as a prayer praising God at the end of every service
kinder—children
kineahora—phrase to ward off the evil eye

kosher—foods that conform to Jewish dietary laws, legitimate or genuine
krenk in the kopf—sick in the head
kuchlech—Jewish cookie
kurveh—prostitute
kvell—feel happy and proud
landsmen—people from the same town
landsmannschaft—an association of people from the same town
mann—man
mazeltov—congratulations
Mein Gott—my God
mein kinder—my children
mensch—a worthy person, a real man
meshuggeneh—crazy
minyan—required quorum of 10 Jewish males required for religious service
mitn drinnen—right in the middle
mitzvah—a good deed
naches—joy in the accomplishments of a loved one
nu—so? What do you think?
oy gevalt—oh, how terrible!
oy vey'z mir—woe is me
oyf kapores—good for mothing, a big mess
payos—sidelocks
pekl—bundle
pilpul—a small point
pushke—container kept in the home for charitable donations
reb—mister
schmutzig—dirty
shadchen—matchmaker
schlaft—sleep
schliemiel—a dolt
schlimazl—unlucky and inept person
schmooze—a long and intimate conversation, gossip
schnorrer—beggar
shayner Yid—a Jew of exceptionally good character whom other Jews esteem

shikker—drunk
shiva—week-long mourning ritual
sholom aleichem—hello, peace unto you
shtarke—criminal
shtetl—little Jewish village in Eastern Europe
shul—school or synagogue
shvester—sister
tahara—ritual burial rites
tochter—daughter
trayf—food that doesn't conform to Jewish dietary laws
tsedakah—charity
tzitzit—fringes on the corner of a prayer shawl
vilde chaya—wild animal
yarmulke—small round cap worn by Jewish men
yeshiva—religious school
yeshiva bocher—a young student of the Torah
zayde—grandfather
zuhn—son

Made in the USA
Lexington, KY
19 June 2014